I, Victoria

I, VICTORIA

Cynthia Harrod-Eagles

St. Martin's Press ❧ New York

Library of Congress Cataloging-in-Publication Data

Harrod-Eagles, Cynthia.
I, Victoria / by Cynthia Harrod-Eagles.
p.   cm.
"A Thomas Dunne book."
ISBN 0-312-13516-5
1. Victoria, Queen of Great Britain, 1819–1901—
Fiction.   2. Great Britain—History—1837–1901—
Fiction.   3. Queens—Great Britain—Fiction.
I. Title.
PR6058.A6945I19   1996
823'.914—dc20   95-39786   CIP

First published in Great Britain by Macmillan London

First U.S. Edition: January 1996
10 9 8 7 6 5 4 3 2 1

Contents

THE CHILDREN AND GRANDCHILDREN OF QUEEN VICTORIA AND PRINCE ALBERT

1 VICTORIA (Pussy, Vicky) The Princes Royal b. 1840

m. 1857 Fritz of Prussia 1831–88 (Emperor of Germany
March–June 1888)

1 Willy b. 1859   2 Charlotte b. 1860
3 Henry b. 1862 m. 1888 Irène of Hesse, Alice's daughter
4 Siggie b. 1864 d. 1866 of meningitis   5 Moretta b. 1866
6 Waldie b. 1868 d. 1879 of diptheria   7 Sophie b. 1870
8 Margaret b. 1872

2 ALBERT EDWARD (Bertie) The Prince of Wales b. 1841

m. 1863 Alexandra of Denmark (Alix)

1 Albert Victor (Eddy) Duke of Clarence b. 1864 d. 1892
of pneumonia   2 Georgie b. 1865 m. 1893 May of Tech –
David b. 1894 Albert b. 1895 Mary b. 1897 Henry b. 1900
3 Louise b. 1867   4 Toria b. 1868   5 Maud b. 1869
6 John b. & d. 1871

3 ALICE b. 1843 d. 1878

m. 1862 Grand Duke Louis of Hesse (who d. 1892)

1 Victoria b. 1863 m. Louis of Battenberg   2 Ella b. 1864 m.
Grand Duke Sergei of Russia   3 Irène b. 1866 m. Henry of Prussia,
Vicky's son   4 Ernie b. 1868 m. Ducky, Affie's daughter
5 Frittie b. 1870 d. 1873 of haemophilia   6 Alicky b. 1872 m. Tsar
Nicholas II of Russia   7 May b. 1874 d. 1878 of diphtheria

4 ALFRED (Affie) Duke of Edinburgh (1893 Duke of Saxe-Coburg) b. 1844 d. 1900

m. 1874 Grand Duchess Marie of Russia

1 Young Affie b. 1874 d. 1889 of pneumonia   2 Marie (Missy) b. 1875   3 Victoria Melita (Ducky) b. 1876 m. Ernie of Hesse, Alice's son   4 Sandra b. 1878 m. Ernst Hohenlohe, Feo's grandson   5 Beatrice (Baby Bee) b. 1884

5 HELENA (Lenchen) b. 1846

m. 1866 Prince Christian of Schelswig-Holstein

1 Christian Victor (Christl) b. 1867 d. 1900 of enteric fever 2 Albert b. 1869   3 Thora b. 1870   4 Marie-Louise b. 1872 5 Harold b. & d. 1876

6 LOUISE b. 1848

m. 1871 Marquess of Lorne

7 ARTHUR Duke of Connaught b. 1850

m. 1879 Louise of Prussia (Louischen)

1 Margaret b. 1882   2 Young Arthur b. 1883 3 Patricia b. 1886

8 LEOPOLD Duke of Albany b. 1853 d. 1884

m. 1882 Helena of Waldeck-Pyrmont

1 Alice b. 1883   2 Charlie b. 1884 (from 1900 Duke of Saxe-Coburg)

9 BEATRICE (Baby) b. 1857

m. 1885 Henry of Battenberg (Liko) (who d. 1896)

1 Alexander (Drino) b. 1886   2 Ena b. 1887 3 Leopold b. 1889   4 Maurice b. 1891

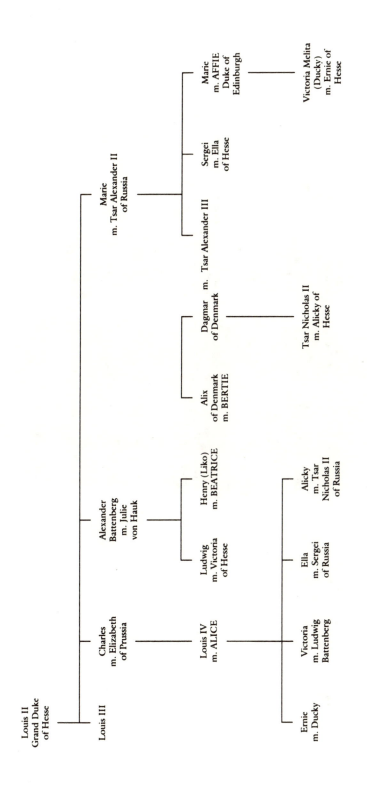

THE RUSSIAN AND HESSIAN CONNECTION

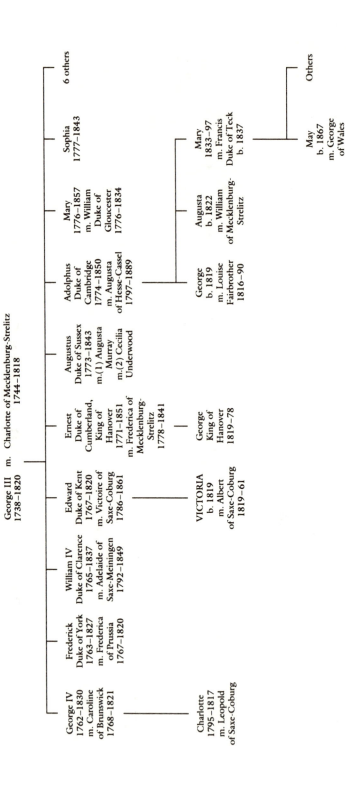

George III   m.   Charlotte of Mecklenburg-Strelitz
1738–1820   1744–1818

George IV
1762–1830
m. Caroline
of Brunswick
1768–1821

Frederick
Duke of York
1763–1827
m. Frederica
of Prussia
1767–1820

William IV
Duke of Clarence
1765–1837
m. Adelaide of
Saxe-Meiningen
1792–1849

Edward
Duke of Kent
1767–1820
m. Victoire of
Saxe-Coburg
1786–1861

Ernest
Duke of
Cumberland,
King of
Hanover
1771–1851
m. Frederica of
Mecklenburg-
Strelitz
1778–1841

Augustus
Duke of Sussex
1773–1843
m.(1) Augusta
Murray
m.(2) Cecilia
Underwood

Adolphus
Duke of
Cambridge
1774–1850
m. Augusta
of Hesse-Cassel
1797–1889

Mary
1776–1857
m. William
Duke of
Gloucester
1776–1834

Sophia
1777–1843

6 others

Charlotte
1795–1817
m. Leopold
of Saxe-Coburg

VICTORIA
b. 1819
m. Albert
of Saxe-Coburg
1819–61

George
King of
Hanover
1819–78

George
b. 1819
m. Louise
Fairbrother
1816–90

Augusta
b. 1822
m. William
of Mecklenburg-
Strelitz

Mary
1833–97
m. Francis
Duke of Teck
b. 1837

May
b. 1867
m. George
of Wales

Others

MY FATHER'S FAMILY

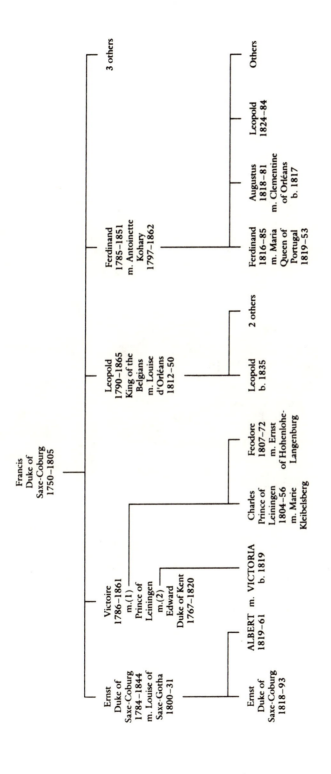

MY MOTHER'S FAMILY

I, Victoria

WINTER

One

28th January 1900, at Osborne

I NEVER really *liked* having my photograph taken, even when I was younger – it always seemed so much pain for so uncertain a pleasure. I have always had the greatest difficulty in suppressing fits of giggles on occasions when I am meant to be solemn, and in the early days of photography one had to keep still for the camera for such a very long time. So of course one always came out looking stiff and grim, and I am not a grim person, as anyone will admit. I love to laugh, but one cannot laugh in a photograph, even nowadays when they have improved the apparatus so much. One cannot even really smile, it looks so very odd – especially when one is Queen and has a certain dignity to uphold.

I suppose if I had ever been beautiful, like dear Alix, I should not have minded being photographed. It's a great comfort to me to have such a beautiful daughter-in-law: she always looks lovely and serene, like an alabaster statue. She will make a dignified queen one day. (What sort of king Bertie will make is another matter – but I won't think about that now!) I have such a great love of physical beauty – indeed, Albert thought it excessive, but having so much of his own, he was inclined to undervalue it. Mamma was pretty when she was young – regular features, dark eyes, pink cheeks, glossy curls – and my sister Feo was the image of her. But I, I must needs inherit my father's looks, especially his nose – large and long, jutting uncompromisingly outward and curving over at the tip – and his receding chin and heavy underlip! (Often and often when I was young I was scolded because my mouth always hung a little open, but I say when a person has a heavy underlip and a particularly short upper lip, what is a person to do?) Dear Papa's features were well enough for a man – indeed, he was thought quite good looking for a prince – but they

1

never sat happily on me. It seems that in my physical self, as well as my inheritance, I am all Hanoverian. The slender, beautiful Coburg looks from my mother's side passed me by entirely.

Yet one can sometimes make a surprising impression! When my granddaughter, sweet little Sophie (Vicky's seventh), came to visit me for the first time, she described me afterwards in her journal like this: 'My dear Grandmamma is very tiny – a very, very pretty little girl – and she wears a veil like a bride.' Sophie was four years old then, and I was fifty-five! It was very gratifying. A woman, even if she is a queen and has more important things to think of, always wants to be pretty.

So it was with mixed pleasure that I spent this afternoon looking over old photographs with Thora. (Dear Thora, the most useful of my grandchildren! Lenchen is lucky to have such a daughter: she has never given anyone a moment's anxiety in her life!) The weather today is vile, real January weather – strong winds and a heavy, sleety snow. Even carriage exercise has been impossible. It is a rare thing for me to be put off going out by the weather, but it really was impossible today – we should never have got the ponies along. Besides, it would have been sheer cruelty to make any of my ladies accompany me: they are all such hothouse flowers! and poor Jane Churchill has a nasty cold in the head. I have had a troublesome cough lately, but that is more from the damp than the cold. The damp has got into my poor old knee, too, and it aches like the memory of an old grief. Oh, the complaining flesh! The greatest tragedy about growing old is that our outsides cease to match our insides. The spirit remains willing, but the flesh shrinks back at the door and yearns towards the comfortable chair and the fireside!

Osborne has always been a cold house in winter. Even with the most extravagant fires lit, a northeaster coming off the sea penetrates the shutters and chills the rooms, except for a little rosy space around each fireplace, where the dogs collect. Well, after all, it was intended as a summer palace, a Marine Residence to replace the Pavilion at Brighton. Albert's clever heating scheme – blowing hot air through grilles to warm the corridors and bedrooms – was meant for counter-acting the cool of a summer evening, but it does little against the icy draughts that racket about the house in winter. But I never mind the cold; in fact the older I get, the less I can bear too much heat. I know very well what my ladies think about that! I tease them sometimes, just for the fun of seeing their dismay. Once at Balmoral on a *really* cold day, I came down at the usual time for my outing to find them all blue-nosed and huddling together like mountain ponies, so I looked grave and wondered aloud whether it might not be too warm for going out. The silly geese took me quite seriously!

We never had a Christmas here while Albert was alive, which is a pity. At Christmas and for weeks afterwards the house smells so beautifully of the pine and myrtle we cut to decorate the rooms, of the applewood burning in the grates, of oranges and cinnamon and cloves. Smells are the most vivid keys to memory, I always find: one sniff of this or that, and one is actually *there*, reliving some long-lost time as though transported bodily. Thank God I have kept that sense intact at least, though my wretched eyes are getting very bad, even with my 'specs' – horrid things! how I hate to wear them! If only people would write more distinct, we should get on better. I have spoken to Ponsonby again and again about it: as my secretary he should look to it. My hearing is not what it was, either – not that I am deaf by any means, but I used to be able to hear the bats shriek, when my darling and I went out walking at dusk; and I could hear a whispered conversation on the other side of a room (an ability which has often stood me in good stead: it is surprising the number and variety of things people decide one ought not to know!).

My earliest memories are connected with smells. I can remember crawling across the carpet at Kensington Palace – a yellow carpet, with red lozenges, and worn patches where the cord was showing through – and it smelled of dust and dogs. (I learned to walk long before I was a year old, so that may well be my very earliest memory of all.) I remember sitting on the floor (cold under my bottom, through a thin muslin dress – we wore so little in those days – I wonder if that is why I feel the heat so much in these better-clad times?) and holding Aunt Adelaide's purple cloth reticule with the gold thread embroidery. The purple was so soft and the gold so harsh to my baby hands, and it smelled of peppermint, which was why I was trying to find out how to open it. Aunt and Mamma chattered in German above my head meanwhile – a sound like birds, like starlings roosting, full of little clicks and whistles, and *zo!* and *ne?* and *ach!* and *scha-a-ade!* Poor Aunt Adelaide always smelled of peppermints: she had bad teeth, so she tended to swallow great lumps of food whole, which gave her indigestion. Now I think of it, it shows what strength of character she had, to remain always so good-tempered while a martyr to dyspepsia, which is a most disagreeable affliction, and one very hard to obtain any sympathy for. A fever or a wound always arouses tender interest, but the workings of the alimentary system one would always rather not think about, especially someone else's.

Having an iron digestion myself, I'm afraid I was not always very sympathetic in the early days when poor darling Albert suffered. He and food were never really intimate friends. They tolerated each other at best.

Aunt Adelaide was a frequent visitor in the first years of my life. When Mamma was first widowed, Uncle William encouraged my aunt to visit her every day to console her – he said that as they were both German, they would be able to talk and pray in the same language. That was like him, my blunt, kind, practical uncle! But sadly the intimacy did not last, owing to a Certain Person, who poisoned Mamma's mind against my dear uncle and aunt. From the time I was about six or seven, I hardly ever saw them, though they continued to write to me and send me presents, and whenever I did see them, they were as kind and loving as ever towards me. But when I think of the opportunity lost – however, it's of no use to repine over what might have been.

Another early memory I have is of the odour of camphor enveloping me as Papa's sister, Princess Sophia, swished past me along one of the garden paths. I must have been very small then, for I remember her black skirts scratching my face as she went by and rattling the gravel against my shoes. A faint smell of camphor always hung about her clothes, and later it was a smell I always associated with melancholy, for poor, sad Princess Sophia – one of the many 'living ghosts' of Kensington Palace – was in permanent mourning for her own life, her long-ago lover and her lost, secret baby. (I was not supposed to know about that, but servants talk all the time – one only has to listen.)

Kensington Palace was a sort of royal asylum for poor relatives in those days, where they could be boarded out of the way at as little expense as possible. Uncle Sussex was another of Papa's relatives who lived there, an extremely eccentric man who lived a life of fierce seclusion and talked to himself all the time. I remember him rushing along a passage, waving his hands as he expounded some serious point to himself (he must have been finding himself hard to convince, for he sounded quite heated!). I was terrified of him as a child, not because he had ever done anything bad to me, poor old man, but because he had been held up to me as the ultimate penalty. An earlier generation of nurses had threatened their charges with Boney, the wicked Corsican who ate little children; when I was naughty and unrepentant (which, alas, was very often!) I was told that if I did not stop screaming Uncle Sussex would come and get me!

There was such a gust of wind just then that it made all the shutters bang against their fastenings, as if the windows behind them were nothing but space! When Beatrice was a little girl, she was once asked what windows were for, and the saucy thing answered promptly, 'To let the wind through.'

I wonder if she remembers that now! Poor Baby! She is sitting opposite me, her feet lifted out of the draught on a little foot-stool, knitting something in khaki. (We have all been knitting as though our lives depended on it: there is so little else one can do for our brave men at the Front.) She looks very handsome still, with her nice neck and pretty hands (though really I do not like the present style of dressing hair, with that front of tight curls, just exactly like a poodle and not at all flattering). It pains me to see her in her blacks, and to know that she, my youngest child, is a widow. It is so very dreadful and pitiful, though she bears it with the greatest fortitude, and her children are, of course, a great comfort. I love to hear them running about and laughing and chattering, to know the old nurseries are inhabited again: it made me very sad when they were closed up, when Baby herself grew up and there were no more brothers and sisters to come after her. It is surprising how much noise just four children can make. If Liko had lived, I expect he and Baby would have gone on to have more, for they were very much in love; but he took it into his head so strongly to go off and fight in Ashanti (the second war in 1895, that was, of course, not the first. It seems that nothing but trouble ever comes out of Africa – so unlike dear India!). I told Liko at once that it would never do, but he would not take 'no' for an answer, and reminded me that he came from a family of soldiers, and that it was a worthy cause to force the King of Ashanti to give up the Slave Trade. In my anxiety I even had Reid put the medical argument to him, that the climate of the Gold Coast would certainly undermine his health; but still Liko would go, and Baby supported him, though she wanted him to go as little as I did. I was right: he lasted only a few weeks, poor creature. He took malaria in those dreadful, fever-haunted jungles, and died on the journey home. The fact was, of course, that he yearned for something noble and useful to do, and one ought not to repine when men seek the service of honour; but his loss was such a dreadful blow to me! I loved him as dearly as my own son, and he brought such *enjoyment* into my life, as though every day were a champagne day. Baby was not thirty-nine years old when he died, younger even than I was when I was widowed. Fate is very cruel, and one never gets used to it.

She hears my thoughts and looks up at me as if I have spoken out loud. When people live together a great deal that is often the way. I can see that she wonders what I am writing, and whether she will be wanted to take dictation – she has done so once or twice recently when my eyes have been too tired or my hands too stiff. Yes, now she has asked would I like to dictate my journal to her, or will I write it myself? No, I say, I will write it myself. There is not much to tell today – just the weather and my health, no news of the war – but I must keep it up-to-date. She smiles and goes back to her work.

My journal! I was thirteen when Mamma gave me a blank book for my very first journal – very handsome it was, too, fine cream-laid paper, leather binding and marbled end-papers. We were just about to depart on the first of our tours of England (what my uncle William, who was King by then, called 'royal progresses' – how angry he was with Mamma for not asking his permission for them! And how mad it made him that she allowed our party to be greeted all round the country with gun salutes as though I were already Queen – 'That infernal pop-popping!' he would bellow. 'It must stop!'). Mamma gave me the blank book to keep a record of every day's happenings, as a discipline of mind and as an exercise in composition. A very useful discipline it was, too; and I have kept a journal ever since, missing only a very few days in my long life – those terrible, black days in 1861.

Of course, that journal was intended for Mamma to read, so I could only write what I knew she would approve of. And so, in a way, I have been writing it ever since for her approval, though I never let her read it after I became Queen, and she has been dead almost these forty years. But all my life I have written for other people: for Mamma, for my children and grandchildren, and for my wider family, the people of these islands and beyond, my subjects who are also my children. And what one writes for other people is never quite, *entirely*, the truth. My writing has always been trimmed to suit them, cabin'd, cribb'd and confin'd so as not to offend – not even, I fear, very much to surprise!

I am very old now, and though I do not feel an imminent dissolution, I cannot suppose God will keep me here very much longer; so I feel it would be a good time for me to tell my story. When my beloved Albert died, Sir Theodore Martin wrote a very careful Life, making sure I approved and agreed with everything, mentioning nothing which he could not praise; and when I die I suppose there will be a polite public biography of me, over which Bertie will hover with his censor's pen in case of any indiscretion. Between the two, many truths, I dare say, will fall like the sparrow.

Poor Bertie was so very much shocked when I proposed to write a Life of my dear John Brown! (There was so much opposition to the idea that in the end, realising how the drawing-room tabbies would chew up my faithful friend and spit him out, I decided to give it up.) If I were to write my own Life now, and tell the whole truth, it would contain many things that would never get past Bertie's pen; or Beatrice's for that matter – the younger generation is so much more censorious than we were. One or other of them would be sure to burn up anything I wrote that came near the truth. Well, they will have to live in the world when I am gone, and I have no wish to make things more difficult for them than they will be in any case. I will do the job for them.

But even if I destroy it before anyone reads it, I should still like to tell my own story. It will be a large undertaking (it has been a very long life!) and perhaps I shall not see the end of it; but I shall make a start, at least. It will be something to do in those restless hours at night when I am alone in my room and cannot sleep. I was always such a good sleeper, it is quite dreadful to wake after an hour or two and know I shall not be able to get off again. And when one has been asleep, the world takes on an odd, disquieting unfamiliarity, a sort of emptiness that has no right to be there – like feeling hungry immediately after a meal. Sometimes I ring as soon as I wake, but a person who has been roused unwillingly from a satisfying slumber is not a sympathetic companion for someone who cannot enjoy the same blessing. Those warm, flushed faces and sleepy eyes bring out the worst in me, I'm afraid, and at my proximity to Judgement I really ought to avoid the occasions of sin when I can!

So I shall take, instead, to the pen, in those haunted hours – and whenever I have a moment through the day. I shall have the rare satisfaction of writing for my own pleasure, something which no-one else will read or criticise, something that is for me and for me alone – for the Victoria who lives inside the Queen Empress; and who, despite the stout, black-clad, old-woman exterior known to half the world's people from a multitude of lithographed reproductions, remains a young girl – painfully shy, embattled, and very much alone.

The inside does not match the outside – never did, but does so much less now than ever. I sit at the centre of a crowded world, the focal point of it; my every whim is consulted, my every word recorded for posterity; I am surrounded by children and grandchildren and great-grandchildren, faithful servants, respectful ministers, adoring subjects; and I am *lonely*. When one has been denied love as a child, no amount of love given later on is ever, quite, enough. And they all left me, one by one, all those I depended upon, all those who loved me and whom I loved. Dear, dearest Beatrice sits opposite me, keeping me company and waiting to do my bidding – my companion and amanuensis – my Benjamina, as I call her – and I am truly grateful, and know how lucky I am in her. But the love and companionship of women and children can never replace that special intimacy, with the one person who is all things – father, brother, friend and lover, the other half of one's soul. When you have once known it, nothing else will really do; and even with a glorious fat great-grandchild chuckling on one's knee, one is still, stubbornly, alone.

31st January 1900 – one o'clock in the morning

I DREAMT that I was back in the old bedroom in Kensington Palace, which I shared with Mamma when I was a child. I was in my little white bed, and the reading-candle was lit, and I could hear the ticking of Papa's silver and tortoise-shell repeater, which Mamma kept on her bedside table – the sound I went to sleep with every night of my life until I was eighteen. Lehzen was sitting on the hard chair beside my bed reading, as she always did until Mamma came up, because I was never allowed to be alone for a single instant, day or night, until I became Queen. Lehzen always sat very upright – she said that no part of a lady's back should touch the chair she sat in – holding her book up to catch the light; but sometimes she dozed a little, and then the book would gradually subside into her lap, her long chin would sink on to her chest, and the ribbons on her cap would fall forward over her cheeks, and flutter in the little puffing breaths from her lips.

But in my dream it was not Lehzen sitting there beside my bed. I knew it was not my good, kind governess, even though I could not turn my head to see who it was. No, it was Someone Else; and in the dream it seemed terribly important that I should make them aware that I knew they were there, that I knew who they were – that I was not, actually, asleep. But all the time I was sinking into sleep, struggle how I might, and I felt such a sense of despair and sorrow, knowing that if I slept, I would wake to a different world and a different person, and that the chance would be gone for ever.

What did it mean, I wonder? It was so vivid I feel it must be significant – but then, I have always had such vivid dreams. When I was first married I used to tell them to Albert in the morning, as I always told him everything that happened to me; but he hated it so, I had to learn to keep my dreams to myself. Poor darling, for a man who believed in logic and order and rationality he was quite dreadfully superstitious. He was a child of the Enlightenment, and a Protestant too, and he always held that belief in signs and omens and portents was wrong – pagan and idolatrous. Yet they worried him far more than they did me. I found such things interesting, and really rather cheering. I liked the thought that there was an unseen world all around us, lapping over the edge of ours like the sea lapping over the shore. I shouldn't have minded at all if I had seen a ghost – in fact I hoped quite hard for it when I was younger, especially when I first went to live at Windsor, where surely there ought to have been ghosts if there were to be any anywhere. (When I discussed ghosts with my dear Lord Melbourne, he said he often saw them, but had never met one whose conversation was worth a damn!) But Albert found even the hint of a portent unsettling, the more so since he could not admit to it. My poor darling had so much more ethereal a nature than mine, more sensitive to spiritual things. What little sleep he was able to get was probably so much troubled by dreams, it is no wonder he did not want to hear about mine. He was all of the spirit, while I was of the earth. Now I come to think of it, he probably had to live with ghosts all the time, poor man.

Now, I wonder if the Person in my dream could have been my papa? I sometimes think that I remember him, though he died when I was eight months old. When I told Mamma once that I had a memory of him, she shook her head and said it was impossible. But I do remember being lifted up by someone and held above his head, up near the ceiling, and I remember the rushing, disturbing sensation of soaring upwards and dangling helpless, combined with the feeling of being absolutely safe. There was something strangely delicious about the contrast between my precarious position and the strong, male hands holding me so securely. As long as he held me, I knew nothing bad could ever happen to me.

I remember it so vividly that I don't think it can have been a dream. I am sure it must have been my father. I can't remember his face (though I've seen portraits of him, of course) but I have thought about him, I believe, every day of my life. When I was a child I used to lie in bed waiting to fall asleep, and listen to the light, swift tick of his repeater, and think how it sounded like hurrying feet. Oh, how he hurried away from me, my papa! – gone before I could even learn his face; yet the spirit of him has been always, always with me. How different my life would have been if he had not died – abandoning me, who was so little and helpless and needed his protection so much! I felt the lack of a father every day of my childhood, and things that happened in those years, which he would have prevented, have moulded me (or marred me, perhaps) in ways that I still feel and cannot control, even here at the far end of my life. My character was altered by those years in which I had to struggle to stand alone, and I have spent the rest of my life searching for the strong arm and wise heart of which I was deprived so very young.

It is very certain that my *fate* would have been different if Papa had not died when he did. For one thing, it is most likely that he and Mamma would have gone on to have more children, the son that she hoped for and had promised him. If they had given me a brother, I should not have become Queen of England – and how would I have liked that, I wonder? How wonderful it would have been to have lived out of the spotlight's glare, without this constant burden of cares and the mountain of work which never gets any smaller no matter how long and hard one 'pegs away' at it. To have lived retired, far away from the prying eyes and critical tongues; to have spent my life as a private person, an ordinary wife and mother – ah, to have been Albert's wife and not Queen, how delicious that would have been!

Well, yes. But as I am to tell the truth in this account, and there is to be no-one but Victoria to read it, I may as well say that the thought of *not* being Queen fills me with horror! How could I ever have endured to be someone else's subject, to come second – or worse – instead of first in everything? And how could I ever have trusted anyone else to do the job properly? (As it is, the idea of leaving my kingdom to Bertie fills me with foreboding.) And as to Albert, if we had married at all (which is unlikely, for if Papa had lived he would have chosen my husband for me, and I doubt if his choice would have been the same as Mamma's) my darling would have carried me off to Germany to live, and there he would have been master in his own house, there is no doubt about that. His will was always to rule, my own dear, beloved domestic tyrant! I adored him, and it pleased me to yield to him, but it is a very different thing to be *obliged* to yield rather than to *choose* to. If I had not had the unassailable power of my sovereignty to hold up against him, I think it would have gone ill with me. As it was we had mighty quarrels, but if I had really been nothing but his *kleines Frauchen* he would have won them all; for he had intellect, while I had only temper, and as his wife in his house in his land, I would have had no right to be heard. No, Victoria would not have had much of her own way – and I suspect, too, that Albert would not have been half so patient with her many shortcomings, as he was obliged to be with those of the Queen of England.

No, no, I think it is a very good thing indeed that I became Queen. However heavy the burden – and it *is* heavy, no-one can know how much so – I would not wish to change that fact, at least. God knew what He was doing; I only wish there could have been some other way to do it. One should not question God's will – so Albert always told me – but there is that in me which always *will* question things, and struggle against fate, and rail at it. Well, perhaps that is no bad trait in a Queen. When I am dead, that will be time enough to 'lie still and slumber'. And if my darling had had a little more of my stubbornness, perhaps he might have been here still, and we could have been old together, as he promised me we should. I believe one should always keep promises, however small or lightly made. One should always keep one's word.

1st February 1900

To RESUME: that I became Queen at all takes a little explaining from the historical point of view, for Papa was only the fourth son of King George III, and in his youth he could not possibly have thought a child of his could ever succeed to the Throne. He went into the Army, as younger sons do, and made his career there. (I have always liked to boast that I am a soldier's daughter, and I think our brave Men have always appreciated my special interest in and understanding of them.) Papa was a fine soldier, brave and honourable, and he served with distinction, particularly in the West Indies and Canada. He brought to his commands a painstaking attention to detail and the same unbending discipline that he applied to his own behaviour. He detested slovenliness, unpunctuality, drunkenness, untruthfulness, and punished them severely – which did not, of course, make him popular with the culprits. Also his openly expressed disapproval of gambling, drinking and fornication set his own family against him – at least, the male half – and sadly he was much hated by his brothers and a large part of society. The gentle side of his character I think he revealed only to women: with them he could be charming, witty, attentive, affectionate, a great talker and a gifted mimic. Mrs Fitzherbert (my uncle the Regent's unofficial wife) was Papa's devoted friend, and Princess Charlotte called him her 'favourite and beloved uncle'; and since no-one has ever denied they were both intelligent women, I think their opinion may be trusted.

I am glad to have inherited some of his qualities: he loved music, and had a band of wind instruments which he took everywhere with him; he loved horses, and detested cruelty to them, or indeed to any animal; he was utterly truthful, and scorned ever to tell a lie; he loved order, and never shrank from hard work; and he was faithful and loyal to those he loved. In the latter context I have now to mention Madame de St Laurent – Julie – a French lady whom Papa met in Gibraltar in 1790, and took with him when he was sent to Canada. Mamma always thought I did not know about Madame Julie. She never spoke of her to me, partly from propriety, but mostly, I think, because she loved Papa so much and she thought I might disapprove and cease to revere his memory if I knew he had had a mistress. But I knew, of course I did! Servants' talk, I suppose – and dear Lord Melbourne told me all the details of Papa's history when I first became Queen. Really, I don't think Madame Julie was anything to be ashamed of. She was charming and witty and honest, and she and Papa lived together in love and trust, in all climates and all adversities, for twenty-seven years. If she had been a princess, or if he had not been a prince, I am quite sure they would have been married: but then, of course, I would not have been born, for Madame never had a child.

Papa's real failing was his extravagance. He liked to live in royal style, but his pension from Parliament was not sufficient for his tastes, and instead of curtailing his spending, he borrowed money and ran up debts. He was no gamester, and he ate and drank sparingly, but he loved fine art and furniture and high-bred horses, and he collected books. Furthermore, he had a particular love of architecture, and liked nothing better than to be building or refurbishing houses. It pains me to have to admit it, but he had no scruples at all about ordering things he had no means of paying for, and his debts mounted and followed him wherever he went. Then in 1803 disaster overtook him. He was sent to Gibraltar to restore order to the garrison, which had got out of hand; and this he did with such severity that there was almost a mutiny. One man was flogged to death, another severely crippled by the lash, and such was the outcry against him that he was removed from command and told he would be given no more active duty.

So Papa was forced to return to England, and was left on a reduced income with nothing to do but spend money (he bought a country house in Ealing, and extensively altered it, besides decorating and furnishing it and filling the stables), evade his creditors, and try to work out ingenious schemes for borrowing enough money to clear his debts and set himself up comfortably. But by 1816, without either career or prospects, he had got so far into debt the situation was hopeless, and his only resort seemed to be to take Madame Julie and go into exile, to live in Brussels (where living was cheap) until a committee of trustees, appointed by his creditors to handle his income and make him an allowance, had paid off his debts by instalments. This he expected to take years; he was forty-eight years old, and for this restless, energetic, ingenious prince it must have seemed like a sentence of doom.

Papa left England in August 1816; but before he departed he was able to rejoice at the marriage of his beloved niece, Princess Charlotte of Wales, to the handsome Prince Leopold of Saxe-Coburg, with whom she had been in love for two years. She had met him in London at the peace festivities in 1814, which he had attended as a member of the suite of the Tsar of Russia; but Charlotte's father, the Prince Regent, had opposed the match (he called Leopold a 'penniless princeling' and a 'dam'd counter-jumper', amongst other things) and had forbidden them any correspondence. Papa, keenly interested in Princess Charlotte's happiness, had acted as go-between for the lovers and passed their letters to each other, and they now regarded him with profound gratitude as the chief promoter of the marriage.

It was a blissfully happy marriage, but tragically short. Eighteen months later the handsome, intelligent, deeply beloved Heiress of England died, on the 6th of November 1817, after labouring for two days to deliver herself of a large, perfect, but dead baby boy. What her sufferings were every mother can imagine, and no man can know; there must have been some mismanagement in the case, for the doctor who had attended her took his own life three months later. England's grief was overwhelming. Even the Duke (I mean Wellington, of course – such was his pre-eminence at any time after Waterloo that he was always simply referred to as the Duke, *tout court* and without qualification) said, 'Her death is one of the most serious misfortunes the country ever met with'; and he was notoriously unsentimental.

The fact was that quite apart from her personal qualities, which made her beloved of all who met her, her dynastic importance was unparalleled. England had just emerged, weary and bankrupt, from twenty-two years of European War, to face unemployment, soaring prices, a failed harvest, and the rumblings of revolution amongst the poor. Stability, strong leadership and a popular monarchy were what was needed; but Princess Charlotte was the only legitimate grandchild of the King, the sole heiress to the kingdom, and her loss created a situation of the utmost gravity and uncertainty.

2nd February 1900

AT DINNER Sir John McNeill said that he believed the situation in Ladysmith to be hopeless, that they cannot break out and must be overrun by the Boers at last. I was obliged to tell him pretty sharply that I do not like such despondent talk: no-one in *this* house is downhearted. Dear old General White reports from inside Lady-smith (by heliograph – such a boon!) that they are now reduced to eating their horses (which information is *not* going to be allowed into the newspapers!). But even so, if they have sufficient ammunition they may hold out for six weeks more. I am disgusted with the Government, they are all delay and bungling; though I don't at all blame Salisbury, whose hands are pretty well tied. But the rest of them care for nothing but votes, and won't take my advice or the advice of experts about the Army, and civilians *cannot* understand military matters. I am furious with the Press, too, who are being very disloyal and unhelpful. I have felt obliged to ban the *Morning Post* from the house altogether – though I fear there may still be a secret copy smuggled into the equerries' room, for they all seem to regard it as the oracle. The worst thing is having no reliable news. It is like the Crimean War all over again – one would hardly think half a century had gone by!

I wrote myself into sleepiness last night, so the 'medicine' seems to work! I shall resume now where I left off, and hope that writing can keep my thoughts away from this wretched war.

I was writing about the death of Princess Charlotte. I never knew her, for she died before I was born – indeed, had she not died, I would not have been born at all. Perhaps for that reason I have always felt strangely attached to her, as if there were some essential connection between us. It may well be that I heard Uncle Leopold and Mamma talking about her when I was a child. Uncle Leopold had adored his young wife. He was with her all through that dreadful labour (just as Albert stayed with me through each of mine – they

14

made tender husbands, those Coburg men!). He held her hand, whispering words of comfort, sometimes lying down on the bed with her; and when she died his heart broke. Now I wonder, was it from him that I learned so early to be afraid of childbirth? Always, even before I could really know the significance of it, I feared that dark side to married life with a deep and instinctive dread. Were there whispered conversations, perhaps, when they thought I was not listening, or too young to understand? Did their words slip into my mind like carelessly dropped seed, and take root? Children do absorb all sorts of things one is not aware of, sometimes remembering them only years later when they have grown old enough to understand ideas that they acquired merely as meaningless sounds.

Princess Charlotte lives in the back of my mind, like the memory of an older sister, loved in childhood, and lost untimely. There were similarities between us: both of us Hanoverians, both heirs to the Throne of England, both expected to make good the damage done to monarchy's reputation by our uncles; and we both married Coburg princes, whom we adored. It was almost as if the accident of her death had not been intended by God, so that He had been forced to begin again with me. If that was so, I need never have feared to suffer her fate: mine was her life fulfilled. Is that being too fanciful? I can't be sure. It is a fanciful time of night, and lamplight always leaves shadows in the corners of rooms, like a speaker's unexplained hesitations which hint at unrevealed truths. I don't think it is fanciful to assert that God has a purpose in everything, and that He had to go to a great deal of trouble to bring me to the Throne of England, none of which would have been necessary if Charlotte and her infant son had not died.

How did it come about, then, that she was the sole heiress? It was not my grandfather's fault. King George III had done his duty amply by the royal nurseries: fifteen children he had fathered, of whom twelve were still living in 1817. (Fifteen! When I think of my poor grandmother, my heart aches for her! She must have had the constitution of an ox, for she lived into her seventies even so.) But among his daughters, the three who were married were all childless and the two unmarried ones were over forty. As for his seven sons – Papa and my Wicked Uncles – well, the Duke once said they were the veriest millstone ever to hang about the neck of a government, with their extravagance, their political wranglings, and above all their irregular private lives!

It was the fault, according to Lord Melbourne, of the Royal Marriages Act, which said that any marriage contracted without the

King's consent was invalid. The intention of the Act was to keep the royal line free from unsuitable blood, by preventing the princes from being trapped into marriage by wily adventuresses, or scheming mammas; but in reality its effect was to allow the princes to behave as badly as possible by all manner of young women, without ever having to face the consequences.

'I don't wonder they ran a little wild,' Lord M. told me. 'There they were, princes, all very handsome men, and the women would hang upon their necks, you know – ' (with that little nod of his, as if, indeed, I *did* know – entrancing suggestion to a girl barely out of the schoolroom!). 'The Marriage Act may have been a good thing in many ways,' he went on, 'but still it sent them out like so many wild beasts into society. In general it is a check on a man, that if he feels too much about a girl he must marry her; but they were, as it were, quite untouchable. They made love where they would, and then said oh, they were very sorry, they couldn't marry.' His droll look as he imitated an apologetic prince in that situation made me laugh very much.

In fact, four of my uncles *were* married; but the Prince Regent, father of poor dead Charlotte, hated his wife (the strange, unwashed, pipe-smoking Caroline of Brunswick) and had been separated from her for years. He had actually tried to divorce her, but Parliament still remembered the embarrassing saga of Henry VIII's children and did not want to go through all that again; so he could not remarry, and he would certainly never breed from Caroline again. Uncle York, the second son, had married a perfectly respectable Prussian princess, but they were childless and she was past childbearing now. She had become very eccentric, lived alone in the country surrounded by hundreds of pet animals and birds and, they said, never went to bed; but Uncle York was fond of her, and would not think of divorcing her.

Wicked, violent-tempered Uncle Cumberland, the fifth son, had married a twice-widowed woman who was rumoured to have murdered her previous spouses and was – fortunately perhaps! – so far childless. Uncle Sussex, the sixth son, had actually married twice, and even had children by his first wife, but as he had done it both times without the King's permission, neither marriage counted and the children could not succeed.

So that left the three unmarried princes. There was my uncle William of Clarence, the third son, who had served in the Navy and was Nelson's friend, and had lived comfortably in extremely domestic sin for twenty years with an actress, Mrs Jordan, and their ten lusty bastard children, my Fitzclarence cousins. There was my uncle Adolphus of Cambridge, the youngest son, who had lived mostly in Hanover to avoid running up debts; and there was Papa, the Duke of Kent, driven by debt to live in Belgium (horrid fate for any man of taste and intelligence!) with his fond and faithful Madame Julie.

Poor Julie's fortunes, however, were already on the wane. Papa hated living in Brussels so much that he had been driven to contemplate a desperate expedient. He could not go home without clearing his debts, and the only possible way left open to him to acquire money was to marry. If he married in accordance with the Royal Marriages Act, Parliament would be forced to increase his allowance, and perhaps give him a capital sum to discharge his debts as well. My uncle York had been given £25,000 on *his* marriage; surely, Papa reasoned, they could not give him less than that? So without mentioning it to Julie, he began discreetly to look about him for a wife.

At that time, in 1817, he was still in regular communication with Princess Charlotte, and he confided his problem to her. Since her marriage, Charlotte had struck up an affectionate correspondence with her husband's sister, the widowed Princess Victoire of Leiningen, who lived in seclusion at Amorbach with her two children, Charles and Feodore. The princess was thirty, said to be pretty, with fine dark eyes and a fresh complexion, and Charlotte assured Papa that she was warm-hearted, honest, affectionate, and of a generous and unselfish nature. What could Papa want more? Armed with a letter of introduction from Charlotte, he travelled to Amorbach in August 1817 (while the unsuspecting Julie was visiting her sister in Paris), met the Dowager Princess, found her charming, proposed – and was refused. Disappointed, he returned to Brussels and his companion and resumed his futile life. Princess Charlotte was with child; the odds at that time must have been heavily against my ever being born, let alone coming to the Throne.

But three months later Charlotte and her child died, and the constitutional crisis filled all the newspapers. Either Papa, or Uncle Clarence, or Uncle Cambridge *must* now marry and get an heir: it was not a matter of expedience any more, but of duty. Poor Julie, all unknowing, opened the London paper one Sunday morning and read an editorial urging the three Dukes to marry, and fainted dead away beside the breakfast-table. Papa tried to comfort her, and – being so very fond of her – put off pressing his suit at Amorbach; but when he learned that Uncle Cambridge had already been accepted by

Princess Augusta of Hesse-Cassel and was thus a good length in front in what the newspapers called 'The Succession Stakes', he dared not delay any further. He wrote again to Amorbach pressing for an immediate answer. This time it was favourable. (Grandmamma Coburg once told me, with her usual frankness, that the case was very different on this second application: before, Papa had been only a balding, penniless, middle-aged duke deep in debt; now he, or at least his son, might be King of England one day. But they were her words, not Mamma's.)

Lord Melbourne told me that Papa was very sorry indeed when he was obliged to put Madame Julie away. 'But it couldn't be helped, you know.' I was glad to hear from Lord M. that Papa behaved very properly by her, providing for her retirement to Paris as generously as he was able, treating her with tact and affection, and continuing to oversee her welfare until his death. 'But in any case, royal mistresses know what they are going in for,' Lord M. said. 'They begin with their eyes open.' I suppose that is true.

So Papa and Mamma were married by the Lutheran rite at Amorbach on the 29th of May 1818, and then Papa brought Mamma home to England for a second ceremony. It was a double wedding at Kew Palace in the presence of my grandmother (my poor grandfather, of course, was hopelessly mad by then, and was kept shut up at Windsor). The other couple were Uncle Clarence and the Princess Adelaide of Saxe-Meiningen – my dear, dearest aunt Adelaide, who was so fond of me, and was as kind to me in my childhood as a Certain Person would allow her to be. The Prince Regent gave the brides away and provided the wedding breakfast at Carlton House, which, considering how much he hated Papa, was probably the most that could be expected.

After a short honeymoon at Uncle Leopold's house at Claremont, Mamma and Papa returned to his apartment at Kensington Palace and waited for Parliament to announce the increased pension. It was a deep disappointment. Instead of the £25,000 a year he had hoped for, he was awarded only £6,000, and no capital sum at all. Marrying Mamma had already increased his debts: she was extravagant, and he was generous and fond, and he had spent heavily on hats and gowns, jewellery, horses, perfume, and a pianoforte for his charming new duchess. Creditors began pressing, the Prince Regent was hostile, and my grandmother, perhaps fearing Papa might try to borrow from her, suggested firmly that it would be better for him to leave the country. There seemed no alternative, and so in September, much against his will, he took Mamma back to Amorbach.

4th February 1900

WHEN I was grown up and had children of my own, Mamma and I became friends again, and we spent a great deal of time together, talking fondly and without reserve, enjoying the relationship we should have had earlier, if it had not been for a Certain Person. And in those warm, lovely years, she told me about Papa, and her marriage to him, and how I came to be born. I can hear her voice now, if I close my eyes, very German even after thirty-five years in England, interspersed with 'Zo,' a sort of articulated sigh, which did service as punctuation, underlining, and a requisition for missing vocabulary. She had always been plump, and in her autumn years she spread comfortably into a grandmotherly shape; but her little beringed fingers never lost their nimbleness, her sweet, good-natured face remained as smooth as an apple and her eyes were as dark and bright as ever. She had always loved hats – all her early portraits show her dark-eyed and smiling under a wide brim and long, drooping feathers – and in old age she transferred the love to her caps, which were always gorgeous confections of lace and knots and ribbons. 'One wants to eat them,' Vicky once said, and I knew just what she meant.

Mamma's first marriage had been unhappy. The Prince of Leiningen was a great deal older than her, a cold, harsh man who had no interest in her beyond the getting of an heir. He had lived in one palace deep in the heart of the forest where he spent his days hunting, while his young wife lived all alone with the children in another, with nothing to do and no-one to talk to, and without even any control over her own household, for the Prince handled everything, down to the choosing of the servants.

From this isolation, she was rescued by Papa. 'I liked him at once,' Mamma told me. 'How could I not? He was so charming, and he *talked*! Such a beautiful, musical voice, and he had a way of choosing exactly the right subject to interest each person. Oh, I could have chatted to him all day long! After such silences, my Victoria, you can't think how *comfortable* it was!'

She had no English and he had no German, so they spoke in French, in which Papa was fluent – not only in the formal language, but in the things one might say to a lady. (No love is ever wasted, you see: twenty-seven years with poor Madame Julie had given him the skills to make Princess Victoire happy.) 'When he spoke French,' Mamma told me, 'it was like singing.' Papa had a good singing-voice

19

too; they shared a love of music, and of riding. His formal proposal to her, after only two days of acquaintance, was like a poem. She was so charming, he wrote, and her manners and accomplishments were so exactly to his taste, that he would count it the greatest good fortune if she would accept his hand. They would spend the winters in Brussels, where he had an excellent house, the summers in Amorbach, and pay short visits to England; and in each other's company, with good music and good horses, no day would ever be too long. Finally he assured her that if he should have the happiness of possessing her, he would cherish her dear children as his own.

'How could you refuse?' I asked her in astonishment. She put her hands to her face. '*Ach*, I was a villain! How could I indeed? But you know, my first husband was so unkind, and I hardly knew Papa then; and I would have lost my pension, which was £5,000 a year of my very own, and Papa had nothing. But love will out, you know. It was meant to be.'

'Were you happy together?' I asked, not doubting it, but wanting to be told.

'Oh, so happy! He was so very *kind*, and not at all the sort of husband men usually are. He was a companion to me, you see, not holding himself aloof, but always interested in what I did and said, and how I felt, and whether I was happy. From the day we were married until the day he died we were never parted, and there was never a cross word between us. I adored him, and I felt I was so lucky to win a man so clever and wise, who had seen so much of the world, who could *manage* things so cleverly; but he said *he* was the lucky one, being nothing but an old soldier, and most unfit to win the heart of a beautiful young princess nineteen years his junior.' She drew out her handkerchief and touched away a tear from the corner of her eye, and added earnestly, 'But I never felt the difference in our ages, you know – except that he took care of me, took all the decisions, and made me feel so *safe*!'

So as Duke and Duchess of Kent they arrived back at Amorbach in October 1818. Charles was away at school in Switzerland, but Feo was at home, and Papa soon won her heart too. 'He was always good with young people,' Mamma said. 'It was so pretty to see them together. Feo adored him.'

And their happiness was crowned in November, when Mamma knew for sure that she was with child. 'So soon,' she said to me, with a nod and a blush, and I understood what she meant: that Papa was her lover as well as her husband – anyone who has known the blessing of that will understand the distinction. Some of the tenderness between them is revealed in a letter she showed me, that he wrote to her on New Year's Eve, 1818. I have it still, and treasure it; some phrases I know by heart now, after reading it so often.

> This evening will put an end, dear well-beloved Victoire, to the year 1818, which saw the birth of my happiness by giving you to me as my guardian angel . . .
>
> All my efforts are directed to one end, the preservation of your dear health and the birth of a child who will resemble you, and if Heaven will give me these two blessings I shall be consoled for all my misfortunes and disappointments . . .
>
> I would have wished to be able to say all this to you in pretty verses, but you know that I am an old soldier who has not this talent, and so you must take the good will for the deed . . .
>
> Remember that this comes from your very deeply attached and devoted husband, for whom you represent all happiness and all consolation . . .
>
> So I tell you in the language of my country, *God bless you, love me as I love you* . . .

As soon as he knew of Mamma's condition, Papa was determined to bring her home to England. Amorbach was not a healthy place for a confinement – badly ventilated and fifty miles from the nearest town; and besides, Papa was determined that his child would be born on English soil. It could perhaps be the heir to the Throne, and if it was born on foreign soil, its legitimacy as heir might one day be questioned.

'He was always quite sure in his own mind that his child would succeed to the Throne,' Mamma told me. 'He used to say to me, "Victoire, I am the strongest of the family, and I have lived a regular life, not like my brothers. I shall outlive them all, and the crown will come to me and my children."' She sighed. 'He expected to be King himself one day, you see, poor Edward!'

It should have been a blow to his hopes when the news arrived from Hanover, where the Clarences and Cambridges were all living, that both duchesses were also with child, and due to be confined in March or April. Papa was only the fourth son, and although the Regent and my uncle York might be discounted as providers of heirs, and any Cambridge child would come after Papa's, still my uncle Clarence's child would come before his.

'All the same,' Mamma said, pursing her lips, 'childbirth is always an uncertain thing; and I had already had two healthy children, while the Duchess of Clarence was approaching my age and quite untried. Twenty-six is a great age for a primipart after all. Without wishing her ill in any way, one never knew what might happen. Papa believed it was essential we go back to England.'

It was easier wished than done, for a man deep in debt. Papa wrote frantic letters to everyone he could think of to try to raise the necessary money for the journey, but it was not until March 1819 that he had managed to collect enough. Then he wrote in triumph to the Regent to say that they would be arriving at Calais on the 18th of April, and requesting the use of the royal yacht to make the crossing, and the use of the apartment at Kensington Palace which had formerly been occupied by Caroline of Brunswick. Since it would cost him nothing, the Regent agreed, though reluctantly, adding that he deeply regretted his brother should have decided on such a journey so late in the day. He had some reason for his objection: Mamma was only eight weeks away from the date of her confinement.

Two

15th February 1900, at Osborne

A MUCH better day today, the storms all cleared away; even a little sunshine, so we shall have a pleasant drive this afternoon. Georgie and May and the little boys are to come to luncheon. Of course I could never say so in front of them – indeed, I would never say so to anyone, though I'm sure many people must think it – but I can't help feeling it is a good thing for my country that the Throne will go to Georgie at last, after Bertie, instead of to Georgie's poor brother. I grieved when Eddy died, and truly I was very fond of the poor boy, but there was something unsatisfactory about him all the same – slack-twisted, they used to say when I was a girl – and I doubt whether he would have made a good king. God arranges these things for the best, though one does not always see it at the time. One must have faith. Georgie will be a hardworking, conscientious king, and May is a very sensible, clever girl and will make the most of him. She is my poor dear cousin Mary Cambridge's daughter, but could not be more different from her ramshackle, hoydenish mother!

Those tight little, plump little hands of May's will never throw money about as Cousin Mary did. (When Mary died just three years ago it was discovered she had not even made a Will, which caused a great deal of trouble. And then the embalmers did not do their work properly which was shocking and *most* disagreeable! It upset me so much that I at once made very detailed arrangements for my own funeral, and made sure that copies were distributed to several people so that there can be no mistakes when the time comes.)

Mark you, Georgie, for all his sensibleness now, has had his wild moments. Once when he was a little boy he was being so naughty at the luncheon table that I told him he must sit *underneath* the table until he could behave himself. He disappeared under the cloth and was very quiet for a while, and then his little voice piped up, 'I'm good now, Grandmamma. May I come out?'

'Very well then, my dear,' I said, and he lifted up the tablecloth and clambered out – stark naked! He had taken off every stitch under the table, and capered before me now displaying the wide grin of one who knows he has just played the ace of trumps. I almost choked with laughter, and had to put my napkin over my face so that he shouldn't think I was encouraging him. I can never see him now, so solemn and bearded and grown up, without remembering that glorious moment and seeing in my mind's eye that little naked, knock-kneed imp! He must wonder sometimes why I smile so broadly when he appears!

Georgie's eldest, David, is a fine little boy too – such a friendly, intelligent child. He doesn't like to see me in my chair, and cannot understand why I do not get up and run about and play with him. He takes hold of my hand and tugs at it and says, 'Get up, Gangan! Get up!' and then tries to push my chair himself – but of course it is too heavy for him. So he looks about for a servant, and has a wonderfully imperious way of ordering them to push my chair for him. There is no doubt whose blood he has in him!

I have done my 'Boxes' and written my 'duty' letters, so I have a little time to go on with my story. Really the sunshine today is so pleasant after the storms that I am quite rejuvenated. When Reid came up for the usual morning consultation, I felt so benevolent I allowed him to listen to my heart, just for a treat. He seemed considerably impressed with it.

What a journey that must have been for Mamma! No railway trains then, but four hundred and fifty miles by carriage, and the Continental roads indescribably bad (indeed, they are not much better now in my opinion), and then at the end of it a sea-crossing over one of the worst stretches of water in the civilised world!

'Weren't you afraid?' I asked Mamma.

'Not very much,' she said. 'The eighth month is safer than the seventh, you know, and I trusted Papa. He would not have asked it if he thought it was too dangerous. And he thought of everything for my comfort. No woman could have taken more tender care of me than he did.'

Papa drove Mamma himself in a light phaeton, which he thought would jolt her less over the frightful ruts than a heavier closed carriage; he was a fine whip, and the phaeton was drawn by his own pair of beautiful, silken-mouthed black mares, whom he knew to a hair. Such an extraordinary caravan followed in their wake: a landau carrying Feo's attendants and the English maids, then a travelling barouche with Mamma's woman, Baroness Späth, and the midwife, then the post-chaise, empty, in case of bad weather; another chaise carrying Feo and her governess, a cabriolet with two cooks, a cart loaded with plate, a spare phaeton drawn by Papa's second pair, a gig carrying Papa's valet and Mamma's footman, another carrying the clerks (Papa's correspondence was always very heavy); then a curricle driven by Papa's physician (Dr Wilson, late of HMS *Hussar*) and finally another cart carrying Mamma's bedstead and bedding.

'How people stared as we passed! And how hard it was to find a place every night with room for us all,' Mamma exclaimed to me. 'We went by very easy stages, for Papa was afraid of tiring me too much – though indeed I was very well, I assure you! – but oh, how sick I was of sitting day after day, for three weeks!'

I knew just how she felt. I always hated travelling in carriages, being bumped and jolted until one was black and blue, aching in every muscle from the effort of keeping upright, and nauseous from the lurching and swaying. The 'royal progresses' I was forced to undertake in my youth were the most severe trial to me. Thank God we now have railways!

They reached Calais safely by the appointed day, and there the news from Hanover was awaiting them: the Duchess of Cambridge had given birth to a healthy boy on the 26th of March, and on the 27th the Duchess of Clarence had had a baby girl, which had lived only a few hours.

My poor, dear aunt Adelaide! How she loved children, and how she longed for one of her own! But God did not mean it to be. It must have broken her gentle heart. I have never lost a baby – thank God! – though I have lost two of my children in adulthood. It is a pain that cannot be healed, to lose a child. But Aunt Adelaide's loss at that time meant Papa's expected baby was one step nearer the Throne, and his strange certainty that his line would inherit was strengthened.

The wind did not come favourable until the 24th of April, and when they at last embarked the Channel was very rough. The strong wind at least meant a short crossing, but Mamma was very sick indeed all the way to Dover. Was I aware of it, I wonder, cradled in her womb? Did I carry the memory with me into the world? At all events, I am always sick on boats – though not, I have to say, as sick as my poor darling Albert, whose delicate stomach seized any opportunity to make its presence known to him. Still at last that evening, pale, weary and heartily sick of travelling, Papa and Mamma arrived at Kensington Palace. And there, a month later, on Monday the 24th of May 1819, I made my entrance into this sinful world.

A chilly morning it was, with a light rain falling, sparrows calling to each other from the dripping hedges, and blackbirds running across the wet green lawns beyond the long windows. In the next room the Duke of Wellington waited, along with my uncle Sussex, the Archbishop of Canterbury, the Bishop of London, the Marquess of Lansdowne, the egregious Mr Canning, the Secretary for War, and the Chancellor of the Exchequer. As the grey dawn broke over Kensington Papa led them into the lying-in chamber in order to sign, in their official capacity and according to custom, the birth certificate and the attestation that I appeared perfectly healthy.

Indeed, there was no difficulty about that: it had been a short and easy labour (in so far as any labour ever is) and I was plainly a lusty child: 'a pretty little princess, plump as a partridge', was how Uncle Leopold's secretary Dr Stockmar described me when he saw me soon afterwards.

'But still, only a girl,' I said to Mamma. 'Wasn't Papa very disappointed?'

'Not at all. He said that the decrees of Providence were always the best and wisest. And besides,' she added with a reflective smile, 'he said that a gypsy fortune-teller he met in Gibraltar years ago had told him he would one day have a daughter who was destined to become a great queen.'

Was it true? When I was young I believed in the gypsy story with all my heart; it showed my destiny was long foretold, and it fitted into the pattern of my belief that God had arranged everything deliberately to bring me to the Throne. But later when I discussed the story with Albert, he pointed out logically that it was much more likely Papa had only said that to comfort Mamma, who had more or less promised him a son, as women do, and must have been feeling disappointed. Of course, I saw immediately that Albert was right and that indeed it must have been so. But in recent years I have returned to my old belief. There are more things in heaven and earth than can be explained by simple logic. After all, Papa did not say, as he so easily might have (and as Albert and I did when Vicky was born) that the next baby would surely be a boy. He mentioned no next child, as if he had always known there would only be the one. From the very beginning he presented me to his friends as the future Queen of England; and he never wavered in his insistence that I should be brought up in England, as an English child, so that I should be fit to succeed to the Throne. I believe now that he knew in his heart I was to be his only child, and was to take Princess Charlotte's place as the Hope of the Nation.

Papa stayed with Mamma every moment all through the labour – as Uncle Leopold had stayed with Charlotte, as Albert always stayed with me. How lucky we were in our husbands, we three women! It is a strange coincidence that these were three constitutionally important marriages between Coburgs and Hanoverians, all marriages of great love and great happiness, and all cut off untimely. There *are* patterns, though we are not always clever enough to see them at the time, or to understand what they mean.

My Coburg grandmother saw and believed. 'Again a Charlotte!' she wrote to Papa in reply to his letter announcing my birth. 'Do not worry that it is not a boy. The English like Queens.'

Now here is another pattern, of which even Albert had to admit the significance: in his letter to Grandmamma Coburg, Papa praised the conduct and skill of the midwife, Madame Siebold, saying no-one could have shown more activity, zeal and knowledge in the care of her patient. When Mamma was out of confinement, Madame Siebold returned to Coburg to take care of Mamma's sister-in-law Louise, the pretty, nineteen-year-old wife of Mamma's brother Duke Ernst, who was expecting her second child. And three months later, on the 26th of August, Madame Siebold delivered the Duchess of Saxe-Coburg of a fine boy, 'as lively as a squirrel'. In due course he was christened with the names Francis Charles Augustus Albert Emmanuel; but he was always known in the family as Albert.

16th February 1900

THE NEWS are much better today, which together with the improvement in the weather makes me feel vastly more cheerful. General Buller is advancing again (though not nearly fast enough in my view), and Lord Roberts' feint to draw the Boers off seems to be working, for we have had reports that they are beginning to melt away in front of Ladysmith. Thank God White refused to surrender! If only he can hold out a while longer, I am sure Lord Roberts' stratagems will work. He has sent French (youngest of our generals and a good, energetic man – I do not hold a man must be ancient to be wise) with the cavalry round to the north to the aid of Kimberley, so we are waiting for news on two fronts now. And orders are to go out at last for the 8th Division – though if I had carried my point they would have been sent three weeks ago and would be on hand already. However if Roberts can take Bloemfontein he will have the advantage of the railway to bring up supplies and men, which will make all the difference to his campaign.

I am godmother now to three little boys whose fathers have been killed in South Africa. Today was the Christening-day of one of them (he is to be called Albert Victor, for my sake, and then Thomas after his father) and the circumstance reminds me of my own Christening, which I will write about to keep my mind off the waiting for telegrams.

Sadly, my Christening was the occasion of a great deal of ill-feeling. The fact of the matter was that the Regent had always hated Papa, and now that his own, only child was in her grave, it must have been gall and wormwood for him to see Papa so happy in possession of a new and vigorously healthy baby – 'more like a pocket Hercules than a pocket Venus,' as Papa once described me. 'My daughter is too healthy to please some of my family,' he said, and the idea that Papa's blood might inherit the Throne certainly seemed to drive the Regent to distraction. Besides, Papa was not the most tactful of men, and he let it be known that he regarded my infant vigour as the just reward for the rectitude of his own life. 'My health remains unimpaired,' he said, 'as I have a right to expect from the life I have always led.' His brother the Regent, grossly fat and unwell, with his swollen legs, violent headaches, and pains in the stomach and bladder, could not have heard such comments with much pleasure.

Papa had asked the Regent to be my godfather, along with Tsar Alexander of Russia, and he had already chosen the names for me:

27

Victoire (after Mamma) Georgina (after the Regent) Alexandrina (after the Tsar) Charlotte (after the late Princess Charlotte of Wales) and Augusta (after Grandmamma Coburg). He submitted the names for approval to the Regent with his usual breezy self-confidence; and as he heard nothing more, he assumed they were acceptable. It was for the Regent to fix the date for the Christening, and he chose Monday the 24th of June, but he did not announce it even to Papa until the Friday, giving him only two days' notice on purpose to annoy. And then he announced that it was to be held in the Cupola Room at Kensington Palace, not in the Chapel Royal, and was to be a private ceremony only. That meant no uniforms were to be worn and there were to be no foreign dignitaries or eminent guests. How disappointed Papa must have been! No gold lace, no swords, no feathers, no glitter, no pomp – just immediate members of the family in plain, dull frock coats, as if I were just anyone's baby being 'dipped'. The Regent didn't want anything to suggest that I was in any way important to anyone but my parents. 'The plan,' Papa said furiously to Mamma, 'is evidently to keep me down. Some members of the family seem to regard my little girl as an intruder!'

A further blow came when as late as the Sunday evening, a message arrived from the Regent that I could not be given the name Georgina, after him, since it would not be protocol for the name to precede that of the Tsar, and he did not care to have it follow. As to the other names, the message continued, the Regent would speak to Papa about them at the ceremony.

That was leaving it to the last minute, indeed! In fact, according to Mamma, it was not until the Archbishop of Canterbury actually had me dangling over the font that the Regent suddenly announced the names Charlotte and Augusta were not to be used either.

'There was a dreadful silence,' Mamma told me. 'Edward looked at me and I at him, both of us very much wounded by the announcement, and by the manner of it. Everyone else avoided each other's eyes in embarrassment, for it was quite plainly just spite and jealousy – he did not want you to have any name that was at all royal.'

After a moment, the Archbishop, feeling things ought to proceed before he dropped me on my head, gently enquired in what name he was to baptise the child after all.

'Call her Alexandrina,' the Regent snapped. 'After the Emperor, her godfather.'

(This may have been spoken in tones of bitter sarcasm. Lord Melbourne told me that Papa had chosen the Tsar as my godfather

28

on purpose to annoy the Regent, who hated him. The thing was that the Regent hated Uncle Leopold and illogically but understandably blamed him for the death of Princess Charlotte; and the Tsar was Uncle Leopold's friend and patron.)

Alexandrina was all very well, but a single name – and not an English, royal name at that – was hardly enough for such an illustrious baby. 'But a second name,' Papa protested. 'May she not have a second name? What does Your Royal Highness say to Elizabeth? Might I urge Your Royal Highness to consider the name Elizabeth for the infant?'

'Certainly not,' the Regent barked (I wonder, were his legs particularly painful that day?). 'That is a name for queens. She shall not have that.'

By this time Mamma was in floods of tears under her large, feathered hat. Uncle Leopold was glaring daggers, and the Princesses Sophia and Augusta were staring hard at the carpet as if they hoped the floor might open and admit them. Still Papa, his face very red as he struggled to keep his temper, urged for a second name. 'She cannot be called Alexandrina only.'

At last the Regent said, rudely, 'Oh, very well, call her after the mother, then.' (*The* mother, you notice, not *her* mother: I was just a disagreeable object to him.)

But Papa brightened, glad to have taken one point at least. 'Victoire, then?' he said. It had been his first choice after all.

'Victoria,' the Regent corrected triumphantly; 'but the name cannot precede that of the Emperor.'

And so it was that I was christened Alexandrina Victoria; and that evening Papa and Mamma gave a dinner-party at Kensington Palace by way of celebration, to which the Regent pointedly refused to come. Three months later he publicly snubbed Papa at the Spanish Ambassador's reception, and the junior members of the family, dependent on his whims, followed suit. Thereafter, it was open season on the Kent family at Kensington. For anyone who wanted the Regent's favour, we were The Untouchables.

But in spite of that, the summer of 1819 was a happy time for my father, probably the happiest time of his life. He and Mamma loved each other more every day, and the pleasant domesticity he had enjoyed with poor Madame de St Laurent was heightened with Mamma by the addition of a pretty and affectionate step-daughter (Feo often told me how much she loved Papa – 'He was always so kind to me!'), and a fat and lusty baby who would very soon, he was sure, be openly acknowledged as the Heiress of England. The royal family might ignore and insult him, but there was nothing they could do about that.

Only my poor aunt Adelaide could prevent it; and that summer she discovered she was again with child. Uncle Clarence, following Papa's example, decided to bring her home from Hanover to have the baby in England, but poor Aunt Adelaide was not as robust as Mamma: she miscarried on the journey. So Papa was safe again, and he and Mamma entertained at Kensington Palace in high good humour, gave dinners and musical evenings, went together to reviews and the theatre, and took us children to visit Uncle Leopold at Claremont.

The only cloud on the horizon was Papa's permanent problem of finance; his income would barely have been enough for a careful and single man, and Papa was neither. He bought with a lavish hand: new furniture and drapes for the apartments, carpets, looking-glasses and pictures; a new carriage, clothes and endless hats for Mamma; fine wines, books and horses for himself – and all without any idea how they were to be paid for. By the autumn his long-suffering creditors were pressing again, and it became clear that both for economy's sake, and to avoid unpleasant encounters, our little family would have to leave London.

It would have been shameful to Papa publicly to admit that he, a royal duke, could not support his family in the style he felt was appropriate; and so to save face, he gave out that he was taking us to the seaside so that Mamma could enjoy warm sea-baths for her rheumatism.

'Which I did have,' Mamma assured me, 'so it was not wholly a falsehood, which he hated; but my aches were more disagreeable than alarming.'

Papa and his equerry went off in October to look for a suitable house. Devon – fatal Devon! – was what they picked on, too remote for creditors to follow them, yet blessed with a temperate climate. After a long search they fixed on Sidmouth, where they found Woolbrook Cottage, a 'cottage orné' only a hundred and fifty yards from the beach, which had a bathing-house for taking warm salt baths. So it was that we left London at last in December, and arrived on Christmas Day 1819, in the middle of a snowstorm, at Woolbrook Cottage.

'*Ach*, it was a dreadful house!' Mamma told me, growing agitated even at the memory. 'So dark and musty – impossible to keep warm!'

A gimcrack place, I imagine it – a cramped thing of low ceilings, inconvenient passages and damp plaster walls; nothing more than a primitive cot with rickety bays and balconies added on after the School of the Picturesque. It was usually let as a summer cottage, but it had been empty for some months at that time, and showed it. The situation would have been delightful in summer – a wooded valley, secluded, green and smiling – but in winter such places become sullen, grey and dripping, cut off from the world by fathoms of mud, and infinitely depressing.

'That was a *schreckliches* winter, so many storms, such piercing winds! Even when the sun shone, the air was so sharp it hurt one's chest; and, oh, the nights were bitter! Papa called them "rather Canadian",' Mamma added with a faint, sad smile.

To add further to the unpleasantness, something disagreed with Papa and he suffered a severe gastric attack, which pulled him down dreadfully. 'The water here plays the very deuce with my bowels,' he wrote to Uncle Leopold. Added to his worries about the future, it did not reconcile Papa to this new sentence of exile. Mamma occupied herself indoors with her English lessons (with which she was not making much progress), obediently took her warm salt bath every day, and took Feo for long walks on the seashore. Papa spent the days writing letters in the hope of bettering his situation, and playing with me in front of the fire (oh, I *wish* I could remember that!).

'You were his whole consolation, my Victoria. You were so strong and healthy – as well grown as a child of a year, though you were only seven months old. You cut your first two teeth without the slightest trouble, and Papa used to love to make you laugh, so that he could see them. Such a sunny baby, you were! But wilful, too. Even at that tender age you showed signs of wanting your own little way – and knowing how to get it!'

Papa was reluctantly coming to the conclusion that there was nothing for it but to go back to Amorbach, which at least would be better than a hovel in Devon; but first there was the Christmas season to survive. We all had colds, and Papa's was the worst, but in spite of it he insisted on going out in the blustery rain on the 7th of January to see to the horses, and came back chilled to the bone and with wet feet. The next day he was feverish.

'Still, it was only a cold, you know,' Mamma told me. 'People had colds every day, and Papa was always so strong, so healthy.' Her eyes grew dark with remembered pain. 'It was the doctors who killed him.'

Dr Wilson, who had accompanied us to Devon, first dosed Papa with the usual remedies of calomel and James's Powder, but they proved ineffective; and when the fever mounted, and Papa developed pains in the chest, he prescribed bleeding. In those dreadful, primitive days, bleeding – either by leech or by knife – was considered the sovereign cure for any fever or inflammation. Indeed, in the eyes of some physicians, it was the specific for every ailment! How far we have advanced since then in medical science – oh, but too late, too late for Papa!

Wilson bled him again the following day, but he was still no better, and now Mamma, beginning to be frightened, sent to London for Sir David Dundas, the royal physician who had known Papa from childhood. Meanwhile she stayed with Papa day and night, nursing him with tender devotion. The house was bitterly cold – that raw, clammy cold which is by far the hardest to bear. No fire seemed to have any effect on the dank atmosphere, and the windows leaked like sieves. Feo had a chill, and I had succumbed to a sneezing cold which gave Mamma some concern, but she could spare little attention for us from her worries over Papa. He now had dreadful pains in his head, as well as in his chest and side, and had difficulty breathing. Dr Wilson applied blisters to Papa's chest; and when that did not help he cupped him all over – an agonising process – even on his poor head, in the hope that it would relieve the headaches; but all to no avail.

'For four hours he tormented my poor Edward,' Mamma said, 'and it nearly made me sick. I could hardly bear to watch, but whatever happened, I would not leave him for a moment.' When the cupping failed to relieve, Wilson bled Papa again.

At last on the 17th the doctor arrived from London; but it was not Sir David Dundas. 'It seemed the old King was very ill and Sir David could not leave him,' Mamma told me, 'so he sent Dr Matet instead, which put me in despair because Matet had little French and I had little English, so we could not talk together.'

Worse than Matet's lack of French, however, was his firm belief in bleeding. Despite the fact that Papa had been relieved already of six pints of blood, Matet applied the leeches once more.

'I protested – Papa was so weak, I said surely it could not be right to drain him further – but Matet said on the contrary, he had not been bled enough, and that as he was of a full habit and high constitution he could bear much more.'

And so it went on like a mediaeval torture, the cupping and bleeding, until there was no part of Papa's body which did not bear the marks.

'He bore it all so patiently, but he was so white he was almost blue, and getting weaker and weaker, having such pain just to draw his breath.'

away from St James's for its inmates to be conveniently forgotten. My feelings about the place were tainted so much with the unhappiness of my last years there, that having left it when I became Queen, I neglected it for many years, and it almost fell down. But I visited it last year when the restoration work was finished, and had to admit that it was a very pretty building after all – though for me still haunted. I could not look at it without painful recollections.

Yet I had happy times there too – the first six or seven years of my life were almost entirely happy, I suppose. Our apartments were on the ground floor, which meant damp and black beetles and mice. In winter the rooms had that mushroomy, cellary smell, and sometimes we would find mould growing on clothes which had been hung up and not worn for some time. I didn't mind the mice particularly – I am not squeamish like some women – but they sometimes ate our shoes and books, and we were never wealthy enough for that not to matter. But being on the ground floor gave us the advantage of the gardens beyond the long windows, which, seeming to belong peculiarly to us, became like extra rooms in the summer. I remember lush lawns, gravel walks, handsome trees, and of course the pond, called The Basin, where Feo and I used to feed the ducks. Adult life, I suppose, has few pleasures which come close to the childhood delight of throwing bread to ducks. God might have created a more absurd and endearing creature, but it's very sure He never did!

When I was a child Kensington was still a country place, rich in orchards and market gardens providing food for London, and very quiet except for the mail coaches passing on the turnpike to Uxbridge and points west. Hyde Park in those days marked the western edge of London. North of the Uxbridge turnpike was open country and farmland; south of the Kensington road, where now the Albert Hall and dear Albert's museums and institutions stand, were large country residences of noblemen; and beyond them small, neat fields dotted with villages – Earl's Court, Old Brompton, Little Chelsea, Walham Green – linked by muddy country lanes.

Strange to think that there was a time when there was no street, square, house or memorial anywhere in the country named Albert, no single little English boy named Albert (for it was a strange, foreign, *German* name then) – and no little English girl named Victoria, either, except for me. England was a very different country then, only just beginning to be industrial, and London was more like a county town than the centre of an empire. Strange as it seems now, sheep, cattle and huge flocks of geese were driven along the roads to London and herded through the crowded streets to market. There was no electricity, no telephone, no modern conveniences; there were no railway trains (and *no* horrid motor-cars!) – only carts, carriages and dashing, dragonfly post-chaises; and everywhere the noble, the beautiful horse.

I loved horses, always, and so much enjoyed riding! When I first became Queen my delight was to ride out with Lord Melbourne and one or two gentlemen, to taste the freedom of going right out into the country – I would have spent all day in the saddle if I could. The countryside, of course, came right up to our door in those days: we had only to cross the road to be in open fields. Now they are all gone under rows and rows of identical terraced houses, packed tight like herrings in a box. In my Journal I recorded one day that we rode over the fields right out as far as Acton; today that would be impossible. The streets of houses stretch unbroken all the way to Ealing, where once Papa bought a secluded country villa!

When I was young I preferred a spirited horse that gave me something to do, and liked nothing better than a good gallop. I suppose I must have been a sadly wild young thing! Certainly under Albert's influence I came to see that it is not at all the thing for a young woman – indeed, for any woman – to ride *ventre à terre* like a Hussar; and I scolded Vicky quite fiercely after her marriage for rushing about the countryside on big, strong horses, instead of confining herself to a ladylike amble in the park. And Alice's daughter Victoria was another who liked to ride men's horses, which I told her roundly was neither seemly nor good for a woman's health. Yet sometimes I still have wistful dreams about galloping full out with the wind rushing past my cheeks and the exhilarating sound of drumming hooves beneath me. Plainly there is a wicked, unrepentant part of me somewhere that my darling did not quite manage to reform!

But such galloping was all in the future. My early life at Kensington was marked by austerity, to which I have always attributed my distaste for grand occasions, gorgeous robes and glittering palaces. And yet, since the purpose of this essay is to be honest with myself, I must admit I did not show any great dislike of fine clothes and grand occasions when I first became Queen. Banquets and balls and ceremonials and dressing-up seemed very fine to me for the first two years of my reign; it was only after I married that I began to yearn after the simple life of a private citizen. Ah, that was all my dear, dearest Albert's influence! How he did improve and refine me, to be sure!

In Mamma's household we lived simply, and the nursery food

was always very plain. Mutton and rice pudding featured so much on the menu, that by the time I became Queen I vowed to myself I would never have mutton on my table again, and I still can't care for it, though I will eat lamb if it is young, and roast. The sweet and the exotic – rich sauces, made dishes, cakes and custards and jellies – oh, all the things the palate delights in – these never appeared before me. That of course is just as it should be, and how I brought up my own children. Once I was Queen and could have what I liked, I indulged my thwarted appetite to the extent that within a year I was having my dresses made a size larger; and as I am a very short person, not even five feet in height, the full-bodiedness has in time rendered me almost *spherical*. Reid tries to tell me now and then that I should eat less, or at least avoid the richer dishes, but I ignore him. I have not reached eighty years of age to be told – even by my personal physician – to eat dry toast and milk-pudding again?

Now here is a thought which has just come to me: if I had been more indulged at the table in childhood, would I have been more rational about food in adulthood, and not rushed helter-skelter after all the sweetmeats and delicacies I had been denied? Bertie, who was brought up by the same spartan rule of mutton and rice-pudding, has also turned out a prodigious eater of dainties, and perhaps if they had not been 'forbidden fruit' he might not care about them now? But no, it does not follow, now I think of it, for Albert was brought up under a spartan regime, but he never came to care about food. And anyway, it would not do for children to be allowed to have everything, for what would there be then to look forward to? And since it seems we must always rebel against *something*, we would undoubtedly embrace some far worse sin than gluttony if nothing were forbidden us in our childhood!

I was a naturally good-natured child, I believe: certainly my desire was always to love and please those around me, and I had always sooner laugh than scowl; but I was born with a strong will and a passionate temper. A child born into a large family has to learn to share everything, but I had no-one near me to dilute my infant conviction that I was the centre of the universe. All in my circle were grown-ups, except for Feo, and she was twelve years older than me; all adored me and conspired to spoil me by consulting my whims and placating my temper. In consequence my wilfulness grew unchecked like a Russian vine, and if I were crossed in the slightest thing, I exploded in a tantrum. Mamma, my nurse Boppy (Mrs Brock), dear sentimental Späth (Mamma's lady-in-waiting), sweet, loving Feo, and of course all the servants, tended and watered my natural obstinacy, and my predisposition to want my own way. I could hardly help knowing I was important, when my every appearance in public aroused such interest. Whenever I played on the lawns at Kensington, an admiring crowd would gather beyond the railings to stare and murmur and applaud; and I, conceited little wretch, would bow and smile and kiss my hand to them, and if I could escape Boppy's clutches I would scamper across to them and let them make love to me, which they were much disposed to do. I adored attention, and I was an attractive child, fat and fair, rosy-cheeked and blue-eyed, always wreathed in smiles (as long as I was having my own way); and especially interesting to my future subjects by virtue of my obviously Hanoverian looks.

By the time I was five years old, therefore, I was almost beyond governing, and Mamma, who was not a very determined person, often despaired of me. She would wring her hands and cry, 'Vickelschen is so *ausgelassen!* The ladies of the household *will* spoil her, and I do not know how to stop them. Brock cannot manage her, and when she screams my poor nerves are all to pieces.'

Screaming was my most effective tool, and hardly to be borne in the confined spaces of our small apartments. Some of my own children turned out to be roarers, too, but in Buckingham Palace and at Windsor it was possible to get far enough away from them for it to be ignored. I can quite understand Mamma's placating me, though it was the wrong thing to do. In later years she told me of a significant exchange we once had when I was a very little girl. 'When you are naughty, Victoria, you make me and yourself very unhappy,' she said reproachfully. 'No, Mamma,' I said promptly – and probably smugly, for I was an abominable child, though very truthful – 'I don't make myself unhappy, only you.'

But when I was five I came under a new influence which was the saving of me: the influence of one who was not in awe of my Hanoverian temper, and who loved me well enough to understand that the greatest unkindness would be to give in to my rages. Baroness Lehzen had come to join our household in 1819 as Feo's governess, and so had known me since I was a few months old. Now that Feo was seventeen she no longer needed a governess; so after consulting with Uncle Leopold, Mamma sent Boppy away, and Lehzen took me into her charge. It was the beginning of a relationship which had a great effect on my character. Lehzen, intelligent, sensitive, principled and determined, devoted herself to moulding me into a rational, useful human being. It was not easy at first. The storms did not cease overnight. I did not take easily to lessons or to discipline, and I was often naughty and defiant. Once in a fit of rage I even threw a pair of scissors at her – point first! – which might easily have blinded her. But she was always calm, always just, and though she was very strict with me, I had wit enough to see that hers was a truer love than that of those who spoiled me. I was a good deal in awe of her at first, but I came at last not only to mind her but to love her; and for her part, she devoted herself entirely to me, and in the thirteen years she was my governess she never once left me. She never took a day's holiday, and never – despite her susceptibility to migraines and (at female times) dreadful abdominal cramps – absented herself from duty one day on account of sickness.

Three

26th February 1900, at Windsor

I HAVE just had my little 'nightcap' of whisky-and-polly, to help me sleep – although it won't. Dear John Brown introduced me to whisky (I never liked the taste of brandy) and I've always been grateful to him. He called it John Begg's Best, or the Water of Life – and so it was for him in the end, poor man, the water of his life, and probably the means of his death too. In the beginning he used to put a 'grand nip' in my afternoon tea without my knowing it: it was years before I realised why he was the only person in my service who could make a good cup of tea! There is a very strong Total Abstinence movement in the country now, and I expect the good burghers and their wives would be shocked to learn that their Queen partakes of strong liquors. They have a way, the respectable middle-classes, of taking over: their ideals, their tastes, their morality, must be the rule for all. They mount my picture on their parlour walls, and think they own me; but *I* am not to be judged by *their* standards – and nor are those whom I choose to protect. It was the whisky that killed my John in the end, but I would not have separated him from the second greatest love of his life, even if I had been able. People are what they are.

39

How I miss him, my dear John! He had such a cheery, original way of saying things, and such a warm sympathy no matter how large or small one's trouble. And he was the great debunker: he observed no distinctions of rank except mine. For him there was the Queen, and then everyone else. How he annoyed them, the high-borns, with his refusal to accord them the deference they thought their due! But all who were not the Queen were equal in his eyes.

I remember hearing a story that once when he returned to Balmoral after being in London, a villager of his acquaintance asked wistfully if Brown hadn't been meeting a powerful lot o' grand folks in London. Brown put on his loftiest look. 'Aye, it's so,' he conceded, 'but me an' the Queen pays 'em no regard.' It amused me enormously, but it was not an attitude likely to commend him to my Household, or those who were tender of their precedence. Once when we were at Osborne I sent him to inform the gentlemen which of them were to dine at my table that evening. Great was the resentment when he poked his head round the billiard-room door, scanned the company briefly, and bawled, 'All what's here dines wi' the Queen!' Another time when he had brought to me a request from the Mayor of Portsmouth to attend some or other review, he carried back my answer to the Mayor verbatim: 'The Queen says sairtainly not!'

It made me laugh very much to see my blunt-spoken Highlander take the proud folk down a peg or two. He did it not to mock, or to set himself above anyone else, but because in his eyes he was simply my mouthpiece, so he issued my commands without dilution. The high-borns did not understand: they thought it arrogance. And they called familiarity what was single-minded devotion, and impudence what was lack of servility. Servility is not in the Highland people, though they understand service very well. John served me because it pleased him to, and because he loved me, and he did it whole-heartedly. He devoted his whole life to me, night and day, body and mind, without reserve, and only 'sickness unto death' was able at last to keep him from my side.

Well, well, I am now both sleepless and alone; so I shall lift my glass in a toast to my old friend, and continue with my story.

Papa's death left Mamma in dire financial straits. His entire estate was taken up by the creditors, who had removed even the basic necessities of establishment. When Mamma came back from Devon to Kensington she had no furniture, plate or linen, not a spoon or a napkin to call her own. Her sole income was the £6,000 a year settled on her by Parliament at the time of her marriage, and that was not enough to keep her, her children and her servants – let alone to pay the interest on the capital sum of £12,000, which she had to borrow straight away to buy those necessary napkins and spoons.

The new King felt that in granting us rooms at Kensington Palace, he had done all that was necessary, and he refused to consider giving Mamma so much as a sixpence to enable us to remain in them. His great desire was to drive Mamma – and therefore me – back to Germany in the hope that he would never see us again. Lonely and miserable, Mamma longed for Amorbach, and for a while considered how she might manage to go back there; but the problem was money, always money. Even if she could find enough for the journey, Papa had run up debts at Amorbach, too, which she had no means of paying off.

Then just a month later, in the February of 1820, while everything was still in a state of uncertainty, my uncle the King fell desperately ill with pleurisy. For some time his life was despaired of, threatening both to make his reign one of the shortest in English history, and to place little Vickelschen, as Mamma called me, within two elderly lives of the throne. After (or perhaps in spite of) a great deal of bleeding, the King recovered; but Uncle Leopold took the occasion to remind Mamma how important I was in the succession, and how it had been Papa's urgent desire that I should be brought up in England as an English child. There must be no possible excuse, on that day which was to come, to deny me the crown Papa had wished for me.

So there was no more talk of Amorbach. Regretfully Mamma gave up her regency on behalf of my brother Charles and tried thereafter to think of England as home. That still left the problem of money. Uncle Leopold could not see his sister and nieces starve, and generously made Mamma an allowance of £3,000 a year. Unfortunately, when Parliament met in July to consider the pensions for all the royal family, they declared that since Prince Leopold had taken our support upon himself, there was no need for the House to vote us anything more. The fact was, of course, that foreigners were always disliked in England, and at that time Germans were the most hated of all. Englishmen of every degree begrudged the £50,000 a year voted to poor Uncle Leopold for life when he married Princess Charlotte, and deeply resented the fact that it could not be stopped now that she was dead. All that good English gold going into German pockets! The least he could do, they thought, was to spend some of it on his sister's baby. As my uncle King said, 'Her uncle is rich enough to take care of her. I'll be damned if I agree to a pension for her.'

So Mamma was left to struggle on with an income of £9,000 a year. Of course it wasn't enough: Mamma was a royal duchess, and had to keep a certain degree of state; and she had two daughters to rear and a household to maintain. Besides, much as I came to love her in later life, I have to admit that she never had the slightest understanding of the value of money, nor the least idea of economy. To Papa's mountain of debt she began adding promising foothills of her own, and it was hand to mouth with her from then onwards. (There was also, though we did not know it at the time, a further drain on her finances which meant that she could never have kept out of debt even if she had been as frugal as a nun.) All she could hope to do was to hold on, and wait for the day of my succession, when everything would be put right and all debts paid. It is hard to blame her, outcast that she was, if she watched the lives of those between me and the Throne with hungry eyes.

In the early years her fortunes ebbed and flowed like the tides. In August 1820 the Duchess of York died, leaving my uncle York free to marry again. He was fifty-seven, but quite hale: our tide was out and Mamma was on tenterhooks. Uncle King urged him with all his skills of persuasion to marry: he and York had not always seen eye to eye, but anything was better than his brother Kent's child succeeding. But Uncle York told him firmly that he was absolutely determined not to remarry, and would never change his mind.

So our fortunes were on the flow again; but four months later it was slack-water, when in December 1820 Aunt Adelaide gave birth to a baby girl, premature but healthy. Mamma was in despair: it was the one thing that Papa had known might spoil his plan, and Uncle Clarence having amply proved his fertility, it was to be expected that a string of Clarence babies might now follow. The King made no effort to hide his delight that I was no longer the heiress, and nothing could have been more pointed than his behaviour over my new cousin's Christening. I had been roughly forbidden any name that had the slightest royal ring to it; but the Clarence princess, with the King's fervent agreement, was given the names Elizabeth and Georgina to add to her mother's name.

But the tide turned again in March 1821, when my little cousin Elizabeth of Clarence, only three months old, died at St James's Palace of a twisted bowel. I was heir again. Poor, dear Aunt Adelaide! It is a measure of her great goodness that only two months after the death of her own baby, she sent me a birthday present together with a note (which I have still) which opens: 'My dear little Heart, I hope you are well, and don't forget Aunt Adelaide, who loves you so fondly . . .' She longed for children of her own, though no more fervently than the King longed for them on her behalf. Well, she was only twenty-nine, and Uncle Clarence was enormously robust, and so the King did not yet despair.

He continued to ignore Mamma and me; and in August 1821 he must have thought himself quite safe: his estranged wife, Caroline of Brunswick, died unexpectedly, and he was free to marry again and get an heir of his own to 'wipe the Duchess of Kent's eye'. In spite of his age – he was fifty-nine – and his growing infirmities, he set off in high good humour on a trip to Ireland and thence to Hanover (where he was also King, of course) and afterwards to Vienna, where, it was popularly supposed, he would 'pick up something in the princess way' and bring her back before Christmas.

He didn't. A fall from horseback in Hanover gave him a swollen knee and brought on painful gout, and anyone who has ever suffered from that will tell you it is not possible to go courting under its influence. He hobbled home to England, and putting the idea of nubile and probably temperamental young princesses gratefully aside, resumed his peaceful life of domesticity with his elderly mistress, Lady Conyngham (Lord M. most improperly used to refer to her as the Vice-Queen, which I'm afraid made me laugh very much!). It's an odd thing about my uncle King that from his young-manhood he only ever fancied women much older than himself; and in my opinion it is a great pity that he was not able to marry Mrs Fitzherbert (whom he was sincerely attached to) in the proper manner, for he might then have led a more regular and satisfactory life. The Royal Marriages Act, again! But of course, I was forgetting that Mrs Fitzherbert was a Roman Catholic, so he couldn't have married her anyway unless he had given up the Succession, and I can't believe any Prince of Wales would do that.

27th February 1900

STILL NO reliable news from Ladysmith, which is very nerve-racking. I have seen Salisbury, who is looking very old and quite 'played out'. It is too much for him to be Foreign Secretary as well as Prime Minister, but who can one trust? I try to keep cheerful however, and to encourage an optimistic spirit about the house, which I think is most important in time of war. God knows I have had enough practice. What a troubled century this has been!

I visited the Military Hospital at Netley again with Baby and Lenchen. It was so very interesting and moving to talk to the sick and wounded. Some of their stories rend one's heart so, and their loyalty and affection is so very touching. Baby and I spoke to the committee about some ideas to help those who have been too badly wounded to work again, and about a fund for all the families. It is particularly sad to see so many of them suffering from heart disease from overwork and hard marching, which one feels could have been avoided with better management – although the African climate is very trying, I know, and there is nothing one can do about that. The news have reached the men that they are each to be given a tin box bearing my portrait with a slab of chocolate inside, which is my Christmas present to them. They talked more of that than of their wounds, in fact, which is so typical of their courage and chivalry. One man who had lost a leg said he would rather give up his other leg than go without his chocolate! I am very glad that I can be sure this at least will get to them. During the Crimean War I was often arranging for little things to be sent out for the men, only to find that the officers had got them all, which was not at all what I intended.

I thought I would be very tired after the visit, for I was out more than six hours altogether, and two walking round the wards and talking to the men, which is something at my age. But I feel such a keen interest in them and their circumstances that I have no attention to spare for fatigue. I felt sleepy enough after dinner, however, to go to bed early, but having slept two hours, I am now wide awake again, and so I shall take up the pen and go on with my story.

In May 1825 I had my sixth birthday, and it prompted a new debate in Parliament about my establishment. The Prime Minister, Lord Liverpool, proposed that I should be voted £6,000 a year for my support and education, and in a rare burst of unanimity, both Houses agreed, with no single dissension. Lord Eldon and Lord Brougham even used the occasion to pay some very pretty compliments to my mother on her exemplary conduct in bringing me up, and I imagine the praise cheered Mamma almost as much as the money, for she must always have been aware that in spite of my father's Will, it was possible for the State to take me away from her if she was judged to be an undesirable influence over me. Hitherto she knew that the royal family hated and disapproved of her, and had no reason to think that Parliament did otherwise; now suddenly I was being referred to as the Heiress Presumptive, and she as a Devoted and Virtuous Mother.

What had caused this strange *volte-face*? I believe it was my uncle King's doing. His attitude towards me had been changing gradually. Since my cousin Elizabeth of Clarence had died in 1821, Aunt

Adelaide had had only one pregnancy, which had ended sadly in miscarriage, so it was beginning to look very much as though there would be no live child from the union. (This must have struck him, or at least Aunt Adelaide, as being horribly ironic, given the existence and rude health of the ten Fitzclarences. But man proposes and God disposes after all.) Since the King himself and Uncle York were both unmarried, I was third in line to the Throne, and that was a fact like a quickset hedge: not to be got over.

I know now that at that time Uncle King had begun to feel a marked decline in his health, which must have brought the question of the Succession to the front of his mind. He may have felt that as his heiress I was far too much under Coburg (that is, German) influence – being in the sole charge of my mother and supported by my uncle Leopold – and that he ought to do something to ensure my loyalties were in the right place. But I like to think also that his better nature at last rebelled against continuing to ignore and insult his own niece, even if she was the child of his most disliked brother. He *did* have a better nature, no matter what people say of him; and I think the more he saw of me the more he recognised that I was a true Hanoverian. We were alike, and not only in appearance. Whatever he was, he was a king, and that is something no-one who has not experienced it can understand.

The first time I remember noticing his changed attitude was in the summer of 1826, when I was seven years old. Uncle King was staying at the Royal Lodge at Windsor with his mistress Lady Conyngham and her husband and children (such an odd set-up! Did Conyngham know, I wonder? But surely he must have!) and he invited Mamma, Feo and me to stay at Cumberland Lodge for a few days. You may believe Mamma went very unwillingly to visit the man who for so long had snubbed and insulted her, refused her financial aid and obliged her to live in a ramshackle palace away from all the fun; but an invitation from the King is by way of a royal command, so she could not refuse. Feo and I went in a daze of excitement and anticipation of better food and far more diversion than we ever had at home.

On the day after we arrived I was taken up to the Royal Lodge to be presented. (I had been presented once before, when I was four years old, but did not remember it, so for me this was the first meeting face to face with my illustrious uncle.) Though I was naturally nervous of meeting so eminent a personage, and though it had been impressed upon me that I must please, my curiosity and excitement were greater than my fear. This was something new, after all, and I relished new experiences, having so few of them in everyday life. Besides, as I walked towards him, clutching Mamma's hand tightly, I could not help knowing I was the centre of attention, and that always pleased me. The King was sitting down, for his legs were swollen with gout and his feet, which were small for a man of his size, hurt him if he stood for long. I am told that he looked old and unwell, and even to me he was certainly an extraordinary sight. His bloated face appeared between his high, choking stock and his wig like a full moon that had got trapped between banks of clouds. He had always been a tall, big man, but now he was enormously fat as well, and his tight corsets had the effect of moulding the excess flesh into a unified vastness, like the façade of a building, which seemed to have little to do with the human form.

And yet he seemed to me very grand, in his silk and jewels and snowy linen, brilliantly coloured, deliciously scented; the very type of an oriental potentate in a fairy story. As I paused before him, gazing at him with interest and astonishment, he seemed to exude both majesty and a strangely luminous charm, as though there were a lamp inside him, which he could unmask when he wished for the dazzling of willing little moths like me. He beamed at me, with a smile that seemed new-minted for me and me alone, stuck out his large fat hand, glittering with rings to the knuckles, and said in a blunt and friendly way, 'There you are! Give me your little paw!'

Reminded by the downward pressure on my shoulder of Mamma's hand I curtseyed and said, 'Good day, Your Majesty,' as I had been taught. But rising from the curtsey I looked up into his face and reserve melted like frost in the sun of his kindness. I put my tiny hand into his, and as it disappeared into his grasp I found myself returning his smile quite naturally.

That seemed to please him. 'What a smile she has!' he chuckled. 'Showing me all those pretty little teeth! Pray God you keep 'em, niece: pretty teeth are a woman's best asset, especially when she knows how to use 'em. Well, Victoria, you ain't afraid of me, then? Come, come, will you sit on my lap, hey?'

I put up my arms and was scooped up and placed on that plump, well-filled bolster of a knee. A moment's anxiety struck me as I felt how slippery it was: I could get no purchase on it, and it would not be protocol, I was sure, to dismount before I was ordered to. But a strong, bulky arm came round my waist and held me firmly, an arm which knew its business, and which I knew instinctively I could trust. I relaxed against it, and my uncle said comfortably, 'That's right!' The face I found myself in close proximity to was painted all over with maquillage, which struck me as strange, though on consideration really rather a jolly idea. Why not use the bare face as a canvas for painting on? I was of a nature to be stimulated rather than repelled by oddness; and though I was shy, I was always quick to sense good will in others, and I felt only kindness coming from this large, brightly coloured man. The pale, china blue eyes blinked, and a kiss was demanded of me, which I gave heartily. The cheek felt oddly slippery under my lips from the maquillage, but it had a nice smell, like beeswax and roses, which along with the other smells of lemon-water, cedar and lavender which were engulfing me were beginning to make me feel rather drunk, like a bee in a rose garden. *Silk and satin, lace and lavender, that's what kings are made of*, I thought tipsily.

He asked me a question or two about my lessons and my likes and dislikes, which I answered easily, and with a certain frankness that made him chuckle once or twice. And then, as if it were a concluding question which arose out of all the others, he asked me suddenly, 'D'you like peaches, hey?'

'I don't know, sir, for I've never had one, but I think I should,' I answered judiciously.

He chuckled. 'I think you should too, puss! You shall have as many as you can eat from my succession-house. D'ye hear that, ma'am?' he barked suddenly at my disapproving mother. 'Let her gorge herself for once! And now,' he added to me, 'I have something to show you – have you it there, Maria?'

Lady Conyngham stepped forward and handed him something, which he held up before me. It was an oval miniature, set in gold with diamonds around the rim, and fixed, like an order, to a square of blue ribbon.

'It's a likeness of me. What d'you think of it, hey?' said the King.

'It's very beautiful, sir,' I said sincerely.

'My sisters each have one just like it. They wear it on the left shoulder as a mark of their rank and my favour. It is a great honour to wear it. I was thinking of giving one to you. Do you think you deserve it?'

I pondered a moment. 'Yes, Uncle,' I said at last. The only other possible answer was 'No, Uncle', and that did not appeal to me at all, besides being, in my view, untruthful.

The King roared at that, pinched my cheek, and set me down off his knee, saying that I was a clever puss, but deuced heavy. He sounded suddenly tired. He handed the miniature back to Lady Conyngham and directed her to 'pin it on, Maria'. Lady Conyngham stooped and pinned the ribbon on to the shoulder of my white muslin dress, but I hardly noticed her: it was the King who held my attention. As I received the honour of his order, he held my eyes with a serious, yet kind look, which made me feel that I was sharing something particular with him; that he and I were connected in a way that was different from everyone else in the room. *He has chosen me*, I thought with pride, *and not Mamma*. Abominable, ungrateful little wretch that I was, I was glad to be more important then her!

We were dismissed then, and I was taken away by my mother. But the King had not forgotten his promise: very soon a page arrived to take me to the succession-house, and there I crammed my little face with delicious peaches, by the King's express orders. Quite well aware that for once no-one could deny me, and that the chance was unlikely ever to come again, I did full justice to the royal command. The experience was made all the more wonderful by my usually plain diet, and by my mother's evident disapproval of such sensual indulgence. I had never before, and don't think I have ever since, found anything so exotic as those plump, delicately flushed and meltingly juicy fruit!

But that was only the beginning. The next day, while we were out walking, the King's phaeton overtook us. It was a beautiful, glossy thing, black paint shining like glass, and drawn by the most magnificent chestnuts I had ever seen (and despite my youth, I already had my father's eye for horses). The footmen behind wore glorious scarlet liveries; my uncle King was driving, clad in a splendid, caped greatcoat and an old-fashioned, low-crowned beaver, with Aunt Mary Gloucester sitting beside him. The phaeton rushed past us with a hissing of wheels and a spatter of gravel, blowing Mamma's feathers over her face. I gazed after it longingly, and as if my thoughts had power, it suddenly drew to a halt a few paces on, the horses snorting like dragons and champing restively at their bits in disapproval of this check. Lehzen was holding my hand, and I felt her grip tighten as though some danger had threatened me, and when I looked up at her, her expression was at its most forbidding. But Aunt Gloucester was beckoning to us, and Mamma was already hurrying forward, and we could only follow. As we reached the side of the phaeton, the King, craning round Aunt Gloucester, shouted perfunctorily, 'Morning, madam. I trust I see you well.' He gestured towards me with his whip. 'I dare say the princess would like a spin. Pop her in!'

I heard the words with a thrill of excitement. Mamma and Lehzen exchanged an alarmed and disapproving glance, but there could be no possibility of disobeying the King, and so I was lifted up by them, got my foot on the step, and scrambled aboard into Aunt Gloucester's arms. She tucked me down unceremoniously between her and the great bulk of my uncle, who today smelled of leather and wool, starch and delicious bay rum; and almost before I was seated my uncle dropped his hands and the horses dashed off, and I was pressed back in my seat by the forward momentum. It all happened in an instant, but I had one glimpse of the consternation on Mamma's face as she was left behind us by the track. In my innocence I thought *She is afraid I will fall out and be killed. How silly! I am perfectly safe.* We drove at a rattling fine pace, and I was thrilled with the speed and the fine action of the horses, the wind dashing past our faces and the deer scattering like blown leaves as we flew past their resting-places. There's little to compare with a well-sprung phaeton and good, forward-stepping horses for smoothness and speed, and Uncle King was an excellent whip, knowing exactly how to get the best out of his beasts. When we had gone a good way, he slowed them to a walk to breathe them, and engaged me in delightful conversation which seemed to treat me as an equal. He neither peppered me with questions nor lectured me, but chatted as though I were a friend and as though I understood all he said. It was a delicious experience, and by the time I was restored to my mother I was half in love. What else could one do but admire the man who had once driven a three-horse rig to Brighton in under five hours, including changes (a record no-one to my knowledge has ever broken)?

The whole week was full of delights for me: an expedition to the Fishing Temple on Virginia Water, where everyone went on board a barge and fished, while another barge floated nearby with a band playing on it; a visit to the King's menagerie at Sandpit Gate; an entertainment by a troupe of Tyrolean dancers; a picnic luncheon on a boat on the Thames; a drive to Eton to have tea and pastries at a tea-shop by the river. Novelty and pleasure undiluted by lessons would have been delightful in any circumstances; but the best of all for me was the King's interest in me, his obvious desire to charm me.

I was quite ready to be charmed, and to charm in return. After dinner one night I was taken down to the Conservatory, which was splendidly decorated with coloured lights, to hear the band playing. The King called me over during a pause and asked me what tune I would like the band to play next.

Even at seven, I was quick-thinking. 'If you please, Uncle King, I should like *God Save the King* better than any other tune,' said I.

His face creased into an appreciative grin. 'Oh-ho, Miss Politic, who taught you to flatter?' he said. 'Well, you shall have it then, and you shall sit with me while they play it.'

It was very agreeable to find that I knew just how to please him: it gave me a sense of power, which is something I think children often feel the lack of; and it was agreeable, too, to feel that my approval was something valuable to him. At the end of the tune he kept me by him, chatting, and under cover of the next piece asked me which of the week's treats I had most enjoyed. I had no hesitation in answering, 'The ride I took with you in your phaeton,' and it was not politic, but the plain truth.

He looked at me then without smiling – almost sadly – and yet I knew he was pleased with me, that my answer had given him pleasure. 'I have a gift for you,' he said, 'which I shall give to your mother before you leave. It is a pair of diamond bracelets.'

I couldn't think of anything to say. Diamonds? I was only a child, but I already understood that the financial value of a gift from the King was taken by the world to demonstrate the strength of the King's regard. Diamond bracelets would be useless to a seven-year-old child, but I understood what was being offered me, and was grateful.

'You have not been often enough at Court,' he went on, with a serious, kindly look, 'but that will change from now on. You and I must get to know each other much better. I want everyone to see you at Court in future and to understand your position. What do you think about that, hey?'

'I shall like to see you again, Uncle,' I said hesitantly. I could not help thinking Mamma would not like it. 'I wish I might stay here always.'

At that his lips moved in a faint smile, and he stooped his head to kiss me. 'You and I are of a kind, little Victoria,' he whispered, his breath tickling my ear. 'We know something *they* do not.'

At first I thought by 'they' he meant merely Mamma and Lehzen; then I thought he meant the rest of the royal family, my uncles, aunts and cousins; and that the 'something' was our friendship. That was intoxicating enough. But later, at home, when I recalled his words and his look and went over and over them in the quiet moments before sleep, as I did in the weeks and years to come, I concluded that he meant something else: that he and I were different from all other people in the country, because we shared a special destiny. It thrilled me and pleased me, but at the same time it made me feel very solemn, as though a heavy yoke were being placed on my neck. It was a burden which I would gladly never have been given, and yet which, being mine, I would not have dreamed of trying to avoid, even if such a thing were possible.

28th February 1900

BERTIE AND Alix called today, and Alix stayed to luncheon, though Bertie had to rush away as usual. She is very beautiful still, in spite of the passing years, and there is something added now of remoteness and serenity which suits her style very well. She seems like a creature from another world. Little Alicky, Alice's girl, has it too, as I noticed last time she visited – with Nicky in 'ninety-six. But with Alicky it comes from a remoteness of spirit which started when her mother died. Before that she was a bubbling, merry little creature (her mother used to call her 'Sunny') but she became very thoughtful and, I'm sorry to say, very religious after she lost her mother. I am all for people having a faith, but that very intense piety, which gives itself to 'adoration' and 'contemplation' and a preoccupation with beads and candles and so on, is most unhealthy, and can prove very inconvenient to other people. Back in the year 'eighty-nine I hoped she would marry Eddy (she was always a favourite of mine, with such a look of Alice about her, and I'd have liked to keep her near me) but she couldn't fancy him. It probably wouldn't have worked out well, though. If Eddy had lived, I expect he'd have made her very unhappy – though she'd have made a beautiful queen.

Alix's remoteness, however, comes from deafness, which is as inconvenient in its way as piety but not half so dangerous. I am quite worn out with shouting. Poor Alix had rheumatic fever after the birth of Louise in 1867 and it left her as deaf as an adder, but she doesn't like to admit it, so conversing with her can be tiring. She answers what she thinks you've said, and you then have to decide whether to go on with what you were saying or to change to her subject.

Deafness can give rise to amusing situations sometimes. I remember once at Osborne I was entertaining to dinner a very deaf old admiral who was in charge of salvaging a ship which had gone down in Sandown Bay. After he had talked about it for a while, I decided to change the subject, and asked after his sister, who had been a lady-in-waiting of mine. The old sailor replied, 'Well, ma'am, we've had her up on the beach, rolled her on her side and had a good look at her bottom, and now we're going to scrape it.' I thought I should choke to death, trying not to laugh! I had to pretend to have a fit of coughing and rummage in my bag for a handkerchief.

I was looking through some old papers after luncheon, trying to find a letter I wanted to show to Alix, and I came across the famous account, written by my dear old Lehzen, of how I came to learn that

I would one day be Queen. According to her it happened on the 11th of March 1830, when I was not quite eleven years old. My tutor had gone home for the day, and I opened Howlett's *Tables of the Kings and Queens of England* to begin my history lesson with Lehzen, to find that (with Mamma's agreement) she had slipped in a new page – an up-to-date genealogical table of my father's family.

'Why, I never saw this before,' said I.

'No, Princess, it was not thought necessary that you should,' said Lehzen.

I then studied the table, which had had the dates of death written in by hand beside the names of my various deceased relatives, and I saw that only my uncle Clarence stood between me and the Throne (Uncle York was dead by then, of course).

'I see that I am nearer the Throne than I thought,' I said in surprise.

'That is so, madam,' Lehzen confirmed, and as the realisation of what it meant sank into my consciousness, I burst into tears.

After some moments, when I had regained my calm, I studied the table again and said, 'Now, many a child would boast of this, but they don't understand the difficulty. There is much splendour in the situation, but there is more responsibility.' And then I placed my little hand in hers, gazed up at her earnestly, and vowed, 'I will be good!'

It is a poignant story, written by my old governess after she had left my service and gone back to Germany, and sent to me by her for my approval; and in the margin of the original there is a note in my beloved Albert's hand saying, 'The Queen perfectly recollects this circumstance, and says the discovery made her very unhappy.' Well, I must have told him so – and indeed I have always publicly agreed with Lehzen's account of the momentous occasion. I even allowed it to be included in Martin's Life of my darling as a true thing, and it makes very pretty reading. But the fact of the matter is that dear, sentimental Lehzen, lonely in her old age, living a life of dull seclusion, banished far from me and my Court and all she cared about, wanted to make herself important again, even if only in memory. I don't say she made up the whole thing, but I certainly do not remember the incident, which does not have the ring of truth to me – and if it happened as she says, surely I *would* remember it. I would not have dreamed of owning as much to Albert, however. Much as I adored him, I would not expose poor Lehzen to him: she deserved my loyalty for the long and bitter years when she alone stood by me. So I let her have her moment of triumph, as the one who revealed the Truth to me. I owed her that much.

But the knowledge did not come to me suddenly one day like that. How could it? How could I have grown up, even secluded as I was, without understanding what my position was in the family? I knew my uncle was the King. I knew my father had been the fourth son and that the second and third sons were childless. And I could not possibly have studied the history of England as I did and not have understood the rules of succession. Queen Elizabeth was a great heroine of mine, and the Tudor period is riddled all through with questions of genealogy and succession – and particularly with the position of females in the succession.

Then again, from my earliest childhood servants had been calling me Princess and Your Royal Highness, curtseying to me – a little child – and treating me with a respect bordering on reverence. Strangers addressed me as Ma'am, and gentlemen doffed their hats to me, though they did not do so to Feo who was older than me and almost grown up; and when on rare occasions I was allowed to play with another child, they were sternly invoked not to call me by my Christian name, though I might freely use theirs. I don't know when it was that I fully understood my destiny, for I suppose it must have come upon me gradually over the whole course of my life, but certainly I understood well enough, that summer at Windsor, what it was that I shared with my uncle the King – that solemn, thrilling, fearful thing that I saw recognition of in his eyes.

Yet if Lehzen had made occasion to inform me of it openly, there is nothing more likely than that I would have burst into tears. When you are a helpless child it is one thing to know something formlessly from your own observation, and quite another to have it confirmed officially and irrevocably by your own ultimate authority.

In her account, Lehzen went on to say that she reminded me that my aunt Adelaide was still young and might yet have children; and that if she did they would ascend the Throne instead of me. I am supposed to have replied that if it happened so, I should not be disappointed, for I knew how much Aunt Adelaide loved children.

The last part is certainly true – I loved her dearly, and grieved sincerely for her childless state. Thank God that it was God's business to bring me to the Throne, for I could never have been hard-hearted enough to eliminate all the lives and hopes between me and it.

But not be disappointed? No, no! Though my sovereignty has not always been a pleasure to me – though it has been a heavy burden, heavier than anyone can know – I would not have changed it for any consideration in this world or the next. I was meant to be Queen of England, and I could not contemplate any other life for Victoria, and that's the truth of it. That is why I said earlier that I could not imagine any Prince of Wales giving up his place in the succession for the sake of marrying an Unsuitable Person. Kingship is everything. Papa, who went to such lengths to secure me the Throne, even giving up his own life, understood that; and I was Papa's true daughter.

I am tired, and must stop and resume tomorrow. I think I will sleep now.

1st March 1900

I WROTE a good deal last night, being unable to sleep, though I doubt whether anyone will ever be able to read it. I had a 'fine, free' hand once, carefully taught by my writing-master; now it is excessively free and not at all fine – it has deteriorated with my eyesight and the increasing stiffness of my fingers. Well, perhaps I shall not need to destroy this essay after all: my horrid old scribble is as effective as a cypher! But this insomnia is a great nuisance, for I fall asleep at last in the early hours and then do not wake at my usual time, which puts me behind all day. I have so much to do, and have become a creature of habit, and I dislike my routines to be put out. Indeed, bowed under the burden of sovereignty, and with no-one to help me now, it has been routine that has saved me – that, and the ability to apply myself.

Application did not come naturally to me. It does not to most children. But Lehzen instilled it into me. She was quietly insistent that what I began I must finish – a most valuable lesson to learn. My formal education began in 1827 when George Davys was appointed as my tutor. He was an evangelical clergyman, though not of the campaigning sort: I have never liked evangelicals, but he was a liberal and tolerant man, and most careful not to indoctrinate me. He was a quietly spoken, truly good person, who was very fond of me, and once I had got over rebelling against his discipline (for wilfulness was always my strongest fault) I came to appreciate his excellent qualities. When at last I became Queen, I was glad to be able to reward him by advancing him in his clerical career: I persuaded Lord Melbourne to make him Bishop of Peterborough (what Lord M. used to call 'the dead See'!). When Davys died in 1864 *The Times* said of him, 'His ambition through life was to be good rather than great.' A muted epitaph, perhaps, but I do not know what truer praise anyone who loved God could want.

Davys taught me English, poetry, history, geography, use of the globes, Latin, and of course Scripture and the Catechism. My writing-master, Mr Steward, also taught me mathematics, and found me very quick at it: I always had a good understanding of numbers (and consequently of money, something both my parents would have benefited from).

Other tutors came in to teach me singing, drawing and dancing, all of which I enjoyed and consequently excelled at. My dancing mistress, Madame Boudin, taught me to move gracefully – something strangers always notice about me, and which has allowed me, in spite of my small size, to display the bearing of a queen. That grace of movement did not, thank God! desert me even when I grew old and stout, although now, alas, I do not do much of any kind of movement, graceful or otherwise! But as recently as October 1891, despite being seventy-two and rheumatic in my legs, I danced a reel with poor dear Liko at Balmoral, and Sir Henry Ponsonby marvelled at my light, airy steps, and said he wished he could move as well himself, though eight years my junior! (That was at the ball to celebrate little Maurice's birth, of course – Beatrice and Liko's youngest – one of those impromptu affairs that dear Liko so loved to organise. He was truly my Master of the Revels. I grieve for my own loss as much as Baby's. How little any of us thought on that occasion how soon we would have to do without him!)

The other thing that strangers have always noticed about me is my clear speaking voice – silvery, I have heard it called. It has stood me in very good stead over the years. Someone, I cannot now remember who, once said I spoke English like a foreigner – by which I think he meant more carefully and distinctly than a native-born English person would bother to. I'm sure it stems from those early singing lessons I had from John Sale. He was the organist of St Margaret's Westminster, and he gave me a very thorough grounding in how to control my breathing, project my voice, and enunciate clearly. These are valuable assets to someone whose speeches must always be listened to!

But I think I may also thank the fact that Mamma was German for my good diction. It is not true, by the way, that I spoke German at home as a child: I learned it, as I learned French and Italian, from a tutor, as a foreign language. Indeed I was much more fluent in French and Italian than in German, and when Albert and I were first betrothed we had to speak together a good deal in French. Mamma was determined that I should be brought up in every respect as an English child, and so all conversations with me at home were held in

English. But Mamma and Späth (her waiting woman) both spoke with strong accents, and I believe that because of that my own accent became more consciously correct than it would have been had they been native English speakers. This clarity of my diction has always been a great asset on public occasions, as I have said, and it has been particularly useful when meeting foreign dignitaries with imperfect English. I've always found they understand me far better than my ministers, who will swallow their consonants and use colloquial phrases!

Altogether my education was well planned and carefully undertaken; and I did try hard to apply myself, but dear Mr Davys said my besetting sin was 'absence of mind', a tendency to drift away into my own thoughts. This, I must say in my own defence, did not stem from laziness but from the peculiar circumstances of my upbringing, the lonely isolation of my existence – especially after my darling sister Feo married in February 1828 and left me to go and live in Germany.

By that time the happiness of my early childhood had already melted away, and together with Feo I had entered a dark period which was to change my life, my character, my fortunes – everything! Some years afterwards Feo wrote to me, 'When I look back upon those years, which ought to have been the happiest in my life, I cannot help pitying myself. Not to have enjoyed the pleasures of youth is nothing, but to have been deprived of all intercourse and to have not one cheerful thought in that dismal existence of ours was very hard. My only happy time was driving out with you and Lehzen; then I could speak and look as I liked. Thank God I am out of it! I escaped some years of imprisonment which you, my poor dear sister, had to endure after I was married.'

She escaped – the word is not overdrawn – into marriage with the nice, handsome Prince Ernst of Hohenlohe-Langenburg, and I am glad to be able to record that they were very happy together. 'Often I have praised God that He sent me my dearest Ernst, for I might have married I don't know who, merely to get away.'

They were as poor as church mice, and the court at Schloss Langenburg, a desolate, echoing place of huge empty rooms and icy corridors, was isolated from society and exceedingly dull. It is sad to think of lovely, vivacious Feo living a life of dreary economy, with no dancing or fun or pretty clothes; but though she was plagued by the lack of money all her life, she and Ernst loved each other dearly, and his death in June 1860 was a great grief to her. They had five children, and it was joy and satisfaction to me when Feo's grandson Ernst

56

recently married my granddaughter Sandra (Affie's daughter) thus uniting our blood-lines.

'The misery of our lives at Kensington,' Feo's letter continued, 'was almost as nothing compared with the observation of the error – almost the impropriety – into which our mother was led by a Certain Person.'

There is no getting round it. I shall have to speak of him if I am to tell my tale. Name him, Victoria! The Mephistopheles of our household – my mother's evil genius – my tormentor – destroyer of our household peace and of my childhood's innocence. The evil creature who estranged me from my own mother and kept me from the right and proper relationship I should have enjoyed with my uncle King and my uncle Clarence.

Name him: John Conroy! There, it is out, and I wonder the page does not sizzle under the ink of those two words!

1st March 1900 – later

THE WONDERFUL news we have waited for have come at last, and are confirmed by telegraph from Buller, who has been into Ladysmith, and reports the Boers all gone like mist sucked up by the sun! The besieged are in poor case, all hungry and many of them sick after living on their horses and mules for weeks past, and White's soldiers are not fit to campaign again until they have had some nursing – but the relief and gratitude is enormous, and our joy not to be measured. There is to be a thanksgiving service on Sunday and I have told the Dean to choose a cheerful hymn: we are all in need of some cheerfulness after weeks of worry. Hundreds of loyal telegrams have arrived from people of all degrees. I am to go to London, drive about the streets, and be received at Buckingham Palace by both Houses, who will assemble in the courtyard to give me a hearty cheer. This will be a very novel proceeding! With all the excitement my private writing must be put aside for a while.

Four

10th March 1900, at Windsor

I HAVE had my two State visits to the capital, on Thursday to Blackfriars and yesterday a drive through the streets of West London, and the crowds lining the routes on both days were quite astonishing, even greater than for my Diamond Jubilee. The loyalty and affection the people displayed was most thrilling and touching. It is a great and glorious privilege to have won the devotion of so many millions.

The only inconvenience I encountered was that the horse trotting just behind my carriage would keep tossing its head and throwing foam over me. It reminds me of the drive to St Paul's during my Diamond Jubilee celebrations: Lord Dundonald was riding just behind me, and he kept shouting out, 'Steady, old girl! Keep calm, old lady!' It was only when I turned round to glare at him that I realised he was addressing his rather frisky mare, and not me!

Despite the pleasure of the last few days, I am suffering under a personal disappointment: I am not to go South this spring after all. After the long, dark winter all my senses yearn for the sunshine, the bright air, the clear colours of the flowers, the smell of pine! It will be the first time for fourteen years I have not gone; but the French have behaved so badly, supporting the Boers all along against what they choose to call our 'oppression'. Not a day goes by without some scurrilous abuse of us, and even of me, in their newspapers, and on that account, and with the war still going on and so much still to be settled, it does not seem wise or even safe to be going abroad. The saddest thing is that I was to have met darling Vicky at Bordighera, and now I shall not see her at all. I have begged her, if she can, to come to England and visit me. If she made the journey by easy stages it might be done, though this wretched pain of hers makes it hard sometimes for her to move from her bed. The doctors don't seem to know what causes it, and another reason for wishing to get her here is to consult an *English* doctor. I hope she will come. I am very uneasy about her health.

Instead of the dear South of France I am to go to Ireland next month, on the 4th of April, for a short visit – the first in many years. This was entirely my own idea, and is intended to thank the Irish people for all their wonderful service in South Africa. I hope it will do much good and give satisfaction. I hope also to enjoy myself very much!

With all the excitement, I am quite unable to sleep, so I will go on with my story. I had just got up to speaking of Conroy.

John Conroy was my father's equerry. He was the same age as Mamma; a tall man, not ill-favoured, but with the sly, slippery, self-satisfied look of a bad dog who has been in the larder and now comes to fawn over you and make believe he has not eaten in days. He had wits, in short, but no scruples. He was a man of superficial charm, but his mind was vulgar through and through, and though he could play the gentleman when it suited him, his manners were over-familiar, especially towards women (for whom he had a deep, if largely hidden, contempt).

His family came from Ireland, and he had chosen a military career, as so many of them did. He acquired a commission in the Horse Artillery, and advanced, I believe, more because he was good with horses than because he was a good officer; but by luck and the exercise of his tongue he made an advantageous marriage to the daughter of Major General Fisher, who happened to be an old friend of Papa's. Fisher and Papa had served together in Canada, and because of this connection, Conroy looked to my father for patronage when Fisher died in 1814. Out of respect for his old friend, Papa tried to get Conroy a preferment somewhere, and when he failed, he good-naturedly took Conroy into his own household as equerry in 1817. Fatal decision! If Papa had known what was to come of it, he would have run the man through rather than employ him.

Conroy was a greedy, ambitious, self-seeking man, but also an impoverished one, with six children to maintain, and his private income from his Irish estate amounting to no more than £100 a year. When Papa died in 1820, Conroy must have believed his hopes of fame and fortune had died too; but more than that, it left him desperately short of the very necessaries of life. He was at Sidmouth with us when Papa died, and lost no time in offering his services to Mamma in order to secure himself and his family some kind of a home. I believe he meant Mamma to be no more than a stop-gap, but when Mamma, desperate in her bereavement for a man's arm to lean on, asked him to be her Comptroller, he began to think more carefully about what opportunities might be offering right under his nose. Mamma was all alone, ignorant of business and out of favour with her late husband's family. She was of a timid and confiding nature, always doubting her own powers, which made her easy for him to dominate; and intensely loyal where she had once given her trust, which made her easy to bamboozle. She was also – her most attractive attribute as far as Conroy was concerned – the sole guardian of a child who might one day be Queen of England.

Conroy soon managed to make himself indispensable: he made all the decisions and told Mamma not to worry about anything, advice she was only too glad to take as long as it was presented by a man, and with an air of assurance. 'I don't know what I should do without him. His energy and capability are wonderful,' she wrote to my grandmamma in Coburg.

Once they were settled at Kensington, Conroy also managed to ingratiate himself with my aunt Princess Sophia, who lived in the next set of rooms to us. Princess Sophia and Conroy were soon thick as thieves; she liked him so much that she made him her Comptroller too and in 1827 begged my uncle King for an honour for him. The King was very fond of Sophia, and also had a weak spot for adventurers and 'likeable rogues', so he made Conroy a Knight Commander of the Hanoverian Order. It was not much of an honour, but it was twice ten times what he deserved, and it also gave him, as *Sir* John Conroy, a superficial and completely spurious respectability.

Conroy's plan was to have complete control over Mamma, by running her affairs, holding her purse-strings, and keeping her isolated from the rest of the royal family. Through her, of course, he meant to have complete control over *me*. Sovereigns come of age early, at the age of eighteen; but my uncles were elderly and not of sound health, and as it grew apparent that I would eventually succeed to the Throne, it also seemed likely that I would succeed as a minor, which would mean a regency. If that were the case, Sir John meant to ensure that Mamma would be made sole Regent, so that, through her, he would virtually be King of England. Contemplation of the power and riches that would then be his must sometimes have made him almost sick with excitement!

If anyone were to scotch Conroy's plans, it should have been Uncle Leopold, my mother's own brother, and her paymaster into the bargain. He took a brotherly interest in her and a fatherly interest in me, and his visits to us at Kensington every Wednesday afternoon were the high moments of my week. How kind he was to me, how affectionate! I used to wait with my nose pressed to the window for the first possible hint of his arrival, and run into his arms to be embraced! He brightened our drab apartments like an exotic bird of paradise – for I have to admit he was eccentric in appearance, bewigged and painted and perfumed, with his coloured silk clothes, high-heeled shoes, and long, trailing feather boas. He used to invite us to stay at his country house, Claremont, near Esher, where I tasted a little of luxury and felt free as I never did at home. There was amusement there and no lessons, Mamma was always in a good humour, and Conroy was banished to the outer sphere of servants where he could not trouble us. Those visits to dear Claremont, for Feo and me, were the happiest memories of our childhood. 'I always left Claremont for Kensington in tears,' Feo said later. We both did.

Uncle Leopold was a man of intelligence and great abilities, but unfortunately Mamma did not get on with him, grateful though she was for his money and protection. The death of Princess Charlotte had made him rather 'dour', as the Scotch say. He was clever, but talked very slow and solemn, and took a long time to make up his mind, which Mamma found tiresome. (Princess Sophia called him *Monsieur Peu à Peu*.) His advice was always sensible, and therefore unpalatable to Mamma. Conroy, on the other hand, filled with the optimism of fecklessness, offered her extravagant hopes and rosy fool's apples, much sweeter to the taste of one who had never had the slightest notion of economy.

Conroy missed no opportunity of poisoning Mamma's mind against Uncle Leopold, so that from finding him rather glum and tiresome, she soon started to regard him with suspicion. Unfortunately, just at the time that Conroy was beginning to put his plan into action, of isolating us from all influence but his, Uncle Leopold disappeared from the scene. He had long tired of living a life of idleness as a private gentleman, the pensioner of the British Government (which made no secret of its resentment at having to keep him). He wanted a situation where he could exercise his considerable abilities, and in 1829 he was offered the throne of Greece, which had just separated from Turkey. He was tempted by the offer, but Parliament and the King were much against it, so he declined; but in 1830 the Belgians, having won their independence from Holland, asked Uncle Leopold to be their king, and this offer he accepted. He left England for Brussels in July 1831 and went out of my life for four years.

He made an excellent king for the Belgians, capable, liberal and just, and they never had cause to regret their choice; but the effect on me was disastrous. Mamma would never have fallen so completely under Conroy's spell if Uncle Leopold had been at hand to guide her; and I should not have been subjected to so many years of misery.

Deprived by accident of a father's love at birth, I was further denied a mother's love by the actions of that wicked man, Conroy – and for that I could never, never forgive him.

Conroy's plan was to isolate us from all influences but himself, to make a separate court at Kensington (the Conroyal Court, as Wellington's friend Mrs Arbuthnot described it), where he alone would choose the courtiers. To that end he must, of course, cut us off from the real Court, and this became especially necessary as my uncle King began to show an interest in me. Conroy worked on my mother's fears by telling her that Uncle King meant to take me away from her. There was probably a grain of truth in it: Uncle King wanted me to gain experience of Court life, and to get to know my paternal relations better. But Conroy convinced my mother that there was a plot afoot to murder me.

His story was that the King had hated Papa, and therefore hated me, and wanted my uncle Cumberland (who now had a son, George, to follow him) to have the Throne. Mamma was in any case afraid of Uncle Cumberland, who combined a fearsome temper with a sinister appearance (owing to a scar across his face, got quite honourably in battle) and a reputation for extraordinary wickedness (most of it probably undeserved). Naturally Mamma believed everything Conroy told her. He said that Uncle Cumberland meant first of all to weaken me over a long period by bribing a servant to put small doses of poison in my bread-and-milk, so that it would get about that I was a naturally sickly child. Uncle Cumberland would feed those rumours, and then at the right moment Uncle King would take me away from Mamma to live at Court, where after a few weeks no-one would be at all surprised to learn I had died.

Poor trembling Mamma believed all this, and was only too willing to follow Conroy's advice. She cut me off from any contact with my relations, refused all invitations to Court, and kept away all visitors but those Conroy approved. To guard against assassination I was never to be left alone, day or night, but must always have either Mamma, Lehzen, or some other trusted person with me. My food was tasted to guard against poisoning; and to prevent murder *à la* Amy Robsart, I was never allowed to walk down a flight of stairs without someone holding my hand. I was never to be in company with a third person without supervision; and I was not to meet or play with any other children, except for Conroy's own daughter Victoire. She was a girl just my own age and was brought to play with me once or twice a week, but I disliked her intensely. She was her father's puppet, gave herself his airs, and by reporting to him everything I said, made trouble for me with him and Mamma.

This, then, was my existence – my dreary, unnatural existence! No fun and no visitors; no companions of my own age, no play, no romping and laughing, no simple childish jollity. I was so much with adults, I often forgot that I was young. That was hard enough; but yet never to be left in peace to read or daydream and know oneself quite private and unwatched – free to think and feel as one pleased – that was still harder. It was the bitter irony of my fate, to be always lonely, and yet never alone. And how often I longed to be alone, to be safe from the intrusions of That Man!

How can I describe the slights and humiliations he heaped on me? He was a natural bully, a short-tempered, self-satisfied, swaggering man with a harsh, hectoring voice; the sort of man who finds out a person's weakest or most vulnerable point and makes cruel remarks about it – and then derides his victim for being upset. 'What, can't take a joke? Tears again, you ninny? What a simpleton you are!' He was like the little boy who enjoys pulling the wings off flies and laughs to see them crawling about helpless. To him, power was the power to torment and humiliate, to aggrandise himself at others' expense. The idea that power might be used to the good of the helpless would have been quite foreign to him.

Oh, how miserable he made me! I was a proud child, and he trampled that pride mercilessly. He laughed at my appearance, always a sensitive point with me: he abused my short stature, my lack of chin, my uncompromising nose. He sneered at my carefulness with money (so different from his own attitude!) and called me 'old snuffy', a reference to my grandmother, Queen Charlotte, who was supposed to have been extremely mean. I had always comforted myself secretly that although I was not pretty, it was because of my royal blood, because I strongly resembled my father's side of the family. Conroy somehow found that out, and claimed that the relative I was most like was my uncle Gloucester, the least prepossessing and also the slowest-witted (known in the family as Silly Billy). Conroy worked up the joke about my supposed stupidity, until many people believed on his authority that I was mentally retarded and incapable even of looking after myself, much less ruling the country.

But it was he who was stupid. His aim was to rule England through me, but he could not see that whenever he bullied or insulted me, or indulged his ill-judged witticisms at my expense, he was knocking another nail into his own coffin. One day I would be

Queen, and did he think I would then keep him at my right hand in love and gratitude? He saw me as a helpless child; and since he controlled my physical self, he assumed that he controlled *me*. But I was born with a strong will, a Hanoverian will, and every slight and cruelty I suffered at his hands only strengthened it. I could never endure to be ruled, and thwarting me only makes me more determined. However miserable he made me, even if he had had the most ingenious imagination in existence, there is *nothing* he could have done to me to break my spirit.

He took my apparent submission at face value. If I had had anyone to turn to, I would not even have appeared submissive; but there was no-one. Mamma was completely under his thumb, and the more I saw that she acquiesced in his treatment of me, the more I was convinced that she did not, could not love me. Though she could not have been in any doubt as to how much I hated Conroy, she never doubted that he was right and that my hatred was unreasonable and the fault of my temper. She became so identified with him in my mind I thought of them as 'they'; and as I hated him, so I hated her.

Oh, that is a bitter thing to have to say! But it is true. My world was divided quite simply into those who belonged to him, and those who did not: 'them' and 'us'. 'They' included my mother, of course; my brother Charles, who, himself a rake, was deeply admiring of Conroy's *panache*; and Princess Sophia, who was so taken with Conroy that she called him her *cher ami* and willingly 'spied' for him on the King and the Clarences.

The 'us' camp, once Feo had left, was reduced to Lehzen, and my mother's woman Baroness Späth; and was soon to be reduced still further. Conroy, though not a sensitive man, could be observant where his own advantage was concerned. Späth and Lehzen loved me, and did not admire him; therefore Späth and Lehzen must go.

His first success came in the autumn of 1829, when Mamma dismissed Baroness Späth from her service. How Conroy worked on her to do it I can't imagine, for Späth had been with her for twenty-five years, all through the miserable years of her first marriage, through her first widowhood, and the happy revival of fortunes of her second marriage. Späth had crossed the Channel with Mamma, suffering tortures of seasickness, had attended her in childbirth at Kensington, had watched beside her at Sidmouth through Papa's last illness. And afterwards she had not hesitated to stay with Mamma, often without wages, bravely sharing her exile in a foreign land, whatever hardships it might bring. Späth was not a woman of great intelligence, but was a dear, good, kind, and utterly loyal servant and friend.

This good person was now to be dismissed because, it was announced, she was too German, and the Duchess of Kent wished to be surrounded by high-ranking English ladies. The very shallowness of the excuse reveals its origin. Conroy had never loved anyone in his life, so he could not imagine that such a pronouncement would seem anything out of the ordinary!

It was received at Court with surprise and considerable speculation – so much so that Conroy, taken aback, went on to provide a string of further unconvincing reasons: Späth's manners were not suitable to English society; her behaviour was not acceptable in a lady-in-waiting; she received too many visitors; she talked too much; she spoiled Princess Victoria by too much uncritical adoration; she had criticised the Duchess of Kent's method of bringing up the child.

Of these only the last had any truth to it. Späth had made the mistake of allowing her dislike of Conroy to show, of openly resenting his treatment of me, of objecting to the airs he put on – he talked insolently of her, and insisted on his wife taking precedence over Späth and Lehzen, who were both baronesses. Finally Späth had committed the crime of scolding Victoire Conroy for some pertness or other. In short, she had shown too clearly that she was not in Conroy's camp – that was her real sin.

Her dismissal caused a scandal. No-one could believe Mamma would put away her intimate companion for the reasons given, and so the rumour grew up that Späth had been dismissed because she had witnessed 'familiarities' between Mamma and Conroy. Society at that time was so loose in the haft that members of the *ton* could not believe a man and woman could live under the same roof without bedding each other, so Mamma and Conroy must be lovers. It was a wicked lie, of course, and must have hurt Mamma's feelings dreadfully, for she was a woman of the strictest propriety, and though she was undoubtedly fond of Conroy, and was probably injudicious in her familiarity with him, she would never, never have behaved improperly with him.

But I have to say she did wrong by Späth; and no doubt would have allowed Conroy to deprive me of Lehzen too, had not Lehzen been too clever for him. Conroy wanted to be rid of Lehzen because she was so friendly with Späth that he could not trust her; but she had seen long before how things were, and had been careful to give no cause for offence, concealing her hatred of Conroy and securing the approval of my uncle King and Uncle Clarence. When it was announced, obliquely, that Mamma intended to send Lehzen away as well, the King obliquely but very firmly responded that it was not to be.

Poor Späth departed, red-eyed and bewildered, to find a home with kind Feo at Langenburg, where she remained for many years as her lady-in-waiting, and probably never understood why she had been so callously dismissed after such long, faithful service. Lehzen and I drew closer, like birds huddling together in winter, intent on surviving. The events were not discussed between us – Lehzen would not have thought it proper – but I knew well enough what was going on, and I was very frightened. Now that Feo and Uncle Leopold had gone, and Mamma had sided against me, Lehzen was the only person in the world I had to depend on, and despite my fear, my heart swelled with rage and indignation at the attempt to deprive me of my only refuge.

I knew where to lay the blame; and I silently saluted Lehzen's restraint in Conroy's presence, and tried to emulate it myself. She would become quite colourless when he was in the room, like a toad pretending to be a stone. She would say yes and no and little more, and nothing betrayed her hatred of him but a slight tightening of her lips, and a sparkling look in her eyes when he left us again. For myself, I was too young and my character too straightforward to pretend to accept him, but under his goad I was learning to deny him the satisfaction of my pain, assuming a grim expressionlessness which was very foreign to my nature.

Stone by stone I erected a wall between myself and him, and consequently between myself and Mamma. It is a hard thing for a child to think ill of her mother, a bitter thing to be brought to such a pass. The wound of it went deep; and though in later years I came to love Mamma, and to enjoy with her the proper warmth and intimacy of our relationship, I bore and still bear the scars of being bent out of my nature in those Kensington years.

The dismissal of Späth had one further evil consequence. Aunt Adelaide, partly on her own account, and partly at the prompting of the King, wrote to Mamma a very blunt warning about Conroy:

It is the general wish in the family that you should not allow Sir JC *too much* influence over you, but keep him in his place. He has never lived before in good society, so naturally he offends sometimes against the traditional ways, for he does not know them. In the family it is noticed that you are cutting yourself off more and more from them with your child. This they attribute to Conroy, whether rightly or wrongly I cannot guess; they believe he tries to remove everything that might obstruct his influence, so that he may exercise his power *alone*, and alone one day reap the fruits of his influence. He must not be allowed to forbid access to you to all but his family, who in any case are not of so high a rank that they *alone* should be the companions of the future Queen of England.

This, and much more. Mamma must have been mortified to receive such a letter; but Conroy must have been even more taken aback, to discover that what he had thought of as his secret plan was completely transparent even to such a simple woman as Aunt Adelaide. He dictated a reply for Mamma to send, something very angry and insolent, as I understand, which very much hurt Aunt Adelaide. Uncle Clarence adored his wife, and could not bear her to be upset, and so was furious with Mamma and Conroy. From then on, it was open warfare between the two camps.

This was a very unfortunate circumstance, because at this time my uncle King was sinking under the weight of his ailments, and only five months later, on the 26th of June 1830, he died, and Uncle Clarence became King William IV. Aunt Adelaide, as can be seen from the letter, had ceased to hope for a child of her own, and my uncle was therefore the only life left between me and the Throne. This was the point at which I ought to have taken my place at Court, to learn its ways and get to know my future courtiers; and my bluff, kindly uncle and gentle, pious aunt would have been glad to have taken me to their hearts like their own daughter; but with the prize so nearly in his grasp, that was the last thing Conroy would permit.

12th March 1900

OF MY uncle King George IV, Greville wrote, 'He had not been dead three days before everyone discovered that he was no loss.' When you are Queen of England, it is a disagreeable fact that you are thought of as public property, and however little you like it, you have to accustom yourself to a certain amount of unjust criticism of yourself and abuse of the relatives you love. Uncle King was very kind to me, and I cried very much when he died. Oddly, it was from a Frenchman, Prince Talleyrand, that he received the most sympathetic treatment: Talleyrand called him *un roi grand seigneur* – 'There are no others left.' That was true. George IV had surrounded himself with splendour, ostentatious extravagance, gorgeous display – almost like an oriental despot of old; and in his time, that was what was expected of a king. But times change, and our century was more critical and down-to-earth than the eighteenth. If monarchy was to survive, it had to change with the times, and prove its worth.

The new King, my uncle William, was a hearty, kindly old gentleman with a loud, quarterdeck voice and a disposition to be friendly towards everyone. He suited the new thinking, for he disliked pageantry, ceremonial, elaborate clothes, 'fal-lals' and French food. He adored his wife, was fond of and badgered by his brood of illegitimate children, and liked nothing better than a simple dinner and a quiet evening at home, dozing in front of the fire while Aunt Adelaide knitted. He was a tallish, stoutish, pink-faced man with the family bright blue eyes, and there was nothing odd about him except the shape of his skull, which sloped rather towards the crown and had given him the nickname, in his Navy days, of 'Coco-nut'.

He had never expected to be King, and took a little while to adjust himself to it. Once, in the early days of his reign he slipped out of St James's Palace and went for a walk about the streets as he had been used to doing as Duke of Clarence. Of course he was soon recognised, and collected an excited crowd about him, who followed him in noisy admiration which his natural friendliness did nothing to dampen. When at last he was kissed on the cheek by a cheerful prostitute on the pavement before White's Club, the scandalised membership came out in a body and escorted its sovereign back to the Palace; where his household, frantic with relief, tried to convince him that kings simply could not 'pop out' and walk about London alone like that.

Uncle William couldn't see what the fuss was about. 'Oh, never mind all this,' he said, waving his hand towards the hilarious mob lingering in the street in the hope of another excursion. 'When I have walked about a few times they will get used to it and take no notice.' It was left to Aunt Adelaide to tell him severely that he must not do it again, whereupon he hung his head meekly and said, 'If *you* say so, my dear . . .'

I *love* that story! It is so exactly the Uncle William I remember. But though he had not expected to be King, now it had happened he was determined to do the thing properly. He had a very strong sense of duty (one of the traits I'm glad to say we shared), and a methodical way of going about things. The Duke spoke very highly of him: he rose early and worked long hours, left nothing undone at the end of the day, and when presented with business he did not understand, asked questions until he *did* understand it. 'Which was in distinct contrast with his predecessor,' said the Duke (though not to me, of course), 'who was at pains never to acknowledge ignorance on any topic!' The Duke found he was able to get through as much business in ten minutes with Uncle William as in ten days with his late master; and was particularly impressed with the way Uncle William tackled the mountain of business left over from the previous reign, including the signing of some forty thousand documents George IV had 'put off'. Sir Herbert Taylor, Uncle William's secretary, said that Uncle sat up late night after night, signing away until his chalky old hands were aching with cramp, in order to catch up and 'make everything ship-shape'.

Unkind and very unfair legends have grown up that Uncle William was stupid – which was very far from the case, though his bluff and simple manner could not have recommended itself to the languid sophisticates of society – and also that he was a thoughtless reactionary, which was likewise untrue. He had a strong sense of what was due to the Crown, but he also believed that the King owed absolute loyalty to his ministers, who were there to advise him. When the Government told him there must be Parliamentary Reform to get rid of the nomination seats, he accepted it; and though he disliked the idea very much, he never wavered in his support of Lord Grey until the Act was through, even though it meant upsetting Aunt Adelaide, who was far more strongly against it than him.

That was the Reform Act of 1832, of course, which was only the beginning of a process I have seen continue throughout my reign; and I don't suppose it is over yet. The franchise has been extended twice – in 1867 and again in 1884. I am 'all for' giving the vote to decent, hard-working, God-fearing men like my dear John Brown, but there is agitation now to enfranchise every man over twenty-one, no matter how little he contributes to the common weal. It has always seemed to me that the vote ought to be a privilege, that one should do more to deserve it than simply be born. Well, it will not be my problem, thank God! Bertie, I expect, will hold out against it (he is much less democratically minded than I am: I think secretly he would like to rule absolutely like a grand seigneur of old!). But in the end the universal franchise will come. Over a long reign I have come to see that there are things which happen not because anyone in particular wills them, but because the tide of history is flowing in that direction. We may choose to act Canute, but we can only expect the same degree of success.

But I digress. The new reign was not a day old when Conroy fired his opening salvo. He wrote a letter, which Mamma signed and sent to the Duke, with demands to be laid before the new King: that I should be acclaimed as Heiress Presumptive, and Mamma made sole Regent by Act of Parliament; that a noblewoman, preferably a Duchess, should be appointed my official governess in recognition of my status; and that Mamma should be given the title of Dowager Princess of Wales (to which she had no shadow of a claim, I might mention!) and an income suitable to her rank. No extra grant should be made to the Princess Victoria, added Conroy unblushingly under Mamma's hand: until she was of age, it was in the Princess's interest that all her affairs were handled by her mother.

The Duke was taken aback by the effrontery of the letter and declined to lay it before the King. Probably guessing its true authorship, he told Mamma warningly that he would not even mention its contents to his colleagues, but treat it as a private and confidential communication. The affairs of the Duchess of Kent and her august daughter, he said, would come before Parliament in the next session, and it was far better that they should be dealt with through the regular channel than that a claim should be put forward by Mamma.

A sharp reply to this went back to the Duke: Mamma insisted on the Regency against her own inclinations, purely for her daughter's good; and if she did not put forward her feelings, she was not likely to be asked for them, undervalued as she was by the whole Court. The Duke replied that there was no-one in the country who had any idea of injuring her interests or those of the Princess, and he entreated her 'not to allow any Person to persuade you to the contrary'. This obvious reference to Conroy angered Mamma, who saw him as her only true friend and champion. She could not understand why other people slighted him and tried to turn her against him, and for a long time thereafter she refused to speak to the Duke or to receive him.

Conroy need not have worried, however. When the question of the Regency came up in Parliament in November 1830, it was unanimously recommended that it should be vested in Mamma. By precedent, the next heir after me had the right to be named Regent, but in my case that was my uncle Cumberland. He was feared and hated by nearly everyone at Court and by the population at large, and a pretext was hastily found for denying him the Regency. The Throne of Hanover, joined to that of England since George I, could not come to me because Hanover operated under Salic law, by which only males could succeed. Therefore when Uncle William died the crowns would part company, and Uncle Cumberland would become King of Hanover. It was plainly impossible for a foreign ruler to be Regent to the Queen of England, and so Uncle Cumberland was passed over and Mamma nominated as sole Regent, to everyone's great relief.

Fortified by this triumph, Conroy and Mamma settled down to a campaign of increasing their own prestige and royal style, and thwarting and insulting the King and Queen on every possible occasion. Isolated in the schoolroom, I did not witness much of the action, though I was aware, of course, that I did not see Uncle William and Aunt Adelaide as often as I would have liked. Loving me as they did, they would have overlooked many of the Conroyal insults, but Mamma carried the war into their own front parlour by her attitude towards my Fitzclarence cousins. Uncle William was a fond father, and since Aunt Adelaide accepted his *bâtards* wholeheartedly into her home circle he saw no reason why my mother should do otherwise. But she refused to acknowledge them, and even if she met them under the King's own roof she ignored or snubbed them. Poor Uncle William! When I became Queen, I made a point of being civil to them, confirmed them in their Court posts and continued their pensions – though it was too late to make amends to *him*, of course.

The squabbles between the Court and Kensington Palace continued, and although they stopped short of open breach, they made life very unpleasant. Together with my continual persecution by Conroy, they began to damage my health, and during the years of my 'teens' I suffered recurrently from headaches, backaches, biliousness and insomnia – all attributable, I'm sure, to the miserable and unnatural life I was leading.

There were breaks in the monotony, as welcome to me as they were infrequent. Mamma and Conroy wished me to be presented to society, and so I was brought down to the drawing-room to curtsey to the company when Mamma gave a great dinner. And there were invitations to court functions which it was not possible for Mamma to refuse on my behalf – like the juvenile ball Uncle William gave in honour of my fourteenth birthday in May 1833.

I opened that ball (as I did others in subsequent years) with my cousin Prince George of Cambridge. It was a funny thing about poor George – we were, of course, just the same age, and there was a general assumption on the part of many people that we would eventually marry. It seemed a good solution, particularly to my paternal relatives, of what might otherwise be a vexed question; Aunt Adelaide especially would have liked it, because George was her particular pet. But George and I both hated the idea. We never discussed it with each other, of course; the whole thing was completely unspoken; but whenever we were brought together at balls and such-like, we would grow very cold and distant, and treat each other with a wooden civility intended to convince onlookers that there could be no question of our ever being in love. I firmly believed that I disliked him very much, that he was ugly and stupid; and he thought pretty much the same about me. But as soon as I was engaged to Albert, and we were safe from each other, our manners towards each other changed, and I found him an agreeable person and grew quite fond of him. He became rather a rake, and was sent into the army (he was my Commander-in-Chief until 1895) to keep him out of trouble, but when he was twenty-eight he married an actress, Louise Fairbrother. It was a shocking *mésalliance*, of course, and pretty well drove his father, my uncle, to his grave; but it was a love-match, and it had the effect of settling him down. He was devoted to Mrs Fitzgeorge, as she became known, and she gave him three Fitzgeorge sons. When she died in 1890 it broke his heart.

That birthday, in 1833, was also the time when I was allowed to adopt as my own the King Charles spaniel, Dash, that John Conroy had given to my mother a few months before. Every child needs someone on whom to bestow caresses, and though I loved Lehzen dearly, I was also in awe of her. She was not physically affectionate, nor would she have permitted me to touch her: she would not have deemed it proper. So it was dear little Dashy who received my kisses and cuddles. I adored him, and a better-natured, more faithful dog there never was. He was and remained the only thing I ever had to thank John Conroy for. Dash was with me from 1833 until he died, in the year Vicky was born; and a very handsome marble monument he has now over his grave in the garden of Adelaide Cottage, here at Windsor.

14th March 1900 – near midnight

VOICES, VOICES . . . When I close my eyes, they come to me, faint and echoing, like dry, dead leaves blown rattling across a pavement.

The King's, pitched for the open air, a kind of muted roar, with those old-fashioned vowel sounds you never hear any more, except perhaps in parts of Norfolk and Lincolnshire. 'Ha! Don't you worry, m'dear! I may be a simple fellow, just an old sea-dog, but these eyes of mine have always been sharp, and I can see what's goin' on under my own nose, dammit!'

Mamma's, soft and sibilant, turning upwards at the end of each sentence like a question-mark, so that even her firmness became strangely hesitant, as though she were saying things against her will. 'Zo, Victoria my love, you must not tsink zat I am angry with you, when I only try to show you where you are wrong? You know you can be headstrong and wilful? Your mother must know better zan you what is good for you, *nicht*? You cannot understand as I do what your position demands?'

Conroy's, loud and hectoring, with a hint of Irish in it, like sour milk in tea, and a hint of temper under it that might erupt at any moment. 'There's nothing worse than a young female setting up her own opinion against those of her betters. That's a thing I can't abide, now! I won't have it in my own girls, and I tell you, Duchess, wherever I see it, it makes me want to stamp it out, double quick!'

Now there is another voice, added in the summer of 1834 – the vinegar tones of Lady Flora Hastings, eldest daughter of the Marquess; a clever, sharp woman of twenty-eight, elegant, not ill-looking, but with a mind that would have done better in a man's body, and a disposition soured by the realisation of the same. She came as my mother's lady-in-waiting, but it was not long before I understood that her arrival marked the beginning of a new phase in the battle to rid me of my one protector, my dearest Lehzen, and put me under the complete control of Conroy. Soon my drives out with Lehzen ceased to be little havens of peace in the storms of my life, for on Mamma's instructions Lady Flora came along too as an unwelcome third, stifling intercourse between Lehzen and me by our rapid realisation that she was Conroy's spy. She and That Man soon had an excellent understanding between them, and a mutual respect that bordered almost on affection. I believe she was ambitious, and saw Conroy as the way ahead, while he saw such a useful tool in her that he was almost willing to forgive her for being female. Certainly his usual coarse manner was modified in her case, and though he still treated her familiarly, there was less of the patronising tone he used with other women.

Lehzen and I soon learned to guard our tongues in her presence, for every word was reported back; but all our care could not protect us against the twist an ingenious mind could put on an innocent word or phrase. Moreover, she joined Conroy in treating Lehzen with such harshness and contempt that it was plain they hoped to make her so miserable she would leave of her own accord. They missed their mark, for Lehzen's hide had been toughened by long exposure to Conroy's insults; but I didn't know that then. I was afraid, and I hated Lady Flora with all the hidden bitterness of the helpless.

A new move in the campaign against me was now being planned. In the summer of 1835 Conroy told Mamma that as I entered on my seventeenth year I no longer needed a governess. My official governess, the Duchess of Northumberland, had proved a disappointment to Conroy since her appointment in 1832. He had wanted her name only, simply to confer status on the household, but she had shown a disconcerting desire to enquire into my well-being and to quarrel with the harshness of my regime. The Duchess and Lehzen should be sent away, said Conroy, and I should become my mother's companion, with a Lady of the Bedchamber of my own. This lady-in-waiting must be Lady Flora Hastings. (I was too old for a governess, be it noted, but not old enough to choose my own attendants!)

The scheme would need the approval of the King, and I had no way of knowing that it would have been angrily rejected by him: he and Aunt Adelaide liked and approved of Lehzen, and if she could endure the discomforts and humiliations of her post, she was quite safe in it as long as they lived. But isolated and ignorant as I was, I suffered agonies that year as I watched the manoeuvres in the campaign to rob me of her. I grew stonier and Lehzen grew grimmer, but the situation was not discussed between us. To the pains and trials of being sixteen were added these terrible anxieties, and all were shut away inside me, with no outlet except in my dreams, and the fits of hopeless weeping I indulged in in bed when Mamma was asleep.

In the middle of all this came my Confirmation, on the 30th of July 1835. I knelt before the Archbishop of Canterbury in the Chapel Royal, St James's, dressed in my new white lace gown and a white crêpe bonnet with a wreath of roses around it. My dear, good tutor, Mr Davys, assisted in the service, and I tried to concentrate my thoughts on the significance of this most solemn ceremony for which he had long been preparing me. It should have been a joyful and spiritual occasion, but I was in a state of nervous exhaustion by then. Uncle William had led me into the chapel, and when my hand trembled on his broadcloth sleeve, he had laid his own dry, large-knuckled hand over it and patted it reassuringly. But a moment later he had spotted John Conroy amongst my mother's attendants, and with a mighty roar, like a goaded lion, he had ordered him out of the chapel.

Conroy went, with a black and bitter look for my uncle which boded me no good; and when a few minutes later, the Archbishop began his address to me on the subject of my future responsibilities, miserable tears began flooding over my cheeks. I was right to be apprehensive: as soon as we returned to Kensington Palace, Mamma handed me a long letter – a favoured method in the Coburg family for delivering important but unpleasant advices. I read it in the exhaustion of tears: my attitude towards Lehzen, Mamma said, must change. I had now reached a period of my life that brought changes with it, and henceforward I must place my attendant at a distance. I must always confide first in my mother, who was devoted to me, and whose sacrifices on my behalf had been so numerous and so great. I was to remember that I was entrusted to the guidance and control of that affectionate mother until I reached the age of either eighteen or twenty-one.

I wept on reading that letter, and went on weeping for a very long time. They meant to separate me from Lehzen. Papa had left me almost at birth; Mamma had abandoned me for John Conroy. Feo had gone away to be married, Uncle Leopold to be King of the Belgians. Even poor old Späth, who had loved me 'not wisely, but too well', had been punished for it and sent away. My uncle King was dead, I was not permitted to see Uncle William and Aunt Adelaide, I was allowed no friends but Conroy's daughters who were his spies. There was only Lehzen whom I could trust, who had been with me from the beginning, who had never let me down. Prisoner that I was, she shared my cage willingly, and placed herself between me and the worst excesses of my gaolers. Without her I felt I could not survive.

And here was a new idea in Mamma's letter: the question of my majority. Royal persons came of age at eighteen, but here was Mamma hinting at twenty-one. I had been dreaming of freedom two years hence; was my prison sentence now somehow to be extended? Most of all, it was the thought of three more years of this existence which broke down my resistance that day and brought me to helpless tears.

15th March 1900

GOD KNOWS each of His creatures individually, and He will never send you more than you can bear. At that darkest hour, help was on the way to me, in the form of my uncle Leopold, who paid his first visit to England in four years in September 1835. Mamma and I were staying at Ramsgate for a holiday, and he came to us there, bringing with him his new young wife, Princess Louise of Orléans, the daughter of King Louis-Philippe of France. She was pretty, vivacious, gay and warm-hearted. I loved her from the first moment she put her arms round me, kissed me, and cried, 'But it is so absurd that I am your aunt, when I am only seven years older than you! You shall think of me, if you please, as your elder sister, and then we shall be quite comfortable!'

Dear creature! Who could not be at ease with her? She managed to combine a natural sagacity with the bubbling high spirits of a sixteen-year-old, despite the fact that she had borne her second son in the April of that year. She laughed, and talked, and took a great interest in everything I did, admired my drawings, and played draughts with me after dinner. And when I shyly proffered admiration for her exquisite toilette (she was the best-dressed, most elegant woman I ever knew) she took me up to her room and let me go through her wardrobe, trying things on.

Women who have had a normal upbringing cannot imagine how this little attention thrilled me. No-one else had ever discussed clothes with me – I had no friends, and it was not a subject to interest dear Lehzen – or treated the topic as something delightful and amusing. But Aunt Louise chatted to me as if we were the same age, shook out her lovely Parisian gowns and held them up against me, told me what would suit and how I might make the best of myself.

'Now *this* one, the white moiré – ah yes, you have the bosoms for it! I, alas, am as small as a child. It will look better on you than ever it did on me. You have very pretty shoulders, my dear: you should make the most of them. And look, this silk rose goes with it – in your hair – so.'

'Oh, Aunt! How pretty!' I gazed in the looking-glass at the smiling young woman who had for a moment replaced the sad child.

'Do you like it? Then it is yours. Yes, yes, I insist! *Ma chère*, it is a trifle, not worth half so many thanks!'

Thereafter a number of little exquisite items seemed to find their way from her boxes into mine: brown silk ribbons, a spangled scarf, a charming lace *pèlerine*, a pair of lavender gloves, embroidered slippers, a painted fan, a fur tippet. As I warmed before her charm and wholehearted interest, like a frozen kitten placed before a kitchen stove, I began to confide in her some of the deeply personal doubts I had about my appearance, which I would have been ashamed to own to anyone else, feeling they must be frivolous in someone in my position.

But Aunt Louise did not think it frivolous to care about one's appearance. 'It is natural to love what is beautiful; and that love must come from God, don't you think? The ugly toad and the little bird may be equally dear to Him, but we cannot help loving the pretty bird more. And I think it pleases God, *ma chère p'tite Victoire*, if we try to make ourselves more like the one than the other.'

'Do you really think so?'

'*Bien sûr*. We must all live together in this world, and it is right to make ourselves as agreeable to each other as possible, and not offend our neighbours with ugly clothes or untidy hair.'

And there was more reassurance waiting for me from Uncle Leopold: he had come to Ramsgate for the express purpose of advising me. In the years of his absence we had corresponded regularly, but letters could be – indeed, in my case certainly were – read by other eyes, and Uncle had long been growing uneasy about the situation at Kensington, which he learned about from a variety of sources. Only by coming to me in person could he be sure we would have a completely private and frank conversation, and this duly took place on the second day of their visit, when he came to me quite alone and stayed with me talking for almost an hour.

It was the most inexpressible relief to me. He confirmed my fears about John Conroy, but by exposing the man's entire, petty and misguided plot to me, he took away a great deal of the terror with which I had invested him. I had made him a monster in my mind, with almost supernatural powers; Uncle Leopold showed me a greedy, ambitious, but fundamentally stupid man, plotting to advance himself through a weak, misguided, but fundamentally good woman. (It was then that I gained the insights into Conroy's motives which I have given in this account of my childhood; and though Uncle Leopold could not then alter my hatred of both Conroy and Mamma, he laid the foundation on which I was later to be able to forgive her and come to love her again.)

Best of all, he reassured me as to the future. 'If you hold out against them, there is nothing they can do to force you,' he said. And, 'Trust Lehzen completely. She has the confidence of the King and Queen, and of the Government, and of me; and she is a shrewd and sensible woman. She will sustain you.' And again, 'I will always support you. I am on your side, and you may always look to me for help and guidance.'

'I have *complete* confidence in you, Uncle,' I said. 'You are the best and kindest adviser in the world.'

He looked grave then. 'I hope I may be. You know at least that my advice is always impartial. My one wish is that you should fulfil the high position to which you have been called with the utmost integrity. It is a grave responsibility, Victoria. You must not allow your mind to be taken up by frivolous amusements. All pleasure is transitory except that which comes from doing one's duty.'

I thought guiltily about the pleasant evening I had spent last night with Aunt Louise, and how often our laughter had been heard over the draughts board. 'I do study very hard, Uncle,' I murmured in self-defence.

'I know. You are a good child. But as I have frequently told you, these are hard times for royalty. You must fit yourself for government not only by preparing your character, but also your mind. Honesty, straightforwardness, absolute probity, dedication, diligence – these you must have. But you must also have patience, wisdom, and sound judgement. You will be called upon to make decisions: you must have the knowledge and sagacity to make them well.'

I said nothing, thinking deeply about his words.

'It is a heavy burden, my niece; but you will be strong enough for it. And I will always help you in every way I can. I emphasise these things now not to frighten you or cast you down – quite the opposite.' I looked up, and saw that his stern gravity of expression had given way to kindness. 'I wish you to see that the troubles you are suffering at the moment, heavy though they seem to you, are unimportant compared with the task ahead of you. One day soon you will be Queen of England, my child, and then these unpleasantnesses – the Conroys of the world and the deceitful webs they weave – will be as nothing. Your real life will begin, and this will seem but a dream – a bad dream, which dissolves at daybreak and is forgotten.'

I stared into the empty air, seeing then, for the first time, a shape to my life, and a life beyond the wretched imprisonment and torment which had been my whole view until then. I wanted to be a good Queen, the best England had ever known. I felt filled with a spirit and a strength beyond my own.

'I will do my best,' I said.

'I know you will,' he replied gravely. Then he stood up, and I with him, and he took my hand and pressed it kindly. 'You have a good vein of stubbornness in you, my dear. Use it wisely. Hold out against Conroy – but try to stay on good terms with your mother. It will not be for much longer.'

Ah, but when you are sixteen, a year is a very long time, a hundred times longer than the same year when you are sixty. And when I had said goodbye to my dear uncle and aunt on Wednesday the 7th of October, and seen their boat steam away from Dover, I felt myself very alone again, and the prospect of returning to my prison with Conroy my gaoler filled me with despair.

Five

19th March 1900, at Windsor

WHEN MY uncle and aunt left England we did not leave Ramsgate, for I fell desperately ill with typhoid. I did not leave my room for five weeks. I grew thin and pale, and so weak I could not sit up without support; and my beautiful hair – my one great attraction – which had been so long and thick one could scarcely take it in one's hands – began to fall out in handfuls. As a last desperate measure to save it, Lehzen cut it almost quite off, which left me looking like a plucked crow – a most depressing sight. I was so very ill that eventually even Conroy was convinced I was not shamming, and tiptoed round the house with an expression of anxious concern which would have been touching, Lehzen said afterwards, if one had not known he was only worried about losing his investment.

He showed his true colours when the crisis had passed and it seemed that I would not die after all. While I was still on my sick bed, thin and white as a peeled stick, he persuaded Mamma that it would be the perfect opportunity – while I was in a weakened state, you understand! – to coerce me into agreeing to appoint him as my personal secretary whenever I should finally become Queen. This was the measure of the man. Day after day he came up to my room, that hateful bully, and stood over me, hectoring me in his loud, coarse voice until my head ached and I trembled with exhaustion. Mamma added her softer pleas to his, and cut me with reproaches and accusations of ingratitude and unfilial coldness; but she did not see the half of it – how he worked away at me, wearing me down, telling me again and again that I *must* agree, tormenting me as he knew so well how to do.

But I did not yield. Uncle Leopold's words were fresh in my mind, and I knew that the one thing I must never do was to give Conroy *any* position in my Household. Once I was free of him, I would banish him from my court and send him as far away as it was in my power to do; all I had to do was to hold out for another few years. So even though he reduced me to tears every day, though I sobbed and turned my face into the pillow to escape the sight of him; though he thrust his hated face so close to mine I could feel his spittle on my cheek; though he called me names and threatened me with dire punishments; though at last he forced a pencil brutally into my fingers and commanded me to sign the paper he held before me – yet weak and sick as I was, I would not yield.

I was a Hanoverian, and stubborn from birth. But now there was a core of iron in me, forged in the fire of That Man's mistreatment of me. Did I say that my dear spaniel Dashy was the only thing I had to thank Conroy for? That inner strength of mine perhaps is another. What Conroy could not do to a convalescent girl of sixteen cannot be done. I will never be bullied, as various people later – Sir Robert Peel and Sir William Gladstone, for instance – have had good cause to know.

We left Ramsgate at last on the 12th of January 1836. I was completely recovered from the typhoid, and was looking forward to going home. We stayed at an inn on the road overnight, and arrived at Kensington Palace on a bright though bitterly cold day, some three and a half months after we had last quit it. As I was about to go in, Mamma laughed and caught me back.

'I have a surprise for you, Victoria,' she said. 'We do not go back to our old apartment. To see where we live now, you must go up two staircases.'

I stared at her in astonished delight. 'We have our new apartments after all?'

'Yes, and all the alterations are done just as we wanted, and the rooms new-papered and with fresh drapes.'

'Oh, Mamma, how lovely! Oh, I can't wait to see them!'

I raced away like a ten-year-old up to the spacious second-floor suite with the wonderful views over the lawns and flowerbeds. Our old rooms on the ground floor had been cramped, dark and damp, with no space for formal entertaining. Here on the second floor, next door to Uncle Sussex, we had two large rooms with magnificent pillars and fine carvings for receiving, reached by a handsome Kent staircase. Our bedroom was large and lofty, and beyond it came a little room for the maid and a dressing-room for Mamma. Beyond that the old gallery had been divided by new false walls into three handsome, cheerful rooms, a sitting-room for me, a study and an ante-room. The workmen were still busy in the study, and making a dreadful noise.

I ran from room to room, admiring the new drapes and furnishings, and exclaiming to Lehzen, who was observing everything with her most tight-mouthed expression, evincing only a kind of dour amusement. I was surprised to find ourselves there, for three years ago, in 1832, Mamma, tired of our cramped quarters, had drawn up ambitious and expensive designs for these very rooms, and presented them to Uncle William with a bald demand for them to be carried out. Irritated with her on various counts, he had refused; and when Mamma had pressed him, he had finally written, 'The King says NO!' in his own hand across the plans.

And now here we were in the very apartments! Uncle William must have relented, I thought – and if he had, it must be for love of me, for he and Mamma–Conroy were still at daggers drawn. What a good, kind uncle he was!

'Oh, it is all so lovely!' I cried, whirling on the spot with my hands clasped ecstatically before me. 'No more mould in the cupboards! No more black beetles! But how did you manage to persuade Uncle William, Mamma? Why did he change his mind?'

Mamma hesitated for a moment, and I saw Lehzen looking at her grimly, as though she, too, wanted to hear the answer.

'It was for your health,' Mamma said at last. 'Doctor Clark says you must have dry, airy rooms if you are not to get ill again. The ground floor apartment was very bad for your health.' I would have asked her more, but she went on quickly, 'Why don't you run down to your old room, my love, and begin fetching up your books and dolls?'

'Oh, yes, Mamma!' I cried, and rushed away, too pleased and excited to notice that there was something a little strained about Mamma's voice, as though she had been reluctant to answer me.

20th March 1900

AFTER THE excitement of settling in, I returned to my dull life. My health improved, thanks to a new regime instituted by Dr Clark. He decreed that I was not to work for too long together, that I should do some lessons at a standing-desk to vary my position, that I was to have plenty of walking exercise in the fresh air (especially in bracing air – the air at Kensington he thought too relaxing), and that I should have exercises with Indian clubs to improve my figure and circulation. The walks prescribed were taken in Hampstead,

Highgate, Finchley, Harrow and such places, and I enjoyed the variety of scene and the air and views from these high places very much. But though Clark prescribed the air, Mamma prescribed the company for the expeditions, and between Lady Flora Hastings and Victoire Conroy there was not much recreation for a gregarious soul. I was a normal, lively, passionate girl of seventeen and I longed for amusement and gaiety and fun and oh! for pleasant company! I wanted bread, and they gave me a stone.

For the rest, I continued with my lessons with Mr Davys – the Dean of Chester as he was by then – and law and constitution were added to my curriculum, and a regular reading of the newspapers, which I regret to say did not much interest me. The news of this thrilling period of history were of small moment to me beside my longing for balls and parties. Every evening I sat down to dinner with Mamma, Sir John and Lady Conroy, and Princess Sophia – which was rather like an oyster sitting down to dinner with the Walrus and the Carpenter. This tedium was interrupted by a fortnightly visit to the theatre or the opera, and occasional attendance at a Court function.

At one of these latter, my kind uncle took my hand in both of his (he had developed chalk deposits in his knuckles, and they were growing pitifully crooked) and with an earnest look told me that he meant to 'hold on' and reign until I reached my majority.

'I hope, indeed, sir, that you live many years,' I said falteringly.

'Ha! Don't you worry, m'dear!' he replied. 'I may be a simple fellow, just an old sea-dog, but these eyes of mine have always been sharp, and I can see what's goin' on under my own nose, dammit! I shall hold on as long as I can.'

These few words brought tears to my eyes, as did any hint of sympathy in those days; but also alarmed me, as they reminded me that he was seventy years old, and suffering from asthma and gout. His death was no remote possibility; and if he died, what would become of me?

It was that year, 1836, which witnessed the dreadful scene at Windsor. Aunt Adelaide's birthday was on the 13th of August, and Uncle William's was on the 21st, while Mamma's fell between them on the 17th. Uncle William, with more propriety than Mamma showed, did his best to remain on terms with her, and he invited her with a very cordial note to come to Windsor for Aunt Adelaide's birthday celebrations on the 13th, and remain until after his own on the 21st. Mamma replied coldly that she preferred to spend her birthday at Claremont but that she would come to Windsor on the

20th; of Aunt Adelaide's birthday she made no mention at all. For arrogance, rudeness and tactlessness this letter hadn't its equal, and the astonishing thing is that Uncle William, who fiercely resented any slight to his Queen, did not erupt at once.

It happened that on the 20th of August Uncle William was in London for the proroguing of Parliament, and afterwards, on his way back to Windsor, he broke his journey (prompted by who can say what demon?) at Kensington, where he made a tour of inspection of the palace. At ten o'clock that evening Mamma and I were assembled after dinner with the other guests in the drawing-room at Windsor when the King arrived. It was plain from the moment he appeared in the doorway that something was wrong, for his pink face was a darker shade than usual, and his bright blue eyes seemed to bulge slightly under his frowning brows. He swept a glance round the room, and then came straight towards me. I was alarmed, but his expression cleared as he approached me, and he took both my hands in the most cordial way and said, 'Ha! There you are, m'dear! I am pleased to see you, very pleased indeed. We don't see enough of you at Court, your aunt and I, not by a long thought.'

Then he released my hands and turned to my mother. His expression underwent an alarming change: the smile disappeared, and the thunder clouds drew down over his brows. Mamma made him the shallowest curtsey she could have got away with, to which he responded with a slight bow. Then he said in a loud and angry voice, plainly meant to be heard by all, that a most unwarrantable liberty had been taken with one of his palaces.

'I have just come from Kensington, madam. What have you to say to that?'

A most unpleasant sensation began in the pit of my stomach. I looked towards Mamma, and though she was wearing her loftiest expression, I could see that she was apprehensive.

'Why, sir, what should I say to it?' she replied frigidly.

The King simply roared. 'By God, madam, do you pretend not to know? Seventeen rooms have been stolen from me – yes, *stolen* I say! Apartments taken possession of without my consent! Walls put up, walls taken down, workmen instructed, bills run up, all without consulting me – indeed, contrary to my *express* commands! What are you about, madam? I cannot understand such conduct!'

Mamma had blanched, but she was not half so white as I felt. So that was it! I had been rejoicing in our new accommodation, never dreaming that I was a usurper – and I had a brief, ignoble sense of relief that I had never happened to thank my uncle for giving them to us and thus brought the storm down on my own head. I was trembling so much with anxiety now that I did not properly hear what Mamma replied, except that it was something about me – the necessity on grounds of my health and what was due to my station.

Uncle William was not placated, but he seemed disinclined to continue the quarrel at that moment. He muttered under his breath, like thunder fading over the horizon. 'Station, eh? Whose station I wonder? But it is all of a piece, all of a piece!' And then one last shell burst over Mamma's unrepentant head: 'I will no more endure such disrespectful conduct towards me! Mark me, madam!' before he turned away to speak to his other guests. I felt weak with distress and shame, but Mamma seemed not to have any such feelings in her. Her eyes were bright and her lips compressed with anger, but there was also something of satisfaction in her expression. Considering what she had gained by way of accommodation, that short outburst was a small enough price.

But she underestimated my uncle's irritation against her. The Birthday Dinner the next day was called a private one, but still it involved about a hundred guests – relatives, courtiers, and prominent local dignitaries. Mamma was placed on the King's right hand, and I had the seat opposite him – the positions of honour. At the end of dinner the loyal toast was drunk, in the form chosen for the occasion by the Queen: 'His Majesty's health, and long life to him!'

The King's part should then have been to respond with gracious thanks, but instead his pent-up rage seemed to burst from him in an uncontrollable tirade, provoked by those unlucky words.

'Long life? Aye, long life indeed! I trust to God that my life *may* be spared, at least for nine months longer, after which if I die there will be no cause for a Regency! I should then have the satisfaction of leaving the royal authority to the personal exercise of that young lady opposite' (he pointed at me where I sat as though nailed to my chair-back with astonishment), 'the Heiress Presumptive of the Crown, and not in the hands of a Person now near me, who is surrounded by evil advisers and who herself is incompetent to act with propriety in the station in which she would be placed.' His voice rose now as he went on, 'I have no hesitation in saying I have been insulted – grossly and continually insulted – by that Person, but it has gone past all endurance, and I will not stand it any longer. No, by God!' He thumped his fist down on the table, making the glass drops of the epergne nearby ring like little protesting voices. His glaring eyes now fixed on me, and I shrank into myself in distress, though his rage was not directed towards myself. 'Aye, aye, and amongst the many offences of that Person, I have particularly to complain about the way in which she has kept that young lady away from my Court! She has been repeatedly kept from my Drawing-rooms, at which she ought *always* to have been present, as befitted my niece and my heiress – but I am fully resolved this shall not happen again! I would have that Person know that I am King, and that I am determined to make my authority respected, and in future I shall insist and command that the Princess shall on all occasions appear at my Court, as it is her duty to do!'

The Queen had her eyes downcast, her lips trembling with distress. Mamma seemed to have been turned to stone, and was facing straight before her with her eyes fixed rigidly on the empty air. I could feel the helpless tears slipping down my cheeks, though I struggled with them desperately, not wishing to add any further breach of etiquette to the already shattered occasion. Perhaps Uncle William was moved by the sight of them, for his voice softened, and he said, as though placating me, 'Well, well, it is only what is right and proper after all. The Princess must be seen at Court, for she will reign over you all when I am gone – and a fine Queen she will make, too, for she is a very good girl indeed, as I have often had cause to tell her, both as my niece and my heiress – or I would have done, had I been given the opportunity. And that's all I have to say.'

All! The half of it would have been twice too much! But there was only a moment or two more to endure, of feeling the eyes of half the company on me, and then the Queen stood up, rather unsteadily, I thought, and at that signal all we ladies rose to follow her out of the room. As soon as we reached the drawing-room, Mamma came up to me and seized my arm in a grip so hard that I found a bruise there next morning.

'Come, Victoria,' she said in a voice meant to penetrate to all parts of the room, 'we are leaving. I shall order the carriage, and we shall go at once. I will not remain under a roof where I am so publicly insulted, and for no reason whatever. It is not to be borne.'

Aunt Adelaide, I could see, was almost in tears at these words, and I wanted most of all to withdraw my arm from Mamma's heedless grip and run across the room to her. Publicly insulted, yes, and that was bad – but for no reason? My gentle aunt who had always been so kind to me, who had befriended Mamma when she was first widowed, and had never offered the least offence, had been continually snubbed, slighted and insulted by Mamma and Conroy. Uncle William's conduct had been hasty and injudicious, even unmannerly, but it was not unprovoked. It was agonising for me to be caught between them, and I felt the misery acutely; but behind my present mortification was a deeper sorrow from the knowledge that after this, Mamma would be doubly determined to keep me away from Court, and prevent me from having anything to do with my dear uncle and aunt. The King might be determined to command my presence, but when it came to determination, he was the merest tyro next to Mamma and Conroy. An essentially kind and easy-going person will never win against the malicious, the self-seeking and the bad-tempered.

Fortunately there were enough well-wishers amongst the assembled ladies, who surrounded Mamma in the drawing-room and persuaded her that we must not leave until the morning, when we had planned to end our visit, or there would be the most dreadful public scandal. Later, as we walked along the corridors to our bedchamber, Mamma gave me a dreadful scolding for 'making up to' Uncle William and taking the part of someone who insulted my own mother, and my tears flowed again. The next morning we left early and went back to Claremont, and as our chaise pulled away I felt I would have been glad never to see Windsor again.

22nd March 1900

THE YEAR of 1837, in which I would attain my majority, opened in a suspenseful quiet, like the oppressive silence that sometimes comes before a thunderstorm. Lehzen and I huddled together and kept as still as possible, like fieldmice, in the hope of escaping attention. It was one of the worst aspects of my childhood that in order to survive the intrigue and duplicity with which I was surrounded, I was obliged to practise what was foreign to my nature. I was by nature straightforward, open, candid; I had to learn to dissemble, to hide my feelings, to be guarded, discreet – *secretive*. By the age of eighteen I could hold my tongue and control my features like an elder statesman, and though they proved valuable skills for a monarch, still they had their price. For one thing, I am sure the worry and torment I endured stopped me growing, as I told Lord M.; and for another, because I had so little opportunity of meeting other people, I never outgrew my childhood shyness. I am still, to this day, paralysed by shyness when I meet someone new; and I have no small-talk. (Lord M. gave me valuable advice on that head – the more one tried to think what to say, the more tongue-tied one became, he said.

Better to say anything, however foolish or commonplace, than silently to search for something witty or wise.)

The weeks passed, and everyone waited and watched the calendar and the King. Bulletins filtered through Princess Sophia to Mamma, and through Lehzen to me. He was seventy-two, and growing feeble, but though his asthma was troublesome he seemed otherwise in no immediate danger. In April my brother Charles arrived for a visit, with his wife and two children – after raking about the Continent for some years, he had married beneath him, to the family's distress, to one of Grandmamma Coburg's ladies-in-waiting, a woman of no lineage and no fortune. His wild and profligate lifestyle kept him in continual debt, which he applied shamelessly to Mamma to pay off, and this importunity and propensity to sponge on others led him into a natural alliance with Conroy. They were always muttering with their heads together, and bending over sheets of paper on which they sketched out, I suppose, ever more fantastic schemes for subordinating me to their wills. Charles had much to gain from promoting Conroy's cause, for if Conroy held the purse strings, he might hope to be able to dip his hand pretty freely.

On the 18th of May the unsettling report reached us that the King had received sitting down, both at the levée and the drawing-room held that day – a circumstance which could only mean he was more than usually weak, or unwell. His doctor, Sir Henry Halford, reported that his health was 'in a very odd state' and that his breathing difficulties precluded his going to bed. 'I trust he may get over it, but he is seventy-two.'

Perhaps his brush with the Great Determiner alarmed my uncle. The next day Lord Conyngham, the Lord Chamberlain, arrived and announced that he had a letter for me from the King. Conroy, who was with Mamma, of course, stepped forward and held out his hand for it, but Lord Conyngham kept a tight hold on the letter and said – with some satisfaction, I imagine – that he must deliver it into the Princess's own hand.

'By what authority?' Conroy demanded sharply.

'His Majesty's,' said Conyngham, and displayed the Sign Manual on the letter.

Mamma and Conroy exchanged a sharp, dismayed look. There were only a few days of my minority left – and now what new trouble was come to plague them? Mamma held out her hand now. 'You may give the letter to me, my lord. I will see that my daughter receives it.'

Conyngham bowed. 'I regret, madam, that I cannot comply. My

instructions from His Majesty are quite specific. I am myself to place the letter in the hands of the Princess and of no other person.'

'Then you shall do so,' Conroy said magnanimously, since there was no help for it, 'but it must be in the presence of her august mother. The Princess does nothing without her mother's help and advice.'

Thus I was fetched into the presence, and Lord Conyngham, with look both kindly and respectful, handed me the letter with a verbal assurance of my uncle's goodwill and affection towards me. I trembled a little as I opened it, for Mamma and Conroy stood by, their hands hooked to tear the letter from me at the first opportunity, their eyes greedily fixed on my face as if they might read the contents reflected there, as in a glass.

I trembled a great deal more when I had read the letter, both in gratitude towards my uncle, and in fear of my enemies' reaction. Dear Uncle William had held out to me the golden key to my cage! This is what he wrote: that when I came of age to reign on the 24th of May, he proposed to ask Parliament for an income of £10,000 a year for me, to be entirely at my own disposal. I myself was to appoint my Keeper of the Privy Purse, who was to be responsible solely to me, and I was to form my own separate Household if I wished it and appoint my own Ladies. Lord Melbourne, he added, had suggested Sir Benjamin Stephenson as a suitable Keeper of the Privy Purse. (Sir Benjamin was a great favourite of the King and Queen, but much hated by Mamma.)

Oh, Uncle! What a prospect to hold out before me at a moment like that: my own establishment, money enough to do as I liked, no Mamma nagging me, no Conroy doing hateful things in my name, no Victoire Conroy or Lady Flora amongst my Ladies! What caged bird has ever pressed itself so eagerly against the bars as I did with that letter in my hand? So eagerly, but so hopelessly – for the next thing I must do is to hand it to Mamma to read.

She paused only to get rid of Lord Conyngham, who, his duty done, could do no more to save me from my lawful guardian. When he had left, Mamma perused the letter eagerly, and Conroy leaned most familiarly over her shoulder and read with her. Their faces grew longer and longer as they read, and I hastened to put my word in before they could speak.

'I think I should answer the letter straight away, do not you, Mamma? I know well that Sir Benjamin will not suit, so perhaps I should ask the King if the Dean of Chester might be named Privy

Purse – just for the time being.' I added this last as the thunderclouds gathered over Mamma's face.

'Absolutely not!' She read the letter again, seeming fascinated by the horror of it. 'Impossible! Outrageous! I have never in my life seen anything to equal it!'

'It is very kind of my uncle to—' I ventured; but Mamma cut me off.

'Kind? *Kind?* It is a deliberate insult! Every feeling must be wounded! To pass over me at such a time, in such a way – your own mother, in whom the country reposes *every* confidence – and when I have sacrificed my whole existence for you! To suggest that I do not know what is right for my own child, when every moment of my life is devoted to my duties to her and to the country—' She choked herself with emotion, and Conroy took up the theme for her.

'Everyone knows, Duchess, that you are the very pattern of motherhood! Only an imbecile – or a malicious schemer – could think there could be two minds on the subject, between you and the Princess. Old Tarry Breeks is getting senile, and that's the fact of it.' (Tarry Breeks was a vulgar nickname for Uncle William, because he had been so long in the Navy. It was a measure of Conroy's insolence that he would use it to my mother and before me.) 'It's the family illness coming on, you know,' he added with a leer at me. 'Remember how the old King ended up, dribbling and talking to himself? He's senile, that's what it is.'

'Senile?' Mamma cried. 'No – he hates me, that's all. And *she* encourages him. Why I put up with that woman – !'

There was much more of the same, aimed partly at me but mostly at my uncle, with a side-stream or two of lava for poor Lehzen, as though she had anything to do with this. I watched the golden key disappear like mist, while the bars of my cage remained too, too solid. 'Might I not have a private conversation with Lord Melbourne on the subject?' I asked at last – a thin, vain hope. 'He would be able to advise me what best—'

'Certainly not!' Mamma snapped. 'What could he tell you that *I* cannot? Do you suppose your own mother does not know better what is good for you than a complete stranger?'

'There's no knowing what *she* supposes,' Conroy said grimly. 'Such whims and inconsistencies are a sign of immaturity, coupled with a weak mind – if not something worse. We must hope and pray it isn't *that* – but whether or not, it's plain such a little nodcock as her could never govern the country without supervision. I've always told you, haven't I, Duchess, that she's not up to scratch? Every day and every word she utters proves it more. Without us, she wouldn't last a minute, and the country'd be in the devil of a stew.'

I could feel the familiar tears rising, but I choked them down to ask, 'What must I do then? I must reply to a letter from the King.'

They exchanged a speaking glance, and then Mamma said, 'I shall draft a reply for you. Leave me now – go back to Lehzen. I am quite overset by this. I think I have one of my headaches coming on.'

I left them, feeling so miserable and agitated that I did not even go down to dinner that evening, though food was usually one of my comforts. Whether Mamma got her headache or not I don't know, but I got one for her, and retired to bed early and exhausted.

The next day there was a flurry of letters between Lord Melbourne and Mamma as she sought to discover how far the Government was involved with the offer, and how far it was Uncle William's own plan. When finally I was called into Mamma's presence, there was a letter – not a draft but a finished document – which I was told I must copy out and sign. I read it with dismay. It was in Mamma's hand, but it was all Conroy's doing. In his words I thanked Uncle for his offer, but said my youth and inexperience unfitted me to enter into the details of the subject (as if I had not thought about my future establishment! As though I did not understand the use of money a hundred times better than either of my gaolers!) I went on to declare that my only wish was to be allowed to remain as I was, under the care and protection of my dear Mother, and that, on the subject of money, I should wish any additional amount that was necessary to be given to her for my use, as she had always had command of my affairs and freely did everything I wanted.

They made me copy it without amendment, and sign it, and send it. It was the only time I yielded on any material point; but afterwards I went straight to my room and had Lehzen witness a statement that the letter was not composed by me, and that I had signed it under duress.

The King was not deceived, however. When he read the communication, he growled, 'Victoria has not written that letter!' He would have pursued the matter, but Lord Melbourne, as he confessed to me later, persuaded him not to. My dearest Lord M. told me, after I became Queen, that he had not the least idea of the misery and bullying I endured at Kensington, 'otherwise there would have been a blow-up'. As it was, he warned the King that the Whigs were not doing well, and that another quarrel between him and Mamma, especially on such a point, would give the Tories useful material. He pointed out that Mamma was on strong ground, because in all respects except for succeeding to the Throne I would still be a minor until I was twenty-one; and that Mamma would be sure, if she were crossed, to appeal to public sympathy by portraying the King's offer as a deliberate attempt to separate a helpless, tearful child from her devoted, self-sacrificing mother.

Sir Herbert Taylor agreed with Lord Melbourne, and told the King that it was worth making almost any sacrifice to avoid another embarrassingly public quarrel in the royal family, and the King wearily agreed. 'The fact of the matter,' Uncle said, 'is that the Duchess and King John want money. She has thrown off the mask – but I will defeat her.'

We defeated her (or rather Conroy) together. My poor uncle was plainly ill by this time, but still for my sake, he hung on to a life which must have become tiresome to him, and in the midst of the quarrel over control of my purse my birthday arrived, Wednesday the 24th of May 1837, and I came of age. Now there could be no Regency; but Conroy still pinned his hopes on keeping control of me for another three years, keeping me in Mamma's care as a minor, and forcing me to make him my Privy Purse and Personal Secretary. I think he had convinced himself by that time of his own lies – that I was backward, flighty, and even a little simple-minded.

After the business of the letter to the King, I refused to talk to Mamma unless it was absolutely essential, kept myself apart from her whenever I could, and when in company with her spoke as little as possible to anyone. The tension was almost unendurable. I had thought my majority would solve everything, but the days that followed it were if anything worse. The King recovered a little towards the end of May, but then on the 2nd of June fell ill again. Conroy grew frantic, and together with Mamma and my brother Charles worked on me every hour, intimidating and bullying, cajoling and threatening, doing everything they knew to make me promise to give Conroy the appointment he wanted when I was Queen. Tossed and battered like a piece of flotsam on a stormy sea, I yet found the strength to stand fast by my refusal – thinking always of that gallant old man at Windsor, holding on for my sake as hard as he could with his twisted, painful hands to the last threads of his life.

On the 14th of June the King was gravely ill, and although the Dean of Chester still came each morning, my outside lessons were discontinued. I remained in my room with Lehzen in hourly expectation of a summons, took my meals there, spoke only to her and the Dean. Beyond the door the old palace seemed to twitch and jump like a dog with fleas as Conroy, Mamma and Charles discussed endlessly what they might still do to further their cause. I learned later from Charles that Conroy had proposed locking me up and starving me until I agreed to make him my Private Secretary and Privy Purse, but Charles intervened, feeling it had gone too far; and speaking in German so that Conroy might not understand, he warned my mother earnestly against such an action. (Charles told me this later to try to gain credit with me, but I doubt whether his opposition had any effect. If Conroy did not persist in that particular scheme, it was probably because he doubted Mamma's resolution in carrying it through.)

On the 17th of June, I am told, my poor uncle whispered to Sir Henry Halford, 'Tomorrow is Waterloo Day, ain't it?'

'Yes, sir – the twenty-second anniversary of that glorious day,' said Sir Henry.

'I should like to last it out. Tinker me up, can't you, Halford, to get me through it? I should like to see the Waterloo sun set.'

Sir Henry did as he was bid. On the 18th, Waterloo Day, the Duke came to see the King, and brought to the bedside the tricolor which had been captured in the battle. By then approaching death had made the King almost blind. 'Unfurl it and let me feel it,' he whispered. He ran it through his hands, and a smile glimmered on his tired face. 'Good, good. We trounced 'em all right, hey, what? By God, that was a glorious day, Duke!'

England's Hero murmured an agreement.

The King turned his head on the pillow, seeking his face in the darkness which surrounded him. 'Look after the gel, Duke!' he whispered urgently. 'See she gets fair play.'

'I will do my duty to the country and crown, sir, as I have always done,' said the Duke.

'Aye, aye,' said the King, comforted. 'I know you will.'

On the 19th in the afternoon, Ernst Hohenlohe, Feo's husband (who was Queen Adelaide's cousin and had been staying with her at Windsor) came to Kensington Palace to see me. In Mamma's presence he told me that the King was sinking fast, and the Queen had been told that he could not last the night. I wept, for although his death would mean release for me, he had always been kind to me and I did love him, the good, brave old man. I had had precious few people to love in my life. Afterwards Ernst contrived to speak to me apart for a moment, to tell me that Queen Adelaide had sent me her love, and thought about me very often (how like her it was, to think to send *me* a message at such a time!).

'But listen, Victoria,' he added, speaking low and quickly, 'there is something else – for you alone – Mamma must not hear!' I checked my tears, and he went on, 'The King bid me tell you, that he cannot hold on any longer, and that when you are Queen, you should send straight away for Lord Melbourne and tell him that you mean to keep on with him and his ministers. He says you may trust them, and they will protect you against Someone.'

'Yes,' I whispered – all I could manage to say, for my throat ached dreadfully with tears. Dying, he still thought of me, and of the country. He was a worthy king. I prayed I should be like him in that respect, and be as brave when my time came.

He died during the night. I was not even able to say goodbye to him, or tell him that I understood and appreciated all he had done for me.

26th March 1900

I MUST have slept heavily that night, for I did not hear Mamma get up early in response to a summons from below: visitors had arrived at five o'clock in the morning and the porter had not wanted to admit them. Mamma was likewise unwilling to admit them to me: it was six o'clock before she came back into the bedchamber and shook me gently.

'Wake up, child. You must get up, Victoria. The Archbishop of Canterbury is here and wishes to see you.'

'The Archbishop?' I said sleepily, sitting up.

'Yes, and Lord Conyngham. Come, we must not keep them waiting.'

I was wide awake then. A cold sensation settled in the pit of my stomach, for I knew what it must mean. I looked past her for Lehzen, and she was there, drawing back the drapes on one of the windows. Outside it was daylight, of course, for it was midsummer; I could see the pale morning sun slanting across the window and hear a thrush somewhere out of sight trying out his phrases. Mamma turned back the covers, and I slipped my legs out, shivering as my bare feet touched the floor, searching for my slippers with my toes. Lehzen came back and met my eyes, but there was nothing to read in her expression, neither agitation nor triumph. She took up my cotton wrapper from the end of the bed and held it out to me, and I turned and put my arms into the sleeves, and put it on over my nightgown, feeling her hands drawing the length of my hair out to hang loose down my back.

'Come, child,' Mamma said, and there was an edge to her voice – impatience? or perhaps apprehension. She took up the candle in the silver candlestick which she had put down to wake me, and took my hand and led me towards the door. 'Lehzen – bring the vinaigrette,' she said over her shoulder. 'Just in case . . .'

Just in case? But I should not swoon, I thought, not today – though I felt very apprehensive indeed, almost sick with it. I was about to experience something quite new, something no woman had experienced in more than a hundred years. It made me feel hollow – and yet excited, too, in a strange, tremulous way; an excitement that seemed to me just then somehow almost sinful – almost sensual. We passed through the anteroom to the backstairs, dark, steep and narrow, the stairs I had never been allowed to walk down unaided. Mamma held my hand tightly, and hers was as cold as a river-washed stone. I held up my white nightgown with my free hand and did not look at the steps of the staircase, though the candle-shadows flowed treacherously across them. There was no ghost of Amy Robsart here. I knew I could not fall. I was in the grip of a powerful force, which bore me towards the one meeting that could never have been prevented. My feet glided blindly and surely, hardly seeming to touch the ground.

Near the door of the sitting-room I paused. The door was open, the drapes had been drawn back, there was sunlight in the room. Three male figures stood there, tall (all men were tall to me, who was less than five feet above the earth) and black, their legs looking endlessly long in their narrow pantaloons, their bare heads grey, their grave faces pale. The third man was Sir Henry Halford, the King's doctor. He must have been with my uncle when he died, I thought.

All this took no more than a second to absorb; and now I turned back, took the candlestick from Mamma's hand (an automatic gesture, for it was not needed) and said, 'I will go in alone.' It was a short sentence, but my voice lifted triumphantly between its beginning and its end, and I saw realisation come into Mamma's eyes that she had lost me; finally, at the last ditch. With one fleeting glance for Lehzen, I left them – as I now could, now and for ever more – and entered the chamber alone.

The three men saw me, and in a graceful and terrifying movement like horses dying all three sank to their knees – grown men, kneeling before *me*!

Lord Conyngham, the Lord Chamberlain, it was that spoke.

'Madam, it is my sad duty to inform you that your uncle, the King, is no more.' His voice wavered at that point, and I saw that there were tears on his face. 'He breathed his last at twelve minutes past two this morning,' he went on, 'and consequently you are from that moment Queen of England.'

The words struck me to the vitals like flame, like a sword of fire, and I thrust out my hand, my arm straight, like a messenger from God. Lord Conyngham took my hand and kissed it, and I felt the brush of his hastily shaven lips and a touch of dampness from his tears; and the knowledge became real, sank into my bones and became part of me. This dignified person, a marquess, the Lord Chamberlain, a grown-up man – was kneeling before me, *me*, and kissing my hand in homage. Now it would begin, my real life. I was free at last, Queen of England, and nobody would ever – *ever* again – make me do anything I didn't want to do.

27th March 1900

I HAVE been looking at my journal for that day, the first day of my reign; and I see that every entry records how I did this and saw that person alone, and *alone*, and *ALONE*! From the time that I left Mamma at the sitting-room door until the moment when I went briefly to say goodnight to her at half past ten that night, I barely set eyes on her. It grieves me to think of it now, but if I had known then how much it pained her to be cast out from my presence, I should only have felt she deserved her punishment. As it was, I didn't think of it at all. Conroy, of course, I would not permit to come near me; one of my greatest satisfactions of that crowded day was in dismissing him instantly from my Household. I could not, of course, dismiss him from Mamma's; and that she retained him when she knew how much I hated him was a great factor in our continued estrangement for the next three years.

What did the Queen of England do that day? She went first to her room and dressed – in mourning, of course, for Uncle William. The only black dress I had was an old one which had been dyed – not very successfully, I thought – for the last bout of Court-mourning, when Aunt Adelaide's mother had died. How Mamma had resented putting on black for the mother of the woman she hated and despised! I think that's why she dipped our dresses, rather than ordering new – for though we were always short of money, she didn't normally mind spending on clothes. I was too excited that day, however, to care what I wore. When I was dressed I went to breakfast, for I was extremely hungry – pausing only to give terse instructions for my bed to be moved from Mamma's room to a room of my own, along with my china, books and dolls. What did she think when she saw that evidence of our separation? I'm afraid the triumphant new Queen neither knew nor cared.

I had breakfast with the good Dr Stockmar (Uncle Leopold had sent him over some weeks earlier to try to mend matters between me and Mamma, but without success), who gave me some very sound advice and steadied my nerves, which had begun to jump a little. After breakfast I took time to scribble two letters, one to Feo and one to Uncle Leopold (and how much I enjoyed signing the latter 'your devoted and attached Niece, Victoria R!) and then at nine o'clock I was ready for my first audience with my Prime Minister, Lord Melbourne.

I received him alone, as I promised in my Journal 'I should *always* do with all my ministers'. He bowed very low and kissed my hand, and then straightening up he looked down into my face and into my eyes with such a clear, direct, and *comfortable* look that I loved him from that very moment. I have always had the knack of judging people quickly, finding out in a single glance or a few words the true worth of their character and their ruling motives, and I am hardly ever wrong. I saw in that first look, felt in the first touch of his hand, that he was straightforward, honest, clever and good; and since he was, besides, an extremely handsome and attractive man, and I was a passionate young girl who had had hardly anyone to love, I gave him my heart on the instant – as indeed he gave me his.

I told him that I had long decided to retain him and his ministry at the head of affairs, and added that I felt it could not be in better hands than his, which I saw pleased him. He explained to me that there was to be a meeting of the Privy Council at eleven o'clock – 'If it pleases Your Majesty' – told me what would be discussed there, and gave me a draft he had prepared of the declaration I must read to them. We talked a little more, and I saw his approval of me growing with every sentence; while the simple, candid warmth I felt emanating from him bathed me in a delicious sense of security I had never known before. I felt that here at last was one who took my part, understood me, and would protect me: a man not only with the heart and the will, but with the power also to act as my champion and my guide. I felt that I could lean on him with absolute confidence; with him beside me I could negotiate all the difficulties and hazards of my new position. There would be ceremonies and protocols and etiquettes, and I was painfully shy and inexperienced in the ways of the world (and of the Court, which was worse); but he would steer me through them safely.

Before I went down to the Privy Council meeting, I took a moment to write a note to my dear aunt Adelaide (who had not neglected to send *me* a message while her own husband lay dying). I addressed the outside to 'Her Majesty the Queen at Windsor Castle' and handed it to Lehzen to dispatch. She bent to murmur in my ear that I should properly have addressed it to the Queen Dowager.

'I am quite well aware of Her Majesty's altered status,' I said quickly. 'She must know it herself – but *I* shall not be the first to remind her of it. Send it as it is.'

And then I went downstairs to the Red Saloon.

A multitude seemed to be gathered there as I stepped in through the double doors quite alone, and for a moment I felt very small and vulnerable, and I felt myself blushing at so many male eyes being fixed on me, who had never before today been allowed to be unchaperoned in the presence of any male thing over seven years old. But then my eyes found Lord Melbourne's face, and he gave me a comfortable look and a little nod, and I suddenly felt quite calm. In fact, my very femaleness suddenly seemed to me a point of strength rather than weakness, and I revelled in being the only woman in the room, and the one on whom they must all bestow their attention.

The first to advance upon me were my old uncles Sussex and Cumberland – frightening enough figures to have bearing down on one, had one been faint-hearted! They took my hands and led me to my throne (in fact one of Mamma's dining-room chairs) and Lord M. told me afterwards that Greville thought the three of us presented a most bizarre appearance, like Beauty and Two Beasts. When I was seated I read the Declaration, and any last trace of nervousness left me, for I knew my voice was sweet and clear and carried to the furthest and deafest ears: it is always a great comfort to do something one knows one does well. After that came the swearing-in, and there seemed a great many of them to kneel to me and kiss my hand – some of them, like the Duke and Lord Palmerston, so eminent they seemed almost figures out of history – but always, whenever I had the slightest doubt what to do, Lord Melbourne was nearby, his face and his eyes ready for my seeking.

When it was all over and I withdrew, I waited impatiently in my room for him to come to me, so that I could ask him what they were saying of me.

'Well?' I demanded when we were alone together. 'Were they satisfied with me?'

I saw there were traces of tears on his cheeks. In those days it was not considered unmanly for men to weep, and Lord M. was always easily moved to tears. 'Satisfied, ma'am?' he said with a tremor in his voice. 'They would *die* for you!'

I felt my cheeks grow warm. 'Truly?'

'Most truly. You had not passed out of sight before your praise was spoken on every side.'

'Tell me what they said of me,' I demanded. What a vain little creature! But I had never heard compliments from male lips before, and I was as ready for them as a monkey for nuts.

'Sir Robert Peel, ma'am, was deeply impressed by Your Majesty's dignity and firmness. Croker admired your clear and beautiful voice, and Greville your complete self-possession – most interestingly mixed, he said, with a graceful diffidence.'

'Oh,' I said, almost speechless with pleasure. 'Tell me another.'

'The Duke said that Your Majesty not only filled the chair, but the whole room.'

'Did he *indeed* say that?' The Duke of Wellington, the Hero of Waterloo, virtually a National Institution, to say such a thing of me!

'He did *indeed*, ma'am,' Lord M. said, his eyes twinkling. 'He said that if Your Majesty had been his own child, he could not have wished to see you perform your part better.'

My cup was full. I said to my Prime Minister, 'I wish you will *always* tell me, Lord Melbourne, what is said of me on such occasions – freely and frankly. I wish to do everything properly. You must not be afraid to be frank with me.'

'I will always tell you the truth,' he said seriously. 'Your Majesty may ask me anything, and I will do my best to give satisfaction.'

'I am sure you will do that,' I said warmly; and I was right.

The rest of my day was wonderfully busy, and I enjoyed so much the sense of purpose after so long in idleness – and the sense of importance about what I did. Other girls might work screens or make purses, sketch or play the piano; I gave audiences (to the Archbishop of Canterbury, the Home Secretary, and the Master of the Horse amongst others), made appointments (Clark to be my physician, Lehzen to be Lady Attendant to the Queen – a position without a post, which would cause no-one any jealousy), and gave orders (for instance that the name Alexandrina should be dropped from all official documents – henceforward I would be Queen Victoria, and would be proclaimed as such the following day). I wrote some more letters, completed my Journal, and dined alone in my room; spoke again to Stockmar, and had a fourth, very comfortable conversation with Lord Melbourne; and then at last at half past ten I retired to my bed, to sleep in a room on my own for the first time in my life. Between the sheets I stretched out my limbs luxuriously, and felt the benison of space all around me – not just in the room, but in my mind, my heart, my whole being. I had been caged and cramped all my life, in a space too small for me even to open my wings, far less use them. They would not hold me down now!

That first day was the antithesis of everything that had gone before: my waking hours had been busy, purposeful, filled with company and conversation; my sleeping hours would be solitary and private. Oh, it was utter, utter bliss!

SPRING

Six

WHEN I began this account of my life, I said that I was writing it for myself alone, and that no one else would ever see it. But reading back over the last few episodes of my childhood, I discover that I still seem to be addressing it *to* someone. When Beatrice came up to me the other day, plainly wondering what I was writing, I found myself putting my hand over the page to stop her reading it. This automatic reaction of concealment showed me who I am *not* writing for. People do not want the truth, when it touches on themselves: it is too uncomfortable. We assemble half-truths around us like our familiar possessions, and we do not at all like a stranger to come romping through the house and moving the furniture around.

Which very much begs the question, who am I addressing? If not my immediate companions, then perhaps some future generation, who will be born when I am long dead and forgotten. Well, no, not quite forgotten, perhaps. I am Queen of England – I shall be in the history books. But though the Queen will be remembered, Victoria will be forgotten. When the last of the people who have known me have died, I shall become as remote as all those other characters in history, brightly coloured, resembling humanity, but unreal – like the Staffordshire figures of Famous People.

Perhaps after all I shall not burn this when it is finished. Perhaps I shall just hide it, and hope that it is discovered one day a long time into the future. Of course, if the wrong person finds it, it will probably be burned anyway, but it must take its chance. Nothing in life is certain, as Lord M. used to say, except death and taxes.

Suddenly, how I miss him! The Queen lives on a lonely eminence, and what she values most of all are those rare few who can bridge the

101

gulf. Lord Melbourne was the least obsequious of courtiers. Wise man, he knew that sovereigns are always surrounded by flattery and deceit, and he determined, as he promised me that first day, that he would always tell me the truth, even when it was not what I wanted to hear. Well, in my old age I have become as fond of having my prejudices confirmed as anyone, but if there is an unclouded eye in me still, that sees without self-delusion after sixty years of being always right, it is Lord M.'s doing. He loved me intensely, but never blindly; curbed my excesses without damping my enthusiasm; and with his own honesty confirmed me in my love of candour, while tempering it with a little (sadly, only a little!) of his tact and tolerance.

'If you want to influence a person you must begin by finding something to praise,' he told me on one occasion. 'You cannot make a friend by reprimanding him.'

We were talking about one of my courtiers – Lord Lyndhurst, I think. 'But I don't like him,' I said, as though that were the end of it. 'He is a bad man.'

'That places him in a category which embraces most of mankind,' he said, smiling. 'It does not embrace *you*,' I said warmly. 'That is not to my credit, ma'am,' he said with a deep sigh. 'I am only too indolent to be wicked. Sinning is such an energetic business, and you know I am always falling asleep in public places.' Only the day before I had reprimanded him for that fault, and so the lecture ended in laughter, as it usually did.

Parliament would not allow me a private secretary such as Uncle King and Uncle William had had, for fear of the influence a person in such a position would have over me. According to tradition, the Prime Minister was the Sovereign's private secretary, though in practice he did not actually carry out the duties; but Lord M. did so for me, advising me, drafting my letters, and wielding the blotter for my signature. So he was always at my side. How he filled my days, guiding, educating, amusing me – approving me, too, so that my poor parched nature straightened up and blossomed under his loving attention! There came a moment when Mamma, consumed with jealousy, hissed a warning at me, 'Take care that Lord Melbourne is not King!' What she was afraid of was never a possibility: I grew up too much under threat of a King John ever to yield the least part of my prerogative to anyone. But there was a sense in which Lord M. *was* King. As Prime Minister, my secretary, my closest companion, and my tutor in statecraft, he wielded an extraordinary degree of power. But there was never, even from his political opponents, the slightest objection to his uniquely privileged position. He was a man of whom it was impossible to believe ill, and he could no more have abused his power than fly in the air.

30th March 1900

THERE SEEMS to be a disgraceful tendency amongst some of my ministers to blame Buller and the other generals for all that has gone wrong in South Africa. It does nothing but harm to lower the officers in the estimation of the men they command. I have had to speak to Balfour pretty sharply about it, for what is said in the House and at dinner parties soon gets about, and it is both unpatriotic and unjust to pillory poor Sir Redvers. No-one who was not there can know the truth of it, and as I have said before, civilians cannot understand military matters. Besides, in time of war it is most important to keep up public morale, and though Kimberley and Ladysmith have been relieved and the Boers seem to be on the retreat, Mafeking is still under siege, and they say the new Boer leader, Botha (what names these people have!), is much more able than his predecessor. So we have a long way to go yet, though the supply problem should be eased now that Roberts is in Bloemfontein.

I feel rather ruffled, and turn to my writing for solace. There could be nothing more likely to soothe me than describing those happy early days of my reign with my dear Lord M. I remember one evening, after dinner, I was seated on the sofa in the drawing-room, with Lord M. in a chair drawn up close to me. Islay, my newly acquired Highland terrier, was curled up beside me, while dear Dashy lay at our feet, his head resting on Lord M.'s feet and his feathery tail curled over mine. Between us we held a book of engravings which we were leafing through, but the book was only an excuse for what we liked best to do – chatting. How comfortable they were, those long, rambling conversations about anything and everything! We talked together by the hour, joking, gossiping, imparting all those minutiae of our lives which are so unfailingly interesting to those who care for each other. We were, in fact, 'having a comfortable coze' as it used to be called in those days. It was a delight I had never known before – and now I come to think of it, have never known again in exactly the same way, for my closeness with Albert was of a different order. I have seen young girls chat together in that way – but I never had a female friend of my own age.

Across the other side of the room Mamma was engaged in a game of whist with my other guests, which satisfied the etiquette which said I must be seen with her, but prevented my having to talk to her. It did not always prevent her from falling asleep in the evenings, I have to say – but who am I, now, to cast that particular stone!

I turned a page and pointed to the next picture. 'Who is this man? He looks amusing.'

Lord M. leaned forward and nodded. He hardly ever let me down – I think he knew something amusing about everyone in the world.

'Oh, that's Cambacérès – he was Boney's Second Consul under the Constitution of 1799. You remember, ma'am, the Triumvirate?'

He had been instructing me recently on the history of the French revolutionary wars. 'Oh yes, I remember. Tell me about him.'

He leaned back in his chair and prepared to be expansive. It was a gesture I loved to see. Usually he sat very upright with his feet together, as was proper, but sometimes when he warmed to a story he forgot himself and stretched out his legs and crossed his feet, so that I could imagine him in his Cambridge days, sprawling on a sofa, or lolling with his feet in the fender and talking, talking, talking. He was said to have been amazingly handsome as a youth, and though I often longed for a time-machine, so that I could travel back and see him as he was then, I could not conceive that he had been any more handsome than he was now, with the warmth and charm and wisdom of maturity added to his physical perfections. His features were strong, his figure elegant, and his eyes were so beautiful – large, blue-grey, fringed with long lashes any woman would have given a fortune for, and full of light and expression.

'Oh, Cambacérès was a down-the-road man, an amazing dilettante, very fond of the opera and painting and so on. But above all, he was a great gourmet, dedicated to the arts of the dinner-table.'

'Like you, then,' I said quickly. 'You had three chops *and* a grouse at breakfast this morning – I saw you.'

He bowed ironically (not an easy thing to do in the sitting position, but he was graceful in everything) and said, 'My dear ma'am, I am flattered you noticed! But I am quite a novice compared with Cambacérès: the delicate flavouring, the exquisite sauce – they were his passion. His cooks were the highest paid servants in France, and they say a spoiled dish could reduce him to tears.'

'I wonder he found time to be Second Consul, then,' I remarked from my recently acquired knowledge of the demands of government. 'I am so busy I arrive at my dinner-table each evening with very little idea of what I will find there.'

'But you must remember, ma'am, that he was a mere cypher. It was Boney who wielded the power. Of course, Boney never cared two hoots for *haute cuisine*: his mind was on higher things and more distant horizons. He used to drive poor Cambacérès to despair by holding meetings of state just before dinner time, and keeping everyone from their dining-tables.'

'Did he not complain to Bonaparte about it?' I asked, fascinated.

'One didn't complain to Boney about a dried-up *ragoût* when he was planning to conquer the world. But on one occasion the Corsican, in the middle of a long meeting about the constitution, saw Cambacérès scribbling a frantic note, and demanded to see what it was he had written. Cambacérès was very reluctant to show it up, and Boney, always afraid of treachery, as your dictators are, rushed down the table and snatched it from his hand.' He paused tantalisingly.

'Well, well, what did it say?' I cried.

'It was addressed to his cook, ma'am, and it said, "*Sauvez les rôtis; les entremets sont perdus*".' We both laughed very much, and Dash lifted his head and looked up at Lord M., smiling and waving his tail.

I turned another page. 'This must be the Empress Josephine,' I said. 'Was she very beautiful?'

'Not beautiful so much as bewitching. *Plus belle encore que la beauté*, she had grace. She moved as though she was floating, and she had the most beautiful voice.'

I was pleased with this, for two things I knew I had were grace of movement and a beautiful voice. 'Was she tall?' I asked.

'Moderately so.'

'I'm sure it must help, when one is an empress – or a queen,' I said wistfully. 'I am so very short of stature. Everyone grows but me. I think I shall never be taller.'

'I think you are tall enough,' he said judiciously. 'Your lack of inches will not prove a disadvantage. As it is, everyone notices your dignity and queenly presence, whereas if you were a tall woman, they might dismiss them as being a part of your tallness.'

'Do you mean it?' I asked.

'Certainly, ma'am. You know I never flatter.'

I regarded him carefully. 'I have often wished I had better features, though. My nose, for instance – '

He did not try to tell me it was beautiful. 'It is very like your royal father's nose.'

'I know, but it's too big for my face.'

He smiled and shook his head. 'I have often noticed, you know, ma'am, that people with small features and little squeeny noses never seem to accomplish anything.' And he turned his head sideways and ran his finger down his own nose, which though extremely handsome in my opinion was certainly not small.

I returned to the engraving. 'Do you like the name Josephine? I think it is rather masculine and hard.'

'It sounds better when one says it in French.'

'Like Victoire?' I said slyly, but he was not caught.

'No, I don't like the name Victoire.'

'What name do you like?' I asked. 'What is your favourite?'

He thought for a moment. 'Alice,' he said at last. 'Alice is a pretty name for a girl.'

I felt a pang for a moment, that he did not say Victoria; but then it was not my favourite name either. I longed to ask him about his own child, as I longed to ask him about his marriage, but though we talked quite freely to each other, I knew they were subjects too sensitive to be broached. His wife was dead – the infamous Caroline Lamb who was really half crazy and had made such shocking scenes over Lord Byron – and even while she was alive she had driven him to distraction by her mad and wicked behaviour. In the end he had had to lock her up, and she had died of complications of drink and laudanum. I learned all this from Lord Palmerston, for I could never have asked Lord M., who had loved her dearly and borne with her excesses with extraordinary patience and tenderness, and had even hurried back from Ireland to be at her deathbed. Caroline had given him one child, a son who turned out to be feeble-minded, suffered from fits, and had died just the year before, in 1836. I could see how lonely Lord M. had been. He had always had a great many friends, of course, including many female friends, often the wittiest and most sophisticated women in society, but that was not enough for a man with a talent for loving and no-one to love. He wanted one special person to devote himself to, and pour out all his affection on – and that was just exactly what I wanted, too.

We talked instead about his days at Eton (where he had known 'Beau' Brummell) and the best way to educate a child. Lord M. was not an advocate for overmuch education: he said it could not change a person's basic character; and besides, he said, look at the Pagets – none of them could read or write and they did very well. We discussed whether large families were better than small ('Where there are a great many in a family, they seldom have anything the matter with them; too much attention brings on ailments') and doctors ('English physicians kill their patients; the French just let them die') and thence to teeth. Teeth were a plague, we both agreed; but it was important to look after them, he said. Poor teeth meant poor digestion, and that could cause global reverberations.

'Bonaparte suffered from bad teeth; so did Queen Mary Tudor; and look at all the trouble they caused. One tried to make us all French, and the other tried to make us all Papists.' And then he reminded me of Mrs Sheridan's Four Commandments to her children: 'Fear God. Honour the King. Obey your parents. Brush your teeth.'

I laughed very much at that, and said, 'I shall teach them to my children. And if I have a daughter,' I added generously, 'I shall call her Alice.'

'If you have a daughter, ma'am, I suspect you may be obliged to consult your husband about her name,' he said.

'I am the Queen. I shall not be *obliged* to do anything,' I said grandly.

'But you will not marry a man you do not love,' he said, 'and if you love him, you will *wish* to consult him.'

'I suppose I shall,' I said, and for a moment our eyes met, and I felt a warm, fluttering sensation in the pit of my stomach which made me feel quite disturbed – and yet delightfully so. 'But I do not wish to marry yet,' I added quickly. 'There is no need, not for a long time.'

'No need at all, ma'am,' he agreed warmly.

It was my first experience of being in love – and yes, from my present distance I can see that that is what it was, though I could never have admitted it to anyone before now. Of course, it was only the foretaste, the rehearsal for what was to come; and after my marriage to Albert I found myself ashamed of the enthusiasm with which I wrote about Lord M. in my Journal. I loved Albert so much I did not want anything to detract from it: I wanted him to be the only creature I had ever loved or ever would love. The nakedness of my recorded passion for Lord M. embarrassed me, and I repudiated it, for fear that it would upset Albert – and Albert *was* jealous, not least because my dear Lord M. was not the sort of man Albert could ever approve of: too sophisticated, too cynical, too much a man of the world. The qualities Albert valued were serious and weighty, and he would never have believed that my former Prime Minister had those too. When he told me that my feelings for Lord Melbourne had been overdrawn and foolish, I agreed with him, and wrote a note to that effect in the margin of my Journal. I even went so far as to destroy a great deal of my correspondence from those three years before my marriage, feeling that I had been a very unsatisfactory person to make such a fool of myself.

So I repudiated my first love in memory just as I did in fact. My dear Lord M. warmed my poor chilled heart and prepared me for the great love to come, and when that love arrived, when Albert came, he stepped back and let me go with all the generosity of his true, good heart. It was he who advised me to put myself henceforward under the Prince's guidance because Albert 'understood everything so well and had a clever, able head'; and I followed his advice, gave my whole self to Albert, and let Lord Melbourne go.

Lord M. was my first love, but I was his last; and when I forgot him, it broke his heart, and he died.

30th March 1900 – near midnight

UNABLE TO sleep again, so I shall go on with my account. On the 13th of July 1837, I left the poor old Palace at Kensington, and moved into Buckingham Palace. I was the first reigning monarch to live there. It had been bought as a dower house for my grandmother, Queen Charlotte, and was then a simple, red-brick mansion house; but in 1825 my uncle King had set Mr Nash on to it to rebuild it in grand style as a royal palace. The scheme was too ambitious and the money ran out, and when Uncle King died it was still unfinished and stood empty, a reproach to the Crown on account of all the money that had been spent on it. Uncle William, when he succeeded, engaged another architect to finish it, or at least to make it habitable; but the critics never thought much of the architectural style, and Uncle William guessed, shrewdly, that it would not be *gemütlich*. He refused to move out of St James's, and when the Palace of Westminster burned down in 1834, he even went so far as to offer the building as a new and permanent home for both Houses of Parliament. 'It would be the greatest thing of its kind in the world,' he said temptingly. But it seemed that the Lords concurred with his opinion of the place, and the offer was hastily and rather rudely refused.

Uncle William was quite right. Uncomfortable and inconvenient it did turn out to be. The chimneys were so ill-designed, for instance, that it was often impossible to light fires in many of the rooms (and quite impossible to clean the flues without using climbing-boys, which made things very awkward when the legislation was passed). More seriously, the palace was a veritable sink of typhoid, built over the most inadequate drains, badly ventilated and full of dreadful smells; and the worst slums in London crawled right up to its walls, providing an endless supply of urchins and madmen to break in and roam its labyrinthine corridors. But at eighteen I cared nothing for any of this – and having been brought up at Kensington, my standards of comfort were not high. It had all been hastily redecorated for me, and the rooms looked to me lofty, pleasant and cheerful. The gardens seemed attractive too, and Dashy plainly felt quite at home in them, rushing about and barking at the ducks and butterflies, so I was content.

In making the move, I scraped off my poor mother like a barnacle on a rock. Though my dear Lehzen had a room adjoining mine with a communicating door, I deposited Mamma in a suite as far as possible from my own, which she soon complained bitterly was too small to hold all her belongings. I should have liked to banish her altogether for refusing to dismiss Conroy from her household, but Lord M. advised against it. Though he agreed with me that Mamma was foolish, deceitful and hypocritical (how I enjoyed hearing him say those reprehensible things!) he warned me against an open breach with her.

'The people will expect you to be chaperoned by her while you are so young, and unmarried. It would cause a very unpleasant scandal if you were to part company with her.'

'But I need not see her, need I?' I begged.

'You must have her accompany you in public sometimes, for form's sake, but you need not see her privately. I suggest you tell her that she must request audience with you whenever she wants to see you. That way she will not burst in on you when you are not prepared.'

The thought of Mamma having to *ask* to see me pleased me. 'Well, but I shall not be nice to her,' I declared. 'She has behaved abominably by me.'

Lord M. shook his head. 'The more credit to you, then, ma'am, if you are seen to be gracious and attentive towards her. I would not have you do anything that might expose you to the reproach of littleness. Let it always be said that the Queen's behaviour to her mother is impeccable.' And when I still looked rebellious he added delicately, 'To snub her entirely, Your Majesty, might bear the appearance of ill-breeding.' After that I had no more to say; and following what I conceived to be his plan, I amused myself by behaving in public with the prettiest civility towards that poor woman, while banishing her from every corner of my private life and feelings.

Mamma, though, was not guiltless by any means, and in the first years of my reign behaved as badly as she could, nagging and complaining and making scenes, reproaching me for my coldness and – infatuated woman! – for my 'ingratitude' to Sir John for 'all he had done for me'. Conroy himself, with a slightly better grasp of reality, was ready to acknowledge defeat. On that very first day of my reign (after I had dismissed him from my Household) he waylaid Baron Stockmar and gave him a letter for Lord Melbourne, containing his demands. The good Baron trotted off like the obedient go-between he was; but when my poor Lord M. read the demands he was so outraged he dropped the paper several times in his agitation. A peerage, the Grand Cross of the Bath, a pension of £3,000 a year, and a seat on the Privy Council: that was Conroy's price for going away and leaving me alone. Did I say Mamma was infatuated? 'No, really, this is too bad!' Lord M. exclaimed. 'Have you ever heard such impudence?'

Lord M. was for an indignant refusal, but Stockmar persuaded him that there would never be peace at the palace until Conroy left, and so on the 26th of June he offered, with my approval, the pension, a baronetcy, and the promise of an Irish peerage should a vacancy occur while Lord M. was Prime Minister. Here is the mark of That Man: he accepted the offer, but did not resign from Mamma's Household. When Lord M. *via* Stockmar demanded to know why, Conroy replied that he had not yet got his peerage, and until I had fulfilled all parts of my bargain, he did not feel obliged to fulfil his. (When eventually an Irish peerage fell vacant, my dear Lord M. was out of office, and the then Prime Minister, Sir Robert Peel, felt justified in refusing to give it to Conroy. Conroy was very bitter about it and accused us of sharp practice, but still he died at last no more than a baronet, which was more than he deserved; but that was a long way ahead. Meanwhile he hung around the palace like an evil spirit, making trouble and causing misery as was his nature.)

Mamma, pressed by Conroy, continued to importune me on his behalf: to give him a peerage, to invite him to Court functions, to receive his family and to give his daughters positions. 'I have the greatest regard for Sir John,' Mamma wrote. 'I cannot forget all he has done for me and for you – although he had the misfortune to displease you at last. The Queen should forget what displeased the Princess.'

I wrote back, 'I am astonished that you should ask me to receive him, considering his conduct towards me for some years past, and still more the unaccountable manner in which he behaved towards me a short time before I came to the Throne. I imagined you would have been *amply* satisfied with what I have done for him, by giving him a pension of £3,000 which normally only Ministers receive, and a baronetcy. I should have thought you would not expect more.'

She replied, 'Sir John has his faults, he may have made mistakes, but his intentions were always the best. You do not know the world, Victoria. This affair is much tattled about and makes me very unhappy. I appeal to your love for me. For the sake of your mother, relent in your line of conduct towards Sir John and his family.'

And thus it went on, the nagging letters freely interspersed with horrible scenes whenever she could get access to me. Sometimes when she wrote requesting to see me, I would simply send back a note saying 'Busy'; at other times, when a more than usually emotional demand was sent to me, Lord M. advised me to let him reply to it formally (though that did not always work: once Mamma responded to one of Lord M.'s letters by writing again to me saying, 'My appeal was to *you* as my Child, not to the Queen.'). The scenes were exhausting, and sometimes Mamma's language could be immoderate. There were times when I was forced to the horrible necessity of reminding her Who I was.

There were other subjects besides Sir John on which she was unreasonable. She wrote to the Speaker demanding to be given the rank and precedence of Queen Mother (reminding me of her previous demands to be called Dowager Princess of Wales, another title to which she had no right). The Speaker, polite but puzzled, referred the request to me, and I refused it, saying that it would do her no good and annoy my aunts. She also complained about the precedence given her at State functions, and went into minute details about the relationship of every person placed near me and why they should not have been put where they were. And she demanded that I pay off her debts, amounting to more than £55,000 – first that I should pay them all, and then that I should make myself personally responsible for more than half of them, leaving Mamma to pay the smaller proportion, which she said she would undertake to do provided her income were suitably increased.

I did not need anyone to help me detect Conroy's hand in this, nor did I need the Chancellor's indignant advice to refuse. Lord Melbourne suggested that I ask Parliament to increase Mamma's pension by £8,000, bringing it up to £30,000, so that she could gradually pay off her debts herself. This was done, and Parliament, Lord Melbourne told me afterwards, voted it through solely out of respect and consideration for me. It was not two months, however, before I was receiving dreadful letters from Mamma revealing that the increase in her allowance had already been swallowed up, without any of the debts being discharged. Indeed, the sum of them was now revealed to be more than £70,000, and since the tradesmen's bills were as enormous as ever, it was plain that the extra money granted by Parliament was going 'elsewhere' which made me very angry. I see no reason why honest tradesmen should suffer on account of greedy and profligate people who should be their betters. It made me especially furious because during my uncle William's lifetime she and Conroy had sworn they had no debts and that accusations that they owed money were malicious lies put about by the King.

Lord Melbourne said that it was deplorable that I should be subjected to such annoyance and importunity from one who ought to be giving me only help and affection; and the quarrels and Mamma's indebtedness cast shadows on the happiness of my first two years, and did nothing to improve my temper. All my life I have been of a passionate nature, and the inclination to fly into rages has been very hard for me to control. Control it I must, said Lord M., and I did try, but sometimes I even lost my temper with him, kind and patient as he was. It does no good to remember that some of my storms were provoked by jealousy: I hated him to be away from me, even for one evening, and when he dined with Lady Holland I would demand to know whether he liked her better than me, and accuse him of disloyalty. I suppose I feared that spending so many evenings with me bored him, although when I asked him the question, he replied with tears in his eyes, 'Oh no! No!'

But Mamma made me so angry that sometimes I would even snap at the servants, which made me very ashamed, for they were not in a position to defend themselves. I always apologised afterwards, and I think they did not mind it as much as I did, but I knew at whose door to lay the blame. If Conroy had been trustworthy with money, I might have forgiven him much, for waste and disorder in financial matters was something I could not endure. But then if he had been an honest man where money was concerned, he must have been a different person altogether.

I should mention here that though I would not give Mamma–Conroy a penny from my Privy Purse, I did use it to discharge Papa's debts, which I regarded as a matter of honour, since as his heir I stood in the position of his son. I had always been careful with money, and before I came to the Throne managed very nicely on an allowance of £10 per month, so the economies were not hard to sustain and out of the £60,000 granted to my Privy Purse for the first year, I discharged £50,000 of Papa's debts. The rest I paid off by October 1839, and at that time I received formal thanks from his creditors for my actions, which pleased me very much.

During this period, Conroy put it about that the reason Mamma was in financial difficulties was that she had been obliged to pay off Papa's debts. I hadn't told Mamma what I was doing, so she had no way of knowing that I *knew* that was a lie; but all the same she let Conroy say it, and didn't refute the story. Is it any wonder that I hated her at that period?

31st March 1900

GREVILLE SAID (most improperly I'm afraid, but his words probably reflected the feelings of a number of my subjects) that before I came to the Throne the country had been ruled successively by an imbecile, a profligate, and a buffoon. Much as I disapprove of these descriptions of my poor grandfather, my kind uncle King and my good uncle William, they go to explain why it was that there was such excitement over my Coronation, which was held on Thursday June 28th, 1838 (I think they are always on Thursdays, I cannot tell why). Those were, as Uncle Leopold had warned me, testing times for kings. Monarchies all over Europe were being weighed in the balance and found wanting; countries hovered on the brink of revolution, and even our own land was restless, because of the changes brought about by industrialisation and war. Now a young girl of nineteen had appeared to save England from being ruled by the Duke of Cumberland – the most hated man in the kingdom – and I should have had to have done something amazingly wicked to have avoided the measureless popularity which I enjoyed that summer. 'All London went raving mad about the Coronation,' one Londoner famously recorded.

Lord Melbourne knew how much the popularity of the Crown needed reviving, and at his instigation Parliament decided to make a very grand affair of it indeed. They voted £200,000 for it – four times what was voted for Uncle William's. The traditional Coronation Banquet had been abolished by Uncle William, and it was decided not to revive it, but to substitute instead the State Procession, which had last been carried out at my grandfather's Coronation. In the robes of state, crowned and carrying the orb and sceptre, I was to be driven on a circuitous route through the streets to allow as many people as possible to have a glimpse of me; and afterwards there were to be band concerts, illuminations, firework displays, and a two-day festival in Hyde Park with balloon ascents, music, theatres, taverns, and every kind of side-show and jollity. It was to be the People's Coronation; and the people responded with all their hearts.

For days beforehand London seethed. There was a tremendous din of hammering and cursing as stands were erected all along the route and bits of wood and masonry fell on the pedestrians beneath; the Park was an encampment, trains and coaches every hour disgorged their passengers from all over the country to swell the throng of Londoners, every ale-house and inn bulged with uproar and excitement, and every pavement was a slow jostle of gaping, gazing sightseers. The roads were crammed with horsemen and carriages jammed tight and frequently unmoving for half an hour together. Windows along the route were being hired out for absurd sums of money, and when the word got about that there were tickets for the Abbey to be had at the American Legation, the place was besieged and several people fainted in the crush. Indeed, it was a wonder that more people were not injured, so vast was the throng – London's population quintupled, they say; but everyone was very good-tempered and well-behaved, despite the vast quantities of beer and gin that were consumed by the lower orders that week.

For days beforehand I was in a state of agitation approaching terror, but, 'You'll like it of all things once you are there,' my dear Lord M. assured me lightly. He kept me going from day to day with little stories and jokes; telling me, for instance, how when the Tories had threatened to boycott Uncle William's Coronation, Uncle had simply replied, 'Good. There will be less heat and more air in the Abbey,' which so took the wind out of the Tories' sails that they had attended after all – 'For there is no point,' said Lord M., 'in making a protest which upsets no-one but yourself.' Of my Coronation, he told me that only two peers knew how to put on their robes properly, and that was because they had taken part in country-house theatricals. He explained that during the ceremony each peer had to pay homage and in turn touch the crown. 'But you are to be sure they do not go away with anything. We have the jewels on loan from Rundell and Bridge. They must all go back on Friday, you know.'

This made me laugh, because there had been a dreadful quarrel between the Keeper of the Jewel House at the Tower, Mr Swift, and Mr Bridge of the famous jeweller's shop on Ludgate Hill, over the new crown. The great Crown of England, St Edward's Crown, had been made originally for King Charles II, who was six feet five inches tall and strong to boot. It weighed over five pounds and if pressed on to my head during the ceremony by the Archbishop, 'I fear would snap Your Majesty's neck like a stick of celery.' There was another crown, the Imperial Crown, which had been made for Uncle King and worn by him and Uncle William, but it was thought unsuitable for me, and so a new crown was made especially for me, using the jewels from the Imperial Crown. It weighed only two and three-quarter pounds and was called the Crown of State.

The jewels in it were magnificent, including the Black Prince's Ruby which was worn by Henry V at Agincourt, the sapphire from the ring of Edward the Confessor, and the huge Stuart sapphire which had been taken from England by James II when he fled and was bought back years later from his grandson Henry Benedict, who was a Cardinal in Rome. Interest in the new crown was intense, and Mr Swift looked forward to a period of prosperity. He received no salarium for his position but depended on showing the crown jewels to visitors at a shilling a time, and he had a large family of hopeful children to provide for. But Mr Bridge, of Rundell and Bridge who had made the crown, put it on display in his shop from the middle of June, and was besieged by such crowds that policemen had to be posted on the pavement to regulate the flow. Poor Mr Swift wailed that his business was being taken away and that by the time the Coronation was over, everyone in London would have seen the Crown and no one would pay him to see it again. He begged the Lord Chamberlain to forbid Mr Bridge to show the crown; but though Lord Conyngham sympathised with Mr Swift, he was only too glad of the public interest, and declined to take any action.

I hardly slept the night before the great day, partly from nervousness, and partly because London was so noisy – they say thousands slept out in the streets that night so as to secure a good place. I kept waking up with an awful sense of foreboding that something dreadful was going to happen on the morrow; and then I was woken at four o'clock by the sound of guns firing in the Park. I fell into a doze at last, but woke every few minutes with a jerk thinking that I had overslept and no-one had called me. By seven o'clock I was glad to get up and go to look out of the window. What a disappointment! It was overcast, and a fine, chilly rain was falling, and the trees were blowing in a gusty wind. Still it did not seem to be deterring the spectators, who were milling about in Green Park, buying hot pies and sausages from the vendors for their breakfasts, and listening to the bands who would surely be out of breath long before events really began. There were crowds already all the way up Constitution Hill, patiently holding on to what they thought might be a 'good spot', and the soldiers were already on duty, lining the road both sides and keeping it clear. The sight of all the people enjoying themselves cheered me, and I felt strong and well despite my sleepless night, though I was too excited to eat much breakfast.

'Try again after you are dressed,' Lehzen said firmly. 'It will be a very long day, and Your Majesty must eat something or you will faint away.'

'I shan't faint today,' I said, and flung my arms round her in a sudden hug, which took her by surprise. 'Oh, my dear Daisy, I am so very, very happy!' I cried. Daisy was my new pet name for her.

'You have deserved this day,' she said, her thin lips curving in a rare smile. 'I hope you enjoy every minute of it, dear Majesty.'

The maids came and I was dressed in a white satin petticoat ornamented with gold, and a red velvet kirtle, my hair was dressed securely behind, but low on the neck to allow for the Crown; and a circlet of gold set with diamonds was placed on my head. At half past nine Feo came in – she had come to stay for the Coronation – and we had a precious half hour together before it was time to leave. I bent to kiss dear Dashy's nose and promise him a walk when I came back. 'For I can't take you with me today, my dear,' and then at ten o'clock exactly I set off from Buckingham Palace in the State coach. It was drawn by six cream horses brought over specially for their size from Hanover 'because anything else would look like rats or mice,' Lord M. had said. And wonderfully, the clouds had all cleared away by the time I entered the coach, and glorious golden sunshine was pouring down to warm the chilled spectators. (Indeed, I have always been lucky about having sunshine for my special occasions, so much so that it has come to be called 'Queen's weather'.)

The processional route was up Constitution Hill, along Piccadilly, down St James's Street and Pall Mall, across Trafalgar Square, and along Whitehall; and every inch of the way was crammed tight with cheering people, filling the pavements and the stands, hanging from every window and even perching perilously on the roofs, waving whatever they could get hold of by way of flags. With all those pink faces and their coloured, festival clothes, each street looked like a long box packed with flowers. I had never seen or dreamed of such crowds before, and their joy and goodwill was palpable. I was so proud to be Queen of such a nation, and to hear them cheering as I bowed and waved to them. All this for *me*! My heart was full to overflowing.

At the Abbey I was met by Lord Conyngham and my dear, dearest Lord M., and I was taken to the robing room where the

Parliament Robes of crimson velvet lined with ermine were fastened on me with the heavy, gold-tasselled cords. Then my eight train-bearers took their places around me – all unmarried girls, in gowns of white satin and silver tissue, their heads dressed with wreaths of silver corn-ears and pink rosebuds. I was anxious about these gowns, for the Duchess of Richmond had designed them with trains, and I feared the girls would not be able to manage their own trains while successfully carrying mine. But Lord M. was there to reassure me. 'Will it be all right?' I whispered: how terrible if I should stumble or fall!

'Yes, don't be afraid. I will be walking before you with the Sword of State, and I will go slowly.'

'*Very* slowly,' I urged anxiously.

'It cannot be otherwise,' he said. 'The Sword of State is excessively heavy, you know.' And then he gave me a smile so comfortable and loving that it melted all my fears. 'The effect is so very beautiful,' he said with a nod towards my train-bearers. 'It looks as though you floated in a silvery cloud.'

The girls took hold of my train, four to a side, with Lord Conyngham holding it up at the tail, and we stepped into the Abbey. The first sight of it made me pause, and I drew a breath and clasped my hands, trembling with awe. The soaring pillars were gloriously hung with crimson and cloth-of-gold, the floors covered with rich Turkey carpets, the bishops were robed in magnificent copes, and the altar was almost covered with gold plate. The congregation, ten thousand strong, packed every inch of space, glittering with jewels against the glowing colours of their velvet and satin. Prince Esterhazy was the most magnificent of all, I am told, and wore so many diamonds that when a ray of light struck him one had to turn one's eyes away from the refulgence. Beams of sunshine were pouring in through the great windows like blessings, and I felt so small, so humble – and yet uplifted. It was not for me, all this, not for Victoria the girl: it was for the Queen of England, chosen to stand for the people before God, to be His vessel, to rule them for His glory. I understood then what my uncle King, for all his profligacy, understood, and what he recognised in me. I understood the glory and the gravity, the yoke that is placed upon one's neck, which might never be cast off. My Ministers now who wish me to abdicate in my son's favour do not, cannot understand. It is not a thing from which one can retire, like a profession or a Court position, because one is old or tired; it is a Holy thing, between oneself and God, and until He calls, one may not take one's hand from His work.

At the same instant that I paused, the orchestra burst into a tremendous crash of music, and there seemed to come simultaneously from every throat in the Abbey a gasp of indrawn breath, as though they had seen the same thing that I had seen, the glory of it, and the awfulness. And then I walked forward to meet the ceremony.

It was not a thing, of course, that one could rehearse; and unfortunately the Dean of Westminster, who had conducted the last two Coronations, was now too infirm to assist at mine. He had delegated his duties to the Sub-Dean, Lord John Thynne, who was the only person who actually knew what to do. The Archbishop had only a hazy idea, and the Bishop of Durham was always in the wrong place. It was a long, complicated, and frequently incomprehensible ceremony, and a great many things went wrong; but I was determined, as I was at the centre of the stage, that I would remain calm and behave with absolute dignity whatever happened; and so we got through.

We had the Recognition and Acclamation, the Litany, and the Oath (I swore to maintain the Protestant Reformed religion as established by law, as I later had to remind Gladstone, who wanted me to disestablish the Church, as if an Oath were nothing. I have always kept my promises, even the smallest ones.) Then I withdrew to the little dark Chapel of St Edward where my robes were taken off and I was dressed in a linen shift trimmed with lace, and then the supertunica. This was a magnificent thing of cloth of gold and silver, lined with scarlet silk, trimmed with gold lace, and embroidered all over with roses, thistles, shamrocks and palms. Lord M. said that it suited me best of all of the robes. I took off my circlet, and then, bareheaded, returned to the Abbey, where I was seated on St Edward's Chair for the Anointing while a canopy was held over my head by four Garter Knights to emphasise the sacredness of the moment. The touch of the chrism on my forehead, breast and hands made me shiver, for it was a very strange and moving thing, mysterious, almost magical.

And then came the crowning itself. The Dalmatic robe was fastened round my shoulders, the sceptre placed in my hand, and the ring put on to my finger. (Unfortunately the Archbishop put it on the wrong finger, for which it was too small, and the force he used to drive it over the second joint made me almost scream with pain; but I could not protest at such a moment – I had to endure it in silence. It took half an hour and a great deal of ice-water after the service to work it off again, and my finger was painfully bruised for two days.) And then Lord John Thynne handed the Archbishop the crown, and he stood before me, lifted it high, and placed it slowly on my head. At the same instant the peers and peeresses resumed their coronets with a flashing of gold and gemstones, the trumpets shrilled out a triumphant peal, and far away I heard the thump and crash as the guns fired in the parks and the Tower, to tell the waiting capital that I had been crowned their Queen. It was a supremely moving moment. I looked instinctively towards Lord Melbourne, standing just to the side of me, and read in his shining eyes the awe and wonder and love he was feeling.

The cheering that followed might well have lifted the roof; from outside we could hear the echo of the cheers from the rest of London. Inside people shouted, wept, waved scarves and handkerchiefs, bawled themselves hoarse, while the saints in their niches looked down, it seemed, in faint and petrified astonishment. The Homage came next, with each peer, beginning with my uncles, kneeling in turn before me to swear fealty, kiss my hand and touch the Crown. When Lord Melbourne took my hand, he squeezed it gently, and I returned the pressure fervently, so glad to be reminded of his personal love in the midst of all this impersonal homage; and he looked up at me then, and gave me, oh, *such* a smile! It was like a draught of cordial, warming me and strengthening my limbs.

Poor old Lord Rolle, who was over eighty and quite infirm, had a sad accident during the Homage. As he was being helped to mount the steps to the Throne, he caught his foot in his robes and fell, slipped through the hands of his supporters, and tumbled in an alarming way to the bottom, to lie all tangled in his velvet and fur. He struggled slowly to his feet, amidst frantic cheering from the spectators, to make another attempt, but I could not bear to see it. 'May *I* not go to *him*?' I whispered urgently to Lord M., who glanced at Lord John, and then replied that he thought I might. So I rose from the Throne and reached down to him, and let him kiss my hand there, and told him he need not bother to touch the Crown. There was a perfect frenzy of cheering for my action, but indeed I was only thinking of him: I feared for his poor old bones if he fell again, as well as for his dignity. (I heard afterwards that some American ladies, guests of the American Ambassador, thought that the accident was a regular part of the ceremony, some quaint and obscure old English custom, and that Lord Rolle's name was in fact the title attaching to the hereditary performer of this function at coronations!)

The Homage took a long time, but there was music playing, and a less solemn spectacle to keep the spectators amused: the Coronation Medals of gold and silver were distributed by Lord Albemarle by the haphazard method of scattering them broadcast. The assembled company was treated to the sight of distinguished peers, generals and statesmen scrabbling on the floor like children for them, and even trying to snatch them from one another's hands. My maids of honour, I'm sorry to say, were particularly active in the scramble, and didn't seem to find their trains any handicap in pursuit of gold.

After I had taken the Sacrament, alone and bareheaded, I resumed my crown and the service continued. I was beginning to feel a little tired, and so, I assume, were some others, for the Bishop of Durham suddenly thrust the orb into my hand and told me that I must hold it, which turned out to have been quite the wrong moment in the ceremony; and Bath and Wells turned over two pages at once and missed an entire section of the service, which caused great confusion. Lord M. was for leaving it out (I think he was getting tired by then) but Lord John insisted we must go back, and I endorsed this view firmly. I didn't want anyone to be able to say we had not done it all properly. However, at last the choir began the Hallelujah Chorus, and at that signal we all withdrew to the St Edward Chapel.

It presented a strange appearance, for the altar had been turned into a buffet, and was covered in bottles and plates of sandwiches and cakes. Lord Melbourne came to me to say, 'I believe you may take off the Crown now for a little, Your Majesty, if you wish.'

'Thank you, I will. It hurts a good deal,' I said. The pressure even of two and three-quarter pounds across my brows was making my head ache. I placed it carefully on the chair beside me. It was good to be out of the public eye for a few moments.

'Will you take a glass of wine?' he suggested, but I did not think I should have wine on my breath on such a solemn day, and I refused.

'But perhaps you should, my lord,' I said, for I noticed he was looking very tired – quite grey in the face, poor man.

'The sword is heavy,' he said with a wry smile. He had been carrying it all through the ceremony, and in the upright position, which required a considerable effort of the muscles of the arms and shoulders; and after all, he was almost sixty, though one tended to forget it. He bowed and went off to refresh himself at the altar, and the Archbishop approached me looking worried.

'According to Sir John, Your Majesty, I am to give Your Majesty the Orb at this moment, to carry in the procession, but I fear I cannot find it.'

'The Orb? I have it already,' I said, indicating where I had placed it on a chair beside me. 'The Bishop of Durham gave it to me some time since.'

'Oh!' said the Archbishop looking rather blank, and then, 'Ah!' He looked around. 'Where is Durham?' he muttered; but Durham had disappeared. Still looking perplexed, he bowed and wandered away. I think he hardly knew where *he* was any more; Durham and the Orb were quite beyond him.

It was time now to change my robes again. I put on the royal robe of purple velvet lined with ermine; and then I resumed the Crown, took up the Orb and Sceptre, and thus *loaded* went out into the Abbey for the last procession, down the aisle and out to my carriage for the drive back to the Palace. We returned by the same route, and the cheers were if anything greater than before. My tiredness disappeared like magic before this enthusiastic demonstration of the great love and loyalty of my people, and by the time we reached the Palace I had revived enough to run up the stairs to my suite, where I made up to Dash for having missed everything by giving him a bath. My headache had quite gone, and I felt fresh as a daisy. Daisy, who had wanted to pet me and bathe my forehead in lavender-water, was quite put out!

In the evening I presided at a State Banquet. Afterwards, amongst the many compliments, I was particularly pleased to receive those of Count Sebastiani, who was the French Ambassador and whose opinion must therefore have been impartial. He said that he had been at the Coronation of the Emperor Napoleon, who had had the Pope to officiate (though when the moment came he ignored the Pope and put the crown on his own head!). The Count said that though he had been impressed by that ceremony, it was not nearly so imposing as the one he had just witnessed.

A little later I received the praise and assurance I wanted above all others. My dear Lord M. came up to me, and when I gave him my hand, he held it a moment to smile and congratulate me on this most brilliant day. 'It all went off so well!' he said.

'And I – was I satisfactory?' I asked shyly, my hand safe and warm in his.

'Oh more, so much more!' he said. 'You did it beautifully, every part of it – and with so much taste! That is a thing you can't give a person advice on; it must be left to a person.'

I was too pleased to reply. Instead I said, 'I think you are tired, my lord.'

He admitted that he was feeling very tired. He confessed that because of the strain and nervous anxiety he had been suffering from diarrhoea for several days, and he had had to take a dose of laudanum that morning to get him through the ceremony. No wonder he looked so worn! I seemed to feel a chill, as though cold air had touched my bare neck. I did not know it then, but I have felt it often since, and recognise it now – the breath of mortality. 'But you must be exhausted too, ma'am,' he said, turning the attention from himself. 'You will not wait for the fireworks afterwards?'

'But I must,' I cried, 'I cannot miss the fun! I am not so very tired after all.'

'Depend upon it,' he said kindly, 'you are more tired than you think you are.'

But I stayed up and watched them from the balcony rail, and they were very good fireworks indeed – like Sodom and Gomorrah, as one of my maids said afterwards, when she thought I was not listening.

Seven

28th April 1900, at Windsor

I AM back from Ireland. My visit was a triumph, and the Irish people showed themselves wonderfully kind, loyal and affection- ate – indeed, Ponsonby (who has accompanied me often enough to know) declared he had never seen anything to approach the 'frenzy' with which I was greeted whenever I went out in my carriage. Such real affection as I was shown by these warm-hearted people amply repaid me for the considerable but unavoidable fatigue of being so often in public. I arrived at Kingstown on the 4th of April and left on the 26th, a visit of three weeks, but really I feel quite sorry now that it is all over. I have decreed that from now onwards there is to be a gift of shamrock in my name to all Irish soldiers every St Patrick's Day, and there is to be a new regiment of Irish Guards to commem- orate my visit and their gallantry in South Africa.

I find the season really well advanced here, and the primroses are all finished, which is a pity. I love to see them each spring – they were a special thing to Albert and me, and he was always able to find the very first of them for me every year, knowing the places where they nestle. I used to send a box of them from Windsor every year to dear Disraeli, who liked them best of all flowers. He said they had a sweet perfume, though I could never detect it. He was altogether a most refined creature!

I have got over the fatigue of the journey very well, and really am quite looking forward to going on with my Life. I really don't want to write about Lady Flora Hastings, but I suppose that if I am to be honest, the honesty must extend to the bad things as well as the good, and it was, after all, rather a crucial incident in the first part of my reign.

When I look back on it now, it seems as though a kind of madness seized me. Perhaps I was a little mad: when a girl of eighteen is pitchforked from the deepest obscurity of semi-imprisonment into the hot-house situation of Queen of England, she might well lose her head a little. If you add to that my deep hatred of Sir John Conroy, the existence of two mutually hostile Courts under one roof, and the probability that Sir John himself kept stirring the brew for his own purposes, it is hardly to be expected that we would have got by without trouble. What happened was unfortunate and unpleasant, and I felt very bad about it for a long time afterwards. How many of my subsequent actions were affected by my feelings of guilt and anger I cannot say, but I was certainly very much disturbed by the whole thing.

I hated Lady Flora with the violence I reserved for Conroy's creatures. She, like Conroy, had remained in Mamma's Household, and that in itself was offence, for from the moment she had come to Mamma she had joined with Conroy in persecuting me. She had spied on me, tried to come between me and Lehzen, plotted with him to get rid of my faithful friend. Lady Flora was a clever, educated and not unattractive woman, but she combined a spiteful wit and a sharp tongue with an extreme of piety which I regarded as blatant hypocrisy. I always had a very English dislike of Enthusiasm, in which Lord M. agreed with me. He warned me equally against bigotry and any excessive display of religious fervour. 'After all,' he said, 'it does not much matter which church one belongs to. The Anglican church is the best, because it is the least interfering.' Though my faith is deep and strong, and nothing can shake it, I do not see any reason to thrust it on other people against their will, and I have always hated intolerance. Quakers, Jews, Roman Catholics ('Nasty Beggars', poor Brown used to call them!), even Hindus and Moslems can all be just as good people as us, in their own way. Equally, I do not believe that attending punctiliously to the forms of religion necessarily makes one a more worthy person. It is the heart, after all, into which God looks.

The atmosphere at Court was not happy from the beginning, and after the Coronation it deteriorated into a brooding tension interrupted by sharp squabbles. My ladies did not consort with Mamma's. They told Lehzen that they went in fear of 'Scotty' (as they called Lady Flora) because of her sharp eyes and censorious tongue. Other members of the royal family joined the hostilities, and lines of battle were drawn. My brother Charles changed over to my side after my Accession (though I fear it was only because I had more to offer than Conroy) while the Cambridges changed to Mamma's. My cousin Augusta Cambridge, three years younger than me, with whom I had been quite friendly, was now forbidden to drop in on me alone, as she had been used to do, for a chat. Mamma bombarded me with demands that I invite George Cambridge to Court, which, believing she wanted me to marry him, I refused, thus setting up my aunt Cambridge's back. Meanwhile Lady Flora, who always attended Mamma when she came to my drawing-room of an evening, spied on me and reported everything back to Conroy, who made what he could of it and circulated *his* rumours through my uncle Sussex.

I had other troubles too. I was receiving hurt letters from Uncle Leopold (whose advice I had begun to rely on less since my closeness with Lord M. began), reproaching me for disloyalty and ingratitude. There was a growing hostility in Court to Stockmar, who was seen as an undesirable foreign influence (*that* idea, I'm sure, was Conroy's doing!) and eventually I was obliged to send him back to Brussels for the sake of peace, which upset Uncle Leopold. And I went constantly in fear of losing Lord M., for his government was shaky, and he often dropped hints about preparing myself for his eventual departure, which only made me mad.

In all this unpleasant ferment it is not surprising that I began to feel unwell and out of sorts. My temper suffered, I was often cross and low, I had bursts of irrational tears. I suffered from fatigue, backache and sick headaches – the latter particularly alarming, for I had understood that it was how my grandfather's madness had begun, and I had a deep, unspoken dread of inheriting his madness along with my other Hanoverian traits. Another trouble was that I was putting on weight – which I suppose was not surprising since I have always tended to turn to food for consolation, and it was now available to me in limitless quantities. I even became irritable with my dear Lord M. I had become so nervous that I could not bear the slightest criticism – it made me feel as though I was being attacked, and he attacked me on my most sensitive point.

'I heard in Paris that Your Majesty's dresses are being made larger this year,' he said to me one day.

'It's true,' I said quickly, 'but only because I can't bear anything tight around me.'

He looked doubtful. 'You do seem to be more robust than a year ago, ma'am,' he said. 'A fine, full habit of body is what I like to see in a woman, but those who hold your health dear cannot wish it any fuller, and it seems to me—'

'Well, well, perhaps I am a little fatter,' I snapped, 'but there is nothing to be done about it after all.'

'I'm afraid you eat too much,' he said frankly. 'It is a failing of all the Hanoverians.' This was sugaring the pill. He knew I liked to be told I resembled Papa's side of the family. 'But it is not good for you. These sick headaches and fits of irritation you have been suffering from recently – I am sure they would be cured by a strict attention to diet. And your complexion seems yellower, too. Your liking for sweet ale and negus, for instance, is very ill-advised. You should never drink beer, ma'am. I have told you so before.'

'Well, but I cannot drink tea. It does not agree with me,' I said crossly. 'What am I to do?'

'Take a little wine instead,' he said. 'A little sound wine every day is essential to good health. It was too little wine that destroyed Princess Charlotte's health: a Hanoverian cannot thrive on a low diet. But you must eat less, or you have a good chance of getting very fat. It is not good to eat just because food is there. One should only eat when one is hungry.'

'Then *I* should be eating all day long,' I retorted, 'for I am always hungry.'

He was not deflected. 'If you ate more slowly, you would not feel hungry when you rose from the table. Your Majesty does tend to gobble, you know. I have often noted it with sadness.'

I felt myself blushing. I knew it was a failing of mine (and indeed, to this day I still tend to eat very fast. I certainly do not mean to correct myself now, however, for it affords me a great deal of amusement when there are guests to dinner. The rule of etiquette is that as soon as I lay down my fork to signify I have finished a course, the plates are cleared away, whether everyone else has finished or not. It is great fun to see the expression of dismay on their faces as the food is whipped away from them before they have had more than a mouthful or two – especially as they are obliged to talk politely to one another, which slows them down. It is amusing, too, to see the 'old hands' at the game, who know better than to converse, and concentrate on rapid fork-work, keeping one eye on me and trying to match me for speed!).

Lord Melbourne went on. 'And you must take exercise – you must walk more,' he said. 'You walk so little, I fear you will soon lose the use of your legs.'

I was not to be bought off by pleasantries. 'I hate to walk,' I said. 'Walking for the sake of walking makes me sick!'

'Nevertheless, the only way to prevent getting fat is to eat less and walk more.'

'When I walk I always get stones in my shoes,' I complained.

'Then you must have them made tighter.'

'My feet swell. You have seen how swollen they get.'

'That is because you don't walk enough. You have poor circulation. If you walk more they will not do so.'

'I hate walking!' I snapped. 'I won't do it.'

'You must!' he snapped back.

'I won't!' He opened his mouth to reply and I got in first. 'The Queen of Portugal is hugely fat, and yet she does so much exercise! What have you to say to that?' I said triumphantly. For the moment my kind friend was silenced, and then he changed the subject. But these arguments did neither of us good, and I always felt bad afterwards.

To this burden of tension the Lady Flora affair added the final straw. She had spent Christmas with her family, and came back into waiting in January 1839, and straight away Lehzen and I noticed that she was decidedly plump in the stomach – without having put on weight elsewhere on her body. Indeed, her face was thinner, while her front protruded noticeably under her gowns. Lehzen and I concluded at once that she must be pregnant, and I was delighted at this downfall of my enemy who had always made such a parade of her piety and virtue. Unmarried, and pregnant! Moreover, I knew exactly who had put her in this condition. A few months earlier she had travelled down from Scotland in a post-chaise – alone with Sir John Conroy for the whole journey! My two enemies shot with a single arrow: it could hardly have been better!

It could hardly have been worse. Gossip of that kind can never be kept down. By the end of the month the whole Palace was buzzing with it, and it could only be a matter of time before it jumped the wall to the world at large. Some of my ladies, worried that their own reputations would suffer by contamination, appealed to Lady Tavistock, the senior Lady of the Bedchamber, to do something, and she in turn appealed to Lord Melbourne, who consulted Sir James Clark. (He was my Court Physician, but he was also still Mamma's.) Clark told Lord M. that Lady Flora had consulted him about her health several times, complaining of pains in her side, nausea and a derangement of the bowels. Clark had prescribed rhubarb and ipecac and such homely remedies; but he said that in his own opinion, Lady Flora was probably pregnant. The best thing was to wait and see, he said, which Lord M. agreed with, and so advised me. 'If you remain quite quiet,' he told me, 'you will get through it very well.'

But the gossip went on fizzing and spluttering like slow-match, my ladies feared for their virtue, and Mamma's ladies accused Lehzen of starting the rumours to discredit Mamma. The situation ought to have been sorted out quite simply by a consultation between Mamma and me, but of course we were barely on speaking terms, certainly not intimate enough to discuss anything so delicate; so when the rumours refused to go away, another of my senior ladies, Lady Portman, went to Mamma, told her what was being said (apparently she had not heard it yet) and said that Lady Flora must either submit to a medical examination to clear her name, or leave the Palace.

Mamma, it seems, was horrified; and Lady Flora indignantly refused to submit to the humiliation. But at last she saw there was nothing for it; so on February 17th she allowed herself to be examined in the presence of Lady Portman (who kept her hands over her face the whole time) and her maid, by Sir James Clark, assisted by a specialist in women's diseases, Sir Charles Clarke. It must have been a frightful ordeal for her; I hate to think about it; but when it was over, both doctors signed a certificate to say that she was still virgo intacta, and that though there was considerable enlargement of the stomach, there was no reason to suppose that a pregnancy existed or had ever existed.

On hearing the verdict Mamma dismissed Sir James from her service for having encouraged the false rumours; and, considerably chagrined, I sent my regrets to Lady Flora, and offered to see her as soon as she liked. She replied that she was too unwell and upset to avail herself immediately of my offer, and it was not until a week later that I did see her. Then I was struck with pity at how very ill she looked, so wretched and yellow and trembling with nervousness. With tears in my eyes I took her hand and kissed her and said I was very sorry for what had happened. She thanked me, and agreed at least to forgive, if she could not forget, for her mistress's sake.

That ought to have been the end of it; but a few days later Sir James Clark, perhaps annoyed at having been dismissed by Mamma, told Lord Melbourne that his certificate might prove to have been misleading. He and Sir Charles agreed that there was an enlargement of the womb very like a child, and that though Lady Flora was a virgin, strange things had been known to happen, and it might still prove to be a pregnancy. Lord Melbourne of course passed this on to me, and we both reverted to our former, more comfortable belief that Lady Flora was guilty. I am ashamed to think now that I had learned nothing from what had passed; but I had had so little experience in loving, and so much in hating, that forgiveness did not come easy to me.

Meanwhile the lady in question had written to her elder brother complaining of her treatment at Court. The Hastings family were rabid Tories, and hated Lord Melbourne (who had often said publicly that there wasn't an ounce of sense between them all), so now the fat was in the fire. Meanwhile Conroy took the story to the Opposition press, and urged them to make good use of it; and he persuaded Mamma to urge Lady Flora to demand compensation for her trials. So it all blew up again, with accusation and counter-accusation, rhodomontades from the Tory Press against Lord M. and Lehzen (whom they conceived to be the prime mover), Lord Hastings plunging about London like a fire-breathing dragon and threatening to call Lord M. out, and Lady Flora's brother in Brussels busily spreading the story as lavishly as he could around the courts of Europe. The longer it went on the more I hated Lady Flora, and the more I hated her the more convinced I was that she was with child. I have to say the only person to come well out of the business was Mamma, who loyally stood by her lady-in-waiting through everything, and maintained from first to last that she was innocent.

At last the good Duke of Wellington, alarmed for the reputation of the Crown, restored an element of calm by persuading the three of us at least to appear in public together, which we did, though I must say it almost killed me to be civil to them. The Duke only managed to persuade me at all by assuring me that he knew who the real villain of the piece was, and that he intended to persuade Conroy to quit Mamma's service. The idea was like a promise of Heaven to me.

'But he will never manage it,' Lord M. said sadly when I told him what Wellington had said. 'Conroy will never obey the Duke, and the Duchess will obey no-one but Conroy.' I feared he was right; but somehow the Duke did the trick. He would never tell anyone what he had said to Conroy to persuade him – 'Plenty of butter,' was all he told Lord M. – but years afterwards Mamma told me that the Duke had come to see her, too. He talked to her 'pretty roundly' about

Conroy, saying that if the Queen disapproved of him, she needed no other reason to dismiss him. Mamma cried and trembled, for there was nothing more awful than the Duke in spate; and though she did not promise to dismiss Conroy, the weakening of her resolve to defend him may have been what finally persuaded him that the game was up.

Whatever it was, the fact of the matter was that on the 10th of June 1839 he dismissed his servants, and left with his family for Italy. It was the lifting of a weight from my shoulders. They stayed in Rome for a few years, and then came back to England to live in style in a large house near Reading. He never stopped corresponding with Mamma, nor pestering successive Prime Ministers for a peerage, but in 1850 the secrets of his appalling mismanagement of Mamma's and Princess Sophia's financial affairs were discovered, and if he had ever had any hope of preferment, it died then. Vast sums of money had 'disappeared' under his stewardship, including a draft for £16,000 from Uncle Leopold to Mamma which was simply never paid into her bank; and when Princess Sophia died, she was found to possess nothing but her household goods, though she should have been a wealthy woman. It was thought in the end that he had stolen some £60,000 of Mamma's money and £400,000 of Princess Sophia's, quite apart from the day-to-day spending of their incomes which he had benefited from. He died suddenly from a heart attack in 1854, and I would have been glad to witness his arrival at the Throne of Judgement and hear what he had to say in his own defence. I doubt it could have been much.

But back to 1839: Lady Flora had been growing more and more ill, while Lord M. and I discussed the wickedness of 'that nasty woman' and her 'wretched family' who were making such a fuss in the newspapers about her. Mamma's championing of her I saw as a treason against me, and I complained bitterly to Lord M. of her harbouring my enemy. 'I begin to dislike Ma amazingly,' I told him, and he nodded gravely. 'It is not to be wondered. Your Majesty is served very ill by them both.' Then a few days after Conroy's departure I received a stark message from Mamma that Lady Flora was mortally ill, and could not last the week.

I was shocked, and yet still a part of me resisted the inevitable conclusion, that I had been wrong about her. There was a stone lodged in my heart that would not yield to reason or experience; but I knew what I must do, in all decency, and I cancelled the ball which should have been held that night, and sent word that I would go and see Lady Flora whenever she liked. The summons came the next day.

I went alone to her chamber, and what I saw there shocked me so profoundly that it was like a douche of icy water. A sickly smell hung on the air, sour and pungent, which was not masked by the roses in a bowl near her head – white and yellow roses, their petals beginning to be limp. She was stretched out on a couch looking as thin as anyone could be who was still alive, the flesh wasted from her bones so that she seemed literally a skeleton; yet her stomach was very much swollen, like a person who was with child. Oh, but her face, her face! Yellow, it was, the skin drawn tight and shiny over the bones, the orbits of the eyes so marked, like the empty pits of a death's-head. She had no eyebrows or eyelashes, for all her hair had fallen out, and there was a horrid emptiness to the cap tied over her head, where the springiness of her locks ought to have been.

I spoke to her – I don't know what I said – and she answered. Her voice was much as usual, and there was a good deal of strength in her hand as she took mine. I made myself hold it, though I wanted to cast it away from me in disgust, for it was nothing but bones, like a handful of bare twigs – a horrible, unnatural feeling. Her eyes scanned my face searchingly.

'How – how are you, Lady Flora?' I said weakly. 'I hope you have everything you want.'

'Thank you, I am very comfortable,' she said. There was a silence. I longed to go, and could feel damp patches of fear growing in my armpits. Then she said, 'I am very grateful to Your Majesty for all you have done. It is most kind of you to have come to see me. I am glad, indeed, to see you looking so well.'

'I am – I shall – I do hope to see you again, when you are better,' I stammered; and she only looked at me, and pressed my hand a little, and then turned her head away wearily, as if to say, 'I shall not see you again.' I could bear it no longer. I muttered something by way of farewell, released myself, and ran all the way up the stairs to my own apartments again, trembling with fear and disgust like a horse that smells lightning.

I had seen Death in there, I had smelled it. It had come into my own palace, forced itself upon my notice in the most violent way, when I had been thinking of quite other things. *I am always here, even when you cannot see me. I will seek you out, I will have you; there is nowhere to hide, nowhere safe from me. Cover me with fine cloth, cover me with roses, it makes no difference. I am the great determiner, and I have already written your end.*

And worst of all, I had wronged her. To fear and disgust were added guilt and self-loathing, and all I could do was to face it out defiantly and admit no fault. A few mornings later Lehzen woke me with the news that Lady Flora had died in the night 'without a struggle, poor thing. She only just raised her hands a little and gave one gasp.' I received the news stonily. I said again and again in the days that followed that I felt no remorse about her death. *I* had done nothing to kill her. It was none of it my doing. She had behaved abominably to me when she had me in her power, while I had graciously gone to visit her when she lay on her deathbed. *Anybody* would have thought she was with child, seeing the shape of her. It was not I who had started the gossip; it was not I who had stirred up the newspapers. Why should I feel any remorse? And so my arguments revolved in my thoughts. Outwardly I was cold and stubborn; inwardly I raged with hatred against Mamma, Lady Flora, the Hastings, and all who sided with them; and underneath it all, I whimpered with fear and guilt, and my nights were hideous with frightful nightmares.

Two days before her death, Lady Flora had made her family promise they would order a post-mortem examination to prove her innocence. This was carried out by Sir Benjamin Brodie and four colleagues, and they concluded unanimously that Lady Flora had died of a tumour on the liver, which was grossly enlarged, causing a displacement of the other organs giving the appearance of pregnancy. The uterus and its appendages, they said, presented the usual appearances of the healthy virgin state.

I was very glad that custom forbade ladies to attend funerals. I sent a carriage, as did Mamma and Queen Adelaide; though the press had been so hostile to me since Lady Flora's death that Lord M. feared mine might be stoned. A force of police was laid on to line the route to St Katharine's Wharf (she was to be buried in Scotland) in case of trouble, but there was none, only a sullen silence and a few mutters. The muttering went on in the press, too, kept alive by the Hastings family (I sent Lady Flora's maid £50, but old Lady H. sent it back), and of course the *Morning Post*'s deep desire to see off the Whig government. It was a great pity, Lord M. said later, that Lady Flora had died in July, for there was nothing much for the newspapers to think about through the summer months, with Parliament in recess and the *ton* out of town. They would forget all about it in September, he assured me; and counselled me to foster the detachment that shrugs off calumny and flattery alike.

But I felt low and wretched, and everything in life seemed to have lost its savour. I did not even care about riding any longer. 'Tired of *riding*?' Lord M. said in astonishment. But he felt guilty too. 'I could have averted the worst of the scandal. Why did I not tell Lord Hastings that it was I who had spread the rumours? I should have told him I was responsible for it all – as, indeed, I was.'

'Oh no!' I said, very much touched.

'Yes,' he said, his eyes filling with tears, 'for I am your adviser, and I have not advised you well in this matter.'

My eyes filled too. 'You are the kindest and best of friends—' I could speak no more. I took his hand and pressed it, and we sat in silence for a while, like castaways on a rock, alone in the middle of the world's greatest metropolis.

2nd May 1900

ONE OF the reasons for the coolness which had sprung up between Uncle Leopold and me was that since I had become Queen I had rather gone off the idea of marrying. It was a long time since I had understood that Uncle and Grandmamma Coburg had planned almost from our births that I should one day marry my cousin Albert; but it was entirely an unspoken understanding. I had seen him only once, in 1836 when we were both seventeen, and he had come to visit us at Kensington with his father, the Duke of Coburg, and his elder brother Ernst. We had liked each other well enough, but at the time I was so wild for company and dissipation I should have liked anyone half as amiable. We certainly had not fallen in love, however. At that time Albert was much shorter than his brother, and rather fat, and he had not been in the best of health and spirits. He had suffered dreadfully from seasickness during the crossing, and had difficulty in shaking it off, and I was always impatient of ill health, being so robust myself. Moreover, I adored banquets and parties and dancing, and would have danced until dawn if the orchestra had gone on playing; while Albert had difficulty in staying awake after nine o'clock in the evening, found rich food indigestible, and preferred solitary reading to dancing or noisy parties. Nevertheless, he could be very amusing at breakfast-time, had a sweet voice, and a great talent for mimicry, which often made me laugh very much. When he went away I was quite willing to accept him as my future husband at some distant date, provided it remained distant.

The difficulty came when, after my accession, Uncle Leopold began pressing me to name that date. I had only just escaped from prison, and had given all my pent-up love to the man who had helped unlock my gaol. There were balls and parties and handsome young men vying for my hand at the dance. My lightest word was law, and, safe in the warm haven of Lord Melbourne's constant attention, I had discovered the delights of flirting. The last thing I wanted was to harness myself to a dull, pudgy, sleepy-head cousin who went to bed at nine o'clock, who would doubtless object to every scheme of irrational pleasure I devised, and would be jealous of my admirers. Having so recently quit my cell, I was not eager to be locked up again, and so when Uncle Leopold enquired, I replied that I was too young to marry, and so was Albert: he needed more experience of the world – and his English was far from perfect. Uncle Leopold must have been alarmed to see his darling scheme slipping through his fingers. Though I did not know it, he had supervised Albert's education specifically to fit him to be consort of England; and though *I* had not promised myself to Albert, Uncle Leopold had. When he relayed, as delicately as he could, my reservations to Albert, Albert expressed some of his own. He would not wait much longer for me to make up my mind, he told Uncle rather crossly. Suppose he held himself in suspense for three or four years, and then I decided against him – he would have wasted half his life. If there was to be no English marriage, he wanted the chance to settle his career in another direction, and choose a bride elsewhere before all the best princesses were snapped up.

In this unsatisfactory state things stood in 1839, in that miserable summer of Lady Flora. One day Lord M. and I sat very glumly together, sighing over my lot.

'I am sadly changed since last year,' I said. 'I was so merry; I enjoyed everything so much, but this year the same pleasures seem like nothing.'

'You will enjoy them when they come, when the Season starts,' he assured me kindly. 'It is the time of year. Everything is dull in July.'

'And then there's Mamma,' I said. 'I hate having her under my roof. Look how she retained a Certain Person, though she knew he was my enemy. And Lady Flora—' I shivered even mentioning the name. 'Everyone thinks I should make it up with Ma now, but I can't forget how she sided with her straight away, instead of with me.'

'It was very shocking,' he murmured sympathetically.

'But she never loved me,' I added, working myself up to a pitch of self-pity. 'She never cared the least bit about me. It's hateful to think of all the years of torment ahead, having her living here. There will never be a moment's peace or comfort.'

133

'It's very dreadful,' Lord M. said, 'but what can be done?'

'I would give anything to have her go away.'

'But that would be very shocking,' he said. 'You cannot live here alone.'

'I know,' I said gloomily, 'and she swore years ago that she would never leave me while I was unmarried.'

'Well then,' he said, raising his eyes to mine, 'there's that way of settling it.'

I felt myself redden. 'That is a shocking alternative,' I said, and I got up and walked to the window to cool my cheeks. Marriage? I could not bear to think of it. I wanted to stay as I was for ever, safe with Lord M., and never have to grow up. I knew what marriage meant: it meant having babies, and the idea horrified me. And what one had to do to get the babies I did not know, but I could guess that that was shocking and horrible too, or why was it kept such a secret? And yet the alternative was to go on living with Mamma, which I hated. Besides, I knew that I could not *really* remain single. I was Queen of England, and my duty was to produce an Heir for the Throne.

Yet even to discuss the possibility of marriage seemed impossible: it was a subject of such delicacy that my maiden modesty retreated before it. I stood there in silence for a while, until I felt it was really too silly to be frightened of opening the subject with my kind friend. We had always been quite frank with each other. And after all, I only wanted to *talk* about it now, not *do* it.

I turned back to him. He had stood up, of course, when I did, but now I signalled to him to sit. It made me feel more comfortable to have him fixed in a chair while I moved about. 'I don't know whether you know,' I began hesitantly, 'that it is my uncle's great wish – King Leopold, I mean – ' he nodded helpfully; I screwed up my courage – 'that he has always wanted me to marry my cousin Albert; but I am not sure about it. I have only seen him once. He was not so very handsome, then, and he fell asleep a good deal.'

'That is not a very appealing trait,' he agreed carefully.

'I cannot bear an arranged marriage. I love my country and I am ready to do whatever is for its good, but when it comes to a choice of husband, my own liking must be the principal thing.'

'I think you have the right to expect that,' he said comfortably. 'No-one would wish you to marry where you had no liking. It does not conduce either to happiness or propriety for any person to marry without affection.'

'I'm sure you're right,' I said eagerly.

'But a *little* guidance can be to the good. Much must depend, I think, on what sort of person your cousin is.'

'I hardly know. And I could not decide anything unless I saw him again,' I said anxiously. 'But I hear Albert's praises on all sides.'

'How would it be with the Duchess?' he mused. He was trying, I see now, to gauge my feelings and accommodate his words to them; but I was so chronically in two minds on the subject he had not much hope of doing that! 'If you were to marry him and then he sided with her against you, it would be dreadful. You would be worse off than before – it would make her so strong.'

'Oh, there is no chance of that,' I said, taken aback. I could not imagine anyone of my generation siding with Mamma. 'You need have no fear on that score.'

'Very well,' he said, as though he doubted it, 'but I wonder if you should marry a Coburg at all? They are not much liked here, ever since your uncle was awarded such a large pension. The quickest way to a person's dislike is through his purse, you know! And they are unpopular abroad. The Russians in particular hate them.'

'I don't see why they should be so disliked,' I said, a little nettled on behalf of my own family.

'Do not you? But your mother is a Coburg – a good specimen of the breed, I should think.'

I burst out laughing at that, and came to sit down opposite him. 'Yes, Mamma is all Coburg! But the men are better, I assure you!'

'I hope so indeed,' he smiled. 'It is well known that German men smoke excessively, and never wash their faces.'

'Oh, but I have met several of my cousins – male cousins – and they have been charming!'

'Ah, there you have it,' he said seriously. 'Cousins! I would not be doing my duty if I did not warn you that it is a very bad idea to marry one's first cousin. There is no religious bar to it in this country, but a cousin is a very near relation, and there can be consequences – I think you understand me. It can happen that the children of such a union are – not quite the thing.'

I blushed again, and said, to change the subject, 'Well, then, but who else is there?' Together we went through all the other eligible princes, but not one of them would do. 'There are objections to all of them,' I said mournfully.

'And a foreigner would be unpopular in England,' he agreed.

'But I could never, *never* marry a subject!' I said quickly. 'It would be making yourself so much their equal; and then you would come so much into contact with all their family; and their most distant connections would put on airs and demand to be recognised, and it would be nothing but jealousies and impertinence.'

'Oh, it would never do: the Court would be full of rustics,' he said with a shudder, which made me laugh. 'But still a foreigner would not be popular in England,' he insisted.

'For myself, my feeling is quite against marrying at all,' I said, beginning to feel cross, 'only my uncle presses me so about it.'

'It is a great change in the situation,' he agreed. 'It is a very serious thing.'

I remembered his own, unhappy marriage. He was a warning to me. 'I need not come to a decision now, need I? Why need I marry for three or four more years? Except—' I remembered, my mind swinging back again like a pendulum, 'that this present state with Mamma is so dreadful.'

'Always on the verge of a quarrel.' He nodded. 'It would try the patience of a saint.'

'To be frank,' I said with a burst of confidence, 'I dread the thought of marrying. I am so accustomed to having my own way, you see.'

'But you would have it still,' he said. 'You are the Queen.'

'But it is ten to one that I should never agree with him – whoever he was. And even if I got my way in the end, how could I endure the terrible scenes beforehand? I am so passionate, we would be worn out with storms.'

There was a silence. Then Lord M. said thoughtfully, 'Is not your cousin coming to visit some time this year?'

I nodded. 'Uncle Leopold wants Ernst and Albert to come to Windsor in the autumn.'

'There can be no harm in just seeing them,' he said agreeably. 'Nothing could be more natural than cousins coming to visit; but as to marriage, it is not necessary.'

His willingness to accommodate my fears seemed only to irritate me. We were circling the problem without ever addressing it, for if I did not marry, I must continue to live with Mamma, and that was where we had started.

'For myself, I don't care if they come or not,' I said with a burst of petulance. 'The whole subject is *odious* to me! I would sooner never marry *at all*!'

'Well, I don't know about *that*,' said Lord M., with such a droll look that my crossness dissolved and I began to laugh. 'But there is no public anxiety about your marriage. It may be better to wait until some such demonstration is shown.'

I could have flung my arms around his neck in gratitude. There he had given me the perfect excuse for fending off Uncles Leopold and Ernst, if they should press me to what I did not like. I was the Queen of England: I could not go marrying my cousin, just because my uncles wanted it!

So things were left for the rest of the summer, and I tried to put it out of my head.

Thursday the 10th of October was a day which I never forgot. It began strangely, for during the night a madman had thrown stones through some of my windows, breaking several panes of glass – a most disagreeable and upsetting thing. We never discovered who had done it, or why. Lord M. and I in any case felt rather cross and headachy, for we had eaten pork the night before, which had not agreed with us. Later we went for a long walk to clear our heads, and as we were returning along the Terrace (we were at Windsor) a page came running up to me with a letter just delivered. I examined it, and glanced at Lord M. nervously.

'It is from Uncle Leopold,' I said. It was quite short. 'He says that my cousins will arrive this evening.' He nodded, but I could see he didn't like it, and I understood why. He was afraid that our comfortable times together were drawing to a close, and I had the same foreboding myself. Growing up was upon me. Very soon – in a matter of hours – I would see Albert again, and be forced to come to a decision. The worst thing, I thought, would be if I didn't really either like him or hate him. If I were merely indifferent to him, what then? 'They say he is grown quite handsome lately,' I suggested nervously.

Lord M. met my eyes. 'Does he stay awake in the evenings now?'

But I didn't laugh. 'I don't know,' I said. 'I suppose we shall soon find out.'

At seven-thirty that evening we were warned that the carriage had arrived, and I went with Mamma to the top of the grand staircase to receive them. The crossing had been bad, and their luggage had gone astray. They would appear tired, pale, and seasick, I told myself, and I must make allowance for that.

The two figures appeared and started up the stairs, and I was almost too nervous to look at them. Ernst was a step in front, and seemed not to have changed at all; but Albert – *could* it be Albert? He was tall and slender and – those who had said he had grown quite handsome had lied damnably. He was *beautiful*!

He stood before me, looked down into my eyes, took the hand which I had held out almost without realising it. I gazed up at him, speechless, and my heart left by breast there and then to fly to his, never to leave it. It was my *coup de foudre*. I looked, and loved him utterly.

The next evening we had an informal dance, and for once I did not mind the etiquette which forbade me to join in the more intimate dances, for I was quite happy to sit out and watch Albert at the waltz, the quadrille and the galop. He was so graceful, and held himself so well, and his figure was perfect – tall and fine, but strong, with broad shoulders and a narrow waist. I had seen him in the saddle that day, and had observed the good calves which filled out his long boots, and the muscularity of his thighs, clad in fine cazimere pantaloons, skin tight, with *nothing underneath them!* The very *maleness* of this young man thrilled me; and yet there was a quality of spirituality about him which made him seem at the same time a creature from another, higher plane. His face was the work of a master artist and tinted by the most delicate hand: blue eyes of the most glorious colour, blue that would make the summer sky swoon with envy; an exquisite nose, fine and straight, a delicate mouth, sweet and expressive. His hair was about the colour of mine, light brown with golden lights here and there, and he wore a fine moustache and very delicate side-whiskers. They say he was the image of his mother, who had been a great beauty; and certainly he looked nothing like his brother, who was very dark, with black eyes, and nothing delicate about him. I was glad that Albert was nothing like him in character either. Their father, the Duke, was a profligate, both expensive and immoral, and Ernst had taken after him. When they visited that October he was already suffering from the syphilis that was eventually to kill him – though I did not know it then, of course! His frequent fevers while he was at Windsor, which made him take to his bed, were explained away as biliousness and jaundice.

I had always longed to be beautiful, and knew I was not, but I had always loved beauty in others. At St George's Chapel on Sunday I was able to observe Albert's delight in the music, and see how his beautiful face grew quite radiant when he listened, as though his soul had drifted close to the surface just for a little while and become visible. Music meant a great deal to me, and I was glad to feel I had something in common with this heavenly creature. He played the piano with great skill and execution, and sang in a sweet tenor voice. We had sung one or two duets, and he had praised my voice, and said – I treasured the words! – that we sounded remarkably well together.

He could be merry, too. At luncheon he made us laugh with anecdotes about his student days at Bonn, and his clever, funny mimicry of various professors and eminent men. He had brought his dog to England with him, a beautiful greyhound called Eos. (He explained to me that 'eos' meant 'dawn', which suited her because she was as black as night, with one silver streak, like the first approach of sunrise.) People are said to be like their dogs, and Eos was exactly the dog I would have picked for him, slender and elegant, gentle and good, and with such a melancholy way of looking at you – not jolly and noisy like my little fellows! She was so well behaved and clever that at his command she walked round the table and gave the paw to each of us in turn. He showed us how she could jump immense heights, and was so dainty she could eat off his fork without spilling. Eos evidently adored him, and I thought *that* the most natural thing in the world!

The next day I sent for Lord Melbourne, while Ernst and Albert were out shooting, and told him that my feelings about marrying had undergone a change.

'It is very natural,' he said, and gave me a significant look. 'Prince Albert is a very good-looking young man.'

'You guessed, then?'

'I could see that he interested you. Yesterday when you sat on the sofa with him, looking at the book of etchings, your eyes were more often on him than on the drawings.'

'You are very clever,' I said, feeling my cheeks glow. 'You will perhaps have guessed, then, that I have quite made up my mind – that is, about marrying Albert.'

Was there the slightest pause? Did he seem to shrink a little under my gaze? At the time I was too full of my own feelings, but looking back I seem to see the blow it must have been to him. Young people are sadly heedless; now I am old myself, I can appreciate his self-restraint.

'I am very glad of it,' he said warmly. 'I think it is a very good thing, and you will be much more comfortable. A woman cannot stand alone for long whatever her situation; and yours is a particularly difficult one.'

'I do feel the need of someone to support me,' I admitted. 'And he is so very beautiful, and so amiable and good-tempered. I have such a bad temper, that must be an advantage, don't you think?'

'He is a very fine young man in every way,' he said kindly. 'And have you thought about the time, when you will do it?'

'I don't know. In a year, perhaps?'

139

'Too long,' he said, shaking his head. 'Parliament must be assembled, in order to make provision for him – his pension and so on – but it is best not to leave it too long after that, to give no opportunity for talk. Preventing talk prevents objections – though I don't think there'll be much. On the contrary, I think it will be very well received, for I hear there's an anxiety now that you should be married.' We talked a little, and decided on February as a suitable time. 'As to titles, he should be made a Field Marshal, of course. That is a usual thing.'

'Yes, and he must be given the title of "Royal Highness" – no more of that horrid "Serene Highness", which always sounds so second-rate!'

'No pinchbeck for the Prince; only solid gold,' Lord M. said, and we laughed.

'As to making him a Duke—' I began, but Lord M. interrupted.

'No, no, certainly not! It would be most unwise. It would raise a great deal of resentment in the country, for I'm afraid everyone would accuse him of meddling in politics if he had a seat in the House of Lords.'

'I was about to say that I don't at all wish him to be made a Duke,' I said with dignity. 'It is not by any means high enough for him: I wish him to be made King Consort.' I saw Lord M.'s jaw drop with horror, and added hastily, 'Not straight away, perhaps, but in a little while – a year or two – when everyone has come to see his worth.'

He found his voice. 'No, no, ma'am, for God's sake put that out of your head! Not King, never King! It would not do at all.'

'But Princess Charlotte promised to make Uncle Leopold King when she came to the Throne. He will expect the same for Albert. And indeed, why should it not be? My power is not worth having if I cannot give my husband the rank he ought to have.'

'It is not in your power to make him King,' he said firmly. 'It would take an Act of Parliament. That is what happened with William III and Queen Mary.'

'If they had one, then I shall have one!'

'Not by any means! Do you not see, if Parliament once gets into the habit of making Kings, it can get into the habit of *un*making them too! We will do nothing to encourage such pretensions, if you please.' I did not please, and was silent for a while, scowling. Then he added gently, 'There will be no difficulty, of course, in awarding him any precedence you wish. He will be first of all men.'

'Before my English relations?' I asked sharply.

'Of course,' he said, and smiled. 'He will have the position in society that he holds in your heart.'

I melted, and reached out and took his hand. 'Thank you! Oh, you have been so very kind to me, so very *fatherly*! I quite thought you would dislike it amazingly when I told you!'

'Dislike what makes Your Majesty happy?' he said, pressing my hand. 'How could that be?'

Dear, kind Lord M.! He must have known how it would be afterwards, and that our happy, intimate days were over. But he never by the slightest word or gesture cast a shadow over my sunlit prospect.

'I think you should tell the Prince of your feelings as soon as possible,' he said, his voice very slightly unsteady.

'*I*, tell *him*? Good heavens, what a strange reversal! How awkward I shall feel!'

'You must be the man in this case,' he said smiling. 'That is another penalty of being Queen – you will be deprived of the privilege of being proposed to.'

I laughed. 'I would think that no privilege! I would far rather be doing, than waiting and hoping for an offer without any way of hastening it on.'

'Oh, females usually manage to make their wishes felt, one way or another,' he said lightly.

We parted soon afterwards, and when he had made his leg and kissed my hand he asked, 'When will you speak?'

'Tomorrow,' I said.

'The 15th of October,' he said. 'It will be a date to remember.' And he went away, tall, leonine, handsome still – but an old man from then on, stepping into the shadows and leaving the stage empty for the new actor who was to play the hero from tomorrow onwards.

Eight

4th May 1900, at Windsor

To RESUME: the next morning, which was Tuesday the 15th of October, Albert and Ernst went out hunting, and when I had done my boxes I went to the Blue Closet, which I used as my private sitting-room, and walked about the room, fretful with anxiety. I loved him, of that there was no possible doubt; but would he, *could* he love me? There had been encouraging signs: he had been very attentive to me – but then I was the Queen, who else should he notice? He was kind and charming and made me laugh – but then who didn't he charm? (Lady Cowper, Lord M.'s sister, said he had very pretty manners, that he was charming and gay and just what a young man ought to be.) On the previous evening, when we stood in the corridor saying goodnight after the dancing, I had given him my hand and he had squeezed it affectionately – oh, but that was slight evidence on which to risk my all!

I paused and stood on tiptoe and looked at myself in the glass over the chimneypiece. A smooth, plump face with a fine complexion, and smooth, light-brown hair. I had abandoned my side-curls now, and wore my hair drawn back to a chignon, with two side-pieces braided, and pinned in a loop over each ear, which Lehzen said made me look more dignified, and rather Plantagenet – like Queen Philippa. I stared at that familiar reflection. Item, two eyes sufficiently large, pale blue, but rather protuberant. Item, a nose quite beyond redemption. Item, two lips, indifferent red, the lower one drawn down by the lack of chin so that my teeth showed – quite nice teeth, small and even, but no-one falls in love with teeth! I had a 'silvery' voice, and I moved gracefully – those were my only assets.

My only assets? Well, I was Queen of England, the matrimonial 'catch' of all Europe, I thought; he knew why he had come to Windsor – Uncle Leopold had assured me of that; he was not very likely to refuse me. Oh, but I was not beautiful, as he was, and I loved him so dreadfully much! If he should accept, but not love me, how would I bear it?

I had told Lehzen to send word for him to come to me as soon as they got back from the hunt, and at about half past twelve I saw them come galloping up the slope. Already I could pick him out from a hundred horsemen: he and Ernst were riding side by side, racing each other; I could imagine their shouts and happy laughter, though they were too far away for me to hear them. *Oh happy horse, to bear the weight of Antony!* I thought. They disappeared from view, and there was a wait, while in my mind's eye I followed him as he dismounted and handed over his horse, walked up the stairs, was met by his valet and given my message. He would want to change his clothes and wash his hands, of course. Would he be as nervous as I was, knowing what was to come? Or would he be cool and indifferent, secure in his superiority to me and all living things?

When the tap came at my door, I jumped almost out of my skin. I called, and he appeared, my most beautiful angel, his eyes bright and his cheeks still flushed from the exercise – I suppose!

'You wished to see me?'

'Oh! Yes – yes, Cousin! Come in.' He came in and shut the door behind him, and stood waiting with an enquiring look for me to speak. He did not seem at all conscious; I might have been going to secure him as my partner for a game of Tactics after dinner. The nervousness was all mine. I twisted my hands together to stop them shaking and tried to speak naturally, though I'm afraid my voice came out rather higher than usual. 'I – I saw you coming up the hill. Did you have a pleasant ride?'

'Very pleasant, thank you.'

'And have they given you a nice horse?'

'A delightful horse, indeed.'

'The weather is rather warm for riding, however.'

'Perhaps it is a little, now. It was cooler when we set off.'

I racked my brains for something else to say, and cursed my unready tongue for offering me no words. I had never had any small-talk, as I often complained to Lord M. 'Say anything rather than nothing,' he always told me. And suddenly, thinking of him, I felt quite calm. It was absurd to be hunting about for trifling things to say, when our lives were waiting to be determined. I lifted my eyes to his, and though I could feel my cheeks burning with consciousness, I said bravely, 'I think you must know, really, why I have asked you to come here this morning. There is something that I must ask you.' Now I saw a blush rise from his collar and rush up to his cheeks, and the realisation that he was shy, too, strengthened me. I would have died to save him the least embarrassment, and my heart overflowed into words – ardent, simple words, the best, really, if I had thought about it. 'Dearest Albert, I am so *very* much in love with you that I can hardly bear it! It would make me really *too* happy if you would consent to what I wish – that is, to marry me!'

143

It was like the breaking of a dam. I saw his cheek pale, and then somehow or other he had crossed the space between us without my knowing how he did it, had taken me in his arms, and was kissing me again and again, my cheek, brow, lips. A few words escaped him, all in German: *'Liebe Kleine* . . . darling Little One . . . I love you too, so much!' I was stunned, dazed with happiness; I clung to him, returned his kisses with ardour, astonished to know that my love was returned, and by such an angel as Albert. He loved me! He *did* love me, and how was that possible? In a little while he took my hands and led me over to the sofa, and we sat down together, gazing at each other, laughing now with relief and happiness.

'Will you really marry me?' I asked incredulously. *'Really?'*

'It will give me the greatest happiness I can imagine on this earth,' he said, 'to share my life with you.'

I felt so humble, so glad. 'Oh, you are too good! I know I am not worthy of you, dearest, dearest Albert, but I will try so hard to make you happy!'

'No, no, it is I who must make *you* happy! It will be both my duty and my pleasure.'

I lifted his dear hand to my lips and kissed it, and laid it against my cheek. 'You are making a great sacrifice, I know, but I will strive to make you feel it as little as possible.'

'It is no sacrifice,' he said earnestly. 'You must believe me.'

But, 'It is, I know it is!' I cried. 'You will give up so much for me, and I—'

'Victoria!' My name, spoken by him for the first time without qualification, shocked me into silence. Now he had my attention, he took my face gently between his hands, looking down seriously into my eyes. 'You must believe me, I make no sacrifice. I love you very much, and we will have a most fortunate life together.' And then, still holding my face, he lowered his head and kissed my lips. 'Dearest little one, I love you so very much!' he whispered. He kissed me again, but now it was different. A stillness seemed to come over me; I tasted him, and it was strange and exciting, something outside my imaginings. *The taste of a man!* His lips parted, I tasted his mouth, and it seemed some essence of him was passing into my body, and I could feel my heart beating against my ribs like a captive bird, almost frighteningly hard, as if it wanted to get to him. When his mouth left mine at last he clasped me close, resting his cheek against my head, and I could hear him breathing quick, as though he had been running. My body was a torrent of excitement. *What was happening? What would happen next?* 'Is it love?' I asked wildly. 'Yes, yes, it is love,' he replied almost gruffly; and he sounded as if he, too, was astonished. 'Will you love me for ever?' I cried. 'Oh yes, for ever!'

At last we were able to separate ourselves (not very far, only far enough to hold hands and look at each other) and talk a little about what we should do. I told him that I thought we should marry in February, and what Lord Melbourne had said about Parliament.

'He knows then? Lord Melbourne knows?'

'Dear love, he is my Prime Minister. I had to speak to him – but no-one else, I promise you.'

'Yes, yes, I must not forget that you are the Queen. Who else must you tell?'

He sounded upset by the idea. 'No-one!' I cried hastily. 'No-one at all. I wish it to be our secret, to keep as long as we can.'

'You will want to tell your mamma?'

'No,' I said sharply. 'Not her.'

He sighed, I think. He was not unaware of the state of things between Mamma and me. 'Uncle Leopold, then?'

'Oh yes, we must tell him. How happy he will be! Wise, wise Uncle! He knew from the beginning how it would be.'

'We should both write to him,' Albert said, lifting my hand and kissing it. 'Separately.'

'And show each other our letters.'

'If you wish. I shall never have anything to hide from you, dearest Victoria.'

'Nor I from you, dearest Albert. Let us write at once, after luncheon. But we must ask him to keep it the strictest secret. I don't want to share you with anyone yet. Oh, what a pity we have to go down to luncheon! I could sit here with you for ever!'

'We have a little time more,' he murmured, putting his arms round me, and we kissed again, as if he could never tire of it.

We were not able again that first day to be alone together; but I was so happy I walked as though on a cloud all day, and though I said nothing to anyone about what had happened, I think my eyes must have betrayed me a thousand times. He came down to dinner that first evening of our love in the Windsor uniform of dark blue with the red facings and cuffs. I had once written in my Journal how well Lord Melbourne looked in it; when I saw Albert I could barely keep from crying out. His eyes met mine, and a most loving look passed between us, and I delighted in the warmth of having that secret with him, the best secret of all!

When I was about to retire for the night, my dresser gave me a note which had been passed to her from Albert's valet.

Dearest, greatly beloved Victoria, how is it that I have deserved so much love, so much affection? I cannot get used to the reality of all I see and hear, and have to believe that Heaven has sent me an Angel whose brightness shall illumine my life. I am bewildered by the suddenness with which my situation has changed, from being alone in all I did to being the object of such full, generous, and joyous love as you give me. With your hand and heart I shall have achieved the height of my desire. You are so good and kind to me, that I feel I can never repay you, except with my absolute and lifelong devotion. Good night, God Bless you. Ever, in body and soul, your slave, your loyal, *Albert*.

Oh Albert, my own, my dear love, all I have of you now is your letters! Holding that one in my hand – the first you sent me in our lives together – I kiss your dear name, remembering that the pen that made those strokes was held by your warm and living hand, your strong, young hand! Your warm, moist tongue dampened the wafer that sealed it! You were alive, flesh and pulsing blood, with me in the world, there to be seen and touched and held! How little I thought then that I could ever be without you! Why did you leave me here alone? It is a cruel and bitter thing to be without you, even now, all these years later. When I remember that first time that you took me in your arms, I would give anything I have to go back, just for a few moments, and taste that joy again.

But it is impossible, of course; and even if it were not, I have nothing to give that would be enough. Time makes no bargains with us, for Time holds all the high cards.

Later

I HAD to break off for a while. It astonishes me a little that I can still weep, all these years later. But oh, my loss! Well, I can think, I can remember, and it will have to do. Those days of our courtship, how heady they were! What perfect, perfect happiness! Even being separated from him for a few hours was a joy, because of the thought of reunion, and how sweet it would be, the anticipation of his kisses made sharper by waiting. We lived only for each other, and when we were in company and could not touch each other, I touched him with my eyes, and felt him caressing me with his. When he danced with me, we locked our hands tightly together; and when he danced with someone else, I felt the imprint on my own hand of the long fingers I saw folded so indifferently round another's.

But when we were alone together – and it happened more and more often as poor Ernst ailed and hardly left his bed – we flew together like magnets, and I was crushed in his arms and kissed and kissed until I was breathless. Though in his shyness he had few words, he told me everything with his body. Now when I attended to business in the Blue Closet, he was there with me, to wield the blotter for me and correct my spelling. He laughed very much to see that I wrote 'schocking' instead of 'shocking'. *'Was für ein' vierkliches Alpenblümchen bist du!'* he chuckled. When he sat to scratch out my mistakes, I leaned on his shoulder, and dropped kisses on the top of his head. 'Your hair is so fine, so beautiful, I love it so!' 'Can you love even the top of my head?' he asked, half laughing, half in wonder. 'Every single part of you, from the crown of your head to the tip of your toes.' *'Liebes Kleinschen! Du bist so zuss!'* 'In English!' 'I cannot in English! I have not the words.'

Little one, little one! He called me that so often, as though my smallness were in itself something lovely. Once when I was writing and he was hovering over me with the blotter, he suddenly took the pen from my hand and lifted my fingers and kissed them. 'Your little fingers are so small, I can hardly believe they *are* fingers! Look how I can cover your hand completely with one of mine. It astonishes me.' He shook his head in smiling wonder. 'The only other hands I have ever held until now are Ernst's, and they are like a giant's compared with these fairylike things!' There was no more writing then. He led me to the sofa, and took me in his arms. 'I love you so much, *ich kann nicht sagen wie!'*

One day I asked, as lovers do, 'When did you guess that I loved you? Did you know what I was going to say, that day I called you here?'

'No, I was taken completely by surprise. I did not expect it all to happen so quickly. The last I had heard, you were wanting to put me off for three more years. I came prepared to tell you I would not wait – villain that I am, to think of threatening such a thing!'

'Oh, but how wicked I was to think of making you wait so long! But it was only because they kept teasing me and pressing me so much, and I can never bear to be forced to anything. And I hadn't seen you then, dearest, dearest love. Now you are here, now I have seen you, all I want is to be yours instantly!'

'Can you really love me so much?' His eyes filled with tears, and he pressed me to his heart and cried, *'Ich habe dich so unausfrechlich lieb!*' and then covered me with kisses. (Torture to remember, but sweet, so sweet. Anyone who has loved will have known such moments; and I am glad there are new lovers in the world every day, who can feel as we felt, and touch, and know. Nothing dies for ever; all things are renewed. But love while you can, young lovers, for it will be meagre comfort later, to watch those who come after you as I watch you.)

In those long talks we had that autumn at Windsor, he told me about his childhood in the Schloss Rosenau, four miles from Coburg, a small palace, not grand so much as *gemütlich*, he said, built in the Gothic style with a mock battlemented tower, lots of decorated stonework, and a vast corby-stepped (as the Scotch call it) gable. Rosenau sat in the foothills of the Thuringian mountains; the River Itz flowed through its flower-bright meadows, and the music of a waterfall tumbling into a grotto could be heard from its terraces. This paradise was at the heart of the green forest, and at night cruel nature would creep right up to its walls, and the child Albert would hear the scream of rabbits, the soft, deadly rush of owls' wings, the fantastic barking of the stags challenging death. But in summer the liquid cooing of wood-pigeons perching on the window-sill in the early sun would wake him; and through the open windows he would hear the splash of the fountain in the courtyard and the chack-chack of jackdaws echoing amongst the chimneys.

He told me about his own little room, with the green wallpaper all patterned over with convolvulus, and the cedar chest which gave such a wonderful aromatic smell to his clothes – 'as though the forest had come right into the house'. He told me about riding with Ernst, about the green, spicy smell of the woods, and the particular soft sound of horse-hooves muffled by thick layers of pine-needles. He told me about the little gardens he and Ernst had created and tended themselves, and the bathing-house built for them on the lake, where they learned to swim. He told me of the collections they had made of minerals, pressed flowers, stuffed birds, and insects, and the miniature wooden house, like a Swiss cottage, where they had kept their 'museum'.

He told me a little, just a little, about his mother (the rest came later, in the safe, warm darkness of a shared bed, where the best and saddest secrets are told). She had been married as a romantic girl of sixteen to his father, a man fourteen years older with already debauched habits, who had neglected her shamefully while running after other women of the lowest sort. Princess Louise had been a tiny creature of fairylike, golden beauty and bubbling high spirits, gentle, charming and warm-hearted. Albert had adored her; but when he was four she had been sent away, and he had not even been allowed to say goodbye to her.

'Ernst and I had whooping-cough. We were isolated in the nursery, we didn't even know she was going. I heard the horses' hooves crossing the courtyard, and though I didn't know what horses they were, I had such a feeling of foreboding that I cried out. I cried and called for *her*, but she didn't come.' He paused, and added after a moment, 'I never saw her again.'

The fact of the matter was that, neglected by her unfaithful husband, the Princess had sought comfort of her own with a gentleman of the court, a Baron von Meyern. Duke Ernst discovered the affair and sent her away; two years later they were divorced and she married her lover, but died at the age of only thirty-one after a long and bitter illness. Albert never forgot her. On the day he left me to go back to Coburg, he gave me a little turquoise pin which had belonged to her, and I knew what a treasure he was bestowing on me.

After his mother's departure Albert and Ernst had been taken from their nurse and given into the care of a tutor, Herr Florschütz, and had been brought up from that time entirely by men. (I think perhaps that may have been why Albert never cared for women's company, and was always very shy and reserved with them. After our marriage, when I first introduced him to my ladies, he found it a great bore and had the greatest difficulty in remembering one from another. He had learned his manners, of course, and could be attentive, but he never really *liked* women – except for me – and of course they instinctively knew it.) He also had a deep horror (engendered by the activities of his father and brother) of infidelity and sexual adventure, which he condemned utterly. That accorded wholly with my own wishes with regard to him, of course! I had never been particularly censorious about such things in others (society in those days was so loose that it would have done me no good) but as far as my own husband was concerned, I would never have tolerated the least deviation; and it was good to know that I never could have had the slightest reason for unease on that score. Albert loved me, and was interested in no-one else, and that suited me perfectly.

He told me that when he had met me in 1836 he had thought me amazingly sophisticated, because I knew how to go on in company and did not seem to feel shy and ill at ease, as he did! (I naturally told him how far that was from the truth; that I was desperately shy in company, but in view of my position had had to learn how to hide it.) He said he had had no idea how unhappy my childhood had been, and pitied me greatly, for he had always loved his father (in spite of his wickedness) and had been gently treated by him; and of course he had had Ernst for a companion, and they had always been very fond brothers.

'I hate to think of you so lonely, my Victoria,' he said. 'I shall see to it that you are never lonely again. I shall be everything to you – father, mother, brothers and sisters.'

'And lover,' I suggested slyly, and he laughed and kissed me. '*Zelbsverständlich!*'

We exchanged locks of our hair, and marvelled at how close in colour they were; we sang duets together, and our voices blended into a single strand; and one day he taught me to waltz. We moved so well together, like one creature with four legs! It was a delicious feeling to have a man's arm so strongly round my waist, and to whirl and whirl about the room with him. The motion was so exciting, I could see why the waltz had been banned for so long from polite society! We had an informal dance on the last day of his visit, and waltzed together in company for the first time, to show everyone how well we suited.

'I like the thought that you will never waltz with anyone but me,' he murmured into my ear.

'I like the thought that this will be my last dance of any sort as an unmarried girl,' I whispered in reply, and I think we both blushed a little.

By that time I had told my mother the secret that everyone else must already have guessed. Albert insisted that I must tell her, and so on the 10th of November I sent for her and told her that I had something to say that I was sure would please her, namely that I had chosen Albert for my future husband. She stared at me for a moment as though she could not believe her ears, and then her face crumpled and she burst into tears. She put her arms out to me and cried, 'Oh Vickelschen, oh I am so glad, so very glad!' I allowed her to embrace me, and, moved by her evident delight, even patted her back a little, awkwardly. Then I put her away from me, and she dabbed at her eyes with a scrap of lace handkerchief, and putting her head on one side a little, in that birdlike way she had, she said, 'Well, my child, though you have not asked me for it, I give you my blessing, my best blessing to the marriage. It is what I always hoped for, ever since you both shared the same midwife.'

There were things about this speech which gave me foreboding, which I didn't want to think about. I hastened to call in Albert, who had been waiting in the next room, and Mamma flung her arms around him effusively, and broke into a stream of German. She was so happy, she said, so delighted; she would bless the day when she could call him 'son'; she was as anxious for his happiness as for mine (or perhaps a little more so, I thought sourly, watching her face); and she begged him to call her Mamma from that day onwards.

Albert said everything that was proper, and I was proud of him. But Mamma showed her true colours afterwards, for the very next day she wrote a letter to me of bitter recrimination, saying that she, my own mother, was the last person in the Palace to know about the betrothal, that even Albert's valet had been told before her (which was not true, though I should have thought him a simpleton not to have guessed – but then she might have guessed just as well). She plagued Albert with letters, too, begging him to appoint her friend Lord Dunfermline as his personal adviser, and saying that she wanted to go on living with us after we were married – which I'm glad to say struck Albert with as much horror as it did me. Of course, I wrote back with great firmness saying it was impossible; after which she sent me endless tiresome, complaining letters, saying that she was being turned out of her own home, that it would break her heart to leave me, that Albert and I were so young we must have an older head to advise us, that she could not afford a separate establishment, and so on and so on. I think it was a revelation to Albert to see what I had had to put up with; but he dealt with his part of the business with great tact and kindness, and began to lay the foundations of a better understanding between Mamma and me – though that was not to be for a few years yet.

Other members of the royal family were told by letter of our betrothal, and I was gratified by the cordiality of their good wishes for us. Some of them called with their congratulations – amongst them my cousin George Cambridge, whose chilly reserve towards me was quite melted away now that he was safe from having to marry me. We shook hands warmly and became good friends from then on.

Albert and Ernst were to leave for Coburg on Thursday the 14th of November, and that day dawned heavily for me; but Albert cheered me at once by sending Eos in to 'say goodbye' to me while I was dressing. She gave me her paw, and when I caressed her silky, bony head she licked my hand affectionately. Later Albert and I had our private farewell in the Blue Closet, where we had spent so many hours of blissful communion. He gave me his mother's pin and promised to write every day.

'Only three months – not even quite three,' he said, 'and I shall be with you again.'

'And you will come to me then as a bridegroom, not a cousin,' I replied. He drew me to him, and I rested my cheek against his. 'I don't know how I shall get through the time.'

'You will have so much to do, it will pass in a flash,' he said. 'As I will, saying goodbye to everything.' And then he put me gently from him. 'Let me look once more into those beautiful eyes before I go,' he said. He looked down gravely into my face. 'So clear, like pools of pure water. I love that honesty in you, Victoria. Don't let anything ever change that.'

'I shan't change,' I said. 'I love you, Albert.'

'I love you, too.' He kissed me once more, and then it was time to go. I went with him to my dressing-room, where Mamma and Ernst waited, and then escorted them to the top of the staircase, kissed Albert one last time, and watched them go down to their carriage and drive away. Then I could only run away to my room and cry – wretched to have parted with him, and yet happy to think that we would meet again so soon, and be united then for ever. When I was able to stop crying, I wrote a letter to him, and then spent the afternoon in the indulgence of talking about him with my kind Lord M.

7th May 1900

I HAVE got out the letters he sent me from Coburg during those three months. They were my comfort then, and touch me still, speaking as they do of his love and joy. 'I have your dear, loving letter before me, and rejoice to read over and over again the intimate outpouring of your warm and tender heart. It is my greatest delight to see there in your own dear words the thing which is of the greatest importance to me – that you love me. How often I wish I had that same passionate nature! It pains me to think how cold and stiff my letters to you must seem in comparison with yours; for though I love you deeply, I have no words to express my feelings about you, however much I try to look for them. Dearest, most greatly beloved one, I can only trust that you do know how truly I am devoted to you; that you recognise that only the thought that I exist for you gives meaning to my life.'

And another: 'Your dear picture stands on my table in front of me, and I can hardly take my eyes from it. I imagine you there in the little blue sitting-room where we were so happy, sitting together on the little sofa. How I wish I could be transported there by magic, to cheer your loneliness.'

And another: 'My desire is to walk through the whole of my life, with its joys and storms, with you at my side! Where love is, there is happiness. Love of you fills my heart.'

I read them over and over again until I feared my eyes must wear the words from the pages. To be loved by him – by this perfect angel, so beautiful, so intelligent, so good – seemed too fortunate to be true. I could scarcely believe myself so blessed; and in just a few weeks I would be joined to him in matrimony, and he would be entirely mine, all my own, for ever. I could only vow to strive to make myself worthy of him.

It must be said, however, that the rest of the country did not at that time see my beloved in the same light. Lord M. had warned me how it would be, but I was not then to learn that foreigners were unpopular. It was a time when Chartism was on the rise, and poverty and unrest were rife; the wealthy believed all foreigners were fomentors of revolution, while the working classes believed they imported notions of absolutism and repression and the Divine Right of Kings.

Of all foreigners, Germans were the most disliked, and of German states, Coburg. 'Lucky Coburg', they said, had once again allied itself above its station. It was a nothing of a country, a tin-pot place with a population no bigger than that of Bristol, and an income not half as big. Albert was handsome, but he was just another penniless princeling. Why should England be expected to keep supporting these nobodies?

Lord M. had told me that there would be no difficulty in getting the usual pension of £50,000 per annum for Albert through Parliament – after all, it had been recognised as the appropriate income for the sovereign's consort for more than a century, ever since Queen Anne had married George of Denmark. However, when Lord John Russell rose to propose it in the Commons, the Radicals and the Tories spoke out against it. The country was in a poor way, they said, and people were starving. Did the House not remember that when the grant of £50,000 to Prince Leopold was proposed, the feeling had been that it was too high? How much more so was it now, when times were bad! And besides, it was known to be a very dangerous thing to set a young man down in London with so much money in his pocket. Colonel Sibthorpe, a rabid Tory, proposed £30,000 instead, and the motion was carried by an insultingly large majority

(Sir Robert Peel voted for it, something I found it difficult to forgive him for later!). It meant that my beloved angel was valued at £20,000 a year less than stupid, insignificant George of Denmark! I was furious, and blamed the Tories bitterly. Lord M. tried to persuade me it was because of the economic state of the country, but I knew what was at the bottom of it.

'As long as I live, I shall never forgive those infernal scoundrels, those abominable, infamous Tories!' I wrote in my Journal. 'Poor dear Albert, how cruelly they are using that dearest angel! Monsters! You Tories will be punished! Revenge! Revenge!'

The next struggle with Parliament was over the question of Albert's rank. I had reluctantly given up (for the time being, at least) the hope of having him made King Consort, but Lord M. had promised me that there would be no difficulty in giving him the precedence I preferred, which was immediately after me. However, when this was proposed, as one of the clauses of Albert's Naturalization Bill, the Opposition began rumbling again. The Duke objected to this 'controversial issue' being 'smuggled in' in a Bill on nationality; Lord Brougham maintained that it was for Parliament to propose the Prince's rank, not the Crown. My uncle Cumberland, who was now King of Hanover, of course, declared he would not give place to a 'paper Royal Highness', and bullied my uncles Sussex and Cambridge (who would have agreed to anything for an increase in their pensions) into siding with him. Finally the Duke pointed out stiffly that if Albert were given the rank I desired, he would take precedence over his own eldest son, which would be constitutionally impossible. And what if the Queen should die without producing an heir? The Prince would then rank higher than the son of the King of Hanover, the Heir Apparent himself.

In the end, the Bill went through with the question of precedence still undecided, and I added the Duke to the list of 'nasty wretches' on whom I cried revenge. Indeed, when Lord M. produced a list of guests for my wedding, I took up a pen to strike out the Duke's name, declaring that I would not invite that wicked, foolish old man to the Chapel Royal.

'I must beg you to think again,' Lord M. said, sounding quite alarmed. 'By reason of his age, station and position he cannot be omitted. It would be the gravest insult.'

'I mean it to be an insult,' I said. 'He has insulted my beloved Albert.'

'He did not mean it so. He only did what he thought right according to his conscience,' Lord M. said anxiously.

'I don't believe it. He hates us; and this is *my* wedding, and I will only have those who sympathise with me. Why should I surround myself with enemies on this day of all others?'

'I do assure you, ma'am, the Duke is not your enemy. One of the reasons he is so highly respected is that his disinterestedness in matters concerning the well-being of the nation and the Crown is beyond question.' I knew this was true, but it only made me feel crosser and more sulky. 'And since he is so well respected, his supporters will expect him to be at your wedding.'

'Let them expect!' I snapped. 'Tories to a man! And what do I owe them? Nothing but hate.'

'The whole country will expect it,' Lord M. said inexorably. 'The Duke is a great hero, the saviour of England in the late wars, and our most eminent statesman. If you leave him out, there will be a dreadful scandal which will certainly damage the Crown. I cannot allow you to risk that.' He smiled at my scowling face. 'Would I insist on it if it were not so important? I know how important your wedding day is to you as a woman; but you must also see how important it is for the Queen of England to do her duty.'

'Very well,' I snapped. 'If I must have him to the wedding, I must, but I will not invite him to the breakfast afterwards.' And then, seeing his careworn face, I realised how much I had been vexing him lately, after neglecting him the whole time that Albert was in England. I softened. 'Tell me the truth,' I said hesitantly. 'Do you think I am growing obstinate?'

'Well, rather,' he said with a crooked smile, and then we both laughed.

The next difficulty arose over the question of my bridesmaids. That they must be young women of good character was certain; but Albert wrote to say he felt I should strike off anyone whose mother had had a chequered history. I was doubtful about this, for in the past – in Lord M.'s heyday – different standards had applied to the ladies of the aristocracy so it would hardly be fair to judge them, as it were, in retrospect; and besides, if people were to be blamed for the sins of their mothers, my own Albert would be sent to the right-about. However, I wanted to please him, so on his urging I presented the suggestion to Lord Melbourne.

Lord M. was taken aback. 'My dear ma'am, it will not do! One might ask for references when engaging a cook or a footman, but one can hardly do the same for people of rank. To enquire into the conduct of a Duchess would be the most frightful impertinence.'

'But can there be one rule for the low and one for the high?' I said. 'The Prince believes I should be surrounded only by the morally irreproachable.'

'That would be a very difficult feat to manage,' he said wryly. 'Which of us, indeed, is beyond reproach? I must tell you, ma'am, that Lady William Russell said of the Prince that his character was such as would be highly approved at a German university, but somewhat ridiculed at one of ours.'

'No, really,' I said, 'it is too shocking that morality should be ridiculed in universities!'

'One should not ridicule what is truly good,' he agreed, 'but the persecuting of everyone's little peccadilloes is not what I would expect a monarch to stoop to. One looks for a certain greatness in one's sovereign, a certain being above noticing such things.'

I should have been angered at the implication, but the image he conveyed rather tickled my imagination. 'I believe, my lord,' I said teasingly, 'that you do not like the Prince as much as you would if he were not so strict.'

'Oh! no, I deeply admire his strictness in respect of himself; but one ought not to judge other people too severely, or one is liable to make all sorts of mistakes. Remember the lamentable case of Lady F. H?'

'Pray do not remind me of that!' I said hastily, feeling myself blush.

'I do so not to give you pain,' he said, 'but to warn you against finding fault too readily. In this country all should go by law and precedent. If someone should ask you to sit in judgement upon accusations or reports against anyone's private character, you should advise them that you do not care to pronounce a verdict where you are not the proper Court of Appeal.'

This seemed to me to be excellent advice, and as far as I could, I lived by it afterwards. Albert, having been brought up differently, and with such an example always in his mind from his own parents, remained a great stickler for spotlessness of reputation. For myself, I would always sooner not enquire into people's pasts, as long as they behaved themselves while in my service.

While we were wrestling with these difficulties, Mamma was still being as troublesome as she knew how, demanding to be given precedence of my aunts at my wedding – 'Surely the mother of the bride has some importance? I know I am nothing to you, Victoria, but the people will expect it. It is you alone I think of. I would not have them accuse you, dear love, of cold-heartedness towards your own mother' – and demanding not to be 'sent away' and 'exiled from you' after the wedding. Neither Lord M. nor I could seem to convince her that she would not be allowed to live with Albert and me afterwards, and I began to have dreadful visions of her having to be dragged away bodily, clinging to every door-frame and shrieking murder!

With all these frustrations and annoyances, it was hardly to be wondered at that I quarrelled at last even with Albert. He wrote to me demanding to be allowed to choose his own Household, and to include some of his compatriots in his staff; and I was obliged to be firm with him. 'As to your wish about your gentlemen, I must tell you, my dear Albert, that it will not do. You may entirely rely on me that the people around you will be absolutely pleasant people of high standing and good character, not too idle and not too young. Lord Melbourne has already suggested several to me who would be entirely suitable.' Lord M. indeed had suggested that his own secretary, George Anson, should become Albert's private secretary, and it was a choice I thoroughly approved, Anson being a good, gentle, intelligent, hard-working and completely amiable man. 'I know you will deal excellently together.'

Albert wrote back his dismay. 'I am sorry you have not been able to grant my request, for I know it was not an unfair one. As to your suggestion of Mr Anson, I give you to consider, dearest love, if my taking the secretary of the Prime Minister would not make me seem like a partisan in the eyes of many? As to his character, I know nothing of him except that I have heard he is addicted to dancing. I entreat you to allow me to appoint men of my own country – high-minded, virtuous and non-political men, of the stamp of our dear Dr Stockmar – to my Household.'

Lord M. was horrified by that idea. 'It will only draw attention to the Prince's foreignness, which is the last thing we wish to do. And it will be said that *you* are ruled by him and *he* is ruled by Germans.' Remembering some things that had been said about dear Lehzen, I agreed with him. 'It is my greatest wish to do everything most agreeable to you, my dearest Albert, but I must differ with you respecting Mr Anson. It is for the Queen to choose your Household, together with her principal minister – a very clever, honest and impartial man – and between us we must know better than you who will be acceptable not only to yourself, but to the people at large. What you suggest would not do at all. Pray do not tax me again on the subject.'

To my astonishment he did not yield. I next received a quite harrowing letter, appealing to the heart, speaking of his anticipated isolation from everything familiar. 'Think of my position, dear Victoria: I am leaving home, with all its associations, all my bosom friends, and going to a country where everything is new and strange to me – men, language, customs, modes of life, position. Except yourself, I have no-one to confide in. And is it not even to be conceded to me that two or three of the people who are to have charge of my private affairs, should be persons who already command my confidence?'

I also received, which annoyed me very much, a letter from Uncle Leopold, supporting Albert's claim and attempting to make me take a 'correct view' of my duties as a wife so that Albert and I could live peacefully together. How peaceful would it be, I demanded hotly of myself, if it was not made clear from the beginning that I was the Queen, and that where my authority ran it was not to be questioned? I wrote back to Albert, 'Dear Uncle is given to believe that he must rule the roost wherever he is, but that is not the case. I am distressed to tell you what I fear you do not like, but it is necessary, my dearest, most excellent Albert. I do it only as I know it is for your own good. I shall choose your people, and once more I tell you that you can perfectly rely on me in these matters.'

Albert yielded at last, but the near-quarrel left me feeling very low. 'This marrying,' I said to Lord M., 'is a very hazardous experiment. What a dreadful thing it would be if the Prince tried to oppose my will in everything.'

'It is only nervousness – very natural,' he said. 'Everyone feels it before their marriage. And you have had much to vex you.'

(I should mention here that Albert took to George Anson instantly, as I knew he would. They became the most thorough friends and Anson remained his secretary until his tragically early death. Albert trusted him completely, and loved him like a brother, and his early reluctance to accept him became quite a joke between them. I am *never* wrong about people, as Albert came to learn, though he didn't like to admit it at first!)

I was so worn out with worries that just a week before the wedding day I went down under an atrocious cold. Clark frightened the wits out of everyone by diagnosing it as the measles, but the truth soon became apparent, and I spent two days in bed feeling very sorry for myself, and that seemed to do the trick. I rose for dinner on the second day feeling almost myself, and very much more cheerful. Wedding gifts were arriving: a pair of diamond bracelets, a pearl and turquoise set from Aunt Adelaide, a new dog – a Scotch terrier called

Laddie – and from Albert a superb brooch, an immense sapphire set round with diamonds.

On Friday the 7th of February I was further cheered by the arrival of Eos with Albert's valet, ahead of the main party. Lehzen departed for Windsor to see that all was in readiness for our honeymoon, which was to be only three days. (Albert had hoped we might retire from the world for a fortnight, but I told him, proudly, that business, for a Sovereign, stopped for nothing and no-one, and a few days was all that could possibly be spared from affairs of State. What a little fool I was!)

I was now in a state of acute nervousness, which was hardly relieved by a letter from Albert saying that he had arrived safely at Dover. He had suffered most dreadfully during an appalling crossing, and told me his face was still the colour of a wax candle, but that he had been greatly heartened by the warmth of his welcome. Despite the wind and driving rain, thousands had been waiting on the quayside to cheer, which made him feel the nation was not so hostile to him after all.

That evening, Lord M. and I shared what was to be our last *tête-à-tête*, the sort of 'comfortable coze' I had almost forgotten about in the recent hectic months. Dash and Laddie were curled up between us by the fire, while Islay sat at Lord M.'s feet, gazing up at him unwaveringly. (It was an odd thing about Islay, that like a jackdaw he liked to play with bright, glittering objects. Once Lord M. had let him play with his glasses, and ever since Islay would sit in front of him all evening if need be until the desired object appeared.) In the pleasant, rambling way I remembered from before, we talked about my feelings, and marriage, and what sort of societies Albert ought to agree to address ('Nothing to do with bridges and engineering; people who are interested in engineering always turn out to be Radicals!') and whether it was possible to have too many dogs, and whether costume balls encouraged immorality ('Ballrooms are like churches: I frequently come out worse than I went in,') and the value of employing Dissenters as gardeners. ('They are so very reliable: they don't go to the races, they don't hunt, they don't engage in any expensive amusements.')

He made me laugh very much by telling me about the new full dress coat he had had made for my wedding. 'In point of work and trouble it was like building a seventy-four-gun ship. My tailor had to employ a clerk from the ordnance office to take charge of the quantity of buttons,' he said with his drollest look. 'I firmly expect it to be the thing most observed about the ceremony. I shall quite put Your Majesty into the shade. Pray do not expect anyone to be looking at you in the Chapel Royal.'

And thus, with laughter subsiding into smiles, back to my marriage. 'You are doing the right thing. Depend upon it, it is right and natural to marry,' he said comfortably. 'And I know enough of the Prince's character to know he is decent, honourable and conscientious. You could not have chosen better.'

'You do not think we are too alike, too stubborn? After the difficulty over choosing his Household, I worry that we may both want our own way, and quarrel dreadfully.'

'There will be squalls, of course, but you will weather them. It is impossible to predict the future, to guess what effect new situations, interests, passions may have on young and plastic natures, but I feel much assured of a good and happy result. And I believe *you* will find the means of doing that which is not altogether easy – of reconciling the authority of a sovereign with the duty of a wife.'

I was much comforted by that. 'I have learned so much from you,' I said gratefully. 'If I have learned any patience and tact, it has been from you.'

His eyes filled with tears at that, and he took and pressed my hand tenderly. 'All will be well,' he said.

The next day, at half past four, the light was fading and the cold greyness of a February dusk was drawing the comfort and the colour out of the day. Behind the wintry trees the last of the sun showed a blurred, smoky red, and the upper branches were filled with huddled starlings, roosting together against the chill of darkness. For the last hour I had been running, most un-Queen-like, from window to window, to catch the first possible sight of Albert's carriage; but as soon as I saw it pull into the yard, I was seized with the irrational fear that something would have changed, that he would love me less, or that I would discover I had mistaken my heart. The differences we had had by letter had frightened me: I was so young, and so new to love, that I could not conceive one might disagree about things and still be wholehearted about each other. I almost wished the carriage would turn and go away. What was I doing, pledging myself to marry this stranger, a foreigner from a distant land about whom I knew so little?

Mamma and the Household were assembled at the top of the stairs, but as the doors were flung open I could not bear to wait any longer; I must get it over with. I left them and ran down to the door, and reached it just as he did. We stopped face to face, and my heart seemed to come to a halt. He was pale, like an alabaster statue, gleaming strangely in the wintry dusk, his eyes shadowed, swaying a little on his feet, still half sick from the frightful journey. My lips parted to speak a welcome, but I had no words. The first glance at his dear, dear face had banished all my fears and agitation. He was his own, beautiful self, so familiar, seeming already something that I knew better than myself; something that belonged to my life – not owned, or possessed, but like a lovely wild animal who chooses of its very freedom to come to your hand and rest beside you. I knew then that I had made no mistake, that I loved him truly; as Lord M. said, that *all would be well*. In a silence as profound and as speaking as my own, he smiled at me; and I took his hand and led him into my house.

Nine

9th May 1900, at Windsor

GEORGIE AND May and the children will be arriving this day next week, in the evening, for the Christening of their new baby, which they are calling Henry. Arthur and Louischen are coming too, with Young Arthur and Margaret and Patsy – how I long to see them again! When Louischen went to join Arthur in India, she left them with me, and I did so love having them around me. Margaret was always a 'handful', but it was hard to be stern with her because she was so funny. She's quite a young lady now, of course, and a credit to us all. Louischen has proved *such* a good mother, which when you consider what a brute *her* father was is quite an achievement.

I do like a Christening – almost more than a wedding, because with a wedding there is always someone going away, and I dislike very much for people to leave. My own wedding was different, of course, because Albert was coming to me. I remember it so well, every detail – better, indeed, than some things that happened only last week.

Monday the 10th of February 1840 was my wedding day. I was to be married at one o'clock in the Chapel Royal at St James's Palace, and when I woke at about half past eight I thought with satisfaction,

'That is the last night I shall ever sleep alone.' I wondered what it would be like to share a bed with a man. Then I wondered if Albert was awake yet, and realised that I would never have to wonder that again, for I would *know*! It seemed strange, but delightful. Mamma and Lord M. had both tried to persuade me not to let him sleep under my roof the night before our wedding. 'It is against tradition,' Lord M. said, and 'It will bring bad luck,' said Mamma. I waved their objections away. 'Narrow-minded nonsense,' I told Lord M.; and to Mamma I said, '*I* am not afraid. I will show you how lucky our marriage will be!'

I stretched a little under the covers, feeling well, and strong, and rested. My cold seemed to have disappeared with my anxieties; I had no fears for the day. Last evening Albert and I sat down and read through the Marriage Service together, so that we should be familiar with it, and had tried how to manage the ring. He had seemed a little subdued, but assured me it was only the remains of his sea-sickness. He did seem very tired, which was only natural after such a journey; but he had been as kind and sweet as I could have wished, and kissed me very often and very tenderly.

I was thinking about those kisses when Lehzen came in to draw my curtains. 'What a smile!' she said. 'You are greeting the day as you should, Majesty.'

I sat up. 'What kind of a day? Tell me the worst, Daisy dear.'

'As bad as can be,' she said, looking out. 'Wild, wet and windy.' Even as she spoke, a gust hurled a hatful of water at my window-panes and rattled them like an impatient hand at a gate. Well, it was February after all! Lehzen tutted, but I only laughed. 'It can storm all it likes today, it cannot spoil my happiness!'

The maid came in with my hot water and towels, but I sent Lehzen first for pen and paper, and still sitting up in bed with my hair about my shoulders I wrote: 'Dearest, how are you today, and have you slept well? I have rested very well and feel very comfortable. What weather! I believe, however, the rain will cease. Send me one word when you, my most dearly beloved bridegroom, will be ready. Thy ever-faithful, Victoria R.'

It was despatched, and I got up and washed, had my breakfast (a large one, as it was to last me until two or three o'clock!) and was dressed. My wedding gown was beautiful, white figured satin, cut low across the shoulders as was the fashion then, with tiny puffed sleeves. It had a deep flounce of Honiton lace of an antique pattern – though it was not old lace. I had bought it the year before (before I had had any idea of marrying, in fact) to help the unemployed lace-makers of Devonshire; a whole length of it, enough to trim the dress lavishly, and to form my veil. I put on my Turkish diamond necklace and earrings and Albert's beautiful sapphire brooch, and then dear Lehzen came back in to dress my hair, and gave me a dear little ring as a keepsake of her own. My hair was coiled behind and on it I wore a wreath of orange-blossoms and the lace veil. Lehzen kept talking as she worked, more I think to stop herself crying than to comfort me, for I was in a dream of bliss. 'There are bigger crowds out there even than for your Coronation, despite the weather; they say the biggest crowds since the Allied Sovereigns visited London in 1814 – though who could be sure, and how they could be sure, I do not know,' she added in her logical way. 'The trees down Constitution Hill are all full of boys hoping for a view, and every now and then the branches snap and down they come tumbling, like hard little June apples on the heads of the unfortunates below! No-one seems to mind, though. Everyone is very good-tempered, in spite of the rain . . .'

When I was dressed, she turned me round to look in the long glass, and I seemed, even to myself, transformed, my cheeks and eyes so bright with happiness that I was almost beautiful. I want him to see me like this, I thought – here and alone, before it all belongs to the world at large.

I told Lehzen to send for him; and he came to me alone, looking slim and tall in glorious scarlet, the uniform of a British Field Marshal, with the white, tight net pantaloons that outlined every muscle of his thighs, white silk stockings and flat buckled slippers. He had not yet put on his sash and sword, of course, nor the diamond Garter Star and jewelled Garter I had given him the day before; and his hair had not yet been pomaded – it looked soft as a brown mouse's fur. I longed to touch it, but instead I spread my arms sideways, displaying myself like a little girl, and said, 'I wanted you to see.'

He was pale, and his eyes seemed to flinch as they touched me, as though he tried to look at a light that was too bright. 'You are beautiful,' he said in a faint voice, and for once I did not deny it.

'For you,' I said. 'Only for you.'

He nodded, seeming to have nothing to say.

'Did you sleep well?'

'Not very well.'

'But you are happy?'

He smiled suddenly, and it was like sunshine enhancing all the colours of a garden. His eyes seemed bluer, his hair more golden, his

163

cheeks not pale but delicately pink. 'Oh yes! I can't tell you how much! But I had better go now – you see I am not quite ready. And you will want to compose yourself beforehand. Are you nervous?'

'Not at all.'

He smiled at that. 'But you are trembling. I can see your pretty blossoms trembling.' And indeed I was, though I think it was not with nervousness.

He was to leave the Palace at midday; I set out at half past twelve in the carriage with Mamma and the Duchess of Sutherland (Mistress of the Robes). It was still raining in torrents, with horrid gusts of wind that drove it in the horses' faces and made them flinch, but the wintry weather did not seem to damp the enthusiasm of the crowds, who cheered me down the Mall, and waved their sodden hats above their dripping heads. Lord M. met me at the door of St James's Palace, again carrying the Sword of State, with which he would precede me down the aisle. He was wearing his splendid new dress-suit, whose buttons gleamed like lamps on a dark night, and we exchanged a smile of pleasant recollection of our shared joke over it. I was to be given away by Uncle Sussex, and he smiled at me unexpectedly kindly and even patted my hand as it rested on his arm, though even for this special day he had not been persuaded to remove his comfortable black skull-cap.

My twelve bridesmaids were waiting in the dressing-room, look-ing beautiful and innocent in white satin and gauze, the overskirt caught up in front with white roses, white roses at the bosom, and clusters of white roses in their hair. Our procession formed up in the Throne Room, the doors were flung open, the trumpets sounded, and the organ began to play, and we walked forward into the Chapel. The room was packed full, and every eye turned to me. I saw members of my family crowded together at the front: red-faced Uncle Cam-bridge nodding like a parrot and talking to himself; Mamma, a drift of scarves and feathers, already snuffling into a handkerchief; kind Aunt Adelaide in purple velvet beaming and fluttering her fingers as though she would dearly love to wave to me; various cousins craning their necks and trying to elbow each other out of the way. Amongst the non-royal guests I saw the Duke, gaunt and as upright as ever, which always made one forget that he was not a tall man; kindly Lord Liverpool, who had befriended my childhood; and Lord Ashley, who had married Lord M.'s niece Minney Cowper – these the only three Tories I had invited (for which I remain unrepentant, in spite of criticism. It was a private wedding after all; the Coronation had been another matter.).

And then I had eyes for no-one but my bridegroom, waiting for me in that place where we were to be joined together for ever. He had turned to look at me, and the diamonds of the Star on his breast were not brighter than his brilliant eyes. The service was beautiful, and imposing in its simplicity. There had not been a wedding of a Queen Regnant for three hundred years, and Mary Tudor's had been by the Catholic rite anyway, and provided no precedent. So it had been decided to follow the ceremonial used by my grandfather and grandmother, George III and Queen Charlotte. But despite my exalted rank, the central part of the ceremony was simplicity itself: the Archbishop asked me quietly and in the plainest language, 'Victoria, wilt thou have this man to thy wedded husband?' and I felt that I stood as humble and naked before God as the least of my subjects. I could not believe it possible for anyone to do other than keep the promises they made in such a way and in such a place. Albert spoke so clearly and beautifully, and put on the ring with such gentleness and yet such a wonderful air of triumph that I felt I had been claimed indeed before God and in front of all the world.

But it was not all solemnity: when he spoke the words about endowing me with all his worldly goods, we both remembered the story of how Princess Charlotte had burst out laughing at that moment of *her* wedding to penniless Uncle Leopold, and we both smiled.

Then we went to sign the register (the Duke of Norfolk made such a bustle, insisting that he must sign first, as Earl Marshal of England, and then keeping everyone waiting because he could not find his spectacles) and then we walked back down the aisle to tremendous fanfares and more music, in the same order as before – except that now my hand rested not on the broadcloth sleeve of Uncle Sussex, but, trembling like a bird, on the arm of my *husband*. There were smiles and kisses and congratulations from those closest to us, and then alone together we went out to the waiting carriage, and like a miracle the rain stopped and a watery sunshine reflected from a million puddles and ten million suspended raindrops. Such a shout went up as we appeared! We were cheered wildly all the way home: royal weddings had always before taken place at night, so it was a new thing for the people to be able to see a Queen in her wedding gown; but there were cheers for Albert, too, and he waved on his side of the carriage as I did on mine, and I think found it an agreeable experience.

Back at Buckingham Palace, we had a precious half an hour alone together in my dressing-room; we sat on the sofa and talked, and I gave him *his* ring, which he put on at once. I put my hand in his, and he turned my wedding ring round on my finger (an absent little gesture I was to come to know very well) and said, 'Now we are man and wife, nothing must ever come between us. There must never be a secret which we don't both share. Promise me that.'

'I promise,' I said. Looking back, I wonder why he asked for that, of all the things he might have had from me in those euphoric moments. Was he already worried about his position? Did he think that he had married the woman but not the Queen? But at the time, it seemed quite a reasonable request to me, and I was willing to promise him anything in the world he wanted. If I took it to mean personal secrets rather than State secrets – well, as it happened, there proved to be no need to keep the latter from him; and the former question never arose. He knew my whole heart, then and afterwards; and I believed I knew his.

After the wedding breakfast, and the toasts, and the cutting of the vast cake – nine feet across and weighing three hundred pounds, decorated with a model of Britannia (instead of the traditional Hymen) blessing the bridal pair, and a vast quantity of turtles and cupids, one of whom held an open book inscribed with that blessed date, the 10th of February 1840 – I went upstairs to take off my wedding dress, and put on one of white silk trimmed with swans-down, and to exchange my lace veil for a white bonnet with a sprig of orange-blossom pinned to the ribbon. When I was ready, Lord M. came in to see me alone.

When we had covered one or two matters of business, we talked of the wedding feast and of the cake: 'It couldn't have been any smaller,' he commented. 'Little pieces are being sent to the farthest corners of the earth, you know. I believe the American diplomatic circle in particular has been urgent for slices. Countless little girls in Boston and Connecticut will be ruining their digestions and dreaming of white satin, thanks to you.'

Then I spoke of the ceremony. 'The Duke of Cambridge would keep talking – and so loudly,' I complained.

'His comments were very good-natured,' Lord M. replied. 'And it's by way of a family trait, ma'am: your royal uncle King William was famed for commenting aloud during Divine Service.'

I laughed at that. 'Well, I suppose it was not so disconcerting as my uncle Sussex sobbing all the way through my wedding,' I said.

'No doubt he was deeply affected – as I was. I must admit to calling on a second handkerchief when Your Majesty spoke the responses so clearly and with such feeling.'

I was pleased. 'Well, I do think it went off well.'

'Nothing could have gone off better,' he said. 'It was the most complete thing; and the people were in such good humour.'

'I'm glad the sun came out for them,' I said. 'Poor wet things – waiting so faithfully just for a glimpse of us.'

'Happy is the bride that the sun shines on,' he said.

I reached for his hand. 'Yes,' I said earnestly, 'and I *am* happy. From the very first moment of my marriage, I felt it must be a foretaste of Heaven. God allows us this, so that we shall know just a little what is to come.'

His large, dry hands folded over mine, and for an instant I saw him tremble on the brink of disintegration. 'Oh my dear—' he said in a breaking voice, his eyes shining with tears; and then he caught himself back, and caught up the improper address. 'Oh my dear ma'am, I pray you will find marriage a great comfort.'

The clock struck the three-quarters, and there was a scratching at the door. 'I must go,' I said.

He nodded. His eyes held mine for one moment more. 'God bless you,' he said, and then released my hand.

The door opened, and Albert was there. 'The carriage is ready,' he said.

Lord M. stood aside, and I put my hand through Albert's arm and he led me towards the stairs.

'Such a brim that bonnet has!' he murmured to me. 'I can hardly see your dear little face hidden inside. How shall I manage to kiss it, I wonder?'

'Do you mean to kiss it?' I asked, laughing.

'As soon as we are in the carriage,' he said.

'That would be most improper, to kiss a lady in a post-chaise,' I said demurely.

'But you forget, you are not a lady now, you are my wife,' he said, and we both laughed heartily.

Downstairs we said goodbye to Mamma, and hurried out to our carriage. We set off just about four o'clock, and the clouds were banking up again and making it seem darker than it should be. It was an eventful drive, for there was an immense crowd of people outside the Palace, which hardly lessened all the way to Windsor, for the road was lined almost every yard with people waiting to get a glimpse of us. We were not a very grand sight, for unlike most newly-weds in those days, we did not have a shiny new chariot for the occasion: we rattled along in one of the old but comfortable travelling-coaches, with postilions in undress-livery and only a small escort. But from the first we were joined by the most enthusiastic amateur outriders anyone could have wanted, young men in gigs and men of all ages on horseback, galloping along beside us, hooting and cheering and waving their hats, disputing possession of the road with us and putting themselves in strong danger of finishing the day in a ditch. They only dropped back when their horses foundered, and their places were immediately taken by other cavaliers with fresher mounts and ever louder halloos. Albert thought it rather impertinent that they peered in at us through the windows and called out our names, but I thought it all the best fun, and a nicer escort by far than a staid troop of uniformed cavalry would have been. When we passed through Eton, although it was dark the boys were all out, lining the road with torches and giving us the most touching welcome. And then at last, at seven o'clock, we arrived at Windsor Castle.

First we explored the suite of rooms that had been prepared for us, admiring the little personal touches Lehzen had provided, of flowers and books and favourite music on the piano-top. Albert seemed as excited as I that this was to be our very first home together, and we ran from room to room like children, with the dogs, whom we had found waiting for us, racing and jumping around us excitedly. Then we separated to change our clothes, and when I was ready I went to our sitting-room and found Albert there in his Windsor coat (which suited him so well) thoughtfully playing the piano. There was something so ethereal about the cast of his beautiful face as he bent over the keys, that for a moment my heart drew breath, with a feeling of awe that was touched with fear. It could not be that this loveliness was for me; it would be taken from me, I thought; I had not deserved it. And then Dash, who had brushed past me in the doorway, ran over to him and barked, and the spell was broken. He looked up and smiled at me, and I knew all was well.

'Oh, don't stop,' I said as he pushed back the seat and stood up.

'I have something better to do than play the piano,' he said. We met in the middle of the room, and he took me into his arms. 'Now at last I have you to myself! What a hard thing it is for a man to contrive to be alone with his own wife on his wedding day!'

'Well, and now you have me, what will you do with me?' I asked.

'I shall show you,' said he; and he did. After a while he broke off from this activity, of which I felt I could never tire, and cupped my face in his hands (I loved him to do that! I loved the touch of his hands on me, those lean, strong fingers, and to have them touch my face, the centre of consciousness as it were, seemed the most intimate thing of all.). He looked down at me searchingly, and said, 'Dear, sweet, sunny face! What a lucky man I am! And how glorious it is to be quite, quite alone with you – no courtiers or well-wishers or servants or friends. Just myself and my *kleines Frauchen*. Do you like being alone with me, Victoria?'

What a question! Absolute privacy – to know I was not being watched and spied on – was what I had longed for all my childhood; but even better was the sense of not being lonely any more, of having someone with whom I could express myself freely, not have to watch my words and guard my conduct. From now on it would be I and Albert alone. His words 'alone with me' might have been held to be a logical contradiction; but in fact to be with him and with no-one else was the best and truest solitude.

He was kissing me again, but suddenly I was feeling dizzy, with that awful black rushing inside the head, like a sandslip, that was the forerunner of a fainting-fit. He must have felt something, for he drew back his head and said, 'What is it? You have gone quite pale.'

'Dizzy,' I said, and staggered. His arms were round me at once, and he almost carried me to the sofa and sat me down, put his strong hand on the back of my neck and bent my head down to my lap. In a moment I felt better, and was able to sit up. 'I don't know what came over me,' I apologised. 'I'm not usually so missish.'

'You have been through a very tiring day,' he said, and then smiled suddenly. 'We must also remember that I am a great deal taller than you, *kleines blümschen*. You had been standing for ten minutes with your head tilted as far back as it would go, like a visitor to the Sistine Chapel! No wonder you fainted. In future we must do our caressing sitting down!'

'In future,' I said wonderingly. 'Oh, to think that we can kiss each other whenever we want! No-one to stop us, or say it is not proper! We can be completely free with each other!'

That seemed to give him pause. He possessed himself of my hand and looked at me thoughtfully, turning my wedding ring on my finger as if it helped him find the right words. 'What is it?' I said after a moment, when he still seemed not to know how to begin. 'Is there something wrong? You must tell me, beloved, if there is. You must keep nothing from me.'

'No, nothing wrong,' he said, and I thought his cheeks were perhaps a little more pink than before, and understood what we had come to. 'I wanted to speak to you about – tonight.'

'You mean – what will happen later?' I said, as diffident as him.

He nodded. 'It will be something very new for you, and perhaps – perhaps a little surprising. Will you be afraid?'

'Oh no!' I cried at once, pressing his hand. 'I could never be afraid of anything with you!'

'You know that – that I would never do anything to harm you?' he said anxiously. I understood what his trouble was. He was afraid of offending my maiden delicacy, and perhaps making me dislike him afterwards; afraid that I would find it so distasteful that it would spoil our perfect love. I wanted to tell him that where he was concerned I had no maiden delicacy, but I thought perhaps they were not quite the right words.

'I trust you completely, dearest love,' I said, 'and whatever you do, I know that it will be right.' He still looked troubled, and I said, 'You will not be all alone, my love! Whatever it is, we will be doing it *together*, because we love each other.'

That seemed to please him. 'Yes, of course we will,' he said; and then, 'It's just that I believe – I understand – it may not be quite *comfortable* – just at first, for the – for you. The first time, you understand—'

A thought struck me. 'You do know what to do?'

'Of course I do,' he said quickly. He sounded almost indignant, and it tickled my unruly sense of humour.

'Dear love, I know you are the most thorough scholar! But have you—?'

'No,' he said, holding my gaze steadily, though his cheeks were warm. 'I could not have done that, knowing I was pledged to you.'

I was brought to silence. I took his hand and lifted it to my lips and kissed it fervently. I had no words for the feelings that rushed through me, the adoration, the gratitude. It was not a thing I could ever have asked him afterwards, but oh, I was *glad* to know! and *glad* that no doubt or memory would ever have the power to come between us! In the society in which I had grown up, women of nobility had been expected to turn a blind eye to their husbands' peccadilloes; but I could never, *never* have been one of them!

The long day and the excitement and agitation had had their effect on me. Dinner was served to us in our sitting-room, but when I got up from the sofa, I felt dizzy again, and by the time I was sitting at the table I had developed a sick headache, and the very thought of food was too much for me. I could not eat a thing, and was obliged to lie down again on the sofa; but ill or not, I never, never spent such an evening! Albert sat beside me on a footstool the whole time, and his kindness and affection gave me such feelings of heavenly happiness that I could never before have hoped to know. To look at his lovely face and know he was my husband, to be kissed and held in his arms, to be called by the names of tenderness that I had never heard used to me before, was bliss beyond belief. When we finally rose to go to bed, I had no thought in my mind other than the joy of knowing that the being together did not have to stop there.

I woke in near darkness, and to a kiss on my cheek. For a moment I was bewildered; then I realised he had got up and drawn back the curtains, letting in the first poor light of dawn, and had paused on the way back at my side of the bed to kiss me.

I had been looking up all the while into his beautiful, beautiful face, and now he said, 'Well, little wife, do you know me?'

'Husband,' I said, and smiled. 'Come back to bed.' He came back and wriggled down under the covers, drawing me into his arms, and I nudged and snuggled like a puppy until I was as close to him as I could be, arms and legs interlocked, my head on his shoulder and his cheek resting on my hair.

'Oh, this is good,' he said. 'This is the best of all.' In the blissful heat of our intertwined bodies, in the safe dimness of our bedroom, I could not but agree with him. He smelled so nice, too, like sun-warmed wood, a safe, homelike smell. I pressed my nose against the skin of his neck and drifted a little while on a sea of bliss. 'Darling little wife,' he murmured, far away and close, drifting on the same warm swell, 'I love you so much. Darling, delicious little wife.'

The proceedings of the night, I reflected, had certainly been bewildering, and if it had been anyone but Albert I might have been tempted to suppose he had got it wrong. How God could have ordered things so unecstatically was a puzzle to me. But yet at the heart of my half-indignant surprise there was a lack of surprise, as when one comes to the end of a mathematical calculation, knowing the answer has been correctly arrived at. There was a sort of inevitable logic to it. And as things went on, it did occur to me that although Albert was too much a scholar and a gentleman to have approached this ceremony without having read through the service, there might yet be something owing to skill which could not be learned from a book. Certainly we managed better the second time; and when we woke again in the early hours of the morning, I was even able to help things along. I began to see how it might be possible for me to become more a *partner* and less a *patient*, as it were – to carve myself out a more active rôle; for I have never liked to be idle and passive. And it did seem to me that my first tentative moves towards partnership were well received by my beloved, who kissed me afterwards with great fervency, and held me very tightly for a very long time.

There is a curious idea at loose in the world that Queens (or Kings) are blind, deaf and dumb, that they do not know anything beyond what is explained to them in official communiqués. Sometimes we go along with the fiction, for there is a great deal that it is more convenient for us not to admit to knowing, and an even greater deal which we are far above noticing, or caring about if we do notice. Into this latter category comes the idea which has been put up from time to time (I think the Duchess of Bedford may have been the first, but she was by no means the last) that Albert did not really love me, that the passionate devotion was all on my side. I have never cared a straw for that opinion, utterly misguided as it was, and based most often on jealousy, but I may as well take the time here to record its falseness. Albert's nature was even more shy and reserved than my own, for where I was able to express my affection only for those closest to me, whom I knew very well and trusted completely, he was able to show it only for me and the children, and even then only in private. His natural diffidence, shyness, and pride made him seem stiff and cold to outsiders, though he was the warmest and also the *funniest* man in the bosom of his own family. Those observers too dull to see past the ends of their own noses, and those who believed a woman's worth could be measured by the length of her eyelashes, concluded he could not possibly love me as much as I loved him.

Let them think it. It never troubled me in the least, for I knew the truth, and only I knew *all* the truth. To the end of his life, until his last illness, we repaired at the end of each day to our bed, as to a ship in which to fly away across the waters of the night and escape from the world and all its vexations; and in its warm darkness, with our arms locked about each other, we could talk and touch and be free as nowhere else. The Albert I knew then, the captain of my dark ship, was mine alone; and my heart lifts in triumph even now to think of the great love he bore me, undeserving as I was. In me alone did he find comfort, pleasure, peace, meaning for his life. The rest of the world was variously a cold and hostile place, threatening, without colour; a place where, like an animal in the wild, he could never be entirely off his guard. But when he sank into my arms he took off all his armour of reserve, and was as tender and undefended as a naked child.

People always came more easily to me than to him: I judged them by instinct, knowing within a very few minutes if they could be trusted or not, if they were 'for me' or not; and my miserable childhood had given me a tough hide, flexible, but hard to penetrate. I had been abandoned by my father, betrayed by my mother, bullied and harassed by all those around me, and it had left me longing for love, needing it, craving it. But there was, by nature it seems, a core of steel in me that would never let me be defeated, that would always hold on; some part of me, I suppose, that always knew I would have what I wanted in the end. But Albert's childhood grief – the sudden and violent loss of his mother – had only made him brittle. He did not easily understand, and therefore did not trust people; and people will not give where they do not receive. His judgements, coming from the head, took no account of the irrationality of humankind, so he was often hurt. *I* hurt him, God forgive me, many and many a time! But it was not my fault. When we quarrelled (as we did often, and mightily!) it did not touch more than the surface of me; I knew, because I did not think about it, that it was possible to go on loving deeply and surely through the most violent altercation. It was as though my ship had a deep keel, which passed through the agitated squalls of the surface and steadied itself in the always-calm water far below. But my poor beloved Albert did not *know* these things with his heart, but with his head, and had to think them out afresh and painfully every time. It was only in the safe darkness of our night-winged ship that he could put intellect aside and assure himself without words of the great love we had for each other.

And even that very first night, when I understood very little of what was going on, I knew with the instinct of my love that there was for him in what we did a great and terrifying release, a yielding of self that was almost painful to him, and yet which left him redeemed and restored. I understood the greater meaning behind his words, that he could not have done it before, knowing he was pledged to me; and I knew how perilous it was for him even with me, how little defence it left him, who needed so much protection. But I had told him from the beginning openly of my love; from the day that I proposed to him had showed it without hesitation, poured it out for him unstintingly, enough to waste half, if he had a mind, and still be satisfied; and coming with dread to be married to me, like a lamb brought to the sacrifice, he had found not pain and death but safety and life, with the one woman in the world he could truly repose in.

God brought us together for His purposes, knowing how we would suit, and how well we would work together for His greater glory. (Uncle Leopold, of course, claimed exactly the same credit to himself; but I am not such a simpleton as to mistake the tool for the Carpenter!)

11th May 1900

THE THREE days of our honeymoon passed in a whirl; a blissfully happy one for me, a mixture of deeply satisfying moments alone with Albert – waking, breakfasting, working, walking on the Terrace – and in the evenings all the jollity of company to dinner, of mirth, jokes, and laughter. On the Wednesday I sent off to London for one of my favourite Pagets (they were such a large family, they always provided one with a choice for every occasion!) and instructed him to organise a ball at Windsor that evening, with as much company as he could possibly come by. He performed this task with a relish, and we had the most tremendous evening, though poor Albert was still rather under the weather, and disappeared at about eleven o'clock. When I went up at ten minutes after midnight I found him fast asleep on the sofa in our bedroom, looking as beautiful as an angel and as innocent as a child. I roused him with a kiss, and we went in great good humour to bed, where he comported himself neither as angel nor child, but to the great satisfaction of us both.

On the Thursday evening we had another ball, though a smaller one, and Albert danced a galop with me, which was delightful; and the next morning, Friday the 14th, we went back to London.

'It has gone by so quickly, I can't believe it's over,' I said as the carriage bowled us back towards the capital.

'What is?' Albert asked, coming back from a reverie.

'Our honeymoon,' I said.

He smiled slowly, and reached out for my hand, carrying it back with him into his lap. 'Oh, that! You are mistaken, *liebe kleine*. That will never be over.'

The first months of our marriage were so happy! Back at Buckingham Palace (which had been redecorated for my marriage, with new chintzes, fresh paint, and lots of gilt) we settled to a delightful routine. We breakfasted together, and then took a walk in the gardens with the dogs, where Albert began to transform my lamentable ignorance about things natural. Before I married him, I could hardly have told one tree from another; now I began to learn the qualities of the different plants and the habits of the bees and butterflies. He had such a clear way of explaining things, and I have always loved to learn; teacher and pupil took equal pleasure in the lessons.

The morning was devoted to work, and while I read despatches and State papers, Albert stood by to blot my signature, or wrote letters of his own at a desk placed alongside mine. I was very jealous of my prerogative, and in those early days did not fully appreciate what a treasure I had. I did not think to share my official work with Albert, and in my still-fresh pleasure in my own powers did not notice that he, too, hated to be idle, and would watch me with a sad, patient look as I did alone what could so much better and more easily have been done by two.

Luncheon we usually had with a small party, perhaps eight or ten close friends or relatives, and in the afternoon, if I had no official engagements, we would ride out, or walk again, or sketch, or play duets on the piano. In the evening we might go to the theatre or the opera (Albert loved the opera as passionately as I did) or entertain at home with a dinner. I loved the jollity of a large company to dinner, but I have always disapproved of the dreadful custom of the men remaining at the table after the ladies have withdrawn. What happens over the port and brandy is seldom edifying (I have Albert's word for it!) and I have always frowned on the 'stayers' who do more than bow to the convention. Albert, I'm glad to say, disliked the custom as much as I did, and never stayed more than five minutes before joining me in the drawing-room, where he would take the seat beside me and we would laugh and talk so comfortably together. When the rest of the company joined us, we would have music and sing duets, or sometimes he would play chess with Anson while I talked to Lord M.

Sometimes on 'company' evenings we would have an informal ball afterwards. Albert was such a splendid dancer, and I loved to whirl around the room in his arms to the intoxicating rhythm of the waltz. But when the warm weather came, I found it just as intoxicating to slip out with him on to the terrace, and stand with his arm round my waist and my head on his shoulder, listening to the nightingales in the Palace garden. But of course it mattered very little what we did – it was the fact that we did it together that made every activity a joy.

Sometimes in those early days I would wake up with the old fear, which had afflicted me when I first became Queen, that it would all prove to have been a dream. But as soon as I opened my eyes, the first thing I would see was Albert's lovely face hanging above mine, as he leaned up on his elbow, watching me.

'I have been waiting for you to wake up,' he said once.

'You said you would always wake me with a kiss,' I pointed out.

'Ah, but I would sooner you were awake just *before* I kissed you. There would be so much more pleasure in it.'

'For you or for me?'

'For both, of course.' And he kissed me. 'You see?'

There seemed no end to the pleasures he could create for me. One morning he said he did not want to separate from me even for the time it took us to dress, and so he appointed himself my lady's maid, and helped me very neatly, even putting on my stockings for me, though he made me almost helpless with laughter by his mimicry of a most *affected* and mincing young female. He was such a talented clown! He invented two comic characters called Herr Pamplemus and Herr Zigeuner, and drew a series of caricatures of them in absurd situations; and sometimes when we were in the middle of a conversation he would suddenly jump up and *be* one of them, and strut about the room in character until I was almost *sick* with laughing.

Most of all, my husband was my friend, the one above all others I liked to be with, with whom I never tired of talking, who could unfailingly cheer me and make me laugh, and bring the world to life and colour with his presence. Every morning he woke me with a kiss; every time he looked at me, his face lit in a smile that ravished my heart. If he went somewhere without me, he never went out or came home without coming through my room or into my dressing-room to see me; he never passed me without taking the opportunity to touch me or, if that were not possible, to salute me with his eyes. He was in everything my true companion; and with the joy of that came the blissful feeling of safety, for he was my husband, my very, very own, and would therefore never leave me. One of my greatest delights was to go into his dressing-room in the morning and watch him shaving. That seemed to me the very *essence* of intimacy and security. A mistress might bed with a man, but only a wife would see him scrape the bristles from his chin.

The only thistle in our bed of roses was Mamma, and she proved a problem not easy to solve. She continued to be extremely unwilling to leave us, and though Albert was kind and patient with her, and by his tactful behaviour to her in the drawing-room avoided many of those scenes I had always found so exhausting, he was as determined as I was that she should go. The difficulty lay in where to put her. Lord M.'s first suggestion, of which I approved, was that the King of Hanover should be given Kensington Palace in return for giving up his suite at St James's Palace, which he never used, to Mamma. I thought this an excellent idea, but both parties refused indignantly, and so Lord M. said sadly that there was nothing for it but that I must rent a furnished house for her out of my own purse. I was furious. Mamma's income had been increased specifically so that she could live within her means and begin to pay off her debts, but she had done neither, and still applied to me for money all the time. Now I was even to be forced to pay for the privilege of being rid of her! In the worst of bad grace I agreed to pay a maximum of £1,500 a year, and for four years only, 'after which she will have to find for herself'. A pleasant furnished let was found for her, Ingestre House in Belgrave Square, and on the 15th of April 1840 – 'sad and momentous day' as Mamma described it – she left Buckingham Palace, complaining bitterly, to take up residence there.

It was not many days before she was complaining that it was too small – 'no better than a little *dog-house*' and too out of the way. Should the Queen's own mother, who if things had been only a little different might have been Queen Dowager herself, live no better than a merchant's wife? This went on at tiresomely regular intervals until September, when the death of my aunt Princess Augusta released her two residences, Frogmore House at Windsor, and Clarence House in St James's (where Uncle William and Aunt Adelaide had lived before his succession). I gave both of these to Mamma, who was finally appeased, and once certain essential repairs and refurbishments had been carried out, she moved into Clarence House on the 21st of April 1841.

It was not only in finding her a place to live that she gave me trouble: there was also the question of her comptroller. Conroy, of course, had resigned and gone to Italy, and if ever a woman needed a good man in charge of her finances, it was Mamma. Lord M. suggested Colonel George Couper, who had acted for Lord Durham in Canada and given great satisfaction, and I thought it an excellent choice: he was a man of great ability, hard working, and with very pleasing, gentle manners; and above all, he was a man of unimpeachable integrity. Mamma, however, was still pining after Conroy (with whom she did not cease to correspond) and wanted one of his sons to take his place. Colonel Couper, she complained, lacked presence, fire, brilliance. Lord Dunfermline, her only trustworthy friend, tried patiently to explain to her that a woman who had been already burnt needed emollients, not more fire, and assured her that no-one of the name of Conroy would ever be considered for an instant. Mamma continued to drag her feet, until finally Lord Dunfermline was forced to threaten her with being turned over to the Duke if she did not accept Colonel Couper.

She yielded reluctantly, but under the advice of Rea, her Clerk of the Works (who was one of Conroy's creatures), she stipulated that Couper must have no dealings with her affairs prior to the date of his appointment (officially the 1st of January 1840, though he did not join her until she left Buckingham Palace) and she locked all the papers up in two large commodes, of which she alone had the key. Colonel Couper, who early confided in me that Mamma's affairs were in a great state of confusion, may have been relieved at first not to have to delve into the secrets of Conroy's stewardship, but as time passed and he and Mamma grew fonder of each other, he grew more and more apprehensive about what those commodes contained. It took him ten years to persuade her to give up the keys, and when he did finally open the commodes, the contents proved as shocking in their way as those of Bluebeard's closet.

However, that was all in the future: in April 1840 I was merely deeply relieved to be rid of Mamma at last, and to have put her finances in the hands of an honest man. But I was simultaneously discovering that while married life was a bed of roses, there were also thorns to be contended with. For one thing, Albert was beginning to show jealousy of Lehzen; and for another, I had discovered I was pregnant.

Ten

14th May 1900, at Windsor

IT HAS always seemed to me a wicked thing that women should have to bear all the disagreeable, agonising and really *dangerous* part of providing a family, while men have nothing but pleasure and convenience in it. My feelings on discovering, only a month after my wedding, that I was pregnant, were not of gratitude to a beneficent God. I knew there had to be children, but if I had only been able to have a year of happy enjoyment with Albert, having him to myself, how thankful I would have been! But no, I was in for it at once, and furious I was to have been caught so soon! Years later I wrote to Vicky (herself then married, of course),

> The first two years of my marriage were utterly spoiled by childbearing. I had constantly to bear with aches, sufferings, miseries and plagues of all sorts. I could enjoy nothing – not travel

or go about with dear Papa – enjoyments all to be given up – constant precautions taken. That is the yoke of the married woman! Without that, certainly it is unbounded happiness, if one has a husband one worships. But I had nine times for eight months to bear real misery (besides many duties) and I own it tried me sorely. One feels so pinned down – one's wings clipped – in fact, at the best, only half oneself. If I could only have waited a year, as I hope you will, it would have been very different.

(My poor Vicky, like me, fell pregnant almost at once, and her first child was born just a year and two days after her wedding day. She had a far worse time in giving birth than ever I had, and was in labour two days in agony that not even vast doses of chloroform could do away with. I had sent one of my own doctors, Martin, to attend her, but the idiot German doctor did not send for him right away, and when Martin did arrive it was to be told that there was no hope, and that the Princess and her child were both dying. Martin thrust him aside, took charge, and working furiously for the next twelve hours managed to save them both. The baby eventually emerged bottom foremost (which is a sad trial to a woman), and was alive but damaged: in the struggle to bring him into the world, his arm had been torn out of its socket, and was blue and lifeless. This I did not know at the time. The first reports spoke only of a live boy, and Arthur, who was eight at the time, raced up and down the corridors at Windsor shrieking, 'I'm an uncle! I'm an uncle!' as if it were some grand title or honour which had been bestowed on him! We were all tremendously thrilled at the arrival of the first of the new generation. It was only later that I learned of my poor child's suffering and the state of the baby's arm. Vicky and Fritz called the boy Frederick William Albert Victor, but he was always known as Willy in the family. The doctors prescribed all the wrong treatment for the arm, claiming it would improve with massage and hot fomentations, but it remained useless. I sometimes think that the unsatisfactory way Willy has grown up has something to do with that useless arm, for he hates to have it mentioned or stared at. At all events, after that Vicky had no more opinion of German doctors than I had, and her other – far too numerous – confinements were all attended by English doctors.)

Childbearing had always been the one thing I dreaded; and there had been before me all my life the example of my cousin Princess Charlotte. I had always felt peculiarly attached to her, as though by some spiritual thread, for her death in childbed had been necessary for me to be born. If our fates were linked in one respect, might they not be in another? The thought of her great suffering and death was always in the back of my mind.

A few days after my condition was confirmed, on the 21st of March, I felt really unwell, and I lay down on the sofa and cried bitterly, to think that this was only the beginning, and there were eight interminable months of it still to come. Poor Albert was distressed, and greatly perplexed besides, for what could he say, after all, to comfort me? What was done could not be undone; he could not even give me the verbal sympathy of wishing it had not happened. I believe if asked he would have said that he would gladly have suffered the whole thing for me; but my view is that if it were men who had to have the babies, the human race would have been extinct long ago.

Meanwhile I lay on the sofa and railed at Fate in a mixture of fury and apprehension.

'All my pleasure ended!' I sobbed. 'No more riding or dancing or doing *anything*! I was so looking forward to the summer with you, and now it is all ruined!'

'There will be pleasures still,' Albert said coaxingly.

'For you, perhaps,' I said passionately, 'but I shall be blown up like a balloon by midsummer, fit for nothing. It's too horrible!'

'But it won't be for ever, dearest love.'

'Eight months is for ever! And everyone will stare at me.'

'They won't stare. And afterwards, think of having a baby – a boy – our son, my darling. Won't that be wonderful?'

'I don't like babies – horrid, bald things, gaping and paddling like nasty little frogs!'

'But the wonder of it,' Albert said wistfully. 'The miracle of life – God's great gift – to bring into the world an immortal soul—'

This head-in-cloud sentiment got short shrift from me. 'Well enough for a man to talk! It's not you who will have to bear the pain and suffering and all the awfulness! And women often *die* in childbirth! You don't think of that!' And I burst again into weeping. He hung over me affectionately, soothed me, stroked my hands, bathed my temples with lavender-water. 'You won't die, my darling. You are thinking of Princess Charlotte, I know, but it won't be like that for you. Hasn't your old friend Lord Melbourne always told you that her troubles came from being kept too low, with a starvation diet and constant bleeding? That won't happen to you. Look how rosy and healthy you are, beloved! Your own hearty appetite and good spirits will see you through.'

The tears began to subside – for now. 'You won't let them bleed me?' I said quaveringly. 'They killed my father with bleeding him – Uncle Leopold said so.'

'Of course not. You will have a happy, healthy pregnancy, and nothing will go wrong. You know you are never ill.'

'Well, that is true,' I said, mollified. I was proud of my robust health.

He grew tender. 'And you know also that God would not separate us now, when we have just found each other. You have told me so often you believe we have a task to do. Don't you think that He remembers that?'

Still hiccuping a little, I put myself into his arms and rested my hot face on his shoulder, and he stroked my head and kissed whatever bits he could reach of me. After a while I said in a more steady voice, 'I wish we could have gone on as we were a little longer. I wish it had not been so soon.'

He tightened his arms around me. 'We are too good lovers for that, my little flower.'

I kept pretty well through that first pregnancy, and though I had fits of lowness and misery, and more than a few bouts of weeping, I could not be miserable all the time. I still had a husband whom I adored, and who dedicated himself to me, cheering my sedentary hours, singing with me, playing to me, reading aloud, playing foolish games to amuse me. I am naturally passionate, and when I am depressed I believe I will always feel so, just as when my spirits are high I cannot believe I was ever miserable. My journals are full of *always*! and *never*! – that is just my nature. But it must have tried poor Albert, who believed in rationality and control, to keep up with me; to dry my floods of tears one minute, and dissuade me from going out for a walk in a violent hailstorm the next.

There were times (I can't deny it) that I felt pleased and excited about the prospect of a child being born of our love, but my anticipation was always of the time when the child would be two or three years old. The intervening business was a disagreeable and degrading process to be got over somehow. In fact, the only advantage I ever discovered in being pregnant was that for a few months I could leave off my stays. All through my life women have been so tightly corseted that I have sometimes looked back at unlaced periods of history with acute envy (though to be sure loose lacing and lack of corsetry does seem to be somehow allied to loose morals and lack of personal restraint: look at Charles II's reign!). I am sure the tight constriction of the upper body was the cause of much of the fainting that went on amongst gently born females; for the lower classes didn't do it nearly so much. I know one was supposed to attribute it to sensibility, which the poor didn't have, but I should not be surprised if it turned out to have been stays after all.

Being in an interesting condition did not mean that I could retire from the public gaze, or from my public duties, which was very trying. When one's ankles are swollen and one's back aches, the last thing one wants to do is to stand for hours and hours at an audience, or be smilingly polite to foreign diplomats. Nor did it make me blind and deaf to the tension within my own Household, between the two people closest to me. Looking back I can see how difficult it must have been for Albert, miserably homesick and struggling to find his place, and how resentful he must have felt of Lehzen, who already had hers. I had been careful not to give Lehzen any official position which might cause public resentment (which was her own advice), but since my accession she had been in charge of my private correspondence, and of the Household arrangements, keeping my quarterly accounts and countersigning the bills for my Privy Purse to pay. This, of course, gave her a sphere of influence and a certain amount of power; and my affection and gratitude gave her access to me on privileged terms. But Lehzen was not one to abuse her position, and I had *never* discussed politics or matters of State with her, as some jealous people thought.

All the same, Albert had been trained by Uncle Leopold and was fitted by his own abilities and wishes to govern alongside me, and now he found that he was not allowed access by me to any State papers, nor given anything to do beyond blotting my signature; and I suppose it was natural for him to feel jealous of Lehzen, and in his jealousy to blame her for his enforced idleness. He thought she had warned me not to let him interfere in matters of State.

But the truth is that it was not her doing, but my own. When I was a little girl at Kensington, lonely, miserable and oppressed, my one sustaining thought was that one day I would be Queen of England, and then I would be above everyone, and beyond torment-ing. It was my consolation and my pride; and to that pride had been added something else which I learned from Lehzen, and from Uncle Leopold – a deep sense of duty and responsibility. The two things together made it impossible for me to share my power with anyone, for not only was it the central pillar of my being, but the proper application of it was a solemn duty laid upon me by God which I could not – and still cannot – lightly set aside. If God had not especially wanted me, Victoria, to be Queen of England, He would not have gone to so much trouble to arrange it.

Also, to be completely honest about myself, there is a stubbornness in me, which was nourished by the long campaign of a Certain Person to usurp my prerogative; and having fought for it so long I was not likely to give it up now to anyone, not for the asking – and certainly not for the pressing. My reasons were sufficient for me, and since I was the Queen, I felt it was not for anyone, even my husband, to question them. So I would give no explanations; I merely said this is what I will have, and that must do for you.

Albert, however, saw things differently. He was a man, and he was a German, and the combination does not make for submissiveness. It was as natural to him as breathing to command, to rule, to decide, to protect: to him the husband was master, and the wife must yield and obey. Not only was that the natural order, ordained by God, but it completely coincided with his own wishes; and his homesickness only emphasised for him how different things were from his ideal, from the way it would have been at home in beloved Coburg. It must have seemed to him that I wanted to keep him as a pet, and it offended his manly pride and made him mad. But I was Queen and I made the rules, and there was nothing he could do about it; and he was wise enough to see that pressing me only made me more stubborn. He felt his powerlessness very much, poor darling: it was his nature to rule the roost, and here he was in a position where he not only did not rule it, he did not even provide it.

He bore it very patiently at first; but when my birthday came around in May, he gave me the present of a large brass inkstand, and as soon as the celebrations were over asked me when he might have an inkstand of his own, and be allowed to use it.

'You do not trust me on even the most trivial matters to do with the Household,' he complained, 'and on matters connected with the politics of the country, where I might be of real use to you, you do not consult me at all.'

'But I love you so much,' I said, hoping to sweeten him, 'I don't want to waste our precious time together discussing politics, when we might be kissing and playing and talking love.'

He looked grave. 'This is not treating me as I deserve,' he said. 'I have a mind, you know, as well as two lips. Do you not value it at all?'

'Of course I do,' I said. 'I think you the cleverest man in the world.'

'Then why do you keep me idle? *"Ein unnütz Leben ist ein früher Tod"*,' he added, quoting Goethe: a useless life is an early death.

Feeling threatened by the mention of death – which I also thought introduced an unfair element into the argument – I'm sorry to say I 'flew off the handle'; and then I flew off to Lord M. for advice. 'What am I to do? I have kept him from affairs of State as much for his own sake as mine, for people do still think of him as a foreigner, and if he is seen to advise me or help me, there will be resentment, and accusations of meddling.'

Lord M. listened, and nodded sympathetically, but said, 'He could be such a help to you, ma'am, in carrying the heavy burden which has been laid upon you. I do think you should acquaint him with everything – perhaps not all at once, but gradually, so that people get used to the idea. People can get used to anything in time, you know, even foreigners. There was a time – you will hardly believe it – when I did not at all like lobsters.'

I laughed, but pressed him anxiously, 'Now do, do be serious! I have always thought that God sent the prince to me for a purpose, but surely he should be my helpmeet in social matters, not political – in the same way that a Queen Consort would help a King.'

'Yet your situation is not quite the same as that of a King. You have more burdens laid upon you than a man would have in the same position, for you must be King and Queen. You cannot give the female part of your royal duties to anyone else,' he pointed out with a kindly look, 'therefore it is only reasonable that you should have help in other spheres, to lighten the load.'

'So you really think I should discuss State business with the Prince?'

'I think you should not deprive yourself of a valuable resource. He has such well-informed and steady opinions, and his good sense greatly impresses those who have the honour to converse with him. Holland was saying to me only the other day that it is now all the fashion to praise the Prince.'

'Is it so?' I said, pleased. 'Well, I do think he is excessively clever. But here's another thing: if I ask for his opinion and it does not agree with mine, I cannot act on it, for I am the Queen, and the responsibility is and must be mine. I cannot be acting against my conscience just to please him! But if I do not *take* his advice once I've asked for it, there will be such resentment! He will feel worse than if I did not ask him at all, and we shall quarrel.'

'As to a conflict of opinions,' Lord M. said calmly, 'Your Majesty has ministers to advise you, which the Prince knows very well. It would not be all between you and the Prince, and if your ministers agree with you, there will be nothing more to be said. He will understand that.'

I remained doubtful. 'He blames Lehzen,' I said bluntly. 'He thinks I tell her things I won't tell him and that she tells me not to trust him.'

Lord M. nodded. 'So I have understood.'

'But it isn't true! You know she does not interfere. She has always been on our side. And *you* have never had any difficulty with her.'

He smiled a crooked smile. 'I am not Your Majesty's husband. And there are those who think the baroness does influence you, perhaps without either of you knowing. It would be natural now that you are married, for your intimacy with the baroness to lessen as that with your husband grows.'

It was gentle, sensible advice, but my resentment flared all the same at what seemed a sidelong attack on my old favourite. 'I know who says so,' I said hotly. 'It is Stockmar! He still thinks of me as a silly child, incapable of seeing what is going on around me. Lehzen influence me without my knowing, nonsense! It is another plot to rid me of her, and I won't have it!'

And so my determination hardened, and Albert's position did not improve. He remained idle and frustrated, condemned to a life of frivolity which had never been what he liked, even in his bachelor days.

15th May 1900

IN THE June of 1840 a very frightening thing happened. I was in my fourth month of pregnancy, and feeling pretty well, the sickness over and the other discomforts not yet too great. At six o'clock on the 10th Albert and I set out to pay a visit to Mamma in Belgrave Square. He was determined that I should at least do my duty by her, and show her the attention the world would think proper; and as long as she was not under my roof, I was willing to be civil, especially when he was beside me to charm Mamma and keep her endless complaints at bay. (She and Albert got on very well, each being the only person the other could talk to about beloved Coburg!)

It was a lovely summer evening, so we had taken an open carriage, the Russian-style droshky, and my favourite greys. As we drove up Constitution Hill the heat was just going out of the day, leaving a warm and balmy evening. The sunlight had taken on that lovely golden tone, throwing the long shadows of trees black across the gilded grass of the Park. The swifts were hurtling and shrieking across the pale bowl of the sky, the warm air was brushing our cheeks, and I felt well and happy.

Albert and I had been talking about horses and I had just turned my head away from him to look at a horse going by, and was saying, 'There, now, what do you think to that chestnut? Do you not think there is something excessively showy about four white socks on a chestnut?' when suddenly there was a tremendously loud report close at hand. Indeed, it was so close that I hardly knew it was a report, for it made my ears ring, and was, in a contradictory sense, too loud to be heard. The horses flung up their heads and stopped, and at the same instant Albert seized my hands and cried out, 'My God! My darling, are you all right? I pray the fright has not shaken you!'

I looked at him, laughing, for his alarm seemed so comical when I saw nothing to be alarmed at. 'It is nothing, dear love, just someone shooting birds, I suppose. They should not shoot so close to the road—' But at that moment I looked past him and saw, standing on the footpath opposite the carriage, a strange, swarthy little man holding a pistol in each hand, his arms folded across his breast in the most affected and theatrical manner. And then, quite slowly it seemed, he unfolded his arms, extended his right hand, and pointed the pistol straight at me. It was an extremely horrid thing to see that black muzzle, like a little, evil eye, come round to stare straight at me, picking me out from all the people in the world for death. My stomach seemed to sink away from me, not so much with fear but with the nastiness of knowing that someone meant quite deliberately to put a ball through my head and kill me. To be made suddenly aware of that degree of hatred is the most unsettling thing in the world.

It takes time to write, but it took no time to happen. I saw him point the pistol at me and I instinctively ducked, at the same instant as Albert, who had also seen the movement, thrust me downwards, covering me with his body. There was another violent explosion, and I think that time I heard the ball whistle across the carriage above my head. The passers-by, who had been frozen into horrified immobility by the first report, were unfrozen by the second, and flung themselves upon the little man. He was only a puny undersized thing, and he completely disappeared under an enthusiasm of well-fed Londoners, some of whom were shouting, 'Assassin! Kill him! Hang him!' and other such loyal phrases. I sat up, straightened my bonnet, smoothed my mantle, and looked at Albert, who was quite white.

'Are you all right?' he said, his eyes scanning my face as though he expected to see I know not what signal of doom writ there.

'Yes, I am not hurt,' I said.

'But the fright – your condition – ' he said in a low, urgent voice. (It was still meant to be a secret, but I don't suppose there was anyone in London by that time who did not know about my 'condition'.) 'We should go back home perhaps. You should lie down and rest.'

I shook my head. I felt a little dazed, though I think that may have been the concussion of sound as much as anything. 'We must go on to Mamma's. She will hear of this and fear the worst if we don't show her we are not dead. Tell the postilion to go on.'

The colour was returning to his face. 'How brave and sensible you are,' he said. 'Very well, we shall go on,' and he called out the order. An enormous cheer went up as our horses moved forward, and I smiled and acknowledged it with a wave and a bow. 'There are enough people to call a constable, or take the villain to a magistrate,' I said. 'What on earth could have possessed him to shoot at me? He must be insane.'

But Albert looked grim. 'He is a vile traitor. He will hang for it,' he said firmly.

When we had spent some time with Mamma, we left again in the carriage, and drove a long way round, partly to give me some air, and partly to show the people I was not hurt, for rumours get about in the most astonishing way, and I would not have been surprised to learn that half of London by then would be willing to swear they had actually seen me carried away lifeless and bleeding. The drive home saw us attended by every rider and driver in the Park, both male and female, gathering around our carriage and forming the most enthusiastic escort all the way back to the Palace. Everyone seemed enormously relieved that I had come to no harm, and the cheers and hat-waving warmed my heart and made me feel that the would-be assassin must indeed be mad, for I was not so unpopular after all. 'I think they know about my condition,' I murmured to Albert as I waved and bowed. 'It makes them happy because they don't want my uncle Ernest on the throne. What a comforting thing it is to have an unpopular Heir Presumptive!'

Albert secured my other hand and pressed it. 'How can you joke?' he said. 'It is over now,' I replied. I think he was more upset than I was. It is being at a distance and now knowing what is going on that upsets me; danger does not unnerve me as long as I am in the centre of things (and well that it doesn't, for that was not the last attempt on my life by any means! Most of the madmen had pistols, but the assault that upset me most happened in 1850, in the gateway to Cambridge House, when a man stepped from the crowd and struck me in the face with a walking-stick. The brim of my bonnet broke the force of the blow, which might otherwise have cracked my skull; but I was knocked unconscious and my forehead and eye were badly bruised and swollen. I carried a scar from that attack for ten years. I found it far worse than being shot at. As a soldier's daughter I can accept that sometimes to face fire is the price of holding high office, and such attacks seem in a way ideological rather than personal. But for a man to strike any woman is brutal and wicked, a most cowardly attack upon our weaker frames, and I felt the upset of it very much).

But although it was over, there was a consequence yet to come. A few days later Albert showed me the pistols which might have finished me off, and very horrid things they were to contemplate. I handled them as one might a dead snake, with flinching, uncertain fingers. One's life hangs by such a tenuous thread as a madman's whim, and there is nothing one can do about it, which is most disagreeable. Albert must have been preparing me, for that afternoon, at the regular audience, Lord Melbourne spoke to me with unusual hesitancy. 'There is a subject which I must raise which is of great importance, and one of great emergency; perhaps you may anticipate what I mean?'

'No, not at all,' I answered absently. 'What is it?'

He looked profoundly uncomfortable. 'I wish I need not mention it to Your Majesty, but it is about having a Bill for a Regency.'

For a second time I felt such a sinking sensation in my stomach. It is not pleasant to have one's death adverted to in such a way. Yes, I might have been finished off by the little madman's pistols, but even given my eminent position, it was far more likely that I would die in childbed than under an assassin's fire. The woman was more vulnerable than the Queen; but the Queen's dispositions were what mattered.

'You are in the right,' I said. 'It must be talked of.'

'And if talked of, ma'am, it must be acted on quickly. We ought to get a measure through before the House rises.'

'Yes, I do see the necessity,' I said wryly. 'But will the Opposition?' Since my marriage, Lord M. had been encouraging me to make friends with the Tories (his ministry was in a bad way, and I think he was preparing me for the possibility of a fall). I had done a little in that direction, though with inward reservations: I never forgot that Peel had voted for the reduction in Albert's pension.

Lord M. said, 'I think they will, ma'am. This is a matter of national emergency; and there can be only one choice for Regent. The Prince as the natural guardian of the child is beyond question the right choice.'

I smiled. 'Well, I think so, of course. But the King of Hanover, as next heir, might not agree.'

'No-one would want the King of Hanover for Regent. They did not when a Regency for you was in question, and nothing has changed. Nor, I am sure, will your uncles Sussex and Cambridge be favoured. If you will forgive me, they are too old and set in their ways.'

But I knew what would be said. 'They will think the Prince too young and inexperienced in this.' They might even think him too *foreign*, I thought, but I did not say so aloud. There was no need with Lord M. to spell every word. 'Even if the Tories agree to make him Regent, they may want him only to be Regent in Council.'

He smiled comfortably. 'We shall see, ma'am. But we will have the newspapers on our side, especially after the incident in the Park, and that always helps.'

In the event he was right. The Tories were very generous about it. Sir Robert Peel said he could not see the practical utility of a Council; the Duke said plainly that it could and ought to be nobody but the Prince. Uncle Sussex rumbled that he could not allow the rights of Family to be passed over, and that he would oppose the Bill in the House, but his was the lone voice of dissent. The Regency Bill went through in July unanimously in both Houses, naming Albert as the sole Regent; and all the newspapers, even the *Chronicle*, praised the decision. Albert was quietly delighted, of course, and I was radiantly happy, as I always was at any mark of respect for my beloved.

'Three months ago they would not have done it for him,' Lord M. told me with a pleased nod. 'It is entirely his own character.'

Then in August came another mark of respect for him. I was going to prorogue Parliament, and the question arose of Albert's proper place in the procession and at the ceremony. 'I suppose we must see what happened with that infernal George of Denmark!' Lord M. muttered (every question of precedent was always referred back to Queen Anne as the last Queen Regnant, and very tired we grew of the comparison!) and went off to look it up. He discovered that by the Gospel according to Queen Anne it would be permissible for Albert to ride with me in my carriage to Parliament, and sit beside the Throne during the ceremony, and so it was ordered. I was delighted to have him near me, supporting me with his beautiful presence, for I was always nervous at such official ceremonies; but I was even more pleased with the cheers he received that day, which proved that the country was accepting him, and taking him to its heart.

When the time came for me to retire into that dreadful birth-chamber, he would have to deputize for me at least for a week or two; and if I died for very much longer. The Regency Act meant that if I died in childbed leaving a living child, Albert would be King in all but name for the next eighteen years. But though I dreaded the forthcoming ordeal, I did not really believe that I would die. I was by nature incapable of conceiving of such a thing. A world with Albert but without me? Impossible! And so although I did discuss the current affairs with Albert more as I grew more sofa-bound (or perhaps I should say he discussed them with me) I still did my Boxes myself, and did not yet let him read State papers. I was the Queen; and I felt he ought to be content to be my consort in the same way that I would have been his if he were King.

Although I love my children and grandchildren dearly, I have never much liked small babies, and cannot understand the craze for baby-worship which has come over this country in the last fifty years. It seems to me the worst kind of sentiment. When children grow rational and one can talk to them, they can be charming and amusing; but the gulping, slobbering things one gives birth to are entirely disagreeable. Most of all, I can never understand those women who rejoice in the actual business of giving birth, and claim to feel themselves uplifted by it. Quite apart from the pain, it seems to me a perfectly revolting process, putting one in the most degrading positions, and I really cannot see that God could have arranged it worse from a woman's point of view.

And I cannot see anything 'natural' or 'beautiful' either, in breast-feeding one's babies. To turn oneself into an animal in that way, as if one were a cow or a sheep, is not beautiful but lowering, and does not befit creatures who have the God-given powers of higher thought and self-determination. I was shocked when I learned that my own daughters, Vicky and Alice, fed their babies themselves; and when once Vicky suckled one of Alice's because Alice was ill, I could barely contain my disgust.

Still, as November 1840 passed, I knew I was in for it, and there was nothing to be done about it. That inevitability is a frightening thought, and I veered from wishing one minute that it would hurry up and start, so as to get it over with, to hoping for a long postponement the next. The accoucheur, Dr Locock, had paid me his preliminary visit (how embarrassing that was!) and said that he thought I should have no difficulties, which was comforting as far as it went; but what man can really understand a woman's fears? Albert did his best to keep my mind occupied so that I had no time for morbid thoughts, and to keep all morbid shocks from me. (In September, when Princess Augusta was dying, he took me to Claremont to be out of the way, in case it upset me, and the oddest rumours began to circulate, which now at a distance I can see were really very funny. It was said that I had had a premonition that I was going to die like Princess Charlotte in childbed; I had gone to Claremont to furnish the lying-in chamber exactly as it was for her confinement, and when the last object was in place, I would follow my cousin to the grave!)

Finally there was no more putting it off. On the 21st of November, in the early hours of the morning, I woke feeling uncomfortable and strange, and though Clark's date for the birth was still a fortnight off, I knew instinctively that it was time. I woke Albert, who got up at once and fetched Clark to me; and Clark said that to be on the safe side, Locock should be sent for. This was done, and Albert advised me to try to sleep again, but though I dozed fitfully, I was feeling too bad to go off completely. Locock arrived at four o'clock, and needed only to lay hands on me to say that the baby was coming, and that everything seemed quite normal. So there was no more sleep for anyone after that: the awful paraphernalia of childbirth had to be assembled round me, and the proper attendants fetched from the four corners of London.

The most shocking thing for a Queen giving birth is the lack of privacy. Ever since James II and the Warming-Pan Plot, the nation has been terrified of having an impostor thrust upon it (though I simply cannot believe in that story for an instant. The idea that his Queen gave birth to a girl and that they exchanged it for a boy smuggled in in a warming-pan could only be credited by a simpleton who knew nothing of childbirth or babies). Still, to ensure fair play the birth-chamber of a Queen has to be crowded with state officials –

191

and in previous times, there were hordes of sightseeing courtiers, too! I had told Lord M. in the roundest terms that I would not put up with any of it, and he replied anxiously that the law required at least some of it, so a compromise had been struck. It was still in my view a shamingly public process: the officers of state were to wait in an ante-room rather than the actual chamber, but the door between the two rooms was to be left open so that the bed could be seen, and the infant was to be brought in to them immediately the cord was cut. But in the birth-chamber with me there was no-one but Locock and Mrs Lilly, the midwife – and Albert, of course, who did not leave me for an instant, held my hand through the pains, and wiped my brow and talked cheerfully to me in between. The throng in the next room comprised the Cabinet, the Archbishop, the Bishop of London, and Lord Erroll, the Lord Steward of the Household. I only wonder there were not hawkers selling pies and hot chestnuts!

My pains were very great, but once I was embarked on it and there was no going back, I found I was not at all nervous – indeed, I think Albert was more afraid than I was. It was hard work, really, rather than suffering, and I have never minded hard work. At last at two in the afternoon the baby was born: I heard an amazingly virile squalling, and shortly afterwards Locock said in a voice brimming with commiseration, 'Oh, madam, it is a princess!'

Albert pressed my hand comfortingly, and was looking at me with such a disappointed expression that I thought it rather hard on the poor baby, who could not help being a female after all. 'Never mind,' I said, 'the next will be a boy.' It was rather a bore, I thought, not to have got a boy first time, and the country would be disappointed, but I was too relieved to have got it over to care much just then. 'Is the child healthy?' I asked.

'Perfect, madam. There is not the slightest reason for anxiety,' Locock said.

'Good. Then you had better do your duty,' I said. He bore the little thing away, stark naked as she was, into the other room, to be laid out on a table for the inspection of those men of state. I found myself thinking that if I had been humiliated in giving birth to her, she had been worse humiliated immediately afterwards; but then she would not remember hers. Albert was looking exhausted, much as if he had been doing the hard work himself. He leaned over and kissed me now, and said, 'How do you feel, darling little one?'

I considered, searching my body for sensation. The pain was all gone, and though I felt weak and tired, I was quite comfortable. No, not quite comfortable – there was one thing. 'I'm hungry,' I said.

16th May 1900

WE VISITED Netley again this morning, and were back for luncheon. There is just time, I think, to finish this episode of my story before the children arrive.

So: after a snatched luncheon, Albert hurried off to represent me at a meeting of the Privy Council – the first time he had done so, and a landmark, though I did not see it so at the time, in his career. He told me when he returned that everyone had been tremendously excited about the baby. Lord Palmerston had pointed out that I had made history, for never before had a Queen Regnant of England given birth to an heir. And Lord M. had told Albert in his droll way that no-one in the country would mind its being a girl, as long as it was another life between the Throne and the King of Hanover.

Because of Clark's muddle over the dates, the wet-nurse we had engaged was not in residence, and a page had to be sent to fetch her from Cowes, where she lived (rather appropriately, as I said to Albert). She arrived at two the next morning, and the baby took to her at once and throve; and when I woke a few hours afterwards, I felt extremely well, and thoroughly enjoyed a large breakfast, so it could be said with truth that mother and child were doing well.

Albert behaved quite perfectly while I was confined: no woman could have been more gentle, no mother more tender in her care. No-one but him ever lifted me from my bed on to the sofa, or wheeled the sofa from one room to another. It was he who adjusted the firescreen, moved the candles, placed my shawl over my shoulders; and so that he should always be within call if I should need him, he refused to go out anywhere, even to the theatre, and most evenings dined alone with Mamma. He was perfectly happy to stay with me hour after hour, reading to me, writing my letters for me, or just holding my hand and talking; and that was the first joy I had in the baby, chatting to Albert about her future. He was plainly quite enchanted at being a father; and to tell the truth, I don't think he minded at all that it was not a boy. Apart from the dynastic significance, I think a girl suited his ideas much better, and in planning her education and recreations, clothes and friends and eventual marriage, he was losing his heart to her every moment. If his tenderness and love for me had not been so plainly expressed, I should have been quite jealous.

One odd thing happened while I was still lying-in. At half past one in the morning one day in early December Mrs Lilly was awakened by the creaking of a door. She sat up and called out 'Who's there?', waking me up. I raised myself on my elbow sleepily, and then was suddenly wide awake, the hair rising on my neck in horror as I saw the door to my dressing-room slowly opening. Mrs Lilly called out again, 'Who's there? Who is it?' her voice sharp with fear; and the door was pulled smartly closed from the inside. With great presence of mind Mrs Lilly jumped out of bed and ran across the room to bolt it from our side, and then she ran to the other door, calling for a page. Kinnaird was on duty, and came to her call, looking as though he had been asleep; but while Lilly was still explaining to him what had happened – and he was being painfully stupid about understanding her – my dear Lehzen came rushing in, aroused by the sound of voices and all anxiety for me.

'What is happening here?' she snapped at Lilly. She understood the situation in a few words, and took hold of Kinnaird's arm with fingers of steel. 'What are you waiting for, boy? There is someone in Her Majesty's dressing-room. Go and catch him!' She pushed the reluctant Kinnaird towards the door, and while he was unbolting it took a moment to fling a reassuring smile at me. 'Do not be afraid. We will catch him, whoever he is.' I was contemplating whether her assumption that the intruder was male was really very tactful when Kinnaird unbolted the door and went in, with Lehzen following close behind him.

'There's no-one here, ma'am,' I heard him say after a pause; and then Lehzen's voice, 'You have not looked under the sofa. Don't you see there is something there.' Another pause, and then, 'Oh, don't be such a coward! Stand aside, I will do it myself!'

There was a sound of scuffling and surprised exclamations, and a few moments later they reappeared in the doorway: Kinnaird looking shamefaced at having the better part of his valour exposed, and brave Lehzen, who cared nothing for her own skin when mine was threatened, holding grimly on to the collar of the intruder – a dirty little boy!

Despite the outcome, I was very much alarmed by the incident. So soon after the assassination attempt in the Park, it struck me forcibly that the boy had been hiding under the very sofa on which I had been sitting but three hours earlier. Perhaps he had actually been there then, crouching under my very legs; and suppose he had come into my bedroom, how frightened I would have been! It was shameful that he had been able to get so close to me without anyone preventing him. Albert was particularly struck by this aspect of it, and though the boy had no weapon or stolen property about him, a thorough investigation was ordered. The boy's name was Jones (he was actually seventeen years old, but was stunted and looking much younger) and he said he often came to the Palace, and got in quite easily over the wall on Constitution Hill and through a window (the newspapers fastened on to this and called him In-I-Go Jones!). He said he had sat on the Throne, heard the baby princess crying, slept in one of the servants' beds, and helped himself to food at night. When asked why he had come at all, he said he wanted to see how great people lived, for he thought he would write a book about it. He was obviously simple, and was sentenced to three months on the treadmill at the House of Correction; but the Palace plainly fascinated him and he kept coming back in spite of stern sentences, until at last we were forced to send him to sea to keep him out of the way. (Over the years the Palace has proved not only attractive but vulnerable to many such intruders, and the fortunate thing is that they have all proved *harmless* lunatics, for it has been impossible to keep them out.)

Lehzen was plainly the hero of this episode, but it did not endear her any further to Albert. I had hoped that being with me so much during my confinement would have soothed his jealousy, but whenever he went from me, he was convinced that Lehzen came rushing in as soon as he was gone and poured poison into my ear concerning him. I resented very much the inference that I was too simple-minded to resist the poison, and that my love for him was so frail a plant that it could be blighted by mere talk, but as I did not discuss him with Lehzen, so I refused to discuss Lehzen with him, and the problem continued to grow underground. I did hint at the general tension to Lord M., who equally obliquely hinted that I ought to give Albert more responsibility, and that if he saw himself trusted with state matters, he would not care about the domestic ones.

'The Prince has conducted your affairs in Cabinet in the most excellent manner during your absence,' he told me, 'and he has an immense capacity for taking pains.'

'Yes, I know that,' I said. 'Nothing could have been clearer or better than his reports to me.'

He looked at me shrewdly and came at the heart of my difficulty, for he knew me very well; better, at that time, than anyone else. 'Anson, as you know, thinks very highly of the Prince,' he remarked, as though casually. 'He says that it is the most remarkable good fortune for the country that Your Majesty has chosen a Prince whose desire is to aim at no power for himself, but to sink his own individual existence in that of his wife, solely in order to be able to assist and advise her.'

But I was not ready for such a compounding of identities, for I had a strong suspicion it would be mine which would be required to do the sinking!

I recovered so well and so quickly that the Court was able to move to Windsor for Christmas. It was a happy season, with the present tables and the German Christmas tree with its radiant candles (Queen Charlotte was the first to bring this German custom to England, I believe, but it was I and Albert who made it popular) and great feasting with meats and pies and sugar plums, and merry games. Our new baby, Vicky – or Pussy as we called her at first – was healthy and lively, and Albert proved especially adept at handling her and soothing her crying. It was he who carried her on Christmas Day to look at the Tree, and he remarked with pride that her lovely blue eyes shone like stars as she stared at the glittering, glowing thing. Mamma, I need not add, was already besotted with Pussette; and even I was finding her an agreeable subject for sketching.

The season was marred only by the death of one of my dearest childhood friends. We buried him with many tears, and raised his likeness in effigy in marble over his grave. A tablet below was inscribed,

HERE LIES DASH, THE FAVOURITE SPANIEL OF HER MAJESTY QUEEN VICTORIA, IN HIS 10TH YEAR. HIS ATTACHMENT WAS WITHOUT SELFISHNESS, HIS PLAY-FULNESS WITHOUT MALICE, HIS FIDELITY WITHOUT DECEIT. READER, IF YOU WOULD BE BELOVED AND DIE REGRETTED, PROFIT BY THE EXAMPLE OF DASH.

It seemed that Time was detaching me from my old life and old ties, pushing me out on to the stream of a new one, and it made me a little nervous. I adored Albert, would have gone to the ends of the earth with him, but still I felt an insecurity; and the year that followed was to be a particularly trying one.

SUMMER

Eleven

26th May 1900, at Balmoral

IT HAS been quite a time since I had the leisure to take up my pen, for we had Henry's Christening on the 18th, and then on the 19th the wonderful news came that Mafeking had been relieved. A flying column under Colonel Mahon, which had been told off for the purpose, had joined up with Plummer's detachment and had driven off two thousand Boers and marched into Mafeking on the 16th to lift a siege of two hundred and seventeen days.

To say the news was well received would be an understatement! The people really went 'raving mad' with delight, the papers were full of nothing else, and General Baden-Powell's picture appeared everywhere as the hero of the day: dogged, resourceful and brave, the very stuff of which our great Empire is made. I was visiting Wellington College on the 19th (Drino has just started his first term there – poor Liko would have been so proud!) and when we got back to Windsor the streets were full of shouting, cheering, singing crowds, and all the Eton boys were out – many of them, I fear, in a reprehensible state! The patriotic fervour of our people led to some indescribable goings-on in London (and I dare say in other places too) and the people were so thoroughly *ausgelassen* that I have already heard a new word being used – mafficking, meaning to celebrate wildly and without restraint.

And after all that, we came up to Balmoral in time for my poor old birthday on the 24th – my eighty-first, which is very hard to believe. There were more than four thousand telegrams, so touching! and some of them quite amusing. One, unsigned, simply read, 'Sincere congratulations. Poem follows.' I await it still, with bated breath!

I am feeling very well and cheerful in spite of the difficult times we have had over the winter and spring; though I'm not looking forward to Baby's holiday next week – she is going to the Scilly Isles, and I do not like to do without her. But I shall have Thora here, and she is a dear girl, and keeps me very much amused. Last night she read to me very nicely from one of Scott's novels. The book she read from once belonged to Albert, but Thora is very good with books and handles them so carefully I had no fears for it. I once knew a chaplain who used to lick his fingers before turning a page – a disgusting habit, as I had no hesitation in telling him. I expect he came to a bad end. I often warn the children of that – a person who has no respect for books is not one to be trusted. We give away our deeper characters in all sorts of little surface ways that the wise person can discern.

I like to have her talk to me, too, for she tells me all about what young women like and do in these modern times. Their lives are so much more full and varied than in my young day, what with bicycling and tennis-parties, roller-skating, tea-dancing, and riding about in motor-cars (I have just banned them from Hyde Park, much to Bertie's annoyance, but they frighten the horses, and besides, one must draw the line somewhere!). Thora was quick to remind me of the modern inventions which I make use of myself, like the telephone and telegraph and electric light; and the 'rising room' (what the Americans amusingly call an 'elevator'!) – which I have had put in at Osborne for taking my chair up and down; though I don't use it often, preferring to be carried. And that led us to talk of the last visit Alicky and Nicky spent here, at Balmoral, in 1896, when they brought their first child, Olga, to see me – the most gloriously fat and rosy-cheeked baby I have ever seen, a positive bolster of a baby, with a row of tiny teeth like seed-pearls! (They have two more daughters now, but no son still, which is a worry to them, Russia being what it is; but they are young yet, and healthy.) I found Alicky sadly changed from the dear, friendly child who used to spend long holidays with me: she seemed so remote as to be almost a stranger. And Russian ways are peculiar – they brought the most enormous retinue, including such a number of detectives and policemen I felt almost offended – what did they think could happen to them here, on my own estate? Bertie did his best to be hospitable by taking Nicky out stalking every day, but Nicky only complained that he never got a stag (which was hardly Bertie's fault!) and said he would sooner have spent the time in his wife's company, which was not tactful. He also complained that Balmoral was colder and bleaker than Siberia; but when they went, he left a 'tip' of a thousand pounds to be shared out amongst the servants! However, the subject of the visit came up in my conversation with Thora because on the last day we all went out on to the terrace and were photographed by the new 'animatograph' process, which makes moving pictures by winding off a reel of photographs all joined together. We had a viewing of it later, in November at Windsor, and there we all were walking up and down and the children jumping about, just as if we were alive! Thora and I agreed it is a very wonderful process, and wondered how it would have been if it had been invented sooner. The photographic process has already changed the way we all think about war, but imagine seeing the charge of the Light Brigade on animatograph!

I have a little cottage here where I work – it used to be the gardener's cottage – and where I come to be alone, and since it is a fine day today I have brought my 'magnum opus' down with me, to take up where I left off – which I see was the Christmas of 1840. At the beginning of 1841, it was plain that my Government was in difficulties, though 1840 had ended in triumph with the successful resolving of the Middle Eastern crisis. Lord M. had been reported at Woburn after Christmas 'like a boy escaped from school, in roaring spirits'. But there is an adage that the People have no interest in foreign affairs, and will always judge a government by its performance at home. I have always found that to be very true (except in times of war when a different sort of spirit prevails, and a multitude of domestic sins can be covered by one glorious victory of our men abroad).

At home things did not look good for the Government. The harvest of 1840 had been bad, which meant hunger and unrest amongst the poor. Tea and sugar prices were unusually high, which upset the middle classes. Trade with both America and Europe was slack, and – most serious of all – government expenditure had outstripped revenues by a frightening one-and-a-half million pounds. I did not understand how a government could spend money it did not have in the first place, but I knew all about debt from members of my own family, and I knew it meant nothing but misery, and must be corrected with all haste.

Lord M., in his droll way, put the blame for the budget deficit on the introduction of the Penny Post.

'But I thought the Penny Post was supposed to pay for itself?' I said indignantly. 'You told me it was a good idea.'

'Oh, certainly, ma'am, it is; and it will – in time,' he replied. 'Once it works itself out, it will generate enormous revenue. But it is like all new ideas: someone must pay to set it up and get it going.'

As well as the money troubles, there was trouble from the

Chartists, the Irish (as usual), and the Anti-Corn Law League, which was stirring up the industrial areas. Then three by-elections in February and another in May went against us, and Lord M. was plainly beginning to feel the strain. He looked tired, and suddenly frighteningly old. 'I'm nearly sixty-one – many men die at sixty-three,' he said to me one day. 'People like me who have been rather young for their age, grow old all at once.' This sort of talk frightened me very much; I was terrified of losing him. But when the Government was defeated in the spring over the Irish franchise, Lord M. said comfortingly that 'they would not go out on such an issue as this.' But the comfort was spoiled when he added that if they were beaten on the budget, it would be a different matter.

It was about this time that Albert sent George Anson to have secret discussions with both Lord M. and Sir Robert Peel about the likelihood in the near future of a Tory Government led by Peel, and what could be done to ensure a smooth changeover. If I had known about these negotiations I would have been very angry indeed; and in a way, that was one of the reasons the negotiations were kept secret.

The fact was that there had been a previous occasion, two years ago, when my Government had been badly defeated. That had been in May 1839 in the middle of the Lady Flora Hastings scandal; and when I had been told that the Whigs must go out and the Tories come in, I had fought it tooth and nail. I could not bear the thought that my beloved Lord M. was to be replaced by the horrid, frozen-faced industrial baronet Sir Robert Peel (someone once said Peel's smile was like the silver fittings on a coffin!). I absolutely refused to change my Ladies of the Bedchamber, as Peel demanded, for his own appointees, and Peel gave the ultimatum that if I did not accept new ladies, he would find it impossible to form a Government: it would, he said, appear that I had no confidence in him. The last thing he expected me to say was that indeed I *had* no confidence in him; but he mistook his mark, and within a week he had admitted defeat and I had my Whigs and my Lord M. back again.

At the time I felt very strongly that I had acted within my rights: my ladies were Whigs, but they were not *political* Whigs, nor did I *ever* discuss politics with them. However, what I did in effectively refusing the change of government was really shockingly unconstitutional; and if my Prime Minister had been anyone but Lord M. there would have been a dreadful uproar and scandal; but everyone liked him, and no-one could believe for a moment that he had anything but the country's good at heart, so we escaped only a little tarnished.

All this had happened before Albert arrived in England, of course, but he had heard about it from Anson and from Stockmar, and he thoroughly disapproved. He believed that the Sovereign should be above party politics, and deplored my open favouring of the Whigs, which he thought lowered my standing to that of a grubbing political patron. He had advocated from the beginning that my Household, or at least the senior appointees, should be a balanced mixture of both parties, so that the Court could be seen not to be partisan, and was also not dependent on the parliamentary distribution.

All these were admirable ideas, and I came in time to accept them as right and proper, likely to strengthen rather than weaken the Throne. Moreover, once I had accepted Sir Robert Peel and got used to his very different manner, I found him an excellent man, with fine qualities, and in some ways he was my best Prime Minister. (Dear Disraeli once said to me it was a mystery how Peel ever came to be leader of the Tories, for he was a natural-born Whig by inclination, which I suppose helped me to become reconciled to him.) But I never loved him as Albert did, and at first I did not find him easy to trust: in the early years of my escape from Conroy, I was always on the look-out for double-dealing, plots and deceit, and anyone whose manner was not open, frank and confiding (and Peel's certainly was not!) I suspected of duplicity.

So when it looked as though the Whig Government must fall, Albert wanted to ensure that there was no repeat of the 'Bedchamber Crisis', which he believed would be very damaging to the Crown. This was the overt reason for his sending Anson to Lord M. and Peel behind my back; but in retrospect I can see that Albert welcomed the change of government because he wanted to be rid of Lord M. He liked Peel (whose manner, being reserved like his own, did not offend him), and admired his intelligence and integrity; but he always undervalued Lord M.'s abilities, simply because *his* manner was not such as Albert could ever take to. That lounging grace, that levity, that sly, cynical humour, that apparent indolence, were all incomprehensible to my darling, who took them as signs of degeneracy.

But more than that, most of all, Albert wanted to rid us of Lord M. because he was jealous of him; because he wanted me all to himself.

At this distance from events it is hard to say how much I appreciated at the time what was really happening. When one is young, one is so much more attached to one's body. One lives inside it, seeing through it with a natural distortion like the refraction of water; affected by its ebbs and flows, like a sea anemone on a rock

201

swayed this way and then that by the great sighing tides. In old age, one wears one's body more lightly, for all its aches and pains, and as it becomes less important, so it becomes more transparent. I can see now many things about myself, and about Albert, which I did not know, or only dimly sensed when I was young. It is a great pity one cannot go back in time, armed with that disembodied wisdom, and correct the mistakes that were made when one was, shall I say, physically distracted.

And I was very distracted by my body that year, which was another reason that Albert and Anson were anxious to have a smooth transition, should it come. Hysterical scenes must be avoided; I was not to be upset if possible, because I was pregnant again. Peel, who had locked horns with me once and lost, was ready to compromise and sent word to Lord M. that if I would 'spontaneously' give up my three most senior ladies – the Duchesses of Sutherland and Bedford, and Lady Normanby – he would forgo any further changes.

So one day at his regular audience Lord M. told me that I must be prepared for a change in government. His budget, he was sure, would bring him down; and when the time came, I must not hesitate to send for Peel.

I trembled a good deal at the thought of a change, but kept control of myself pretty well, though I said at once that I had sooner send for the Duke. 'I have come to like him really very well,' I said. 'In fact, I think he is a good friend to us.' He had stood proxy for Albert's papa as godfather at Pussy's Christening in February, and had unbent sufficiently to smile and say she was a beautiful and intelligent child, which had warmed me towards him. 'And I know he is honest, that is the greatest thing.'

'Why, ma'am, so is Sir Robert,' said Lord M. 'And you know the Duke will not do it. He will give you the same answer as he gave in 'thirty-nine – that he is too old and much too deaf.' He smiled. 'A little political deafness can be a great advantage to a Prime Minister – I enjoy it myself from time to time – but the real thing is a great drawback.'

I did not respond to the smile. 'I do not like Sir Robert,' I said, clenching my hands. 'I do not *like* him. And he will take away all my ladies and leave me with no-one, and I shall be quite forlorn.'

'Well, as to that,' Lord M. said casually, 'I think there will be no difficulty. In fact, I know it. Sir Robert has very chivalrously declared that three new appointments will quite satisfy him – and I think, ma'am, you may change *three* without feeling too forlorn.'

'Do you mean you have seen him? You have asked him about it?' I said in surprise.

There was the slightest hesitation. 'Anson has seen him – spoke to him yesterday, in fact.'

'*You* sent Anson?'

'Not I, ma'am. It was the Prince, anxious for your comfort and security, who asked Anson to sound out Sir Robert on the subject. And Anson was so eloquent on the Prince's behalf that Sir Robert's eyes filled with tears. He exhibited, I'm told, the most proper feeling!'

This image so caught my attention that I quite forgot to be angry. 'Did he really? But whenever I have seen him he has always shown me a horrid, cross face. It is the case with all the Tories. I do not want cross-faced ministers about me.'

'I think, not *cross*, ma'am. Most probably they were shy and embarrassed. Strange faces are apt to give the idea of ill-humour, you know; but once you are used to them – and *they* are used to you, which is more to the point – you will find them as agreeable as anyone. You know that to be true in the Duke's case,' he pointed out coaxingly. 'There was a time not long ago when you disliked him amazingly.'

I sighed, conceding the point. 'But I do not want you to go out, my lord. I cannot do without you. And I'm sure you will not like to go.'

He sighed too. 'Nobody likes going out – but I am a good deal tired, and it would be a great rest for me.'

I looked at him in dismay. Could it be that this was not just another crisis, but really the end of things? '*Must* it be?'

'I will not go unless I have to, you may be sure; but if I do, you will have an excellent man in Peel, whom you may absolutely trust.'

'I may grow to trust him, but I could never confide in him as I do in you. He could never be a friend to me as you are.'

His eyes grew moist, and he leaned forward confidingly. 'As to that, I see no reason why we may not continue to meet, and to correspond, if it is Your Majesty's wish.'

'It is – it is!' I said, feeling enormously relieved at the prospect. 'If I could see you – write to you – have your opinions, I should not feel so alone.'

Lord M. nodded. 'I have touched on it with Sir Robert, and he has said most generously that he has no objection whatever to a continuation of purely social intercourse between us – indeed, he said that he would be glad of whatever gives Your Majesty comfort. You see how properly he speaks of you! But, of course, we would not discuss politics together any more.'

'Of course not,' I said more brightly, meeting his eyes, and seeing in them the same conviction – that no-one would dictate to *us* what we should and should not discuss. 'It would make the change-over much less disagreeable to me if I might not lose my friend as well as my Prime Minister.' But I still did not really, at bottom, believe it would come to that.

The defeat of my Government in June over the budget was brought about by a remarkable combination of what ought to have been conflicting interests. There was a strange alliance between the West India sugar merchants, who objected to new duties on sugar, and the anti-slave-traders, who objected to the fact that slave-grown sugar was now more freely imported than free-grown. The Chartists, who Lord M. said ought sooner to have voted for the Anti-Christ than the Tories, voted against the Government on the grounds that no-one was going to give them what they wanted anyway, so they might as well have a change just for the variety. And tinkering with the Corn Law scale of duties annoyed everyone – the agriculturists because they wanted more protection, and the industrialists because they wanted none.

The Corn Laws were a great cause of dissension throughout the early part of the century. As Lord M. explained it to me, the arguments for and against the protection of corn prices were roughly these: the free importation of foreign corn, it was said, would reduce home production and cause a dangerous dependence on other countries which could be fatal in time of war, and would make us vulnerable to blackmail by foreign governments. The contrary argument was that the competition of free trade would reduce the price of corn which would make bread cheaper for the lower classes, for whom it was the staple diet.

Lord M. dismissed this latter argument as sentimental nonsense: if bread were cheaper, he said, employers would simply feel justified in cutting wages, and the poor would be no better off. Besides, when the harvest was good at home, very little foreign corn was imported anyway, and when it was bad at home, it was usually bad abroad too, and foreign corn was both so scarce and so expensive that the import duties made little difference. Lord M. was largely against changing the law simply because it would cause such disruption and set one class against another. He always thought change should be avoided unless it would bring some definite good.

(The Corn Laws were finally repealed by the Tories under Sir

Robert Peel in 1846, and in justice to Lord M. I can't see that it made very much difference either way. The repeal did, however, make poor Peel so unpopular that he was forced to resign immediately afterwards, so if the Corn Laws can be said to have defeated Lord M. in 'forty-one, they did the same for Peel five years later.)

After the Government's defeat in June 1841, Lord M. was persuaded, somewhat against his better judgement, not to resign, but to go to the country in the hope of getting an improved majority. I was very glad of this decision, which gave me a respite, and I was such a fervent Whig I was sure the country could not be so infatuated as to prefer the Tories; but the elections were an embarrassment for the Whigs, and in August the Government was defeated heavily in both Houses. The crisis I had dreaded ever since I first came to the Throne was now upon me.

I wrote to Lord M. on a black-bordered paper (the Court was in mourning for the Queen of Hanover) which I thought only too appropriate. 'The sad, sad event has taken place at last. I have dreaded it for so many months, and the reality is so *very*, very painful and dreadful to believe!' He wrote back, 'I also feel deeply the pain of separation from a service which has now for four years been no less my pleasure than my pride.'

I felt I was abandoned amongst my enemies, and no amount of reassurance by Albert would convince me that I should like Peel just as much one day. Lord M. did all he could before he left to reconcile me to it, and to make me accept Albert and Peel in his place as my mentors; but though I loved Albert dearly, I did not yet want him as my partner in government; and Peel I neither loved nor trusted.

My last audience with Lord M. as Prime Minister took place on the 30th of August at Windsor. After dinner we went out together on to the Terrace and walked a little, quite alone, talking of old times. We had so many happy memories; and after a while it was necessary to change the subject, for we were both close to tears.

'What will you do now?' I asked him.

'Oh, this and that,' he said lightly. 'I shall cultivate the habits of a country gentleman. I think I shall buy some horses – I haven't done very much riding lately.' We talked of horses, and of rides we had taken together in the past. 'I hope I shall see a little of the bloom of spring and summer which I have missed for so many years,' he said. 'There will be compensations, you see, to being out of office.'

'In or out of office, I shall always regard you as my most dear and valuable friend,' I said. My voice shook as I spoke, and we stopped of the same impulse and turned to each other in the starlight. His kind, dear face was almost hidden in shadow, but it was so familiar to me I did not need light to see it. 'For four years I have seen you almost daily,' I said in a low voice. 'I do not know how to contemplate the change. I have not said much – I have not made a fuss as I did last time – but that is because I feel it so much more.'

'I know,' he said. 'I have observed your courage, and admired your efforts at control so much.' He stopped abruptly, and I put my hands blindly into his, feeling them, large, dry, comfortable, close round mine as on so many occasions before, when I had been afraid or lonely. He had been not quite father, not quite lover to me – a little of both – the first love of my lonely life, and he was very, very dear to me still. We were not parting because our love had ended, and that is the hardest sort of parting of all.

He bent his head and spoke softly. 'The time of my service to you has been the proudest and happiest part of my life. For four years I have seen you daily, and liked it better every day. It is as if—'

He stopped again, and I said, 'Oh, don't! My heart is breaking!'

He made a strange little sound like a sob, and lifted his head a little, and I saw the tears on his cheeks glint in the starlight. He had tilted his face back so that his tears should not drop on to my hands, which would have been *lèse-majesté*, and I would have smiled at such consideration if I had not been crying too by then.

'I shall not be far away,' he managed to say after a while. 'I shall still see you.'

'But it won't be the same,' I said despairingly, and he did not argue. We both knew it.

'You must rely on the Prince now. Lean on him, seek his advice. He must be everything to you. And trust Peel. He is a good man.'

'Yes,' I said; but in my heart I said no. In my heart I said, I don't want Peel, I want you! I wanted things to go on the way they were. All my life people had been leaving me, and I hated change, it frightened me. And Lord M. had always been on my side, my one true friend and supporter. Albert was still in some ways an unknown quantity. Albert was already on terms with Peel, whom he liked far more than I ever should, for they were alike in their tastes and their temperaments. And now Peel was being foisted upon me as my principal minister. Suppose he and Albert worked together to push me aside, took over government from me piecemeal until I was nothing more than a cypher, a consort to be paraded on public occasions for the people to cheer at? I had grown up in an atmosphere of conspiracy, and it was hard for me not to see it all around me, even in the one I loved best – oh, especially in him! For where one loves, one has the most to lose, and trust has the greatest territory to cover.

And I knew that as Queen Regnant I had a great weakness which Albert and Peel could exploit if they wished; for what could be easier than to use my periods of confinement in childbed to weaken my position and take away my power? And who could more easily conspire to do so than my husband and my Prime Minister?

'I wish you would not go!' I sobbed at last. 'Oh, I wish you would not!'

'It has to be,' he said, and there was a world of sadness in his voice.

28th May 1900

TWO DAYS later Albert and I went to Claremont and it was there that I had my first audience with my new council of ministers. My heart was very full, and I spoke little, knowing that I would easily be tipped over into tears; but I kept my composure and behaved, I think, with dignity. My visible condition – for I was seven months' pregnant by then – must have affected the ministers, for they behaved in the gentlest way, speaking softly and showing me every consideration. Even Sir Robert's manner was softened, and he assured me with an unexpected tremble in his voice that he considered it his first and greatest duty to consult my happiness and my comfort in everything; no person, he said, would be proposed to me in any capacity who was in the least disagreeable to me. In my heart I answered, 'Then take yourself away and bring me back Lord Melbourne!' but outwardly I was all complaisance, and said what I must. I must have performed well, for afterwards Peel said that I had behaved perfectly to him, and the other ministers all agreed that they had the fullest confidence in my intended fairness towards them.

Ah, but what about fairness to me? The longer this pregnancy went on the more ill I felt, and the more nervous and alone. Lord M. was gone; Albert had aligned himself with the enemy; I had only Lehzen left.

That awful pregnancy ended at last, on the morning of the 9th of November 1841, when after severe suffering I gave birth to a fine, large boy. Albert stayed with me throughout, holding my hand, wiping my brow, supporting me with his love. I don't know what I would have done without him. But though I had now fulfilled the promise of a year ago and given the country and my husband an heir, my troubles were not over. Soon another attack was to be mounted, and by the one nearest me, who should have loved and sympathised with me most, to deprive me of the last support of my early life. Albert had seen off Lord M.; now he had to remove an even more hated rival for my attention, before he could reign alone. He was king of my heart already, but he knew, as I knew, that I had not surrendered everything to him yet, and the last battle was about to be joined.

Sunday the 16th of January 1842 – oh, how I remember that date! We had been to Claremont for a few days, for I was badly in need of rest and change. My second child had been born less than a year after Pussy; I had had a wretched pregnancy and a difficult birth; and having had two children in twenty-one months of marriage, I was exhausted and depressed, and my poor nerves were so chafed that I could hardly bear myself. Since the boy was born, everything seemed to irritate me, and though I tried so hard to control my temper, it only made it worse when I lost it – as if every annoyance was stored up like an explosive shell in a magazine, which all finally went off together.

When we reached the Palace that Sunday we went straight up to the nursery to see Pussy. She had been a lusty baby for the first nine months of her life, but in the autumn of 1841 she had begun to ail and lose weight; her food disagreed with her, she was often sick, and cried and was fretful. She was given the very best of everything: Clark decreed she should be fed none but asses' milk – which was the richest, richer than Jersey even – together with chicken broth and the finest arrowroot. As the food was so rich, to avoid overloading her little stomach it was measured out carefully to her in small amounts and at long intervals. But still she did not thrive.

The nursery was stiflingly hot, too hot for my comfort, but it was the understanding in those days that cold air was fatal to babies, so I did not question it. Certainly the new baby seemed to like it: he lay quietly in his cot, staring ahead of him with those dark-blue eyes, peacefully blowing bubbles and moving his limbs slowly like an underwater creature. (Even now poor Bertie reminds me somewhat of a large fish – slow-moving and glassy-eyed.)

Pussy was a different matter. As soon as we came through the door we could hear her whimpering, and as I bent over the cot, I could smell by the sour odour that she had been sick again. I turned to the nurse, who had got up hurriedly from the fireside at our appearance.

'How has the Princess Victoria been, Roberts?'

'Much the same, madam,' Mrs Roberts said, curtseying. 'She brought up her last feed, I'm afraid.'

Albert bent over the cradle and stroked his daughter's hollow cheek with the back of one finger. 'How pale and thin she is,' he said, and I could hear the anxiety in his voice. 'Poor little Puss!' The baby whimpered again, turning her eyes up to Albert's face as if in appeal. 'See how she looks at me! Poor baby, she's so hungry.' He looked at me accusingly. 'This regimen does not suit her, you know.'

I knew – he made no secret of it – that he did not agree with the nursery regime laid down by Clark; but what irritated me most was the insinuation that only *he* cared about Pussy, that I, her mother, who had borne the suffering and inconvenience and downright danger of giving birth to her, did not mind seeing her unwell.

'When is her next feed due?' I asked Roberts tersely.

'Not for another two hours, madam.'

'So long?' Albert looked up sharply. 'But she's hungry! A child so thin can't be getting enough to eat.'

'She's fed according to Doctor Clark's instructions, sir,' Roberts said, resentfully. Albert did not like pertness from servants, and I saw the corners of his nostrils whiten.

'You make her wait, although she's hungry? Ah, she is so helpless that all she can do to tell you her trouble is to cry, but you ignore it.'

'The food is rich enough, sir. She doesn't need more,' said Roberts. She looked at him with a narrow, sidelong glance. 'I'm afraid gentlemen don't understand babies. It does them no harm to cry a bit.'

Albert turned sharply away from her and muttered to me, 'Now that is a spiteful remark. I know who has been at work here.'

It was not much, but it was enough to touch off my temper. 'Oh, and what would you do?' I enquired angrily. 'Feed her every time she cries? That would be a splendid thing, would it not? She'd be dead inside a week – and much you would care!'

'Please, Victoria, let us not argue,' he said in a low voice.

But I was in a passion now. 'Oh, no, let us not argue, let us do exactly as *you* say! You know all about babies, of course! What you would like best, I suppose, is for me to leave the nursery altogether so that you can get on with murdering my child in peace!' I saw him grow pale, and felt that strange, perverse thrill one has when one lets go of oneself and says the unsayable. The words seemed to leap out of my mouth with their own power. 'Yes, you would murder her if I let you! You've never cared for her, I know that. You were sorry she was a girl, and now you have a boy you'd be happy to see her dead!'

A dreadful shiver of excitement surged through me as I passed beyond the bounds of control. I had said monstrous things; I had struck him, with my words, as hard as I could; now I waited, vibrating with the lust for battle, for him to strike back. But at the last moment he caught himself up, remembering what I had ceased to care about – that Roberts was listening to every word, and that it would be all round the Palace by evening. '*Liebe Gott*, I must have patience,' was what he did say – muttered rather – and he swung on his heel and went quickly away, closing (not even slamming) the door behind him.

My unexpressed rage almost choked me. As I stared at the closed door I could feel it like a lump jammed half-way down my throat, immovable, and my stomach lifted for an instant as though I really might retch. It was not the first quarrel we had had, for my nerves had been in a state of irritation all through my second pregnancy, but Albert would never quarrel properly: when rational argument failed, he would withdraw himself, first verbally and then, if I persisted, physically. I ought to have taken warning this time from many little storm signals, in myself and in him, but it always maddened me to have him walk out of the room in the middle of a quarrel, and just then I felt I must have it all out or die from rage. Trembling with the effort of control, I said something neutral to Roberts, I know not what, and went to look for Albert.

He was in his dressing-room. I had never seen him so angry. He was walking up and down with a snatched, angry gait; his eyes blazed, his face was white except for two small red spots over his cheekbones, his lips were pressed hard together. The look of him made me shiver inwardly with something that was not aversion. I was both excited and angry, but there was something else in me, too, something that licked its lips at the sight of him.

As I came in and shut the door behind me, he turned and looked at me with a sort of grim relish. 'Ah yes, here you are,' he said. 'I expected it. I knew you would not be able to leave it there.'

'Leave it there? No, indeed!' I retorted. 'The health of my child is not so unimportant to me as it seems to be with you!'

He boiled over. 'How dare you say that? How *dare* you? It is you that cannot see what is under your nose! The child is starving! The food Clark orders for her is too rich and she cannot keep enough of it on her stomach to nourish her. I have told you so before, but you won't listen to me. And Clark doses her with calomel, which is too powerful for such a tiny child. Good God, it's meant for overfed aldermen after civic banquets, not frail little babies with empty stomachs!'

'Oh, you know better than the doctor, I suppose? I wonder you do not prescribe for everyone in the Palace, if you are so skilled in medicine! Clark has been a physician for thirteen years, but don't let that consideration trouble you!'

'I know Pussy is not well, and I can see he is making her worse. How can you see her and hear her cry and not know that? Your heart must be as hard as flint. But no, you won't even accept the evidence of your own senses if your precious Lehzen decrees otherwise!'

I was stung. 'Lehzen has nothing to do with this,' I began, but he overrode me.

'Lehzen has to do with everything in this house! You are besotted with the woman! And not content with letting her rule you, you hand over the nursery to her as well.'

'Mrs Southey is head nurse, as you know very well. Lehzen merely takes a kindly interest in the babies, which is perfectly natural.'

'She is never *out* of the nursery! Every time I go to see my children I see her and Southey sitting by a great roaring fire, far too hot for the little ones, and gossiping together like a pair of *tricoteuses* at the guillotine! And don't tell me she and Clark are not hand and glove! She supports him in everything – which is why you can't see how wrong he is about Pussy. It's Lehzen who orders everything in this house, and I'm sick of it!'

'Yes, I know about your crazy jealousy of her,' I snapped. 'All it is is that *you* want to rule the roost. You think no-one but yourself should ever be considered or consulted. You think *I* am nothing—'

'On the contrary,' he said fiercely, 'I know very well who and what you are. It is you who forgets. Because Lehzen was your governess you treat her like an oracle. You think every good quality you have comes from her—'

'I know how much I owe her, which you seem to have forgotten! If it had not been for her I should not have survived the misery of Kensington – but perhaps you don't care for that. It's all one to you what I suffered – and do suffer still! Lehzen endured miseries for my sake, and stood by me when there was no-one else to help me. She has never asked for anything for herself, but because I don't turn her out to starve like an old dog now that I don't need her help any more, *you* think yourself slighted.'

Albert rolled his eyes. 'You are irrational about that woman! You think she is the fountain of all virtue; but the truth is she is a crazy, stupid intriguer, obsessed with the lust for power! She sees herself as a demi-god – and anyone who refuses to acknowledge her as such, you treat as a criminal!'

'She does not lust for power! She thinks only of serving me!'

'She serves herself, Victoria, can't you see that? When you married me she was afraid of losing her power, so now she seeks to keep control of you through the nursery, and by turning you against me, whispering lies and dripping poison into your ear.'

I was maddened by the unjustness of this attack on my dear friend. 'She does not!' I panted. 'She never speaks ill of you, though God knows you deserve no loyalty from her, the way you hate her and vilify her!'

'I don't hate her, though I have every reason to—'

'You do! It is you who are irrational about her! I hardly ever see her now, but you are ate up with jealousy over her.'

He boiled up again. 'Hardly ever see her? The moment I am out of the house she comes creeping into your room—'

'She does not!'

'And when we disagree about something you go running to her to complain about me – and she magnifies every little difference between us and makes it into some great offence!'

Oh, this was so unjust! I lashed out with all my strength. 'At least she truly loves me, which is more than I can say for you! You might learn a thing or two about loyalty from her!'

He seemed to grow still. 'What do you mean by that?'

'I mean what I say. You are cruel and unjust and utterly selfish, the most selfish man I have ever met! You think of no-one but yourself and your own advancement! Your position in Court is not high enough for your ideas of yourself – that is what it is really about!'

'You are not in earnest.'

But I was soaring now, on wings of pure fire. 'But I am!' I said triumphantly. 'I'm sick of your ingratitude, and I wish I had never married you! You have brought me nothing but misery with your jealousy and disloyalty and greed for power! In fact I wish I had never even *met* you! I was far better off without you!'

'Then the situation is easily rectified!' he snapped, white with anger, and stalked out of the room. I celebrated my victory by bursting into tears, and running into my own room, where I flung myself down upon the sofa and wept until I felt sick. Oh, it was dreadful, dreadful! I had never seen him so angry, for he had always held back, as I knew instinctively, from the brink over which we had both just plummeted. How could I have said those things to him? I had *seen* them hurt him, but I didn't mean them. If only he would trust me! He was wrong about Lehzen. He had no cause for jealousy, but he would not let me love anyone but him, and wanted me to get rid of her. I was angry with him for that, for I would not have wished to deprive *him* of anyone he loved or found valuable; but I had wept myself into penitence now, and my bruised heart was crying out for him. I wanted his arms, his warmth, his kisses. Now the heat of my anger had drained away I felt cold, and lonely for him, and I wanted to forgive and be forgiven, to be enfolded, to be close.

Ah, but this was not like our other quarrels. This one had gone deep with him, and while I was still lying tear-stained on my sofa, wondering where he was and what he was thinking, I received a note from him – a bitter, unforgiving, cold little note.

> Doctor Clark has mismanaged the child and poisoned her with calomel and you have starved her. I shall have nothing more to do with it. Take the child away and do as you like, and if she dies you will have it on your conscience.

Oh, that was cruel! When I am in a passion I say things in the heat of the moment, hurtful things that I don't in the least mean. But I could never, never have written that note: such calculated anger is not in me. Words spoken can hurt, but they dissipate on the air like soap bubbles; words written are etched on the mind and the heart for ever. I felt myself wither under that frosty touch. He was angry still, and I was not forgiven. He had withdrawn from me not only his presence, but his love, and without it I knew I would die, as a plant dies without the sun.

Twelve

1st June 1900, at Balmoral

THAT DREADFUL quarrel with Albert: I can never forget it. When I received his letter, I knew I was alone again, with everyone against me, as I had been at Kensington. But this time it was worse, for then at least I had Lehzen; now I could not turn to her for support, because she was the cause I was fighting for. Out of old habit, I turned to Stockmar as mediator. I sent him a note, asking him to tell Lehzen that something had happened to upset me and that I could not see her for a few days: I knew if I saw her she would have it out of me, and not for anything would I tell her what had happened between Albert and me. I am loyal, you see, even when most wounded.

I knew every hand was against my old friend. The men who ruled my life were her enemies: Albert, Anson and Stockmar. Mamma, even had I wished to confide in her at that time, regarded Lehzen with loathing as the person who had made me hate her. Lord M., who always understood, was no longer with me, and I could never have confided in Peel; who, besides, would certainly have taken Albert's part against Lehzen. I had long known that no-one liked my old governess except me; but I was bewildered and hurt by the eagerness of everyone to take her away from me. If I loved her, that should surely have been reason enough to leave her alone.

The next day I felt so forlorn and bewildered, as though I had had a dreadful dream; I could not stop crying, and crying gave me a headache and made me feel sick. Albert was still angry, and punished me with a cold formality of manner as though I were a stranger. He would not speak to me except of necessity; and when he looked at me, his eyes went straight through me. I was desperate for reconciliation, but he had slept in his dressing-room last night, and that meant I had no way of reaching him. Bed was the one place all quarrels could be resolved; and to be banished from sharing it with him was desolating.

If emotion could not reach him, I thought, I must try to sway him by his own system of ratiocination. He had to go out that morning to open the new Stock Exchange, and when he was gone I rushed to my desk and penned a sad little note to Stockmar, begging

214

him to go between us and pacify Albert. 'He seems so very angry still. I am not. If only you will impress upon him the importance of speaking up when he sees anything amiss, I will try to improve it. But he must listen to me, and believe what I say, and not credit stories which help to make trifles seem like serious affairs. As to the thoughtless words of yesterday, I forgive them; they were said in grief and anger and vexation.'

Stockmar, at least, was obliged to answer me! The Prince had been writing to him, he said (I guessed he would – it was the Coburg way to resort to pen and paper in times of vexation, and Stockmar was Albert's mentor); he knew about the quarrel, but he had not written to me before because he wanted to be sure all tempers had cooled and everyone was on an even keel again. The quarrel between us had shocked him dreadfully. He could only undertake to try and help us if such violent emotions were kept in check in future; indeed, if there were more such scenes, he would not be able to remain at Court.

This stern warning was the covering letter to the two Albert had written to him, which he enclosed for me to read. They were a dreadful shock to me. The first was a long tirade of hatred of Lehzen, and the words seemed to sear the page with their anger. Lehzen was crazy, jealous, power-mad, an intriguer, self-seeking – and so on, and so on.

> All the disagreeableness I suffer comes from one person, and that is precisely the person Victoria chooses for her friend and confidante. She tells her everything, discusses everything with her, accepts her opinion as though it came from the oracle. Up to now I have suffered in patience, and will go on doing so for love of Victoria, if she wishes; but there can be no improvement until she sees Lehzen as she is. I declare to you as my and Victoria's true friend that I will sacrifice my own comfort, my life's happiness to Victoria in silence, even if she continues in her error. But the welfare of my children and Victoria's as sovereign are too sacred for me not to die fighting rather than yield them as prey to Lehzen. It seems like a curse on our heads that everyone in the world sees the truth, and only Victoria regards the object of her infatuation as an angel and the world as suspicious, slanderous, envious . . .

But it wasn't true, none of it was true! It was like seeing a familiar face in a distorting mirror, something comfortable and everyday made twisted and frightening and evil. How could he hate Lehzen so much?

215

What had she ever done to him? And how could he trust me so little? There was arrogance there, too, which stiffened me for a moment in anger; but only for a moment, for I turned to the second letter, and there had the glass held up to my own reflection.

> You ask me why I have not spoken out before now, why I let things go on until they reach this pass. But Victoria is too hasty and passionate for me to be able to speak of my difficulties. She will not hear me out but overwhelms me with reproaches of suspiciousness, want of trust, ambition, envy and so on. There are therefore two ways open for me: either to keep silence and go away, in which case I am like a schoolboy who has had a dressing down from his mother and goes away subdued; or I can meet her violence with even more violence of my own, in which case we have scenes (like that of the 16th) which I hate, because I am so sorry for Victoria afterwards in her misery; and besides which it undermines the peace of the home.

Oh, my temper, my awful temper! Here I knew I was at fault. But I had had provocation! It had built up over the past year, bringing me at last to a pitch of misery; for when I had discovered, back in March, that I was with child again, I was sunk in despair. I was only twenty-one, I had been married but a year, and already I was pregnant for the second time. Was this what my life was to consist of, this endless round of childbearing, until I was worn out with it? I had been so happy to say goodbye to Mrs Lilly and get back to normal, so delighted to resume the interrupted embraces of my beloved husband – and it was all to do again! Albert had not helped by being so thoroughly besotted with Pussy, and so pleased at the thought of a second episode of fatherhood: to him it was a natural state of affairs that his wife should bring forth his children, and he had no objection at all as to numbers. He was a natural patriarch, and though he loved me, and tried to sympathise with my objections, it was only intellectual; in his heart and his bowels he was *glad* I was pregnant. No matter what he said, I knew really how he felt, and I blamed him bitterly and unreasonably for my condition.

It had been a bad, wretched year. I was unwell from the beginning of the pregnancy, easily tired, my emotions perpetually in a ferment, suffering from bouts of depression and misery so intense as to be frightening. Albert seemed strange to me, a stranger, out of reach, out of sympathy, even hostile. Though he did not mention it, of course, he was afraid for my reason. My grandfather, George III, had

216

died mad; my temper was so wild and my fury so ungoverned that he was afraid I had inherited that taint, and he watched me like a cat at a mousehole, while he did everything he could to keep me calm. I do not blame him now – I can see that he had no choice – but it was just the wrong thing to do. I am not out-of-the-ordinary intelligent, but I am very quick to sense things; I perceived his guarded watchfulness and interpreted it as coolness and indifference to my state. Why, he did not even love me enough to quarrel with me!

When I was so desperately miserable, he seemed so calm and distant that I wanted to shake him off his cool, airy mountain-top and make him come down to the hot and dusty place where I was and share my suffering. I wanted the satisfaction of a violent quarrel, followed by tears, hugs and kisses – thunder and lightning, followed by cool, healing rain. I felt separate from him, and I wanted to be close. But his temper was not like mine, and when I raged he only withdrew; when I grew heated, he grew cooler. When I hurled abuse at him, he quietly left the room; and when I longed for his arms around me, and passionate kisses to stop my mouth, he sent me unemotional, neatly written notes showing how I had been at fault.

Now I ask you, who was the more cruel to whom?

No, no, I was at fault, I own it completely! My poor Albert was simply not made by nature to storm as I stormed. As I read that second note, I saw the situation for a moment as though through his eyes, saw myself in one of my rages cutting off his measured sentences, lashing out at him with whatever words came to mind. For that instant I felt how helpless he must feel, afraid to provoke me more, yet too proud to let me win on what he thought were unfair terms. We were both proud, and that was the fact of the matter; but I would show him I could also be generous and yielding. I swallowed my hurt and wrote a letter for Stockmar to give to Albert, taking pains to set it out rationally and coolly, playing the game according to their rules, humbling myself, though I was the Queen, for the sake of the great love I bore him.

Albert must tell me what he dislikes and I will try to remedy it, but he must also promise to listen to me and believe me when I tell him the truth. Lehzen was perhaps my confidante before my marriage, but she has not been since. Everyone acknowledges her past services to me, and my only wish is that she should have a quiet home in my house and see me sometimes. Albert surely cannot object to that? I assure you upon my honour that I see her very seldom now and only for a few minutes – Albert often and often thinks I see her when I don't. And I only ask her questions about my papers, and my *toilette* for which she is of the greatest use to me – nothing else. I never speak to her about what is decided for the Nursery, and I never go to her to complain, which I fear Albert suspects I do – no, never!

The second thing is my being so passionate when spoken to; I fear this is irremediable as yet, but I hope in time it will be got over. There is often an irritability in me (like last Sunday) which makes me say cross and odious things which I don't mean and which I fear hurt Albert, but which he should not believe. I will strive to conquer it, though I knew before I married this would be a trouble, for the two years and a half when I was so completely my own mistress made it difficult for me to bend to another's will. But I trust I shall be able to conquer it. Our position is very different, though, from any other married couple's: Albert is in my house and not I in his. But I am ready to submit to his wishes as I love him so dearly. His position is difficult, Heaven knows, and we must do everything we can to make it easier.

So I waited for the knock on the door, for the open, smiling face, the proffered hands, the forgiveness and kisses; but there was none. I was still left outside, in exile; and back from Stockmar came the ultimatum – Lehzen must go. Albert would forgive me and take me back into favour, but only if Lehzen left my service, and left the Palace.

I saw how it was. Albert's rage had gone beyond governing, and he was so little in the habit of losing his temper that having lost it, he could not easily find it again. I had humbled myself, offered an olive branch, and I had been snubbed. His pride would not bend even a little to accommodate mine. All the faults were to be mine, and he was not to be in the least to blame for any friction there had been in the house, or between us.

The tears rushed up my throat as I realised all this, and a feeling of sick misery swept over me. I felt so desperately alone that I thought I should die of it. I had chosen this man, had given him my whole heart, had borne two children to him, but it was not enough; where I had given my love completely, he did so only conditionally. He wanted my capitulation, complete and utter. I understood instinctively, without words, what was at the heart of this, and it was not really to do with Lehzen. I was the Queen of England, and I had not yielded that citadel to him: he had the woman, but the Queen was not his, and his pride could not bear it. If I wished him to stay with me, love me, support me, hold me through the dark hours as before and fill me with his warmth and life, I must humble myself before him. I must share my prerogative with him, ask his advice and take it, consult him in everything, give him the keys to my Boxes, to my Household – to my whole life, in fact, to everything. Otherwise he would withdraw into his citadel, and I would die of cold outside.

When my tears had subsided I lay on the couch, face down, his letter in my hand trailing over the side. I rested my wet face on my folded arm, and felt my tears slowly cool and dry on my cheeks, and I considered the alternatives. I was a proud person, and I was Queen of England, and those two things were tightly bound up with each other. I was the anointed of God, and I had made solemn vows which I could not break. It was no small thing he wanted, but something immensely important and greater than myself; it was something that was not my gift.

But the alternative was no alternative. I loved him so much, and I knew I could never bear the pain of losing him. To live with him year after year and never have him – never to know again the bliss of that particular smile, that look of absolute love which he gave me and me alone, never to share that sweet, intimate intercourse of unfettered trust – no, that would be impossible, quite simply impossible!

But how could I ever yield him enough to satisfy him, without breaking something essential in myself? Would he not go on demanding further sacrifice until I was no more a person? And if I was not true to myself, I would not be able to love him.

Besides, he had no right to demand such sacrifices from me. I could not give him what was not mine to give, and he must acknowledge it. But I knew he would not, and that it was the end. Wearily, miserably, I got up; I washed my face, tidied my hair, straightened my gown; and looked at myself for an instant in the glass, saw myself pale and shadowed about the eyes, floating in the twilight like a severed head. *It is the end of everything*, I thought. I walked slowly, as though to my execution, along the corridor, paused outside the door of his dressing-room, then raised my hand and rapped upon it. The hollow sounds were like sods of earth falling on a coffin.

'Who is it?' I heard his voice from inside.

'It is the Queen,' I said, and opened the door. He was at his desk, his little student's lamp with the green shade throwing a pool of light on to the sheet of paper before him. A pen was in his hand, but the paper was blank, and something in the way he was sitting told me he had been staring at that blank page a long time. I looked at him, at the weary stoop of his shoulders; at the soft, shiny hair already – yes, it was true! – receding from his brow and growing a little thin on the top. I looked at his profile, the lovely straight nose I so admired, the mouth, drooping a little with unhappiness, the smooth plane of the cheek and the glitter of the fine whiskers, like thin copper wires, the neat convolutions of his ear. But more than that, I looked at him, the being of whom this was the outward shell, and I discovered something wonderful and important, so important I wanted to cry out with it: that it is perfectly possible to love someone absolutely and unquestionably and consumingly, even though you disagree with them about something fundamental, even though you might be fighting with them for your very life. I loved Albert, and nothing could change that, even if we fought from that moment until the day we died; even if I disagreed with everything he ever said or did, I would still love him unquenchably.

And realising that, I found myself full of happiness and relief. 'Albert!' I said.

He looked up, and I saw in his unsmiling face not anger or stern sorrow or determination, as I might have expected, but apprehension. His eyes were full of the fear of loss; he had made his stand, and did not in the least know what I would do, or how he would cope with my decision. But he was my own darling, still my beloved Albert, always, always! Why did he not know that? How could he doubt his Victoria? And I saw also my own folly. He wanted me to yield, and yield I must, for he was at the end of his endurance, and he could not get back from the far place he had taken himself to. My pride must give way to his, not because that was just, or right, or proper, but *because I could do it*, and he could not. Nothing I might do to make him lord and master, king of the house and king of my life, could diminish me or touch the inner sureness of myself; but he had no such sureness. I must give him everything, hold nothing back, let him see he had me completely; and as to my vows before God – well, I would find some way to keep those, and keep my husband too. There was nothing I could not do. I was strong – strong enough to lose, and still to win.

'Who is it?' he said again. Foolish question! But no, I understood him.

'It is your wife,' I said. I saw the skin around his eyes relax a little, but he was still wary. 'I came to say, Lehzen shall go,' I said.

'You will dismiss her?'

'If it's what you want. I don't care about her. I only care about you.' I waited for the smile, the capitulation, the open arms, but he only went on looking at me. Was it still not enough? Did he still not believe that he had won? Impulsively I held out my hands to him, and said the words which for him, I realised at last, would mark the final citadel taken. 'I'm sorry. Please forgive me.'

'Oh, my love!' he said. It broke from him like water breaching a dam. He stood up, thrusting back his chair violently, crossed the two steps between us, and took me in his arms. Oh, the bliss of being there again! I pressed myself to him, to the familiar, beloved shape, felt his strong arms tighten round me. 'Oh, Victoria, say you love me!'

'I love you, Albert! Always, always. I shall love you for ever.'

I felt him shudder with relief. 'I love you too. Dearest little one, I love you so much!' He hugged me convulsively; and then I turned my face up to him, and we were kissing, kissing as though we should never stop. Everything is all right, I thought. I am home again. All is well.

We did not talk much on that evening of reconciliation: there was a great deal of kissing and hugging and not a few tears, and then we retired of one mind early to bed, where there was a glorious resumption of our married intercourse. If the awfulness of that quarrel had any good side to it, it was in the intensity of emotion we both felt in each other's arms that night. Whatever it had cost me, I was repaid, for in a sort of agony he yielded to me as much and more than I had yielded to him. It seemed to tear at the roots of his spirit, that strange release which he both desired and feared; and afterwards he was so vulnerable, as if his very soul lay naked and helpless against my breast, so that even a wrongly drawn breath might have mortally wounded him. But I had only tenderness for him. I held my lover close to me as a mother cradles an infant; and my heart sang with triumph, for if I could not live without him, far, far less could he live without me.

The next day we had our talking. Lehzen, a little to my surprise, was not mentioned: it seemed that having won that point he did not find it necessary to press it. What Albert wanted to talk about was his own position.

'From the beginning you have kept me out of affairs – Household and State – and it has been the most severe trial to me. I must *do* something, Victoria,' he said, clenching his hands with the urgency of it. 'I can't be nothing.'

'Well, tell me what you want, and you shall have it,' I said soothingly. I thought he would name specific tasks, positions, powers – but his eyes were full of a visionary light, and he was surveying a wider landscape.

'I want to bring Enlightenment to this country, as we have it in Germany. I want to bring England into the nineteenth century.'

'Are we not in the nineteenth century?'

'No! By no means!' he said eagerly. 'We are trapped in the cobwebs of the eighteenth century, and the Court and the Government are the worst examples of what is wrong. Oh, I hate what I see – corruption, jobbery, privilege! Great men occupy positions of responsibility and deputise the duties to a lesser man, who pays an even lesser man, and so on – until you come to some wretched, shabby underling who needs the money, and he does the job, without care or skill. So nothing gets done properly – and meanwhile at every stage someone is making a corrupt fortune by exploiting his position.'

'Well,' I said fairly, 'I suppose there is some truth in that. But what would you do?'

'Sweep away all the Spanish practices. Scour every department clean of jobbery. Above all, make sure the right men come to the fore. Everything in England works on the coffee-house system – friends recommend friends, and those who have none don't get on.'

'But surely if they have no friends, there must be a reason,' I said, 'and they ought not to get on.'

'Oh, Victoria, how naïve you can be! Do you think being likeable makes a man worthy?'

'Yes,' I said firmly. 'For if I don't like someone, he always turns out to be bad and untrustworthy.'

'But if you like someone because he is amusing and charming, it does not necessarily mean he is the right man for a position of responsibility,' Albert said. I tightened my lips, knowing we had come to Lord M., and not wishing a new quarrel to break out. Albert went on, 'I want to see a system which advances men of serious purpose and philosophical bent – not those who ride best to hounds, or who have the nicest arrangement of neckcloth. When I see the business of the country carried on in the clubs of St James's, by languid cynics who smoke and drink and keep mistresses, who would far rather be thought witty than virtuous, it makes me so angry!'

'But you don't understand,' I cried. 'Men like – like our top people – they like to seem nonchalant, but they really do care about things, and take their duties seriously. They don't think it good form to appear to, that's all. Ever since Bloody Mary we distrust enthusiasm. In England a man must appear to be lounging when he is working his hardest; he must speak wittily and lightly of what he cares for most profoundly.'

Albert shook his head gravely. 'I can't approve of that. It is wrong to talk lightly of serious subjects, to joke about what is good, to appear to condone what is evil.'

I remembered Lord M. saying to me that sinners were much more amusing company than saints, and shook the memory away. Being amusing would not seem a virtue to Albert at this moment. 'But that's the English way,' I said, rather apologetically.

'Then we must change it,' he said firmly. 'We must introduce the German way. In Coburg we do not admire levity. Punctuality, diligence, economy, humility: those are the qualities we expect a great man to display; and above all, gravity. *Il faut être sérieux*, my love! Those who are honoured with the highest positions in the land must be men of high intellect, serious purpose, and scrupulous personal morality. Then we shall see progress!'

'Well, yes,' I said doubtfully, 'but I do think on the whole we have such men in the Government, though it may sometimes appear—'

But he was in full flow, his blue eyes blazing with enthusiasm. 'Yes, and there is another thing! There is too much pragmatism in government here – doing what seems practicable, just because it works. That is not the proper way to run a country! You must have moral direction. First your ministers decide the principles and goals, then your philosophers devise a system to bring it into being.'

I was beginning to feel lost. 'But our system has always worked well enough here,' I said feebly.

'*Laissez-faire* is not a system! To avoid trying to change something because it will be difficult is not government but indolence! Everything is capable of improvement – if we don't believe that, we have no business being here on earth. We must strive to improve human nature, not wallow in its imperfections and tell ourselves nothing can be done about them. Men must be made better than they are – and we at the top must set the example. You and I, Victoria, have the greatest opportunity and the greatest responsibility of all! The monarchy must be seen above all to be the guardian of morality, the personification of justice, virtue and honour!'

Well, it certainly had not been that for some time past, I acknowledged to myself. I noticed that for some time Albert had been speaking in German, slipping into it naturally as his words became more inspirational. And it was a stirring vision he presented! I saw him in shining armour, holding aloft a bright sword, marching into battle against the forces of evil. How I loved him! How beautiful he looked! But it was a stern vision, too, and the practical part of me suspected that it might be rather uncomfortable for a permanency.

'You are right, I know you are,' I said, 'but is there to be no laughter in your brave, new world? No amusement or pleasure?'

The tension slid out of his face and he smiled at me in that tender, sweet way that ravished my heart. 'Of course there is, foolish little one! Innocent laughter, homely amusements, and virtuous pleasure – much the best sort! And we shall gather around us all the best people, the greatest thinkers, poets, artists, musicians; we shall have intellectual, improving conversation at our dinner table instead of trivial gossip.'

(This part of the programme rather daunted me, for although I do not approve of harmful gossip, I do love to 'chat'. I am naturally interested in every detail of the lives of people about me, and like nothing better than to discuss their houses, children, daily routines, ailments and pleasures with them. But Albert had no interest in the 'small change' of people's lives. Trivial talk – what was not intellectual or improving – bored him, and many a time I have seen his eyes glaze in the drawing-room, or seen his nostrils stretch and whiten as he conceals a closed-mouth yawn.)

He was continuing. 'We shall patronise the arts, gather the treasures of the world about us, promote philanthropists, scientists, explorers. England will lead the world in everything that is good and fine, everything that advances mankind in purity and wisdom – and we shall lead England. *You* will lead England!'

His enthusiasm was intoxicating. I clasped my hands together and cried, 'Oh, yes! Yes! But it will be all your doing! Your name will resound throughout the world; there will be statues raised to you in every city!'

'I want no statues,' he said gravely. 'I want only your love and trust.'

'I do love you!'

'And trust me?' he said gently. 'Will you share everything with me?'

I was brought up short; but I answered steadily and promptly enough. 'Everything,' I said. 'Did I not tell you so last night?'

'You did not speak the words,' he said, and as I continued to gaze levelly at him, he smiled and said, 'Yes, yes, you did. I must not be less generous than you have shown yourself. I don't deserve you, Victoria. You are so open and generous and warm and loving, and I am always so suspicious.'

'But not of me?'

'No, not of you. Never again of you,' he said, and he lifted both my hands to his lips and kissed them almost reverently. '*Hertzliebste!*'

2nd June 1900

IT WAS not long after our great reconciliation and my decision to submit that we celebrated the Boy's Christening. Being so much in love with Albert, I naturally hoped our son would resemble his father in every particular, and I did my best for him from the beginning by naming him Albert for his father, and Edward for mine. Albert had no objections, but Lord M., when I told him, asked if the names should not be the other way round. 'Albert is not an English name,' he said. 'I don't think the people will like it.'

I thought 'King Albert' had a wonderful ring to it. If Parliament would not allow me to make my Albert king, at least I could ensure that the Throne went to an Albert after me. I did not say this to Lord M., however, but simply pointed out firmly, 'It is an old Saxon name.'

He smiled gently. 'But it has rather fallen out of use since Saxon times. Now Edward is a sound English name, much in use, and has a high degree of popularity attached to it from good associations from the past.'

'He is to be Albert Edward,' I said immovably. 'And he will be like his angelic father in every respect, in both body and mind. And from now on,' I added, to make sure he understood how serious I was about it, 'I shall insist that every one of my male descendants bears the name Albert, to show that a new dynasty began in 1840, when the Prince and I were joined in wedded bliss.'

(When Georgie and May's first boy was born, I naturally wanted him to be called Albert, as he will one day be King of England. They, however, vexed and disappointed me by insisting they wanted the boy christened Edward. What was worse, they tried to wheedle me by saying that they were calling him after Georgie's brother, poor Eddy, who they know I was very fond of. I pointed out with some triumph that of course Eddy's name was not Edward at all, but Albert Victor – Eddy was only his pet-name. I thought that would be the end of the matter; but they went ahead and christened the boy Edward anyway – which proved to me that bringing Eddy into it was nothing but a subterfuge. I dislike that sort of dishonesty very much. I'm afraid it must have been May's influence, for though she is a nice, good girl in general, there is occasionally just a little commonness about the cast of her mind, a carelessness in some matters, which comes from her upbringing, I suppose. And as it happens, they call the boy David anyway, so they might just as well have christened him Albert in the first place and saved all the unpleasantness.)

Lord M. tried one last protest. 'But how will you manage with two Alberts in the family?'

'The boy will be called Bertie,' I said simply.

Royal babies had always been baptized privately, but after all the uncertainty over the Succession for so many years past, it was decided to have a public Christening for the boy, in St George's Chapel, Windsor. It was to be a grand affair, and the organist composed a special anthem for the occasion and submitted it for our approval. Albert read it through and pronounced it tedious.

'We can hardly ask someone else to write one,' I said. 'It would be such an insult when he has composed it specially – and on his own organ.'

'Then we shall have no anthem at all,' Albert decided. 'No-one likes them anyway, and no-one remembers them a week later. If we end the service with an anthem, we shall all go out criticizing the music and feeling bad.'

It was so true, I laughed. 'Well, what then?'

'We should end with everyone singing. Something devotional, but something we can all join in.' He frowned a moment, and then, 'Yes, of course! The Hallelujah Chorus: we can all join in that, with all our hearts.'

I opened my mouth to protest, for I have never liked Handel's music, and all my life I seem to have been haunted at every occasion of a remotely celebratory nature by that wretched *Hallelujah! Hallelujah!* business. But then I remembered I was now a submissive wife, and closed my mouth again. In the event it worked very well, and we were praised for the innovation (and as it was played while we walked out, I did not have to hear much of it). As on so many occasions, I discovered that Albert was right after all. The Christening went off very well, the baby behaved perfectly, and the Dean of Windsor made it memorable for me by solemnly congratulating the Queen for 'saving the country from the incredible curse of a female succession'. I had the misfortune to catch Albert's eye at that moment and had to bite my cheeks to stop myself from bursting out laughing.

It was a tremendous occasion, with well over six thousand people travelling up from London for it. The Great Western Railway ran trains every half hour, and had to fit out two new waiting-rooms at

Slough Station for the accommodation of distinguished persons, with crimson carpet, marble fireplaces, and vast gilt-framed looking-glasses. I had never used the railway at that time – it was not until June of that year that I ventured, very nervously, for the first time upon it; and then I could not conceive how anyone could prefer the roads. When I and Albert travelled by chaise, we were forced to gallop along as fast as possible to avoid being surrounded by inquisitive horsemen and gig-drivers, which jolted me quite frightfully and frequently resulted in the most interesting bruises. Besides that, there was the inconvenience of the dust; and every time we did stop, we were besieged at once by crowds all wanting to stare and poke their heads in at the windows.

But the railway train was utter, utter bliss – so fast and so smooth, and giving us absolute privacy, so that it was like being transported along in one's own drawing-room. I adored the speed, and would have liked to go 'flat out' as they called it, but Albert was made very nervous by the countryside whipping by – 'Not zo fast please, Mr Conductor!' he muttered once, and obliged me to send a message forward to slow down – so afterwards I made it a rule that the Royal Train should never go at more than forty miles per hour. Even so, it was four times the speed of a carriage on the road, and I believe that the railways, along with photography, were the best and most universally beneficial of the many inventions of this century.

The Duke, I should say, hated the very idea of railway trains, ever since the horrid accident he had witnessed at the opening of the Liverpool and Manchester Railway in 1830, when William Huskisson had been run over and killed by a locomotive engine. The Duke absolutely refused to travel by train until, accompanying me on a journey in August 1843, he could not help himself and was forced despairingly to climb up into a railway carriage again. I must say he saw immediately the advantages he had been forgoing, and was quite reconciled to the mode of transport from then on.

But to go back to the Christening, *The Times* complained the next day that the guests had been almost all German, which was aimed at Albert's choice of the King of Prussia for a godfather. (Albert felt that Prussia was a natural ally for England, and longed to see a united Germany under Prussia's leadership, with Pussy on the throne. The King of Prussia's marriage was childless, and his brother, the Crown Prince, had a son who was only ten years older than Pussy, so it was not beyond the realms of possibility.)

After the Christening, there came the reorganisation of the Nursery. Mrs Southey was not proving satisfactory: she seemed unhappy in her work, could not keep order amongst the servants under her, and was frequently absenting herself, so that the children were left in the care of lower people for long periods. I asked Lord M.'s advice, and he suggested that we should appoint a lady of rank as Governess, not just as a figurehead, but genuinely to take charge.

'At all costs let her be an aristocrat,' he wrote to me. 'Women of the middle rank have frequently little education and less sense. They are possessed by strong prejudices, and they are more liable to have their heads turned by their elevation. And they always seem to have innumerable low connections who press them for their interest at Court and force themselves upon your notice, putting you at the inconvenience of driving them off and being rude to them.'

Albert agreed (nobly, since it came from Lord M.) that this was sound advice, and our choice fell upon Lady Lyttleton, who had been one of my Ladies of the Bedchamber since 1838. She was a Spencer by birth, a Whig lady of the old school, tolerant, liberal, well educated, and devoted to children (she had five of her own whom she had been left to bring up alone after the death of her husband in 1837). She remained as Governess until she retired in 1851, and the children all became devoted to her and called her 'Laddle'. She said from the beginning that she did not believe in punishments for small children – 'One is never sure that they are fully understood by the children as the consequences of their naughtiness' – but by some means or other she soon got Pussy to mind her, and after that there could be no difficulty with the others when they came along. Under her influence there was a little more of common sense and a little less of theory brought into nursery practice, and Pussy soon threw off her troubles and began to thrive as before, becoming, in Laddle's own words, 'a fine, fat, fair, royal-looking baby, and too *absurdly* like the Queen'.

When I do something, I like to do it thoroughly. If Albert wanted a meek and submissive little *Hausfrau* in the German style, I decided, he should have it – and we'd see how he liked it! Oh yes, I'm afraid there was a little spirit of perversity in me, which, disagreeing with his view of things, wanted to give him so much of it that it made him sick! I would be clinging and frail and helpless, have no opinion of my own, show him that I was incapable of so much as choosing a bonnet without his guidance; and when the full weight of my dependence finally broke his arm, I would tell him so!

But that was only one small and very reprehensible corner of my mind. There was a great deal of me that wanted a man to guide and support me – as my dependence on Lord M. had shown. I had lost my father in earliest childhood, and had searched ever since for someone to replace him, someone wise and strong to care for me and keep me safe. Yielding to Albert of necessity, and somewhat against my wishes, expecting to dislike it, I found it in the end almost entirely delightful.

The yielding did not come all at once, of course. There were still quarrels, disagreements and hurt feelings; I could not change my spots in one day – and some spots, I have to admit, never completely disappeared. But over the years I became a better person for submitting – more rational, better informed, and above all happier. To have someone else make the decisions and take the responsibility has a wonderfully liberating effect on the spirit, and if I was obliged to change myself, it was almost always for the better. For his part, Albert, finding himself at last in what he felt to be his natural and rightful position of authority repaid me with devotion, tenderness, and a warmth of perfect companionship which I guess few people are lucky enough to experience in their lives. I found a deep and quiet content in the safe fortress of his care which made me look back in amazement at the Victoria who had so bitterly refused to enter it.

But the most obvious immediate change in my life was that, once I had given Albert the keys to my Boxes, he became in fact, though never in name, my Private Secretary. It was a decision I never regretted, and my deep-seated fear that my power would be usurped was shown to have been completely foolish and groundless. No-one could have been better served by any secretary than I was by Albert, who read State papers for me, prepared synopses, marked my reading, wrote drafts of my official statements and letters, recorded important conversations, researched the backgrounds of people and situations in order to advise me, and kept all the resultant papers in meticulous and catalogued order. It was a monumental task, and grew greater year by year as ever more State departments looked to him as my right hand.

I came to rely more and more on him in matters of government as in domestic things; and burdened as I was by almost continual pregnancy and childbirth, I cannot see how I could possibly have managed without him. Indeed, if he had not been there to share the work with me, the exercise of my power must have suffered, and perhaps fallen into other hands, hands from which I would have been puzzled to wrest it later. Far from usurping my prerogative, Albert preserved it; and he did it not for himself or his own glory – for there was no glory in it for him – but solely and unselfishly for me and for the country. Anson had spoken truly. Of all the princes in Europe I might have married, I do not believe there was another such as him – hardworking, dedicated, and utterly selfless. Is it any wonder that I raged sometimes that the country he served so tirelessly did not appreciate him? Or that since he has left us, I have strived to raise his monument in every corner of the land?

As to the overt cause of the quarrel, Lehzen did not actually leave my service until September. The date of her retirement was agreed between her and Albert without consulting me (which I suppose he felt was a kindness) and I was told about it in July as a *fait accompli*. My dear Lehzen behaved in the matter of her leaving just as she had in everything else – unselfishly, considering only my welfare. She gradually handed over her duties to her successors, and finally slipped away quietly, early in the morning of the 30th of September, in order to spare me the ordeal of a formal goodbye. She retired to Hanover to live with her sister, and I gave her a new carriage and a pension of £800 a year to make her comfortable. Sadly her sister died not long afterwards, and my poor old governess lived alone for the rest of her long life. I wrote to her once a month, but only saw her on two more occasions, though she lived another twenty-eight years. She died in 1870, within a month of her eighty-sixth birthday, and they say the last word on her lips was my name. As I sit here, almost as old myself, and surrounded by children and grandchildren, I contemplate the loneliness of her old age with enormous pity and not a little sense of guilt.

On the morning after her departure I woke having dreamed that she had come back to say goodbye to me, and the realisation of the truth was very painful. But Albert was there beside me, to take me into his arms, to listen to my trouble and soothe it away with reason and kisses. It was the beginning of a new era. Now all the old influences on me had gone, the stormy seas were negotiated, and I had sailed into a safe haven. From now on there would be only one influence, and that both benign and unfailing: my beloved husband and friend. But when a person makes another creature completely dependent on them, be it child, spouse or animal, it behoves them to make sure they will always be there. Albert brought me to a state where I could do nothing without him, and then most cruelly abandoned me to struggle through an endless desert of years alone. But of course neither of us thought of that then. We were only twenty-three years old, and when you are young, you naturally assume that you are immortal, and that everything will go on just the same for ever.

Thirteen

5th June 1900, at Balmoral

I HAVE been obliged to telegraph to Salisbury to warn him against withdrawing our troops too soon from South Africa. It is natural for the lower classes to believe, on the strength of our recent successes, that the war is all but over, but it is my experience that too much enthusiasm at moments like this makes us relax our guard, and then fresh troubles arise and more troops have to be sent. I remember how it was in the Crimea! But Salisbury is a good man, and will listen to me. He was the first of my Prime Ministers to be younger than me (in fact he was a page at my Coronation, as I remember!), but when he came in in the year 'eighty-five I was so relieved to be rid of Gladstone I was like a child let out of school! He – Salisbury – has now been my longest-serving Prime Minister, and apart from the subject of ecclesiastical patronage, we agree so well on everything that it has been a most tranquil period of my life – in politics, that is.

The weather has been atrocious since the 2nd, and I have felt out of sorts, disliking the curtailment of my carriage exercise and missing having Baby about me. Also Georgie feels obliged to leave on Saturday, for reasons that seem wholly inadequate to me; I dislike having people go away. May and the children stay on, however. The new baby thrives, but little David has been fretful, and we only just got to the bottom of it yesterday. It seems that when Henry was born, Georgie told David that his little brother had 'flown in through the window' and that they had 'cut off his wings so that he couldn't fly away again'. It seems that since then, the boy has lived in fear of stumbling across the horrid, bloody things, and has been having nightmares about finding them under his pillow or in his bed. Really, as I told Georgie, I can't approve of lying to children like that. He meant no harm, but it is better if they are too young to understand something that they be told just that – that they are too young. David has an over-active imagination which hardly needs feeding with horrors!

I have always had a good imagination, and in writing, these last few months, about my early life, I have been able to make myself *feel* what it was like to be young and untried and ignorant, and write accordingly. But now I come to write about my children, and it is

231

rather different. For one thing, one changes so much oneself through their lifetimes, that to pick out the way one felt about them at any particular time would not be to give a true picture. Perhaps there is no true picture of motherhood. The odd thing about having children is that they don't really grow up. My children as they are today seem to me to be quite separate individuals from the goggling, squalling babies they began as, and yet both exist together in my mind. It is as if a new child comes into being at each intermediate stage of growth – so that on that reckoning I have had not nine children but something like sixty-three.

Children are supposed to be a blessing, and so they are of course in many ways; but they diminish one. Little pieces of one's clay are pulled away and rolled into new shapes, and though one sees a likeness here and a likeness there, the newness is always greater than the similarity. Suddenly you find that there is a full-grown stranger in the room, and you have grown old. They take away your young, strong life in the service of their own, and when they hand it back and go off independent at last, you find it shrunken, damaged and ill-fitting, all the nice shiny youthfulness gone.

Probably it is different for a man. Albert used to talk a great deal about the children perpetuating our love, being living monuments to our wonderful union, the eternal proof to future generations that he and I had loved, and so on. Well, he always had the wider vision. Mentally he lived on a mountain-top with great vistas spread all around him. I seemed always to be toiling up the slope behind him, carrying the picnic basket and the rugs, and stubbing my toes on the rocks in the path!

I had nine children in seventeen years – seven of them born in the first ten years – and though I loved them and cared for them, and often had great pleasure from them, they kept me from Albert, and they had from him some of the love that should have been mine. Often I resented that. I expect I would have felt quite differently if Albert had lived, if I had been allowed to enjoy long years of quiet intimacy with him after the children were grown up. I think that I could watch him now playing with his grandchildren and feel nothing but pleasure, and spare them his attention and smiles and kisses without jealousy. But Baby was only four years old when he died. All of our life together – oh, so horribly short as it turned out to be! – was taken up with parenthood. There was no time, only that pitiful one month in 1840, for me to be a wife and not a mother.

Would I have had it any other way? Well, there had to be children, of course, given my position; and even if it had not been a necessity,

I think I would not have wanted to deprive Albert of the joys of fatherhood, which evidently meant so much to him. Perhaps if we could have stopped after four, that would have been just right. Vicky, Bertie, Alice and Affie – the Big Four, as we used to call them because they gravitated so naturally together – they would have provided us with the dynastic replacements we needed, without wearing me out and keeping me from my beloved husband.

Oh dear, I ought to strike that out! It sounds as though I don't love my younger children, which is far from the case. And Baby, dear Baby, how could I ever have borne my miserable widowhood without her? She is my constant companion, thoughtful and kind and diligent – no, I could never have done without her! It must stay as it is: I could not part with any one of them. But I shan't strike out that paragraph, for this is meant to be my utterly truthful account, and I shall make sure that no-one will ever read it who can be hurt by it.

The Big Four came tumbling into the world almost on top of each other. The year 1842 turned out to be one of respite for me, and desperately I needed it after the first two pregnancies and the marital storms I had endured. But the new closeness and trust I shared with Albert after our reconciliation, and the help I now allowed him to give me with my public duties, meant that my nerves were much improved by the time I discovered, in the autumn of 'forty-two, that I was pregnant again. I took the news calmly; the pregnancy was straightforward and the birth relatively easy, and our second daughter arrived on the 25th of April 1843. We called her Alice. It was a nice old English name, I told Albert, and he agreed; but I had not forgotten that it was Lord Melbourne's favourite name, the one he had said he would give to a daughter, if he had one. It was, I suppose (though I did not think of it that way at the time), a sort of farewell gift to him, for after Alice's birth our old intimacy was much diminished. I hardly ever saw him, and though I continued to write to him, it was more for his sake than for mine. Albert was everything to me now.

When she was born, we thought Alice would be the beauty of the family. She did not quite fulfil that promise (her face was too long and her eyes just slightly too close together, which gave her a rather horse-like appearance – oh, but a dear, gentle, fine horse!) but she was the child of ours who looked most like Albert, and therefore I thought her beautiful. She grew up to be exceptionally graceful, with a gentle charm and a sweet, silvery voice very like my own. I have such a lovely portrait of her at the time of her wedding, all in white gauze with a black lace shawl and a wreath of roses round her head.

That sweet, sad expression on her face reminded me so much of him. Her eyes and eyebrows were shaped just like his, and she had the same delicate, porcelain skin. Alice had much of Albert's character too: she excelled at music and painting, and had besides what is most unusual in a child, a selflessness, a dedication to others which made her a treasured child and an exemplary wife and mother. (Laddle called her 'an angel in the house'.) She adored her father, and dreaded parting from Papa when it came time to marry, though she loved her Louis of Hesse dearly. But in the event, it was Papa who left her, and her marriage took place just a few months after his death. She was with him all through his last illness, and devoted the rest of her life to living as she thought he would have wished. She worked herself nearly to death on behalf of her new people, supporting Hessian hospitals, lunatic asylums, orphanages, and pursuing better education and housing for the poor (oh, how like Albert!).

Poor, sweet Alice, gentle Alice, was the first of my children to die, of that awful curse diphtheria. Nursing had been her first love since her father's last illness, and during the Franco-Prussian war she turned her own house into a hospital and dressed wounds and emptied slops with her own hands. So when her children went down with diphtheria she insisted on nursing them herself. She tended them devotedly, but still the youngest, little May, died. Her only son, Ernst, was too ill to be told of his favourite sister's death, and when he asked his mother to give May one of his books to read, she was overcome with pity, covered his poor face with kisses, and took the infection herself. Oh, I still remember the horror of that dreadful, dreadful morning when they handed me the incoherent telegram from Louis at breakfast! 'Poor Mamma, poor me, my happiness gone, dear, dear Alice!' Bertie, weeping brokenly, said, 'It is always the good who are taken.' (There had always been a special tenderness between him and Alice.) Loving her father above all mortals, she died, like him, on the 14th of December, on the seventeenth anniversary of his death. It was too, too awful and mysterious!

To lose a child is a terrible grief, for we are not designed by nature to outlive our children. But there, I have her still in my mind as she was when a baby – quite a different Alice, so different that they cannot be the same person. The baby we used to call 'Fat Alice', or 'Fatima', for she was a complete little barrel – I have sketches of her I made when she was eighteen months old, looking like a square stuffed pillow with a stout little limb sticking out at each corner. She was full of chuckles, Fat Alice, and full of mischief. I firmly believe it was often her who led Vicky into their naughty escapades rather than vice versa – such as the time they found a housemaid black-leading a grate in a remote part of the palace, and daubed the blacking all over the unfortunate girl's face. I marched them down to the kitchens and made them apologize when I found out about it – I would never tolerate unkindness to servants – but by far the worst punishment to them was to witness their papa's disapproval, his sadness at being 'let down' by them.

After Alice I actually managed to go for seven months before falling pregnant again, and Alfred was born on the 6th of August 1844. We had needed a second son, for Albert had long anticipated that his reprobate brother would not produce an heir (not a legitimate one, at any rate), in which case the Dukedom of Coburg would pass to Albert. Self-evidently Bertie could not go to Coburg, so Albert would need a second son on whom to devolve the dukedom. Affie was a very good child, handsome and clever, passionately musical – he taught himself secretly to play the violin and surprised me one day on my birthday by playing me a composition of his own, which was very pretty (though I think Affie thought more of it than anyone – he always had a very good conceit of himself). For as long as any of us could remember, Affie was mad to go to sea, and when he was only fourteen Albert, much against my will, arranged for him to go into the Navy. I was very angry about it at the time, for he was really much too young to leave home; and afterwards he was to all intents and purposes lost to me. I saw him only when he came home on leave, and when he grew older he took to spending his leave as often as possible with Alice at her married home in Darmstadt. He and Alice had always been fond of each other, but I think the main reason he went there was that being away from home had given him a taste for freedom, and he knew I would not approve of the bad habits he had picked up from the other sailors, such as drinking, smoking and consorting with women. There was a scandalous *affaire* with a young woman in Malta in 1862, for instance – but I will not dwell on that. He did not marry until 1874, and then he must needs (as if on purpose to annoy me) pick on a Russian princess, Grand Duchess Marie, daughter of the Tsar (whom he met at Alice's – her mother was a Hessian princess). I have never liked or trusted Russia, but Affie was in love, so I grumbled but did not oppose it. But the Tsar was against the match, behaving as though it were disgraceful for a Grand Duchess to marry the son of the Queen of England! (Marie herself has always given one to understand that marrying poor Affie was a great condescension on her part. However, they settled down together in the end, and I must say she has been a good wife to him, and a good daughter to me, though offending many by her pride and display. It must have been a terrible grief to her to have lost her only son last year in such painful circumstances. He shot himself after a violent quarrel with her, and when she defied the doctor's advice that moving him might be fatal and sent him to the Tyrol to recover, he died a few days later. Well, they say pride goes before a fall, but surely that is too great a price to pay for a little common conceit.)

12th June 1900

IT IS good to remember our little ones when they *were* little ones, and their troubles all unimagined and far in the future. Vicky and Alice were Albert's favourites; he always got on better with his daughters than his sons. Vicky particularly was his pet. We knew from the beginning she would be intelligent, but she surprised even our particularity, growing up so quick and clever (and pretty and charming too) that it seemed as if our very first effort had produced the perfect child. Certainly Albert felt he could not have got one better suited to him if he had ordered it from a shop! Vicky had my ear for languages (and my voice too – everyone said we sounded absurdly alike) and by the time she was three she could speak French and German with fluency. Standing one day on a hilltop, she remembered and quoted a line from a French poem: *Voilà le tableau qui déroule à mes pieds!* which I thought remarkable in a three-year-old. Her grammar was sometimes a little shaky, but she used French with the readiness of one to whom it is not a foreign language. One time when she was in one of her rages I heard her scream at poor Lady Lyttleton, '*N'approchez pas moi, moi ne veux pas vous!*'

She inherited my temper too, you see – indeed all the first three were much given to tantrums and 'roaring' which put poor Laddle, who would not whip them, in a quandary. Pussy, being clever and the firstborn, and thinking quite as well of her own abilities as Papa did, was convinced for many years that it was she who would inherit the Throne, and not Bertie. She told him so many times, and poor dull Bertie, who freely acknowledged her superiority, was perfectly willing to believe it. (He was not disabused until he was twelve years old, and then, when we realised how things lay, it took a great deal to convince him that she had been mistaken. He cried dreadfully about it and wished it need not be, which annoyed his father considerably, for he liked fine, manly little boys who stood up to responsibility.)

Believing herself to be the Heiress, Vicky had a very strong sense of her own importance, and would not let anyone behave towards her with what she considered familiarity; while towards people beneath her station she could sometimes show an unbecoming arrogance. She referred to my younger maids-of-honour as 'these girls', for instance, and even expected my senior ladies-in-waiting to fetch and carry for her. I was quick to stamp on that sort of thing. At one time she refused to call Doctor Brown (who attended the nursery and some of the servants) by his full name – she had heard me call him simply 'Brown' and took to doing the same herself. I rebuked her several times, and told her if she did it again, she would be sent to bed. The very next day she came into the room while I was talking to him and greeted him breezily with 'Good morning, Brown!' and then catching my irate eye the naughty girl curtseyed and said quickly, 'And good night, Brown, for I am going to bed,' and took herself off. I was very angry, but had difficulty all the same in not laughing at Brown's expression of bafflement, for he hadn't the least idea of what was going on!

But it was high spirits with Vicky, not vice, and she had the warmest heart in the world. As soon as she had enough to do to occupy her mind, these little awkwardnesses were smoothed out (though her quick temper remained, along with her argumentativeness). She loved to learn, and devoured mathematics, philosophy, chemistry, history and political economy the way lesser children do stories. She spent all her pocket-money on books, and by the age of ten was better educated than most adults. Albert said she had 'a man's head and a child's heart', and we loved to see newcomers to the palace fall under the spell of her astonishing mind and her sparkling charm – beginning by treating her as a child and ending by falling in love with her. Certainly it was so with Fritz, the son of the Crown Prince of Prussia, whom Albert had picked out from the beginning for her future husband. I was very glad of it, for I would never have forced a child of mine into a marriage without love; I always wanted them to know the same sort of absolute confidence and intimacy that I had with my husband. So my plan has always been to make sure they meet the right people, and leave the final choosing to them, which I think is the right and proper way for a parent to go about these things.

But when we invited the Crown Prince and Princess with their family to London in 1851 for the Great Exhibition, dear Fritz tumbled head-over-heels in love with Vicky, for all that he was twenty and she was only ten. 'You cannot form an idea of what a sweet little thing she was,' he told me many years later. 'Such a childlike simplicity, combined with a woman's intellect. She seemed almost too perfect.' They walked together about the exhibits at the Crystal Palace, and she explained them all to him, engaged him in witty, lively conversation, and flashed her dazzling smiles at him until I think the poor young man had no idea if he was on his head or his heels. He went away prepared to wait for as many years as it took to gain Vicky's hand, and spent the interim in studying politics and the British Constitution in order to make himself more worthy of her.

After their marriage he told her that he had fallen in love with more than just her: he thought England the most enlightened country in the world, Albert the best and wisest man alive, and had been glad and astonished to see what a happy family we were. The Prussian Court and his own family circle was full of acrimony, bickering and intrigue; but Albert and I, he said, were so devoted that it might be supposed we had only just married; while he had never seen children before on such affectionate terms with their parents. (Poor Fritz lived to see his own son Willy turned against him by court faction, taught by his grandparents and Bismarck to despise his father and scorn his mother, and espouse the illiberal, 'blood and iron' policies which were everything gentle Fritz was against.)

13th June 1900

THE WEATHER vastly improved, and everyone's temper with it! I am out in my little hut again, going on with my writing, and with the door and windows open, to enjoy the delicious air. The white rose outside the window is in full bloom, and smells almost too sweet. It makes me want to cry: beauty can affect one so, almost like sorrow. If my darling could only be here to share it with me! 'They are not long, the days of wine and roses' – no, no, I must think of bright, happy things on such a lovely day. I resume my story.

It was always our intention that the children should have a happy childhood.

'Yours, I know, *Liebling*, was unhappy,' Albert said to me one night as we lay in bed together, face to face and holding hands – our 'discussions in the dark', he called them – 'and though I cannot say mine was so, I lost my own mother, and did not enjoy the kind of tender intimacy with my father I would have liked. I should wish our children to grow up frank and unafraid, able to talk to us freely, regarding us as friends rather than gaolers. I want to guide them and mould them, of course – but I also want to play with them and hear them laugh.'

'You will amaze everyone,' I remarked. 'In this country children live apart from their parents, in nurseries tucked away at the top of the house, and only see them on formal occasions. And the boys are sent to boarding-schools, and never see them at all.'

'But that is so wrong!' he cried. 'Who in that case will influence the child? Not his own parents, but the servants who attend him and the hirelings who teach him. As well not have a child at all, as give its shaping over to inferiors!'

'Well, I agree with you,' I said. 'I do not think being shut up and kept silent and ignored makes a person better. Happiness is the best teacher. I want my little ones to laugh and romp, as I was never able to do.'

'You want to laugh and romp with them,' he said teasingly. 'You would have them be the brothers and sisters you never had.'

'*They* will not grow up suspecting their mother of plotting against them,' I said firmly. 'But Albert, there is one aspect of my childhood which I think Mamma got right, and that was the simple, domestic background I had. No hint of the purple, no luxurious surroundings and elaborate dinners – everything as plain and economical as possible. I don't want them to grow up filled with pride and contempt of others. They will be exposed to flattery enough when they get out into the world – let them be humble while they are with us.'

'By all means,' he said easily – for things of the flesh had little weight with him anyway – 'but I think you may have your labour in vain. Our children cannot help knowing they are the sons and daughters of the Queen of England. If they learn not to be above their station, it will be because of what is put into their hearts and heads, not on their table and on their backs.'

But I had my way, and my nursery must have been one of the plainest in the kingdom. Clothes were unadorned and made for wear, and when outgrown were passed on to younger members of the family, or put into mothballs for the grandchildren. And the nursery food was of the boiled beef and boiled mutton, rice pudding and semolina order. (Affie once complained that the hands on board ship had better food than he had at home! And in more recent times Ena, Baby's daughter, has complained that visiting children get meringues and éclairs while they, the resident children, get only plain biscuits. Once when it was her turn to say Grace she folded her hands and said, 'Thank God for my dull dinner!' and was sent away from the table in disgrace and without it.)

But I wanted to be sure that they would not develop luxurious tastes which might run them into debt later in life; and that whatever station in life they were called to, they would be able to survive. I must have forgotten by then how much I had disliked the regimen when I was a child; or if I remembered, thought it would be good for them, as I assumed it had been good for me. But from the other end of my life now I am not so sure it was a good plan. Certainly in my own case, I like rich food, and especially the pudding and cake, chocolate ice, apricot tart, macaroon, trifle and syllabub part of the meal – and I have done ever since I was released from the tyranny of boiled mutton in 1837. Reid says I overload my stomach with rich things, and just lately he has persuaded me to try Benger's food. I was reluctant at first – I cannot bear the idea of 'slops' – but once I tried it I found I liked it. So I have started to have a large bowl of it before meals – and now Reid says that he meant me to eat it *instead of* the rich food, not *as well as*! Lenchen and Louise both had a word with me about it – but I am the Queen after all, and there's not much point in being Queen of England if you can't at least eat what you like.

I sometimes think I have not been quite fair to Bertie. The trouble is, I think, that I always wanted him to be like his father in every respect; and since, as I have often stated, Albert was both perfect and unique, Bertie was bound to fall short. But how far he fell short! To begin with the poor unfortunate child quite soon began to look like me rather than like his papa – no heavenly porcelain beauty, but the bulging blue eyes, curved-over nose, pendulous lip and receding chin I had mourned in the looking-glass day after day. When I looked at him I saw my Hanoverian blood peeping back, I saw my Wicked Uncles thinly disguised in a child's frame.

And then instead of being gentle, obedient, scholarly, and full of noble purpose like his father, he displayed a violent temper (oh dear, where had he that from, I wonder?), an immovable stubbornness, a deep loathing of lessons and books, and a desire for nothing but what was idle, useless and naughty. And yet he *had* good qualities: he had an affectionate heart, an incorrigible honesty, and a strong bent for loyalty. He was fond of animals, displayed much tenderness towards his little brothers and sisters, and when he was away from us, he had considerable charm and the knack of making himself liked – a useful thing for a future monarch. Unfortunately, these were not qualities that I was prepared to praise then (being on the whole what he had inherited from me), when he showed himself so ungrateful as to have inherited nothing from his father. He was a caricature of me: that was the trouble, and his whole misfortune.

If he had only been the third or fourth son, instead of the first, we might have done more kindly by him in bringing him up. But we knew, you see, Albert and I, how much depended on him. He was to be King of England one day, and if Albert succeeded in realising his vision, he would be the political, philosophical and moral leader of the entire enlightened world. It was the heaviest of tasks, and nothing, we felt, must be omitted from his training that might help to make him fit for it. Not a week, not a day, not an hour of his precious childhood could safely or properly be wasted. Every detail of his physical, intellectual and moral training must be mapped out and rigidly adhered to. He must be watched day and night, and the slightest spot or deviation instantly rubbed out or corrected.

Is it any wonder the poor bewildered child rebelled? It was all he could do – bent out of his nature, forced against his will and against all possibility of success, into his father's exquisite mould. Either the mould would break, or he would (and he was my son in this respect, that he would always survive against all odds). But we did not see it at the time – indeed, Albert never lived to see it. Only in more tolerant old age have I come to see that almost everything we did with Bertie was wrong and bound to achieve the very opposite of what was intended (and even now I cannot admire him much, poor creature! though I love him, of course, and acknowledge his many good qualities).

Part of the trouble was in the reputation of those same Wicked Uncles he so tauntingly, if fleetingly, resembled. I had inherited a tottering Throne, and a Crown brought to its lowest ebb of respect by the behaviour of my family, whose blood I was only too well aware of in my own veins. This blood flowed also in Bertie's, and that we were so constantly aware of it was mostly Stockmar's fault. He never missed an opportunity of impressing on us that the future of the Crown in England depended on a moral foundation: the least sign of depravity would inevitably pitch us into revolution and republicanism. Albert did not need to be convinced. He told me from the beginning that his object was to make Bertie as unlike as possible to any of his great-uncles, and I agreed with him whole-heartedly. (Looking back now, I do think it was decidedly odd that we did not worry about the Coburg blood in Bertie's veins, considering the licentiousness of Albert's father and brother. Now I come to think of it, Albert was the first virtuous Coburg for generations – and indeed it was his reaction to his father's behaviour and his brother's awful fate which gave him such an unconquerable horror of debauchery. Why was it that we felt Albert's individual goodness was sufficient barrier against an inherited Coburg taint from Albert's father, while my virtue was not able to protect Bertie from the indirect blood of my uncles? I really can't say. It seemed at the time a very simple equation – Coburg good, Hanover bad – and I went along with it unquestionably.)

Stockmar assured Albert that my uncle King's weakness was due to a faulty education, and said that it was imperative that the Prince of Wales should lead a life of utter purity, and be educated on a rational plan. Bertie must be surrounded by none but the morally spotless; and since Albert knew (and I believed) what depraved little beasts boys are, and how they corrupt each other and tell each other disgusting things, he was not allowed to mix with other boys. All his childhood he had no friends to play with other than his own brothers and sisters. Did I not remember how I had hated Conroy's system at Kensington – the loneliness and boredom, the longing for company of my own age? Well, well, it seems not – or at least I assumed that the benefits to Bertie would far outweigh the pain. The trouble was, of course, that we had forgotten the principle of inoculation, which Lord M. had long ago propounded to me: a boy unexposed to even the mildest form of depravity has no resistance, and is likely to fall victim to the first infection that comes his way. (This is in fact what happened in Ireland in 1861, with such appalling consequences. Lord M. was always right.)

And as to education, Bertie was unfortunate in having our brilliant Vicky ahead of him. A schedule of lessons was worked out for him which she would have found challenging: poor Bertie, who was not above average clever, found it impossible. When he did not advance, and showed a great aversion to his lessons, we called it wilfulness and responded by lengthening the hours of study and making them harder; and when he grew pale and languid with exhaustion, his anxious, concerned parents decided that he was suffering from a natural laziness which needed to be driven out of him. Poor Bertie was watched, guarded and checked every moment of the day; and when the baffled creature erupted in fury, roared, spat, swore and threw things, it seemed to us that the Devil was winning, and that we hadn't been beating him enough.

'Why must I always be good?' he cried out one day. 'Other children are not always good!' We did not hear the plea, only the defiance. I think now that the whole system was wrong, of trying to make all children alike, instead of bringing out what was best in each, like a carpenter working with the grain of a piece of wood instead of against it. But it was the way we thought in those days: all children could be perfect, if only they would. I should have done better to remember what Lord Melbourne – wiser than his generation – had said to me: 'Do not be over solicitous about education. It does not do so much as is expected from it. It may mould and direct character, but it rarely alters it.' We wanted to make Bertie a scholar and an aesthete like his father, but deep in his nature he was a thorough sensualist. Even as a young man Albert scorned physical discomfort, and was never happier than when studying alone by the light of his green student lamp, pursuing some challenging intellectual objective. But Bertie at the same age liked comfortable chairs, fine clothes, good dinners with plenty of wine, pleasant conversation, and something jolly at the theatre with friends. We might as well have tried to teach a pig to fly.

14th June 1900

IT IS odd that it was Sir Robert Peel who first drew our attention to Osborne House. When I think how amazingly I disliked him in the early days, it seems strange that it was with him that Albert and I naturally discussed our desire for a house of our own. But Lord M. had been right in that, as in so much: once I got used to Sir Robert's odd manner, I found him absolutely to be trusted. Though his way of speaking seemed stilted and pompous to me at first, I noted that he had a good voice, and his opinions were sensible; and when he grew less shy (for he was shy, though few people realised it) he proved to have a very colourful and lively way of describing events in the House and so on, which made me feel as though I was really there. (Dear Disraeli also had that talent, though it was more to be expected in him, since he was a novelist: to listen to his account of the goings-on in the House was almost like watching one of those 'animatograph' films! I never had such a complete picture of everything as when he was my Prime Minister.)

Much of the trouble, I think, was that Peel was very proud, and being only the son of a cotton-spinner he had met with many slights and snubs on his way up through society. Now, I despise that sort of snobbery: it doesn't matter to me what a man's father was, only what *he* is; and I was proud of Sir Robert for refusing, like Lord M., to accept any honours for his services. But most of all I liked him because he really appreciated Albert, and praised him warmly to me.

It was in October 1843 that Albert and I took a stroll with Sir Robert, after his regular audience, in the garden of Buckingham Palace. The dogs were rushing about nose-down under the bushes, my hand was tucked where it liked to be under Albert's arm, and the soot was gently falling on the privets and laurels all around us. We soon got on to the subject of houses. 'It seems astonishing to me,' I complained, 'that the Queen of England should be the one person in the land who cannot have a comfortable place to live. Buckingham Palace is a disgrace! Windows that won't open, doors that won't shut, fires that won't draw, bad smells in the corridors—'

'The sanitary arrangements are very bad,' Albert joined in. He was particularly interested in sewerage. 'Do you know, there is a closet waste-pipe which discharges itself on to the leads immediately outside the Queen's dressing-room window?'

'That is very bad indeed,' Sir Robert said gravely.

'But worst of all, we have no privacy,' I said. 'Here we can walk in the grounds, but you know, Sir Robert, how often people get over the wall. One can never feel quite safe from interruption. And a few turns about a sooty London garden is not enough for the Prince: he needs peace and quiet and real country air. And at Windsor the public can come almost right up to the door. We have no privacy there at all – and surely even a Queen is entitled to that!'

'I think Your Majesty is right to wish for it,' Peel said, circumspectly.

'What one wants is a place of one's own,' I said mournfully, 'quiet and retired, where one can enjoy the solace of family life.'

'Preferably a marine residence,' Albert added. 'The sea air is so beneficial to lungs which have been starved by London fogs.'

'A marine residence?' Sir Robert said, surprised.

This was a new interest of ours, after a summer spent sailing up and down the south coast. 'We *so* enjoyed our cruising this summer,' I said, 'but the drawbacks of the Pavilion are too severe. It will not do.'

I and Albert and the children had based ourselves at Brighton, and taken excursions of varying lengths in our new steam yacht, the *Victoria and Albert*. (On a summer holiday the year before I had discovered it took three and a half days to sail to Scotland but only half that time to steam back, so I had asked Sir Robert to request Parliament and the Admiralty to provide us with our own steam-powered vessel. The *Victoria and Albert*, launched in April 1843, was a paddle-driven steamer of 1,049 tons, and I had appointed as commander Lord Adolphus Fitzclarence, one of my uncle King William's *bâtards*. I never forgot my debt to my kind uncle, and helped his children when I could.) It had been a very happy holiday, but neither of us liked the Pavilion. Uncle King's sumptuous oriental fantasy struck Albert with horror, though it represented some of the world's finest work in that taste; but it was all too sensual and decadent for such a Child of Reason as my beloved. I thought the interiors interesting and amusing, but they would plainly not do for family life, and the place was not at all *gemütlich*.

Besides that, the environment of the Pavilion presented us with severe problems. When Uncle King had settled in Brighton is 1787 it had been a tiny fishing village, and the Steyne, where he had elected to build his palace, had been surrounded by open downland and commanded a fine view of the sea. But he had made it such a popular resort, and sea-bathing had become so fashionable, that the open ground was now all built over, and houses crowded right up to the Pavilion door. No glimpse of the sea could be caught from its windows, only the crowds milling by and peering in at us, and the moment we stepped out of doors we were surrounded by a mob. They followed us everywhere, and once when we tried to stroll on the beach they had the impudence to come up and peer under my bonnet to see what I looked like. Wherever we went they treated us just as they did the Town Band when it went on parade. Lord M. used to say the people of Kent were the worst in the country, but I am not sure the people of Sussex weren't worse – loyal, certainly, but so vulgar and impertinent!

'I imagine it would not be difficult to find another house somewhere along the coast,' Sir Robert said, 'but whether it would be sufficiently large and imposing for a Royal Residence—'

'But I don't want it to be large and imposing,' I said quickly. 'You know, Sir Robert, if it were not my duty to be on public display and give great banquets and receptions, I would most gladly retire to the country, and live quietly in a cottage with my husband and children. London and the excitements of the Season would be no loss to us, I assure you.' And my words were rewarded by a squeeze of my hand against Albert's ribs. 'What we want is just a dear little place of our own where we can be snug and cosy.'

'*Gemütlichkeit*,' Albert summed up, with a nod.

'Exactly!' said I.

'In that case, ma'am,' said Sir Robert, 'there could be no difficulty in finding a suitable house – indeed, I think I have one in mind that might do admirably – but I have the gravest doubts as to whether Parliament would sanction any further expenditure at this moment. Things, as you know, are bad, uniformly bad.'

At this Albert was indignant. 'Something will have to be done sooner or later, about Buckingham Palace at least. It is a national disgrace that the Sovereign's family should be so badly housed! Our children, you know, sir, have nothing but an attic that was meant for servants – low and dark, no ventilation, and too small already. If our family goes on increasing—' He broke off at this approach to delicate matters, and he and Sir Robert gave identical tactful coughs. 'The State Apartments are quite inadequate for the sort of receptions we must give,' Albert went on. 'There is not even a ballroom; and the kitchens cannot provide anything that is edible. It is a wonder we have not poisoned some visiting head of state by now!'

Sir Robert had put on his most wooden face. 'Nevertheless, sir, you must know that the country is deep in recession, and the Exchequer could not bear the strain of it.'

I cut through the argument. 'But we are not talking about Buckingham Palace at the moment,' I said firmly. 'We are talking about a new marine residence for my family, and I must tell you, Sir Robert, that I do not *wish* Parliament to buy it for me. I want a place that is all my own, so that I can do as I please *in* it and *with* it. If I can buy it with my own money, out of the Privy Purse, Parliament can have no objection, can it?'

'Why, no, ma'am,' Sir Robert said, looking as surprised as his inexpressive face allowed, 'if indeed there is enough in the Privy Purse for such a purchase.'

'You perhaps have no idea of the extent of the Prince's economies, Sir Robert,' I said proudly. 'He has been reorganising the Household, and we are very well beforehand with the world, I assure you! A house of our very own is what we want; and I shall be very glad to be free of those tiresome Woods and Forests, and all the other charming departments, which really are the plague of one's life!'

Everything that had to be done in and around the palaces had to pass through some or other department – the Lord Chamberlain's office, the Lord Steward's, the Clerk of the Works, the Master of the Horse – all of them cumbersome and dilatory; but the Woods and Forests were the worst of all. Chancery itself moved with indecent haste compared with them! And since nothing seemed to be governed by one department alone, and none of them was willing to co-ordinate their activities with the others, it was maddeningly difficult to get anything done at all. Fires, for instance, were laid by the Steward's office but lit by the Chamberlain's, so frequently we had no fire at all, and each blamed the other while we shivered. Windows were cleaned on the inside by the Lord Chamberlain's Office, but on the outside by the Woods and Forests, and since the Woods and Forests could never be brought to clean their side on the same day, we lived in a permanent fog and had to open a window to see what the weather was like.

Sir Robert said thoughtfully, 'If you are determined on this course, what does Your Majesty say to the Isle of Wight? I happen to know that Lady Isabella Blatchford is anxious to sell the Osborne estate.'

'Osborne? Oh yes, I know it,' I said, and turned eagerly to Albert. 'You remember I told you we stayed several times at Norris Castle when I was a girl, and how I wished I had been able to buy it when it came on the market in 'thirty-nine? Well, Osborne is the next-door estate. I was never in the house, but I cantered my pony over its grounds many a time.'

'The Isle of Wight is very pretty,' Albert said. We had sailed past it that summer, and I had pointed out some of its glories to him.

'Very quiet and rural, sir,' Peel said. 'An excellent climate, I believe, and with the railway service quite conveniently reached from London.'

'The sailing would be good from there, ' Albert said. 'How big is the estate?'

'I believe it is about a thousand acres, sir,' said Peel. 'Parkland, woods and a farm, or perhaps two.'

'What do you think, my love?' Albert said to me in German. 'Does not the Isle of Wight have some bad memories for you? You will not associate it with a Certain Person?'

I don't know whether I had told Albert or not, but in fact Conroy and his family had stayed at Osborne while Mamma and I were at Norris Castle – not in the house but at the Lodge; but I tossed aside that memory. I had had happy holidays on the Isle of Wight, and was now all eagerness to buy a house there. Once I get an idea I want to steam full ahead with no deliberation or delay. 'No, no, I am sure it will be perfect,' I said. 'You must go down at once and see it, and tell me what it's like.'

He smiled and pressed my hand again. 'We must go about this in an orderly fashion, my darling. There is much to discover before anyone goes to see it. It may not be suitable at all.'

'But I tell you I know it, and it is perfect!' I insisted.

'You will leave it to me, if you please,' Albert said firmly, and turned back to Peel, who did not speak German and was politely pretending that we were not. 'I hope you will be willing to forward some enquiries to Lady Blatchford for me, Sir Robert?'

'I will be happy to communicate on your behalf with Lady Isabella,' Peel corrected gently. (Albert was not very good on English titles – he had a very German contempt of the English aristocracy, and I think this was one of his ways of expressing it. It was a great trial to me sometimes at receptions.) 'You will wish to know the purchase price, of course.'

'And so much more. The water supply and drainage, the access to the sea, whether or not there are any rights of way across the land – a public footpath through the grounds would be fatal to our privacy. And we had better have an Ordnance map showing the farms and woods and so on – the exact extent and make-up of the estate. I will write a detailed letter about it, and give it to you in a few days.'

Between Albert's 'orderly fashion' and Lady Isabella's awkwardness, the delay seemed interminable to me. She wanted £30,000 for it, which Peel thought too much; and Albert was not willing to spend money on something that might not completely suit, so when the preliminary enquiries were complete he went down, on the 18th of March 1844, to see it. Between the railway train and the steam ferry, it was by then possible to go to East Cowes and back in a day, with plenty of time between to look round (a far cry from the journeys I had made in my childhood!) and getting up at dawn, Albert was back by the evening with a good report. 'The house is very good, the estate is excellent, and we shall have all the privacy we want; but there will need to be some alterations to make the house completely comfortable.'

'What sort of alterations?' I asked dubiously. I hate a put-off, and I could see one looming.

'Some extra rooms will be needed. New kitchens are essential, but there is a good site for them in an open yard near the present offices. And a dormitory for the servants can be added over the stables. You see now, my love, how important it is not to rush into things? We shall want time to work out how much needs to be spent on it and whether it is worth the expense. The Privy Purse is not bottomless, you know.'

Disappointment welled up in me. I was by then pregnant again, and longing for a house of our own in which to 'settle down'. 'You don't like it?'

'Yes, I do. The land is particularly good – fertile farmland, neglected at present, but capable of much improvement. But we must proceed cautiously, my love. I recommend that we propose to Lady Blatchford to rent it only, for a year, with an option to purchase at the end of that time. We might argue to have the rent deducted from the purchase price as well,' he added thoughtfully.

'How long will it all take? I had hoped to get there this summer.'

'We shall see,' he said, annoyingly. 'These things cannot be hurried.'

In the end it was not until October that I finally got to visit my new home, and then only as a tenant. How well I remember that first visit! It rained on and off all the way down to Gosport, and even the crossing to East Cowes was attended by violent showers; but as we drove up to the house the sun suddenly came out, lighting the façade so that it was like someone smiling a welcome at us. Such a nice house it was, too! Handsome and plain in the Palladian style, a three-storeyed, rectangular eighteenth-century stone building, with a handsome fanlight over the door and a classical pediment. All houses have a 'face', and there was something open and honest and friendly about that one. Handsome tall trees were dotted all about, with a good sweep of lawn surrounding the house, and beyond it gentle rolling parkland and hayfields sloping down to the sea. Taking my hand, Albert led me inside, and we walked together from room to room, discussing and admiring. It reminded me of our wedding night, when we had run like children from room to room of our new suite at Windsor; we did not run now, but we were just as excited – more so, for this would be our own, not the State's.

Everything was delightful. It was exactly what I wanted. The rooms were smaller than at Windsor or Buckingham Palace, but beautifully proportioned, as they always are in that style of house. It was light, cheerful, dry and warm; and handsomely decorated, if a little shabby with wear in some places. There was a library, a drawing-room and dining-room, two halls and two ante-rooms on the ground floor, and sixteen bedrooms and dressing-rooms above. Nothing could have been more complete and snug! It wanted nothing, from wine-cellar to nursery, from ice-house to piggery, to make it a comfortable residence for a gentleman and his family.

'It is exactly the thing!' I cried to Albert. 'This is true *gemütlichkeit!*'

We wandered outside, and strolled along the lawn to admire the view. The watery clouds were dispersing and the sun was shining strongly now, and below the wooded slopes the Solent lay sparkling, blue as chicory-flower, dotted with tiny white sails and black steam-ships. We could see quite clearly across to Spithead, and the bare masts of the warships at anchor there, and beyond in the hazy distance the gentle swelling curves of the Downs. The air came up to meet us, clean and balmy, with an autumnal hint of leafmould and a tang of ozone in it – I have always loved that first, intoxicating smell of the sea! All around us was a riot of birdsong. There was no other sound – no soot or smoke – no other person or building within sight. We might have been Adam and Eve in the Garden. Albert's fingers locked through mine, and I felt his joy tingling through me.

'It is like the Bay of Naples, you know,' he said; and I could hear the lilt of happiness in his voice. 'The gentle slopes, the colours, the soft air. It is hard to believe we are in England.'

'We shall be quite, quite private here,' I exulted. 'No more jostling and peering. We can walk about and sit and romp just exactly as we please, like ordinary people.'

'There is a beach, too, did you know? A dear little sandy cove, with sea-shells and rock pools, where the children can bathe.'

'A private beach of our own?' It seemed too good to be true. Perhaps I might even learn to swim. I had never been in the sea before – much too public for the Queen of England!

'All our little ones must learn to swim; and row a boat. And we can build a landing-stage, you know, so that we can embark and disembark for our pleasure cruises from our own grounds, with no one staring at us—'

'No bands and speeches! No welcoming committees!' I said, laughing. 'Oh, Albert, it is perfect, isn't it?'

'Perfect,' he said. 'And there is more land adjacent we might be able to buy too, to make sure we are completely private. We can make a proper, working estate of it. I have lots of ideas for rational farming I would like to try out.'

'The children can grow up here, and play, and be healthy and happy. And it will be something to leave to them when we die.'

'When we die?' He turned me round and drew me to him, folding my hands in his against his chest, and smiling down into my face. I gazed up at him, my heart quickening. I had never seen him look so happy; he was so beautiful, he almost stopped my breath. 'Who talks of dying? I think here we shall live for ever, love of my heart.'

'I think we may,' I said, my voice rather faint. He stooped and laid his lips against mine so tenderly, and the touch of them pierced me like a sword of flame.

'I love you, *kleines Frauchen*,' he whispered.

I could not speak, only press my cheek to his in reverence.

And then he straightened up. 'Shall we walk down to the woods?' he said cheerfully. 'It is the wrong time of year now to hear them in daylight, but I think we may find there will be nightingales there.'

Fourteen

13th July, at Windsor

I HAVE not written anything for several days because we have been rather *occupé*, with a garden party for five thousand at Buckingham Palace on the 11th, amongst other matters, for which we went up from Windsor and found London *abominably* hot! I wore white roses in my bonnet and white feathers, and wore my large pearls and carried a fringed parasol – black and white silk – and thought I looked rather well for such an old lady. Everyone was very kind and attentive. I find I am become a sort of war-hero, which is rather amusing and touching.

One lady talked to me animatedly for some minutes, evidently quite unaware that she had forgotten to take the price ticket off her hat (it was quite small and discreet, but definitely a price ticket, tucked into the band, like the illustrations in the book of the Mad Hatter). It reminded me of that wonderful occasion in the early years of my reign when I attended a ball and was chatting to a duchess, who shall remain nameless. She was showing her young sovereign how tremendously sophisticated and tonnish she was, when a footman came across and bowed to her, holding out a horrid-looking sausage of horsehair and canvas with cotton tapes, one of which was broken. 'Pardon me, Your Grace, I think you dropped this.'

It was a bustle, of course, what we wore under our skirts in those days to give us interesting shapes behind. The poor woman turned scarlet with embarrassment and hotly denied ownership – I suppose she had felt it fall and had quietly walked away from it, hoping no one would notice. Now she was being confronted with it in the very presence of her Queen! The footman bowed and went away; but returned a few moments later, still dangling the object of shame. 'I beg your pardon, Your Grace,' he said, 'but I've just spoken to Your Grace's maid, and she says it is certainly yours.' I was obliged to feign a coughing fit to hide my uncontrollable giggles.

The weather has now turned stiflingly hot even here, which I find very trying. Reid has ordained that I am to rest for an hour after luncheon, which is supposed to be good for me, but loses time. Even at this time of year I am not free from business, and I cannot afford to be put behind. However, I can use the time to go on with my writing. Sleep is out of the question after luncheon as I am rather *souffrante* these days: my cast-iron digestion seems sadly to be deserting me, and when such an old and faithful friend leaves you, it is thin times indeed! Well, we shall soon be moving to Osborne, and it will revive me to be there, as it always does. My darling always seems closer to me at Osborne.

To resume, then: I sometimes regret that little house, Old Osborne House, as it was when first Albert and I visited it in 1844. It was so perfect and complete in its way, its proportions so satisfying to the eye of the artist – even an amateur like me. Though it is not much admired these days, classical architecture at its best cannot be bettered, both for beauty and comfort. But there was no doubt that the house was too small for a Royal Residence. Though it was a private home we wanted, wherever the Queen goes there is a court, and courtiers and politicians and ambassadors come and have to be housed – *and* their staff *and* their servants! And there have to be Privy Council meetings, which means not only an audience room but an ante-room in which the ministers can wait; and they have to be fed, and their secretaries entertained, and sometimes they have to stay overnight which means more beds and more servants.

So from the first we knew Old Osborne House would have to be enlarged, and Albert's first proposal was to add a new wing. 'But we will *not* go through the Office of Works,' he said.

'I should think not!' I laughed. 'We shall want it finished before the Millennium.'

It was Anson who suggested we approach Thomas Cubitt, the builder. Cubitt was one of the new sort of speculating builders (though he was now so well established it was hardly speculation in his case) who bought up tracts of land and built streets of houses and then rented them out or sold them. Whole areas of London were already bearing his imprint – Belgravia was sometimes called 'Cubit-topolis' – and his success was certainly deserved, for unlike most builders, he paid attention to two essential points: he built houses that people liked to live in, and he never exceeded his estimates. Anson himself lived in a Cubitt house in Eaton Place, and was full of praise for its arrangements and comfort, and when he effected an introduction between us and the builder, we liked him at once. Cubitt was then in his fifties, a compact, neatly built man with a fine, open face, deep-set, clear eyes, and an impish sense of humour. He was at the zenith of his career and comfortable with his powers and his position in society, which meant he was neither overawed nor overfamiliar – a thoroughly sensible, kindly, likeable man.

We had him down to Osborne, and he and I and Albert walked and talked and measured and sketched, and then I went in and he and Albert walked and talked some more. When we were together again, Cubitt, expressing his admiration for the situation and the fall of the land, said, 'There is a great opportunity here, which it would be a pity to pass up. I can do the alterations you require, and I can build you a new wing, too, if you like. But it would be infinitely better to pull down the old house altogether and build a new one. Start from 'scratch', and have it exactly as you want it.'

I could see Albert's eyes kindle at the idea. 'But such a scheme would be far too expensive. Our resources are not unlimited,' he said doubtfully.

'Mr Cubitt is perhaps giving us the advice that best suits his business,' I remarked drily.

Cubitt turned his honest face to me. 'I cannot deny, ma'am, that I would relish the chance to build you a new house. It could not but enhance my reputation to be honoured with such a commission; but as to the expense, I believe in the long run a new house would prove less expensive to you than repairs and alterations to this – and would be much more satisfactory.'

'You must not forget, Mr Cubitt,' I said, 'that we have had experience in our family of building schemes that failed. My uncle King George IV had plans for Buckingham Palace that could never be finished for want of time and money.'

Now he smiled, and his eyes twinkled engagingly. 'Ah, but His Majesty did not employ me! The mistake, if I may be so bold, ma'am, was that His Majesty began with an architect.'

'You do not approve of architects, Mr Cubitt?' Albert asked, raising a cool eyebrow. There could be no belittling of one of the learned arts in Albert's presence.

'I regard 'em as I do physicians, sir: they are sometimes necessary, but I would sooner do without 'em.' We had to laugh at this, and

Cubitt went on, 'You see, ma'am, when you employ an architect, he then contracts out all the other parts of the work to a multitude of individuals, and there is no firm hand on the reins. Now my system is different. I like to do the whole job myself. I have my own masons, carpenters, draughtsmen, blacksmiths, glaziers – everything. When a patron is so kind as to employ me, I see to every part, from the digging of the foundations to the painting of the ceilings. That way I control the quality of the materials and the work, the time it takes, and the cost.'

'Time is another matter of concern,' Albert said. 'We came here seeking a peaceful retreat. We would not want to have to go away again, and not be able to return for years and years.'

'As to that, sir,' said Cubitt, 'I do not see why anything you may decide on may not be built in discrete units. That way you would never be without a house to live in.'

'What do you mean?' I asked him.

'Well, ma'am, to begin with I can do the necessary alterations here in a couple of months. Then you can live here in comfort while I build the new house next door. Oh, there would be some inconvenience of noise and dust, but it can be managed so as to upset you as little as possible. A house of, say, equal size to this I can build for you in not much more than a year.'

'So little time?' Albert queried.

'I have my own systems, sir. I manufacture many of the elements in my own workshops and simply assemble them on site, which is much quicker, as you can imagine. And since I use all my own workmen I can ensure they work quickly and well, and that one team is not kept waiting because another has not finished its part of the work.'

'But you said a house of this size – and we have already said that it is too small,' I objected.

'Quite so, ma'am. My idea was to build in sections: make the first part complete and habitable while you live here, and then add further wings joining the new house to this, and finally pull this down and build the last section. Another advantage to that scheme,' he said, with an eye on Albert, 'would be that the cost would be spread out, and not fall in all at once.'

Albert thought for a moment, and then he declared, 'Mr Cubitt, you sound to me like a very enlightened man. I think we should talk in more detail about your plan. And if you would permit me, I should like to visit your workshops when we return to London.'

And so the death sentence was pronounced on the old house

almost without consulting me. When it was finally pulled down, I felt a pang of sadness; but the whole Osborne scheme was so exciting and pleasurable to Albert that I could not repine, and the new Osborne House is so completely identified with him, so redolent of his spirit and his vision, and so full of happy memories of him, that I have to love it.

So we went ahead and bought Osborne, which passed into our hands in May 1845, after Sir James Clark had visited to give his opinion of the air (very good and wholesome, a thought too relaxing perhaps at some times of the year, but the most bracing in the north of the island, where Osborne is situated, and therefore quite acceptable). And on the 15th of May I said goodbye to the old place as it was, and as I had seen it with Albert that October day; for on the following day they were to cut down the nearest trees to clear the site, and begin digging the foundations.

Osborne was all Albert's from the start to finish: he and Cubitt discussed and contrived between them, and then Albert would explain to me what he had decided on. I understood quite well why it had to be done this way. Albert was putting right the one thing that had been wrong for him from the beginning of our marriage – his position as my pensioner, living in my houses and by my provision. Now he was doing what men had done for countless generations: providing a home for his bride. He brought me each new addition to the scheme, each idea, each stage finished, as gifts to lay at my feet; and I would have been churlish indeed to object to such chivalry, such care from the man who was my knight and my protector.

Everyone knows now what Osborne looks like: the Italianate, three-storeyed stone building with the twin campaniles, and the great bow window on the seaward front of the Pavilion. On that first day of our first visit together, Albert had said that the view reminded him of the Bay of Naples; and so he had built me a Neapolitan villa to suit. When it came to the interior, he filled it with marble pillars and statues, arched niches and coloured tiled floors. Italy was come to the Isle of Wight – even down to the word *Salve* inset into the floor of the Grand Corridor – and though some of the intelligentsia deplored the taste (of course! for we had done something different without consulting them!) the fashion for Italian villas soon began to spread throughout the country.

The house had very much Mr Cubitt's stamp – 'rather Londony', one of my ladies called it – and incorporated many of his clever contrivances. He was very concerned about the danger of fire (not unreasonable in those days of lamps and candles) and so he built the house on a framework of cast-iron girders instead of wooden beams. This had the advantage also that they could be manufactured in his workshops and bolted together on site, and made the house very strong. The floors were further strengthened by brick arches, and layers of cockle shells were put down between floors, both as insulation against sound and to prevent fire spreading upwards from storey to storey. The skirting-boards were not of wood, either, but of concrete – though that was partly to accommodate Albert's idea for heating the corridors by blowing hot air into them through iron grilles, as the Romans did. I think it was Cubitt's idea to cover the shutters on the inside of the house with looking-glass, so that when they were shut at night they reflected the interior and made the rooms more spacious.

But the sanitary arrangements were all Albert's, though of course Cubitt had to engineer them. But I can say we had a great number of extremely *modern* water-closets, and no smells (unlike either of the royal palaces); and we enjoyed the inexpressible luxury, for those days, of baths that were not only supplied with hot water, but which were also fitted with drains for emptying themselves.

Cubitt's greatest virtue in my eyes was in working to budget. Because he had control of all parts of the process, he was able to furnish exact estimates at every stage, and I must say he never once exceeded them. I appreciated very much the accuracy of his accounts; I have no respect for those who are careless with money. And Cubitt did not hesitate to suggest several clever contrivances to keep down the cost for us. Portland stone, for instance, was horribly expensive, and it was his advice that we used it sparingly, only where it would really be noticed, as in the grand entrance. For the rest, though the house appears to be stone built, it is really made of bricks, and covered in Roman cement which has been moulded and coloured to resemble stone. Again, the 'marble' pillars inside are concrete, plastered for the finish and then painted to resemble marble – and few there are who can tell the difference. Cubitt had a marble-painter of his own amongst his employees, and the man was certainly an expert. I loved to watch him work.

The work went on with amazing speed. On the 23rd of June 1845 Albert and I, with Vicky and Bertie, had a little ceremony of 'laying the foundation stone'. First the children brought a little glass box containing coins from my reign and an inscription of our names and the occasion, and this was put into a hole and cemented over, and then the huge foundation stone was lowered on top, and we all walked around it and hammered on it for luck. It was a solemn and joyful occasion, half holy and half pagan, and I added a fervent prayer, that God would bless the work, and that we would spend many happy years in this house with our children and our children's children.

That was, as I say, June; only three months later the main bulk of the first wing of the new house (which we called the Pavilion) was up, though it lacked a roof. By November the tower was up, and I was relieved to see that it did not look out of proportion, for I had feared from the drawing it was too tall. On the 1st of March 1846, Albert and Cubitt took me on a tour of the interior, and I was astonished to see how much had been accomplished, for now the ceilings were in. There was a surprise for me when we reached the staircase hall: I had always admired the grand cantilevered staircase at Claremont, and Albert had had Cubitt copy it (only a little smaller) in Osborne House in order to please me.

The Pavilion was finished in September 1846, just less than a year and three months from the laying of the stone – fast work indeed! (The Household Wing, containing accommodation for the House-hold, the offices and the servants' quarters, was finished by August 1847. The old house, which stood between the two, was demolished the following year, and all that now remains of it is the fine front door with its fanlight, which were incorporated into the wall of the kitchen garden, as a memento. The Main Wing, joining the Pavilion and the Household Wing, was built on the site, incorporating the foundations of an even older Osborne House uncovered by the demolition. It was finished in 1851, and the house as Albert envisaged it was then complete.)

The arrangements in the Pavilion were *gemütlichkeit* itself. It was a horseshoe-shaped building, with the staircase in the middle, and the rooms leading one out of another around it. On the ground floor were the living rooms: the dining-room, the drawing-room with the bay window facing the sea, the billiard room, and a small sitting-room. On the first floor were Albert's and my apartments: our bedroom above the dining-room, then my dressing-room, then our sitting-room above the drawing-room, with the bay window and a little balcony outside from which we had a beautiful view of the sea, then Albert's dressing-room, and then the rooms for his valet and my dresser. On the second floor, where we could reach them easily, were the nurseries: the nursery bedroom was above our sitting-room, and Lady Lyttleton's apartments were over the dining-room.

It was all as snug and neat as could be, and on the 15th of September 1846 we spent our first night in our new house. It was light, clean, and airy, but gave the feeling of being most solidly built;

and there was, for a wonder, not the slightest smell of paint! What delighted me most was that everything was new, and everything was our very own, right down to the china ornaments, and Albert's Italian Primitives on the walls. As I walked in at my own front door for the first time, one of my younger maids threw an old shoe in after me, for luck, which she said was an old Scotch custom, and made the children laugh very much. They were wildly excited and rushed about from room to room, and only with the greatest difficulty could they be got to bed. Then Vicky took it into her head to be frightened of the newness and strangeness, until I pointed out the statue of her papa, which was placed in a niche at the head of the staircase on the nursery floor, which I said was there to keep guard over them, and then she went off as meek as a lamb. (The truth was that the statue was one we had just been given, of Albert in Greek armour, which I liked a great deal; but he said that the bare legs and feet were indecent and could not possibly be displayed in a public room, so it had been relegated to the nursery floor. The children liked having it there, and every year on Albert's birthday they would put flowers in the niche around those shocking, naked feet.)

As darkness fell we went into our new dining-room for dinner, leaving the shutters open so that the lights from our brilliant chandeliers would be seen right across the water and everyone would know we had come home. After dinner everyone rose to drink a health to me and Albert by way of a 'house-warming'. Albert rose to reply, and gazing down into my eyes he said in his quiet, simple way, 'We have a psalm in Germany, for such occasions as this. It begins: *Gott behüte dieses Haus / Und die da gehen ein und aus.*'

'God bless this house, and our going out and coming in', it might have been translated; the words so fitting, so solemn that my eyes filled with tears. The others around the table were touched too, and murmured approbation to each other. But though the words were for everyone, his look, and the tender, lingering smile that touched his lips, were for me alone.

Afterwards, when we were alone in our sitting-room, we walked out on to our little balcony and stood there, Albert's arm warm around my waist and my head against his shoulder, breathing the soft autumn air, and staring out into the darkness. It was beautifully spangled with tiny lights – of ships on the water, and across the water of houses on the mainland.

'If they can see us, we must look like a great ship floating in the sky, all lit up for a grand occasion,' I said. 'They will think we are having a ball, and imagine the music and the dancers and the lovely coloured dresses.'

'I hope the ships do not take us for a lighthouse and go upon the rocks,' Albert said.

'Oh no,' I said. 'Nothing but good can come of this house.'

Albert squeezed my waist and looked down at me. 'So, *kleines Frauchen*, are you happy? Do you like your new home?'

'So much!' I said fervently. 'More than I can tell you.'

He kissed the top of my head and turned to look out again. 'We will be happy here. The children will run and play, you will sit under the trees and sketch, and I—' He stopped there.

'Yes? What will you do?' I asked contentedly. I did not know why he had broken off, and I looked up at him. There was a strange look on his face, almost of sadness, and I was alarmed. 'Albert? What will you do?'

He looked down, abruptly as if he had been a long way away in his thoughts. 'I will make you a beautiful pleasure-ground,' he said. 'I will dig and plant and "improve", make a vista here and a tantalizing glimpse of the sea there, so that you will think you are in Arcadia. A winding path down to the shore through plantations of rhododendrons and magnolias; fine stands of English oak and English beech; lovely dark myrtles and cypresses clustered against the pale green of the lawn. A terrace, with arcading, and a parterre, and beyond that the land tumbling away so naturally, as if God had indented it with His thumb. The slopes are not right as they are, but I shall reshape them.' He looked at me again, smiling. 'I shall move earth for you, darling one. Not quite mountains, perhaps, but a great deal of earth!'

I laughed, partly with relief that he was not sad after all. 'You will have a new name,' I said, 'Capability Coburg.'

'Down there,' he said, pointing, 'will be the terrace; and in the middle, right opposite our bedroom window, we will have a great fountain like the one at Rosenau, and in the summer when the windows are open we will lie in our bed and hear the sound of the water falling into the basin. We will walk on that terrace, my darling, you and I, and talk of love. The years will pass and at last we shall be two old people, with our children all grown up, still walking there together, with their children running about us just as they once did.' I was picturing it all, and drew a great sigh of happiness. 'But you are getting cold,' he said.

I was distressed that he had misinterpreted my sigh. 'No, no,' I said, 'I am not cold, I am never cold.'

259

'But you are,' he said very firmly. 'What am I thinking about, keeping you standing out here? I must take you in to bed.'

'Oh,' said I, understanding at last, 'I think you must. I fear I can be warm nowhere else.'

And so in our handsome rosewood bed with the nice chintz hangings, all smelling of newness, Albert and I had a second, private house-warming of our own. Long and slow and tenderly did we love each other; and afterwards as I drifted off to sleep in his arms, I thought I could hear the plashing of a fountain below outside the window. My head was resting on his chest, my ear against his heart, and so perhaps I was catching the sound of it from his inmost, half-asleep memory.

20th July 1900, at Osborne

WE MADE the move here yesterday, and already I feel fresher. The journey down was most comfortable, despite the scorching sun. The Royal Saloon was kept beautifully cool with blocks of ice, and buckets of ice surrounded by bouquets of flowers were placed in all the corners. The carnations smelled so beautifully! But poor Marie Mallet, who has only just come into waiting, was quite overcome with the heat and Reid had to help her from the train. She is now confined to her room with lumbago, of all things, a most painful and depressing ailment, especially in hot weather when one wants to be out of doors.

Beatrice and her children are here, of course, and Lenchen and Thora, and the little Yorks come next week. Louise comes next month for a visit, but Affie is not coming over after all, which is a great disappointment because I have seen so little of him in recent years and was so much looking forward to a long visit. It seems his health is a matter for great anxiety. I hope he has been prudent lately. He drinks far too much, as we have all warned him time after time, but men will not be told.

The new Royal Yacht is lying at Portsmouth, and it appears she is rotten from stem to stern. I have told the Admiralty that I will not accept her at any price. I am warned there will be a 'row' about it, and the Government mutters about wasting half a million pounds, but if everyone did their business properly in the first place these things would not happen.

It is impossible to be really downhearted or cross here, though, at

Osborne. It is Eden, this perfect and private garden Albert made for me on the English Bay of Naples, and sometimes, even now, I can still find him here. His quick, light step is in the pattering of the water into the bowl of the fountain; his thoughtful whistle, when he was thinking out a problem, is in the hesitant song of the robin; the touch of the sun on my upturned face is like the benison of his smile, which he never failed to bestow when he passed me.

On warm summer days I still like to breakfast in the alcove on the lower terrace, as we used to; and if I close my eyes I am wrapped in the familiar smell of hot gravel and the deep, heady fragrance of honeysuckle, roses, orange blossom and white jasmine, which deck the walls and clamber over the pergola. Smells, of all the senses, have the strongest power to carry one back, instantly, to a place loved and a time lost. A little breeze rustles the papers on the table, and I know that he is sitting opposite me, turning the pages of a letter propped up against his coffee cup. In a moment he will read out to me some item of interest or amusement – I will hear his voice again! And if I keep my eyes shut, he may reach out, as he so often did, without taking his eyes from the page, stretching between the bowl of fruit and the bread-basket to find me, and I will feel again the shape of the palm and the long fingers which I knew better than any, the smooth warmth of that hand laid over mine, whose touch was one soul saying to another *I am here*. Then someone moves or speaks – a dog sneezes – a cup is set down clumsily in its saucer – and the spell is broken. I open my eyes, and it is only Baby sitting opposite me, or dear Jane Churchill; and I am old. The hand that lies on the tablecloth before me is one that Albert never knew, wrinkled, veined, large-knuckled with age.

I cannot now walk the paths he laid out for me, but I have myself wheeled or driven where we walked together so indefatigably, talking and planning, arm in arm. Beyond the little gardens that the children tended is a meadow, of waist-high grass, tawny-fronded in summer, and bright as a tapestry with wild flowers: purple vetch, clover of three colours, blue and crimson bugle, white and gold moon daisies, green-white angelica, cornflowers the colour of the sky, and the little wild orchids the bees love so, purple and yellow and white like Easter vestments. Here once I remember sitting down with my sketching-book in the shade while he took off his jacket and rolled up his sleeves for the pleasure of cutting grass with a scythe. All the sights and sounds and scents of that day are etched in my mind: the swish of the scythe, the smell of bruised grass; the sleepy drone of bumble bees pottering from one flower to the next, unhurried amongst such summer plenty; a rustling of breeze in the treetops, and the intermittent sound of the children's voices, high and echoing under the summer sky as they played nearby. Behind me was a thicket of bamboo, whose shadows gave off a cold, dark smell of earth and mould, and it came to me now and then when the little breeze dropped, a sharp contrast to the bright, warm scents of the summer meadow.

After a little my darling stopped to rest and came over to me, dropped down on to the grass beside me, pulled out his handkerchief to wipe his brow. I smelled the sharp odour of his sweat, exciting to me, quickening my senses. 'I am not used to such labour,' he said happily, taking off his hat – the low-crowned, wide-brimmed straw hat he wore when he was 'playing the rustic' – and squinted up into the perfect sky, which might have sighed for shame that it was not more blue than his eyes. 'What a day!'

'You should not tire yourself,' I said. 'It is too hot for working in the sun.'

'Who else should I tire?' he laughed. 'I shall sleep well tonight, at all events.' He rested an arm companionably on my lap, and I let my pencil fall idle. I was pressing down the desire to kiss the top of his head, on the place where a glimmer of scalp was beginning to show through his fine hair. He did not like me to notice it – it was his one vanity, his fretting over the thinning of his hair – but that spot was very dear to me. It somehow enhanced his perfection that he had that one little imperfection, and made him more precious and more mine in his vulnerability. Now he felt my eyes on him, and looked up at me. 'Have you been drawing me working, Wifey?' he asked, trying to see my sketch. 'Show me!'

I tried to hold it away from him, but he was too quick for me. My drawing was only of the meadow and the woods behind – 'A landscape without figures,' I said apologetically.

'So, my vanity is well served,' he said, laughing ruefully, restoring it to me. 'You never do draw me, do you? All the children, Mamma, Laddle – even George Anson, but never me. Why is that?'

'I don't trust my pencil,' I said. 'I could not do you justice.' But it was not that. It was superstition. I had drawn him only once, when we were first married, and afterwards, when I looked at it, it made me go cold all over. I felt as if I had put him at some terrible risk; as though I had taken his soul out of his body to look at it, without knowing whether it could be put back.

He only smiled now, as if he knew the truth of it, and got to his feet. 'I had better get back to my work. My half-cut meadow calls me.'

'It is so lovely here,' I said, watching him as he rose up before me, loving his man's shape, the glimpse of his chest under his thin shirt, the play of muscles in his bare forearm. 'We are so lucky.'

'Lucky, yes,' he said, 'but there is nothing that does not have its price.' He had picked up his scythe and was running his thumb along the blade to test its edge. Now he snatched his hand back and drew a sharp breath. '*Ach!*' A bright line of blood, gleaming and dark as ruby, appeared on the ball of his thumb. 'So, you see?'

'No, Albert!' I said in alarm. The back of my knees ached at the sight of his blood. I could never bear him to be hurt.

'It is nothing,' he said, conveying it to his mouth. 'What a clumsy fool I am.' Then he removed the thumb in order to smile at me. 'Even Paradise has its serpent, you see, *Kleinchen*!' I did not manage to smile back, and he stooped to cup my face with his unwounded hand and kiss my lips, keeping the other well away from my white muslin gown. 'Oh, foolish one, you have gone quite pale! It is only a little scratch,' he said. 'It has stopped bleeding already, see?' He made pretence to show it to me, but did not allow me to see it, and as if to forestall any fuss went quickly back to his scything.

I watched him, feeling my heart beat foolishly. It was nothing, it had been a nothing of an incident; but for a moment I could smell only the cold, dank odour of the bamboo's shadows, and I felt a sense of grief I did not then at all understand.

There was an ancient tomb which was discovered in Italy, whose entrance was decorated with a carving of a death's-head, and under it the words *Et in Arcadia Ego*. Scholars have argued long about the meaning of the inscription. Does it mean, 'I, who am now dead, once also lived in Paradise'? Or does it mean, 'Even in Paradise, I, Death, am present'? But it seems to me that the translation does not matter, because both versions mean the same thing: *remember thy mortality*.

Albert made me this garden, this perfect and beautiful Arcadia, and it breathes of him still; his presence is around every corner, near, but mockingly out of sight. For it was here that he first began to withdraw from me, though I saw it only with hindsight. I knew only that he spent too many hours away from me, planting and planning and organising and overseeing the works; working, himself, like one possessed, as if he were afraid that he would not get it finished in time. In time for what? I might have asked; but the answer then was hidden from me.

I have my Arcadia still, and still God spares me to sit in it, and enjoy the beauty He created and His servant enhanced. But the servant has departed, and I am alone, and old, so old.

Nothing that does not have its price.

28th July 1900

WE HAD the Marine Band from Portsmouth to play to us last evening after dinner – quite glorious! And the most tremendous thunderstorm broke, too, which was thrilling, and cleared the air wonderfully, so I slept much better last night. Everything today is glittering with freshness, the sky as limpid as if it had been washed, and the sea sparkles down below so invitingly that I can't help glancing up every few minutes from my writing, as if to exchange a smile with an old friend.

Unlike the royal palaces, Osborne was very much *home* to the children, and so many of my best memories here are to do with them. Albert wanted to recreate for them at Osborne the perfect happiness he had known at the Rosenau in his own childhood. Of course, his childhood had *not* been perfectly happy, but he liked to remember it so, when he was feeling sentimental or homesick. What he really created at Osborne was the parts of his childhood he had enjoyed, but made perfect by loving, devoted, and above all faithful parents.

So our little ones spent a great deal of time with us when we were at Osborne, breakfasting and lunching with us when we had no important guests. Usually at these meals the smallest was placed between his chair and mine, where it could be helped from either side; and Albert kept them all in order, rebuking them if they sat badly or snatched or gobbled their food, but otherwise chatting to them so kindly and amusingly, and keeping us all laughing with his fun and mimicry.

And then there were the outings. Never did children have so much freedom, and fun, and romping! He encouraged them to run about catching butterflies, climb trees, and roll over and over down the slopes (as I had always longed to do at Windsor when I was a child, and never had, and now never would). To facilitate this freedom, they were never dressed formally when we were alone, but had sensible clothes for romping – the little girls in stout Holland frocks, and the little boys in sailors' dresses – 'slops' – which became

264

very fashionable afterwards amongst the middling sort for their children.

A favourite walk was always down to our little beach, when I would sit and sketch while the children and Albert dug extravagant earthworks in the sand, threw sticks into the sea for the dogs, collected shells, examined the rock-pools, paddled at the water's edge, or went right in to bathe. Albert had not forgotten his vow that they should all learn to swim: he had a large floating 'swimming bath' made, a cross between a raft and a sieve. It had a wooden deck with a changing-hut and a water-closet, and the bath itself was made of zinc grating with a wooden, slatted floor which could be raised or lowered. The whole was moored to pontoons, so that it went up and down with the tide and so could be used at any time, and here the children could safely take their first swimming lessons, graduating when they could swim several lengths with confidence to the sea proper. They learned to dive, too – girls included – and in anticipation of the worst, Albert made the boys learn to swim fully clad in shirt, trousers, stockings and boots.

Encouraged by the seclusion of our private beach, I took my first sea-bathe there in 1847. I had a bathing-machine which ran down into the sea on stone rails, and a very kind and experienced bathing-woman. It was the most exhilarating experience (until I grew *too* confident and put my face under the water, whereupon I was convinced I must suffocate!). I never learned to swim, but I did very much enjoy splashing and jumping about in the waves while Albert stood in the water nearby and encouraged me. I stopped going into the sea when Albert died, of course. The pleasure would have been nothing without him.

Another thing Albert had built for the children was the Swiss Cottage, a play house, smaller than a real one, but properly constructed of wood with real fireplaces and chimneys. On the ground floor were a kitchen and scullery, fitted out with a miniature stove and boiler that really worked, and all the equipment they needed to learn to cook and keep house. Upstairs were a dining-room, where the children entertained us and a few favoured guests to meals they prepared themselves, and a sitting-room where they kept their natural history collection. (Albert and Ernst had had such a collection at the Rosenau.) In front of the Swiss Cottage, each child had his or her own garden plot, with tools made to scale for them, where they grew flowers and vegetables. Albert wanted to teach them his own love of gardening; but he also purchased what they grew at the regular price, to help them to understand commerce.

Later, in the same part of the grounds, Albert further reconstructed his childhood with the building of a miniature fort, complete with earthworks and barracks. He and his brother had played soldiers in a mock fort when they were boys. The improving lesson to be learned here was of the classical strategies of war; but such energetic boys as ours did not need any encouragement to play at battles. (It was particularly favoured by Arthur – or 'Arta', as he called himself when he was little – whose godfather was the 'Dook of Wellikon' on whose eighty-first birthday he had been born. He was destined from the beginning for the Army and loved all things military. When he was two he was given the uniform of the Scotch Fusiliers for his birthday, complete down to the bearskin and toy rifle, and he looked so sweet and funny in it. It amused Albert very much, and Winterhalter later painted him wearing it, which became Albert's favourite painting of Arthur.)

These contrivances were the tangible signs of his loving attention to his children, and what other children can boast more? But the memories I cherish are the little fragments of family life, so dear, so private: of Albert playing his organ with a baby on each knee, while the little fat fists tried to add a counterpart to the tune; of Albert swinging a little one to and fro between his legs in a napkin – a process which always gave rise to impassioned pleas from the older ones who were now too big for the treat. I remember picnics and pony-rides and drives in the miniature phaeton; I remember expeditions into the kitchen gardens for all parties to stuff themselves with raspberries and currants to their hearts' desire. I remember Albert lying on his stomach on the floor with Affie and Arthur, laying out an entire campaign of lead soldiers; Albert, Bertie and Affie flying Affie's kite and trying to stop it leaving England altogether; Albert, dogs and boys playing a wild game of hide-and-seek in and out of the plantations.

I remember – oh sweet, poignant memory – Albert teaching Vicky to waltz, circling solemnly while she, heartbreakingly dignified, trying to be grown-up, stared down with concentration at her little slippered feet placed on top of his. I remember him watching, with such an expression of tenderness that it was almost like pain, as dear Fat Alice rushed about one October trying to stick the leaves back on the trees because she didn't want summer to be over.

It was always Albert who arranged the 'birthday tables' and planned the birthday treats. At Easter he hid the painted hard-boiled eggs around the breakfast-room and cried out 'Warm!' or 'Cold!' or 'Hotter!' as the children rushed round hunting for them. One midsummer he turned somersaults in a haystack to teach Bertie how it was done. On a wet autumn day when no one could go out of doors he had them all playing at charades, with the girls acting boys' parts and the boys girls', to everyone's intense hilarity. In winter he built a ten-foot-high snowman for Vicky, and dragged Affie about on a sled while the little tyrant shouted and pretended to crack his whip like a miniature potentate.

But it's the summers that I remember best, when we could be out of doors all day. I remember one warm evening when we sat out on the lawn until after seven o'clock, with Albert and the children playing a game of his invention called 'Naughty Rabbit', a cross between Hot Cockles and Tag, which had them all breathless with running and laughing, until Laddle said she was afraid no-one would sleep. In the event, no-one was sick except Dacko, one of the dacks-hounds we had brought back from Coburg, and that was because he had been eating grass. And that night, after dinner, Albert and I climbed the stair to the nursery floor and walked hand in hand to each bed, to look into each little flushed and sleeping face.

'They are so beautiful,' he whispered. 'God has blessed us.' Lenchen had flung off her covers, and he drew them up, tenderly tucking in her chubby arm, and then stooped to kiss her cheek, a feather touch that did not wake her. 'She smells like hay,' he said, almost to himself.

It was at moments like that, that I did not begrudge the effort and inconvenience involved in childbearing. To have given him such treasure, such joy, seemed a privilege I could not value highly enough.

We went downstairs again, and when I went to my dressing-room to prepare for bed, Albert came with me, and stood leaning against the chimneypiece with his legs crossed in that elegant way of his, chatting to me as my maid undressed me. I had had my hair dressed with white roses and ivy that evening (I usually wore fresh flowers rather than jewels in it when we had no guests), and when it was undone, he reached over and took one of the roses from the dressing-table, and held it to his nose.

'How soon the scent fades,' he murmured. 'It is wilting, poor little rose.'

'It has served its purpose,' I said, and then seeing him still look fixedly at it, I added, 'I could press it for you, if you liked – as a memento.'

He looked up at me quizzically, as though I had made a joke, or spoken in a foreign language; and then, pushing himself to his feet, he stepped across to me, and stooped, laying the rose gently in my hand. 'You keep it,' he said; brushed my bare shoulder with his lips on the way to my ear, and whispered, *'Die Frau hat gar hübsche Schultern.'* My heart beat a little faster at this compliment. He had always admired my shoulders, and it thrilled me that he should desire me still after all those years and all those children. I watched him in the glass as he went through the door into the sitting-room on his way to his own dressing-room. 'Don't be long,' he said, feeling my eyes on him.

The rose I laid aside to be pressed when I had a moment to myself; for now, my maid finished undressing me, and when I was in my nightgown and she had brushed out my hair, I sent her away. Then I touched a little Kölnischwasser behind my ears, put on my favourite brown-and-green silk robe, and with my hair streaming down my back, went to find my husband. He was not yet in the bedroom; nor was he in the sitting-room, but as soon as I entered it I heard the sound of his organ playing, so I knew he was in his dressing-room. I walked over to the door and opened it.

He was seated there in his dressing-gown, staring at nothing, playing. He did not notice me come in. I did not know the piece – if piece it was – but it was so melancholy that it made the hair stand up on the back of my neck; something in a minor key, with no tune, but continually modulating, as though passing through hall after hall of the mind, in which each image and memory was yet more sad. And his face, oh, his face was set and white and expressionless, a stranger's face – a mask. I was so frightened that I shivered, and the movement, small as it was, was enough to disturb him. He stopped and turned to me (I'm sure he did not know what he was playing, but he was too much a musician not to complete the resolution he had been leading towards, and his hands played on two chords after he had turned his head, to bring the music home). Then the life came back into his face. It was like seeing a light kindled at a window in a previously empty house, and I felt my blood rush back into all the places it had abandoned for a moment. Now he looked only tired.

'What is it? Have I kept you waiting?' he said, almost in a normal voice. He stood up, and came to me, and taking my cold hands looked down into my face and said again, 'What is it?'

'Albert,' I said, 'you wouldn't – you wouldn't leave me?' I didn't know how else to phrase the question.

He didn't answer for a moment – for one heart-stopping moment. And then he said gently, quizzically, 'Foolish little one, where would I go?' And then, seeing it was not answer enough, he said seriously, 'It is not *you* I would leave, don't you understand that? There is nowhere I ever want to be, except in your arms. Come, come now, come to bed.'

I did not understand, but I would not resist him, seeing how tired he was, and hoping things would become clear, I let him put his arm round me and lead me away. A few minutes later he put out the light on his side of our bed, and turned towards me, taking me into his arms. 'Now we are safe,' he said. 'Now there is no world, thank God, only us.' I turned my face up to him, and even in the dark our mouths found each other without hesitation, and we kissed with the sweetness of accustomed lovers. Then I felt him reach upwards for the little brass lever on the bedhead that worked the door lock, and my heart lifted as I heard the familiar, satisfying, heavy click as he shut out any possibility of our being disturbed.

Afterwards he slept soundly, with no bad dreams.

Fifteen

7th August 1900, at Osborne

I HARDLY know how I am to write this. Oh God, my poor darling Affie! The news came by telegram at eight in the morning on the 31st of July – the terrible news – and Baby brought them to me after I had dressed. A third child of mine lost! It is so very hard to bear. I did not even know the end was near. Marie gave me no hint of it when she visited in June with Baby Bee, though perhaps she may not have known herself – since Young Affie died she and Affie had hardly seen each other. I see now that Beatrice tried to prepare me for the shock a week beforehand, but even she did not know the full facts, for though the doctors told her he was hopelessly ill, they said he might live six months more. It has been kept secret, but he has been ill for two years with the same thing that took poor Vicky's Fritz, and it seems that for the last two weeks he was being fed through a straw, because the horrible disease had taken such a hold on him. One could not wish him to linger on in such a state, and his death must be seen as a merciful release; but it is hard for a mother to say about her son, Thy will be done, oh God. The end, at least, was peaceful. He was sitting in the garden at six-thirty in the evening,

269

went to bed at nine and was sleeping, 'like a child' they say, when he died half an hour later. I feel so for poor Marie, losing her only son last year, and now her husband; and for her dear daughters, who adored their papa – how they will grieve!

But three children gone before me! And three dear sons-in-law besides! It is very hard at eighty-one. My only comfort has been in talking over my happy memories of his life, his childhood, Christmases and treats, his dear birthdays which he always spent here. He would have been fifty-six on Monday. It seems impossible to believe he has gone! He died at the Rosenau in dear Coburg, of course, where he has been since 1893, when he succeeded to the title. I have seen so little of him in late years, for he was five years in Malta and four at Devonport before that. Lenchen feels it very much, for he was a great favourite with her.

I felt too shaken and broken to do or write anything for days, and the weather as if in sympathy with our tragedy has been frightful, with the most terrible gales I ever remember at this time of the year. There is a great deal of damage to the trees, several ships in the Solent have pulled their anchors, and the poor old swimming-bath has been blown on to the rocks and wrecked, quite beyond repair I am told. And I had only just been writing about it! Life is full of such ironies.

But good weather follows bad, just as bad follows good, and life goes on – ah, how it goes on! One must endure, and bear what God sends with patience and humility. There are still moments of gladness to be gleaned in the acres of sorrow. The children, for instance, were very droll at luncheon. Little David was standing by my chair and telling me about playing football with some of the boys from the village, boasting how clever he was at it. I said, 'That is very well, my dear, but I hope you are clever at your lessons, too.'

'Oh, I am a good boy,' he said. 'I know lots of German.' So then Maurice, who was listening with a superior look from the vast eminence of three years' seniority, challenged him to say something in German; and David of course was immediately struck dumb, cudgelling his brains in vain.

'You don't know any German words at all!' Maurice said triumphantly. 'He doesn't, Gangan! It's all "spoof"!'

David went red in the face. He can't bear to be laughed at. 'Yes, I do!' he shouted. 'I know – I know *lumbago*!' He must have heard me asking Marie Mallet about her attack of it. I did laugh at that – shocking myself for a moment; but children are the strongest goad for bringing one back to life!

And now I am sitting in the sun again and getting on with my writing, which helps to keep my mind off things. I have scribbled off a letter to Victoria Battenberg (poor Alice's eldest), who sent me such a nice photograph of the baby to cheer me up, seven weeks old now and such a big child! When I held him on my lap at the Christening, he flung back a hand and knocked my 'specs' off my nose, and almost blacked my eye into the bargain! To please me, Victoria and Ludwig gave him Albert as his first name (Albert Victor Nicholas Louis Francis is the full set) but it seems they call him Dickie at home, I can't think why.

The three problems which almost from the beginning of the century had made governments' heads ache – the Corn Laws, the Irish, and Chartism – became inextricably tangled together, and reached a crisis in 1848 (the *annus mirabilis* of Europe, as it has been called, when the continent boiled up, spilled over, and eventually settled down in a completely different pattern).

Peel had gradually been persuading me that the Corn Laws imposed an unfair and unnecessary burden on the labouring classes and must be abolished, and the partial failure of the potato crop in Ireland in 1845, and the consequent famine amongst the Irish peasants, finally brought matters to a head. It was not that cheaper corn would help the Irish, for they were so dependent on potatoes that even if they had been given wheat they would not have known what to do with it, and had no machinery for grinding it. But the famine provided a warning that cheap food for the lower orders was pressingly needed, and so Peel introduced a measure for the abolition into Parliament in January 1846. Albert went down to the House to hear the debate, meaning it as a sign that the Bill had my full support. Unfortunately, his presence there gave offence to many, partly, I suppose, because of the old thorn of his being a 'foreigner', but also because the landed aristocracy did not think I had any business supporting a Bill which they thought was directly against their interests. Lord George Bentinck went so far as to write me a very impertinent letter on the subject, which made us both very angry; but on Peel's advice, Albert never went to the House again.

Peel got his Bill through, and the Corn Laws were repealed on the 26th of June 1846, but the disgruntled landowners had their revenge by defeating him immediately afterwards on an unrelated matter, forcing him to resign, and leaving me with no choice but to summon Lord John Russell and the Whigs to form a government. I had grown fond enough of Peel by that time (and trusted him completely, which was more important) to be very sorry indeed at losing him, especially as I did not at all care for Russell, a little, ugly man who was conceited and opinionated (his nickname was Finality Jack) and had very unappealing manners. But I had only just emerged from childbed (Lenchen was born on the 25th of May) and I was rejoicing in being fully reunited with my darling husband; so the change of government, which once would have had me trembling and in tears, now had far less impact on me. The continuity of family life, and my contentment with Albert, made matters of mere politics very much of secondary importance.

In 1846 the potato crop failed again, this time completely, while at the same time cereal crops everywhere were very poor. The winter that followed was one of the most severe in human memory, and the sufferings of the Irish were too dreadful to be imagined. Meanwhile the removal of price controls encouraged wild speculation in wheat, especially since with the scarcity of 1846 the price soared to 115 shillings; then in 1847 the wheat harvest was enormously abundant, the price dropped to 49 shillings, the speculators were ruined, eleven banks failed, and there was disaster in the City. The Lord Lieutenant of Ireland had been begging for money for Ireland, to relieve some of the desperate suffering; but with this new financial crisis, the Chancellor of the Exchequer had to tell him, 'I cannot give you what I do not have.'

So the three threads drew together. Chartism had strong links with the Irish problem, for the leader of the Chartists, Feargus O'Connor, was MP for Cork and also leader of the Irish Nationalists, and many of his lieutenants were Irish Nationalists too. Chartism had been rumbling and grumbling around the country in various forms all my life (the so-called 'Massacre of Peterloo' happened in my birth-year of 1819) but since 1839 it had been consistently demanding the six points of the 'People's Charter' which gave the movement its present name. The six demands were: the vote for every man over twenty-one, regardless of his status; the secret ballot; equal-sized constituencies; the abolition of the property qualification for MPs; payment of MPs; and annual Parliaments. Apart from the fact that the demands themselves were either absurd or undesirable, or both, the greatest objection to the Chartist movement was that it stirred up the lower classes and got them into trouble. Few of the labouring sort had any desire at all for political reform, but when they were out of work or hungry or had some grievance against their employer, there were the Chartists (who were usually educated and comfortably off people of the middling sort) ready to harness the discontent and turn it into violence and civil disobedience for their own ends. I believe that is how the French Revolution of 1789 began – perhaps it is how all revolutions begin. As Lord M. said to me once, all the poor ever want is enough to eat and a little more than enough to drink; but in their ignorance they become sticks with which political agitators (who you may be sure are never hungry themselves) beat governments. And then when things go wrong, it is the poor who finish up at the end of a rope or on the treadmill, while the agitators escape abroad to plot the next rising.

Revolution was in the air. By 1847 we were aware that trouble was brewing all over Europe, and every country was seething with discontent. There was civil war in Spain; in Portugal Queen Maria faced a pretender to the throne and fierce conflict between factions; the Austrian empire was creaking at the seams with the nationalist ambitions of its constituent countries; Italy under a new liberal Pope was preparing to make a bid for independence; Greece was suffering under intense poverty and a corrupt tyrant of a king. Everywhere there was trouble. Only two countries were peaceful: Belgium, industrialized and prosperous, where my beloved uncle Leopold, king by invitation, had modernised the institutions and ruled with justice by a liberal constitution; and Russia, where whatever the sufferings of the people, the great autocrat Nicholas I kept an iron control over everything.

But the first revolution of 1848, the Year of Revolutions, took everyone by surprise. We had known for some time that King Louis-Philippe of France was unpopular: his regime was corrupt, and his principal minister, Guizot, was a hated reactionary. But no-one had anticipated any real danger to the Throne. The ties between our families were strong, for Louis-Philippe, when still the Duc d'Orléans, had been forced into exile during the French Revolution and had gone to Canada, where he had encountered his old friend Madame Julie de St Laurent. Madame had introduced him to my papa, and they had become great friends, and Papa had generously lent the Duc £200 (which he could ill afford at the time) to set himself up as a teacher. (The Duc never forgot the kindness and as soon as he became king he paid back the loan to me, Papa being dead by then, of course.) On his return to Europe the Duc had come to England and become friendly with the Regent, and with Princess Charlotte and Uncle Leopold. The Duc had become King of France in 1830 and Uncle Leopold King of the Belgians in 1831, and Uncle Leopold had, of course, married the King of France's daughter, my beloved aunt Louise.

It was Aunt Louise who had first urged Albert and me to visit the King and Queen of France, and in order not to make it a State visit, with all the political implications, Albert and I had gone to them at their private home at Eu in 1843, as part of our first cruise in our new steam yacht. They gave us a wonderfully warm welcome (and rather touchingly ordered from London vast quantities of Cheddar cheese and bottled beer, under the impression that this was all English people ate! I heard afterwards that Peel, who was not going on the trip, sent a message to Lord Aberdeen, who was, saying he hoped the weather would be calm on the crossing so that he could do justice to all the delicacies that were being laid on!) The King and Queen and their children treated us most affectionately, and we had since quite thought of them as family. Sadly since then diplomatic relations, and my feelings about the King, had cooled because of his increasingly Bourbon attitude to ruling, and especially because of his very bad behaviour over the Spanish Marriages.

The Spanish Marriages problem had been extensively discussed on our second visit to Eu in 1845, and I had thought the King and I understood each other. The situation in Spain was this: King Ferdinand had married for the third time in 1829 after two childless marriages, and had produced two daughters, Isabella and Louisa. But he died in 1832, leaving two-year-old Isabella Queen (with her mother Queen Christina as Regent). It was obviously of the greatest importance to all of us who Isabella eventually married. Albert and I favoured our cousin Leopold of Coburg (younger brother of Ferdinand, who had married Maria of Portugal), which would keep it all nicely in the family.

However, in 1843 a rumour grew up that King Louis-Philippe had hatched a scheme to marry Queen Isabella to her cousin the Duc of Cadiz, and her younger sister the Infanta Louisa, to Louis-Philippe's own son Montpensier. Since the Duc of Cadiz was widely believed to be incapable of having children, this would mean the Throne of Spain would eventually come to the Infanta Louisa and her French husband.

If true, this would have been a shocking thing, for not only did the Treaty of Utrecht forbid the uniting of the French and Spanish thrones, but it also expressly barred any member of the House of Orléans from coming to the Throne of Spain. When we visited Eu in 1845, Louis-Philippe assured us he had no designs on the Throne of Spain, and that he wanted the Spanish marriage only because the Infanta was very wealthy and would make a good wife for his son.

He further promised that he would not pursue the matter until Isabella had made all safe by marrying and producing an heir.

We believed his assurances, and continued to promote the match between Isabella and Cousin Leopold; but the rumours persisted, and suddenly in September 1846 French and Spanish ministers (prompted by the wicked Guizot, of course!) got together and arranged the double wedding of Isabella to Cadiz and Louisa to Montpensier on the same day. We were all very angry about it, and I was especially upset that Cousin Leopold had been treated in such an offhand and really *rude* manner, which hurt Albert's feelings very much. There was nothing for it but to pronounce at an end the special *entente* between France and England – which pleased Russia and Austria no end! (In the event, Louis-Philippe did not prosper by his scheming, for Queen Isabella went on to have five children by the Duc of Cadiz; so he did not gain the Throne of Spain, and fourteen months later he lost the Throne of France into the bargain!)

As I said, we all knew that Louis-Philippe was unpopular, but the opposition in France was understood to be against the regime, rather than against monarchy itself, and Paris was as well defended as any capital could be. There had been a number of anti-government demonstrations, but they had passed off peacefully; but then on the 22nd of February Guizot banned a particular procession in Paris, because the numbers gathering were thought to be dangerously large. Despite the ban the procession still took place, and by then feeling in the city was running so high that the National Guard sent a deputation to the King at the Tuileries saying they could not answer for the peace unless the government was changed.

The King accepted their word and dismissed Guizot, and everything seemed to quieten down. But on the following evening another demonstration formed in the centre of the city. The crowds were huge, but apparently peaceful, until outside the Ministry of Foreign Affairs a single shot was fired. No-one knew who fired it, but the ball broke the leg of a horse. The horse was the mount of a major commanding the line regiment guarding the Ministry, and he was very, very fond of it. On such tiny things the fate of nations can depend! In the heat of the moment, and his anger and grief, he gave the order to fire into the crowd.

They say fifty or more people were hit, many of them women and children, and the crowd ran, dispersing into the *faubourgs* to rouse their friends and neighbours. Gunsmiths' shops were raided, barricades thrown up, and by next morning Paris was in armed revolt, with the National Guard joining the mob. It was 1789 all over again, and the King and Queen must have been terrified as reports came in to them through the night. By the morning an armed mob had surrounded the Tuileries, and a representative of the National Guard presented the King with a hastily drawn up Act of Abdication to sign.

I have to say in justice to him that Louis-Philippe refused at first to abdicate, saying that he would sooner die; but his family did not entirely agree with his sentiments, and at length Montpensier persuaded him to sign. It was only just in time: as the royal family fled through the Tuileries gardens, the mob broke in and ransacked the palace. The old King was hustled away, muttering, '*J'abdique, j'abdique*,' to everyone he passed. In the confusion the family got separated, both from each other and from their possessions, and when they eventually managed to smuggle their way to England, they had nothing but the clothes they stood up in – and in the case of the Duchesse de Nemours, not even those, for they were torn off her by the mob.

Of course, at the time we did not receive the story clearly and concisely as I have just written it. All we had for days was rumour and suspense and false report. We heard on the 25th that Louis-Philippe had landed at Folkestone, and I cancelled our dinner engagement and summoned Russell and Palmerston to request that we might give sanctuary to the French royal family. The report turned out to be false, but it was agreed that we might put the royal yacht at the King's disposal if and when he escaped. We were told, however, that we must be careful how we received the exiles, because the country would not like it, and it might make diplomatic relations difficult in future with the new rulers of France.

'We have family ties,' I said shortly. 'It is a family matter. And as to the country not liking it, what sort of example would I be giving my own subjects if I failed to support a brother sovereign? I will not be seen to encourage revolutionaries. I cannot and will not ignore their plight.'

'Quite so, ma'am,' Palmerston said soothingly, silencing Russell with a glance. (I was heavily pregnant at the time, and I suppose he felt I needed tender handling: Russell was notoriously 'tackless', as Arthur used to say.) 'I would not dream of asking you to do so. But I do recommend extreme caution. Our *entente* with France failed, as you know, because of the King's own behaviour. I think you ought not to invite them here, to Buckingham Palace, at least not to begin with, until we see how the country takes it.'

'Claremont,' Albert said suddenly. 'Why should they not go to Claremont? Will that be "unofficial" enough?'

'Certainly, sir,' said Palmerston, with a nod, and added kindly, 'As for their immediate necessities, I'm sure we can manage something out of secret service funds – we can call it a gift from an anonymous well-wisher, or something of the sort.'

By ones and twos the desperate, heart-stricken French began to arrive; but still not the King and Queen. We began to fear the worst, and Albert, strange to say, seemed to feel it much more than me, and began to look really haggard and careworn. Perhaps I was insulated against the shock by my condition. At last on the 3rd of March we had a letter from Newhaven from the King himself, to say he had arrived safely: the British Consul at Le Havre had rescued him and smuggled him and the Queen across in disguise. It was a very affecting letter, for he addressed me as 'madame' instead of the kingly 'ma soeur', and signed himself simply by his name, with no title.

Albert went down to Claremont to see them settled in, and on the 6th of March Palmerston allowed them to visit us at Buckingham Palace. They came looking very pale, very worn, and very shocked at what they had suffered. They were very conscious of the change in their circumstances – the poor things hardly had the means of living. I had to provide the Queen with some very basic necessities, even with a hairbrush, for which she thanked me tremblingly. She cried a good deal, and I did my best to make her comfortable, and lost any desire to point out to them that the King had brought it all on himself. He looked, indeed, very old, a poor broken old man; and it made us realise by what a slender thread our fortunes hung.

There was one happy footnote to the story: in October of that year the National Assembly – the new ruling body of France – voted almost without a dissentient voice to restore to the exiled Orléans family their private property and incomes. Russell told me that he thought when everything was arranged the King would have better than a million pounds, so they could all live in comfort for the rest of their lives. It was unexpectedly generous of the French Republic, and seemed to show they had no spleen against Louis-Philippe, but simply wanted to be rid of him. It made me remember, with guilty amusement, something that Lord M. had once said to me – that the French could not bear *l'ennui*, and though they would forgive their kings for being wicked, they could never forgive them for being dull!

9th August 1900

THERE WAS no doubt that the revolution in France made us nervous; we had the victims living under our noses, and in those days the memory of 1793 haunted every sovereign's darkest thoughts. Albert was very much cast down by the whole thing, and I grew quite worried about him, but it was not until early April that the danger of our own situation really came home to me. From the middle of March I was too much preoccupied with childbirth to think about anything else, in any case. The new baby – our sixth – was born on the 18th of March; another girl, a large baby who gave me a very bad time. But I was growing used to the business now, and, as Albert said to comfort me, we had been very lucky in six pregnancies to produce six live, healthy babies. It would have been the outside of enough to have had all that labour for a stillbirth, or a child that lived only a few days, which was the experience of so many women.

(We named the new baby Louise, after Albert's adored and lost mother. She has turned out the handsomest of our children, the most vivacious and the most artistic – she is a very fine sculptress – but she has a sharp tongue and a 'difficult' personality. In fact, she has a reputation for being a mischief-maker: Ponsonby – Sir Henry, that is, not Fritz – once said, 'Princess Louise plays old Harry with every household and person she touches.' But she has not had the easiest of lives, poor thing. When she was sixteen she almost died of tubercular meningitis, which we have since learned causes infertility, and I fear that may have been at the bottom of the unhappiness of her marriage. She and Lorne simply couldn't get on together, although I have always said that as long as they keep up appearances in public, I accept their right to spend their time apart. Of course, she can't have been easy to live with – she always was dreadfully contradictory, even as a child – but if what I have heard about Lorne is true, she has had her provocations. But things have been much better between them in the last few years, and I'm happy to see they are rediscovering their common interests, and becoming friends, as husband and wife ought always to be.)

But to return to my story: on the 3rd of April 1848 I left my confinement, and was able to have breakfast with Albert again in our dear old way. No breakfast egg ever tasted so good as that first one after each baby, when I sat opposite my husband again, and had him smile at me across the table.

'Oh, this is good!' I said. 'I feel as though I had been in prison. I can quite see why they call it confinement!'

'It is a prison for me to be without you,' he said. 'But the new baby is very handsome. She has the most remarkably white skin. Perhaps she will be as beautiful as my mother was.'

'She is bound to be something extraordinary, born into such stirring times,' I said.

He gave me a quizzical look. 'I wonder if you know *how* stirring? The Chartists are all stirred up by events in Paris, and there have been parades and meetings almost every day in various parts of London.'

I frowned. 'But it will not come to anything, surely? It is just a few troublemakers. They have no real support amongst the ordinary people.'

'I don't wish to alarm you, my love, but it is more than that. The organisation of these people is amazing. They have secret signals, and spies everywhere, and they correspond from town to town by means of carrier pigeons. There is no knowing how many of them there really are, but they have the support of the Irish Nationalists, who are always looking for a revolution—'

'Revolution?' I cried, not knowing whether to laugh or be afraid. Was he joking me?

But he looked serious. 'The troubles all over Europe have repressed trade, and Europe is our market. With no-one buying our goods, there are thousands out of work and starving. They are the tinder only waiting for the spark.'

I put down my egg-spoon in dismay. My lovely white Dorking egg was suddenly Dead Sea fruit. 'Have I been living on the moon?' I said. 'I did not think things were so bad – just little disturbances, nothing really to worry about.'

'It was natural for you to be otherwise preoccupied.' He hesitated. 'I have to confess to you that I am very worried. I believe we are in danger.'

Well, I had seen he was worried ever since the news first came from France, and it had puzzled me that he was so much more alarmed than I saw reason for. I think now, with hindsight, that it was a proof of his 'foreignness' which I always tried to deny even to myself, but which every now and again revealed itself in a sort of mutual incomprehension between him and the English. In the present instance I think he was afraid because he did not have the instinctive feeling for the people which I have always had, the ability to judge their underlying mood, which often proves more valuable to a monarch than all the intellectual analysis and ratiocination in the world.

However it was, he was nervous and it communicated itself to me. Later that day it seemed he was not the only one who was worried, for I was asked for a special audience by Russell and the Home Secretary, Sir George Grey, and when they were admitted, their expressions were very grave indeed. They had come to tell me that the Chartists were planning a monster meeting in London for the 10th of April – only a week away.

'Their idea, as we understand it so far,' Russell said, 'is to have deputations from all the different quarters meet on Kennington Common, and then march to Westminster to present a petition of a million and a half signatures.'

Albert paled. 'A million and a half men marching on Parliament?'

'It won't come to that,' Russell said quickly. 'The signatures will have been collected all over the country. But I've heard that O'Brien has said there will be half a million at the meeting.' He shrugged indifferently. 'I dare say he exaggerates. You know what these Irish are like.'

'You do not seem to be taking this meeting very seriously,' I said severely. His attitude to Albert sometimes bordered on the disrespectful.

It was Grey who answered. 'Oh, we do take it seriously, ma'am, I assure you. But we have been given a week's warning, and that is everything. It gives us plenty of time to make our arrangements.'

'The meeting must be banned,' Albert said decisively. 'It must not be tolerated.'

I glanced at him, frowning. That was how the trouble in France had begun, with the banning of a meeting.

Grey said, 'If you will forgive me, sir, that would only add fuel to the flames – give the leaders ammunition to use against us.'

'You should never have let the leaders out of prison in the first place,' Albert growled. I loved him when he was defending me! 'You had them locked up, and you should have kept them locked up.'

Russell answered almost scornfully. 'We don't do things that way here, sir. O'Brien and the rest were imprisoned for public order offences according to the law, and when they had served their sentences they were released according to the law. It has always been my opinion that if these people have real grievances, they have a right to express them; and if they don't, they will not keep their following. Repressing them only makes them struggle harder; very often these things fizzle out if you don't inflate their self-consequence by paying too much attention to them.'

'Evidently you do not think this will "fizzle out", or you would not be here,' I said.

'Well, no, ma'am,' Russell said, raising a cool eyebrow. 'That there will be a monster meeting seems certain. Our business is to contain and control it, not forbid it.'

'There will be no march on Parliament, ma'am,' Grey said soothingly. 'That we can and will prevent. There is a law on the Statute Books dating from the seventeenth century which forbids the presentation to Parliament of a petition by more than ten persons, and we shall invoke it.' (And a very handy law it has proved, too, on several occasions!)

'The law may forbid it, but how will you prevent it?' I said. 'Half a million men will not be easy to convince.'

'I assure you it will not be half so many,' Russell said in his annoyingly lofty way.

'Then you should not have mentioned the figure at all,' I snapped.

He was impossible to snub. 'That is the figure the Chartists are mentioning. I merely thought it my duty to keep Your Majesty informed.'

Grey intervened again. 'Without wishing unduly to alarm Your Majesty, an event of this sort inevitably attracts mischief-makers, and I think it would be wise to be prepared for the worst.'

Now I did begin to feel alarmed. 'Then we must send for the Duke,' I decreed, and about that there was no argument. In any crisis, England always turned to him.

Albert walked off with the two ministers, but did not immediately return, and in his absence his fear began to work on me. Half a million Chartists meeting on Kennington Common? A multitude beyond imagining! I saw them in my mind's eye, brutish, low men, their uncultured minds inflamed by revolutionary language; I saw them marching across the bridge, surrounding Parliament, stones and iron bars ready in their hands, their voices hoarse with animal violence. And Westminster was a notorious slum area, narrow streets of the worst sort of tenements, inhabited by beggars, thieves, prostitutes, murderers, all the dregs of society. Those people would see their chance and seize it, emerge from their rackety hovels like rats surging out of a sewer and overrun the streets, pour like a plague over the houses of the rich nearby, looting, smashing, burning.

And just up the hill was Buckingham Palace, its walls notoriously easy to climb. They would come pouring through the gardens like the Paris mob through the gardens of the Tuileries; they would swarm into the Palace, tearing down pictures and curtains, smashing windows and looking-glasses, ripping the clothes from our backs as we tried in vain to escape, our helpless children stumbling beside us, sobbing in terror . . .

In my own defence, I must say that I had just emerged from a very trying confinement, and my spirits were often low at this point in my recovery. By the time Albert came back, I was in floods of tears and shivering with fear.

'Where have you been?' I cried. 'How could you leave me?'

'I was walking in the garden,' he said. 'My nerves were a little disordered by the news, and I needed to calm myself.'

'*You* needed to calm yourself!' I raved. 'What about *me*? What about *my* nerves? You simply disappear and don't tell me where you are going, leaving me here all alone, to think about what might happen to me! How can you be so selfish? It's me the mob will be after, you know, not you! I am the Queen! And what about my poor children? What about my helpless little baby? Not a month old, and torn limb from limb by revolutionaries! Oh, what will become of us?'

There was more of the same, I'm afraid. When I am in a passion I say anything that comes into my mind, and poor Albert had much to do to quieten me (though perhaps the storm had the advantage for him of taking his mind off his own fears). When I was calmer, he told me that on the way out, Russell and Grey had said that in view of the late events in France, it might be advisable for me and the children to go out of London for a few days.

'They want me to run away?' I gasped. Such a thing would never have occurred to me.

'Oh, not run, I think,' he said in his funny, precise way. 'Just quietly leave, you know, perhaps two days before the meeting, and go down to Osborne. You will be quite safe there with the children, on our own estate, with our own people about you. And it will make the Government's task easier if they do not have to worry about defending you. Of course, it may all come to nothing, but there is no sense in making things difficult for them—'

I had quite stopped crying now. My eyes narrowed. 'You speak of me and the children. What about *you*?'

'Oh, I stay here, of course,' he said lightly, as though talking about taking a bath or going early to bed.

'No,' I said.

'But someone must take care of your interests,' he said, eyeing me cautiously.

'I have a government to take care of my interests. We go together, or not at all. I will not be separated from you.'

'Now, little Wifey—' he began, but I cut him off.

'I will not be argued with. I don't care what happens, we can go or stay, but we will remain together. Good God, do you think I would have a quiet moment at Osborne if you were here? Do you think I would *want* to be safe if you were in danger?'

He saw that it was no use, and shrugged, and left it at that. Perhaps he thought that the Duke might side with him and persuade me, but the Duke, when he came to discuss the arrangements with us, was of my opinion. He brought with him Richard Mayne, the Commissioner of the Metropolitan Police – a very capable, intelligent man whom I liked very much.

'What I think is most important, ma'am,' said the old soldier, standing with his hands clasped behind him (as I'm told he stood when planning many a military strategy), 'is to keep the temperature down. I am at one with Russell in that. To have the streets filled with troops would likely provoke more trouble than it prevented. Besides, it would present a very *off* appearance. We're not Frenchmen, after all.'

'Our idea, ma'am,' said Mayne, 'is to have only police officers on duty, so as to make it appear a purely civil operation. We don't want a repetition of Peterloo.'

'Quite so, Sir Richard,' I said, 'but can your men cope? I understand the numbers involved will be quite extraordinary.' I had had my moment of wild weeping, and was completely rational again. Great events, in any case, make me calm; it is only trifles that irritate my nerves.

'Special constables, ma'am,' said Mayne. 'We mean to enrol as many as we can – a hundred and fifty thousand if possible. Every gentleman in London will be under oath if I have any say in it.'

I nodded. 'Excellent. But is there to be no military presence, Duke?'

'The troops will be there, ma'am, but out of sight until required. I have given my orders, and by the day itself I shall have nine or ten thousand in the capital, including yeomanry and artillery.' He began to walk about, clearly excited by this return to arms, like an old warhorse scenting gunpowder. 'The men will be concealed at strategic points about the city, and there will be a detachment inside every government building, with the windows barricaded. Warships will be commandeered, and moored on the Thames with men and artillery on board ready to come ashore if they are needed. And there will be a battery of artillery stationed at every bridge. The man who holds the bridges holds the town – that is one of my aphorisms.'

I was feeling much more comfortable by now. Somehow one could not be much afraid of anything as long as the Duke was in charge – and the Chartists would know that too, of course.

'The Palace will be well defended,' he went on. 'I shall put a battery in the Royal Stables, and a detachment of foot in the gardens, as well as doubling the normal guard. Your Majesty shall not suffer the inconvenience of so much as a broken window.'

'Thank you, Duke,' I said. 'But as to my own movements?'

'If Your Majesty pleases, we should like you to leave two days before the meeting, on the 8th. A train will be laid on for half past ten in the morning for Gosport, and the party will consist of Your Majesty, His Royal Highness, the royal children, and your personal suites. No military escort or presence, if you please: we wish it to appear that Your Majesty is merely taking a holiday.'

'But we shall have plenty of constables on duty, ma'am,' Richard Mayne put in, 'though I doubt there will be any need of them.'

'You seem to have everything very well arranged,' I said.

'We shall be prepared, whatever happens,' the Duke said decisively. 'Your Majesty may rest assured that nothing will get past *me*. But to make sure no false reports are spread to alarm or inflame other parts of the kingdom, I propose to seize the telegraph system on the day itself, and all transmissions will be passed through me.'

I smiled inwardly at that, for the Duke's reports were renowned for their brevity and lack of emotion. The story has often been told that his first report of victory at Waterloo had been so muted that many had taken it for a defeat!

When my two brave defenders had gone, Albert came to take me in his arms. I rested my head against his chest and we stood like that for a while, drawing comfort from each other's nearness.

'I still think it would be easier just to arrest the ringleaders,' he said at last.

'You can't arrest them until they've done something,' I said.

'*You* can,' he said. 'You could order it so.'

'No, no, I'm sure they're right – Russell and the Duke. If we made martyrs of the ringleaders, the ordinary people would never see how worthless they are.'

'But all this trouble – and danger – '

'Even if the ringleaders were arrested, it would not necessarily stop the meeting,' I pointed out. 'It might even be worse without them.' We were silent a while, and then I said, 'My one comfort is that all this protest is not directed against *me*.' But even as I said it, I knew it was false comfort. Revolution, if it came, might not be against Victoria, but it was certainly against the Queen.

Over the next few days we prepared for our flight, and Albert brought me back reports of the progress of the Duke's campaign and snippets of news. The great landlords who had houses in London were taking the threat very seriously, and many had brought up men from their estates to defend them. Lord Malmesbury, for instance, had six gamekeepers all armed with double-barrelled shotguns on permanent sentry-duty. As it was April and the middle of the Season, most families had been in residence, and there was a considerable exodus of wives and children down to the country, and cartloads of valuables were being smuggled out under cover of darkness. The troops were being marched in in small detachments and stationed very quietly and out of sight; but the artillery batteries on the bridges could not be hidden of course, and their presence had certainly made Feargus O'Connor nervous, for he stood up in the Lower House to assure his colleagues that no violence was intended and that he would not allow the meeting to take place if he thought any breach of the peace was likely to result. Meanwhile there was an enthusiastic rush of gentlemen to take the oath of the special constable: I suppose since we had been at peace since 1815, they were all eager for the chance to break a few heads in a just cause.

(Amongst those sworn, as a matter of interest, was one Louis Napoleon Bonaparte, nephew of the Tyrant, who within a very few years was to make himself Emperor of the French, and who later became quite a friend of ours; and a very fascinating man he was too. When yet another revolution – oh, these French! – drove him from France, I invited him and his Empress to make their home in England. He lived here at peace until his death in 1873, and she is still one of my dearest friends.)

On the morning of the 8th I looked out of my window and saw soldiers in the Palace Gardens. The sight of them brought home to me the danger we were facing, and I found my palms damp and my stomach churning. Only six weeks ago a peaceful demonstration in Paris had turned, at the firing of one shot, into a revolution, and the King of France now languished, a penniless exile, in my uncle's house in Esher. If the same were to happen here, where would we go – always assuming we escaped with our heads still attached to our necks? I most passionately did not want to go into exile, away from my beloved country – and besides, who would take us in? There was only Uncle Leopold, and I didn't want to live the rest of my life in Belgium. Death – as long as it was the death of all of us – would be preferable to that.

Albert and I breakfasted almost without talking, and then we went to see that the children were ready. The atmosphere had affected them, too. They were quiet and subdued, far from their usual noisy, boisterous selves. Dear Lady Lyttleton was a monument of calm. Alice ran straight to her papa as soon as he appeared, but Vicky, for a wonder, remained by Laddle's side, holding tight to her hand. 'Mamma,' she said urgently, 'what if the baby cries? Won't it give us away?'

I met Laddle's eyes above her head. Since the French exiles had arrived, the children had all been playing together, and she had plainly absorbed too many narrow-escape stories of hiding from the *gens d'armes*.

'Don't be silly, Puss, we're not running away in disguise,' I told her. 'We don't have to hide who we are from anyone.'

'But we are escaping, aren't we, Mamma?' Bertie said anxiously. I could not tell if he wanted reassurance, or was hoping we really were having an adventure.

'We're just going in our own carriages to the station, and taking an ordinary train and steamer to Osborne,' I said.

'You will like to see how Mr Cubitt's men are getting on, won't you, my son?' Albert said.

Bertie nodded, though not with any great enthusiasm, but Affie burst in, 'Can we help the man mix the concrete, Papa, like last time?'

'Yes, if you are very good, and do exactly as Laddle tells you all the way down,' Albert said. He drew out his watch. 'The carriages should be ready. I think we should go downstairs.'

A cold rain was falling steadily as the horses trotted out of the gates. Why did these familiar streets seem suddenly threatening, unreal? I stared from the windows, thinking one moment there were more people about than usual, and the next fewer, and finding a horrid significance in either state. Albert held my hand, and I could feel his tension like electricity in the air: I thought that if I ran my hand over him, he would crackle. The scene around the Palace of Westminster looked the same as on any day, the crowds and the traffic, the workmen whistling and crashing about on the scaffolding as Pugin's delicate Gothic spires rose painstakingly towards the skies. It was nearing completion now – but perhaps, I thought with a shiver, it never would be completed. Perhaps the mob would throw it down, set fire to it all over again in their frenzy of revenge. The artillery on Westminster Bridge was both reassuring and alarming, and a frigate was moored just below against the Charing Cross embankment, rocking gently on the flow, looking as if butter wouldn't melt in her mouth – just as if she were not crammed as full of men as an egg is of meat.

We arrived at Waterloo station exactly at half past ten, trotting between two lines of special constables to a welcoming committee of Richard Mayne and several senior officers.

'We thought it as well to clear the station completely, ma'am,' he said. 'The train is ready for you, with steam up. It can depart as soon as you are all on board.'

We walked quickly across the empty concourse, and its very emptiness frightened me, for our footsteps seemed to echo unnaturally, and the silence invited some violent rupture. At any moment, I thought, there would be the loud report of an assassin's gun – I had heard *that* before. A rifleman somewhere up in the rafters might be taking aim at this very instant, looking down on me as the French sniper looked down from the crosstrees at Admiral Nelson on the afterdeck of the *Victory*. The thought stiffened my spine. If there was such a one, he should see a soldier's daughter, not a refugee. I held my head higher and slowed my steps a little. If I was going to die, it would be with dignity!

All the same, I was relieved to find myself aboard the train, and felt so exhausted that I was glad to be laid down on a couch in the royal compartment and propped with pillows. As soon as the last door was slammed, the train jerked and chugged forward, and we were soon racing through the grimy suburbs and out into the fair, green, wet countryside – going much faster than Albert liked. He sat beside me, holding my hand, and for once had no complaint to make about the rushing speed and the frantic rocking of the carriage. Our speed excited the children, who soon forgot their fear and began to be as noisy and troublesome as usual; and then Louise began to cry.

We reached dear Osborne at a quarter past two in the afternoon. It was still raining, the evergreens were dripping most dismally, and the quiet and isolation seemed oppressive after all the excitement and worry of London. To be coming here in this way – not longing for it, and having planned how we would spend our precious time here, but all in a panic, against our will as it were, and leaving behind events of such moment which we could no longer affect in any way – seemed bewildering, almost painful; certainly not pleasant. By the evening reaction had set in. Now that we were all safe, I was feeling very strongly that we should not have left at all.

'My place at such a time is in my capital, alongside my people,' I grumbled at dinner, 'not running away like this.'

'It is your people you are running away from,' Albert pointed out, gloomily prodding at a cutlet.

'Nonsense! My people love me. It is one or two wicked, wanton men – agitators – who are causing the trouble, that's all. I have never run away from danger. What will people think of me?'

'I'm sure they won't think anything, my love,' Albert said.

'They must think *something*,' I retorted. 'What if they should decide it was cowardice? I am a soldier's daughter – I could never bear to be thought of like that. When people are wavering it could be the very thing to turn them against the monarchy.'

'But you said your people loved you,' Albert objected, putting down his fork with a weary air. 'Now you say they are wavering. Are these the same people, or some others, I wonder?'

'Why do you pick at everything I say in that disagreeable manner? You know exactly what I mean.'

'Do I? But I have never claimed to be a thought-reader.'

It was not a good evening.

The following day, in response to an urgent telegraph message from me, Albert's equerry, Colonel Phipps, who had remained in London, went out into the streets to see what people were saying about my departure for Osborne. He reported back, very much to my relief, that 'Her Majesty's reputation for personal courage stands so high, I never heard one person express a belief that her departure was due to personal alarm.' That point settled, there was nothing to do but to await events. For everyone's sakes, Albert and I tried to 'keep up our peckers', but the forty-eight hours between our arrival on the Isle of Wight and the news of the monster meeting were, I think, the longest in my life.

At last, at two o'clock exactly on the 10th of April, a telegraph message was relayed to me from Lord John Russell via the *Victory*, lying in Portsmouth harbour. I opened it with trembling hands, and the paper vibrated so much I could not focus at first on the words. I thrust it at Albert.

'Read it,' I begged him. 'Tell me the worst.'

'For the Queen,' he read, and then, his eye running ahead, he began not quite to smile, but to lighten, like a sky when the clouds roll away. 'The meeting at Kennington Common has dispersed quietly. The procession has been given up. The petition will be brought to the House of Commons without any display. No disturbance of any kind has taken place and not a soldier has been seen.'

By that evening, we had had the full story: the monster meeting had been a complete failure. To begin with, nothing like the numbers O'Connor had expected arrived. Estimates varied, but Russell's figure was about fifteen thousand. (*The Times* said twenty, but that many of them were spectators rather than demonstrators.) The waggon containing the mountain of paper which was the petition set off from Chartist headquarters at ten o'clock, drawn by six carthorses. Shops were shut, special constables lined the roads, but no soldiers were in sight. Through the morning small processions converged on Kennington Common, the Irish prominent amongst them, and the people watched them go by with mild curiosity rather than with any fervent or fellow feeling. When the protestors had all assembled on the Common, a few speeches were made, rather lacking in fire, and then the procession formed up behind the petition waggon and began to roll slowly back towards Westminster.

Before more than a few waggons had even got off the Common, the leading one was stopped by a constable, who asked O'Connor, very politely, if he would kindly come and have a word with Mr Mayne. O'Connor followed him to a nearby public house, where Richard Mayne and Lord John Russell were seated in comfort beside a good fire (and probably with a glass or two of something warming on a table between them!). Mayne told O'Connor that the meeting could continue but that the procession would not be allowed to cross the river, and Russell suggested genially that a cab – or rather two or three cabs – might be summoned to carry the petition to Westminster, if O'Connor was still desirous of delivering it.

O'Connor – looking white as a sheet, Russell said – thanked them, shook Mayne by the hand, and hastened out to tell the meeting that it had much better disperse. A heavy rain had started to fall, and the crowd began to fray and thin at the edges as the less enthusiastic slipped away to seek shelter. One or two formed small groups and tried to get up some speeches, but by a quarter to two the common was almost deserted, and the police allowed the last stragglers, wet to their skins, to cross the bridges and go home.

Three cabs, kindly summoned by a police constable, carried the petition, O'Connor and one or two lieutenants to Westminster, where it was handed over and disappeared at once into some or other anteroom – the equivalent of eternal oblivion. It was later discovered that many of the signatures were patently false (Victoria Rex was amongst them, with Sir Robert Peel, the Duke of Wellington, H. Nelson and Mr Punch) which further discredited O'Connor; and in a few months the movement had entirely collapsed from lack of support and lack of funds.

'All the same,' Albert said to me, 'we must not forget the legitimate grievances of the poor. Some of the working classes live in the most appalling conditions – filthy, insanitary, without education, without enlightenment, without hope. If we are to avert a real revolution, we must show ourselves worthy of our great position by protecting the weakest in our society.'

'You are right,' I said, catching fire from him. 'It is what every Christian should do for his neighbour – and we have more neighbours than the ordinary man. But what must we do?'

'Bad housing in particular is a great evil,' he said, pacing about the room like a cat. 'You cannot think how I long to see all those evil places torn down – like the "rookeries" behind Westminster – and replaced with rational housing. It is a most bitter disgrace that such horrors exist within a stone's throw of Buckingham Palace. Overcrowding alone accounts for so much of the misery and degradation of the poor. How can any family be respectable and decent when all share one room, and do *everything* in it? When they may be as many as seven sleeping in one bed?' I could see that for him this was a particularly horrible idea – but then he craved solitude and space around him. I wondered if sometimes the working classes might not actually like huddling together, especially when it was cold – and as to seven sharing one bed, if they disliked it so much they could surely sleep on the floor? But then when I thought of the happiness and real value of family life, I agreed with him absolutely. A clean, decent house, with sufficient separate rooms to protect the young ones from immorality, ought surely to be the least any family had the right to.

'What must we do, then?' I asked again. It seemed to me such a vast task. There were so many of the poor, and they were so *very* poor. Albert did not immediately find an answer, but it came to me a moment or two later. 'We must have advice,' I said. 'We must send for Lord Ashley.'

So that's what we did. The great philanthropist and reformer (later Lord Shaftesbury) came down to Osborne on the 19th and spent the whole day with us, walking about the grounds and talking about the condition of the working classes and what we could do to help them.

Ashley agreed with me about their disposition. 'They are good people, and very loyal, and all they need is a few comforts and some improvements to make their dwellings more healthy. They want no "Charter" – just a little sympathy and kind feeling.'

As to what we could do, he suggested that the Prince was the one to show the way, as my representative, by putting himself at the head of all social movements in art and science, especially as they bore on the poor; and as a practical beginning he offered to take Albert to visit some of the worst areas in the vicinity of the Strand, and to invite him as guest of honour to a meeting of the Society for Improving the Condition of the Labouring Classes.

This Albert did, with great success and acclaim, and it was the beginning of a new interest in his life. I mean, of course, interest in the active sense, for both of us had long been concerned by the way the rapid advances of the nineteenth century had left so many behind, and outside the scope of the benefits the progress conferred. It had always seemed to me wrong that those who had the most toil had the least enjoyment in this world. The obvious lack amongst the poor was of enough to eat and a decent place to live, of course, but beyond that I felt it wrong that they had so little in their lives except toil. For that reason I have always been very much against our dull, dreary Sundays. It is well enough for the middle classes, who have comfortable homes to do nothing in, to talk about 'keeping the Sabbath'; well for them to say there must be no games on Sundays, no galleries and museums open, no bands playing in the park, no fairs, no dancing – but when else can the working classes have any enjoyment of such things? I would have them go to church, of course – but Sunday ought to be a day of happy amusement for everyone. To deprive the lower orders of their innocent pleasures will not make them better people, or make them more receptive to Christian teaching. Certainly I have always tried to make Sunday a pleasant day in my family, without unnecessary restrictions. (A very impertinent Evangelist once wondered that I allowed my children to play tennis on a Sunday. I replied coldly that I had told them on Sundays they must retrieve their own balls, and not ask a servant to do it for them.)

So to his own concern for rational housing and proper sanitary arrangements for the working classes, Albert added mine for the fuller use of their leisure, and for helping them to better themselves. Public libraries, parks, promenades, museums, reading-rooms, Institutes of all kinds – where they wanted encouragement, Albert gave it. He headed subscription lists, attended meetings, performed opening ceremonies, spoke at banquets for the raising of funds, accepted honorary presidencies. It added another burden to his already over-taxed time, and took him away from me far more often than I liked, but we both knew that we were not put upon this earth merely to please ourselves; and to see the good that we did, and to receive the gratitude of those whose lives were uplifted, was more than ample reward.

AUTUMN

Sixteen

20th August 1900, at Osborne

I DREAM that I am all alone in a vast building stocked with magnificent treasures, walking slowly along the aisles, gazing about me at the white and gold and red, the marble and crystal, all glittering in the radiant air. A luminous mist obscures the distances; the air is mild and perfumed like a day in May; a feeling of delight, and peace, and pleasure pervades the vast spaces around me; and most of all, best of all, his presence hovers over everything. I stroll and stare and marvel, but I am puzzled. Why am I here? Not for pleasure alone, but for instruction. *What do you learn from all this, Victoria?* – his voice, benign, wise, solemn yet touched with joy. I look about me, considering. Yes, I see it now – that nothing is lost.

Nothing is lost. Nothing walks the earth aimlessly. It is all intended, and everything is to God's glory. His dear voice, near and all around me in the vastness; and then the touch of his lips upon my brow, the bliss of his real presence again. *Be at peace – I am near.*

I wake with tears on my cheeks, for it is only a dream, and I am old, and all alone. Oh, Albert, why did you leave me? For a moment, in the agony of my loneliness, I stretch my arms out to the empty air and cry out for him, gone from me so long ago. I know I shall not sleep again, so I climb from my empty bed and go to the window, draw back the drapes and look out. Dawn is coming, and there is a sea mist like thin milk, luminous towards the east, through which the tops of the junipers he planted stand up dark and strong. To every grieving soul morning comes with its small deliverance. And the dream was strangely comforting. If I am quiet, I can still feel his kiss, and hear his dear voice, though they will fade like this mist with the broadening of the day. *Be at peace – I am near.* Yes, it's true, his presence is everywhere to be found, and his influence. I know what it

293

was that I was dreaming of, and it is time now to write about it; and as it was a joyful thing, I must take myself back in time and write about it with a glad heart and a lively pen.

High society – the aristocracy and the idle rich – what I called 'the fashionables' – never liked my darling. It was partly because his great shyness and reserve gave an impression of *hauteur*, and people don't like to be snubbed. But it was mostly because he and they were so very different, and they must have known in their heart of hearts that he was their superior, and resented it. How could he do other than snub those whose roots were deep in Regency profligacy; whose manners were free and easy, and whose morals scandalous; addicted to deep play, hard drinking and sporting prowess; contemptuous of respectability, robust, cynical, sceptical, and tolerant of everything except intolerance? And how could they fail to be annoyed by a virtuous, studious, diligent, patient, painstaking, cultured idealist with a strong sense of duty – particularly when he was German, and had not the least interest in the blood-lines of horses?

As the Fashionables naturally gravitated towards gaming-rooms and race-meetings, Albert found his natural sphere in the learned societies, whose members were – at least in theory – dedicated to the searching out and dissemination of Truth and Enlightenment. In those solid Augustan buildings, with their weighty libraries, dark-panelled lecture-rooms, echoing corridors, marble busts and memorial windows, he found the atmosphere in which his great intellect could flourish. *Es bildet ein Talent sich in der Stille*, as Goethe says – Genius develops in quiet places!

The most eminent of these learned societies was the Society for the Encouragement of Arts, Manufactures and Commerce, familiarly known as the Society of Arts. In 1845 it invited Albert to become its President, and he fulfilled its best hopes by procuring for it from me a Royal Charter. Accepting this presidency led him in the end to the means of annoying more Fashionables at one time than we could ever have dreamed possible! It also had a darker consequence, which we could not have guessed at – but if he had known what was to come would he have altered course? I have to doubt it. Albert saw life from a different viewpoint from anyone else – certainly from me. It was as if his lens had a distortion which enabled him to see round corners, but not straight ahead.

The Great Exhibition was Albert's idea. There are several people – Henry Cole not least nor quietest among them – who have claimed that they thought of it first; but Albert was its 'only begetter', and I can state that positively because it was with me that he discussed the ideas which led up to it. It began in 1848, when Europe was in ferment, nationalism was a new and potent force, and we were all only too well aware that European war on a Napoleonic scale could not be ruled out. We were talking about it one evening.

'It is madness for one nation to pit itself against another,' Albert said passionately. 'No one wins. Everyone loses. War makes nothing but widows and poverty.'

'Lord M. always said that all wars are trade wars, whatever the politicians say,' I remarked over my needle. 'I suppose you can't stop people trying to seize territory from their neighbours.'

He waved a dismissive hand. 'That was one thing when we were primitive tribes competing for hunting grounds. But now we live in sophisticated societies, trading with one another, depending on one another. You cannot rob your neighbour now without robbing yourself. How can men be so infatuated as to believe permanent gain can come from another country's loss?'

I put down my work and looked at him. 'I suppose other men don't think as clearly as you do,' I said, taking his question literally.

But he wasn't listening. He whirled on me, his eyes bright with fervour. 'Do you know, Victoria, I think there is a chance now before us which never existed before – to unify all Mankind. Until this moment in the world's history, the problems of time and space were always too great. How could you regard as your brother a man whom it was impossible to reach or communicate with? But now there are railways, and telegraphs, and steamships capable of crossing vast oceans. Distance is being eliminated, people being drawn together as never before! Now, at this moment in this century, the possibility exists of drawing every nation on earth into a common understanding, a brotherhood of civilization!'

'How?' I asked. Then I wished I hadn't. It was my nature that I always wanted the practical points nailed down, but it tended to end his flights with rather a bump, and I loved listening to him when he talked like that.

'I don't know,' he said after a moment's silence. 'But I tell you this – it has to do with Free Trade. That's where it must all start, with the removal of all trade barriers between countries. The prosperity of each is part of the prosperity of all: *we* have learned that since 1815 – look how every upheaval abroad sends our trade down! England must lead the way. Democracy began here, and industrialisation. England must find the means to show the world that peace and prosperity cannot be separated, and that both depend on free competition and the full exchange of ideas.'

That was the earliest conversation on the subject that I remember, but it was a continuing preoccupation of Albert's. The nations of the world must be brought together – but how to begin it? Some great event was needed, some congruence, some gathering in one place, not of flawed and corruptible politicians, but of manufacturers and traders. The world must be shown, the point made, the new era started rolling – but by what?

The idea of an exhibition coalesced gradually in the opening months of 1849. The French Government was to hold an exposition of art and manufacture in Paris that summer – one of its quinquennial expositions – and the Society of Arts had long wanted to do something similar in England, but the plan had lacked backing, and nothing had come of it. On the 30th of June Albert called to a meeting at Buckingham Palace four eminent members of the society – Thomas Cubitt, the dynamic Henry Cole, Francis Fuller, who had just come back from the Paris exposition, and the Secretary of the Society, Scott Russell.

To these men Albert proposed that there should be an exhibition of works of art and industry in London in 1851, for the purposes of competition and encouragement. But unlike the French affair, the exhibition in London must embrace foreign products too. It must be a completely international affair – the very first such the world had ever seen – and on a vast scale. Every nation must be invited to contribute to it, sending examples of its raw materials, and the very best of its art and artefacts. Thus we would present to the world a living picture of the point at which mankind had arrived, and of the new starting-point from which all nations could direct their future endeavours.

'We will open the great treasure-house of the world and take stock,' he said. 'And we will show the way forward, turn men's minds from military aggression to commercial and industrial competition.'

Scott Russell said doubtfully, 'I don't know that our manufacturers will like it, sir. They may rather want less competition than more. How will it benefit them?'

'Competition benefits everyone,' Albert said firmly. 'And international competition will benefit all mankind. It will stimulate new effort, raise standards, increase output, open up new markets, give new scope to ingenuity and originality – and so produce a higher standard of living for all of the competing nations.'

'But will our factory masters understand that?' said Scott Russell.

Henry Cole answered him cheerfully, 'Even if they don't, they will still want to show off their wares. Depend upon it, they have a very good conceit of themselves. They will firmly expect to be superior to any foreign maker, and carry off all the prizes.'

If the exhibition was to be an international one, it would need the backing of the Government, so that foreign governments could be canvassed for their contributions. A fortnight later a second meeting was held by the same group, to which they invited Sir Robert Peel (who would seem to be Albert's natural ally in the scheme, being himself the son of a factory-master – it was such a puzzle that he ended up in the Tory party, when he ought to have been a Whig) and one or two members of the Cabinet, including Labouchère, who was the President of the Board of Trade.

After the meeting Albert came to me looking down in the mouth. 'We seem to have stumbled into a vicious circle,' he said. 'The Government doesn't want to commit itself to supporting the idea until we find out how much interest there is in the country at large. But I can't see how we are going to persuade the manufacturers of the importance of it, unless we can tell them that the Government is supporting us.'

'You will need a Royal Commission,' I said.

He nodded. 'But Parliament is about to go into recess, and a request for a Royal Commission can't go before Cabinet now until October at the earliest. And Labouchère hinted that we ought to have some evidence of support – especially financial support – before we even propose it.'

'Financial support? Do you need very much money, then?' I asked.

'A suitable building will have to be constructed. Nothing exists that will do – it will have to be a new thing – and Cubitt estimates we will want £75,000 for that. And then there must be prizes, or no one will exhibit – you know how suspicious these manufacturers are, always thinking their ideas will be stolen. The prizes must be substantial to attract the best – another £20,000, Fuller thinks.'

'A hundred thousand pounds, then,' I said soberly. 'Where will you get it from?'

'The society has no funds of its own,' Albert said. 'We must collect subscriptions; but people will not subscribe unless the whole thing is controlled by a Royal Commission. Without that, there will be no respectability, no guarantee of impartiality – no confidence.'

'Yes, I see the problem. You need the Royal Commission to obtain public confidence, and you must prove public confidence to obtain the Royal Commission.' I pondered. 'Do you really think there is enough interest in the country at large for a scheme of this sort?'

'I'm sure of it. Once things are moving, it will all be carried forward by its own momentum. There has been nothing like this, on such a scale, and the excitement will transform men's minds. But how to start it moving – that's the hard part.'

I could see he was growing despondent. I have found it is often the way with men of great enthusiasms, that they are easily set down by little setbacks which do not bother ordinary, dull people like me. 'Nothing can be done about the Cabinet until October,' I said, 'but I don't see why you can't canvass opinion in the meantime. If people know *you* are behind the scheme, they will know it must be respectable and impartial. Send your Society of Arts friends with letters of introduction to talk to the mill-masters and mayors and chambers of commerce. If they do their part well, by the time Parliament reconvenes, the whole country will be talking about the exhibition, and the Government will not be able to hold back.'

It was enough. Albert lifted my hand and kissed it, looking brighter. 'My clear-minded little wifey! Yes, I'm sure you are right. That is exactly what we'll do.'

So Cole and Fuller – the most persuasive and active of the group – went forth on their travels to all the great centres of industry in England, Scotland and Ireland, and by October they had compiled a report which was very gratifying. Interest in the scheme was intense – not only amongst manufacturers but also merchants, traders, bankers, and even members of the public with no direct connection with commerce. And best of all, as far as Albert was concerned, everyone seemed to agree that the international character of the exhibition was of the greatest importance, and to understand the wider significance of what was proposed. The suggestion of prizes had seemed almost irrelevant, Cole and Fuller reported: everyone wanted to show their goods, compare them with those of other nations, and see what improvements could be wrought. 'Give us a clear stage and no favour,' one Lancashire group had said; Edinburgh felt that the competition would 'rub the sharp corners off many nations'; while Manchester said that free competition would benefit all concerned.

Armed with the report, the society held a meeting at the Mansion House to which it invited four hundred great men from the City, and Henry Cole gave a glorious speech describing all the wonders the Exhibition would display, and the fabulous benefits that would accrue from it not only to mankind in general, but to London in particular in being the host to 'an intellectual festival of peaceful industry, a festival such as the world had never seen before'. The speech was received with rapturous applause, and the most influential financiers in the country were converted to the cause. *The Times* at this point took notice, declared itself enthusiastically for the Exhibition and described Albert as his country's benefactor for thinking of the idea. A week later the Government succumbed to the invisible pressure, threw caution to the winds, and agreed to issue a Royal Commission.

From that time the Great International Exhibition was a certainty; all that remained was to organise it. Thus the great boulder of work and worry that was to crush Albert began rolling slowly down the slope towards him.

21st August 1900

THE NAMES of the commissioners were published on January the 4th, 1850, and included Albert as President, Lord Granville as Vice-President, and Peel and Russell, like the two poles, providing impartial political support. There were twenty-four commissioners altogether, but most of them were included for show rather than for any active help they might give. It was on Granville, cultured, tactful, hardworking, good-tempered and utterly imperturbable, that Albert came to rely almost entirely.

Money was the next concern. Albert persuaded the Duke to put his name at the head of the subscription list, and with that distinguished lead money began to pour in. I put myself down for £1,000 and Albert for £500, and in the first six weeks £15,000 was raised, such was the general interest in the business. A working man even sent a shilling, together with a most touching letter of support. Henry Cole, who was immensely active in publicising the affair and coaxing money out of pockets both high and low, saw to it that the circumstance and the letter were published in *The Times*.

As interest at home and abroad increased, it became a matter of pressing urgency to decide on a home for the exhibition. Enquiries were coming in from all over the world, and since it was plainly going to be impossible to assess even roughly how many individuals would exhibit, or how much in bulk they would want to display, the commissioners were obliged to fix on an arbitrary size for the building. They ruled that the exhibition should cover 800,000 square feet, four times the size of the largest exhibition yet held anywhere.

But where to put all these square feet? An area of about twenty acres was needed. Albert put forward the suggestion of Leicester Square – then an open, undeveloped place – but it was surrounded by poor and neglected areas which the commissioners felt might not give the right impression to visitors. It was Henry Cole who put forward the counter suggestion of Hyde Park – the Garden of London, central, spacious, and handsome. In his energetic way he took his wife and children to the Park after church one Sunday and walked about until he had found the perfect spot – the strip of ground stretching from Albert Gate to Prince's Gate, lying between the Serpentine River and the Cavalry Barracks at Knightsbridge. Albert thought this an excellent site, and I approved of it (once it was determined that it would not interfere with the cavalry's movements in any way) and so with Crown permission already secured, we assumed that the matter was decided.

The next stage was for the design of the building to be chosen. A separate Building Committee was formed, consisting of two commissioners, three architects and three civil engineers (including Mr Brunel, the railway man), and they decided that as time was pressing, a general competition would be the quickest way to obtain ideas. So on March the 13th they issued an invitation to the public, at home and abroad, to submit suggestions as to the form the building should take. Anyone might contribute – architects or amateurs – but the time limit was April the 8th.

Despite the tight deadline, two hundred and forty-five designs were submitted, ranging from the preposterous to the Babylonian – and in a very short time two hundred and forty-five designs had been rejected by the Building Committee. They issued a report stating that while some few had been highly commendable, none was quite suitable, and all contained serious flaws of design for an international exhibition. The committee felt itself in a strong position to learn from the mistakes of the two hundred and forty-five others, and intended to provide a plan of its own which would combine suitability of purpose with 'some striking features' to show the current state of the science of construction in England. It then shut itself away to ponder, and we were left waiting in breathless silence outside its closed door.

Would that the rest of the country had also remained silent! While the Building Committee deliberated, a ferocious reaction to the general euphoria over the exhibition set in, and soon the papers were full of nothing else. It began with Lord Brougham (who was growing steadily madder by the month). Having originally spoken out in favour of the exhibition, he now suddenly stood up in the House to launch a violent attack on it. Hyde Park, he declared, was the lungs of the capital, and now it was proposed to choke them with a tubercule – a huge building, paid for by the money out of Englishmen's pockets, put up for foreigners to sell their wares in.

In the Lower House he was joined by another madman, Colonel Sibthorpe, a truculent little man with a fierce black beard and a flashing eyeglass who passionately opposed change of any sort, and who hated any idea that was new since 1815. He had discovered that ten elm trees in Hyde Park had been marked with whitewash, signifying that they would have to be cut down for the proposed exhibition building. These trees, he thundered, were the property of the people – and for what reason were they to be destroyed? Why, for the biggest fraud and humbug ever to be forced upon the people of this country! The Government was going about demolishing valuable public property solely for the purpose of encouraging foreigners, who would laugh at us for our folly while filling their pockets at our expense.

Then *The Times* joined in. Hyde Park and Kensington Gardens would become a bivouac to all the vagabonds in London, it declared. It was bad enough during the Coronation celebrations, but this time the nuisance would last months rather than days. The neighbourhood would suffer dreadfully – the handsome homes and mansions in Kensington Gore and Park Lane would be ransacked. No servant-maid would be safe. Equestrians, who depended on Rotten Row, would be deprived of their daily horseback exercise. Hyde Park would be spoiled, trees would be cut down, children would lose their playground, and no-one would sleep safe in their beds. Prince Albert, it warned gravely, should think carefully before associating his name with such horrors.

In the middle of all this, on the 27th of June, the Building Committee suddenly emerged from seclusion and published its design for the exhibition building. It was received with howls of outrage and mockery from the Opposition, and with a low moan by Albert, for it was a monstrous thing: a long, low building four times the length of Westminster Abbey and surmounted by a gigantic dome somewhat larger than that of St Peter's in Rome. The influence of Brunel was unmistakable: the great arches at the front end were distinctly reminiscent of Paddington Station.

Granville, Albert and I looked at the drawing for a long time in silence, and then Granville sighed. 'It looks,' he said, 'like a railway shed that's collided with an observatory.'

301

'What can the committee be thinking of? They will bring us all into disrepute,' Albert cried frantically.

'It plays right into the Opposition's hands,' Granville admitted. 'We've said all along that the exhibition will be housed in a temporary building, but this thing looks anything but temporary. Brick and iron and stone, as solid as Buckingham Palace: it looks fit to last a century.'

'Nineteen million bricks,' Albert said in agony. 'It will take a year to build at the least – and the cost! Not a penny less than £100,000, or I know nothing.'

'It has to have a separate furnace house,' I said, still examining the report. 'Boilers and chimneys and engines for pumping steam – all in the middle of the Park. Oh, Albert, it will be such an eyesore!'

'It won't do,' he said. 'Certainly it will have to be modified.' But he sounded worried. Time was so short. Here it was, June already, and the exhibition was supposed to be opening in May of 1851 – less than a year away. And what modification could make this monumental railway shed acceptable?

'It's not going to help the cause,' said Albert gloomily.

Letters of protest flooded in, to the commissioners, and most of all to Albert, and alternative suggestions, of varying degrees of unhelpfulness, were published in every newspaper. Both Houses were in uproar with continuous interruptions about the site and the building; and an Association of the Residents of the Environment of Hyde Park presented a Save Our Trees petition to the Commons.

'Things can't get any worse,' said Albert. But they could, and did.

On the 29th of June Sir Robert Peel attended a meeting of the commissioners at Buckingham Palace at midday, to discuss the delicate situation. The debate over whether the Hyde Park site should be sanctioned by the Government was due to begin on July the 4th, and Peel was to be our spokesman – if anyone could influence the Lower House, it must be him. But at this late stage a change of site was considered impossible. The meeting decided that if the site should be forbidden, the whole scheme would be called off.

After the meeting Albert asked Peel to stay behind for a moment or two, and I joined them. They were talking about the provision of a temporary ride in Kensington Gardens, to replace the part of Rotten Row that would be lost to horsemen for the duration of the exhibition.

'I have written to the Woods and Forests – our favourite department,' he added with a smile for me, 'but I'm sorry to say I have had a very curt reply from Lord Seymour. He seems to think the ground would be too soft for riding, and that it would cost too much to fence off the area needed.'

'Lord Seymour is something of a Protectionist, I'm afraid,' said Peel. 'He would be glad to put a difficulty in the way of the exhibition.'

'I don't see that the ground would be any softer than in Hyde Park,' I said, 'particularly not in May, June and July. And after all, outside those months horsemen have to take their chance wherever they ride.'

'Quite so, ma'am,' said Peel. 'Lord Seymour must know it. It simply needs the right person to concentrate his mind on the fact.'

'You will ask Lord John Russell to speak to him, then?' Albert said. 'And as to the expense of fencing the area, I'm sure hurdling is cheap enough.'

'Woods and Forests must have any amount of hurdling in store,' I pointed out indignantly. 'They are always putting it up and taking it down.'

'Indeed, you are right, ma'am,' said Peel. 'And if they have not enough, I am sure it could be bought, or even hired for a few months.'

'In fact,' said Albert thoughtfully, 'there is a quantity of wattle hurdling in St James's Park which ought really in such a place to be changed for iron hurdles. Why not use the iron hurdles first for the ride in Kensington Gardens, and then transfer them to St James's when the exhibition is over?'

I looked at him admiringly. 'How you do think of everything!' I exclaimed. He had even the smallest detail of the business at his fingertips. 'Now, Sir Robert, would not that put Lord Seymour on the spot? He can hardly object to proper fencing in St James's Park, can he?'

'I think, ma'am, that there is a very good chance he will be defeated on that point,' said Peel, but the gravity of his face did not change. 'But I cannot conceal from you that the opposition in general is very great, and I cannot be sanguine about our getting the Hyde Park site agreed on.'

'You must tell them,' Albert said earnestly, 'that if it is not, the whole affair must be cancelled, and that would be a disaster! Speak to Palmerston about it – twenty-three foreign states so far have committed themselves to send exhibits. Speak to Labouchère – two hundred and forty local exhibition committees have set themselves up throughout the country. Speak to Sir George Grey – £64,000 has been subscribed already, and the labouring classes are subscribing their wages to funds to enable them to come up to London to see the exhibition. We *cannot* cancel now! Speak to Russell. You must persuade the House.'

'I assure Your Highness that I will do everything in my power,' Peel said, as earnestly as was in his nature.

Impulsively I held out my hand. 'I know you will do your utmost, Sir Robert,' I said. 'I know we have no better friend than you.'

He bowed over my hand, and a moment later left us. Albert stared at the closed door a moment and then said in a low voice, 'If he cannot help us, then we are done for.'

I was worried by his mood. 'Dearest,' I said gently, 'do not take it so much to heart. You have done all you can – no-one could have done more.' I wanted to add that it was only an exhibition, that it did not matter so very much if it failed; but I stopped myself in time. It did matter to him. He had invested so much time and trouble in it already – but more than that, he had set his heart on it. It was not just an exhibition to him – it was a holy crusade. Instead I said, 'Sir Robert will win over the Lower House. There can be no doubt about it.' Since his resignation over the Corn Law appeal, he had belonged to no party, and so had a unique position and influence in the House.

Albert knew that, and allowed himself to be comforted; and a moment later was talking about his plans for the provision of drainage and water for the site.

The dreadful news were brought to us some hours later – the worst news we could have received at that time. My cousin George Cambridge brought them. On his way home from Buckingham Palace, Peel had been riding his brown cob up Constitution Hill when she shied, slipped, and fell. Peel was caught under her, and as she struggled to her feet, she somehow stepped or kneeled on him. A passer-by at once put his carriage at Peel's disposal, and he was carried to his house and the doctor summoned. It was feared he was gravely hurt.

Albert went at once to Peel's house, and returned much shaken.

'How is he? How is our dear Sir Robert?' I asked him.

'In a great deal of pain,' Albert said.

'Yes, yes, he always was more sensitive to it than other men,' I said. Under normal circumstances he could not bear even the prick of a needle. 'The least thing gives him the most exquisite suffering. Poor man! But what do the doctors say?'

'He is in too much pain for them to examine him thoroughly, but they think a broken collar-bone – or perhaps a broken shoulder. They may be able to say more in a day or two.'

'A broken collar-bone,' I said hopefully. 'If it is only that!'

'We must pray it is no worse,' Albert said shortly.

'He must have the best of attention. I shall send Sir James Clark to him,' I said. 'Oh, what a wretched, wretched thing to happen!'

'There was quite a crowd outside his house when I got there,' Albert said. 'Mostly poor people. They know who gave them cheaper bread. He is well loved.'

'But not only by poor people,' I said quickly.

He gave a brief, pained smile. 'Oh, no. The Duke was there too – he arrived just as I was leaving.'

Clark went to visit Whitehall Gardens, and came back with a cheerful report. It was undoubtedly only a broken collar-bone. Sir Robert was heavy, gouty, and high in blood, but he would recover. I was comforted, but Albert, who went to see Peel every day, remained impenetrably grave. Peel continued to suffer agonies – the slightest ministration was excruciating to him, though he bore it all with desperate patience. The crowds grew outside his house day by day, and a policeman was posted at the door, who passed out regular bulletins to the anxious, waiting supporters. An odd story started up that the brown mare, who was a recent purchase of Peel's, had been sold at Tattersalls because her previous owner could not break her of her habit of shying; and from there it was only a step to rumours of a plot to assassinate the senior statesman. But the fact was, as Palmerston said (and I knew very well from my own observation), that Peel was a very poor and clumsy rider. When he fell, he managed somehow to get himself tangled up in the reins, and so was not able to get clear of her as she struggled to her feet. It was not the mare's fault.

However it was, on the 2nd of July we received an alarming note from Peel's own doctor. He feared that there may have been a broken rib which had now pierced the lung. Sir Robert was in a very poor way; the worst was feared. We had been planning to go to the opera, but I cancelled that. Neither of us had the heart for it, or even to eat any dinner. We sat waiting for news; and at half an hour after midnight a letter was brought. My hands trembled so much I could not open it. I handed it to Albert without a word, and he stared as if he wished to die before he had to read it. Then he tore it open with a violent, despairing gesture. Sir Robert Peel had died just before midnight.

27th August 1900

WE HAD a family photograph taken on the terrace yesterday, to send to poor Vicky. Her last letter was very worrying – she said she was in great pain and could not rise from her bed, and since she always writes very stoicallly, it has put me in a dreadful anxiety. I haven't seen her now since the summer of 'ninety-eight, when she visited us in Balmoral. It was on her return from that visit that she had her bad fall while out riding, and since then she has been suffering from what she calls 'lumbago', but with the terrible news from Coburg fresh in my mind I cannot shake off the fear that it is something worse. I *cannot* lose another child! Would to God she could come here, or I go to her! One is not less a mother because one's child is sixty years old. Oh, my dear Vicky, my firstborn!

Tomorrow the ever-dear day returns on which, eighty-one years ago, my beloved Albert came into the world as a blessing to so many. How I remember the happy day it used to be, and the preparation of the presents for him, choosing what he would like best, and looking forward to his pleasure in them. But of all the things I ever gave him, he always said that my love was the best gift he could ever have had. On his last birthday in this world he wrote to me, 'How many a storm has swept over our love, and still it continues green and fresh and throws out vigorous shoots' – these tender words from the husband of more than twenty years! Oh, I know how lucky we were, lovers to the end – and that love is still green in my heart. Yesterday on the terrace, while we sat still for the photographer, I felt a warm touch on the back of my neck, and knew that he was standing there behind me, taking his rightful place in the family group. Others might have thought it was only the sunshine, but I knew. He is always close at this time of the year.

Peel's death was the most appalling blow to Albert. He had grown more and more fond of him, had relied on him not only for his support over the exhibition, but in every way. They had had so much in common and worked so closely together – Peel above all had been the one statesman of importance to appreciate Albert's talents and put them to use. And the blow was made worse by the fact that George Anson, Albert's secretary and his one intimate friend, had died suddenly of a seizure the previous October. Now with Peel's death, Albert said, 'I have lost my only friend.'

m the Society of Arts; and he was
Exhibition.
ph Paxton, once head gardener to
y more of a friend and colleague to
in the Commons, Paxton remarked
s that the acoustics in the Chamber
nd that he feared another mistake was
bition building.
e problem,' Ellis said. 'The building has
trong enough for the purpose, but how
sufficiently solid?'
on, and proceeded to outline a plan to his
increasing astonishment, and then said, 'I
e Board of Trade. Will you step across with
've just told me?'
sed was nothing more nor less than a giant
be made solely of iron, wood and glass – all
uld be ready at once for use (a building made
could take months or even years to dry out
rts would be manufactured off the site and
ll interchangeable. Thus it could be put up
ape could be altered, or its size increased or
at a moment's notice. When its use had finished,
y be taken down again, and if required erected
as a winter garden or even stored for future exhi-
ll, it would look light and pleasing, entirely suited to
frightening nobody with a permanent appearance;
ould be only half that of the Building Committee's

principle was explained, it seemed so simple and so
o defy criticism. On Granville's advice, Paxton had his
tsworth draw scale plans of his proposal, and only ten
his meeting with Granville he sent them to the Building
e. The Building Committee threw them out – by now they
heir own design or nothing; so on the 6th of July (two days
debate on the site) Paxton by-passed them by having his
published in the *Illustrated London News*. They took public
by storm. Letters poured in, the papers took up the general
ille leaning on their shoulders and breathing in their ears, were
d to give in. On July the 15th they dropped their own plan and
ally accepted a much smaller tender from a contracting company

I h
ha

c
wo

A
Hyde
brief ad
on in the
motion wa
defeated! Eve
and perhaps in
to vote against
Upper House Lor

Two days later
building. The Buildin
loud protest, and thoug
for economy's sake, aban
some of the other 'strikin
too, too solid – quite apar
because of the surgery it had u

The miracle came from an u
minster Palace was largely comple
a trial session had been held in the
the acoustics. One of the Members,
the Midland Railway, had brought wi
on the Midland Railways committee,
interested in the engineering problems of
had himself designed and constructed many
and conservatories, including a gigantic lily-h
had solved many problems of construction, hea
tion and condensation. He had invented an entire

sash-bar which had won a medal fro
passionately interested in the Great
This friend was of course Jos
the Duke of Devonshire but no
His Grace. After the trial sessio
in a conversational way to Elli
were obviously unsatisfactory,
about to be made over the exh
'It seems to be an insolub
got to be large enough and
can a temporary building b
'I know how,' said Pax
friend. Ellis listened with
think Granville is still at t
me and tell him what yo
What Paxton propo
greenhouse. It was to
dry materials, so it wo
of bricks and mortar
properly). All its p
in standard sizes,
rapidly, and its sh
reduced, easily an
it could as quick
somewhere else
bitions. Best of
its park setting
and the cost
railway-shed.
Once the
obvious as
men at Ch
days after
Committe
wanted t
after the
designs
opinio
deligh
Gran
force
form

I had been worried for some time about the amount of work that had been accumulating on his shoulders since the exhibition scheme was started; and he had had so many worries recently. I had given birth to Arthur on the 1st of May, which though a happy event in itself always meant extra strain and worry for Albert. Then in the same month, when I was barely out of childbed, there had been two attacks on me, the first on the 19th by a man with a pistol (which fortunately was loaded only with blanks) and the second on the 27th, that horrid attack by the man Pate, who struck me in the face with his cane. Then there was all the upset over the opposition to the exhibition; and now this most frightful blow. Albert sank into black despair, and I could not comfort him. I worried that he would really make himself ill, and wrote urgently to Stockmar, begging him to come and comfort and advise my poor darling, but he could not, or would not come.

And then on July 4th a miracle happened. The debate on the Hyde Park site opened, and Lord John Russell began by making a brief address to the Lower House about Sir Robert Peel. What went on in the minds of the Members then I can't say, but the opposition motion was brought forward by Colonel Sibthorpe – and heavily defeated! Everyone knew Peel had been in support of the scheme, and perhaps in respect to his memory no-one could bring themselves to vote against it. At all events, the site was accepted, and in the Upper House Lord Brougham withdrew his motion.

Two days later a second miracle solved the problem of the building. The Building Committee's design was still drawing down loud protest, and though the committee had pruned and pared at it for economy's sake, abandoning (probably with relief) the dome and some of the other 'striking features', it was still too expensive, and too, too solid – quite apart from looking more peculiar than ever because of the surgery it had undergone.

The miracle came from an unexpected direction. The new Westminster Palace was largely completed by now, and on the 7th of June a trial session had been held in the new House of Commons to test the acoustics. One of the Members, John Ellis, who was chairman of the Midland Railway, had brought with him a friend who was also on the Midland Railways committee, a man who was very much interested in the engineering problems of new buildings. This friend had himself designed and constructed many new sorts of greenhouses and conservatories, including a gigantic lily-house at Chatsworth, and had solved many problems of construction, heating, lighting, ventilation and condensation. He had invented an entirely new kind of metal sash-bar which had won a medal from the Society of Arts; and he was passionately interested in the Great Exhibition.

This friend was of course Joseph Paxton, once head gardener to the Duke of Devonshire but now more of a friend and colleague to His Grace. After the trial session in the Commons, Paxton remarked in a conversational way to Ellis that the acoustics in the Chamber were obviously unsatisfactory, and that he feared another mistake was about to be made over the exhibition building.

'It seems to be an insoluble problem,' Ellis said. 'The building has got to be large enough and strong enough for the purpose, but how can a temporary building be sufficiently solid?'

'I know how,' said Paxton, and proceeded to outline a plan to his friend. Ellis listened with increasing astonishment, and then said, 'I think Granville is still at the Board of Trade. Will you step across with me and tell him what you've just told me?'

What Paxton proposed was nothing more nor less than a giant greenhouse. It was to be made solely of iron, wood and glass – all dry materials, so it would be ready at once for use (a building made of bricks and mortar could take months or even years to dry out properly). All its parts would be manufactured off the site and in standard sizes, all interchangeable. Thus it could be put up rapidly, and its shape could be altered, or its size increased or reduced, easily and at a moment's notice. When its use had finished, it could as quickly be taken down again, and if required erected somewhere else as a winter garden or even stored for future exhibitions. Best of all, it would look light and pleasing, entirely suited to its park setting, frightening nobody with a permanent appearance; and the cost would be only half that of the Building Committee's railway-shed.

Once the principle was explained, it seemed so simple and so obvious as to defy criticism. On Granville's advice, Paxton had his men at Chatsworth draw scale plans of his proposal, and only ten days after his meeting with Granville he sent them to the Building Committee. The Building Committee threw them out – by now they wanted their own design or nothing; so on the 6th of July (two days after the debate on the site) Paxton by-passed them by having his designs published in the *Illustrated London News*. They took public opinion by storm. Letters poured in, the papers took up the general delight with the idea, and the Building Committee, with Albert and Granville leaning on their shoulders and breathing in their ears, were forced to give in. On July the 15th they dropped their own plan and formally accepted a much smaller tender from a contracting company for Paxton's design. The glorious creation which *Punch*, in November, christened the Crystal Palace, was born.

30th August 1900

IT WAS not the end of opposition. Colonel Sibthorpe continued to fulminate about the enormous cost of the scheme which must inevitably come out of the taxpayer's pocket. *The Times* said that the glasshouse would leak when it rained, and when the sun shone would get so hot inside it would fry the paying customers. Others declared that the vibration of thousands of feet inside the building would shake it to pieces, a gale would knock it down, or a hail-storm would smash it up. As the building rose with astonishing rapidity, glittering and enchanting, above the trees, and the general public fell victim to a first love which quickly strengthened into glass-mania, the opposition gathered their forces in the hope of putting off potential visitors.

The Astronomer Royal was persuaded to write a pamphlet pointing out that Paxton had no formal qualifications so the building must be unsafe and would inevitably collapse on the heads of those foolish enough to enter it. Colonel Sibthorpe entered the lists again to protest about the destruction of the last of the elm trees, but Paxton had an answer for him: leave the elms where they are, he said, and I will build a semi-circular roof to the transept to accommodate them. (Thus these wretched trees became a delightful and most distinguished part of the exhibition itself. Sibthorpe was confounded and, I'm glad to say, very much ridiculed. I hated him particularly because it had been he who first moved that Albert's pension should be reduced, back in 1839.)

Other Members of Parliament declared that the influx of foreigners into the country would start a red revolution, murder the Queen, and set up a republic. Economists calculated that the price of every commodity would increase to astronomical heights, and that the vast concourse of people descending on London would cause a shortage of food which would end in general famine. Doctors predicted that so many different races coming into contact with each other would result in a plague like the Black Death sweeping England. Theologians said that the Crystal Palace was a second Tower of Babel and would draw down the vengeance of an offended God on to the hapless nation of unwilling hosts.

Moralists cried out that English society would be infected by new wickednesses imported by the hateful foreigners, who everyone knew were not civilised like us; and the ratepayers of London predicted that Richard Mayne's tiny police force would never be able to cope with the influx of vagabonds, thieves, burglars, pick-pockets, prostitutes, cozeners, swindlers, sharps, forgers, beggars and drunks who would come from every corner of the country – and indeed the world – at the beckoning of this irresistible bait, and that we should have to declare martial law before the exhibition was well opened.

And all this, of course, was Albert's fault. While the senseless opposition and abuse were poured on his dear, lovely head, he laboured night and day with all the multitude of details that had to be taken care of. The exhibits had to be approved and classified; the space had to be agreed upon and allocated for each State, the punctual arrival of their contributions ensured; communication and transport had to be arranged; endless enquiries answered, jealousies calmed, mishaps dealt with. Russia had to send her contributions early, before her ports froze: where would they be stored? The Swiss republic was eager to exhibit cheeses along with her leathers, silks and cottons, but how were they to be classified? They weren't vegetables, nor yet agricultural machinery – and would they stand up to five months on display? And if they were allowed in, would not English farmers want to put up their own cheeses, with serious consequences for the public nose? (The cheeses were withdrawn.) Then the Chinese government, which had shown utter indifference to the scheme, sent goods enough only to fill three hundred of the five thousand square feet allocated them. The public was eagerly looking forward to a fabulous oriental display: what was to be done? Albert suggested the commissioners scour the private collections of the great houses of England (where indeed more Chinese art had probably accumulated than was to be found in China itself) so as to get together a sufficient collection.

Others worked hard, but none worked harder, or worried more, than my darling, for while they each had their own concerns and areas of responsibility, he was responsible for the whole. He was the only person who had the complete picture in his mind's eye, and yet was still aware of all the detail: a feat of comprehension, memory and concentration so enormous as to defy belief. Without him, Granville said afterwards, the scheme would have fallen to pieces in confusion, bickering, and dreadful damaging muddle; but he held all the threads together, and finally brought into being the greatest expression of human hope, skill, and peaceful endeavour the world has ever seen.

Everything had been thought of: fire precautions, public lavatories, refreshments, ticket prices, floor sweeping, transport, policing – everything. Even through the very day before the Opening, his attention was constantly being sought over some little difficulty or hitch, every moment some new question was being put to him; but though he looked fagged to death, he met every one with the greatest good temper. And though the whole triumph of the scheme must be his, he never spoke a word about himself, but laboured quietly on, satisfied simply to promote the good of the people and the glory of the country.

But at what price?

Seventeen

2nd October 1900, at Balmoral

HOW THIS war seems to drag on and on – and how right I was to warn Salisbury against too much enthusiasm too soon! It is good to know that we have Kitchener out there – his unflagging energy and attention to detail are just what is wanted in this 'cleaning up' phase of the war, which might last for many months yet. All the same, the Government has called a General Election, hoping that the popularity of our victories and the people's relief over the returning soldiers will increase their majority, which has taken rather a 'knocking' over the past five years. It is Chamberlain's idea first and last, and I must say it does not seem to me quite the thing. I am sure Albert would deplore it as not being 'fair play'. Besides, it is surely unwise to presume on the single issue, for the Government can hardly claim afterwards that it has been given a mandate for its other difficult measures – though I don't suppose that will prevent it from doing so!

I have left my writing untouched for some weeks, but now we are back up at Balmoral, and the air is so pure and fresh that I feel a great deal better, and have taken it up again. The colours are so wonderful at this time of year, and sitting here in my little hut I can look up and out of the open door and see purple and green and gold and blue, the colours of nature as sumptuous as any of the treasures of the Orient. It is a Feast for the Heye – as one of my footmen described the display at the Crystal Palace those many years ago.

The Duke's interest in the Great Exhibition had from the beginning been one of apprehension about the number of people who would be gathered in one place, and the inevitability of their misbehaving themselves. Whenever Albert dilated to him on the beauty, harmony and peacefulness of the idea, the Duke would reply gruffly with some suggestion about keeping the roads open to facilitate the passage of soldiers. When Albert said, 'But surely you cannot believe that on such a peaceful, innocent occasion as this there could be anyone bent on mischief?' the Duke would simply stare into the middle distance and say, 'Better to be prepared, sir.'

At all events, the Duke spoke to Lord John Russell, and Russell consulted Richard Mayne and then shook his head and went to the commissioners to say that the opening ceremony had better be private. For safety's sake, he said, I had better declare the exhibition open to a handful of officials, and be got right away before the public was let in. In view of the strange faces seen all around London, the beards and fezzes, the baggy pantaloons and low-crowned hats, I had nothing to say to the decision. I was always ready to take my chance of being shot at in the line of duty, but it was not my business to ignore the advice of my ministers; and Albert seemed relieved that there would not be a public ceremony to organise on top of everything else.

The announcement was made in the press in the middle of April, and at once there was another flood of letters to the commissioners and fierce editorials in the newspapers. It had been assumed all along that the opening was to be public, and eight thousand holders of season tickets had made arrangements to be present. Many, it seemed, were planning to come up from remote parts of the country solely for the purpose of seeing me.

'Listen to this, my love,' Albert said over breakfast, folding *The Times* into a more convenient shape. 'It says, "We believe that Her Majesty would be in no greater danger inside than outside, for Socialists, whether French or German, who intend an attack have no need of entry into the Building in order to carry out their purpose."'

'Well, that's true enough,' I said, 'though I don't know that it makes me feel more comfortable.'

'They are very free with your safety,' he agreed, and read on. '"Is our gracious Queen a Tiberius or a Louis XI that she should be smuggled about under a bodyguard? And what satisfaction would she obtain by entering a monster warehouse of upholstery and machinery attended by none but a few Silver Sticks? The safest place for Her Majesty is where she belongs, in the midst of her loyal subjects."'

'That strikes home!' I said. 'I have always maintained that the people are very good, and that they love me.'

'It is not *our* people the Government fears,' Albert pointed out, taking up another paper. 'Well, they are all at one about this, at all events. The *Chronicle* says that the decision to hold a private ceremony shows an insulting lack of confidence in the public. And the *Globe* believes that the best exhibit of all in the palace of wonders would be the Queen of England displayed in the midst of her people.'

I was indignant. 'They want to sit me on a throne, I suppose, nicely roped off, so that everyone can walk past me and stare!'

He put down the paper. 'Perhaps they would like you to move a little, like one of those automata.' And he lifted a hand stiffly up and down while turning his head from side to side with an idiotic grin, just like a mechanical toy, and it made me laugh very much.

Later that day Granville came to see us. He had been out of London for a few days, and on his journey through London he had heard but one opinion. 'From Bishopsgate to Bayswater it is all indignation and disappointment.'

'Yes, we have been looking at the newspapers,' Albert said. 'The *Globe* actually uses the word "betrayed".'

'Is feeling really so very strong?' I asked.

'They seem to feel, ma'am, that there is little point in a celebration of national pride without the Queen at its centre.'

'It is an exhibition of the skills of *all* mankind,' Albert pointed out sternly. 'It is meant to transcend national feeling.'

Granville smiled his gentle, attractive smile. 'Yes indeed, sir. But our own people can't help wanting to show off a little to Johnny Foreigner – and they have so very much to be proud of, don't you think?'

'Well, Granville, I am willing to do whatever is necessary,' I said, 'but Russell will not have it, you know.'

'Oh, I think he may be persuaded, ma'am,' he said drily. 'He does not at all want to upset the middle classes.'

'That is all very well,' Albert interrupted, 'but there is no *reason* for the Queen to be there – not as Head of State. What ceremonial is to be used? What form of words? She cannot just walk about looking at things.'

'As a matter of fact,' Granville said, 'I have already had a word with Cole, and he has an idea about that. How would it be if the commissioners as a body – with you at their head, of course, sir – handed some sort of official document, a Report, say, on the completion of the work to Her Majesty, indicating that the royal sanction was essential to the enterprise? Something large and impressive with ribbons and seals – and a speech on the importance and true significance of the exhibition, finishing up, perhaps, with a reference to Her Majesty's peaceful and glorious reign.'

I liked the idea of that – my beloved standing forth alone, the centre of attention, the object of every eye, his voice filling the breathless, waiting silence, his ringing words inspiring every heart and mind to a greater appreciation of what he had achieved. 'Yes,' I said eagerly, 'a speech by the Prince. That would sound very well.' And I looked across at him and smiled, and saw that he was reading my mind perfectly: he gave a little rueful shake of the head, as though reproving me for wanting to push him forward.

But the public feeling was so strong on the subject that after a series of agitated letters and earnest meetings, it was arranged as Granville suggested. The ceremony was to be simple and solemn but *not* religious (though the Archbishop would speak a special prayer of thanksgiving) and there would be music. Russell, to save face, said his fears had been about overcrowding rather than any danger to the Royal Person, and asked for admission to be limited to season-ticket holders, which was agreed. When the announcement was made in the press, there was a sudden rush for season tickets, and four thousand were sold in four days, bringing the total to twelve thousand.

'However will so many be accommodated?' I wondered when I heard.

'We will have to have the constructors build stands,' Albert said, with a sigh at the thought of the extra work involved. 'They will have to be taken down again before the general opening, of course. And we will have to decide what to do about the diplomats: a public opening of an international exhibition gives almost unlimited scope for errors of protocol. Oh, and there will have to be an ante-room provided for the royal party – if you will excuse me, my love, I had better go and write some letters.'

There were only ten days to go before the opening day. Everything simply seemed to make work for Albert.

But the great day came at last – May the 1st, 1851, Arthur's first birthday and the Duke's eighty-second – and it dawned fair, rather chilly at first, but broadening as the sun rose higher and the mist burned off into a brilliant early summer day of the best, English sort.

of perpetual summer had
d translucent walls of the
al foliage, trembling palm
with their colours. Before
y decorated with white
ntre of the transept, the
ntain carved out of pure
jets of water leapt fifty
nd the galleries draped
in all the dazzle and
multitude of statues
essive. And standing
e and mysterious to
nt regions far above

together with two
ces, burst into the
st few notes were
which rose from
they had but one
k of pink faces
ng with delight
r celebration –
s, for the glory
rosperity with
the heart of
e world. The
so touching
– filled most
I have ever
y of all the
uthor, my
nd selfless

ed down
ners and
words,
reign.
voice
ment I
in all
here.

'er,
my
hing
were

d Albert
t off up
sun came
were such
ion, packing
rom the win-
w vacant, and
Park there were
pectators on the
oaded down with
down Rotten Row
re us was the great,
f-hidden amongst the
nd the Park so that it
a magic palace caught
ation.

orth entrance and went in
d straighten our dresses. I
with silver, with the Garter
d very well, I thought. Vicky
ath of wild roses on her head
ertie looked very nice in Scotch
Mamma and Mary Teck were
rs of the family, and the Crown
h Fritz – they had been invited to
ts, so as not to annoy the King of

took Bertie and Vicky by their hands,
rward, entering the north nave. There
across the end of it, and the glimpse of
– the waving palms, flowers, statues,
e galleries and seats all around – gave me a
get, and I was much moved. Then there was
pets, and the gates were flung back by the
e Guard, revealing the whole scene.
prehensibly vast, the luminous distances made
unrestricted light and space. The air was warm

and serene, as though by magic a world
been created within the delicate bones ar
palace; and everywhere the eye fell on tropi
trees, banks of flowers drowning the senses
us was a dais under a gold-fringed canop
ostrich feathers, and beyond, in the very ce
heart of the whole exhibition, was a vast fou
transparent crystal, from which the glittering
feet into the air. The stalls had been covered a
in warm red Turkey cloth, comfortingly solic
indistinctness, and against the strong colour a
stood out dead white, most startling and impr
guard over all were the elm trees, soaring serer
spread their lofty canopies of leaves across the luce
us.

As we appeared in the gateway the vast organ,
hundred musicians and a choir of six hundred voi
National Anthem, but nothing more than the fir
heard, for they were drowned out by the great chee
the multitude assembled there as though in their joy
voice. There they were before me, bank upon bar
under tall hats and silk bonnets, and every face shini
and love and goodness, shouting out the joy of the
shouting for me, yes, but more than that for themselve
that was England, her achievement, the peace and p
which she nurtured her children, and her place at
everything that was good and noble and liberating in th
experience of being there was so magical, so glorious,
that one felt – and everyone I spoke to afterwards agreed
of all with *devotion*, more so than at any church service
attended. It was a Festival of Peace, uniting the industr
nations of the earth, and there at the heart of it was its a
beloved husband, my dearest Albert, whose soaring vision a
labour had brought it all into being.

As the noise died away, Albert left my side and stepp
from the dais to place himself at the head of the commissio
read aloud the report, putting his vision into clear and simple
invoking God's blessing on the work, on the people, and on m
When he had done I replied in a few words, hearing my ow
lift small but clear through those airy spaces, and at that mor
truly felt my great and dear country stretching away from me
directions, as though I were at the centre of a vast intangible sp

Albert went early to the Crystal Palace to see that all was in order, and returned in a mood of fatalistic calm, which contrasted with my growing agitation on his behalf. I so desperately wanted everything to go well, and when I remembered my Coronation, there were plainly so many things that could go wrong!

We were in the carriages at twenty minutes to twelve, I and Albert and Vicky and Bertie, and a little rain fell just as we set off up Constitution Hill, but it passed after a few minutes and the sun came out again, and we had 'Queen's weather' all day. There were such crowds everywhere, greater, I think, than for my Coronation, packing the pavements, streaming through the Park, hanging from the windows. Apsley House and St George's had not a window vacant, and every face looked so cheerful and happy. In Hyde Park there were carriages and equestrians, boats crowded with spectators on the Serpentine, and the glorious chestnut trees were loaded down with boys, whistling and waving their caps. We trotted down Rotten Row with our cavalry escort behind us, and there before us was the great, glittering edifice of glass, shining in the sun, half-hidden amongst the trees and with its surfaces reflecting the sky and the Park so that it became curiously hard to take in, as if it were a magic palace caught half-way through some mysterious transformation.

At exactly noon we descended at the north entrance and went in to the ante-room to remove our shawls and straighten our dresses. I was wearing pink watered silk brocaded with silver, with the Garter ribbon, and a diamond tiara, and looked very well, I thought. Vicky was in white satin and lace, with a wreath of wild roses on her head and looked so sweet and pretty, and Bertie looked very nice in Scotch highland dress. In the ante-room Mamma and Mary Teck were waiting for us with other members of the family, and the Crown Prince and Princess of Prussia with Fritz – they had been invited to the opening as our private guests, so as not to annoy the King of Prussia.

Albert gave me his arm, we took Bertie and Vicky by their hands, and our procession started forward, entering the north nave. There were tall, wrought-iron gates across the end of it, and the glimpse of the transept through them – the waving palms, flowers, statues, myriads of people filling the galleries and seats all around – gave me a sensation I shall never forget, and I was much moved. Then there was a flourish of silver trumpets, and the gates were flung back by the attendant Yeomen of the Guard, revealing the whole scene.

It seemed incomprehensibly vast, the luminous distances made soft and hazy by the unrestricted light and space. The air was warm and serene, as though by magic a world of perpetual summer had been created within the delicate bones and translucent walls of the palace; and everywhere the eye fell on tropical foliage, trembling palm trees, banks of flowers drowning the senses with their colours. Before us was a dais under a gold-fringed canopy decorated with white ostrich feathers, and beyond, in the very centre of the transept, the heart of the whole exhibition, was a vast fountain carved out of pure transparent crystal, from which the glittering jets of water leapt fifty feet into the air. The stalls had been covered and the galleries draped in warm red Turkey cloth, comfortingly solid in all the dazzle and indistinctness, and against the strong colour a multitude of statues stood out dead white, most startling and impressive. And standing guard over all were the elm trees, soaring serene and mysterious to spread their lofty canopies of leaves across the lucent regions far above us.

As we appeared in the gateway the vast organ, together with two hundred musicians and a choir of six hundred voices, burst into the National Anthem, but nothing more than the first few notes were heard, for they were drowned out by the great cheer which rose from the multitude assembled there as though in their joy they had but one voice. There they were before me, bank upon bank of pink faces under tall hats and silk bonnets, and every face shining with delight and love and goodness, shouting out the joy of their celebration – shouting for me, yes, but more than that for themselves, for the glory that was England, her achievement, the peace and prosperity with which she nurtured her children, and her place at the heart of everything that was good and noble and liberating in the world. The experience of being there was so magical, so glorious, so touching that one felt – and everyone I spoke to afterwards agreed – filled most of all with *devotion*, more so than at any church service I have ever attended. It was a Festival of Peace, uniting the industry of all the nations of the earth, and there at the heart of it was its author, my beloved husband, my dearest Albert, whose soaring vision and selfless labour had brought it all into being.

As the noise died away, Albert left my side and stepped down from the dais to place himself at the head of the commissioners and read aloud the report, putting his vision into clear and simple words, invoking God's blessing on the work, on the people, and on my reign. When he had done I replied in a few words, hearing my own voice lift small but clear through those airy spaces, and at that moment I truly felt my great and dear country stretching away from me in all directions, as though I were at the centre of a vast intangible sphere.

I felt my people's love curve about me like the petals around the heart of a rose; for the heart of the rose *is* those petals – take them away, one by one, and there is nothing more. It was a moment of great reverence and mystery.

When I had spoken, the Archbishop pronounced his prayer of thanksgiving and then – I might have expected it – the organ, choirs, musicians, two military bands and nine State Trumpeters burst into that infernal Hallelujah Chorus! I cast such a look at Albert, but his in reply was limpid with innocence. Under cover of the noise we began to form our procession for walking round the exhibits – the commissioners, the foreign representatives, the ministers, the Household officers – and here a curious thing happened. A Chinaman in gorgeous silk robes had been moving about amongst the dignitaries – I saw him shaking hands with the Duke and Anglesey (who were standing together) and made a mental note to ask Albert who he was, for I knew China had sent no official representative. A moment later the Mandarin thrust through the crowd and flung himself at my feet in a deep obeisance. It caused a great deal of consternation, for no-one knew quite what to do about him. It was all very irregular, but on the other hand, one did not want to offend China, even if it had broken all the diplomatic rules. Concealing my annoyance, I smiled at the man, and spoke a few words to the Lord Chamberlain, telling him to find a place for him in the procession. The Mandarin was put in behind the foreign diplomats, beside the Duke. The Duke managed however to slip back, and by offering his arm to Lord Anglesey (who was lame, of course, having lost a leg at Waterloo) was able to dissociate himself politely from the unknown. The sight of those two old rivals (Anglesey in his wicked youth had eloped with the Duke's sister) in such friendly converse raised a great cheer from the spectators.

We took our places behind the officers of State and started our walk about the exhibition. I walked beside my darling Albert, who was calm and modest as always, surveying the fruit of all his vast labour as though it had been nothing to do with him. He held Vicky's hand, Bertie walked with me, and both were very excited and impressed with everything they saw – and how could they not be? We took only a brief tour that opening day, but the impression of it on my imagination remains to this day: a fabulous sight, brilliant, scintillating, such as the world had never seen before and has never seen again; the sunlight pouring in through the transparent spaces above and all around, the rich warmth of the hangings, carpets and tapestries, the palms, the flowers, the pellucid, rainbow colours, the music and voices and soft plashing of the fountain in its wide crystal basin; and above all, the sense of wonder, gratitude and love I felt from my people all around me. That day I walked, though a feeble woman, unguarded and unafraid amidst a multitude: no soldiers, no bodyguard, not even a policeman in sight – and what other ruler of what other country in the world could have done the same?

We returned finally to the dais where I gave the word to Lord Breadalbane to pronounce the exhibition open, which he did in a ringing voice, to be followed by a fanfare of trumpets and a one-hundred-gun salute outside in the Park, which raised a tremendous cheer. I think everyone in our party shed a few tears at that point. Then we drove back to Buckingham Palace, through the most colossal crowds, all wildly enthusiastic but keeping perfect order, which was the hallmark of the day. We arrived at twenty past one. As soon as we were through the gates the troops lining the road to keep it clear let the people through, and in a moment The Mall was packed from side to side with a vast throng, all looking towards the Palace as if hoping for something more. It was at Albert's suggestion that we went out on to the balcony in the middle of the main façade and showed ourselves, and it proved to be a very good idea and very well received. We waved to the people, and they cheered and cheered, and I think would gladly have gone on cheering all day if we had stayed there to be cheered at. (Since then we have made it a custom to appear on the balcony on great State occasions, and I very much hope that it will be continued. Love needs the means and opportunity of expressing itself, and our love for each other, Crown and People, is at the heart of everything good in this land.)

Later that day Granville sent us a message about the mysterious Chinaman. He was not a representative of the Imperial Government at all, but the proprietor of a Chinese Junk which was moored at the Temple pier and which he showed people over at a shilling a time. Since all the papers mentioned the affair, it proved excellent advertisement for him, and ensured him a profitable season. I laughed very much about it afterwards, and Albert said that since the Great Exhibition was intended to be a celebration of Free Trade and Commercial Enterprise, the Chinaman's actions were very much in the spirit of the thing, and he ought to be taken up as its mascot!

3rd October 1900

ONE EXHIBIT which properly belonged to the Great Exhibition was not displayed within the Crystal Palace. This was the Model Lodging House, which Albert, as President of the Society for Improving the Dwellings of the Labouring Classes, had designed himself as an example of rational, decent and economical housing for the lower orders. After long wrangling with Horseguards and the abominable Woods and Forests, he had obtained permission to erect it on a piece of waste ground next to the barracks, which he had done entirely at his own expense. It was a wonderful thing, four dwellings arranged on two floors, each storey identical so that further storeys could be added if desired. There was a central, open staircase connecting them, and the whole was built of patent, hollow bricks, with brick arches supporting the floors and roof instead of timbers, reducing the fire risk. (Fire was always a great hazard in 'slum' areas.) Each dwelling had a living-room, three bedrooms, and a scullery fitted out complete with sink, coal bin, plate rack, meat safe, et cetera. A dust shaft for refuse led to an enclosed repository under the stairs, and each apartment had a water-closet with modern Staffordshire glazed furniture, so that the families could live in a wholesome and hygienic atmosphere.

At the end of the exhibition the Model Lodging House was transferred to the edge of Kennington Park (the Duchy of Cornwall owns most of Kennington) where it remains to this day. Sadly Albert was unable to persuade any capitalist to invest in building such houses for the working classes; and the working classes themselves proved equally suspicious of the innovation, and seemed positively to relish the lack of hygiene in which they normally lived. Men are so narrow-minded that Albert's great desire for Rational Housing for the labouring sort is still unrealised, despite the awful death-rate from fever and disease amongst these people.

Albert had decided that it was right to offer refreshments at the exhibition (many people would stay there for the whole day, since there was so much to see, and some of them would be coming from a very great distance), but that there should be no alcohol on sale (which he felt would strike the wrong note) and no hot food except potatoes. This latter rule was partly because of the danger of fire (the potatoes could be cooked safely in the steam provided for working the moving machinery in the Machine Courts) and partly because of the nuisance to other visitors of the smell of hot meats and onions and so on. But there was an elegant supply of sandwiches, patties, cold meats, pastries, fruit and cakes on sale, together with Seltzer water and hot and cold beverages. Messrs Schweppe paid the commissioners £5,500 for the contract to provide refreshments, and a good bargain it proved to be, for they took over £75,000 in all. The quantities they sold over the course of the exhibition were astonishing – a million Bath buns, for instance, thirty-three tons of ham, and eight thousand gallons of cream. In two of the refreshment courts humbler fare was also provided for the poorer sort, in the form of cocoa, spruce beer, bread and butter and cheese: Albert wanted to be sure everyone was catered for. And of course outside in the park and on the streets there was no limit to what could be bought from itinerant vendors, from sausages and hot pies to coconuts and oranges.

The exhibition was, by every possible criterion, a remarkable success, and all those who had fought my darling so long and hard to oppose it were utterly confounded. People came from the furthest reaches of the country to visit it. Mill-masters got up excursion trains for their employees, rectors char-à-bancs for their parishioners; villagers clubbed together and drew lots for who should go; artisans and yeomen brought their wives and children, some of them leaving their home town or village for the first time in their lives. An agricultural implement maker sent his people round by water in two hired vessels which tied up at a wharf in Westminster. One woman walked on her own two feet all the way from Plymouth to see the exhibition; and London residents were besieged by relatives they had never heard of and friends from their childhood long forgotten, all eager to visit London that summer of all times. Everyone came, and no-one was disappointed; those who could came again and again. I myself paid something like forty visits, and delighted in showing a succession of our guests my favourite exhibits; I even paid for my head ghillie (not dear Brown in those days, of course, but Grant) to come down from Balmoral to see over it.

And the Duke, who had been so sceptical of the affair, and so afraid of public disorder, grew remarkably attached to the Crystal Palace and visited it several times. On the last of these visits, four days before the closing, he went quite alone, in spite of warnings, to take a fond farewell of his favourite items. It was a very crowded day, and the small, silver-headed, frail old hero walked up the nave amid a throng of almost a hundred thousand souls, and was inevitably recognised and mobbed by enthusiastic admirers, all wanting to touch him or shake his hand. Those out of sight in other parts of the building heard the uproar and thought it betokened some disaster (perhaps the collapse which Colonel Sibthorpe had been predicting with increasing wistfulness as the season progressed). A panic ensued as thousands ran for the exits, and a large display of French chinaware was overset. The Duke was captured by six constables who had been following him without his knowledge, and he was removed, pale and indignant, almost bodily from the scene.

But when I tell you that in the five and a half months of the exhibition that was the only untoward occurrence, you will have an idea of what a peaceful, orderly celebration it was. More than six million people passed through the entrances to the Crystal Palace that summer; on opening day there was a crowd of half a million surrounding the building; and at all times London was crammed with people of every degree from all over the country and all over the world. Yet in all that time there was no major crime committed in or around the exhibition. Crimes in general over the whole of London were fewer in number than in other years; and Richard Mayne's specially enlarged police force had nothing to do in the environs of the Crystal Palace but to take up a handful of people for pick-pocketing and selling forged tickets. What a nation this is!

And when everyone had been paid at the end of it all, the exhibition was found to have made a vast profit of £186,000. At Albert's instigation the commissioners used it to purchase some eighty acres of land south of the Kensington Road. Here they planned to build museums, gardens and institutes dedicated to Art and Science and the furtherance of knowledge. On the site now, of course, are the Horticultural Gardens, the Natural History Museum, the Royal College of Music, the Royal Albert Hall, and a jumble of buildings known as the South Kensington Museum. Only last year I laid the foundation stone of a new building to house the collections of the latter, which when it is finished will be called the Victoria and Albert Museum, and will be dedicated to the fine and applied arts of all countries, with entrance free to all degrees of people. It will all be as my darling wanted it.

As to Paxton's glasshouse itself, the country had grown so fond of it that it did not want to part with it, and a motion was speedily put before Parliament to purchase it for the nation and turn it into a permanent Winter Garden. The commissioners were pledged, however, to return the Hyde Park site to the Woods and Forests in the condition in which they had found it; and so in the spring of 1852 the great conservatory was dismantled and transported across London to be re-erected in Sydenham, where its sobriquet of the Crystal Palace became its official and permanent name; and I'm told it is still a great attraction.

5th October 1900

WHEN IT was all over, we came up here to Scotland. I had never seen Albert so tired. The work and worry and conflict of the exhibition had worn him to a shadow, and for months he had been sleeping badly, getting up in the night and going to his desk to sit and read, and then returning to lie heavily in my arms for an hour or two before his usual hour of rising drove him away from me again. He had been suffering, too, from violent headaches, intermittent toothache, and stomach and bowel upsets, all of which are grievous troubles to a man with so much business to get through. On the evening of our arrival at Balmoral I found him sitting alone in his dressing-room, crying in an exhausted way which quite frightened me. I could do nothing but put my arms round his shoulders, upon which he turned and seized me clumsily, pressed his face against my belly and wept like a weary child.

But Scotland revived him; the silence and the emptiness of the landscape seemed to fill his spirit as the cold, clean air filled his lungs. When one day we found ourselves on top of an eminence with nothing in view but wild mountains, lochs and heather – no buildings, no people, no symptoms of habitation of any sort – he seemed to find his peace, and I saw his eyes brighten, and his shoulders straighten like a blade of grass that has been pressed down and is now released.

'It is so wonderful here,' he sighed. 'It is just like home!' And by home he meant, of course, not Buckingham Palace or Windsor or even dear Osborne, but the Rosenau. He said the mountains around Balmoral were just like the wooded Thuringian hills of his childhood. Now, I have been to Coburg, and stayed in the Rosenau – slept in the very room Albert and Ernst shared as boys – and I know there is not the least likeness; but I understood, though in a way I could not put into words, what his heart was saying to him. It was all part of a process which had been going on all his life, and which I came to understand only too late – the process of running away.

He had said to me once, 'It is not *you* I would leave; there is nowhere I ever want to be except in your arms,' and I had taken it for

322

reassurance – indeed, there was nothing else I could do. But I came to see that there was a core of him which did not belong to the earth, which was not attached, and struggled always to get away, tugging at him as a kite flown high in a good breeze tugs at your hand. It is fun, when flying a kite, to feel that tug, exhilarating to be connected even if only by a string to something that moves to a stronger wind than that which stirs our earth-bound bodies. But for Albert it must have been exhausting to go on resisting. His soul rippled and dragged in a strong, pure wind none of us understood or even knew about; and how often he must have longed simply to let go of the earth and go sailing away, free at last of pains and trials, to soar into the clear, clean place where he knew he would find his Maker's shining face and loving, soothing hands.

But duty made him stay – hard, heavy, leaden duty. And so he worked, and worked, and waited for release; remained always patient, always diligent, always cheerful (for he believed, as I do, that God loves those who do His work with a glad and willing heart). The tug upon the string manifested itself only in these vain attempts to run away – first to Osborne, then to Balmoral, and then just further and further into the merciful anodyne of work. But it wore him out, of course, the conflict between body and soul. The only peace he had was in my arms, in the certainty of my love for him, and in the release of passion, that strange release he half-feared, but which he never ceased to crave.

He was a man who found it difficult to express affection, and so the loss in quick succession of the two men he regarded as his friends – Anson and Peel – had been grievous for him. Anson was like a younger brother, the only man I ever saw Albert touch spontaneously, though it was only a casual arm across the shoulder, and on a rare occasion. Peel he had liked and trusted, and he had felt – which was more important – that Peel understood him and approved of him. He had lost them both while still struggling with the exhibition; and to those losses had been added two more – not in death, but in the going away of two people he had admired and enjoyed the company of. One was our dear Laddle, who retired in January 1851, feeling that the nursery needed a younger supervisor; and the other was Thomas Cubitt, who finished his work at Osborne, packed his plans, and went away to other schemes.

Those things were the spur, I think, to the Balmoral scheme. As long ago as October 1848, after several delightful holidays in Scotland, we had told Russell that we meant to buy a second home in the Highlands, where the air would be less relaxing than in the south (and, though we did not express it so, of course, where we would be further away from bothersome ministers and reports and Boxes). Lord John had replied somewhat sourly that no Treasury funds would be forthcoming for its purchase or maintenance; and that further, since Aberdeenshire was so far from London, a Minister in Attendance would always have to be with us, and his expenses would have to be met out of the Privy Purse.

These matters did not deter us from taking a lease on Balmoral. The castle, like old Osborne House, was too small and very inconvenient, and Albert wanted to be building, but we could not afford another scheme after Osborne. Then, like a wish come true, in the summer of 1852 I was left an enormous legacy. I have always been given presents, by foreign heads of state and by my own subjects, ranging in value from diamond parures to a giant pumpkin, but John Camden Nield's was the most valuable of all. He was a miser and a recluse, living in dreadful squalor, and no-one knew he had any money at all. But when he died his estate turned out to be worth more than a quarter of a million pounds, and having no family whatever, he left it all to me, with no explanation other than that 'he knew I wouldn't waste it'. Nor did I. I blessed my benefactor, restored the chancel of his parish church and put up a memorial window to him, and gave the rest of the fortune to Albert to buy the Balmoral estate and build his new castle. This time he employed the services of an architect, but Balmoral, like Osborne, was all my darling's own design, and he considered every detail of it. In his building work he was happy; in manipulating materials, dimensions, mathematical equations he found no conflict that he could not solve, no troublesome human inconsistencies or emotions to cloud the issue or falsify his calculations. He was powerful; he prevailed.

Balmoral is Osborne with turrets. Many of Osborne's innovations were repeated here: the hot air system, for instance (though every room has a fireplace as well, because of the greater cold); and the sanitary arrangements (four bathrooms were built – for me, for Albert, and two for the children – and fourteen water-closets, which I believe must be the largest number in any house or palace anywhere!). The house was built all of local stone so that it would blend harmoniously with its surroundings. We loved Scotland, so Albert made everything about the house as Scotch as could be, with tartan wallpaper, carpets, curtains and upholstery, the thistle emblem appearing in carving and moulding in every room, and everything made of stags' antlers that conveniently could be. All the servants were local people, all the estate workers and ghillies were Highlanders, and we attended Divine Service at the local church at Crathie, which we found very simple and nice. Albert thought the Scotch form of Protestantism very like the German, which made him feel at home. (I was under the impression that I was Head of the Church of Scotland as well as the Church of England, and very disappointed I was many years later to be told this was not the case. I wanted so much to belong to them.) I and Albert admired the Highland character – proud, honest, courteous and candid – and we felt honoured to be so well loved by these independent people. I often remembered with a smile and a shake of the head what my wicked Lord M. had long ago said to me about Scotland: that there was nothing to detract from it except the very high opinion the Scotch themselves entertained of it. 'And those Highland Clans are so *very* interesting and romantic,' he said with a droll look; 'What a good thing there are so few of them left!' I truly believe he could never have been to Scotland; but of course he may have met Scotch people in London, and no-one likes to hear another country praised by a visitor to their own.

The time we spent at Balmoral in the summer of 1852, when Albert knew it was to be ours entirely and when he was beginning to plan the new house, was a very happy time for us, and by the end of summer I knew I was pregnant again. Yet in this moment of joy and renewal we were dealt another blow which, though we must long have anticipated it, still set us down dreadfully: on September the 14th the Duke died quite suddenly. I was glad afterwards that he had been snuffed out so mercifully without suffering, but it was hard, very hard, to think of England without him. His position, like his gifts, had been unique, and the whole nation mourned in the most spontaneous and heartfelt manner. The people had loved him, and though he was quite indifferent to their adulation, he would have sacrificed his fortune or his life to preserve them. For myself, I had lost a loyal and disinterested friend. All my life he had been there – indeed he had been witness to my birth – at my Coronation, my wedding, my children's Christenings; and in every crisis both personal and political I had always turned to him. He had never loved *me*, but he loved England and he reverenced the Crown, and I knew that in any circumstances I could rely on him completely, to advise and serve me without fear or favour.

To our troops, of course, the Hero of Waterloo was a legend, and the ideal against which everything military was measured. 'It wouldn't have done for the Duke,' they would say, shaking their heads disapprovingly – and do say still, I'm told, though he has been dead nearly fifty years.

In December of 1852 something happened which alarmed everyone very much, but whose real consequences none of us anticipated at that time. The previous December Louis Napoleon had executed a *coup d'état* in Paris and made himself Prince-President for an initial period of ten years – in effect, dictator. We had thoroughly disapproved of this unconstitutional behaviour, and had instructed the Foreign Office to remain sternly neutral on the matter. But Palmerston had privately told the French Ambassador in London, Count Walewski, that he thoroughly approved of the Prince's actions, and as Walewski had promptly passed on the congratulations, England found herself in the painful position of having both approved and disapproved of the action at the same time.

This was by no means the first time Palmerston had embarrassed us by acting on his own and without or against instructions, but this time Russell, provoked in the extreme, dismissed him, much to our surprise and relief. The absence of Palmerston made everything so much easier and removed such a thorn from Albert's side that it contributed greatly to his contentment that summer (and hence to the new baby's existence – an odd thought that, which I think I shall not pursue!).

However in December 1852, just a year after the *coup d'état*, Louis Napoleon unmasked, and declared himself Emperor Napoleon III – supported, I'm sorry to say, largely by the French army which thirsted for revenge for Waterloo. It was an anxious time, for we all feared a renewal of French militarism, and there were rumours of renewed plans to invade England; but since his removal or death would have caused dreadful chaos in France, and since the new Foreign Secretary, Lord Malmesbury, was a friend of his, I was obliged to accept my ministers' advice and acknowledge him. The new Emperor expressed himself very correctly and seemed anxious for England's friendship – so anxious, indeed, that he made an offer for the hand of my niece Adelaide (Feo's daughter) with the intention of allying himself, however distantly, with the British Monarchy. I had no wish to see Adelaide married to such an adventurer, but fortunately Adelaide and Feo both disliked the match, and it went off. The Emperor soon showed his true colours by marrying Eugénie de Montijo, a creature of great beauty and charm (some say Palmerston was her real father) but with an extremely *colourful* past. In the event, however, she proved a good, virtuous and gentle Empress, and much worthier to sit on the Throne of France than many women of birth and reputation. I came to like her very much indeed, and she had the greatest admiration and respect for me. (I remember one incident when Albert and I visited them in Paris, and we all went to the opera together. Afterwards Eugénie told me that one of her ladies-in-waiting had commented that when we took our seats in the Imperial Box, I had seated myself without looking to see if there was a chair behind me. 'The Queen of England is so royal that she simply *knows* there will be a chair. Any other state of affairs is unthinkable – so she does not look. But you, Madame, you were not born a Queen. You look before you sit.')

The consequence, though we could not then foresee it, of Louis Napoleon's making himself Emperor, was the Crimean War. If he had not had so much to prove to the French army, if he had not needed some military glory with which to bolster his reputation, and placate his subjects by reminding them of his illustrious uncle, he would not have wanted to tweak the Bear's nose. It was with Russia we went to war, nominally to keep Constantinople out of Russian hands, but I don't believe we would have done so without France as our ally, or without France's enthusiasm for the fight.

It was dreadful to be having a war without the Duke, and I think we all felt at a loss. The supreme command was given to Lord Raglan, who had been the Duke's military secretary at Waterloo, where he had lost an arm. (Lord M. used to tell the story of how after the amputation, as the attendants were carrying the arm away, he shouted out, 'Hoi, bring that back! There's a ring my wife gave me on the little finger!') Raglan did his best to think what the Duke would have done in every situation, but on reflection I don't think his mental powers were really up to the job. All through the campaign he kept referring to the enemy as 'the French', quite unable to adjust to the idea that there was anyone else in the world to fight, or that this time the French were our allies!

At a distance I can see that there were good things that came out of that unsatisfactory war, but my heart bleeds when I think of those thousands of British soldiers who died out there, and the widows and orphans at home, left to struggle on in poverty and misery. I, who have lost a husband and two sons, know the terrible pain of that loss, which can never be made right again; and I have said since, to younger, less experienced rulers, that we must be very careful before we commit our soldiers to war. When King Victor Emmanuel visited me in 1855 he said that the only part of kingship he really enjoyed was making war, and

I warned him sharply that Kings must be sure that wars were for a just cause, because they would have to answer before God for men's lives. 'God will pardon our mistakes,' he said; and I replied, 'Not always.'

But there is a mystical relationship between a Sovereign and the Army, which I felt very strongly at the time of Crimea, and have felt since. Those good, brave, uncomplaining men march and fight for their country, of course, but a country is a big thing and hard to comprehend or to love. It is their Queen who is the visible symbol of what they are willing to die for, and many a time I have taken the salute as they march off to war, and felt the great hungry waves of their love wash over me. In my mind and heart I have marched at their head, have fought with them, and taken their wounds for them. If I had not been born into a woman's feeble frame, I am sure I would have led my armies indeed; and I have visited wounded soldiers in hospital and seen the light come into their eyes as I approach, have witnessed miracles as a man despaired of rallies and recovers after I have touched him. I say this not in self-conceit, but to exemplify something which is greater and more mysterious than we can explain with our science and earthly wisdom.

In May 1855, when the war was over, we had a special ceremony at the Horseguards to present medals to the Crimean veterans. I stood on a dais with Lord Panmure (the War Minister) with the medals, which were silver on a blue and yellow ribbon, in a basket between us. There were huge crowds, and several bands playing, and the dear, noble fellows (many of them sporting the evidence of their wounds, some on crutches, some even in wheeling-chairs) filed past and I gave each his medal and a word or two of commendation. Some were so shy they dared not look up, others looked into my face and smiled; all touched my hand, and I saw in their eyes the reverence and love they felt, simple soldiers, meeting their Sovereign face to face for the first time. My hands shook so much with emotion I could hardly keep hold of the medals which shaggy old Panmure (the men called him The Bison) handed to me out of the basket; and I was deeply touched when I learned afterwards that many of the men had refused to give up their medals for engraving in case they did not get back the actual one I had given them.

There is one story about this ceremony which I heard afterwards and which made me laugh very much. A lady of fashion, meeting Lord Panmure at a dinner party, asked him about the ceremony, and particularly about my feelings on the occasion. 'Was the Queen touched?' she asked. 'Bless my soul, no,' said Panmure indignantly, 'she had a brass railing before her, no-one could touch her.' 'I mean,' the lady persevered, 'was she moved?' 'Moved?' said Lord Panmure. 'She had no occasion to move!'

Eighteen

15th October 1900, at Balmoral

THE NEW baby arrived on the 7th of April 1853 – a boy, whom we named Leopold, after our dear uncle. The birth was attended by an innovation which, I am glad to say, has now become quite commonplace. My good physician Sir James Clark – himself a Scot, of course – had been following with interest the work of Dr Simpson in Edinburgh in the use of chloroform. It is astonishing to think now that the properties of anaesthesia had been known about since the beginning of the century, when Humphry Davy, of safety-lamp fame, had written a paper about the effects of inhaling nitrous oxide. Another substance, ether, had first been used in a London hospital in 1846, by the great surgeon Robert Liston who had amputated a man's leg without his feeling anything. And Dr Simpson had successfully administered chloroform in 1847, to a woman whose gratitude was so intense that she named the daughter she bore under its influence Anaesthesia!

Simpson's associate, Dr John Snow, had written a paper on the subject: 'Where the pain is not greater than the patient is willing to bear cheerfully, there is no occasion to use chloroform, but when the patient is anxious to be spared the pain, I can see no valid objection to the use of this agent.'

But if he could see no objection, many others could, and the vast majority of the medical profession refused to have anything to do with anaesthesia. Pain was an essential part of surgery, they said: the 'sting' of it was what stimulated the system and initiated recovery. Operated upon painlessly, the patient would sink into lethargy and death. Outside the medical profession, it was widely believed that pain was the fire which refined the steel of men's souls, and that mankind would grow soft and degenerate if it were eliminated; and the clergy claimed more simply that pain was ordained by God as man's lot, and that to evade it was to resist God's will.

But when Dr Simpson recommended chloroform for women in childbirth, all the various opposing factions joined together in vigorous protest. There could be no doubt that *this* was a sin. Woman was *meant* to suffer in labour. Did it not explicitly state in the Book of Genesis that she should bring forth children in sorrow? In vain did Dr Snow point out that God made Adam fall into a deep sleep before removing his rib, which sounded very like anaesthesia; every man knew with certainty that women had to suffer pain in childbirth, or they would not love their children.

I had heard something of the argument, and listened with interest when my good Clark brought the suggestion to me that we should invite Dr Snow (who had been demonstrating anaesthesia in a London dental hospital) to attend me when my time came. Its use had been sufficiently studied north of the border by then to be sure it was safe and had no deleterious effect on mother or child.

'It is a very simple thing,' he said. 'A little of the liquid is poured on to a handkerchief which is rolled into a funnel and held over the patient's mouth and nose. She breathes in the vapour, which is not unpleasant – it is an ingredient of most cough-mixtures, you know, ma'am – and the pain is softened and sometimes done away with altogether.'

I saw no reason, religious or otherwise, to bear pain that could be softened or done away with, and Albert firmly believed that God had not given man his inventive mind for its fruits to be ignored. And so – a little nervously, I must admit – I gave the word. Dr Snow did not give me so much of the substance as to make me insensible at any time, but just enough to dull the pain, and I found the whole experience delightful, soothing and quieting beyond measure, and only wished it had been offered me earlier in my childbearing career. The news soon got out that I had had the blessed chloroform administered to me, and the sensation in the press was indescribable. All the arguments were rehearsed once again, and there were plenty of old men ready to condemn me for impiety, and worse. But I'm glad to say it was the beginning of the end of resistance to the idea of anaesthesia, and I'm happy to have played a part in the promotion of such a great good. Afterwards, diehards might fulminate in provincial newspapers, but polite society knew where its loyalties lay. If the Queen of England had it, no lady was going to lag behind.

The proof of its value was demonstrated by the fact that I had a much quicker recovery from that confinement than any of the previous ones. The baby, however, did not thrive. He was a fat and jolly-looking infant at birth, though I thought not handsome, with a head too large and rather a common nose. For the first few weeks he seemed well enough, but then he began to lose weight. Clark thought he had a weak digestion and that his wet-nurse did not agree with him, and with some difficulty we procured a different one, which seemed to bring about an improvement. I thought Clark had discovered the trouble, but it was not long before little Leo began to ail again, and eventually the hideous truth was discovered: that my baby was suffering from haemophilia.

The very word has a hideous sound, like an evil magician's conjuration. And indeed, it was as though a dreadful curse had been put upon me. It bewildered me – and does to this day, for the doctors all agree that it is an hereditary disease, but it has *never* been in our family. I know this to be true, for it is not a thing that could be hidden in a royal house, and none of my ancestors has ever suffered from it. Nor, as far as I can discover, has it ever existed in the Coburg family (although records may be less complete on that side, especially with the death of children in infancy, where the cause may not have been ascribed). But neither Mamma nor Albert had ever heard of it on the Coburg side. Yet they say it is passed on through the mother. I *cannot* understand it.

Oh, the feelings of a mother who has infected her own precious child with this hideous disease cannot be described! Every time little Leo ailed, I knew it to be my fault, and felt as though I had driven a knife through his little body with my own hand. And to this torment there could be no end, unless it be in the death of that same beloved little soul. Any blow, any little fall – and what normal child does not spend half its day tumbling down or knocking itself against one thing or another? – could start the bleeding; and then would come the swelling, the fever, the agony – the piercing cries that tore at one's heart – the helplessness of watching the suffering without being able to alleviate it. From those bouts the child might recover, or might die – or might survive permanently crippled. To live with that knowledge day after day is what no mother ought to endure.

Any mother in that situation would be protective, would try to stop the little one from running, from playing rough games, from climbing trees – try to stop the others in the family from wrestling or playing boisterously. Only when Leopold was lying asleep in his bed did I feel safe (and what a precarious safety that turned out to be!). He grew to be the cleverest of the boys, and the most studious; in his mental attributes and ability to apply himself, he was the most like of any of the boys to his dear father. He loved and early learned to appreciate Italian painting, which Albert so adored; his fondness for music was the most passionate of all the family, and his command of languages was extraordinary. Naturally, I suppose, my desire to make him take care of himself fretted him, and made him rebel and do the very things I tried to prevent; but I could not help admiring his spirit, which no illness or apprehension of death could dampen. Though I complained bitterly of his wilful neglect of advice and disregard of his doctors, I would probably secretly have loved him less if he had meekly accepted the restraints I tried to put on him.

In 1876 dear Disraeli, recognising Leo's abilities and his desire to be useful, suggested I make him my political secretary, and he served me well in that capacity, and was immensely proud to have the key to my Boxes which had once been his papa's. We had feared we would not raise him, but in the event he lived to be a man, to serve his country, and even to marry and father two perfectly healthy children. I had been against him marrying at all, fearing the strain would be too much for him, but he insisted in his headstrong way. Helen, on whom his choice fell, proved a good and clever girl, most interesting to talk to, and very fond of mathematics, which endeared her to me. Less than a year after their wedding, she gave birth to a girl whom they called Alice.

(I was so thrilled when I heard the news that in my haste to go and see my new grandchild I twisted my ankle and had to be carried to their room. There was Leo lying on one sofa and Helen on the other, and when I came in as a third helpless person, the effect was quite ludicrous!)

How ironic it was that frail Leo should outlive his own father. All through his childhood I had tried to protect him from falls and accidents, but when he died, a week before his thirty-first birthday, it was not from some violent accident, but in bed, in his sleep, of a burst blood-vessel in the head. (By an awful coincidence, he died on the anniversary of that dreadful day when he rushed into my dressing-room with the terrible news that my dear John Brown had passed away in his sleep.) He was the second of my children to die before me, and bitter was my grief – but for my own loss. For my boy himself I could not repine: there was such a restless longing in him for what he could not have, and it seemed to increase year by year rather than lessen.

Leopold had been married less than two years when he died; his son, Charlie, was born four months posthumously, a dear child of whom I have always been very fond. Helen has done an excellent job of bringing him up, poor fatherless boy; and now that my poor darling Affie has followed his only son to the grave, Charlie is to rule

Coburg, his grandfather's beloved home country. I think Albert would have been glad that Leo's son is to have Coburg after all – a son from the son we never thought to raise.

I was luckier than my gentle Alice, who lost her little boy Frittie when he was only three years old, after a fall from a window. Frittie was the liveliest, most spirited of her children – why is it that haemophiliac sons are so often that way? – and her grief was terrible. As to my own – what words can describe the feelings of a mother who has not only afflicted a son, but has been the cause of a daughter afflicting *her* son?

And yet it was not in my family! Where could it have come from, that hideous disease? When we first learnt that Leo was afflicted, I found myself remembering Lord Melbourne's words: 'It is a very bad idea to marry one's first cousin . . . There can be consequences . . . It can happen that the children of such a union are – odd.' Could it be that Leo's illness was a consequence of my having married my first cousin? I could not bear to think it – could not bear to imagine that anything bad could have come of my love for Albert and his for me – and so I shut the thought away, mentioned it to no-one, not even to my darling. But it was there, beneath the surface, along with my deep anxiety for the child (and another fear which was even less possible to name) and these hidden worries affected my health and my temper. I was by turns depressed, nervous and irritable, and who was to bear the brunt of my passions but my beloved? So once again the blissful stream of our marriage was disturbed by violent quarrels; on and off for four years they broke out, worse even than those we had endured just before and just after Bertie's birth.

I tried so hard to control myself, but one cannot keep hold all the time, and every now and then the dog would slip the leash. I raged; and Albert wrote me letters – cool, calm, mildly reproachful, sympathetic, kindly, *damnable* letters!

'My dear Child, let us calmly consider the facts of the case . . . I am often astonished at the effect a hasty word of mine has produced, though in your candid way you usually explain afterwards what was the real root of your distress. I insist that I am not the cause, though I have often been the *occasion* of your suffering . . .'

'I admit my method of treatment as on former occasions has signally failed, but I know of no other. If I say nothing I am accused of want of feeling, hard heartedness, cold indifference etc. etc. If I leave the room to allow you time to recover yourself, you follow me to renew the dispute and "have it all out" . . .'

'It is my duty to keep calm and I mean to do so, for I do most sincerely pity you in your suffering. But if you were less preoccupied with your own feelings and more interested in the rest of the world you could avoid these outbreaks . . .'

'What are you really afraid of in me? What can I do to you save, at the most, not listen long enough when I have business elsewhere?'

Yes, what indeed? Oh, Albert, Albert, I saw, I knew, though you thought *Kleines Frauchen* was too silly and too selfish a little person to understand. But how could I speak to you on the subject? This was the thing I dared not even think about, dared not admit to myself for an instant. Far less how could I write it down, for written words have power, and come back to haunt you afterwards, and torment you with *what might have been*. But I knew, beloved, and I saw in your eyes that you knew it too. I saw you year after year withdrawing yourself from me, going away from the world, further and further, gradually into death.

When we were in London or at Windsor, business was the excuse. Well, he had enough of that in good truth, enough to leave me alone all day while he attended meetings, made speeches, inspected new schemes, planted trees, laid foundation stones. President of a thousand societies, patron of a thousand charities, every educator's friend, every improver's sympathetic ear – how tirelessly he spent himself, pouring out his hours and days in the service of others, as though he had a limitless store. And my share was to breakfast and dine with him: so, to see him bolt his breakfast while he read papers and reports, spoiling his digestion to save a few minutes for his crowded day; and to see him at dinner too tired to eat, his face pale with fatigue, doing his best to be civil if we had guests, making the family laugh if we had not. My share was to sleep with him, to lie pressed against him in the darkness and feel him ache; to feel him creep carefully from my side in the night, trying not to wake me, to go to his desk and punish his insomnia with study. My share was to pretend I had not wakened, because that was all I could do for him.

Oh, how I tried to get him away from all his cares and concerns; but even away from London he did not stop. At Osborne he left me and went out all day seeing after his improvements about the estate and the farms; and at Balmoral, when he had no building or philanthropic scheme to advance, he would go out all day after the deer, tiring himself out on the mountains.

It was at Balmoral he went the furthest from me, searching in the wild mountains and empty spaces for the Thuringia of his childhood, searching for some essential thing he had lost then which he needed in order to be able to live. I knew that was what he was doing, I saw it, though I think he did not. But he tramped exhaustingly through the rough heather and up the stony paths, always eager on the way out, always disappointed coming home – for the thing he searched for was not there to be found. At first I went with him, hoping to be some comfort to him, but as he went further and marched longer I could not keep up, and had to let him go alone. Then to be able to cover more ground he started staying overnight, at first under canvas, taking no-one but his valet Löhlein, and a ghillie or two; later he had his own bothy built at Feithort – what Brown used to call 'the wee hoosie' – just a single room with a bed, table, chair, stove, and a few shelves, and a second hut nearby for his people. There he stayed for longer, two nights or even three. I think he would not have come back at all, had it not been for engagements and duties.

I was so lonely away from him, worrying about little Leo, about Vicky's engagement to Fritz (she was too young, too young!), about Bertie's lack of progress, about the international situation, about the latest Government crisis – and with nothing to distract me from my worries except the worse thought I dared not think. I fretted for him all day, never entirely at ease except when he was with me; and he would come back tired, with that lost look in his eyes like mist, and ask me polite questions about my day, as though I were a stranger and he would be considerate towards me whatever it cost him. But at least those expeditions helped him sleep. After a long day of physical exertion, he would fold his sad body into my arms and my heart, as if for consolation for that thing he had not found, ready for tenderness and then for oblivion.

Once, in the early days of the Wee Hoosie, I rebelled against being left behind and followed him. Brown went with me to lead the pony over the rough tracks – Brown whom Albert had chosen for me, to sit on the box when I drove out and lead the pony when I rode, because of his magnificent physique, transparent honesty, and straightforward, independent character. It was a thing I always liked to remember afterwards, that it was Albert who had chosen Johnny Brown for my own ghillie, though he could not have known how much his choice would one day come to mean to me. But three years after Albert left me, I brought Brown down from Scotland to be 'the Queen's Highland Servant', and from that time he never left me for a single day until he died. It was because of him that I was able to get through the terrible desert of years. He did everything for me – carried messages, fetched my shawl, blotted my letters, drove my carriage or led my horse – saved my life on more than one occasion – dried my tears on many another. When my steps grew uncertain, it was on his strong right arm that my left hand rested, and I knew he would not let me fall. When my hands grew stiff he tied my bonnet strings and poured my tea – yes, and put a 'grand nip o' whisky' in it, too, to help me through the day! He was mother and nurse and bodyguard and friend – above all, friend – the truest, kindest, most disinterested and faithful friend one could ever hope for. Most of all, he was simply *there*: I did not need to send for him, or even look around for him – I had only to put out my hand.

But that was a long way into the future. On the day I went up to the Wee Hoosie, Johnny Brown was a rather shy young man, unsmiling, and more at ease with horses than with people (he had worked as an ostler before joining our service, and there was no horse that he could not handle – and no dog that would not come to him, ears flattened and tail a-swing, to be petted). It was a long journey, through country progressively wilder, and though the day was fine, there was something forbidding about the purple starkness of the mountains, and the indigo shadows under the outcrops. But the pony, Fyvie, was strong and willing, and Brown strode with his long, springy step in front of it, not really leading it, though he held the bridle, but allowing it to follow him. It was not an arrangement conducive to conversation. Only once, when we stopped at the top of a ridge to let the pony breathe, I said to him, 'Will it rain, do you think?' and he looked around at the sky and seemed to snuff the wind, and then said, 'Not on this side. Over yonder, perhaps.' And so it proved. As we went up the glenside, I saw the rain falling white on the other side of the valley from a plum-purple cloud, even while the sun shone on us. It was the strangest sight, rather awe-inspiring. I had no desire to talk or laugh.

Reaching the encampment at last, we found all the signs of life – ponies tethered, a fire drifting steel-blue smoke lazily through the trees, and two ghillies squatting beside their hut smoking their pipes. They scrambled to their feet as the dogs began barking, and Löhlein came to the door of Albert's bothy, a cloth in his hands and a startled expression on his face. (He had come with Albert from Coburg in the very beginning, and was devoted to him. After Albert's death I kept him on in my service, for he had nowhere else to go. He is dead now too. One of the penalties of a long life is that one outlives everyone.)

'Where is the Prince?' I asked him in German, and he replied apologetically, 'He went out early this morning, Your Majesty – at six o'clock – after the deer. He took Herr Grant and Herr Macdonald. I don't know when he will return.'

It was a blow; but I would not seem disconcerted. 'No matter, I will wait a while now I am here,' I said.

'His Highness did not know you were coming,' Löhlein said, half statement, half hopeful question. I did not answer, but indicated to Brown that I would get down. 'I shall stay a while,' I said to him. 'You may take off Fyvie's saddle.'

He glanced once into my face, with his shrewd, measuring look, and then helped me to dismount. Seeing that Löhlein was still standing there, looking put out and turning the cloth over and over in his hands, Brown said briskly, 'Now then, Meester Lowland, will ye no get Her Mad-jesty a chair tae sit on, seeing I have holt o' the pony and canna dae it maself?'

This provoked Löhlein into action. He fetched a chair out from the bothy and set it up in the doorway, and I seated myself while Brown took the pony away to tie it with the others, and then sat himself down with the other ghillies. After a while they settled down and began talking to each other again in low voices, but Brown, I noticed, did not join in. He sat, his arms clasped lightly round his updrawn knees, watching me without appearing to do so.

I waited, wondering if I had been a fool, wondering how long I should stay there, wondering if Albert did come back, whether he would be angry with me for disturbing him. The longer I waited for him the more I felt like a foolish and lovesick girl, rather than a wife of fifteen years' standing. It was a very still day, unusually in those hills, so little movement in the air that the smoke from the fire hardly rose, and was long dissipating, hanging like muslin in the branches of the trees. The smell of it was autumnal; and behind it I could smell pine resin and the clean snowy emptiness of Highland air – all sad smells. Under my feet was a layer of dead needles, brown and thick as a carpet; the only sounds were the soft, lilting voices of the ghillies talking in Gaelic, the occasional sigh or stamp from the ponies, and now and then a snapping and spitting from the fire.

I tilted my head and looked up at the sky, past a framework of half-bare branches and hanging pine-cones, and it was blue and empty, except for a single dark bird circling high up, so far up I could not tell if it was eagle or kite or buzzard. (When I had first met Albert, I had not known one bird from another, but I knew them all now – and the flowers, and the trees.) What a view it must have from up there, I thought: like God's view of His creation, the sweet, beautiful earth we had been given to look after. And suddenly my heart was aching with the sadness of all beauty, that longing to possess which can never be fulfilled. Perhaps that was Albert's sadness, I thought suddenly, that and nothing else. Perhaps I have been fretting and worrying for nothing, and all he seeks in these empty places is the beauty that walks one pace ahead of us always, and cannot be overtaken. I should not have come here with my foolishness to fret him. I should go, now, at once, and leave him be.

With the thought I stood up; and although he had not appeared to be looking at me, Brown stood too, with that graceful ease of trained strength, like a ballet dancer. And then one of the dogs barked, and moments later the hunting party appeared coming up the path – dogs, ghillies, ponies – and Albert. They had not killed, I saw that at once – the ponies carried nothing across their saddles. Albert walked ahead, wearing the kilt of the grey Balmoral tartan he had designed himself and a heavy tweed jacket, his gun under his arm. He walked into the clearing, came directly towards me, but, whether it was a trick of the light, or whether his mind was on other things, he did not seem to see me. He was looking straight at me, but he was walking towards the hut, and I might have been an insubstantial ghost for all that my presence was impinging on him.

He paused a few steps from me, like a blind man who knows there is something in his path but does not know what, and I looked at him with the sudden clarity of a stranger. A man in his thirties, but looking older; a married man, a family man, with the lines of responsibility and daily cares in his face; a balding head, a double chin, a hint of girth under the waistcoat, a slackness in the cheek muscles, a pouchiness under the eyes. The slender, golden-haired, porcelain-skinned youth whose beauty seemed to have come from another sphere, as though an angel had been caught in human form – where was he? I did not care, I did not want him back – I loved this man standing before me now, whose beauty was *of* this earth, the beauty of experience and compassion, of human love and happiness. I had lived with him and eaten and slept with him and borne his children, and all those years of ours were in the soft wornness of his face. I loved him so much that I felt as though it must burst my heart.

'Albert,' I said at last, softly. 'I hope you are glad to see me?'

He did not reply. It was a mild day, and the air, though still, was fresh; but I felt a cold sweat start up under my arms and down my back – a sweat of fear. His blue eyes were blank, and there was something about the way the light fell that showed me the contours of the socket bones around them, so that it was as if I could see through the skin and flesh to the skull beneath. Beneath every beloved face is a death's-head.

'Albert!' I said in desperate appeal.

I am always here, even when you cannot see me. I will seek you out, I will have you; there is nowhere to hide, nowhere safe from me. Cover me with fine cloth, cover me with roses, it makes no difference. I am the great determiner, and I have already written your end.

There seemed an utter stillness over the encampment. No breath of air stirred. Even the fire did not crackle. *'Was machts du hier?'* he whispered. *'Es ist nicht zeit, nicht zeit.'*

It was not me he spoke to. *'Es ist Frauchen,'* I said desperately. *'Kennst du nicht?'*

Out of the corner of my eye I saw something move on the other side of the encampment; and at the same moment, as though some spell had been broken, Albert blinked and put his hand up to his brow in a bewildered way. When he put the hand down again, he looked at me and saw me, and his eyes were his own, blue, beautiful, all-seeing.

'I wasn't expecting you,' he said. 'My mind was far away. Dearest little one, what brings you here? Not trouble at home, I hope?'

'No, not at all, only I missed you so,' I said, stammering a little. 'I could not wait to see you.'

'Ah, that's so good,' he said, smiling. He took my hands and lifted them, one and then the other, to his lips and kissed them. 'Will you take luncheon with me in the heather? Dare I hope?'

I joined in the play, only too relieved to have him back. 'If there are potatoes, I will stay and eat.'

He laughed. 'There are potatoes. In Scotland there are always potatoes! Did you bring nothing with you? Improvident Queen! Suppose we had not been here, you would have starved.'

'Not at all,' I said loftily. 'Brown would have shot a deer or caught a fish.'

He chuckled – a lovely sound, better than music to me. 'Ah, but not even Brown could have dug potatoes out of this hillside! *Kennst du das Land, wo die Kartoffeln blühn?'* he sang, paraphrasing Goethe. I laughed, and he tugged at my hand. 'Come, then, little darling, let us see what we have that's fit for a Queen.'

It was a lovely luncheon, cooked there in front of the bothy and consumed out on the open hillside, at a cloth spread for us in the heather. Before us a view all purple and rose-brown in the foreground, emerald and indigo and breathtaking steel-blue in the distance; no sounds but the cry of the blackcock and a little domestic chumbling from the bees in the heather. We had excellent boiled potatoes and cold beef, cheese and oat-bread, and a cold tart of cranberries, very good, which Löhlein had baked that morning. He opened a bottle of claret, too, and one of Seltzer-water, and we spent so long over luncheon that we drank both; and then Grant made tea, and offered us whisky with it, which Brown brought to us, carrying away the claret bottle between finger and thumb with a scornful look that made us both laugh. And while we ate, we talked, about everything and nothing in the most comfortable way, and the years seemed to roll back, and we were our young selves again, before the cares of State and family had bent our shoulders.

After luncheon Albert wrote on a piece of paper that we had been there, our names and the date, and put it into the Seltzer bottle and buried it on the spot – something we had been doing for some time now, whenever we had a particularly delightful visit to a place. When we were old, he said, we would come back and dig them up, and relive the happiness.

When that was done, we fell silent for a while, as the afternoon sun grew softer and the shadows less dense.

'So,' I said at last, a little archly, 'are you glad now that I came up here after you?'

'Very glad,' he said – he was holding my hand and thoughtfully turning my wedding ring round and round on my finger. 'But why did you?'

'I felt so very lonely without my dear master,' I said.

'I was only to be away for two days. Other people are often separated for a few days.'

'We are not other people. Habit could never make me get accustomed to it. Without you everything loses its interest. It will always be a terrible pang for me to be separated from you even for two days – and I pray God never to let me survive you.'

He looked at me curiously. 'Why did you say that?'

I felt nervous. 'Because I could never live without you,' I said. I knew that was not what he had asked, but I could not answer the other thing.

'But you *could*,' he said gravely and firmly. 'You always underestimate your powers, Victoria. You could manage very well without me because you have a great strength to hold on with. But I – if anything were to happen to you, it would be all up with me. I could not go on without you.'

Now I felt shy as well as nervous. 'You?' I said in a sort of incredulous tone, and he pressed my hand as though to silence me.

'You know – you must know – it is not in my nature to be able to express my feelings. Sometimes I can write them down – but even then the words are poor, cold things, shadows of what I really feel. But to say – to speak – to tell you face to face all that is in my heart—' He stopped, looking away from me, a spot of red in each cheek. It enchanted and touched me that this man to whom I had been married all these years could still blush in front of me. 'I wish I could tell you, darling little one, that you are everything to me. You are my safe place. You are my castle. Do you know?'

I could not speak at once, which was perhaps just as well; but I pressed his hand fervently, and he squeezed mine in reply. And then he said in a very quiet voice, looking away across the valley, 'So you must be generous, as I know you are, and not ask me to outlive you. If you love me, you must let me go first.'

'Oh no, no,' I cried, and bit my lip to keep it from trembling. When I had control I said, trying to speak lightly, 'You promised me we would grow old together. You said we would walk together on the terrace at Osborne when we were old, and have our grandchildren frolic round us.'

'Yes,' he said, smiling as if he were looking at that charming scene, though it was a heathery slope in front of him.

'We *must* grow old together. Surely God would *never* part us!' I cried.

'Surely He would not,' said Albert. He was silent for a while; and I – I dared not speak, for my heart was too full. Then he said quietly, 'But life here, you know, in this world, is only the beginning. Whatever happens here, we must not forget that it is but a preparation for the life to come.'

I nodded; and swallowed and managed to say, 'Shall – shall we be together there?'

He turned to look at me, and seemed amazed at the question. 'But of course we shall! Don't you believe it?'

'Yes – yes. But I wasn't sure you did.' I had half expected his view of Heaven to be too austere to encompass such gentle joys.

'We don't know in what state we shall meet again; but that we shall recognise each other and be together in all eternity I am perfectly certain,' he said with emphasis. He took my hand and gazed at me earnestly. 'That is why I don't fear death. Do you think I could die gladly if I thought I would be leaving you for ever? The God of Love could not inspire us with a longing to be together if we were not ultimately to be so. That would be too cruel! I could not worship a cruel God.'

His warm, living hand was pressing mine, and the light of enthusiasm which burned in his beautiful blue eyes fired me as it always did. 'No,' I said, agreeing as best I could; there was a part of what he said I could not quite consent to. It was a great comfort to know that he believed so firmly in the afterlife, as I had always done, but I felt he valued the *before*life too lightly. I loved his soul and his mind, but I loved his body too, and I wanted our eternal life together in Heaven to come after a long life together here on earth. I did not want him to 'die gladly' until we were both old and frail, and I could die gladly very soon afterwards and follow him.

31st October 1900

Is THERE no end to the shocks of this year? The dreadful news have come from Pretoria that our darling Christl has died of malaria and enteric fever. He was only twenty-three – a gay, brave, warm-hearted boy – and we were all so proud of his brave exploits. Why is it that God takes the best so young? It is cruel, cruel! In only three weeks more he would have been with us again – he wrote so happily to Lenchen about coming home and seeing all his friends and relatives and his dear dogs again. Thora, poor child, is almost numb with grief – he was her favourite brother, and they were very close. She loved him more than anything on earth. Poor Lenchen bears it very well, but I know what a blow it is to her. She was so proud of him – we all were – oh God, this wretched, wretched war! Well do they call it the Dark Continent! I can't believe he is gone.

Yesterday little Maurice came to me, his eyes red with crying, his little face so solemn. 'Gangan,' he said, 'I have decided that as soon as I am old enough I shall join Christl's regiment. I want to be as good a soldier as he was.' I was so moved I could not say anything. He admired his cousin so much, and his ambition for years past has been to go into the Army, but since he is haemophilic, I cannot suppose it will ever be possible. But one cannot wish to suppress honourable feelings like those.

How many more blows can one take? I am feeling so very low and wretched, my appetite indifferent, and this curse of insomnia throwing all my routines into chaos. And yet even in the darkest hours there are gleams of relief. At Crathie church on Sunday the 'meenister' (as dear Brown used to call him) prayed very solemnly to God to send down His wisdom on Her Majesty's Government, 'because they sorely need it, oh Lord!' Our Maker gave us a sense of humour as His last gift to mankind, to help us through the trials of this world – which are so many, and so heavy.

I must go on with my story. I have come now to feel almost a compulsion to get it down – the legacy perhaps of Lehzen's training, that what one starts one must finish. I don't know how much time is left to me. Well, well, one never does, not the youngest and strongest of us. Oh God, poor, poor Christl! And like our dearest Liko, he fell not to the enemy, but to the hideous spectre of disease! And poor Affie gone. And poor Vicky – the acute attack has passed, but she is still too ill to write to me, only sends her love through Sophie. Oh where will it end? No, I must turn my thoughts in another direction. I must write, write.

It was an odd thing about Lord Palmerston. I found him very fascinating when I was young, in my Lord M. days – and even before, for I sometimes encountered him as a dinner guest before I became Queen, and found him most entertaining and informative to talk to. But as Foreign Secretary he was a crown of thorns, treating the office as his own private kingdom, pursuing his private prejudices, and embroiling us in embarrassment after embarrassment by acting on his own without authority and often contrary to the decisions of the rest of the Cabinet.

But when it came to the Crimean War, we simply had to have him as Prime Minister, firstly because the country demanded it – no one but 'Pam' could win it for us, they thought – and secondly because no-one else could command enough support to form a government. God knows I tried to find an alternative, battling for days, travelling back and forth from Windsor to London in the most appalling weather (this was January and February of 1855) to interview every statesman I thought might have a chance – Derby, Lansdowne, Russell – but it would not do. Even Derby said, 'It must be Palmerston,' though he said perfectly frankly that at seventy-one Pam was past his best. He was half blind, more than half deaf, inefficient and erratic. His supporters called him the Whiskered Wonder; Disraeli in his colourful way called him 'the old painted pantaloon'. But once he was Prime Minister, and hemmed in by good reliable men so that he could not get up to mischief, I found I grew very fond of him again. Albert and I agreed that of all the Prime Ministers we had, the poor old sinner gave us the least trouble, was the most amenable and the most ready to adopt suggestions. Taken out of foreign affairs, and put in charge of the whole, he was sensible and clear-headed, and we were always confident that he had the honour and interests of the country at heart.

I was very much against the war to begin with, but the country was amazingly for it, and 'war fever' was rife. It seemed that the young men – and some not so young ones – were all burning to go out and fight the foreigner, and I don't think it mattered very much who. There was talk of 'glorious hostilities' and fulminations in the press against the peacemongers, as if war were some delightful activity going on abroad that everyone else was getting their share of except us. I came at last to feel that it was better to have the war and get it over with, rather than make do with a patched-up peace which would lead to a worse war later; that if Russian aggression was not nipped in the bud, it would turn into a monstrous flower much less easy to prune.

In that, at least, I feel I was right. I have never trusted the Bear, and Tsar Nicholas (though he had many good qualities, and I had quite liked him when he paid his unexpected visit to England in 1844) was quite mad and not at all clever – a dangerous combination. His sudden death in March 1855 (they say his heart was broken by our victories at Inkerman and Balaclava, which by the logic of numbers and supplies the Russians ought to have won) took the thrust out of the war for the Russians; but from our point of view I fear there was never any chance of doing more than smacking the Bear's paws and sending him back to his cave. No-one could ever conquer Russia – it is too big, too cold, and the population too scattered (and indeed if it were possible, what could one do with it when one had it? It is not a country I would care to have to rule). But the Crimean War ended as unsatisfactorily as it began, for after the long and costly siege it was to the French that Sebastopol finally fell; and I found it hard to bear that the peace should come before our brave soldiers had had a chance to secure the brilliant final victory they so much deserved, and which they had paid for in advance with so many lives. But the French army by then was too riddled with sickness to fight on, and peace was made in March 1856. Palmerston won my admiration for battling tooth and nail to improve the conditions of the peace; and the Russians were at least pushed back out of the Black Sea and Constantinople was kept from their hands.

One good consequence of the war was the spur it gave to the development of the techniques of photography, and to its widespread use, which has been to everyone's advantage. It was the first time ordinary people back home had been able to see exactly what it was like at the Front, and the photographs and reports shocked the nation, and led to an improvement in the lot of the common soldier. This in turn improved his morale and thus his fighting qualities. (The Duke would probably turn in his grave to hear me say that! But it is demonstrable that enabling a serving man to send home part of his pay to his family, for instance, makes him a better soldier, for if he knows his loved ones are being taken care of, he has less desire to desert and go home.) The improvement, too, in hospital nursing was of great benefit to everyone, for it spilled over into civilian hospitals, and the introduction of fresh air and proper sewerage alone must have saved hundreds of lives. I must say I still sometimes feel qualms about women being involved with nursing, but it has become such a commonplace now that one takes it for granted most of the time; and as long as they are *married* women of the decent working classes, there can be no serious objection, I suppose. I met Miss Nightingale several times, and was apprehensive beforehand as to the effect her experiences must have had on her, but I found her a delightful person, sensible and clear-headed but not at all 'mannish', really quite shy, very gentle and *perfectly* lady-like. But she was a very remarkable person and I fear one could not rely on every unmarried girl to keep her head and her modesty in such conditions, and therefore I think it is *not* a good idea in general for young ladies to nurse.

When the war was over I felt every member of the Government must be aware of the great part Albert had played in it. It had made endless extra work for him, and without his clear thinking, strong principles, and immense grasp of detail, I don't know how we would have got through, for government departments were worse then even than they are now for idleness and inefficiency. Granville said that Albert had a better grasp of the management of government departments than the ministers in charge of them; Lansdowne said that Albert had kept the Government out of innumerable scrapes; and Clarendon (who was Foreign Secretary during the war) said that Albert had 'rendered the most important services to the Government' and had 'written some of the ablest papers he had ever read'. Even Palmerston (who I have learned since had no great opinion of Albert before the war, they being of such different temperaments and habits of mind) said afterwards that he thought Albert a great man of extraordinary qualities, and that it was fortunate indeed for the country that the Queen had married such a Prince.

I did not know that at the time, of course; but I had witnessed the better understanding between them, and the increased respect and warmth with which Palmerston addressed my darling, and in June

1856 I wrote a long letter to the Prime Minister, reviving an old question which still rankled with me, and which my little Arthur, in his innocent child's way, had phrased: 'If you are Queen, Mamma, why is Papa not King?'

So I wrote, 'It is a strange omission in our Constitution that while the wife of a King has the highest rank and dignity in the realm after her husband assigned to her by law, the husband of a Queen Regnant is entirely ignored by law. This is the more extraordinary, as a husband has in this country such particular rights and power over his wife, and the Queen is married just as every other woman is, and swears to obey her lord and master.'

I went on to say that initially members of the royal family had resented any defining of Albert's position, but that now they were all dead the matter should be settled for Albert and for all future consorts of Queens. My own preference was for the title of King, but as this was a complete novelty in England and might cause resentment, I had settled on that of Prince Consort; which, together with the highest precedence in the land after the Queen, ought to be settled on the husband of the Queen Regnant by Parliament once and for all. I pointed out the disadvantages of the present system: that my children officially had precedence over their own father, whom *I* was bound by my marriage vows to obey, which was insulting to both of us; that when we went abroad the husband of the Queen of England had no legal position other than that of younger brother of the Duke of Coburg, which was detrimental to the dignity of the Crown and of England; and that in my own country my husband was perpetually presented as a foreigner – 'The Queen and her foreign husband Prince Albert of Saxe-Coburg-Gotha' – which was injurious to the Crown and prevented his very great services to the country from being generally recognised.

I was quite confident now that Parliament would not oppose such a measure, especially if it was made clear to the Lower House that there was no request attached to increase Albert's pension. Albert did not care about it as I did. He agreed with my reasons in theory, but said in practice it made no difference. 'I do what I do because it is my duty, not for recognition – you know that.'

'Of course I do, but you should *have* recognition all the same. And I hate the way the Fashionables go on calling you German.'

'They will do that whatever my title, *Liebchen*,' he said with a smile. 'I shall never be beloved by them. I must make do with being loved by the best little wifey in the world, and the finest family of children any man ever had.'

'Well, at the very least,' I said, wishing I could stir him up to a resentment of his treatment, 'you shall not be slighted again by foreign courts,' remembering 1845 and the behaviour of the King of Prussia, who had given the place that should have been Albert's to the mere uncle of the Emperor of Austria!

'I wish you will not trouble about it, my love,' he said mildly. 'You only court disappointment.'

'Nonsense!' I said; but he was right. First of all the Bill was postponed because of pressure of business; and then when the Cabinet considered it again in March 1857, they raised a completely new objection, which I thought after seventeen years was too much to swallow. They said that the law and usage of England was for a husband to communicate his rank to his wife and not vice-versa; therefore if the husband of a Queen Regnant were treated the same as the wife of a King, he would become King Consort, and if he survived her and married again would make his new wife Queen. Furthermore on the matter of precedence, the proposed Bill would place the consort between the Throne and the Prince of Wales, depriving the latter of the proper constitutional priority of the Heir Apparent, and creating further problems in the case of the Queen's predeceasing her husband.

I was furious; Albert was philosophical; and Palmerston, though he sympathised very warmly and in very proper terms with my disappointment, was adamant that nothing could be done. 'The legal position, ma'am, is so very delicate – the question of the right to sit in the House of Lords and on the Privy Council – the position of the Heir Apparent – I have no confidence at all that I could find anyone to sponsor the Bill, let alone get it through the Lower House.' I raged a little, and when he had heard me out, he said gently, 'The position of a Queen Regnant, ma'am, is bound to be anomalous in some ways; but one of the great strengths of our Constitution lies in what it does *not* specify. His Highness enjoys a degree of power and influence in the country and in the Government which, if it were defined in law, might well frighten a great many people, and lead to our being deprived of the inestimable value of his services.' This soothed me a little, but I was still sore, which the poor old sinner plainly saw. 'If I might be so forward as to suggest it, ma'am, you might give him the title of Prince Consort by Letters Patent. That might be done at once. It would take no longer than the time needed to draw up the document.'

'And his precedence?' I enquired shortly.

'Next to your own, except where otherwise provided by Act of

Parliament,' he said. I heard Lord M. in those words, and smiled inwardly. In seventeen years we had come full circle! But I saw the benefit of the vague wording. It might be stretched a very long way before it broke, and absence of specification could work to one's advantage, if one were clever. 'It will give His Highness an English title,' Palmerston added temptingly.

'His Royal Highness,' I corrected sternly. 'Yes, and it will prevent his being treated by foreign courts as nothing but a junior member of the House of Saxe-Coburg. Well, let it be done, then, and as soon as possible. I want to hear him prayed for as the Prince Consort before the end of the Season.'

We managed it, just: the 25th of June 1857 was the day when my beloved officially received the title that should have been his long before.

By then a further happiness had blessed us. The previous year, 1856, had been a happy one, and the Season remarkably gay, with the relief of the peace and the joy of everyone's sons coming home. London was brilliant with balls and banquets, a delicious season at the opera, and for us the pleasure of witnessing the great affection between Fritz and Vicky, whom we had allowed to become secretly engaged. In the May of 1856 the new ballroom and concert-room at Buckingham Palace, designed by Albert, were finished at last, and we used the ballroom for the first time for Vicky's come-out. I danced indefatigably all through the Season, and had the pleasure of hearing myself described as one of the most graceful performers in the world. With the ending of the war Albert had a little (just a little) less work and worry, and his pleasure over Fritz and Vicky's engagement (which was a stage in his great desire to see a unified Germany under liberal Prussian leadership) made him happy and relaxed. We had a very pleasant visit at Osborne, including the arrival of our new yacht (also called *Victoria and Albert* but one hundred feet longer than the old one, and so grand and spacious I felt quite lost in her); and then we went up to Balmoral to find the new house finished and all traces of the old castle completely gone, which was very gratifying to Albert. So what with one thing and another it was not a great surprise to me to discover that I was pregnant again; and on the 14th of April 1857 – again with the blessed, soothing influence of chloroform – Beatrice was born. From the beginning we felt sure she would be the flower of our little flock. We called her Baby at first, as most families do with the new arrival, but the name in her case took on something of a personal quality, and became our permanent, affectionate nickname for her.

(Some years later Vicky's eldest, Willy, came to visit, and the naughty boy took to calling her Baby because he heard others do so. When he was told sternly that she was his aunt, though only two years older than him, and that he must address her respectfully, he rebelled, and finally wriggled out of the situation by calling her Aunt Baby, which made me laugh very much – though not, of course, in front of him.)

When I was out of childbed, my good physician Clark came to me solemnly to warn me that I must not have another baby. 'Your Majesty's constitution could not withstand it,' he said with awful emphasis. 'I must most seriously advise against embarking on such an adventure.'

The awful vision opened up before me. 'But, Doctor,' I cried, 'must I then have no more fun in bed?'

Clark looked away and went red, as he always did when faced with a question he thought delicate (which made me feel rather impatient with him when I considered what he must already know about my anatomy: if I could bear the thought of what he knew, why could not he?) and he harrumphed a bit and indicated that that was a matter on which the Prince might more properly be expected to enlighten me; but the Prince was not at hand, and it was not until that night that we were completely alone and private, by which time I had spent the day feeling low and miserable at the prospect.

When we were alone I told him first of what Clark had said.

'Why, my little darling, I thought you hated having babies,' Albert said with a tender smile. 'Would you not be glad to be done with it all?'

'I don't like being pregnant,' I said, 'but I like having them once they are had. Do you think me such a heartless mother that I would wish any of my little ones out of existence?'

'No, I don't think that at all. But nine is a good family, is it not? And we have been so lucky not to lose one of them—'

'*Unberufen!*' I prompted quickly, thinking of Leopold, and crossed my fingers, too, for good measure.

'*Unberufen,*' Albert said obediently. 'Nine lovely children is enough, is it not?'

'I don't like to be told,' I grumbled. 'It should be as *I* choose, not Clark.'

'Don't I have any say in the matter?' Albert teased.

'Ah yes,' I said quickly, 'that brings me to another thing.' And I repeated the other part of my conversation with Clark. Albert chuckled. 'Poor man, what a torment you are to him, wifey!' 'But what did he mean?' I insisted. 'What have you to explain to me?'

Now Albert was blushing too. 'Well, my heart's heart, there *are* things one can do – similar to what we do but – not carrying the risk of pregnancy. Things that fall short of the totality.'

I considered, my imagination leaping ahead and supplying me with pictures. 'I don't like it,' I said at last. 'It sounds like false coin. I want everything to be honest and true between us – as honest as daylight.' I reached for his hand. 'Can't we just go on as before, and trust in God? I don't want to think I can never have another child. I don't want you never to be able to love me *fully* as before. Let God decide what happens.'

'It is leaving a lot on God's shoulders,' Albert said doubtfully, turning my wedding ring round and round on my finger. 'We are supposed to take responsibility for our own lives, and make our own decisions.'

'Well, I've made mine,' I said firmly.

'And what about Clark's advice?' said Albert.

'Doctors don't know everything,' I said.

WINTER

Nineteen

12th November 1900, at Windsor

THIS MORNING I had to swear in a new Privy Council: Lord Salisbury has managed to get himself returned again, though the majority is only increased by three. Hardly worth calling an election for, I said to him afterwards (the newspapers are calling it the Khaki Election, and there have been some criticisms, as I expected there would). He – Salisbury – is looking quite exhausted, but is to give up the Foreign Office and take Privy Seal instead, which will be much less tiring. Lansdowne is to be Foreign Secretary, which pleases everybody. There are various other moves which I can't pretend to find very exciting. But I am glad at least to have the Conservatives again, so that I shan't have to get used to a new Prime Minister. Salisbury and I agree very well and understand each other's little ways.

It is Conservatives and Liberals now, where when I was a girl it was Whigs and Tories. Oh, how passionately I was for the Whigs and against the Tories! It is hard to believe now, especially when I consider how little difference there was between the parties: they were all drawn from the same rank of society. It is not so now, since the various reforms. We get some very *odd* people coming into Parliament, though they all seem to behave pretty well once they get there. The House, I'm told, is *much* less unruly than it was back in the 'twenties and 'thirties. This last election has even seen two candidates returned from the Independent Labour Party, which has ruffled a few feathers, but I can't see any harm in it. Provided they *behave* like gentlemen, it doesn't matter a jot who their fathers were.

I remember at my first Privy Council, I had to look to Lord M. to tell me what to do; not one of that first Council is still alive, and these days the new men look to me to guide them through the protocol. I have had ten Prime Ministers during my long reign. Salisbury has in some ways been the best; Gladstone was in all ways the worst – I really sometimes think he was a little crazy, the way he tried to create friction between class and class, and threw our country's honour away abroad. He was always inconsiderate and often impertinent, treated me like a machine and lectured me like a school-girl. And yet he was undoubtedly a man of abilities, though his manner was deplorable. There is a story that a young lady went out to dinner on two consecutive evenings. The first evening she sat next to Gladstone, and rose from the table convinced that he was the cleverest man in England. On the second evening she sat next to Disraeli, and rose from the table convinced that she was the cleverest woman in England.

Dear, dear Dizzy! What an incomparable man: his intelligence, his erudition, his wit were only equalled by his warmth and charm. He never, never lectured or badgered me, like Gladstone, but treated me like a woman, and made me feel strong and beautiful, in a way that's only possible with someone you truly admire. You cannot pretend it. He and I were naturally drawn to each other – two 'outsiders', perhaps – and the longer we knew each other, the deeper and steadier our friendship became.

When he first became my Prime Minister in 1868 I was just beginning to recover from the appalling shock of my beloved's death. It was as though I had been struggling through a dark tunnel all alone. I never stopped working – indeed, I had to work harder than ever, doing Albert's share as well as my own – but I felt an aversion amounting almost to horror to the idea of being seen in public. I could not bear to do alone those things which I had always done with him at my side. I was nothing but a poor, shattered widow, and it seemed barbaric that the world should want to stare at me in my weeds.

But it seemed it was not enough for the people that I should do my duty – I must be seen to do it. The fact that I no longer attended public functions annoyed them: once a 'wag' went so far as to pin a note on the gates of Buckingham Palace saying To Let, Owner No Longer Requires. It was unfortunate that this was also one of those times when revolutionary feeling was sweeping through Europe. I saw the discontent as an impertinent desire to order my life and stare at me like a waxwork, but France had just become a republic for the third time, and there were many who believed that England was in danger of going the same way. There were even questions asked in the House as to whether I was 'worth' my Civil List and whether I performed any useful function – I, who never stopped working from morning till night! (That was Sir Charles Dilke, and deeply it hurt me that he should say such things, for I had known his father, who had worked with Albert on the Great Exhibition. Indeed, I had first met little Charles when he was only eight years old at the Crystal Palace, and had stroked his hair: I can only assume, the wrong way.)

If the Monarchy was really in danger, what saved it, ironically, was a close brush with death – first in the August of 'seventy-one when I became gravely ill with an abscess on my arm, and then in November of the same year when poor Bertie almost died of typhoid. The people soon saw where their hearts really lay: when they almost lost us, they understood how much they wanted us. Still, from then on I undertook more public engagements – never as many as were demanded, and always more than I enjoyed. But when Disraeli came back in in 1874, he found the way to persuade me to do things I would have found impossible otherwise. He had a way of putting his head on one side and saying 'Dear Madam' so persuasively, I found him irresistible! I would always more willingly open Parliament for *him* than for anyone else.

There were those who found it shocking that we should have a Jew for Prime Minister, but I always abhorred such small-mindedness. I loved him for what he was – and, yes, I did love him, and he loved me. I am one who needs to have someone to love, and though nothing could ever replace my perfect union with my beloved Albert, there was great satisfaction for me in the years that Disraeli was my friend. I see, at this distance, similarities with my relationship with Lord M.; but the one was all emotion, while my relationship with Disraeli was a true marriage of minds. He had a bold mind and wonderfully large view, and his vision of the world and England's place in it coincided pleasingly with mine. As with Lord M., I continued to correspond with him after he went out of office, and he continued to enrich and invigorate my experience of society and of politics, but it was not the same as having him in office. The period of his ministry was one of the most vigorous and stimulating of my life. For six years I felt we governed England together, and it was good.

Well, he is long in his grave; Gladstone too. Politicians come and go, with their aspirations and certainties and their little blindnesses, but I am always here, year in and year out, the one Great Continuity. It has come to the stage where I know more about government than most of my ministers. That, of course, is the great value of our constitutional system: in a republic there is never anyone with an overview, or anyone to say, 'We tried *that* in the year such-and-such, and it did not work.' Ah yes, despite my increasing weariness, I must ask God to keep me here a little longer, for my country's sake. When I am gone, who will keep a steady hand on the reins? Not Bertie, I fear: he will be at the races!

I resume: my ninth pregnancy, though it came of such happy circumstances, and though the issue was so happy, was not in itself a tranquil time. I found myself more 'fidgety' (as Albert called it) even than usual, to the extent, I discovered afterwards, that Clark and Albert had great fears for my sanity – that old bugbear of the Hanoverian Inheritance! Indeed, Clark had told Albert some time previously that if I had another child I might well lose my reason, and it is not surprising, therefore, that Albert found my abominable outbursts of temper more trying than ever.

I had provocation. To be carrying a child, with all the discomforts, humiliations and disadvantages it entailed (and at thirty-seven one does not carry as easily as at twenty) is enough, without having to deal with one's own teenage children at the same time, particularly when one of them is engaged to be married. I worried a great deal about Vicky, who was only fourteen when Fritz offered for her. We agreed she should not be married until she was seventeen, but that was still very young. Vicky was mature for her age, and had mental abilities far beyond most adults, but one cannot help thinking of one's child as a child, whatever its age, and to be throwing one's daughter to the wolves of matrimony at such a tender age is very hard. Also the Prussian connection was unpopular in the country in general, and Prussia itself I regarded as a very backward country, especially in maternity, childbirth and child-rearing. So I had deep reservations about committing my darling child to such a fate – and certainly had she and Fritz not been so very much in love there would have been no question of it.

But there was another, selfish reason for my ill-temper. Once we had agreed to Vicky's betrothal, we felt that we could not very well go on treating her as a child, but ought to admit her into our company on adult terms. Albert, too, wanted to give her special lessons, in German history and in statecraft, for he was depending on her very much to further his plans for German unity, and since she was far Fritz's superior in intellect it would have to be *her* who taught *him* and not vice versa. So from six to seven every evening Vicky and Albert had their session; and afterwards she joined us at dinner and spent the evening with us. This was very pleasant in its way; but Albert was away from me all day long as it was, immersed in his affairs, and our *diners à deux* were very precious to me, the only time I had alone with him. Now instead of those precious, tender hours, and the glorious freedom of intimate talk with the soul I loved best in all the world, I had a teenage girl beside me (and one who was in love, moreover, and had developed a devastating talent for turning any conversation round to her beloved) in front of whom one could not be wholly frank and unfettered. And instead of having Albert's attention to myself, I had to share it with Vicky, whom he adored, and whose intellect he admired. He often addressed a great deal more of his conversation on those evenings to her than he did to me.

It is unpleasant to have to note such weaknesses in oneself, but honesty forces me to do so. I adored Vicky and was proud of her, and dreaded losing her; but at the same time I wanted my husband to myself now and then. Add to this the aches and miseries of pregnancy, and it is hardly surprising that I sometimes lost my temper. But when Albert accused me of wanting to be rid of her he was speaking out of his own lost temper (and he *had* quite a temper, though he generally kept a good hold of it) and it was very far from the truth. Once the baby arrived, I felt instantly better, and the rest of the time before Vicky's departure passed happily. The delivery was easier than any before, and I felt better and stronger than with any of the others; and all my sufferings were amply rewarded when I heard my darling say, with that special tenderness in his voice, 'It's a girl!' He was so glad to have another girl. We had sons enough to cover all the constitutional eventualities: girls, in Albert's mind, were for pleasure, and with the prospect of losing Vicky in less than a year's time, he was going to have a vacancy for a new favourite.

Baby was a good candidate for the post. She was lively and quick and full of impishness, and it was impossible to be stern with her, for she made us laugh so much with her droll sayings and the funny things she did. She spent more time with us, I think, than did any of the others when they were little, and since most of her own brothers and sisters were also much older than her, she developed a peculiarly adult way of talking, which coming from the chubby, rosy little thing that she was, was irresistibly funny. When she did something naughty, like knocking something over, or touching something she had been forbidden to touch, she had a way of looking across at you and saying, 'Oh dear, oh dear!' which sounded so funny in a baby's voice that it quite disarmed you. One day she came downstairs to us shaking her head mournfully and saying over and over, 'Oh dear, oh dear,

Baby's been so naughty, poor Baby!' We never did find out what she had been up to.

She adored Albert from the beginning, and her greatest delight was to come down to his dressing-room and watch him shave and dress. While this private performance was going on she would ply him with impossible questions. 'Papa, why wasn't I at your wedding? Was I too little?' 'Papa, was Lot's wife the same salt that I have on my chicken?' 'Papa, where does the flame go when you blow out the candle?' Albert did his best to answer her fully, sometimes sitting down and taking her on his knee if the explanation was to be a long one. (From him she picked up the habit of calling people 'my dear' and of interspersing her sentences with a little pursed-lipped, considering 'zo'.) Sometimes I told him he was wasting his time answering her so fully, for she asked whatever questions came into her head just to get his attention, often without really wanting an answer. But he said, 'One never knows how much goes in and stays. I would not give her short change, for this little head is full of thoughts, and it must have proper sustenance.' And he tapped it tenderly with his fingertip, for she was sitting on his knee at the time. 'Is that not so, my dear?' Full of thoughts it was, more by a long way than we were ever made party to! One day she said to one of my ladies, 'I had such a funny thought this morning, but it turned out to be an *un*proper thought, so I would not let it think.' I'm afraid she 'got away with' a great many things through sheer impudence, combined with drollery.

Often when she was bustling along the corridor bent on some mission of her own and was told she must come and have her hair brushed or her hands washed for luncheon, she would cry sternly, 'No time, no time, I must write letters!' and continue on her way. That was Albert, of course – busier than ever, as Baby grew up and held out for her share of his fractured attention. I am so glad he had her, and that she so often made him laugh; for he loved to laugh. His delightful chuckle was the thing people most often remembered about him. I am glad too that she had him. When I see her now, my good, dutiful Benjamina, a serious, dignified, handsome woman, a mother herself now and – ah, alas! – a widow, it is hard to realise that she is the same Baby that Albert swung deliciously back and forth in his table-napkin, or who brought him a page from a sketching-book saying gravely, 'I drawed a picture of a d'raff today, but I don't believe in it.' When Albert died, something of Baby died too, and in a little while the naughty, lively, impudent thing, always running everywhere, interfering in everything, graceful and light as a butterfly, chattering constantly like a running stream, had turned into a solemn and thoughtful child. She seemed to inherit as a gift from beyond the grave her father's selflessness and devotion to duty; and indeed in later life the only time she ever defied me was when she insisted on marrying Liko. But she was right to do so, for in marrying him she brought me a son-in-law to charm and lighten my sad sufferings and weary hours. His death has been a grievous loss to me, more almost than the loss of my own sons; for he brought a quality of lightness and sparkle to our lives, like a draught of champagne. Without him now there are no more party days.

15th November 1900

A LIX TO luncheon yesterday, and shouting at her quite wore me out. But I slept well last night and felt distinctly better this morning, and was able to enjoy my egg and coffee and white bread at breakfast for the first time in two weeks. The death of our darling Christl quite 'knocked the stuffing' out of me and it has been pitiful seeing how calm and brave poor Lenchen has been about it. We will feel it all so dreadfully when everyone else's sons start to come home, and not our dear boy. But at least the fog has now cleared away, and the lovely autumn colours are to be seen again in the Great Park, the last of the leaves, and the great sweep of coppery bracken, which is cheering. My poor old appetite has been quite deranged lately, but after this morning's better start, Reid seems pleased with me, and says that as there is nothing actually wrong with me, no disease, I should be better by and by.

To return to 1857 – there were terrible news out of India that year: mutiny among the native troops, murders of Europeans at Meerut and Delhi, the hideous massacre at Cawnpore, the siege of Lucknow. As soon as the news of Meerut reached us, Palmerston sent for good old Sir Colin Campbell, hero of Waterloo and the Crimea, who set sail for India the very next day; and every child knows how he and the 93rd Highlanders (the Ladies from Hell, the Russians had called them) relieved Lucknow, marching up in a cloud of dust to the sound of the pipes playing 'The Campbells are Coming, Hurrah!'

The mutiny was over by the end of September. Everyone in England felt terrible rage over the appalling acts that had been carried out during the uprising, and a deep desire for revenge; and dreadful reprisals were carried out by the officers and administrators on the spot, which I cannot bear to write about. But when things were quiet again the truth had to be faced that India had grown too large to be ruled effectively by the East India Company. Combining commercial requirements and those of government had never been easy, and in the last twenty years the territory of India had doubled through annexations. It was time for John Company to hand over the reins. The following year, on August the 2nd, I gave the Royal Assent to the Act which brought India under my direct rule; and Governor-General Canning (known as Clemency Canning, because he had tried to stop the reprisals at the end of the Mutiny) became Viceroy.

The principles by which we were to rule India were set out in a Proclamation, which Albert wrote to my instructions. First, I wanted it clearly stated that I had no intention of interfering with any of the native religions and customs, for I was very much against that proselytising, interfering sort of governance that holds everything cheap but our own home-grown ideas. I knew how much comfort I derived from my own faith, and had no desire to take that same comfort away from anyone else. So I said that my servants in India would be directed to act scrupulously within my orders, and leave the native customs alone as long as they were peaceful.

Second, I wanted it made clear that I meant to relieve poverty in India by the introduction of railways, canals and telegraphs, but that these would be introduced solely to benefit the population, and not to exploit them for profit; and finally, I wanted it stated that my assumption of rule, though rendered necessary by the horrors of the bloody civil war, was made in a spirit of reconciliation. Nothing could excuse the atrocities against innocent women and children, but the peaceable inhabitants, who had always been friendly to us, should be shown the greatest kindness: they should know that there was no hatred of a brown skin, and that the Queen desired nothing but to see them happy, contented and flourishing.

I have always taken the liveliest interest in the governing of India ever since, and have done everything in my power to ensure that the people were ruled as *we* would have wished, in their place, to be ruled. 'We can never keep our 'old upon Hindia by force of harms alone,' one Member of the Commons famously pronounced; and I agreed with him. I have no time for racial hatred or cruelty to supposedly 'inferior' races. The subjugation of one colour or creed by another was never in Nature's plan, I am sure. Since we took over the rule from John Company, I have always had one or two Indian attendants in my suite, and have found them to be excellent servants, and absolutely trustworthy. (Sadly, though, I have had to struggle against that horrid prejudice in my own Household, and even in my own family. I have even had to give instructions that my Indian servants are not to be referred to as 'the black men', which I would have thought ordinary civility would have prevented.)

Disraeli later came to believe that 'one could only act upon the opinion of Eastern nations through their imagination', and for that reason in 1876 he steered a Bill through Parliament to change my title to Empress of India. A hard job we had to get it through – opposed as we were by all sorts of petty minds, too mean and greedy themselves to impute any higher motive to anyone else. (I *never* forgave Gladstone for opposing the Bill in such vituperative terms – horrid, vulgar old man!) But Disraeli and I proved right, and India, the brightest jewel in England's crown, has shone brighter than ever since those dear, good people have been able to think of me as their Empress Across the Sea. The new title was proclaimed in Delhi on the first day of 1877, and that evening I gave a banquet at Windsor to celebrate the occasion. I wore all my Indian jewels, and when Arthur proposed the toast to 'The Queen Empress' it was one of the proudest moments in my life.

Later

I SPENT the evening looking through old photographs, and came across the daguerreotype taken on the morning of Vicky's wedding to Fritz, so I have brought it to my room with me, to look at again: Vicky and me facing each other and Albert between and behind us. Dear, sweet Vicky, with her eyes cast solemnly down, looks so pretty in her wedding gown of white moiré silk, and absurdly like me (except for the prettiness, of course). She is wearing my wedding lace for a veil, held with a crown of white roses and myrtle, and she is trying not to cry. Albert looks at the camera, stern and noble in full dress uniform, beautiful to me, though I can see it isn't one of the best pictures of him; and as for me, you can hardly see me at all, for I was trembling so much my image is quite blurred. Only a diamond tiara tells you who it is!

Vicky's seventeenth birthday came in November 1857, and there was no putting off any longer: her wedding day was set for the 25th of January 1858, and as I said to Albert when we woke that morning, it felt exactly like taking a poor innocent lamb to be sacrificed. He was a little pale himself, but told me briskly not to exaggerate; but of course as a man he had no idea of the physical trials and dangers she would have to face in marriage – and since I *did* know, it seemed a peculiarly horrible thing to be doing, to be thrusting her, however willingly on her part, towards them. Besides, she was going to Prussia, and though I knew Fritz was everything good, kind and liberal, I had no opinion of the rest of his family, or of the Court and the Government in general. Prussia was backward, and her politics reactionary. Everything would be a trial to Vicky, and at the time of her life when she would most need her mother to confide in, I would be far away and unable to come to her.

Still, there was no going back. As soon as I was out of bed I wrote a little note about the solemnity of marriage, and had it sent along to Vicky, together with a very pretty book, *The Bridal Offering*, which I thought would comfort her. I had arranged that we should get dressed together so that we should have those last tender moments as mother and daughter together, and very peaceful and lovely it was. Vicky arrived looking quite composed, and quietly happy. 'Are you not nervous?' I asked. 'I am marrying Fritz,' she said simply, 'so there is nothing to be afraid of. Did you not feel like that when you married Papa?' And I remembered how I had felt that nothing Albert did could ever frighten or harm me, and I nodded. I was far more nervous on her behalf than I had been on my own. 'I pray your own marriage will be as happy as mine has been,' I told her. She put her hands between mine in the gesture of fealty, and said gravely, 'I hope to be worthy to be your child.' I was too moved to be able to speak.

When we were dressed, we sat side by side to have our hair dressed, and then Albert came in to fetch us for the daguerreotype. He met my eyes in the looking-glass and smiled.

'You look very handsome,' he said. 'It is hard to tell which is the bride and which the bride's mother.'

'That is not very flattering to the bride,' I said, but managed a smile. I was wearing a tiered gown of lilac and silver, which I did think became me. As Vicky rose and turned away from the glass, Albert took the opportunity to stoop and kiss my bare shoulder. 'My wife has beautiful shoulders,' he whispered, the old incantation.

Vicky was married in the Chapel Royal at St James's, just as I was, and it affected me deeply to see my own darling Flower kneel on the same spot where I had knelt eighteen years before, and dedicate her life to a man. Dear, kind Fritz wore the uniform of a Prussian general, and spoke his vows in a trembling voice, looking as though he did not know what to do with so much happiness. My sons looked handsome in kilts, my daughters innocent all in white, and my beloved husband, standing beside me, had such difficulty in holding back his tears that it was fortunate he had nothing to say in the ceremony, for I'm afraid the effort of speaking would have broken him down. Afterwards the couple came hand in hand up the aisle to our good friend Mendelssohn's Wedding March (the first time it was used on such an occasion), and Vicky's face was so calm and bright, serious and yet completely happy, that I could have no regrets in allowing the marriage. When we returned to Buckingham Palace she and Fritz went out on to the balcony and received a wonderfully warm reception from the crowds below; and then we went in to the wedding breakfast, where the couple, seated opposite their four parents, were entirely hidden by the gigantic wedding-cake.

The children had a four-day honeymoon at Windsor, just as Albert and I had, and then on the 2nd of February they were back at Buckingham Palace for their departure for Berlin. It was the sort of winter day I have always most disliked, bitter cold, and the sky so low and dark it seems like twilight all day, and the day seems over before it has begun. Poor Vicky's eyes were swollen with tears when she came into the Audience Room with Fritz to say goodbye to everyone; the children all sobbed dreadfully as she hugged them one by one, with a kiss and a whispered word for each. Alice clung to her pitifully, and even Baby cried, as if she understood that her big sister would not be there any more to play with her. I was trying very hard not to cry, for Vicky's sake, but as Albert and I left the children and led the way down the Grand Staircase, I caught sight of his set, white face and my control left me. Tears poured down my cheeks, and as I embraced them both at the door I was unable to speak a word, and my darling child clung to me and wet my neck with her own tears before walking out to the carriage. I thought my heart would break as I watched that little, brave figure, all wrapped in white velour, walk out under the frozen sky and climb into the carriage. She was Princess Frederick now, and belonged to me no more. Fritz climbed up after her, and then Albert, who was to accompany them to Gravesend, followed without a backward glance for me. Theirs would be the hardest farewell, I knew, and I did not begrudge him the extra time with her. Fritz told me afterwards that he occupied himself with staring out of the window so that they could talk together in private.

It began to snow as the carriage turned out of the Palace gates. At Gravesend the *Victoria and Albert*, in which they were to sail to Antwerp, was waiting for them in a strange, white world, the snow falling on the grey water and on the shoulders and hats of the crowds waiting to see her off, the flowers they had thrown lying on the snowy cobbles. 'Be good to her or we'll have her back,' a Cockney drayman shouted as she and Fritz went up the side. On the deck she laid her forehead against her father's chest and her tears ran free as she whispered, 'Beloved Papa!' Albert came back in the gathering gloom of a bitter afternoon to Buckingham Palace and went straight up to his room to write to her: 'I am not of a demonstrative nature and therefore you can hardly know how dear you have always been to me, and what a void you have left behind in my heart.' She showed me the letter years later, and it almost broke my heart. The words were so desolate. If she left a great gap in my life, how much greater a gap in Albert's? For at least now I had a woman correspondent, a married woman to whom I could say anything, without any of the awkward restraints of communication with an unmarried girl or with a man. Our correspondence has been of the greatest importance and comfort to me. We have been writing to each other now for almost forty-three years, often several times a week, and I don't think there is a soul in the world I know better, or love more dearly.

Poor Vicky had a great deal to put up with in her new life. She was known contemptuously as *die Engländerin*, for Prussia was as anti-English as England was anti-German, and she was too straight-forward to be able to hide her natural feeling that England was the best and most advanced country in the world. She and Fritz had no influence and almost no friends at the backward, intensely militaristic Court. Vicky was too clever for them, and Fritz too gentle; the men talked of nothing but manoeuvres and uniforms, and the women of clothes and parties. The King and Queen ignored and snubbed them. The apartments allotted them were damp and dirty, the stoves blocked by twenty years of soot, not a single lavatory or bathroom, and the kitchens so far away that the food was always cold.

Fritz's uncle died in 1861, his father became King, and Fritz and Vicky became Crown Prince and Princess. Vicky used her new position to fight for women's rights, including her own to be involved in politics, but it was an unequal struggle. Almost immediately, Fritz's father did away with parliament and called for Bismarck, and Bismarck brought in repressive measures, including censoring the Press. Fritz, torn between his duty to his father and his duty to his liberal principles, came down on the side of the latter and made a speech condemning the move (Vicky supported him in this). Bismarck never forgave them, and spent the next twenty-five years using his consider-able influence to discredit the Heir and his wife.

Albert had spent his last private time with Vicky in reminding her of her great purpose, to work with Fritz to bring about by peaceful means a united and liberal Germany, and she never ceased to work for it. But it was not to be. It was not until March of 1888 that Fritz's reactionary father died, and Fritz became Emperor of Germany (as the title was by that time), and by then he was already fatally ill with cancer of the throat. His appalling suffering was made worse by the ineptitude of the German doctors (of whom I had *never* had any opinion, as I told Vicky roundly before she ever went to Prussia) and by the knowledge that his son and heir, Willy, had been seduced by the Junker party, by his grandparents, and by Bismarck. They together had set Willy against his own father and filled his mind with dangerous militaristic rubbish. Fritz was Emperor for only three short months, too little time to do anything, especially since the government and the ruling party had long since allied themselves with Willy. On June the 15th 1888 my poor darling Vicky became a widow, the Dowager Empress Frederick, and Willy became Kaiser Wilhelm II, and began polishing up his army and navy and antagonising everyone in Europe.

This has been the end of my beloved Albert's dream. I can't see Willy ever becoming the kind of liberal, improving ruler Albert would have wanted. Though he has his good qualities, and though I have always been fond of him (and I am the only person in the world, I think, that he minds in the least), he is all ate up with Prussian pride, and has always been the sort of boy who pulls off a fly's legs and wings and thinks the fly doesn't mind. Even at Bertie's wedding, on his first visit to England, when he was only four years old, he showed his future character by throwing Baby's muff out of the carriage window, and later during the service, though looking very sweet in Scotch dress, he picked the cairngorm out of the hilt of his dirk and flung it across the chapel with a shocking oath. When Affie and Arthur tried to restrain him he fought like a mad thing and *bit* their bare legs. Later when he was brought before me he addressed me impudently as 'duck' (where he had that from I can't imagine) but I managed to keep my lips from twitching and quelled him with a look. From the first, I never spoiled him or allowed him to 'get away with' anything, which I think was what gave us our better understanding. But even I cannot control him when he is out of my presence, or influence him politically. I fear it will end badly.

17th November 1900

YESTERDAY I met a group of Colonial soldiers returning from South Africa, who are fine men with good, honest faces, though all of them sadly worn and many sick and injured. I made a little speech and then shook hands with them and spoke to them about their experiences. Even their chaplain, poor man, was injured: he had had his foot bitten off in the veldt by a mad horse, a perfectly dreadful fate!

I was very tired afterwards, but am feeling better today, and I told Reid quite sharply this morning that I will not be treated as an invalid. It is the worst thing for me to be petted and cosseted and kept indoors. I have had a pleasant drive out with the little Battenbergs, but it has turned very cold now, so that even I am glad to pull up to the good fire as I carry on with my writing.

With Vicky married, we turned our attention to Bertie. His tutor, Gibbs, had been chosen by Albert for his rectitude and learning, but their temperaments did not suit, and Gibbs had failed to make anything of Bertie, and the lack of sympathy between them was now verging on the improper. So it was decided to change the regime. Bertie was given his own establishment, at White Lodge in Richmond Park, and his Tutor was replaced by a Governor, Colonel Robert Bruce. Bertie was at the difficult age between boyhood and manhood, and Albert was terribly concerned that at such an influential period he made only the right friends. Albert's greatest – though unspoken – fear was that Bertie would be led into sexual error. He wanted him to remain as pure as he, Albert, had, until he could be married happily to an equally pure girl. Only in absolute moral rectitude could Bertie hope to find happiness, and fulfil his duties to the Crown of England.

I understood Albert's anxieties – which, as I said, he never spelled out to me in so many words – in an indirect way. I had not the same obsessive fear, but certainly I wanted my boy to be good, and I worried acutely about what sort of King he would make. Suppose I were to die suddenly, this year or next? Bertie would hardly be fit to rule, and either Albert would do everything, which in his state of health would probably kill him, or Bertie would refuse to listen to any advice and do everything wrong and probably bring about a revolution and lose the Throne.

Three carefully chosen and irreproachable young men were introduced, under Bruce, as Bertie's gentleman companions to set him an example, and Albert set out in a long memorandum exactly what was expected of our son. There was to be no lounging, lolling in armchairs, no placing himself in unbecoming attitudes with his hands in his pockets. There was to be no whistling, no talking slang, no horseplay, no practical jokes. Conversation was to be serious and improving – not idle gossip – and leisure activities should aim to expand and refine the Prince's character – not cards or billiards, but music, sketching, looking at engravings, hearing plays or poetry read aloud, et cetera. Bruce was required to send frequent reports on Bertie's behaviour and progress, and to keep an exact note of everyone he met and what they talked of. Bertie was not to leave the house without reporting to Bruce and obtaining permission.

The following year Bertie was sent to Oxford – which I did not at all envy him, for I have never liked the atmosphere of Oxford. There is something gloomy and monkish about the place. The Dean of Christ Church urgently requested that Bertie be allowed to live inside the college so as to be able to make friends of his own age, not realising that was the very thing Albert wanted to prevent. In a private house, living with his Governor, Bertie would be under much stricter supervision, and Bruce would be able to prevent him falling in with an undesirable set. So it was arranged; and when Bertie went to Cambridge for a spell in January 1861, the same restrictions applied. By that time even Colonel Bruce was pleading for more freedom for Bertie, and looking back, I suppose we did handle the business badly. Lord M. had warned me against watching a child too closely, and I have passed that same warning on to my own children about the upbringing of theirs. But at the time I was unable to see past Albert's fears, born of the behaviour of his own father and brother; and my own worries about the Succession. There was so much at stake with Bertie that I can't see how we could have tried less than everything to make sure it all came out right; and much less than everything was probably the only thing that would have improved him.

Bertie himself had expressed two wishes about his own life – that he should be allowed to enter the Army (which I said that of course he could not, as a profession, though he might spend some time in it in an unattached capacity), and that he should be allowed to travel abroad. So in November 1858 we allowed him to visit Vicky in Berlin for three weeks. Albert wrote warning her that she would find him improved in looks but interested in nothing but clothes – 'Even when out shooting he is more occupied with his trousers than the game!' – and asking her to make sure he had some mental occupation while he was there. Socially Bertie was a great success. Though short and rather knock-kneed (his son Georgie is too, I'm sorry to say) he was at that time quite nice looking, a fine dancer, and possessed of considerable charm. Vicky wrote, raving about him and saying how everyone had adored him.

In the summer of 1860 we sent him with Colonel Bruce on a tour of North America, where he was very successful. His welcome in Canada and the United States was wonderfully warm (surprisingly so in the case of the United States, which had rebelled so violently against Bertie's great-grandpa!) and though the tour was supposed to be a private one, he did a great deal of good as an ambassador for England. It would be impossible to exaggerate, said Bruce, the enthusiasm of Bertie's reception; the men approved him and the women were all in love with him, the newspapers thought him a fine manly fellow, and the whole tour had been one continual triumph.

Returning to the life of a scholar was difficult for Bertie after his success in America, and Bruce in one of his reports urged that an early marriage should be considered for him, before his charm and love of gaiety could get him into trouble. Albert and I had already begun thinking along those lines, but the choice of princess was difficult. He could not marry a Catholic, and had already stated firmly he would only marry for love (which I agreed with), but Albert's first list of eligible Protestant princesses proved them to be very few and very plain. My own stipulations were that she should be reasonably good-looking, virtuous, and if possible have sufficient strength of character to influence Bertie for the good. After all, whoever she was, she would be Queen of England one day.

We asked Vicky to look about for someone suitable, but the only name she came up with was Princess Alexandra of Schleswig-Holstein, who though outstandingly beautiful was still in the schoolroom, and who, because of the complexity and bitterness of the Schleswig-Holstein question, was politically undesirable. (Palmerston in later years said only three people had ever understood the Schleswig-Holstein question. One was the Prince Consort, and he was dead. The second was a German professor, and he had gone mad. The third was Palmerston himself, and he had forgotten what it was! But the core of the problem as far as we were concerned was that both Denmark and Prussia claimed sovereignty over the Duchies. Alexandra's father, the Duke of Schleswig-Holstein, was also heir to the Throne of Denmark; but Albert, because of his plans for a united Germany, had always supported Prussia's claim, which would have made an awkwardness if the Duke became Bertie's 'pa-in-law'.)

However, in the spring of 1861 we learned from Vicky that the Tsar was interested in Princess Alexandra for the Tsarevitch, and had gone so far as to obtain photographs of her to show to his son, which put us on our mettle. Vicky and Fritz met the girl in May, and wrote glowingly of her beauty, charm and goodness, and said it would be a tragedy if we let her slip through our fingers. Given Bertie's susceptibility to the pretty women of the United States, and the plainness of the other possible candidates, Albert decided Bertie ought to be told about Alexandra and given a chance to view her. If he liked her, the marriage might be contemplated on condition that there were to be no political aspects to the match.

It was all arranged quite nicely and privately through Vicky – Bertie was to visit her and Fritz, and they were to make a trip to Speyer, where Alix (as her family called her) was to be brought by her parents. They all met 'accidentally' at the Cathedral on the 21st of September 1861, and when Bertie got back to Balmoral, he told me that he was quite pleased with the princess, her manners, her pretty face and her figure. Vicky, however, wrote rather crossly from Prussia that 'Bertie was extremely pleased with Alix, but as for being in love, I don't think he can be, or that he is capable of enthusiasm about anything in the world.' And certainly Bertie never mentioned her afterwards, nor showed any eagerness to be married to her or to anyone. He even told me in conversation that the idea of becoming a father horrified him, which did not bode well for his or England's future. (Where this attitude sprang from we were later to find out!)

Before that, though, in the spring of 1861 Bruce (by then General Bruce) had been with Bertie in Cambridge, and had urged Albert, in view of the success of the North American tour, to allow Bertie to taste a little of his other wish, to enter the Army. A ten-week course of training at the Curragh during the next Long Vacation, he said, would be very good experience for the Prince. Albert had gone down to Cambridge in March 1861 for a meeting with General Bruce, and it was decided that Bertie should undergo a concentrated course of training for every grade from ensign upwards, moving on every fortnight so that at the end of ten weeks, if he exerted himself, he would be competent to manoeuvre a brigade in the field. Strict supervision was to be exercised, however, to keep Bertie from mixing too much with other young officers. He was to give dinner parties twice a week to senior officers, dine twice a week in his own mess, once as a guest in some other regimental mess, and twice (including Sunday) quietly in his own house.

So Bertie had arrived at Kingstown on the 29th of June 1861, spent a few days at the castle, and then went on to the Curragh. Though he had worked hard, he had not the abilities to succeed in the ambitious training course that had been laid down for him, but he enjoyed himself very much. How much we were to discover in the most painful of circumstances, when we also learned that without locking him up, it is impossible to keep a young man bent on mischief out of it. At the very time he was being brought together with the virtuous Princess Alix for them to take stock of each other, Bertie was harbouring a hideous secret, the discovery of which was to have the most appalling consequences.

In 1860 Alice was seventeen, and stepped into the position of eldest daughter at home, which she very much enjoyed. Though quiet and thoughtful, she had a perfectly natural girl's love of gaiety and balls and reviews, of dancing and spectacle and having compliments paid her and all eyes upon her as she entered a room. It was time to find her a husband. We toyed for a while with the idea of Prince William of Orange (grandson of the William whom Princess Charlotte had jilted in 1814, and son of the William who had been suggested for me without success in 1836 – not a very good omen!) but when he visited us with his brother we found him a very languid, dull sort of youth, and he and Alice did not fancy each other. When we discovered he already had a vicious reputation, we felt we were well rid of him. (In fact he never came to the throne, but died of his debaucheries in 1879 – fancy if we had given him our gentle Alice!) The next candidate was brought before our notice by Vicky, and Uncle Leopold, asked to investigate, gave him a very good report. He was Louis of Hesse, nephew and heir of the Grand Duke, twenty-three years old and intelligent, interested in politics and government – which recommended him to Albert – and of absolutely pure habits, though Uncle Leopold said he was not handsome. He and his brother visited us in the summer of 1860, and I liked him very much, a gently spoken, frank, sensible young man who obviously admired Albert enormously and sought his opinion about the political situation in Europe in the prettiest way. He and Alice were in love almost on the instant. He visited us again in November, and at Christmas they became engaged.

We were not going to let our little girl go so young, though, this time. Albert said she could not be married for at least another year; and we decided, and the young people agreed, that after they were married they would spend half of every year in England. (The marriage was very happy and very successful, and the Hessians proved a good family, and provided us with two other good young men –

Ludwig of Battenberg, first cousin to Alice's Louis, who married her daughter Victoria, and his brother Henry, or Liko as we always called him, who married Baby.)

The only drawback to the House of Hesse was their strong Russian sympathies: Louis' aunt Marie had married Tsar Alexander II (another of my girlhood suitors!). Later Louis and Alice's daughter Elizabeth married Grand Duke Sergei of Russia, Marie of Hesse's son – and so became aunt to her own sister, Alicky, when Alicky married Sergei's nephew Nicky. (Nicky, in fact, used to call Alicky 'Tetinka', which means 'little aunt', when they first knew each other.) I seem to have been haunted by Russia all my life. Alix's sister Dagmar married Tsar Alexander III, which makes another connection – and she is Nicky's mother, so it's no wonder that Nicky and Georgie look so much alike, being cousins on both sides. When Nicky was staying at Windsor once, Georgie's valet went looking for him and coming upon Nicky was quite convinced he had found his master!

19th November 1900

HAD GENERAL Buller to dinner on Saturday, who let out some hints to one of my ladies that he thought Roberts was not the thing and was responsible for prolonging the war in South Africa. So I sent him a message that I would not have him discuss other generals in my presence, but that I should like to hear anything he had to say about dear Christl. At luncheon yesterday he talked most amusingly about liking his pint of champagne every day on campaign to his next neighbour, Lady Erroll, who is a fanatical supporter of Temperance. Thank God that I keep my sense of humour, if not my digestion!

In the autumn of 1860 we went on a visit to Coburg. Albert had taken into his mind a positive obsession to see the old place again; but also it was the only way we could get to see Vicky and Fritz and little Willy without a State visit being organised on one side or the other. Vicky had had a second child in July, much too soon after her dangerous first confinement, but all had gone well this time, and she had a daughter they had named Charlotte. Albert was as eager to see his darling daughter again as to see the dear old Rosenau, and so it was arranged we should all meet there. We took Alice with us, too, to give her her first taste of foreign travel.

Oh, the first moments of meeting were so overwhelming! My dear, sweet Vicky looked so pretty and womanly and well, and after embracing me she flung herself into Albert's arms, and the two wept silently into each other's necks, too overcome to speak. Kind Fritz, with a faint anxious frown which was becoming habitual to him between his brows, shook hands and said everything that was proper and cheerful, but we were both really watching Vicky; the moment came when she and Albert slowly disentangled themselves, and stood back in each other's arms, just far enough to look at each other.

'Papa?' Vicky said, searching his face anxiously. 'Are you well?'

'Yes, my darling girl, of course I am,' he said. 'And you? Are you taking care of yourself? Are you getting plenty of fresh air? After what you've told me about the drains at the Palace, I am so glad to get you away from there, even for a short time.'

And Vicky was diverted from her question, and laughed, as he had meant her to. 'Oh, Papa, what a thing to be your first question!'

'Drains should always be one's first question,' he said, smiling, and released her. 'Now I must let you kiss your sister, who is straining at the leash and thinking you've forgotten her.'

Vicky turned to kiss and hug Alice – the two were always devoted, and nothing was ever to come between them, not even when their respective countries were on opposite sides of a war. I looked at Albert. What had Vicky seen, that he had not wanted her to notice? Albert felt my regard, and met my eyes for a moment, and then turned his attention to Fritz, asking him about the political situation. There was something of embarrassment about the action, and I continued to study his averted face. He looked no different to me – but then I had been seeing him every day, and he always looked to me like my husband and my lover. Vicky, absent for so many months, had seen a change, and Albert knew it. I could not determine what it was.

But then we were disturbed, in the nicest way, by the entrance of good Mrs Hobbs (the English nurse Vicky had had brought over) holding the hand of our darling eldest grandchild. He came walking in, quite steady on his sturdy little legs, and smiling, and looking such a little love! He had on a little white dress with black bows, and looked as fine and fat a child as one could wish, with a beautiful soft white skin, and Fritz's eyes and Vicky's mouth, and very fair curly hair. He was very good all the time we were with him, and never stopped beaming at us, and he understood quite well who we were. His poor, cold, blue, useless arm I did not look at too closely, for I did not want Vicky to worry about it. Clark had told me it would come right in the end, so I wanted her to think I took it very much as a matter of course, and did not draw attention to it in any way.

We visited good old Stockmar while we were there, too, and found him quite himself, as vigorous in his mind as ever, but grown old, of course. Albert said he thought the old man in poor case. 'I had not thought to see him so weak and ill,' he said gloomily; but I said briskly that it was not surprising a man of seventy should have some frailties. 'He seemed very well to me. You must remember that our good Baron was always inclined to exaggerate his aches and pains.'

Albert would not be convinced. 'He can't last much longer,' he said. 'We must accept that we may be seeing him for the last time.' I saw he had got a Coburg Gloom upon him, and said no more. The next time we saw Stockmar, I looked at him very closely, and he did not seem to me in imminent danger of demise.

As it turned out, my darling was in more danger than his old teacher. About ten days after our arrival, Albert went over to Kalenberg to shoot, and Vicky, Alice and I joined him there for luncheon, taking our sketching-books, for there were some lovely views around the castle. A little later Albert said he must go back to Coburg to see some people on business, and Vicky and I, exchanging a rueful glance (for I had already complained to her about how over-devoted her papa was to business), said we would follow at our own pace.

We were walking down to the park gates, carrying our sketch-books, and laughing over the way a fresh-faced peasant woman had scolded Vicky for letting her dress trail on the ground and get dirty instead of looping it up, when a phaeton came bowling towards us, drawn by a very hot pair and driven by a coachman, with Colonel Ponsonby, Albert's equerry, sitting in it. One glance at his face made my heart go cold. Vicky must have seen it too, for she reached at once for my arm and gripped it hard. 'Wait, Mamma, wait and see,' she said; but I heard the fear in her voice.

Ponsonby came striding towards us, his face pale. 'Oh what is it?' I cried before he had even reached us. 'It is the Prince, I know it! Good God, tell me at once, Ponsonby! Don't spare me!'

'He is not hurt, he is not hurt,' Ponsonby cried quickly. 'He bade me tell you so at once – only a scratch on the nose, and the doctor says that's of no consequence.'

'What's happened? There's been an accident!' I said. My heart was beating so hard now I thought I would faint. I could hear it fluttering in my head like a bird in a chimney. Ponsonby reached my side and looked as though he would take hold of my other arm. But Alice was there, calm, steady Alice.

'There has been an accident to the carriage, but the Prince sent me to tell you about it, and to emphasise that he is not hurt, so that you will not be startled or frightened.'

If Albert had sent Ponsonby, he must not be in too bad a case. I took one or two deep breaths, and said, 'Very well, Ponsonby, I am quite calm now. Tell me what happened.'

The story was this: Albert was alone in the four-horse barouche when, about a mile from Coburg, the horses had taken fright and bolted. He did not know what had startled them, but when the coachman ceased to curse and began to pray aloud, he knew they were completely out of control. Up ahead the road crossed the railway line at a level crossing, and Albert saw that the bar was down to signal a train, and a waggon was drawn up in front of it, waiting. The speed of the horses had not slackened a whit, and seeing that collision was inevitable, Albert took his chance and jumped.

He hit the road and rolled over, and though bruised and shaken, with a cut across his nose and abrasions to his hands, knees and arms he was not seriously hurt. But he heard the terrible splintering crash and the scream of horses which told him that he had been right to jump. He scrambled to his feet, wiping the blood from his face, and limped towards the wreck. The coachman was badly hurt, and one of the horses was dead, killed by the impact; the others, struggling madly, managed to free themselves from the wreckage and went galloping off towards Coburg. By chance Ponsonby, who had been out driving in the phaeton, had seen them and recognised them, and had driven straight to the scene of the accident. A doctor, a local man, had already arrived at the scene by then, and Albert, who was helping him attend to the coachman, ordered Ponsonby to come straight to me.

Alice and I went back in the phaeton, Ponsonby taking the box seat beside the coachman. I forced myself to remain calm all the way home, and Alice, though naturally anxious, seemed to have taken her father's words at their face value. But I could imagine the force of the fall my darling had had, jumping out of a carriage at full galloping speed, and I felt sick with fear. I had had many falls from horses and many carriage accidents in my time, but such things do not trouble me, any more than being shot at by madmen or finding my house on fire. My nerves are only affected when I cannot find out what is going on, when I am far from the scene and cannot act or help. But Albert was not like me. He was always badly shaken by accidents, even when he was young and supple. He had taken a fall while out hunting back in 1840, and though hardly scratched he had been very shaken and his nerves much disordered; and the same in 1841, when he had gone through the ice while skating. I had managed to pull him out almost at once, and we hurried him back to the house before he could catch cold; but the shock of the accident made him quite ill with nerves.

So when I saw him lying in his bed, with lint compresses on his nose, mouth and chin, I was not surprised to see his face white as milk and to feel how cold his hands were. He was rigid under the bedclothes, and trembled like a winter sparrow. I kissed his hand and pressed it to my cheek, and said how thankful I was that he was not much hurt. 'God must have had you in His keeping,' I said. I could not see his mouth under the bandages, but his eyes were fixed on mine with a look of weary appeal, like an animal in pain that hopes in its innocence you will make it stop. 'Albert, it is nothing, isn't it? You aren't hiding anything from me?'

'No,' he whispered. 'I am bruised and shaken, no more.'

The next morning he rose at seven, dressed, and was reading at his desk by the time I went to him. 'You see,' he said, smiling at me brightly, 'I am perfectly well. A good night's sleep was all I needed.' His eyes were heavy with shadows, and the skin below them pouchy with lack of sleep. A good night's sleep was all he needed, but had he had one? All day long he behaved normally, spoke cheerfully, took a lively interest in everything that went on around him; it was only when he thought no eyes were on him that he flagged, and the animation drained out of his face, leaving it with that dreadful look of depression and melancholy. But my eyes were always on him, and I saw, and inwardly cursed his stoicism for getting out of bed too soon and not taking sufficient rest. He did not want to alarm me; he did not want to waste any of his precious time with Vicky; he did not want to waste a moment of being in beloved Coburg. Like a condemned man he devoured these pleasures and kept up a cheerful flow of spirits for the sake of his visitors before the scaffold, and it angered me, both his being so upset by the fall and his pretending so hard he was not. They were both unnecessary, and between them they wore him out. I felt he was being melodramatic; and I felt he was pushing me away with his noble-under-suffering act, keeping me at arm's length instead of admitting how poorly he felt and letting me comfort him.

But I pretended nothing was wrong. What else, after all, could I do?

Twenty

22nd November 1900, at Windsor

THE WEATHER remains clear, though wet, which is acceptable – I have never minded rain in the least, but fog is so depressing. I am feeling quite well in myself, though the least thing tires me, and consequently Reid frets me to behave like an invalid and lie on the sofa all day, which I *cannot* bear. Inactivity makes me frantic; and besides, there is so much to do and everything takes longer when I have to have things read to me instead of reading them myself. Baby does a great deal, and reads very nicely, but I fear she doesn't really understand what she is reading, which sometimes makes it hard to follow. Lenchen understands more, but she reads rather too quick. Oh how different it was when my darling and I shared the work, when we sat side by side at our desks, and I had only to turn my head to find him! Was I ever so lucky as to be able to turn to him for every need and comfort? As I am now, all alone and walled up in this failing body, it seems like the most distant of wistful dreams.

The Christmas of 1860 was wonderful. We had crisp, snowy weather and glorious floods of sunshine, and the ponds froze. Albert, Alice and the boys all skated; Louis Hesse flung himself into a wild game of ice-hockey which I'm afraid must have left him black and blue; I stood watching with Leo and Baby, admiring Albert. He had a black velvet jacket on, which suited him so well, and his skates had swans on the upcurving toe ends of the blades, and he glided about so gracefully. I called out a warning to him not to go too near the end where the bulrushes grew, where the ice might not be thick enough, and Baby looked very interested and asked me, 'Is they the bulrushes that Moses lived in?' She had just learned the story.

Louis and Alice shared a present table for the first time, and Alice looked so blushful and conscious it was quite touching. Mamma joined us for luncheon, and the little children came down for dessert, and Baby climbed at once on to my darling's knee and picked up his spoon and cast her greedy eyes about the table for the best thing. She lighted on a very rich iced pudding, and began to draw the plate towards her.

'No, no, Baby mustn't have that,' I said quickly. 'It's not good for Baby.'

'But she likes it, my dear,' the naughty thing said calmly, digging in her spoon, and it was so very droll that we all began to laugh, which was probably very bad for her, but it was impossible to be angry with the funny little thing. After luncheon we played games and Albert romped and was so funny the children were almost sick with laughing. He did conjuring tricks for the little ones, and even Bertie watched wide-eyed. (I remembered the occasion when he was much younger and a world-famous magician had been brought in to entertain us; afterwards Bertie went across to him and said confidently, 'My father understands all those tricks.' He was perfectly sure his father knew everything in the world!) A little later Baby dragged Mamma to the piano and made her sing all her favourite songs. 'I don't know the name but it sounds like this,' Baby would say, and sing the beginning of a song in a husky little voice – what Lady Augusta called her 'pot-room voice'. She knew all the words, though she often got the tunes mixed up. Later when Arthur read aloud from the Bible the story of the Massacre of the Innocents, Baby took the book over and pretended to read. 'Then the Naughty Men killed all the children,' she pronounced importantly, 'and the mothers cried *wipperly*.'

But after this happy time the New Year of 1861 began badly. As I have mentioned, the poor mad old King of Prussia (Fritz's uncle) died on the 2nd of January and Fritz's father became King, and all his reactionary tendencies were given free rein. This meant that endless bitter disputes broke out over the projected unification of Germany, which caused Albert more worry and work, trying to help and advise Vicky as to what she could hope to achieve as the new Crown Princess of Prussia.

Then on the 29th of January there was a railway accident at Wimbledon, a crash between two trains, and by a horrid chance the only person killed was our Dr Baly, who fell through the floor of the carriage and was crushed by the wheels. He was a brilliant young physician who had only been with us a year, but Albert already had the greatest confidence in him. Baly had replaced my good old Clark, who had retired at seventy-three. Now we had to ask Clark to recommend us someone else. It was very upsetting and unsettling, particularly as Albert had begun the year with dreadful toothache which settled down into a constant, painful neuralgia of the upper part of the cheek, due to an inflammation of the nerves. Incision of the gum was tried, in case the imflammation was caused by poison, but there was no draining, and a second operation nine days later gave no relief either. Toothache is a dismal, miserable affliction, which thank God I am not prone to, and when you have it, you can think of nothing else. Albert was very much pulled down by it, and by the sleepless nights he passed, but he would not let up on his work, and at the height of the attack, when his poor glands were very much swollen, he insisted on going to a meeting at Trinity House about new lighthouses, and came back exhausted. It was not until the end of the month that Clark found us a replacement, a Dr William Jenner, who had been a friend of our poor excellent Baly. I liked Jenner's calm, comfortable manner very much, and whether by chance or intervention, Albert's trouble cleared up at last a few days later.

But almost immediately another blow fell: on the 28th of February Sir George Couper died quite suddenly – 'Snuffed out like a candle,' Albert said. Since 1840 he had been Mamma's Comptroller, but had long been more than that to her – her intimate friend, protector and adviser, to whom she referred every decision and every difficulty.

'These are bad news indeed,' Albert said later that evening, when we had talked over our sadness. 'Mamma's health is very indifferent. I'm afraid of what the shock might do to her.'

Mamma had been suffering for nearly two years from attacks of erysipelas (that horrid disease which killed my poor John Brown – though his was exacerbated by too much whisky) but though she was seventy-five now, a great age for those days, I had not anticipated any particular danger. One expects one's mother to live for ever: that is nature in us. 'Surely there is nothing to worry about?' I said.

'You know she has an abscess on her arm,' he reminded me. 'That is the sort of thing that pulls a person down.'

'But it will soon be better,' I said. 'She is very strong. She comes of healthy stock.'

'My love, I think you should not hope too much,' he said gently, looking at me steadily.

I began to be alarmed. 'What is it? Do you know something more than me?'

He nodded unwillingly. 'Clark said – he told me – he said we should be prepared for the worst.'

'*Clark* told you?'

'Yes. He wanted me to decide whether you should be told or not, and I decided against it because—'

'*When* did he say this?'

'About two years ago, when she had the first attack—'

But I interrupted him, laughing with relief. 'Clark told you two years ago to expect the worst? But she is *still here*, you see! Oh, how you worried me for a moment. It is too bad of you.'

He went on trying. 'My darling, that arm of hers is not good, you know. An abscess like that poisons the whole system.'

'It will be better in a week, you'll see,' I said firmly.

It was not, however, and on the 9th of March Jenner said he must open the arm and try to find the seat of the trouble. It was a trying operation – he had to cut right down to the bone – but the relief was only temporary, and a fresh swelling soon started to gather. Still I had no apprehension. On the 15th of March we were at Buckingham Palace, and I was peacefully marking newspapers while Albert wrote letters, when a message was brought to us from Frogmore from Dr Clark (who was still Mamma's physician), telling us that Mamma's condition was desperate.

'It can't be true,' I said, puzzled and alarmed. 'He is mistaken.'

Albert stood up. 'We must go to her at once,' he said. 'Prepare yourself, *Liebchen*. I will order the train.'

No time was wasted. We reached Frogmore at eight o'clock that evening, and I would have hurried straight up to Mamma's room, but Albert put a restraining hand on my arm and said, 'No, let me go first. Wait here, my love.' He seemed gone a long time, and I waited in impatience rather than fear. I should be with her, I thought, it is me she will want, her daughter – but they were words of form, making themselves inside my head like idle spindrift forming. At heart I still did not really believe there was anything to fear. Then Albert came back, and his face was wet with tears. 'Albert?' I said, rising to my feet. 'How is she? Is she awake?'

He stood before me, and looked at me so sadly and kindly. 'She is dying, Victoria,' he said. 'The end is very near.'

'Near?' I stammered, aghast. 'You – you mean – she will not get better?'

'She will not last the night. She is dying, child – dying *now*.'

'Oh, God, it can't be,' I whispered, putting out my hands to him. He nodded, taking them, and turned with me to walk upstairs. I felt numb with disbelief, not knowing what to think or feel; and I clung to my husband's hand as the only thing that made sense to me in a world grown strange. He helped me into her room, and there she was, the little, plump old lady, the Mamma I had grown so late in life to love, the brave, kind, warm-hearted grandmamma to my children – lying on the sofa in a pretty dressing-gown of green silk, with a fresh, lace-trimmed cap over her hair. Her head was propped by several pillows, and she seemed to be breathing rather heavily, but otherwise she looked so normal that my heart rallied. Surely, surely she could not be dying? I hurried to her and dropped to my knees beside her, caught up her hand and kissed it and laid it against my cheek. 'Mamma!' I said. 'Mamma, are you awake?' Her eyes opened, and she looked at me, but she did not seem to know me. For the first time there was no welcoming smile for me. Her eyes looked black and empty, like holes on to nothing. 'Mamma, it's Vickelschen. How are you feeling?'

The hand in mine moved; I laid my other hand on her shoulder, and a frown crossed her face, and she pulled feebly away from me and brushed at the thing on her shoulder as though it were a fly or a fallen leaf.

'Mamma?'

She rolled her head away from me. 'Don't fuss me,' she muttered thickly. 'Where are my glasses? Fetch my glasses, girl.'

She didn't know me. My heart was pierced with despair, and I felt the tears slide like a river out of my eyes and down my cheeks in desolation. She was going to die – not one day, but now, this very night; she was going to leave me for ever, abandon me, her child whom she had loved and now turned away from. I struggled to my feet and ran from the room; Albert followed me. Clark was standing there, my good old Clark, having left the room to give me space, and through my tears I looked appealingly into his face. 'Is there no hope? Oh, say there is hope!'

'Your Majesty,' he said helplessly, looking as miserable as a dog left out in the rain, 'I wish I might say there is. But I fear there is none whatever. Her Grace is very near the end. But it will be easy, we think. She is beyond her pain now.'

Easy? I thought. Death easy? That was doctor's talk, that was Coburg talk. Death was the enemy, to be fought, to be howled at and defied. Death could never be *easy*. I wanted to howl myself, and raise my fists, and scream at the heavens, at God, who had dared to do this; but I was the Queen, and there are things queens don't do in front of doctors. I turned away from him, held out my hand towards Albert, and at once his handkerchief was in my fingers, and his warm hand was upon my elbow, supporting me as I wiped my face. (Oh, blessed time when he was there, always there, when I needed him!) Then I nodded to him, and we went back in.

Oh, what a long and dreary vigil! We sat in silence, for there was nothing to say, watching her sleep away the last dregs of her life, listening to that steady, heavy breathing; and every quarter came the little silvery chimes of the tortoiseshell repeater which I had heard through every night of my childhood, until, becoming Queen, I had left my mother's room for ever. I had left my mother, too, left her in anger and hatred, until Albert came to soften my heart and clear my reason and give me all that could be salvaged from the wreck of my childhood. I had hated her so much, and it is not possible to hate the mother who bears you without hating something of yourself. Now she was leaving me – leaving me! – and I hated her again. How could she do this to me? How could she care so little for me as to die without saying goodbye? As my father's watch picked away at the stitches of that last night, and gave silver tongue after the fleeing quarters, I counted the heavy breaths and willed her to wake and to know me, to smile, kiss me, say she loved me, bid me adieu. I counted the breaths and wondered how many of them there were altogether to be spent, and how many left before the end.

In the early hours Albert made me go and lie down on a sofa and rest, but though weary I could not sleep, only doze fitfully, waking to a sense of unreality which made me more tired and sick. At four I went in to the room again, but there was no change. At six, no change. At half past seven I gave up pretence of sleeping and went back to the room, and sat on a footstool beside her, and took possession of her hand again. Now she was so deeply unconscious she could not object. It was not like sleep, this heaviness – it was like going away. Clark came and looked over my shoulder, reached quietly to feel for the pulse. I looked up at him. His ancient, craggy face was so worn with time it could not look tired, though he had not been to bed; but there were white whiskers sprouting from his chin.

'It will not be long now,' he said softly. 'Shall I call His Highness in?'

'Yes,' I said; and my voice came out so unused it sounded dusty. Albert came and stood behind me. I could not look at him, but I was glad he was there. He had loved her, always, and called her Mamma. But she was not his mother – she could not betray him, having no faith with him to break. Fainter and fainter grew the breaths, and the hand I held seemed unnaturally soft, limp, and smooth, as though receding life had washed it clear like the sand below the tide-line. Now they really were numbered, those breaths, so few left, coming further apart, like clockwork winding down. And then there were none. I listened for the next – surely it would come? I waited past the moment when it might, still listening for it, and heard instead the silvery chimes of the half striking. Half past nine. She was gone. Left without speaking, without moving, without a sigh – just gone, between one breath and the next, as though it were a matter of supreme unimportance. How could death be so unremarkable? And yet as I looked at the thing before me, I knew it was death. I had never seen a dead body before, but now I would always recognise it. They lie, the poets: it is not like sleep. The solemn, marble flesh which no life inhabits is not like a living person sleeping. It is not a human being at all – it is a foul mockery, got up to cheat the heart, to whisper seductively that the beloved might return, if one is only faithful. But one does not believe it. Like all the Impostor's works, it is not a good enough cheat to convince.

Behind me I heard Albert break into terrible sobs, the sobs of a man who has lost one who had been almost a mother to him. *But she was not his mother!* I sat as I had sat unmoving, unable to cry, frozen by the awfulness, the mystery of it, hollow to the depth of my heart with the bitterness of my loss. She had gone, she had left me, and she would never come back, not if I stayed here for ever. Still sobbing, Albert put his arms round me, drew me to my feet, gathered me up to help me from the room. I wished I could cry, but the tears would not come yet, only a savage pain in my breast and my throat as though something iron were being forced into me. Tears would be a relief from that pain, I thought, but for the moment it was Albert who wept, not me. He was not the one betrayed.

26th November 1900

I CAN still remember what a shattering blow it was to me. I had never before had anyone close to me die; and of recent years I had seen Mamma, or exchanged letters with her, daily. She had become to me what mothers ought to be to their daughters, my confidante and adviser, my support in the upbringing of my children, and the person who was interested in all the minutiae of my life – the curl of my hair, the trimming of a new petticoat, the state of my digestion, what I meant to order for luncheon. She was of the fabric of every day, and of late Albert had not been. He would not give up any of his business, though it was making him ill; he was from me for a great part of each day, and when he came back to me he was often too tired or preoccupied to be interested in trivia. Now in addition to everything else, he had Mamma's estate to sort out, for she had made him her sole executor; the demands on his time were enough to drive anyone distracted, and many of the things we had used to do together had now had to be given up.

And so I *missed* Mamma, in the exact sense of that over-used expression. She was not where she had been; and a dozen times a day I began to think, 'I must remember to tell Mamma—' or, 'Mamma will like to hear that—' only to have the horrid truth forcibly 'brought home' to me again. It was the irrevocability that distressed me most; the lost opportunities that could not be caught back, the things not said that could now never be. She had left a mass of papers and letters, and sorting through them with Lady Augusta Bruce I was reduced to tears by the discovery that Mamma had never thrown away a single scrap of my writing, however trivial; she had kept all my locks of hair, even my baby-shoes. In her journal I read her tender observations of my babyhood and childhood: all those years I had been hating her – and I had declared passionately to Lord M. that I did not believe she had *ever* loved me – she had been writing tenderly, affectionately, wistfully about me in her journal. Misguided she had certainly been, but she had never acted from malice or indifference, only from a mistaken idea of what would be best for me. So to loss and grief were added guilt and remorse. Through that dismal, wet, cold spring I mourned, and would not be comforted.

In May, Louis of Hesse came to visit, eager to see his sweet Alice, and was visibly taken aback at the deep mourning and gloom he discovered in the house. But his sympathy for me was intense and practical, and I discovered then what a worthy claimant he was for Alice's hand. He sat with me for hours, talking quietly and sensibly, listening to me with the patience and tenderness of a woman, looked over the new plans for a mausoleum at Frogmore for Mamma's remains with respectful enthusiasm surprising in one so young. Unfortunately he took the measles while he was with us, and pretty soon gave them to our children. Arthur, Leo and Baby all went down with them, and in Leo's case illnesses were never trivial. The poor little boy was very ill indeed, which added to my worries and Albert's weariness.

In August we visited Ireland to see how Bertie had progressed. He was touchingly pleased to see us, and proud of his achievements, and we watched him march past with his company, looking better than I had expected. Then on our return we went to Balmoral. There

381

my spirits revived at last; I was ready to put aside deep mourning and enjoy the good air, and our simple, good people, and the expeditions that dearest Albert planned for my entertainment. I loved travelling incognito, as we did on those expeditions, staying at small inns and eating whatever the landlady had prepared for her 'ordinary' guests. I must admit, though, that the fun was not complete unless a disclosure came at last; otherwise it was like a play in which the highborn heroine takes a situation as a housemaid, and remains unidentified to the end. The best thing was when we were recognised just as we were leaving, and could witness the people's astonishment and excitement as we drove away. I suspect that the reason this so often happened was that the servants grew tired of not having their eminence appreciated and 'told'; but the time I was most pleased was at Grantown when it was Albert who was recognised and cheered. I liked to see all his great work appreciated.

But the best thing about Balmoral was that I was able to detach Albert at last from that work, and see him give himself a little to pleasure and relaxation (not that stalking is not very hard work, but it did not make him sick or give him neuralgia or insomnia). At Windsor and in London he was never still: he had even taken lately to running along the corridors instead of walking, to save time. He rose at seven every day and worked at his desk in his padded dressing-gown for an hour before he even dressed; at breakfast he would read *The Times* as he ate – or rather bolted – his egg and bread and butter, and before the last morsel was swallowed he would be calling for his secretaries to discuss the business of the day. He hated being in the public eye and giving speeches and proposing toasts, yet he never turned down an invitation, if it was for a good cause – and the approach of a speech occasion always brought on the sickness and shivering fits and insomnia. He never cancelled an outdoor appointment on the grounds of foul weather or his own ill-health, and so often came back shivering, exhausted, nauseous, or tortured with rheumatism or neuralgia; he even insisted on keeping an engagement he had made at the horticultural gardens when little Leo was very sick with the measles, which made me very angry. And all this was in addition to the constant flow of questions which were brought to him by every member of the Household and every department of Government. 'Ask the Prince' was the solution to every problem which arose; and the Prince never turned anyone away, and delegated far too little.

But at Balmoral I had him back, and that autumn holiday in 1861 was one of the best I remember. Louis Hesse was with us, and already seeming like one of the family; and Bertie was not with us, which made the household more peaceful. Some of the stoop my darling had got into his shoulders in the last two years went out of them, and something like the old gaiety animated his face. When it was in repose, it had a solemn, grave, dignified cast to it, but no-one who had witnessed it ever forgot his smile, or the delightful, hearty sound of his laugh. We had one or two very good balls, and Albert and I danced several reels, impressing Louis greatly – Albert was still an incomparably graceful dancer, and when I danced with him, I was as light as thistledown. And at night when we retired to our bedroom, I found I had got back my lover again, tender and fond and as passionate as when we had first wed; but now, suddenly, after twenty-one years of blissful, faithful marriage, it seemed that the strange struggle – almost pain – that the final yielding had caused him had gone. He gave all to me as sweetly as fresh, good water bubbles out of a spring, and my heart ached with joy as I held him close to me night after night.

The last expedition we took was on October the 16th, and since once Albert had planned them (which was done with maps and the ghillies and much consultation, down to the last detail) he would never put off, however bad the weather, I was delighted to wake to a perfectly beautiful day. It was one of those windless days you get in October, mild as summer, all blue and gold, and the colours clean and bright and simple, like heraldic painting. There was not a cloud in the spotless, deep blue sky (as blue as Papa's eyes, Vicky used to say). There had been a sharp frost in the night, and as we breakfasted in our room with Alice, Louis and Lenchen, it still lay white and crisp and thick as powder-snow on the lawns where the shadow of the castle fell. The poor trees were almost leafless, but what few leaves remained were gold and crimson and rust-brown against the sky and the rowan berries were a scarlet blaze.

We started at twenty minutes to nine and took carriages as far as Loch Callater, where the ponies were waiting for us – my darling Fyvie whinnied when he saw me; Alice had Inchrory and Lenchen had Alice's grey Geldie, who was very safe – and set off up into the mountains. The day was glorious, the country in such beauty, the heather blooming and the bracken all turned to golden brown; and in the distance the light on the mountains was so soft that the blue shades on them looked almost misty, like the bloom on a plum. Sometimes we walked, and sometimes rode; the men walked mostly, and talked about game, and politics, and such-like. Sometimes Louis came up to walk beside my pony, and we discussed the view, and whether it would make a good sketch, and where it reminded us of. When he went to walk with Alice, Albert took his place, and we exchanged a special smile, and then went on in a companionable silence which, between lovers, can be sweeter than words. The air was very sharp, but so still that where the sun fell on one's head or shoulders it felt very hot. Albert was wearing his cape and deerstalker cap with the laps turned up, and I wondered he was not too hot; but I thought he looked very handsome in them. With the hat covering his bald top, he looked young again, and to me utterly delicious.

We stopped just before two o'clock at the top of the valley of Cairn Lochan, which Grant had told us we should find 'a bonny place', as indeed it was. The hills leading down into it were green and steep, broken in places by grey precipices; and the river Isla wound through the bottom of the valley like a silver ribbon, fringed with trees. We stopped to have luncheon at a flat place right above a vertical drop (which made me nervous about anyone's moving backwards) where there was a magnificent view right up the valley and down into another glen leading off it. The air was very keen up here, and Brown found a little standing pool which was frozen hard as thick as a shilling, and the ice did not even melt when he broke a piece off and brought it to us held in his hand; but the sun was warm on our shoulders, and there were bees in the heather, which was in full bloom around us. The rugs were spread and we sat, and Duncan and Brown served us; we were all hungry after our long ride, and even my dear darling, who sat beside me, ate with good appetite. We had some excellent patties, I remember, and very good potatoes, a fine claret – and, of course, a 'grand nip' of John Begg's finest! Afterwards I made some sketches, and Albert came up behind me to watch. Then he reached over a hand and tore a corner off my page, and resting his cheek against mine he took the pencil from my hand and wrote on it the date and the names of our party, and that we had lunched there. I smiled, and he left the breath of a kiss on my cheek (without anyone's seeing, of course) and whispered, 'Remember!' This note he buried in a Seltzer bottle, like the others.

We went home then by a different route, and it was all new to us, for it was in a different direction from any of our other expeditions. Albert was delighted. 'I wish we could know every inch of these mountains! But it would take a longer expedition than one day, I suppose.'

'Well, we have time,' I said. 'Not this year, but next.' He smiled, but said nothing. We got back down to the road at half past four, as it was growing dusk, and rode back along the side of the river. We startled a stag at one point, but by the time Albert had his gun up to his shoulder it was too far off in that light to shoot. 'Never mind,' he said. 'Let it live. I am too benevolent after such a fine day to wish it ill.' The moon rose in the clear sky, and shone first faintly gold and then blue-white; almost full, and very beautiful. 'There will be another sharp frost tonight,' my darling said; and then putting his mouth close to my ear, so that his moustache tickled my cheek, he whispered, 'It will be a cold night. Will you keep me warm, wifey?' My heart jumped like a startled deer – but with delight, not fear, of course.

We got home at twenty minutes to seven, and did not dress that evening, but dined *en famille*, and afterwards looked at maps of the Highlands, talking over the day and planning where we might go next. Louis asked Alice to sing for him, and she went to the piano and gave us *The Bonnie Lass o' Fyvie*, which is a very sad air, but sounded more like a love-song as Alice sang it, gazing into Louis' face. Albert leaned over the back of my chair while she sang, and stared into the fire. It was burning up bright, with that red heart to it you see on cold nights. 'The frost is in the fire, you see,' he said to me. 'I love snow, and all the forms of the radiant frost – of which this is one.'

I caught the quotation from him. 'I love all that thou lovest, spirit of delight!' I turned my head to look up at him. 'When the song is ended, I think we should say goodnight. It is time the young people were in bed.'

'And the old people?' He smiled. 'After such a long day, an early night is advisable for all, I think. And besides, I have another poem for you, which I can only tell you in private.'

So we went to bed. When I was in my dressing-gown, and my hair was down, I sent my maid away, and Albert came to lean against the chimneypiece in his old way and watch me brush my hair. 'You've been happy today,' he said.

'It was a lovely day, but I'm always happy when I'm with you,' I answered.

'I have been with you these last six months, but you have not been happy,' he reminded me, with gentle reproach.

'Oh,' I said, looking up quickly; but he was smiling. 'I have been better of late, have I not? I have only cried once since we've been here, over Mamma's poor carriage.'

'Yes, I can give you a very good certificate this time,' he said, 'and I'm happy to witness the improvement, and to see *you* witness it. You see it is as I have always told you, that if you will only look outside yourself, you will manage very well. It is because you dwell on your own feelings that you increase your pain to an unbearable degree.'

'Yes, I know you are right,' I said, 'but when I am in the middle of it, I don't want to look outside myself.'

'You enjoy it, in fact,' he said drily.

'Oh, not enjoy it precisely,' I said quickly, 'but it's hard to see beyond it.'

'I think half your grief over poor Mamma was rage, because you would not accept God's will. You like to have your own way, and not even the Almighty is to thwart you.'

I felt faintly shocked. 'Oh! no – but Albert, you grieved too.'

'Yes, for I loved Mamma very much. But I accepted God's will, as I always do – and as you must learn to do for your peace of mind, however hard it is.'

I felt my mouth tighten. 'There are some things one cannot accept.'

'Yes, I know you think death is one of them. But that is not my way. I am happy in my lot, but if God called me home, I would go willingly. You cling to life as something valuable in itself, but I do not set the same store by it. If I had a severe illness, I'm sure I would not struggle, but give up at once. That would be His will.'

'That,' I countered severely, 'would be merely want of pluck.' I thought he would argue with me, but he only looked at me for a moment with an odd expression, almost smiling; his eyes softly gleaming, his mouth under his moustache seeming to curve upwards with a wry humour, as though watching the caperings of an incorrigible but adored child. Then he said, 'Oh my wifey, if you only knew how much I have missed you these past months!'

'Missed me? But I have been here – I mean, wherever you were. You had only to come to me, but you would go out exhausting yourself with business—'

He shook his head and lifted a hand to stop me. 'I am selfish, I know, but what has always kept me going through all my work and worry is the knowledge that *you* are vitally interested in everything I do; you want to know everything that happens to me, everything I've said, everything that's been said to me. I love to tell you things, and see your face alight with passion, to see you angry or delighted or concerned by turns at what I tell you – and all on *my* behalf. But these last months it has been like knocking at the door of a darkened house. No light shows and no-one comes, and you feel that hollow certainty that there is no-one within, and you are all alone with night coming on.'

'Oh my darling,' I said, all contrition now. 'I never thought – I didn't realise—' I rose to my feet and put myself into his arms. He closed his arms round me, and I pressed my face against his neck, smelling the familiar scent of his skin which was bliss and warmth and safety and *home*. 'Oh Albert, I'm so sorry! You will never find the house dark again, I promise! I will always, always answer you! Forgive me, my love. I didn't mean to be selfish; but it didn't seem right not to mourn Mamma. It was her due – don't you think?'

'Everyone should be mourned – but with moderation, as in all things,' he said, putting me back from him to look down into my face. 'Rationality, order, harmony – that is what we should strive for. I hope you remember that, if it comes to mourning me.'

'I should not survive you,' I said sharply, 'so the question would not arise.'

He gave me that strange, half-smiling look, and said in a different voice, a soft voice that thrilled me as though I were seventeen again, 'Don't you want to know what the other poem is, that I said I had for you?'

'Yes, of course. Is it Shelley too?'

He nodded, and ran his hands down my arms to take hold of my hands, and looked into my eyes. 'Shelley again – and most improper, so I'm sure you can't have heard it before:

> *The fountains mingle with the river,*
> *And the rivers with the ocean;*
> *The winds of heaven mix for ever*
> *With a sweet emotion;*
> *Nothing in the world is single;*
> *All things, by a Law divine,*
> *In one another's being mingle.*
> *Why not I with thine?*

'I wish we were only one person, my sweet Victoria! I wish I had your great vitality and courage and steadfastness. But as we are two people, we must do the best we can, and find out if there may not sometimes be some advantage to it. Shall we try now? *Veux tu, mon âme?*'

'*Je veux,*' I said.

A long time later I lay in his arms with my head on his shoulder, in the position I liked best to be, feeling so safe and happy and loved; and I heard him sigh happily, and felt him draw me a little tighter, rather as a cat in a warm basket flexes its paws in pleasure. I smiled into my darling's neck. 'I wish we didn't have to go back to Windsor,' I murmured.

'I wish we didn't, too,' he agreed; and then we drifted off to sleep.

29th November 1900

I WISH that I could end the story there. But like an evil enchantment that hung about the place, as soon as we got back to Windsor, things started to go wrong. The work we had managed to leave behind for a while fell back on to Albert like a boulder, and he staggered under the weight before, agonisingly, taking up the strain. Then at the beginning of November the news came that the Portuguese royal family had all been struck down with typhoid, and that King Pedro and his brother Ferdinand were dead. Albert had loved these cousins almost like his own sons, and he was deeply distressed. I tried to comfort him, but he seemed utterly dejected; and his unhappiness manifested itself in various aches and pains, toothache, backache, headache, and a sharp neuralgic pain behind one eye, which tried him very much.

Then on the 12th November – I will never forget the date – my poor darling came into my room looking utterly miserable, and holding a letter in his hand. 'Oh good God,' I said at once, looking at it, 'not another death! Say it is not another death!'

'It is worse,' Albert said, and his voice was as black and cold as the tomb. 'It is the worst thing that could happen. Death would be a blessing compared with this.'

'But what is it?' I cried. He was near enough now for me to see the writing on the letter – it was from Stockmar. 'From the Baron? What has happened? Sit, sit and tell me.'

He collapsed rather than sat in the chair beside me. He looked more miserable than any creature I have ever seen, before or since. 'It's about Bertie. It's about our son.'

It was the last thing I expected. 'Bertie? What can Stockmar know about Bertie that we don't?' Bertie had been with us only a few days before for his birthday celebrations, and he had seemed perfectly well and in good spirits. Now he had gone back to Cambridge, and I could not see how Stockmar in Coburg could have more recent news than those.

Albert did not give me the letter to read, but staring ahead of him in a dreary way he said, 'The Baron writes to warn me that there is a rumour abroad, a most dreadful story, that while Bertie was at the Curragh he – he committed a most heinous crime.'

'What? I don't believe it!' I cried indignantly. 'Bertie would never, never do such a thing! He is as honest as the day is long! He has many faults, but he is not a criminal. How could the Baron entertain the idea for a moment? I wonder he dares write such a thing to you!'

'No, you don't understand,' Albert said. My anger had not stirred him. He looked blankly ahead of him as though he were facing the end of everything. 'I don't mean that sort of crime.' He shuddered. 'Good God, theft or forgery or even murder would be easier to bear than this! What he has done is much more vile. He has betrayed us, brought shame on the whole family, put the very Throne in danger. He has – he has consorted with a common harlot!'

For a moment I did not understand what he had said; wound up like a spring by his foreboding words, my mind snapped back on itself uncomprehendingly. 'Consorted with –?'

Albert nodded. 'If Stockmar has heard it, it must be all over Europe already. Everyone will know what he has done – and the Baron wonders how it will affect his prospects of marrying Alix of Schleswig-Holstein. Of course, there can be no thought of that now. He has lost her for ever. Penniless her father may be, but he will not relish the prospect of tying that sweet, innocent girl to a hardened rake.'

'Hardened *rake*? *Bertie*?' I felt almost hysterical. 'For God's sake, tell me what he is supposed to have done!'

'I've told you – must I spell it out? You should not be burdened with the disgusting details of his foul misconduct. I will tell you only that while he was at the Curragh, a girl was brought into his bed.' I saw his lips whiten. 'Whether or not he desired it, he certainly did not refuse it, and the rumour the Baron has heard is that he liked her so well he brought her back with him to Windsor.'

I grasped eagerly at that. 'But *that* is not true – we *know* that is not true – so the rest may be false too.'

'Not to Windsor Castle,' he said, 'but there are lodgings in the town, and inns, and who knows what friends he might have who would harbour the girl?'

'Well, we *don't* know,' I said stoutly, 'and until we do we should not believe the worst. Stockmar is not always right, you know, and he is a long way from England – or from Ireland. Until we find out the truth we should accept nothing of this story.'

He stood up wearily. 'I know the truth. I have seen it in him all along – that poisoned blood; the infection lurking, waiting to come out! His great-uncles' inheritance is coming home to roost. Our son is corrupt. It would be better if we had not lived to see this day.'

'For Heaven's sake,' I said impatiently, 'won't you try to find out the truth before you condemn the boy?'

'Yes,' he said glumly; 'but if it is true we must quite give up the match with Princess Alix – and my heart was set on that. Indeed, we will have difficulty in finding any princess in Europe who will have him.' He swayed a little, and I saw his face drain yellow-white. 'I think—' he muttered, and then clapped his hand over his mouth and hurried away. Upsets always went to his stomach.

I don't know, for he never told me, how he went about getting confirmation of the story, but I know where it came from in the end – Lord Torrington, that arch gossip of all gossips. Torrington knew all the details (which Albert did not want to tell me, but which I 'wormed' out of him, for Bertie was my son too, after all) and even said that the story was well known around the clubs, which both depressed Albert and confirmed his opinion of those places.

It seems it had happened on the last night at camp, when there had been a farewell ball given at the Mansion House in Dublin in Bertie's honour. He was very popular amongst the other boys, and they had all had more than enough to drink. They danced, and flirted, and went back to camp very late. When Bertie got into his hut, he found the girl in his bed, naked, and saying that she was 'a present' from his fellow Guards officers. Her name was Nellie Clifden (I wish I had never known her name – it made it worse, somehow) and she was an actress, and very pretty in a common way. Bertie ought, of course, to have turned her out into the night, but he didn't; and it seems that he liked her well enough to smuggle her back with him, not to Windsor, but to Cambridge, where he installed her in lodgings.

Now I have wondered since whether this 'prank' was all indeed just high spirits on the part of Bertie's friends. I know it is the sort of thing boys do, and it was the very reason Albert did not want Bertie to mix with other youths, for they take a delight in corrupting each other, particularly if one of them is more innocent than the others, and they think such escapades are amusing and manly. But there is no doubt that when we were at the Curragh that summer, Albert had made some very searing remarks about the general idleness and profligacy of young officers – 'English youth', he had called them – and how they engaged in idle chatter in the mess rather than serious discussion of military matters. I had seen one or two disagreeable looks amongst those who overheard the rebukes; and I remembered that every time Albert had tried to improve the Army it had been bitterly resented. The Army was the heartland of the Fashionables, and it was the last place they wanted a foreigner interfering – especially a German. Perhaps the Guards officers had not merely carried out a thoughtless prank, but had done it deliberately to corrupt Bertie, so as to 'get their own back' on Albert – for his views on such matters, and particularly with regard to Bertie, were well known.

Twenty-one

3rd December 1900, at Windsor

I SEE now that my darling had it all out of proportion. At any other time, or if his health had not already been impaired, he would not have allowed it to weigh so much on his spirits. As it was, however, he was unable to shake it off. It haunted him with the persistency with which even trifles haunt the mind when the nervous system has been overtaxed; and since I lived so much with him and by him and through him, and had absorbed his thoughts and his preoccupations and his philosophies over such a period of years that I hardly had any of my own, I was haunted by it too. I could not divert his thoughts or give them a more rational perspective. What hurt him, hurt me, and in the state he was in, the story of what Bertie had done caused him, he said, 'the greatest pain that he had yet felt in this life'.

On the 16th of November, having brooded over it for four days, he wrote Bertie a letter. At this distance I sincerely pity my son, who adored and reverenced his father, for what he must have felt receiving such a letter – though at the time I thought it no more than he deserved. It was very long, and the words might well have seared the paper. Much of it Albert would not let me see, saying that it concerned things which were not proper to be mentioned to a woman

(I suppose it was about syphilis and suchlike matters); but I read the last page, and I am glad I never had such a letter sent to me.

'You have become the talk and ridicule of the idle and profligate,' was one of the milder phrases. 'The woman, who frequents the lowest dance halls in London, is already known by the nickname of "The Princess of Wales". Probably she will have a child, or will get a child, of which you will be the reputed father, no matter what the truth of it. If you were to try to deny it, she can drag you into a Court of Law to force you to own the child, and there, with you, the Prince of Wales, in the witness box, she will be able to give before a greedy multitude disgusting details of your profligacy for the sake of convincing the Jury. You yourself will be cross-examined by a railing, indecent attorney, and hooted and yelled at by a Lawless Mob!! Oh horrible prospect, which this person has in her power, any day, to realise! YOU have put it in her power to break your poor parents' hearts!'

The language was impassioned, the grammar shaky, the handwriting violent; my darling was almost deranged with grief that after all his endless care, *this*, the worst thing he had feared, had happened; and with worry as to what it might be the beginning of. Night after night he was unable to sleep, but sat at his desk, his little green-shaded lamp burning through the black middle watch as he sat with his head in his hands and grieved. His father – his brother – my half-brother Charles – and now his own son, in spite of every care, seemed to be going the same way, infected by that fatal tendency he so feared and abhorred. He felt he had failed – he told me so again and again. Once I found him weeping – not violently, but hopelessly, which was far worse. 'I could not even protect my own child,' he said. 'Everything else I have done is wasted, for when he is King he will reverse it all.' In vain I struggled against such terrific ideas. I was worried too, and deeply hurt and disappointed. I could not condone what Bertie had done – it was wrong, both absolutely, and because of who he was. But it was not worth all this grief. Oh my darling, it was not worth dying for!

Bertie's letter came back – shocked, overwhelmed, a letter steeped in misery and contrition. I think he had seen it as a prank merely, in his young heedlessness not realising it was far graver than such misdemeanours as smoking and drinking spirits, which he would also have hidden from his father and me. Albert and I read the letter together, and Albert read it over and over again, poring over it as though it were some rare manuscript, weighing every word and its possible implications. He almost wore the ink from the page in his effort to understand Bertie's heart. But it seemed to lift him, just a little. 'I think he understands his error – do you not think so, my love? I think he shows true repentance. Read here, this sentence. Do you not think he is really ashamed and sorry?'

I agreed heartily, glad to encourage this better frame of mind, no longer – forgive me! – really so much caring about the state of Bertie's soul as the state of my husband's mind and heart.

'I will go and see him,' he said at last. 'If he truly repents, we must forgive him – though no forgiveness can restore him to the state of innocence he has lost.' He paced restlessly up and down as he spoke, unable to keep still under the fever of his thoughts. 'He has thrown away the best gift of youth – its purity. He must ever hide himself from the sight of God.'

I was not so sure about that. 'Surely, if he behaves himself from now on, and marries and settles down – if he proves himself a good husband and father—'

'Early marriage *must* be his only hope now. If Alix will have him. If her parents will agree to it. They must be told – *she* must be told everything. She must not be allowed to bind herself to him without knowing what she takes on.'

So on Thursday the 21st he wrote to Bertie in Cambridge, telling him he would be down on the Monday. 'Those around you will do everything they can to help you, but they will be powerless unless they are met on your part with that openness and honesty which must characterise the dealings of gentlemen with each other.' On the Friday he seemed to be starting a cold, but in spite of that he went to Sandhurst to inspect the new buildings for the Staff College and Royal Military Academy – one of his pet projects – and walking about all day in the pouring rain got soaked to the skin and came back to Windsor shivering and aching. All weekend he was suffering – we had the usual complement of guests and he did not spare himself in his duties as host – and by Sunday night he was obviously feverish and aching all over, he said, with rheumatic pains. But he would not be deflected from his decision to go down to Cambridge on the Monday, and knowing that his body could not be easy if his mind was not, I did not try too hard to stop him.

It was another damp day, not raining precisely, but mizzling on and off, as though the skies were too heavy with water quite to hold it all in – the worst sort of weather, as it happened, for had it been positively raining, they might have stayed indoors. But as it is always easier to talk when walking, and privacy is better served out of doors, where no-one can eavesdrop, Albert and Bertie went for a walk along the deep, damp country lanes about Madingley, where we had taken a house for Bertie, and they talked – very long and very deep. I have always said that Bertie's best qualities are his honesty and his affectionate heart, and both came to his rescue now (from what Albert told me about it afterwards). He was deeply grieved by the pain he had given his beloved papa; had not thought it was so very bad at the time, though he had not liked deceiving us, but saw now that it was very bad indeed; would never, never do such a thing again for the world. He told Albert exactly how it had come about in a very frank way: it had not been his idea at all – he had known nothing of it until he found the girl in his bed; then it had seemed only rather a lark; and even so if he had not been a trifle bosky from the banquet he would have sent the girl packing. But somehow or other, he couldn't say how, he had found himself kissing her, and she was such a nice little thing, and he was lonely and far from home, that matters had got out of hand before he knew it. She was a very nice girl, not the way the rumours painted her, but well spoken and kind-hearted, not at all the sort who would blackmail a fellow or anything of that kind. But yes, he did see that he must have nothing more to do with her, and that such a thing must never happen again.

'He spoke so properly and feelingly,' Albert told me, 'that I was very touched. He said that he loved and respected me so much that it would kill him if I did not forgive him. So I told him, of course, that I forgave him, and that nothing more on the subject would ever be said again. Did I do right?'

'Yes,' I said, 'quite right. If he knows his error, he must be forgiven. He is a warm-hearted boy, after all, and I dare say that's what led him astray, rather than a real addiction to vice. If he marries a good girl, his affections will have a proper outlet, and he will grow steadier. I don't know how I shall be able to face him when he comes home, though. What does one say in such a case?'

'Ah, that brings me to another point,' Albert said. 'He asked me if you and his sisters need to be told about it. He was very anxious to keep it from you and them if possible. I did not tell him that you already knew. I thought it would make relations easier between you if he goes on thinking I have been able to keep the affair from you.'

As the day wore on, the sky grew darker and it grew bitterly cold; and owing to Bertie's taking a wrong turning and getting lost, they were out walking far longer than was necessary or good. Albert had intended to come back that evening, but he had been so chilled and tired by the long walk he had had to stay the night at Madingley, and did not get back to Windsor until half past one the next day. By then he was so exhausted he had to lie on the sofa, shivering and aching, but with a mind so much relieved by the talk with Bertie, it gave me to believe he would soon recover his spirits and his health. But the next day he was no better, and his old gastric trouble returned, so we sent for Jenner. Though we did not say the word aloud, we were both terrified of typhoid; but Jenner pronounced it to be only a feverish cold, though a bad enough one for him to remain at the castle for the rest of the week. Poor Albert could not eat, nor sleep, and the rheumatism in his shoulder was so bad that he could not go out to shoot with Louis Hesse when a party was arranged; he felt so weak he had often to lie down and rest, and he complained of pains in the back and legs. His temper, unusually for him, was irritable, and he tried me sorely by refusing to rest properly and then complaining of weariness. But by Friday Jenner pronounced him much better and said that there was no need for him to sleep at the castle any longer.

Unfortunately the week's end also brought a new crisis to trouble us – and Albert in particular. The Americans had been fighting a civil war for eight months now, north against south, which was nothing to do with us; until the news arrived that one of our mail ships, the *Trent*, had been held up by an American warship. An armed party had boarded her and removed by force four of the passengers, who were gentlemen of the Southern states bound for London and Paris as envoys, and travelling under the protection of the British flag. This was an outrageous breach of international law, and there was an instant clamour in the country for war with the northern states. 'Bear this, bear all!' thundered *The Times*; the Americans, as witness the behaviour of their ministers abroad, their businessmen, even their debutantes at Court, were growing too big for their boots. It was time to teach them a lesson – and incidentally take vengeance for the insult of 1776. Palmerston was snorting like an old war-horse scenting gunpowder; and Gladstone (how I disliked that man!) declared that the country and the Cabinet were as one, and that eight thousand of our troops were in Canada and ready to march into the United States at any moment.

The draft of a despatch from Russell – then Foreign Secretary – to Washington reached us at Windsor that Friday, and it was terse to the point of downright provocation, demanding the instant release of the arrested passengers with full apology and full reparation for the breach of international law, in such tones as to leave the Americans no alternative but to defy us. Certainly they had behaved extremely badly, but did we really want to go to war with them? On the Saturday came further news, in a letter from Palmerston. Two of the passengers on the *Trent* were in London and had said that the officer in charge of the boarding party had told them he had done it on his own initiative, and not on official instructions. On the other hand, a senior officer of the Northern army who was in Paris had stated that the whole thing had been planned by Washington with the intention of provoking war with Britain so as to bring in France on their side with the promise of restoring Canada to them.

'I don't believe that,' Albert said, coughing a little. He had been troubled yesterday and today by the dryness of his tongue, which had turned a horrid brown colour. His eyes were unnaturally bright, and he moved restlessly, but he assured me he had no fever, only the dreadful aches and shiverings. 'I don't believe the Northern states want war with us. They may fancy they could beat us on land, but they can have no doubts about the superiority of our Navy.'

'Whether they want war or not, *we* do not,' I said firmly. 'It would bring us no credit to engage such ruffians; and I do not think matters of this sort warrant spilling the blood of God knows how many of our men.'

'Then Russell must reword the despatch,' Albert said. 'The Americans must be given some means of making their apology without losing face. I must think how it can be done.'

The next morning, which was Sunday, he rose without a word to me at seven, and put on his thickly padded dressing-gown.

'Where are you going?' I asked him. 'Surely you are not going to work today?'

He looked towards me, but his eyes did not connect with mine. 'I am going to rewrite that draft,' he said. 'I have thought how to do it. You remember what Palmerston told us the passengers said? We must say to Washington that we cannot believe they would wish deliberately to insult our flag or jeopardise the safety of our mails, and that we therefore assume it was the action of an over-zealous captain acting without orders, or at least misunderstanding his orders. That way they can apologise and make reparation without shaming themselves.'

'Oh yes,' I said, 'that is exactly right! How clever you are, beloved! But must you do it now? Come back to bed – you don't look well enough to be up.'

'I can't rest,' he said starkly, 'and it had better be done as soon as possible, or between them they will make an international incident out of it.'

'But my darling, a few hours can't make any difference.'

'Don't fret me,' he said irritably. 'I will do it. Leave me alone.' And he went away to his desk. An hour later he returned, bearing the paper, which he presented to me with a shaking hand. 'I am so weak I can hardly hold the pen,' he groaned. 'Here, read it while I dress.'

'You are too ill,' I said. 'Come back to bed and let me send for Jenner.'

'I can't lie down, I hurt too much,' he said fretfully. 'And Jenner can't help. He doesn't understand my disposition as poor Baly did. I wish he had not been killed.' And he went away to dress. The draft was excellent, beautifully worded, an invitation one could hardly refuse to back away from war and negotiate – emollient to the sensitivity of the young country and accommodating to its pride. I could not know as I read it, that it would be the last thing he ever wrote.

He could eat no breakfast, and in desperation to find something that would ease him I suggested a walk on the Terrace, hoping the fresh air would do him good. He came with me to Chapel and knelt with me as usual, but he looked so ill my heart panicked in me, and I found I could not think or pray, only stare ahead of me in a sort of frozen frenzy. He ate no luncheon afterwards, but sat with us and entertained us while we ate, telling us amusing stories and waiting with an odd kind of patience while we laughed, as if our reaction were somehow irrelevant. I laughed with the rest, and watched him painfully, wondering if he really knew what he was saying. In the afternoon Jenner came, with Clark, and I saw their disappointed looks, and their exchange of glances which were almost shrugs. There was no fever, they said, as if to console me; and Albert laughed strangely and said that was a good thing, for he was so ill he would never survive a fever. Don't say such things, I begged him. Say what things? he said, and laughed again. And yet he was not delirious: he looked at me almost with malice, and I could only take refuge from my fear in anger. You know very well, I snapped. My dear, he said, there is no cause for alarm.

He ate no dinner, and went early to bed, but he slept little, lying shivering through the dark hours. I dozed a little, waking sometimes to find him sleeping fitfully, sometimes not. Once or twice I tried to hold him in my arms, to comfort him, but he said his skin hurt and begged me not to touch him. Towards the morning he got up and went to lie on the sofa at the foot of the bed; and when the clock struck seven he sent for Jenner.

That was Monday the 2nd of December. He did not come downstairs again. Oh, I cannot, even now, even at this distance, recount all the agonising hours of the last two weeks. He would not eat, he could not sleep, but wandered from room to room, and I followed him helplessly, brought him drinks, tried to anticipate where he might settle so as to make it comfortable for him. But he looked at me with that strange, blind look I had seen before, up at Feithort, and which frightened me so much; yet, perhaps because I *had* seen it before, I did not, *could* not believe what it portended. Only the young can flirt with the idea of death, speak his name, write poems to him, for the young know they are immortal. When you come to the age of understanding that he might come for you next, you take care not to attract his attention.

So I would not think of death, shut it out of my thoughts, out of possibility. (*I am always here, even when you cannot see me. I will seek you out, I will have you; there is nowhere to hide, nowhere safe from me.*) Albert had a malady, a feverish cold, but he would get well if he rested and did not worry. If only he would eat! He drank a little Seltzer with raspberry vinegar added to cut through the bad taste in his mouth; he ate a few mouthfuls of broth and brown bread, but brought them up again. He walked, he shivered, he moaned. He asked Alice to read to him, but after a few pages he complained she had chosen the most tedious book in existence and bid her leave off. Jenner came and gave him ether and Hoffman's drops, and for a blissful hour and a half he slept quietly before waking to confusion and restlessness again.

On the night of the 6th he slept in his own room, if slept is the right word. Jenner was with him all night, and Clark came and went (his own wife was desperately ill, and he was much distracted, poor man). On the morning of the 7th I went in at eight o'clock while the doctors withdrew to discuss the case, and found him quiet for the moment, only looking so exhausted my heart wept for him. I sat down beside his bed, and leaned over to kiss his brow. The blue of his eyes seemed to have smudged into his eye sockets, and his cheeks were hollow; but he looked at me with recognition. It was like a window opening on to a prison: he gazed out at me hopelessly, and yet with appeal, as though I might bring him out into the sunlit land where I still lived.

'How long will it go on?' he said miserably.

'Not much longer,' I said. 'A week perhaps, then you will be well.'

'What made me ill? Where did it come from?'

'It was overwork, as much as worry and annoyance.'

He sighed, moving his head a little, as though to get away from something. 'It is too much,' he muttered. 'You must speak to the ministers.'

'I am doing so,' I said. I had been discovering in the last few days how much work he had always saved me. 'But it was not only that – it was your own concerns as well. All your societies and projects – the Horticultural Garden – it was all too much.'

He seemed to have wandered away while I spoke. Now he said, 'At dawn, when the birds started singing, I thought I was at the Rosenau. I kept my eyes shut, hoping to make it so.'

'We'll go there when you're well,' I said. 'For a visit. We'll arrange to see Vicky again, like last year.'

He didn't seem to have heard me. 'When I was there last year, I knew I was seeing it for the last time. Ernst said to me, why are you crying, and I said, because I shall never see all this again.' He blinked his eyes slowly, as though blinking away tears, but he had not enough moisture in him for crying. 'What was I talking of?' he said suddenly.

I wanted to give his thoughts a better direction, so I said, 'The birds singing.'

He looked at me blankly. 'When the window is open you can hear them quite plainly. And the fountain, too.' He has gone back to the Rosenau again, I thought sickly. His childhood is all to him, and I am nothing. But then he smiled faintly and said, 'I told you so, didn't I, the very first night we slept there, that we would have a fountain on the terrace, and listen to it in bed.'

'Yes, at Osborne,' I said gladly. 'Oh, darling one, get well quickly so that we can go there again, and sleep in our own dear bed in our own room!'

'There, oh there, my beloved, would I with thee go,' he whispered. His hand stirred on the cover, and I took it, and felt it press mine feebly. '*Gutes Weibchen.*' He closed his eyes and sighed, and I stayed still for a while, my heart in a painful state of uncertainty as to whether these were good signs or bad. Then Clark and Jenner came in, and Jenner made a sign to me that he wanted to speak to me outside. I got up, but Albert did not seem to notice my leaving him; and as Clark bent over him again, I walked out into the passage, and along to my dressing-room, and Jenner came after and closed the door behind him.

'Your Majesty,' he said as I turned to face him, and I saw what was in his eyes, and wanted to scream, *No! Get away from me with your executioner's face! Take off your black cap! I won't hear it!* But no sound escaped me. 'Your Majesty,' he said, 'I'm afraid I have to tell you that this morning a rash has appeared on the Prince's person. It is an indication – it is the confirmation of what we have been on the watch for from the beginning.' He scanned my face for comprehension but I gave him none, setting it stonily against the doom he wanted to pronounce. 'His Highness has the low fever, or bowel fever as it is sometimes called.'

'Typhoid,' I said. The word came out of my mouth as though summoned, and I clapped my hand over my lips, but too late. It had been let loose.

Jenner stared kindly at the rest of my face. 'Your Majesty must not despair. We know all about this disease now. We know exactly how to treat it, and the symptoms are all favourable. Our judgement is that His Highness began the sickness on the 22nd of November, and since it takes a month to run its course, he should be well again in another fortnight.'

He talked a little more, but I could not listen. The agony of hope and despair went on, romping about inside me, and how to contain or reconcile them I did not know.

The next day Albert asked to be moved into the Blue Room (which was also known as the King's Room, because it was the one in which Uncle King and Uncle William had both died). It was Sunday again. Löhlein moved his things and the bed was made up, and also a wheeled day-bed, since he sometimes preferred a sofa; but much of the time he would not lie down, only wandered as he had done before from room to room. I followed him with eau-de-Cologne and smelling salts, and sometimes he knew me and sometimes not. He had fits of irritability, when he would rattle a door-handle, or call for General Bruce, or shout that I had lost an important paper. Once he asked Alice to play for him, and she sat down at the piano and played *Ein Feste Burg* until he called enough; another time he asked for all the looking-glasses to be covered up, because the reflections frightened him: 'It is like Holyrood Palace,' he said. But the worst moments were when he came back to himself and looked at me, not unsmiling and unrecognising, but with those eyes of pleading from within his prison. *'Frauchen,'* he would whisper, as if his gaoler had looked away just for long enough for him to speak that one word to me, to tell me he loved me still, to tell me he could not get back to me. I suffered for him in his torment, but if there had been a way for me to release him, I could not have done it. I could not wish death for him. I needed him so much, even blindly wandering. I needed so much to go on hoping he would get better.

On Friday the 13th he did not wander, but lay gasping, eyes open and fixed. Jenner said there might be congestion of the lungs. I went out on to the Terrace for a breath of air, and walked up and down the pavement in the grey of a bitter December afternoon; bare black trees and dull grass stretching away, and wateriness of mist clinging to the distances. Will it ever be spring again? I wondered. I thought of primroses at Osborne, where they grew in the woods so thickly one could gather basketsful in just a few minutes. I remembered Lord M. saying that he looked forward in retirement to seeing the changing seasons again. It was on this very terrace I had said goodbye to him in the starlight, and he had held his head away so that his tears would not fall on my hands. He had been dead these thirteen years, died sad and neglected because I had my new love who was everything to me, and did not need him any more. And suddenly the tears came, and I wept for him, and for me, and for all who love, because there is nothing else you can do about love but to suffer it, and to cry.

While I was walking, there was a crisis, a sinking, with such shiverings that Jenner thought it was the end, and advised Alice, who was with him (she was always there, good, gentle Alice) to send for Bertie. The telegraph was worded so carefully that Bertie and Bruce did not properly understand, and went to a dinner engagement before catching the last train. They arrived at three in the morning, smelling of fog and cigars and wine and full of cheerful, outside conversation – a sudden gust of normality, of the world beyond our prison, painful as nostalgia, like the smell of cloves and cinnamon when Christmas is two months past.

By then Albert had rallied, and was warm and comfortable, rational but very weak; but Bertie had known nothing about the illness and was shocked to the core by what he found. Alice and I had been sitting by the bed, and I was holding his hands. They gave him brandy every half hour to stimulate him. Kind Jenner said that he had seen worse cases recover, that he never gave up hope in the case of fever; if the Prince lasted this crisis, all might yet be well. I went out to Bertie, and found the poor boy trembling and weeping. 'I didn't know, Mamma! I didn't know! Why didn't you tell me?' And he flung himself into my arms and sobbed.

I was trying to hold back my own tears. 'We mustn't despair. Jenner says there is ground to hope the crisis is over.'

'He must get better, he must!' Bertie cried, muffled, into my shoulder. 'I can't bear it if he dies.'

He wanted me, like a child, to tell him all would be well; but I was more child than him, and had no reassurance in me. 'However frightened we are, we won't give up hope,' I muttered. And then he lifted his head from my shoulder, and the feeling of his arms around me changed: he was no longer clinging to me, but holding me up.

'I will help you, Mamma,' he said bravely. 'I will help you every way I can.'

'My dear boy, I know you will,' I said, very much touched, and I kissed him, and felt him shyly kiss me back. Poor little Bertie! Poor lost soul!

I went to lie down in my own room for a while, and the messages that came every hour were increasingly hopeful. At seven I got up and went to the Blue Room. The watery greyness of yesterday was gone; it was a bright morning, and the sun was shining – a day for hope, for renewal. The door of the room was open, and I saw the sad look of night-watching, the candles burnt down to their sockets and the group of doctors gathered round the bed, with anxious faces and shadowed eyes. There were more of them now – Sir Henry Holland, Dr Watson and Dr Brown had swelled their ranks in the last two days. I walked past them to the bed, and saw my darling was awake, and my heart lifted. *He's better*, I thought. His face was calm, serene, and lit by the morning sun his skin looked almost transparent, as it had done in his youth – like the delicate leaves of ivory the miniaturists paint on. He had never looked so beautiful; his eyes were softly bright, and seemed to gaze on objects unseen by me but which gave him pleasure. '*Hertzliebste*,' I whispered, '*wie geht es dir?*' But he didn't seem to hear me, or see me, only watched those bright visions, and almost smiled.

Through the calm, bright morning hope bloomed, a rose coaxed out by winter sunshine, beautiful but hopelessly fragile out of its season. The bed was wheeled through to the other room, which was warmer in the morning. Jenner and Clark both said it was a decided rally, but they remained anxious about his breathing, which was too rapid. But in the afternoon the fair sky clouded over, the sunshine disappeared, and it grew very cold. The winter rose was pinched and drooped. When the evening came and the lamps were lit, I knew he was sinking. My darling's face grew dusky, his breathing heavy; I leaned over him and whispered, '*Es ist kleines Frauchen*,' and saw he knew me. He turned his head towards me, and then laid it against my hand and sighed – oh, what a sigh! – drawn up shuddering out of the roots of him, not a sigh of pain, but as if he knew he was leaving me, and the leaving was hard, so very hard!

I felt myself trembling on the brink of tears, and went into the next room to compose myself. I sat on the floor for a while, so sunk in despair I did not think I could ever get up again. How could he leave me? How could he? But it had been going on so long, I was numbed to it, I had begun to think the end would never arrive. It was hope of a kind, I suppose.

A clock struck out in the corridor. I heard it too late to count the numbers. A shape moved on the edge of my vision and I lifted my head. It was Alice, standing in the doorway, slender as a wand, faithful as love itself, her neat head bent. 'Mamma,' she said, 'come back. It is time.'

No, oh no! Let it not be! Don't take him from me, dear God! He is my life, I cannot live in the world without him!

I went to the bed, I knelt down and took his hand; and it was already cold, smooth and limp as though the marks of his occupancy had been washed away by the ebbing tide. Oh, yes, this is death! I thought in agony. I had seen it before. The faint, quiet breaths drew in and out, like a quiet tide lapping, going farther out and farther out, so gently. How long did we kneel there, listening, counting out the last breaths? When I heard half past ten strike distantly he was still here, though far away from me. And then there were two long breaths close together, and no more. He had gone. All, *all* was over.

11th December 1900

THEY SAY Charles I walked and talked for an hour after his head was cut off. I have done better than that. I have done it for almost forty years.

There is a numbness that invades one at first – a merciful sleeping of the senses, sent by God to quiet the pain of the amputation. For some days I walked and slept, tried to work, and did not know what I felt, beyond bewilderment. All my instincts kept trying to go back to him, and I went again and again to the Blue Room, like a lost dog returning to the last place it saw its master. But he was not there. I knew *that* quite clearly. Later, much later, I was able to feel that his spirit was near me and watching over me – I have felt it even more strongly of late – but in the beginning there was nothing of him at all, only the void where he had been. Perhaps newly freed spirits rush very far away to begin with, rejoicing in their release from the restraints of the body, and return close to earth only long afterwards when they have refreshed themselves.

But when the numbness wore off, oh, then the anguish began! How could I be alive after what I had witnessed? I who prayed daily that we might die together and I not survive him? I who felt, when clasped in those blessed arms and held tight in the sacred hours of the night – when the world seemed to be only ourselves – that nothing could part us. I had felt so secure, and repeated so often, 'God will protect us.' I never dreamed of the physical possibility of being parted. Now I might weep or be calm, pray or rave, vow whatever future virtue or service to God I might, but it would change nothing. He was gone, and would never come back, and the awful, awful finality of it desolated me.

I don't remember by whose will it was that we went, five days later, to Osborne. Perhaps it was Alice's idea – she did everything for me in those first weeks, tender little nurse. It was a long, dark journey, and I remember rain and storm and a wild crossing, but that may be what was inside me rather than outside me. But that night I was again in the great bed in our own bedroom in Osborne House, which he had designed, with all the little comforts he had thought of; and settling my head on the pillow I turned instinctively to put myself into his arms, just for an instant before I remembered again. That was the hardest thing of all, those continual tiny lapses of memory which caused me a thousand times a day to *re*discover the agony of the truth!

Now I would have to go to bed and get up alone – for ever. Oh, I was driven mad with desire and longing! I was as much in love with him as if we had married yesterday, and I wanted his warm body beside me; I wanted to touch him. I lay looking up at the polished headboard, and at the brass lever he had installed, to lock the door for our privacy when we made love. I should never need it now. I folded my arms across my breast and wept hopelessly – slept at last – woke in the morning from a brief oblivion to the vague, confused sensation that something bad had happened. And then the sickening, crushing weight of realisation rolled on to me like a stone. How many such wakings since? How can any human heart bear it?

As the days passed, oh, so drearily, I began to think that perhaps God would not make me stay here without him; perhaps I should soon die and be with him again. The longing moulded itself into a conviction, and I set myself to put my affairs in order and ensure my darling's last wishes were fulfilled before I left. Alice's marriage to Louis – that had been Albert's ardent desire: that should take place without delay. Tuesday the 1st of July was the date, and the dining-room at Osborne the place – just the immediate families, and the Archbishop reading the service most beautifully, standing below the Family Picture, as we always called it – Winterhalter's group of 1847, in which Albert's outstretched hand seemed to be offering its blessing to his darling child. I allowed the girls and the Household to go into half-mourning for the day; Alice wore white satin and gauze and my wedding lace; I wore black. She used Albert's room to dress. I thought, *She is putting on her wedding gown in her beloved papa's room, while I am having my widow's cap adjusted. It is a dreadful dream!* I managed to keep myself from weeping until the service was over, but Baby kept whispering loudly weren't we going to wait for Papa? and Affie sobbed all through. Poor Alice, it was more like a funeral than a wedding; but she and Louis were happy together. And she is with him now.

Then there was Bertie's marriage to Alix to arrange – a sacred duty, I told Bertie, left to us by his father to perform; and he, grieving, believing he had helped to kill that beloved one, had no more resistance (which was fortunate, for I could not have forced him if he had been really unwilling). Vicky was charged to explain to Alix and her parents about my poor Boy's temptation and fall: I would have all open and above-board. But we need not have worried about their scruples: the future King of England was a prize not to be passed up by a penniless princeling, even if he was heir to the throne of Denmark.

In September of 1862 I went over to Belgium to inspect her for myself, and found a ravishingly pretty girl in a simple black dress, with her golden-brown hair taken back off her fine forehead and falling in curls over her shoulders. I have always been in love with beauty, and hers was angelic. She was besides a very good girl, not clever or well educated, but principled and dutiful, and with a sweet temper and warm affectionate heart. She told me how very sorry she was never to have met Albert, and that it had long been her dearest wish to become his daughter-in-law. I thought she would do very well, if she learned a little firmness and statecraft from me. Bertie came a few days later, and after four hours alone with her, he proposed and was accepted. Thank God! they fell in love with each other in those four hours, for I would not have wished to see a reluctant girl take on an indifferent boy. They were married in St George's Chapel, Windsor, on the 10th of March 1863, and both seemed radiantly happy. The Archbishop complained that we should not be having a wedding during Lent, but I told him sharply that in my young day there was no Lent! It's a High Church thing, an invention of the Puseyites. Keeping Lent does not make you a better Christian: why, the Russians make a great fuss about it, and look at them!

Well, Alix proved a good wife for Bertie, and steadied him a great deal, and if she did not manage in the end to keep him straight, she did the next best thing, which was to behave as if he were. 'He might stray,' she told me once, 'but he always loved me best' – which I would regard as cold comfort, but I suppose we must all get through trouble as best we can. She gave him six children in the first eight years – Eddy, Georgie, then the three girls, and then the boy, John, who lived only a day. All of them were born prematurely and all frail-looking and puny. The girls, with their bulging eyes, sloping chins and quivering nervousness, always reminded me of mice (the House-hold called them Their Royal Shynesses) but it was the misfortune of all of them to look too much like their father and not enough like their pretty mother. Alix smothered and cosseted them too much, to my mind, and kept the boys tied to her apron strings (compensation, perhaps, for their straying father!). Poor Eddy was the strangest-looking of all, with such a long neck and long arms that Bertie gave him the nickname of 'Collars-and-Cuffs'. I think there may have been something wrong with Eddy, for he was always lethargic in his body and slow and dawdly in his mind; but a dear boy all the same, and kind to his sisters – I was always very fond of him, and in his last delirium it was me he called for, not his mother. On the day before his eighteenth birthday, shortly after becoming engaged, he fell ill with influenza, which turned into pneumonia, and six days later he was dead. However, Georgie, who was always the prettiest and most lively of the children, took over and married Eddy's fiancée, May of Teck, and they have now amply secured the next generation. The Throne is safe.

So the first years without Albert passed, and I did not die, though the work was a load which would have killed a horse. Everything Albert and I had done between us, I now had to do alone, for the idiot Government reverted to its previous stand that I might not have a secretary. The Prime Minister was *ex officio* my secretary, they said, just as they had said in Lord M.'s time. That was all very well, but Lord M. had actually *acted* as my secretary, which Palmerston was incapable of, even if I had felt inclined to have the old sinner permanently at my elbow. Dear Sir Charles Grey, Albert's secretary, did all he could to help me, but it was not until 1867 that the Government gave in and appointed him officially as my secretary. But the work was in its way a blessing. Every hour of the day, except for meals and a little walking or carriage exercise, I spent at my desk, labouring through my Boxes, mastering the arcane details of every case, though they were often couched in such dreadful English they were like a foreign language. No beloved Albert to read them for me and *précis* them; no Albert to explain the significance, look up the references, fill in the background. No Albert to discuss them with – my conclusions must be my own now. I vowed at the beginning of the new reign – when he died, that is – that I would always be guided by what he would have done; but as the years carried me further and further away from him, I could not always be sure what that might have been. Looking back now, I can see that I have moved in some cases quite a distance from his ideas, and I sometimes feel a little shy about the thought of facing him again, for I'm afraid I have done many things he will not approve of. When I decided to submit myself to him in all things, to submerge my life in his, it was rather like pressing a foot into a shoe too small for it. Once you take the shoe off, the foot spreads and swells into a quite different shape – different from the shoe, and different from its original self, too. (Not that I mean to suggest that Albert's was a smaller soul than mine – only that his mind was so disciplined it was an ill fit for an unruly one such as mine!)

And suddenly I was two years, three years away from him, and it was plain I was not going to follow my darling to the grave. That was a hard thing to bear, even though I never dreamed at that time how very, very long I would have to stay behind. Oh, I was angry with him for leaving me! Often and often I lay awake through the tedious nights alone, remembering those last years when I had watched him withdrawing, worried about him, refused to allow myself to believe; he died in the end, as I saw quite clearly in the middle watches, because he did not want to live. The load of work and worry had been too much for him, and instead of fighting, he had given up. I railed at him through the darkness, even as I wept: I would not have left you, Albert, no matter how weak, or sick, or tired I was! I would have fought and fought to the last breath to stay with you! How could you desert me? How could you leave me here alone? In the end, he did not fail of love, but of the joy of it. 'It is not *you* I wish to leave,' he had told me; but I was not enough to make him want to stay. I had always wanted to believe him perfect, and it was hard to have to acknowledge that he had a sad want of what they call pluck.

20th December 1900, at Osborne

M AUSOLEUM DAY – the anniversary of the day he left me – with its attendant ceremonies, and then the journey down here, have tired me so much that for days I have been able to do almost nothing but lie about on the sofa and have Thora read to me. She is a dear girl! And when I have a mind she chats to me so interestingly about this and that. I dearly love to chat. Christmas will soon be on us, and when I remember the joyful occasion it has been, with the Tables and the Tree, and all the wonderful smells and good things to eat, my spirits almost fail me. Without him it is like a birthday party where the birthday person does not turn up. I must try to keep up appearances, for the children's sake, but this wretched insomnia disrupts the pattern of my days so much that I find it hard to feel enthusiastic about anything.

I do feel a little stronger today, and I want so much to go on with my story, so I shall scribble away while I can. I can hardly see the page, and I doubt whether anyone would ever be able to decipher this scrawl, but it doesn't matter, after all. I must finish what I began, and then Chance can do what it likes. Perhaps when I have finished I should simply leave the manuscript lying about, rather than hide it. People look for what is hidden; what is obvious they often miss.

In the December of 1864 I had John Brown brought down from Balmoral so that I could take up riding again. Jenner thought I ought to have the exercise, and Baby was learning, and I wished to accompany her; but I should not have trusted a strange groom. I found such pleasure in riding again, ambling about the familiar paths at Osborne on my lovely black Flora, and felt so safe with Brown beside me or at the bridle, that after a few weeks I decided there was no reason not to let him make himself useful in other ways. In Scotland, when one rides out, one's ghillie does everything, acts as groom, butler, cook and lady's maid all in one, and it is incomparably comforting to have one person do everything, if they are a good and devoted person. Brown was, and soon made himself indispensable. He was quiet and quick and had an excellent memory, which made him a good servant; but besides that he was physically strong and very brave, which made me feel safe riding or driving with him.

Looking back, I think it was the beginning of my recovery. Still I laboured through a dark tunnel, but there were moments when I was able to know pleasure, when the children would say something droll, or I would find beauty in a landscape or a sky or a flower. Brown soon came to fill another position in my life, as well as ghillie. When Albert died, so soon after Mamma, I felt very deeply that there was no-one left who was completely mine, whose business it was simply to see that I was happy; no-one with that minute and single-minded interest in all my concerns. My children were a great comfort, of course, but that is not the same as the comfort an adult can give; and when they became adults, they naturally put their own families first, which was right and proper. As to servants, one can be fond of them, but there is always a barrier between, which comes of their dependence, their knowledge that you can dismiss them in a moment if they fail to please; so they are always submissive, servile even, and hide their thoughts and feelings from you.

Brown was not like that. Though utterly devoted to me, and giving his life to serving and obeying me, he nevertheless argued with me if he thought I was wrong, and did not hesitate to let me know his opinion of things. He did not care in the least about the fear of dismissal: though it would have grieved him, I know, to leave me, he did not cower to keep his job. That was what annoyed my family and the Household, who regarded it as arrogance in him, and were offended that he did not 'know his place'. On the contrary, he knew it very well: it was at my elbow! As the years went on and he became less and less like a servant, I permitted him more liberty than most people thought proper, and he often addressed me without the deference that is usually expected by any mistress from a servant, let alone the Queen of England. But he knew how far he was allowed to go, and never went further; and he cheered me up, often and often, when all else failed, with his drollery, and his rough-tongued care for me. 'Whit are ye daeing, wearing that auld black dress again? It's green-moulded!' Ah, I miss him, my good and trusty friend! There's no-one now to care what I wear, or how often!

When he was ill once, and we thought he was dying, I promised him that if he went first, I would have his picture and a lock of his hair put in my coffin with me. 'In your hand?' he insisted anxiously. I held up my left hand, which rested when I walked upon his strong right arm. 'In this hand,' I said. And he had nodded, content. 'There's no-one loves you better than me,' he said. 'Nor serves me more faithfully,' I agreed. 'You are my true friend.'

So I have left instructions: Reid will see it done. It must be done secretly, so as not to offend the family, but I believe one should always keep promises, however trivial they may seem, and I will not break my word to my dear old friend. His picture and a lock of his hair, wrapped in tissue-paper, will be placed under my left hand after I am laid in my coffin. Albert would not mind, I know. He has told me he and I will be together for all eternity, after all: he won't begrudge my good, faithful John his place near me.

14th January 1901, at Osborne

OH, WHAT a sad Christmas! My dear Jane Churchill died on Christmas Day after forty-six years in my service. They kept it from me at first, for fear of giving me a shock, but Beatrice told me the sad news at last. It was a heart attack, and thus quick and merciful, but the loss to me is not to be told. And then the old year went out in a series of storms so severe I could not go out of doors for several days. So I begin a new year, and a new century, but oh, so sadly, and feeling so weak and unwell; though Reid says I will be better in the spring, as long as I let him treat me as an invalid, and do not try to do too much. I saw Lord Roberts for an hour this morning and discussed South Africa with him – I conferred the Garter on him on January the 2nd, for his conduct of the war. He says it is in its final phase now. I pray no more of our men will be lost before the peace is signed. Talking to him tired me, but I went out this afternoon for my carriage exercise, and the air did me good.

I came to bed early, but despite my tiredness, I cannot sleep, so while I can, I will write. It is an effort now; but my mind is still alive and lively inside this 'wreck', and I must, must finish!

I had got up to my dear Brown's death, I think. Ah, it seems so long ago now. I have lived and reigned so long, I have become a legend even to myself; I sometimes catch myself doing and saying things that are purely the Queen Empress, and have nothing to do with Victoria, the Victoria that lives inside this venerable hulk! When Albert died, I longed to die also. At one desperate time, I even thought (oh, wickedness!) of taking my own life; but I felt his spirit bid me, 'Still endure!' – and so I have, year upon year, enduring and outliving everyone. I have reigned longer than any other British monarch; and I believe it has never happened before that there is a sovereign and three direct heirs (I mean, in three generations) all alive at the same time. I have not only grandchildren but great-grand-children now, scattered all over Europe: Albert and I shall have supplied the Thrones of I don't know how many countries.

410

Oh, but I am tired! This last year has been one of such sorrow and weariness – poor darling Affie dying, the third of my children to go; and then dearest Christl – that was such a terrible shock. And my darling Vicky, my beloved Angel's first-born and best-loved: they think I don't know how ill she is, and she tries to keep it from me, but a mother always knows. I think she is dying. One has lived too long when one starts to outlive one's own children.

At other times in my life, even in the midst of sorrow, I have felt my own vigour at the core of me, attaching me to the world; but now I am full of aches and pains which make it hard even to rest. Did my poor darling feel like this in his last weary weeks? If so, I have to take back what I said about his want of pluck. I cannot blame him for not struggling to live in such circumstances.

Not that I would ask it of God, precisely; but if He would like to call me home now, I should go willingly. I have been away from my darling for such a very long time, and I want so much to see him again. Dear Lord, might you not see your way to it? Bertie is not going to get any better or any worse, and my affairs are in order and my funeral planned down to the last carriage, so there will be nothing for anyone to do. I have even ordered my favourite hymn:

Life's dream is past,
All its sin, its sadness;
Brightly at last,
Dawns a day of gladness.

Gladness it will be to me; and I don't suppose Bertie will be sorry to be King at last.

Poor, poor Bertie! I blamed him so bitterly at first for his part in his father's death – and unfairly, too, as I did come to acknowledge to him (though being sorry afterwards is not the same as not doing or saying the thing in the first place, as I know). Unfairly, because my darling had been fleeing from life for a long time, and he would have found the way out sooner or later. Bertie has not turned out the way my darling would have wanted, but there was nothing he could ever have done about it, as I see now. Lord M. was right. What can any of us do, but what we do? We are all God's playthings, hemmed in by our flesh and our blood and our shortcomings, and struggle as we might, we cannot outrun our fate.

Bertie's destiny was to become a man of fashion, the darling of society, a creature of fine clothes and fine wine and expensive cigars, an expert on horseflesh and she-flesh, a spinner-along of motorcars, the man every hostess would give her hair to have at her dinner-table. I dare say he will be a popular King, if not a good one, and one might say a great deal worse than that.

My fate was to become England, a little old woman in a bonnet who rules half the world, a profile on a postage-stamp, a sombre, familiar face in a thousand, thousand reproductions, instantly recognisable to half the world's population, from tall thin Yankees in strange trousers to little hopping brown boys on the shores of the Ganges. All this, Victoria, born to be Queen – she whose legs are too short to reach the ground when she sits on the Throne, and who is so shy she trembles like a cold kitten when she has to meet someone new. Oh, irony! But I am England all the same. That's what the people mean when they talk of me: not the woman but the monument. The woman no-one now knows.

And Albert's fate? Ah, perhaps the strangest of all! His was to change us all, the way we speak, and think, and act, what we believe, what we accept, what we respect. We are all Germans now (except for Bertie's set, but there aren't many of them). I have never liked the High-borns, the Upper Classes if you like; but I can admit now, since it doesn't matter any more, that I've never liked the Middle Classes either – too self-satisfied, too censorious, too intolerant of human frailty. But it is they above all who appreciated my beloved one's qualities; and their virtues, which are his, are good ones – industry, self-improvement, charity, enquiry. And it seems they are the people who count, now and for the future. All England will be middle class one day – when Bertie's day is done, and Georgie and May rule my country. I once said to Lord M. that modern women have more accomplishments, men drink less, and dogs behave better towards the furniture than in the past. It is truer now than ever, and perhaps that is no bad epitaph for a reign.

The odd thing is that I suppose when I am gone they will talk about the 'Victorian Age', as they talk now about the 'Elizabethan Age'; but the things they will remember my reign by will be Albert's achievements. Would he mind? I wonder! I see his face now, and his twinkling smile, and hear his voice, with that lovely chuckle in it, saying to me as he so often did, quoting Goethe, *'Die Tat is alles, nicht der Ruhn'* – the Deed is all, the Repute nothing. All his life he worked with dedication, bowing his back under the stern weight of duty, struggling to bring about the changes he knew were right and good; but he never wanted recognition. The deed is all, he said: I want no statues put up to me.

So, very well, my beloved, I'll take the name for you, and I'll take the blame for you, too, if there's any going about, for that's my privilege. After all, it was I who was Queen of England, not you. You were just a penniless German princeling from a country the size of Bristol! You changed the face of England, and then slipped quietly away in the night and left me to stand alone for forty years under the thousand staring eyes, under the fierce light that beats upon the Throne. But I always knew my duty, and I have done it, and shall do it to the end.

I can write no more: my poor old hand aches so, I can hardly hold the pen. I will stop and resume tomorrow. I really am so tired now that I think I shall be able to sleep.

Postscript

THE DAY after this writing finishes, the Queen was seen driving in the park with her daughter-in-law, the Duchess of Coburg: it was her last outing. On the morning of the 16th of January, the Queen could not seem to wake properly, though she muttered several times that she must get up. Reid decided he must see her even though he had not been summoned, and went to her room. He had never seen her in bed before, and was struck by how small she looked. She seemed dazed and bewildered, and he later concluded she may have suffered a mild stroke.

A London specialist was called in the next day, who agreed there had been some mental impairment. Reid believed the end was near, and privately telegraphed the Kaiser, whom he had promised to forewarn. Arthur was in Berlin at the time, and he and Willy travelled back to England together. They arrived at Osborne on the 21st, with Bertie. The Queen had rallied, but on the 22nd it was plain the end could only be hours away. She died at half past six that evening, with Willy supporting her in his one good arm, Bertie holding her other hand, and Baby, Lenchen, Louise and Arthur at the foot of the bed. Vicky in Germany, dying of cancer of the spine, could not leave her bed of sickness to be there.

The funeral took place two weeks later, all in white, just as the Queen had planned it. Her coffin, so small it looked like a child's, was buried next to Prince Albert's in the Mausoleum at Frogmore, where above the door were the words:

His mourning widow, Victoria the Queen, directed that all that is mortal of Prince Albert be placed in this sepulcre. AD 1862.

Farewell, beloved! Here at last will I rest with thee; with thee in
Christ I will rise again.

After her death, Bertie and Baby between them dealt with her
vast accumulation of letters and diaries. Many of the former were
destroyed, while the latter, after being transcribed in a severely edited
and censored form, were burned.